Ian Irvine was born in Bathurst, Australia, in 1950, and educated at Chevalier College and the University of Sydney, where he took a PhD in marine science.

After working as an environmental project manager, Ian set up his own consulting firm in 1986, carrying out studies for clients in Australia and overseas. He has worked in many countries in the Asia-Pacific region. An expert in marine pollution, Ian has developed some of Australia's national guidelines for the protection of the oceanic environment.

The international success of Ian Irvine's debut fantasy series, *The View from the Mirror*, immediately established him as one of the most popular new authors in the fantasy genre. He is now a full-time writer and lives in the mountains of northern New South Wales, Australia, with his family.

Ian Irvine has his own website at www.ian-irvine.com and can be contacted at ianirvine@ozemail.com.au

Find out more about Ian Irvine and other Orbit authors by registering for the free monthly newsletter at www.orbitbooks.co.uk

D0267363

By Ian Irvine

The Three Worlds series

Ian Irvine

A Tale of the Three Worlds

Alchymist

Volume Three of The Well of Echoes

www.orbitbooks.co.uk

ORBIT

First published by Penguin Books Australia Ltd 2003
First published in Great Britain by Orbit 2004
This edition published by Orbit 2004
Reprinted 2005, 2006

Text copyright © 2003 by Ian Irvine
Maps copyright © 2003 by Ian Irvine

The moral right of the author has been asserted.

A CIP catalogue record for this book
is available from the British Library.

ISBN-13: 978-1-84149-181-3
ISBN-10: 1-84149-181-0

Typeset in Veljovic by M Rules
Printed and bound in Great Britain by
Clays Ltd, St Ives plc

Orbit
An imprint of
Time Warner Book Group UK
Brettenham House
Lancaster Place
London WC2E 7EN

Contents

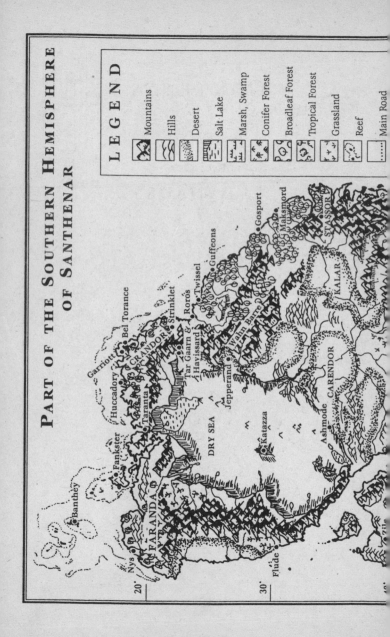

PART OF THE SOUTHERN HEMISPHERE OF SANTHENAR

LEGEND

- Mountains
- Hills
- Desert
- Salt Lake
- Marsh, Swamp
- Conifer Forest
- Broadleaf Forest
- Tropical Forest
- Grassland
- Reef
- Main Road

Banthey

Nys

Fankster

Flude

FARANDA

DRY SEA

Katazza

Huccadory

Garriott

Taranta

Bel Torance

CRANDOR

Srinklet

Roros

Twissel

Tar Gaarn &
Havissard

Jepperand

Walm Barte

Ashmode

CARENDOR

Guffeons

Gosport

Maksmord

KALAR

STASSOR

Maps by the author

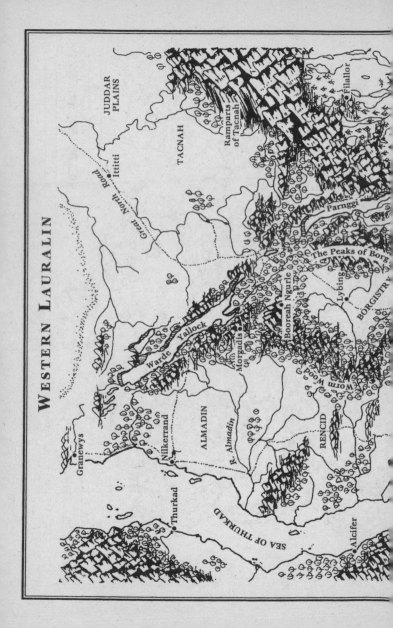

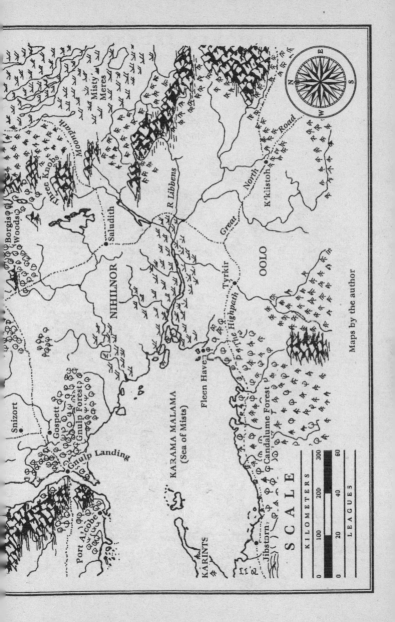

Maps by the author

MELDORIN ISLAND

N

DRY SEA

SEA OF QWALE

Siftah

Zile

Granewys

Ganport

MELDORIN

Chanthed

Thurkad

SILBIS

Shazmak

Flumen

Sith

SEA OF THURKAD

Zarqa Gap

Alcifer

Fiz Gorgo

L. Neid

SCALE

KM

0   50 100 150

0   10   20   30

LEAGUES

Garching

Gnulp
Landing

ACKNOWLEDGEMENTS

I would like to thank Kay Ronai for her initial work on this book, and Nau McNab for taking over so ably.

PART ONE

PHYNADR

ONE

The mud was made from earth and blood, organs and entrails, for the battle had raged back and forth until the dead carpeted the ground. It was the most ghastly sight Irisis Stirm had ever seen, and after a day and a night she was still stuck in the middle of it. The flower of humanity's youth was being slaughtered outside the walls of Snizort, and there was nothing anyone could do.

Dropping her broken sword in the mire, Irisis took up a sound one. There were plenty to choose from. 'Scrutator,' she said as they climbed a little knoll, boots skidding in the wet. The rising sun picked out red eyes in their dirty faces. 'What are we going to do?'

'Die,' Xervish Flydd grimaced. 'This marks the end of civilisation, of everything I've fought for all my life.'

'I won't give up, surr.'

'Very noble of you, Irisis.'

'There's got to be a way.'

'There isn't. There's too many of them and they're killing us twice as fast as we're killing them.'

Irisis looked around. 'Let's try and get to the command post. It's not far now.' It stood on a flat-topped hill away to their right, and the Council flag still fluttered there. 'At least we'll be able to see what's going on.'

'Where's Ullii?' said Flydd, very belatedly.

'Hiding, I expect.'

'Then she's got more sense than the rest of us. What about Pilot Hila?'

'She was killed in the first attack yesterday morning, not

long after the air-floater crashed. You stood over her, holding the enemy off, until she died.'

Flydd shook his grizzled head. 'I don't remember. I can hardly remember anything about the past day.'

'I remember every minute,' said Irisis, 'and I wish I didn't. Come on.'

A lyrinx staggered out of the wallow to their left. The creature stood head and shoulders over Irisis, who was a tall woman, and its great mouth could have bitten her leg off. One leathery wing dragged in the bloody muck; a mighty arm had been severed at the elbow. It slashed feebly at the scrutator, who swayed backwards then lunged, plunging his sword between the armoured skin plates and into its heart.

The creature fell into the red mud, splattering it all over them. Flydd did not even look down.

'Where did you learn such swordsmanship, Xervish?' said Irisis. The scrutator was a small, scrawny man, past middle age. She had seen him fight before, but never with such deadly efficiency as in the past day.

'The scrutators have the best of everything, so I was taught by an expert. Even so, that move wouldn't have worked on an able-bodied lyrinx.'

They passed between two clankers – eight-legged mechanical monsters big enough to carry ten soldiers and all their supplies. The one on the left looked intact, though a headless man lay on the shooter's platform up top, slumped over his javelard, a spear-throwing device like a giant crossbow. Another body was sprawled on the catapult cranks. Once the node had been destroyed its field vanished, and the clankers became useless, immobile metal.

A lone shooter stood behind the loaded javelard of the right-hand machine, training his weapon back and forth across the battlefield. He fired, and the heavy spear was gone too quickly to trace, taking a distant lyrinx full in the chest.

'Nice shooting,' said the scrutator, squelching by.

The soldier shook his head. 'Not good enough to save us, surr.' He jumped down. 'It was my last spear.'

4

'Where's your operator?'

'Dead!'

'What are you like on the ground?'

The soldier turned out the inside of his jerkin. Irisis caught a flash of silver.

The scrutator stopped dead. 'You earned that with a sword?'

'And a long knife, surr. At the battle for Plimes, two years ago.'

'I need a good man with a blade. Find yourself a weapon and come with us.'

Irisis was astounded. The scrutator was known for decisiveness, but to select a stranger so quickly was unprecedented. 'I hope you're a good judge of character,' she said out of the corner of her mouth as they slogged through the bloody mire.

'I chose you, didn't I?'

'That's what I mean.' She grinned. Irisis, with her yellow hair and that long, ripe figure, was a beautiful woman, even covered in mud and gore.

'You didn't see, did you?'

'The badge? No.'

'That was no badge. It was the Star of Valour, and it falls to few living men to wear their own.'

They angled across the field towards the command-post hill, skirting a wallow in which lay the head of a soldier like a single flower in a brown bowl. The eyes stared right at them. Irisis looked the other way. They'd seen a thousand such sights in the past day but still it made her stomach roil.

'Your name would be Flangers, would it not?' said the scrutator.

'That's right, surr,' said the soldier. 'How did you know?'

'It's my business to know the names of heroes. Do you know who I am?'

'Of course. You're the People's Scrutator.'

'Where did *that* name come from?' Flydd exclaimed.

'I can't say, surr,' said Flangers. 'The soldiers have always called you that.'

5

'Disrespectful louts,' growled Flydd. 'I'll have a detachment or two whipped, and then we'll see if they dare such cheek.' There was a twinkle in his eye, though, and the soldier saw it.

Irisis chuckled. Flydd liked to be in control and to know everything; it was a rare sight to see him surprised. 'I'm Irisis.' She offered Flangers her hand.

'You're not from these parts, Flangers?' the scrutator went on as they began to climb the hill.

Flangers shook his head. He was grey eyed and fair haired, with neat, sunburnt features set off by a jutting jaw. Though not overly tall or muscular, he was lean and strong. 'I'm a Thurkad man,' he said, staring blankly at a pair of bodies that lay side by side without a mark on them. The swarming flies were already doing their work.

'Refugee?' asked Flydd. Thurkad, the greatest and oldest city in the west, had fallen two years before, ending the resistance on the great island of Meldorin.

'No. I joined up when I turned fifteen. Six years ago.'

'Did you see much fighting before Plimes?'

Flangers named half a dozen battlefields. 'More than I care to remember.'

'You must be a fine shooter,' said Irisis, 'to have survived all those.'

'Or a lucky one,' said Flydd, slipping in the mud. 'I could use a bit of that now.'

Flangers helped him up. 'It ran out today. I've not lost an operator before.' He was not bitter about it, though many a man might have been. 'We're done, surr. It's over.'

'You're a hero, Flangers. You can't talk like that.'

'I've seen whole nations wiped out, surr. The ancient wonders of my homeland are no more, the millions who dwelt there dead or scattered across the globe. Even Thurkad, the greatest city the world has ever seen, lies empty and in ruins. There's no hope left. The enemy will eat us all.' He gave a little shudder of horror. 'Even our little children.'

'You know the penalty for despairing talk, soldier?'

'For many of the common folk, death at the hands of the scrutators is preferable to being torn apart and eaten.'

'Yet despite your despair you fight on.'

'Duty is everything to me, surr,' said Flangers.

'Then may you take comfort from doing your duty. Give me a hand up here, would you?'

Taking the scrutator by the elbow, Flangers helped him through the steep pinch to the top of the hill. At the edge, Flydd took Irisis's arm and moved away. 'Tell me, Irisis, do you despair as well?'

'No.'

'Why not?'

'I know you'll find a way to save us.'

'Be careful where you put your faith. I'm just a man. I can fail, or be brought down as easily as any other man.'

'But you won't. I know you'll see us through, surr.' He did not reply. 'Surr, what is it?' she went on.

'Flangers has shaken me, Irisis. The people now see death as their only escape. Despair will bring us down more quickly than a horde of the enemy, and how can I counter that?'

'With a bold strike; a miraculous victory.'

'It would take a mighty miracle to save us now.'

'Then you'd better think of a way,' she retorted, 'We're counting on you, surr, and you can't let us down.'

On top of the hill was an oval of cleared land, almost as flat as a tabletop, containing a large command tent in the centre and clusters of smaller ones to either side. A wall of guards lowered their spears to let them through. Inside, a line of crossbowmen held weapons at the ready. The lyrinx always attacked the command post first, if they could get to it.

Flydd nodded to the captain of the guard, then turned to look over the battlefield. A shadow passed across his face and he made for the command tent.

General Tham, a bouncing ball of muscle topped by a shiny bald head, met him at the flap. 'Scrutator Flydd! We'd given up hope of seeing you –'

'Where's General Grism?' Flydd interrupted. 'He's not dead?'

'He's over the far side. Shall I call him?'

'You'll do. What's our situation?'

Tham plucked at an ear the shape and colour of a dried peach. 'We've lost fourteen thousand men, dead, and another six thousand will never fight again. The Aachim have lost six thousand and, even with their grudging aid, we're failing fast.'

'Grudging aid?' Flydd said sharply.

'I – I'd hesitate to call our allies *cowards,* surr, but . . .'

'Spit it out, General.'

'Even before the field went down, the Aachim never gave what we asked of them. They always hung back. And since then, I've seen only defence of their own lines. When we counterattack, they never come with us . . .'

'It's a long time since they've fought to the bitter end,' Flydd mused, 'knowing that, if they lost, all would be lost. Their noble exterior, it seems, conceals a rotten core. More than once they've failed in the uttermost hour, when the difference between victory and defeat was simply the courage to fight on, no matter what the odds. Even so, the Histories tell us that the Aachim have more often fallen through treachery than military might. Well, General, if that's the kind of allies we have, we must fight all the harder.'

'And die all the sooner. I beg you, Scrutator, allow me to sound the retreat or by dawn there won't be a man left.'

'Sound it,' said Flydd, 'though if the enemy *truly* want to destroy us, that will give them the chance to do the job by nightfall.'

'You doubt that they do?'

'It's doesn't seem to be their main objective,' said Flydd.

'Then what are they really here for?' Tham exclaimed.

'That's what we'd all like to know.'

Tham gave orders to his signaller, who ran to the edge of the hill. Horns began to sound. Irisis watched the scrutator from the corner of her eye as he paced back and forth, looking sick. Nothing had gone right since they'd come to Snizort. The Council of Scrutators had ordered him to destroy the lyrinx node-drainer, for similar devices at other vital nodes had immobilised clankers and led to the destruction of the armies they escorted.

Flydd and Irisis, aided by the seeker, Ullii, had stolen into the underground maze of Snizort. Ullii had led them through the tar saturated tunnels to the uncanny chamber of the node-drainer, and Flydd had succeeded in destroying it. Unfortunately that had caused the destruction of the node itself, in a catastrophic explosion. All the fields, weak as well as strong, had vanished, rendering clankers and constructs useless, and leaving the army of sixty thousand men, plus twenty thousand Aachim, unprotected.

Such a force should have been a match for twenty-five thousand lyrinx on an open battlefield, but Snizort was surrounded by a maze of tar bogs, mine pits, windrows made from cleared woodland, traps and ancient tar runs that the enemy had set alight. And when the lyrinx emerged from their underground labyrinth they were far more numerous than expected – near to thirty-five thousand. The soldiers, lacking the armour of the clankers, had been slaughtered.

Flangers stood guard outside the command tent as Flydd and Tham went in. Irisis stalked the rim of the hill, looking down at the battlefields but seeing nothing. After all their work, and all their agony down in the tar pits, the result was worse than if they had done nothing.

Yet she'd had a personal triumph in Snizort. Under extreme duress, and with Ullii's help, Irisis had recovered the talent that had been hidden, or suppressed, since her fourth birthday. Her ability to draw power from the field was back. Irisis was no longer a fraud, but a true crafter at last.

All her life she'd obsessed about getting her talent back but, now she had it, it gave her no joy. Why was that? Was she incapable of taking pleasure in her own achievements? Or was it that nothing would ever come of it?

A shiver passed up her spine. Her life's dream, after the war was over, was to be a jeweller. Irisis had a rare gift for that craft and had been making jewellery in her spare time since she was a child. Once the war ended, and controller artisans were no longer required, she planned to follow her dream. However, from the moment they'd escaped the tar pits, Irisis had been troubled by intimations of mortality. She felt doomed.

Despite her earlier talk, today or tomorrow must see the end of them. Not even the scrutator, wily dog that he undoubtedly was, could get them out of this fiasco. There was no hope of escape in the air-floater, for it had been damaged in the explosion of the node and would take days to repair, assuming it had survived the battle at all.

Discovering that she had returned to her starting point, Irisis sat down on the edge of the hill, to the rear of the tents, trying to get a picture of what was going on. Everywhere she looked, desperate men fought and died. A lyrinx could take on two human soldiers at once and win, and often, three or four.

There were few enemy in the air, though that was not surprising. Many lyrinx could fly, but on this heavy world they had to supplement their wings by using the Secret Art, if they had a talent for it. Even then, flight took so much out of them that they could do little else at the same time. But to fly here, they would have to draw on a distant node, and only the most powerful mancers of all could do that.

Irisis saw a pair directly above, riding the noonday thermals, conserving their strength. They were watching the formations on the battlefield and relaying simple messages to their brethren on the ground.

Scanning the sky, Irisis caught sight of an oddly-shaped speck just above the eastern horizon. It did not look like a lyrinx. Another speck appeared to the left of the first, and a third to the right. The air was hazy; she could not quite make them out. Squinting until her eyes watered, she saw that the specks were slightly elongated, with a smaller mark beneath each.

More specks appeared, until there were a dozen. Irisis ran to the command tent. 'Scrutator! Scrutator!'

He looked up from the map table where he and Tham were moving pointers, planning the retreat. Scribes were taking down the orders and passing them to a stream of messengers outside.

'Go away, Crafter,' he snapped. 'This can't wait for anything.'

'Come outside, quickly! You won't believe it.'

Flydd peered at her from beneath an eyebrow that snaked from one side of his forehead to the other. At the look on her face he dropped his marker and hurried, in that crab-lurch of his, to the entrance.

She drew him around the back of the tent. 'Look!' Irisis threw out her arm.

The shapes were unmistakable now. 'Air-floaters!' said Flydd. 'Twelve of them, and coming fast. So *that's* what the Council was up to.'

'Any reinforcement is welcome,' said Tham, pushing between them, 'though a dozen air-floaters can do precious little to help us now.'

'Let's wait and see,' said Flydd. 'Can you rustle up some breakfast, Irisis?'

In twenty minutes the air-floaters were overhead, flying in perfect formation, four wide and three high. They made a circle over the top of the battlefield and the fighting broke off as humans, Aachim and lyrinx stood by to see what their intentions were. Being so light, air-floaters could be driven by a distant field.

'They seem to be working to a plan,' said Irisis, wolfing down a gritty hunk of black bread. It was tasteless army fare, but she was too hungry to care.

The machines had maintained formation all the way around the circuit. 'It's almost . . . It's as if they're all controlled by one mind.' Flydd carved slivers off a distinctly green cheese and popped them into his mouth, two at a time. 'Though I know that's not possible.'

Flangers came up beside them, one hand resting on the hilt of his sheathed sword. 'They'd better look out!'

The two lyrinx sentries were now converging on the ranked air-floaters. One corkscrewed down to the left side, the other plummeted directly towards the top-right machine. The attack was co-ordinated so they would reach their targets at the same time. And air-floaters were vulnerable. One slash of a lyrinx's claws could tear the gasbag right open. Moreover, an attack from directly above was difficult to defend against.

The air-floaters shifted slightly out of line. Just before the higher lyrinx reached its target there came a flash that lit up the creature. Its wings folded up and it fell out of the air. Rotating slowly, it disappeared behind a boulder-topped hill.

'What was that?' said Irisis.

'I don't know,' the scrutator replied.

The corkscrewing lyrinx beat its great wings, coming out of the dive right beside the gasbag of the air-floater. It gave a measured slash but, before its claws could part the fabric, it too was hit by a flash of light. The lyrinx's wings churned, it somersaulted backwards and fell, upside down. Halfway to the ground it seemed to recover, flapped several times and almost broke its fall, but lost it and plunged into the bloody mud of the battlefield at a speed that must have pulverised every bone in its great body.

'I don't sense the Art,' said Flydd, puzzled. 'What are the scrutators up to?'

The battle had not resumed. The air-floaters pulled back into that perfect formation, now hanging motionless above the battlefield, their rotors turning just enough to counteract the gentle motion of the air.

'I wonder . . .?' said Flydd. 'Who on the Council has the boldness for this kind of venture, and the foresight to know that it would be needed?'

Irisis had a fair idea, but she would just wait and see. From the topmost middle air-floater, rods extended to either side, all the way to the neighbouring machines, which latched on. A roll of shimmering fabric fell, was caught as it passed in front of the middle row of machines, and again at the bottom.

'What on earth are they doing?' said Tham.

No one answered. The air-floaters moved ever so slightly this way and that, bending the rods and pulling the fabric into a gentle concavity. It took a long time, for the slightest change in the breeze tended to drift the machines apart, and much manoeuvring was required to get them aligned again.

'It's a mirror,' said Irisis. 'But what is it for?'

'They're not using the Art at all,' Flydd replied. 'They simply hit the flying lyrinx with a dazzling beam. Lyrinx have poorer eyesight than we do, and their eyes are sensitive to bright light. They only fight in the middle of the day if they have to. The beam disrupted the Art they were using to keep aloft, and they were too close to the ground to recover.'

'They're moving,' said Flangers.

The twelve air-floaters wheeled in perfect formation. The sun flashed off the mirror, the beam lighting up a strip of ground some twenty spans long.

The beam crept across the battlefield, to play on a group of lyrinx attacking a line of soldiers. Irisis focussed on the scene with a spyglass. The lyrinx threw up their arms, trying to shield themselves from the boiling glare, then broke and ran, staggering from side to side. One bold soldier attacked from behind, felling his quarry with a sword thrust between the back plates, but the others escaped.

The beam stepped to another group of lyrinx, who broke like the first. As it tracked across the ground, the mud began to steam gently. The next detachment, some fifty lyrinx, resisted longer than the others, but within a minute they too had fled.

'With a lens, anyone can focus the sun's rays so as to set paper or cloth alight,' said Irisis, 'though I don't think that's their aim here.'

'The beam isn't tightly focussed,' said Flydd, putting down his spyglass, 'but it's enough to dazzle and confuse. And blind too, should you look directly at it.'

The general had a calculating look in his eye. 'Shall I order the counterattack, surr?'

'Wait,' said Flydd. 'If the mirror tears in the wind, or the

13

lyrinx make a determined attack on it, we'll be more exposed than we are now.'

The enemy now attacked desperately, but the beam stopped each onslaught. Within an hour the lyrinx began to fall back en masse, whereupon the beam moved towards the ranks of enemy surrounding the walled perimeter of Snizort.

Suddenly half a dozen lyrinx took to the air, well apart, rising into the path of the air-floaters. 'This'll be interesting,' said Tham. 'They'll never move the mirror quickly enough.'

The air-floaters did not attempt to. The first lyrinx to approach took many crossbow bolts to the head and chest. It tumbled over and over, wings cracking in the wind, before slamming into the ground down the slope behind the command tent. The second suffered a similar fate, for the air-floaters were packed with archers. The other lyrinx flapped away. In the air they were too vulnerable. The mirror beam continued its inexorable progress.

'Something's happening,' said Irisis in the early afternoon. She was watching enemy movements inside the southern wall of Snizort. Lyrinx were running backwards and forwards through the drifting smoke. 'Looks like they're sending out reinforcements.'

'I don't think so,' said the scrutator.

Flangers said quietly, 'They're carrying boxes and bags.'

'Where's my spyglass?' Flydd demanded.

'You left it by the tent,' Irisis replied, passing him her glass. He focussed it and said, 'You've got good eyes, soldier.'

'That's why I was chosen as shooter.'

'What are they doing?' Irisis and Tham asked together.

'A group of . . . perhaps one hundred have formed up behind the southern wall,' said Flydd. 'They've all got big packs on, which is unusual, and they're carrying what appear to be boxes, or cases. Or coffins!'

'The same thing happened yesterday morning,' said a sentry standing nearby. 'Even before the node exploded their fliers were heading south-west, carrying huge packages.'

'Is that so?' said Flydd. 'How odd.'

'The tar's burning underground,' said Irisis, 'and it would be the very devil to put out. They'd have to abandon Snizort, whatever the result of the battle.'

'I wonder if those cases contain flesh-formed creatures?' Flydd gave Irisis a keen glance. 'If we could only . . .'

'I hope I'm wrong about what you're thinking,' said Irisis.

'Regretfully,' said Flydd, 'you're not. They're weapons we don't know how to deal with, but if we had one or two little ones to study, we might be able to find a defence against them.'

The mirror beam now carved across the eastern wall, towards the enemy ranks on the other side. It was not causing as much confusion as before, but the lyrinx were still retreating from it.

Fighting broke out near the northern wall. A band of some twenty lyrinx had advanced in a rush that took them right through a line of human soldiers. The beam did not shift to counter this new threat, but kept moving back and forth across the ranks of the enemy, on the far side of Snizort.

'That was just a diversion,' cried Irisis. 'They're retreating.'

The group of lyrinx carrying the baggage rose into the air together then spread apart, holding low to the ground until they crossed the southern wall, where there was little fighting. There they climbed rapidly, disappearing into the smoky haze that hung over the fortress.

'They're mighty mancers,' said Flydd, 'to fly under these conditions. Whatever they're carrying, it's more important than winning the battle.'

There was no way to bring them down; the lyrinx were out of range of the catapults and javelards, and the fleet of airfloaters did not seem to have noticed. The flying lyrinx reappeared out of the haze, flew into a pall drifting from the molten remains of the node, and vanished.

The scrutator shook his head. 'I think we're going to regret that.'

TWO

Inside Snizort, the remaining lyrinx began to swarm over the western and southern walls. Fighting their way through the few human defenders nearby, they headed south-west down the tar-crusted valley. One by one the detachments outside the walls turned to follow them. Those lyrinx not yet called to the orderly retreat fought on.

The air-floaters turned together, drifting closer so as to direct the beam at a skirmish on the northern wall. The lyrinx must have been waiting for that, for three catapults fired at once and their balls of stone went through the mirror sail, tearing gashes which spread until the fabric hung down in tatters. It was released, the shreds winking in the air like tinsel. Each machine produced many smaller mirrors, the size of large shields, which the soldiers aimed individually. The effect was not as dramatic, but the lyrinx still broke when the beams struck them.

Eiryn Muss, Flydd's personal prober, or spy, came up beside him, whispering in his ear. Flydd looked surprised. He whispered back and Muss, an entirely nondescript fellow in his present disguise, slid away.

'What was that about?' said Irisis.

'Scrutators' business,' he replied tersely.

The air-floaters continued their work for another hour, until, suddenly, it was all over.

'The last of the lyrinx are retreating,' said Flydd. 'We've survived – at least until nightfall.'

'So you think they'll come back?'

'You can't always tell with lyrinx. Since they've had

to abandon Snizort, they may not. But then again, the opportunity to destroy our army in the dark may be too tempting to resist.'

The air-floaters were rotoring towards the command hill, but they did not all make it. A squad of lyrinx catapult operators had remained in position, camouflaged, waiting for just that moment.

A ball went right through the cabin of the lowest air-floater, shattering it into splinters and sending at least a dozen people to their deaths. Another missile struck the ovoid bag of a second machine, deflating it instantly. Fortunately it was, by then, only a few spans above the flank of the hill. The crash made a loud noise, though the machine did not seem to be damaged further. The other ten air-floaters made it to the ground a safe distance from the catapults.

'The lead one's flying the Council flag,' said Flydd, squinting through his spyglass again. 'I wonder who can be in command? Surely not Ghorr. The chief scrutator would never do anything to risk his mangy hide.'

'We'll soon find out,' said Irisis.

'I'd better go to meet them.'

Again Irisis felt that foreboding. She was following the scrutator when he turned and said, coolly, 'You won't be needed, Crafter. Wait here for my orders. If you would be so good as to ask Fyn-Mah to come down?'

The sudden, cold formality was like a slap in the face. He kept going so she headed back to the tents, found Perquisitor Fyn-Mah and gave her the message, then resumed her pacing around the hill.

Flydd did not hurry, for he also had an uncomfortable premonition. Despite their truly heroic efforts, the mission to destroy the node-drainer had been a failure, doomed before it began. The device the Council had given him had been faulty, perhaps deliberately so. Because of that, a third of the army had been lost. Flydd could not avoid the blame, nor would he, had he been able to. The soldiers lives had been in his hands,

17

and he had failed them. Though inured to war, and hardened by it, every death weighed on him.

But another leader might have won this battle, he thought, despite the loss of the node. Another leader might have seen that the mission to the node-drainer was fatally flawed. Another leader might have done a hundred things to avert this disaster. Having done none of them, he could only feel culpable. If duty required him to pay, he would do so.

Nonetheless, his heart lurched when he saw who was getting out of the air-floater that had crash-landed. A tall, deep chested man, apparently in hale middle age, he was broad shouldered, dark haired, full bearded and of noble good looks, except when his smile revealed those vulpine teeth. It was Ghorr, the chief scrutator, and his temper looked fouler than usual. Behind him were ranked the ten other members of the Council of Scrutators, four women and six men. All were bruised, dishevelled and furiously angry.

Though Flydd was still a scrutator, he was no longer on the Council. He ran down to help Ghorr over the side, but the big man smacked his hand away. Blood droplets clustered on his left eyebrow from a gash at his hairline.

'I'm glad you've come,' said Flydd, putting out his hand. 'Your mirror is a fine innovation, though it'll only work once. The next time we meet the enemy they'll have a tactic to neutralise it.'

The chief scrutator ignored the gesture. 'I should never have allowed you back!'

'You should have led by example,' said Flydd, 'and done the job yourself. But that was never your way, was it, Ghorr?'

Ghorr brushed General Tham's hand aside, too, and panted to the top of the hill, where he paused to survey the battlefield. It was a pose, of course – he'd had hours to study the scene from the air-floater.

The other scrutators followed, and not even Flydd's former friend, Halie, the dark little scrutator, had a sympathetic glance for her former colleague. Flydd had expected no less. Though few knew it, the scrutators answered to a higher power – the shadowy Numinator. Someone must take the blame and he was the man responsible.

Ghorr was about to speak when the last of the air-floaters edged up over the hill, to settle directly in front of the command tent. A small man climbed over the side, rather awkwardly, for he had only one arm. Flydd gave an involuntary gasp. If there was one person he had not expected to see, it was this man.

As the air-floater lifted off and headed down the slope, the man turned and the sun caught a gleaming platinum mask that covered the left side of his face. Twin metal bands encircled his head like a helmet, and the hole in the cheek plate of the mask had been repaired. The single eye had the glare of a deranged man.

'You won't get away with it this time, Scrutator Flydd,' said Acting Scrutator Jal-Nish Hlar.

Irisis was catching a moment's rest in the shade behind a tent when Perquisitor Fyn-Mah shook her awake. Fyn-Mah was petite, black of hair and eye, with a stern, frozen beauty that deterred rather than attracted. The perquisitor normally exuded dignity, but now she was flushed as if she had run a long race.

'Get your artisan's pliance and your sword, and follow me, Crafter.'

'I have them,' said Irisis tersely. They did not like each other; moreover, Irisis's sharp tongue had once done Fyn-Mah a wrong and she did not know how to repair it.

'Now!' rapped the perquisitor. 'Scrutator's orders, Crafter.'

Irisis knew better than to question her. A perquisitor, the rank below scrutator, could give orders to the master of a city and expect them to be obeyed without question. Besides, Irisis knew why Flydd wanted her out of the way. Ghorr would not have forgotten her escape from Nennifer, and he still wanted to know how she'd killed Jal-Nish's mancer up on the aqueduct at the manufactory. It was a secret that threatened all mancers.

19

Fyn-Mah reappeared carrying a small pack and they slipped through the guards and over the edge of the hill into a shrubby gully which ran away from the battlefield. Flangers was standing in the shadows halfway down. He nodded to Fyn-Mah, then fell in beside Irisis.

'What's going on?' she said in a low voice.

'I'm to assist you to the limit of my ability,' he said, which was no help at all.

Fyn-Mah kept to the centre of the gully, where the cover was densest, and after ten minutes they reached the foot of the hill. One of the air-floaters was tethered only a stone's throw away. She headed for it.

'Act as if we own it,' Fyn-Mah said over her shoulder.

They emerged from the scrub directly behind the machine. Fyn-Mah stood up and rapped on the side. The vessel suspended from the airbag was about eight spans long and three wide, shaped like a round-ended boat, but flimsy, being made from stretched rope, canvas and light framing timbers. The deck was canvas, the sides just rope netting that served to stop people from falling overboard, while a central cabin about four spans by two provided shelter, sleeping space and a tiny separate galley. It was also made of canvas framed with timber, with a light timber door suspended on leather hinges.

The air-floater was a different design to the one Flydd had brought from the east. A ten-bladed rotor, shielded at the front by a wire grid, was mounted on a stanchion at the stern of the craft. The rotor could be swung on a steering arm, making the big machine quite manoeuvrable. The controller was fixed to the steering arm. Above the rotor, mounted on a bracket, sat a complex mechanism in a metal housing, with a small water barrel on top. A pipe ran from the mechanism up to the airbag, and another out to the rear. It appeared to be a device to create floater gas, which, Irisis thought, was a considerable improvement on having to fly all the way to a suitable mine to replenish it.

A soldier, lounging against the rail, let out a squawk. He

leapt for his spear, let it fall when he saw the perquisitor's badge, and snapped to attention.

Fyn-Mah climbed through the rope mesh and nodded to the captain of the guard. Irisis and Flangers followed. There were ten soldiers on board, counting the captain of the guard.

'We're going to take a look inside the wall of Snizort,' Fyn-Mah said. 'What's your name, Pilot?'

The pilot was a young woman with hair the bright yellow of a daffodil, freckles all over her thin face, and a charming gap between her front teeth. She was small and slender; all pilots were, for the weight mattered.

'Inouye, surr.' The pilot bowed her head, unwilling to look the perquisitor in the face, but cast a pleading glance sideways at the captain of the guard. A young man with sunburnt cheeks and a thin, pointed nose, he would not look at Fyn-Mah either but inflated his cheeks and frowned. He did not want to deny a perquisitor, but he answered to another master. 'We're ordered to wait here,' he said, studying the canvas floor.

'By whom?'

'Acting Scrutator Jal-Nish Hlar. This is his air-floater.'

'My orders come from *Scrutator* Xervish Flydd, the commander-in-chief of all the forces here.' Fyn-Mah showed him a parchment which contained the scrutator's seal.

The captain gulped, nodded and gave the word to the pilot. Inouye slipped an open helm of crystals and wires over her head, took hold of the controller and screwed up her face as she sought for a distant, usable field. The rotor began to spin. The soldiers cast off the tethers and the air-floater rose out of the grass.

'Stay low,' said Fyn-Mah, checking an instrument concealed in her hand. 'Head that way, keeping just above the enemy's catapult height.' She held out her arm, directing the pilot.

The air-floater rotored gently towards the northern wall of Snizort, crossing over a number of smaller tar seeps where the hard resource had been mined down in benched cones, then a valley that had once been full of the same material. Now only black patches remained, some still smoking, for the lyrinx had fired the tar runs at the beginning of the battle. They saw no sign of the enemy.

'You're taking a risk, aren't you?' Irisis said quietly to Fyn-Mah. They were standing up the front by themselves.

'The scrutator has given me a valid instruction,' the perquisitor said stiffly, then, thawing a little, 'Besides, I am incurably identified with Xervish Flydd. If he falls, so must I.'

'You could change allegiances,' Irisis said slyly, to see how Fyn-Mah would respond.

'Change once and you are forever tainted, your word worthless. I have sworn to my scrutator and will not break my oath, whatever it costs me.'

'There are many who would not be so noble.' She spoke without thinking.

'I'll watch my back,' Fyn-Mah said icily. Especially when you're behind me, was the implication.

Irisis had not meant her words the way they were taken, but it was too late to withdraw them.

The wall of Snizort was four spans high and equally thick, topped with thorn bushes scarred here and there by fire, and torn and smashed by catapult balls. The wall had been breached in five places and was unmanned.

They cruised along inside. The breaches, and the smashed gate, were piled with the bodies of the dead, lyrinx and human. Other dead were scattered across the enclosed space. Irisis saw no sign of live enemy, though from a high point she could see columns of lyrinx streaming away to the south-west in the direction of the Sea of Thurkad. Their withdrawal had been astonishingly swift.

Smoke issued from a tarry bog and several of the pits, which would make access to the underground city difficult. The ground above the node-drainer, which had risen up in a red-hot dome just before the node exploded, was now a fractured, fuming hole. Further off, though still inside the walls, the Great Seep formed a bottomless cauldron of tar about a league across. The source of the tar at Snizort, it was steaming gently. The exploded node lay some leagues to the north, and underground, but it was too smoky to see that far.

The sun touched the western horizon. Irisis looked the other way, back towards the command hill. The scrutators must be inside the tent, with Flydd. She turned towards Snizort again. 'There can't be any creature left alive underground,' she muttered. 'The whole place is on fire.'

'That's where you're wrong,' Fyn-Mah replied. 'Tar burns hot, but it burns slowly. Most of the city will yet be untouched. Let's go.'

'*In there?* We'll choke before we've gone a dozen spans.'

'The fire draws air to it. Away from the burning core, the air should be fresh. Our orders are to get inside, if we can, and recover any of the flesh-formed creatures left alive.'

'We may get in,' said Irisis, 'though I doubt we'll ever get out again.' She said it fatalistically. Having expected to die for so long now, in so many hideous ways, she was no longer moved by the thought of danger. She indicated the largest pit. 'That's where the scrutator and I entered last time. Though . . . we had the seeker to find the way for us.'

Irisis wished Ullii were here now. Objects powered by the Secret Art appeared in the little seeker's mental lattice, which was how they'd located the node-drainer. Ullii could also see people with a talent for the Art, and most lyrinx. If she were here now, they would be able to avoid any enemy who remained inside, and quickly find the flesh-formed creatures that were their target. But Ullii had disappeared.

'Go down into that pit, Pilot Inouye,' said Fyn-Mah, pointing towards the largest, which contained only a haze of smoke. 'Soldiers, ready your weapons.'

Inouye's green eyes widened, but she nodded stiffly. The air-floater drifted towards the pit, just a spear-cast above the ground. The soldiers pointed their crossbows over the side while Irisis scanned the black, lifeless terrain. Nothing moved; with luck, all the lyrinx were gone.

They floated over the pit, a conical excavation in tar-saturated sandstone, with a ledge path spiralling down. Inouye vented floater gas. The air-floater lurched, steadied and began to descend through a rising trail of smoke.

'Where do we go from here?' asked Fyn-Mah, at her elbow.

Irisis did not answer at once. The black rock was featureless and it was taking her eyes some time to adjust. Tunnels began to appear, extending off the path. There were a dozen, at least, and smoke oozed from several. How could she possibly tell? It had been dark when she had come down previously, the night before last.

'We went down 741 steps,' she said, counting them aloud.

Fyn-Mah did the same and checked her instrument again. 'There!' She pointed to a tunnel near the base of the pit. 'Take us to that point, Pilot.'

The whirring of the rotor died to a gentle tick as they descended into the black pit. The reek, hanging heavier than air at the bottom, stung their eyes. They came alongside the tunnel and the soldiers tossed out grappling hooks, pulling the air-floater up against the steps.

'We're going in,' Fyn-Mah said to the captain. 'Bring five of your men. Scrutator Flydd has ordered me to recover certain . . . items from inside. The remaining four soldiers will guard the air-floater.'

The captain shuffled his feet. He looked about fifteen years old and Irisis felt sorry for him. 'I have orders to remain at my post.'

'Those orders are superseded.' She stared him down. 'This mission is for the good of the war, soldier, and we can't do it alone.'

He regarded his boots, glanced up at her, then nodded. 'So you won't mind giving your orders in writing.'

Fyn-Mah took a small piece of paper from her chest pack, scribbled something on it and stamped it with her personal seal. The captain read the document and put it in his wallet.

'Wait here,' Fyn-Mah said to Pilot Inouye. 'If there's danger, go up out of range and keep watch.'

'What if you don't come back?'

'Wait until dawn. If we haven't returned by then, you are released back to your master.'

The underground had a different feeling from Irisis's previous visit. Then it had been a vibrant, working city, still occupied by the lyrinx. Now it was a black, reeking hell where the ceilings had collapsed into heaps of rubble, the floors into fuming sink-holes and dead lyrinx lay everywhere. Fumes wisped down the tunnels like black spectres; sudden winds blew hot and cold; and, always in the distance, was the seething, bubbling crackle of burning tar.

They struggled through into a less damaged area, where they sought for the flesh-formed creature pens for hours without success. Fyn-Mah called out each turn and intersection as they passed it, Irisis noting them down so they could find the way out again. The air here was relatively clean, apart from drifting wisps of fume. Some of the tunnels were still lit by lanterns fuelled with distilled tar spirit, giving the air an oily tang, but they were guttering now.

Fyn-Mah stopped where the tunnel split into four. Consulting directions on a scrap of paper, she scowled. 'We must've taken a wrong turn. Do you recognise this place, Irisis?'

Irisis shook her head. 'The tunnels all look the same.'

'You're not much use, are you?'

'Ullii was leading us the other night,' said Irisis. 'It was dark, as I told you.'

'I can find my way around in the dark,' said Flangers. 'You get used to that, up on the shooter's platform. What if I were to take a few soldiers and go that way?' He pointed to the right. 'You could check the other tunnels.'

Fyn-Mah frowned. 'I don't want to split up, but I suppose there's no alternative. Irisis, take Flangers and him,' she indicated a soldier so young that he had no trace of beard, 'and go that way. We'll follow this tunnel. If you don't find anything in half an hour, come back to this point.' She scratched a zigzag mark into the wall with her sword. 'Don't get lost.'

*

'Let's have a look through this door,' Irisis said to Flangers. They'd searched dozens of chambers but had found nothing.

He gestured over his shoulder to the young soldier, a pink cheeked, frightened lad called Ivar. Irisis pushed the door open. Inside, in a damp, mist-laden space, stood three rows of objects that resembled chest-high pumpkins connected by grey vinelike cords.

'What do you suppose they're for?' asked Flangers.

'Something to do with flesh-forming, I expect,' said Irisis.

He swallowed. That dark Art was beyond the comprehension of the greatest hero.

Other rooms contained similar objects, all with a vaguely organic appearance, all equally inexplicable. They passed out into a round chamber with a series of five closed doors on the far side.

'What a warren!' Flangers wiped sweat from his brow.

He opened the door on the left and uttered a low whistle. The room held ten cages, well separated, and inside each was a creature unlike anything he had ever seen: all horns, spines, teeth and armour plating. Each was different, and all were dead, killed by blows to the skull.

Irisis clutched the bars of the first cage, staring at the flesh-formed monstrosity inside. The grey-green, coated teeth were like shards of glass. 'Imagine that beast sticking its teeth into your leg while you're trying to fight the enemy.'

'It could bite straight through bone,' said Flangers. 'And it looks fast. It'd be hard to attack, too.'

'Doubtless they're breeding thousands of them. Ivar,' Irisis said to the young soldier, whose eyes were sticking out like boiled eggs, 'run and tell the perquisitor we've found them. Can you find your way back to the place where we separated?'

'Yes, Crafter.' Ivar ran off, glad to be going.

Irisis continued around the room. She was examining a beast whose maw was half the length of its body when Flangers called out, 'Irisis! This one's still alive.'

The creature, a heavy-headed monster with as many teeth as a crocodile and a row of yellow-tipped spines all the way down its backbone, lay on its side, its head half-covered in blood. The mouth was open and a trickle of grey matter oozed from one rimmed nostril. The chest did not move. As Irisis approached, the yellow and black eye shifted slightly, then the warty lid came down over it.

'It's dead now. We'll leave Fyn-Mah to check them,' said Irisis. 'Let's try the next room.'

It proved much the same as the first, and all the flesh-formed creatures were dead. Irisis shuddered and headed to the third room. Here the beasts were smaller, still spined and fanged but less armoured, more fleet-footed and with larger brain cases.

'These look smarter than the others,' she said, studying a creature the length of a large dog. Even dead, it made her feel uneasy.

'They've not long been killed,' said Flangers.

'They're thick-skulled. It could take them quite a while to die. Let's try the doors on the far side.'

They took the door furthest to the right. It was dark inside, but as soon as she entered Irisis could tell that this was different. There was no smell of blood, and the stench of fresh ordure was strong.

She motioned Flangers to hold up his lantern. The room had the same layout as the others but the creatures were alive. They were smaller still – the size of small dogs – and as the light fell on them they clawed at the bars.

'We'll take one or two back,' Irisis said, walking along the row. She was wondering how they could carry the cages without the beasts inside striking at them.

As she reached the other end of the room, an unseen door opened and a lyrinx stepped in. It was almost as startled as she was.

Irisis took a step backwards, overcome by panic. The lyrinx, a tall female, carried a bloodstained club. For an instant it stared at her, then swung the club. Irisis cried, 'Flangers, look out!' and threw herself behind one of the cages.

Letting out a deafening bellow, the lyrinx swatted the cage

out of the way. Irisis scuttled between two more, knowing she was not going to make it. The lyrinx was too strong and fast. It sprang onto the cages, lifting the club high. The blow would not just cave in her skull, it would splatter her brains halfway across the room.

The bars bent under the weight, one foot slipped through and the fanged creature inside sank its teeth in. The lyrinx tried to jerk free, stumbled and came crashing down on a pair of cages.

One was crushed flat, along with the creature inside. The other burst open, liberating its occupant, which darted into the darkness behind the cages.

Irisis scuttled out of the way as the lyrinx struggled to get up. The little creature was savaging its foot, snarling with bloodlust. The lyrinx roared, found its feet and, with a mighty swing, sent the cage and its attacker creature flying across the room to smash into the wall. It turned in her direction, limping badly. She drew her weapon.

Flangers appeared by her side, sword out. She had never been so glad to see anyone.

'Are you any good with that?' he panted.

'Not much. I normally use a crossbow.' Irisis had done sword training, and had a natural aptitude, but little combat experience.

'Stay to my left, one step back. Keep the point up.'

She moved into position. 'What if we were to smash open a few more cages?' Already she was deferring to his greater experience, a rare thing for her. 'A few of these creatures would give even a lyrinx something to think about.' She had heard tales of the flesh-formed nylatl that had so terrorised Tiaan, and later, Nish.

'We'd want to be sure the beasts would attack the lyrinx, and not us,' Flangers said.

The lyrinx was only half a dozen steps away, advancing slowly. It was a big one, head and shoulders above them, with scars on its right cheek and across its breast plates.

'Looks as though it's seen a fight or two,' she said.

'And won them. It would be handy if Fyn-Mah turned up about now,' he said dryly.

The lyrinx kept coming. With its size and reach, there was no need for subtlety or fancy footwork.

'What's the plan?' Irisis hissed.

'Fight for our bloody lives!'

The lyrinx moved to within striking distance, lunged and slashed with one arm. Irisis barely saw it move, nor the flash of Flangers's sword, but blood spurted from the palm of its hand. It jerked away. The cut was deep, though not incapacitating. They had an instant's respite before the mighty thighs bunched and it hurled itself at him, arms going like scythes.

Flangers threw himself to his right; Irisis went the other way. It ignored her and pursued the soldier, the claws of its bloody hand raking him from shoulder to elbow. Another blow tore the seat out of his pants and four gouges across his buttocks.

Flangers fell to his knees and the sword clanged on the floor. He dived for it. The lyrinx went after him, leaving bloody footprints. Flangers could not reach the sword in time; the lyrinx was going to slaughter him.

Irisis went up on tiptoes, crossed the distance with two strides and thrust at the lyrinx's exposed side. The sword went between two plates, slid between the ribs and jammed. She heaved but could not pull it out. The lyrinx bellowed, spun around and sprang at her, the sword quivering with every movement.

She dived over a small cage, lifted it and in one movement hurled it at the lyrinx's face. It batted it aside like a ball, then tore the sword out and flung it at her. She ducked and scampered up between the rows, not knowing what she was doing, only that she was defenceless. As she approached the rear door, a second lyrinx burst through it. And after it, a third.

THREE

Xervish Flydd knuckled puffy eyes as he prepared to face his tormentors. The Council of Scrutators occupied four sides of the makeshift table in the command tent. He was seated at one corner, which meant that he could not see the whole group at one time. It was a particular disadvantage at an inquisition. And, not having slept for two nights, he was in no condition to match wits with Ghorr.

All eleven members of the Council were present. Their late intervention had only saved the disaster from becoming a catastrophe and it would be a sorry remnant of the army that left here, abandoning thousands of precious, useless clankers. To protect themselves, the Council had to have a scalp. The scrutators looked as though they relished the duty.

Jal-Nish, being only an acting scrutator, was not permitted to sit at the table; though, having an interest in the proceedings, he had been allowed to attend as an observer. His chair was placed directly behind Flydd's, who could not see him without turning his head. He dared not. To look away from the inquisition would be a sign of weakness. Flydd could feel that single, malevolent eye boring into his back.

'Scrutator Flydd,' began Ghorr, without doing Flydd the courtesy of standing or even looking in his direction. It was another bad sign. 'You stand accused of dereliction of duty, fraudulent misrepresentation of your abilities, gross incompetence occasioning a military disaster, exceeding your authority in negotiating with an alien race, corruptly making concessions to that race, contempt of the Council, harbouring a fugitive, wilful assault on the person of an acting scrutator while suspended from the Council, knowingly causing the death of a mancer in the legitimate pursuit of her duties, failure to adequately protect a mine and manufactory under your command . . .'

Flydd's mind wandered. He knew it was a deadly thing to do, but the list of charges made it clear there was no way out. When the Council genuinely wanted to discipline a scrutator, the charges were brief and specific. When they wanted to destroy one, they put down everything they could come up with.

He felt so very tired. He could have laid his head on the table and slept. Was there any point in defending himself? Might it not be better to remain silent, even though that would be taken as an admission of guilt? They might just execute him.

The errant thought made him grimace. The Council would not allow him the luxury of death until they'd wrung such torment from him that sensitives would be having nightmares for fifty leagues around. He knew how they operated. After all, he'd been one of them for decades, and suffered at their hands before.

Besides, he would not be the only one to fall. Ghorr would destroy everyone associated with him – dear Irisis, little Ullii and her unborn child, Eiryn Muss, Fyn-Mah, and all his soldiers, advisers, friends and relatives. When the scrutators made an example of their own it was worthy of a whole page in the Histories.

What could he do to save them, or himself? What defence was there when the Council had covered every eventuality? Xervish Flydd could think of none.

Scrutator Ghorr finished his iteration of the charges, shuffled the papers and turned to his left. 'Scrutator Fusshte?'

Fusshte, acting as recorder, was a meagre, ill-made man. Pallid baldness made a cruciform shape through oily black hair. His eyes were reptilian, while the jutting teeth gave him a feral look. He made a mark on a document, nodded and passed it to Ghorr.

Ghorr cleared his throat and finally met the eyes of the man he was trying. 'How do you plead, Scrutator Flydd? Be swift! Humanity stands in very peril of its survival.'

'In that case,' snapped Flydd, whose only defence was to attack, 'why are you wasting time on farcical blame-shifting? The Council knows I followed my orders to the letter. Your instructions were faulty. You should be on trial, not I.'

'The tiredest ploy in the world,' yawned Fusshte.

Flydd rotated in his chair and locked gazes with the secretary. The game of intimidating an opponent was one every scrutator knew, but Flydd was more skilled at it than most. He'd always detested Fusshte, and had voted against his elevation to scrutator. Moreover, Fusshte had a dirty little secret and Flydd knew it. Its revelation would not be enough to destroy the secretary, but it would taint him in the eyes of his fellows.

Neither could draw on the field here, of course, but scrutators had at hand older, subtler powers, ways of weakening an enemy's will. Flydd used them all. Fusshte's snake eyes defied him. It won't do you any good, Flydd thought. I despise you too much to ever give in to you.

He smiled, grimly at first, but as he saw the first flicker of uncertainty in the eyes of his opponent, Flydd gave a savage grin. The man was weakening. Flydd snorted in disdain and suddenly the secretary broke. Choking back a gasp, Fusshte looked down at his papers and the battle was over.

Such a little thing, but the atmosphere of the room changed subtly. Flydd was not defeated yet. He turned back to the chief scrutator.

'I have a countercharge against Ghorr!' Flydd said flatly.

'We'll hear it after your trial is done,' said Chief Scrutator Ghorr.

'I'll not fall for that one. Once you convict me, as you plan to, I'll have no right to put a countercharge.'

'You were charged first,' said Ghorr. 'The procedure can't be changed.'

'My entire case depends on my countercharge.'

'How unfortunate.'

'I appeal to the Council to set aside your decision.'

'On what grounds?' asked a diminutive dark woman whose cheeks were painted with red wax: Scrutator Halie.

Flydd was pleased to discover that she was the appointed appeals scrutator. Halie had been an ally of his previously in difficult times; he could rely on her to be impartial. 'On the ground that a failure on the part of one or more members of the Council led to the destruction of the node.'

'How so?' said Halie in a dangerous voice.

'My first countercharge is that Chief Scrutator Ghorr provided me with a defective device to destroy the lyrinx node-drainer, and that device failed in use. My second countercharge is this: in commissioning that device, Chief Scrutator Ghorr negligently failed to appreciate that it was likely to cause the destruction of the node itself.'

'These are serious charges, Scrutator Flydd,' said Halie.

'And I intend to prove them.' He held her gaze as rigidly as if she had been his most bitter enemy, then broke it before it became a contest.

'I shall set aside Chief Scrutator Ghorr's ruling for the moment. The Council will hear your charges first. Present them with dispatch, Flydd.'

'Thank you,' said Flydd. He stood up and met their eyes, one by one. 'You have heard my first two countercharges, which relate solely to the destruction of the node. Ghorr's other charges are frivolous and motivated by mischief. He's happy to waste the Council's time, even at this desperate hour, so long as he can bring me down.' He turned eyes like lighthouse beams on the chief scrutator. 'That is my third countercharge.'

'I did not formulate the charges,' growled Ghorr, glancing at the secretary.

'But you gave them your authority.'

'Make your case, Flydd, if you have one.'

'Putting it simply, the device you gave me was defective.'

'On what evidence?'

'It failed when I used it, and led to the destruction of the node.'

'That proves only that you used it incompetently,' said Ghorr.

'Also an assertion that must be proved,' Flydd retorted.

'It's up to the accused to prove his innocence.'

'And I'm accusing you.' Flydd flung out his arm.

The chief scrutator smiled thinly. 'Very theatrical! You were charged first. Your claims are countercharges.'

'Ah,' said Flydd, making a desperate gamble without knowing what the answer was. 'But my countercharges are being heard first, and therefore you must prove your innocence. Is that not so, Appeals Scrutator?'

Halie looked dubious, but reached below the table, brought up a bound volume and began flicking through the pages. After some minutes she put it down again and went into a huddle with three other scrutators. When it broke up, all the scrutators, apart from Flydd and Ghorr, went to the other end of the tent, speaking in low tones with much glancing back at their chief. Ghorr grew purple in the face. Finally they returned to the table.

'Though this question is unprecedented,' said Halie, 'we have reached agreement. Confirm that you have, members of the Council.'

Each of the scrutators affirmed that they agreed. Halie continued. 'We have voted, by a margin of six votes to three, that the countercharges must be defended first.'

'Be damned!' roared the chief scrutator.

'Due process –' began Halie.

Ghorr stood up, and he was a huge, dominating man. 'We've lost a third of our finest army. We may yet lose the war because of it. Flydd led them to disaster and now you call on the evil of *democracy* to let him off!' He spat the word out as if it were heresy, which it was.

'That is the prescribed process, Chief Scrutator!' said Halie. 'Would you care to retire for a few minutes to prepare your case?'

'With the greatest pleasure,' said Ghorr, back in control. He strode out, robes flapping.

The other scrutators gathered at the corner of the tent, talking in low voices. Jal-Nish remained where he was. Flydd moved his chair so he could see the acting scrutator. 'Nice day for it,' he said conversationally.

Jal-Nish shifted in his seat, as venomous and deadly as a nylatl. 'I'll be dancing on your flayed corpse by sundown.'

Flydd felt the touch of fear and was careful not to look into Jal-Nish's eye – it was the one contest he could not win. The man was determined to destroy him, whatever the cost. He could not afford to show his disquiet – not the least trace. Summoning all his strength, Flydd yawned in Jal-Nish's face. 'And you want to replace me, of course.'

'I'll have your place on the Council and crush the lyrinx too.'

'Really?' said Flydd, without bothering to correct him. 'What next? Abolish famine, pestilence, *death*?'

'You won't be sneering when the torturers have their disembowelling hooks in you.' Jal-Nish stormed out.

I've got to him, Flydd thought. Impossible to resist, but was it wise?

After half an hour, Ghorr came through the flap of the tent, accompanied by Jal-Nish and three people in robes. The first was a thin-faced, sallow fellow, the second a grey-haired woman wearing shoulder pads that squared off her stout figure; the last was a sawn-off, good-looking man with regular features, brilliant blue eyes and a leonine head of brown hair, swept back in waves. He had the rolling gait of a sailor and was only half a span tall. Flydd knew him – Klarm, the dwarf scrutator, an honest man, as scrutators went, but as ruthless as any.

Klarm nodded cheerfully to Flydd, who waved back. The other two newcomers, mancers both, did not acknowledge him. Jal-Nish resumed his seat.

'I present my witnesses,' said Ghorr. 'Mancer Vydale and Mancer Lubis.'

The sallow-faced man bowed formally, as did the stout woman.

'You all know Klarm, of course,' Ghorr went on. There were a few nods around the table. 'Vydale and Lubis, you designed the device that was given to Scrutator Flydd in Nennifer, did you not?'

'We did,' said Vydale.

'Each must answer the question, if you please,' said Halie.

'We did,' said Mancer Lubis.

'And you supervised the team of artisans who built it?' said Ghorr.

They both affirmed that they had.

'Was the device tested?' asked Ghorr.

'It was,' each said in turn.

Flydd sat up, surprised, though he should not have been. The scrutators were notoriously thorough.

Ghorr smiled thinly. 'Who supervised the testing?'

'I did!' said Scrutator Klarm.

'How was the device tested?' Flydd asked. 'With an operating node-drainer?'

'How else could it be tested?' said Klarm. 'We rotored to a node in the mountains that had gone dead, located the enemy's node-drainer and fitted the device to it. After some adjustment by the artisans, the node-drainer collapsed and failed.'

Flydd felt his last hope die. 'What about the node?'

'Its field returned to normal the following day.'

Flydd knew that Klarm was telling the truth, and there was no doubt that he would have done his work competently. Flydd's counterattack had been destroyed.

'Mancers Vydale and Lubis,' he said, 'can you confirm what Klarm has told us?'

They averred that they could.

'Any further questions, Flydd?' said Ghorr.

Flydd had none, for he believed them too. Nonetheless, the breaker had been tampered with. But how, and by whom?

36

'Only one. When I began to use the device, it became clear that it was faulty. Someone must have –'

'I saw it sealed in its box,' said Klarm. 'It never left my custody until it was placed in your air-floater, just before you left Nennifer. Were the seals broken when you opened the box?'

'They were not,' said Flydd. 'And no one but myself and my trusted prober, Eiryn Muss, ever had charge of it.'

'Then it can't have been tampered with. No one but a scrutator has the Art to break those seals. They were made with scrutator magic.'

'So if it was tampered with,' Ghorr said relentlessly, 'it happened while you had charge of it. Again, the negligence is yours.' He dismissed his three witnesses. 'We'll take a vote on the countercharges. Yea if they are proven, nay if disproved.'

There were eleven nays.

'And my first principal charge, that Flydd's incompetence led to the destruction of the node?'

Nine yeas and two nays.

'My second principal charge, that Flydd's negligence after the destruction of the node lost a third of our army?'

Seven yeas and four nays.

'It is enough,' said Ghorr. 'The charges are proven. Now, scrutators, we must agree on penalties.'

The scrutators dismissed Flydd ignominiously from his position and broke him to a common citizen. However, after half an hour of acrimonious debate, during which time Ghorr became ever colder, they could not agree on a penalty for the second charge.

'I'll take no more of this!' cried Ghorr. 'The enemy could counterattack at any time. I make the Declaration of Emergency. All rights are suspended, and all privileges, that conflict with my duties.'

He stared around the table. All broke under his stare, even Flydd, though he strove mightily against the chief scrutator. Ghorr had played the unbeatable card. Later he would have to justify the declaration but for the moment he was unassailable. Ghorr could punish him in any way he saw fit.

'I beg leave to address the Council,' came Jal-Nish's voice from behind Flydd.

'The matter is closed,' Ghorr said frostily.

'I do not wish to speak about that.' Jal-Nish glanced idly at Flydd, then away, as if he were of no significance. 'Fault and blame are irrelevant now. Rather would I speak about the war. *And how we might still win it.*'

'Go on,' said Ghorr, showing his canines.

'The enemy have abandoned Snizort in haste, leaving behind everything, including their flesh-formed abominations. They must be dreadfully demoralised by the destruction of the node as well as the loss of their great city. The Histories tell us they are slow to recover from their rare defeats. And they have suffered terrible casualties: twelve thousand dead and half as many unable to fight.'

'Our losses are worse,' snapped Ghorr, 'for we've lost all our clankers as well. It'll take years to replace them.'

'Were we to pursue the enemy now,' said Jal-Nish, 'with our clankers and the constructs of the Aachim, they would be hard put to save themselves. The lyrinx are obscenities that flesh-form their own young in the womb. We must eradicate them to the last child!' He looked as though he would enjoy the slaughter.

'The node is exploded, you fool! The field is dead, our clankers useless metal.'

'I can save them,' said Jal-Nish.

Now he had their attention. 'How?' said Ghorr.

'I would bring in bullock teams,' said Jal-Nish. 'And teams of horses, buffalo and men. I'd put the clankers on skids and haul them to the nearest node field, north-west of here. It's only seven leagues away, I'm told. Then I'd go after the enemy with all our strength and strike them down before they have a chance to recover. From this defeat we can yet snatch victory, and what a sweet victory it will be. It could turn the tide of the war, Chief Scrutator.'

Flydd's voice dropped into the following silence. 'This is folly! The lyrinx are at no disadvantage at all. They don't need supplies – they've enough of our good soldiers in their bellies to do them a week.'

Ghorr turned on him. 'We'll hear no more of your cowardly words, Flydd. As of now I strip you of all rights. You are a non-citizen, and the meanest person in the world may strike you down without penalty. Guards!'

Two burly guards burst through the entrance. 'Take Non-Citizen Flydd to the punishment pen. Guard him well and await my further instructions.'

The guards hauled Flydd off, his legs dragging.

Ghorr turned back to the table. 'Jal-Nish, take Flydd's place at the table. We would hear more of your proposal, though I don't see how it can be done. To move five thousand clankers that distance would take a hundred thousand men, and even then it would be the most spine-cracking labour.'

'We have forty thousand hale troops,' said Jal-Nish, 'plus many thousands of camp followers. And we can conscript half as many again from the towns and villages to the east and south. Adding their beasts of burden, we'll have sufficient, if we drive them hard enough.'

There was silence around the table while the idea was considered .

'I don't see how it can be done before our supplies fail,' said Ghorr. 'And who could pull together such an unwieldy force in the time?'

'I can do it,' said Jal-Nish boldly. 'You know my record, surr.'

Ghorr looked doubtful. 'You have never held such high command.'

'No scrutator has, surr.' Excepting Flydd, but Jal-Nish was not going to mention him, in case the Council had second thoughts about the man. 'We must have courage, Chief Scrutator. We must dare the impossible. What have we to lose? And . . .'

'Yes?' snapped Ghorr, nettled that a mere acting scrutator should lecture him.

'If the enemy should get over their fright and come back, they'll annihilate us.'

'That's my main concern. Very well. I will give you the command, Acting Scrutator. But remember, I'll be watching you . . .'

Jal-Nish went still. '*Acting Scrutator,* surr? But . . . you told me to take Flydd's place on the Council.'

'Flydd was dismissed from this Council months ago. I said take his place *at the table.* The test for scrutator is a stern one. Prove that you are deserving, Jal-Nish, and I will promote you. I may even admit you to the Council, should a vacancy occur. Fail and you may share the rack with Non-Citizen Flydd.'

'I won't fail,' said Jal-Nish with such black-eyed intensity that one or two of the Council members, hardened though they were, shuddered.

They worked for an hour before breaking up with a plan. Then they ran, each to their own duties. It fell to Jal-Nish to visit the guards at the punishment pen, a cage made from stakes hammered into the side of the hill.

'Rouse out the slaves,' he said with a liquid chuckle.

Xervish Flydd lifted his head. His face was bruised all over, for the other prisoners had welcomed the fallen into their company.

'What do you want with us?' he said.

'We don't have enough bullock teams, so men must make up the difference. You're going in the first team, to serve as an example to all. The lash will teach you to do your simple duty, Slave Flydd.'

FOUR

Flames blasted from a fissure in front of Tiaan. Liquid tar, hot enough to sting, dripped from the roof onto her head and shoulders; fumes burned tracks up her nostrils. A red glow lit up the tunnel behind her, for she was trapped in her walker, deep underground in Snizort. Though the lyrinx had repaired her severed spine with their flesh-forming Art, her legs were still too weak to stand on.

There was no field here, and the node was no longer visible. She reached down and felt the amplimet. It was still cool to the touch, thankfully, for heat could destroy such crystals.

The amplimet was powerful enough to draw on a more distant node, so she still had a chance. Tiaan tried to remember where other nodes might lie. In her long flight here in the thapter she had used many, and should have been able to recall them all, those memories were gone.

Everything was strange here; the ethyr was clotted with warpings the like of which she had never seen before. The amplimet seemed different, too. She wasn't sure how, but it was harder to use, almost as if it had grown stronger since the node exploded, or more wakeful and watchful. She did not like the feeling. Fighting down panic, Tiaan sought for a field and, at the very limit of her senses, detected a faint aura.

So far from the node that generated it, the field was tenuous, weak, fragile. She drew power into the controller. One leg twitched feebly but the walker did not move.

Dismayed, Tiaan made another attempt. That was better; she actually got one leg to take a step, though a wobbly, lurching one. She took another. Better still – she was remembering how to manage it.

Ahead, through cracks in the tunnel wall, the flames roared as if pumped by a distant bellows. They died away for the count of nineteen before roaring forth again. If she misjudged the timing, or went too slowly, she would be roasted alive.

Creeping as close as she could get, Tiaan waited for the next exhalation. It was sweltering here. She put her hand over the amplimet to protect it. The cracks flamed, then died to wisps. *Now!* She lurched the walker forwards and they flamed again, right at the controller. The impulse to jerk her hand away was overwhelming. She fought it, enduring the pain as she tried to make the machine go backwards. It shuddered but did not move.

The flames stopped. She tried to move forwards but that did not work either. Blisters were rising on the back of her hand. 'Move!' she screamed. The walker gave only a spastic twitch. Its front feet were stuck in tar which had softened in the heat.

Hot tar ribboned onto her shoulders. She bent the four legs as far as they would go, then straightened them all at the same time. Three legs pulled free, the other did not, and the machine began to topple. Tiaan threw her weight the other way and managed to save it, though it left her directly in front of the cracks. The next blast would burn her to a crisp. She could hear it coming, a breathy roar.

Flexing the legs again, she gave a mighty heave. The stuck leg pulled free and the walker shot forwards and up as the flames roared by. Tiaan felt the heat on her backside.

Further on, she went down into a hollow where heavy black fumes had pooled on the floor. As the walker crabbed through it lifted inky tendrils as high as her head. Eyes stinging, she lurched down the corridor, having no idea where she was going. Since the explosion, Tiaan could not remember Merryl's directions, and most of the wall lamps had gone out. She just kept moving because she could not remain where she was.

Creeping along, breathing through her sleeve, she thought

she heard human voices coming from one of the branching tunnels ahead. 'Hello!' she yelled.

No answer. She moved to the intersection. Definitely voices, from the middle tunnel. She crept up through the gloom, turned a corner into a wider tunnel lit by a single lantern on a pole, and stopped.

Half a dozen people had their backs to her, staring at something that she could not make out. They looked like the human slaves the lyrinx had kept here. The walker's legs clacked and they turned, squinting into the dark. She moved forwards and, with wild cries, they broke and ran. What was the matter? Tiaan realised, belatedly, that she must have made a terrifying sight, half human and half machine, and coated with droppings of tar.

'Wait,' someone yelled from around the corner. 'That's just Tiaan.'

The voice was familiar. 'Merryl?'

He appeared, carrying a lantern. She was so glad to see him. 'The tunnel's on fire, Merryl. I couldn't get through.'

'This passage leads to an exit but there's a construct stuck in the tar and we can't get past it.'

'A construct?' Tiaan edged forward curiously.

He caught her arm. 'Careful. The tar's sticky over there. I've sent people to pull shelves out of a storeroom, to stand on. We may be able to climb over the top.'

'Is there anyone inside it?'

'I don't know.'

The construct, which was just like her own thapter, though only half the size, was two-thirds buried in sticky tar. The former slaves, four men and two women, came panting up, carrying long planks, and began to lay them across the tar. The timber ran out just before the construct; they hurried off for more.

When planks had been laid all the way, they began to scrape the tar off with shovels and mattocks so they could climb over. Being unable to help, Tiaan waited where the tar was firm, working her wasted leg muscles until they hurt.

She had to be able to walk unaided. The planks were too narrow for her walker and she was wondering how she would get across when someone hissed, 'What's that?'

The work stopped. *Tap, tap, tap* came clearly from inside the construct.

Tiaan felt a spasm of fear. The Aachim had chased her halfway across Lauralin. If the ones inside were freed, they would come after her and these unarmed slaves could not stop them.

'Don't let –' Tiaan broke off. She couldn't condemn those inside to suffocation.

'What's the matter?' called Merryl, who was stripped to the waist and covered in sweat. It was growing hotter all the time.

'Oh, nothing.' In her condition, Tiaan was afraid to trust anyone.

She watched as the tar was scraped off the top of the construct. It took ages, for it clung to the tools and they had to be cleaned every minute or two. Someone climbed up, holding the lantern aloft.

'Tunnel's collapsed further along,' the man announced. 'We'll have to find another way out.'

'All the other passages run back in the direction of the fire,' said Merryl.

The hatch of the construct was forced up, tearing the coating of tar into clinging strands. A head appeared in the opening. Tiaan edged back into the shadows, hoping it was some obscure Aachim who had never seen her.

It was Minis. Her heart began to hammer. She had sworn revenge on him and all the Aachim kind, but what was the point of that if they were all going to die?

Another Aachim climbed up beside Minis. Tiaan recognised her too, despite her haggard look. Tirior had also been in on the betrayal. Minis climbed down onto the boards and Tirior followed. A third person emerged, a short, stocky young man with a cap of dark hair that clung to the contours of his skull. Cryl-Nish Hlar, *Nish*. Her nemesis. If there was any man in the world she loathed as much as the Aachim, it was him.

Tiaan sprang the walker backwards, colliding with the wall. She covered her face, peering through her fingers at Minis, and tears sprang to her eyes. She had invested all her foolish, youthful dreams in him, and he had cast her aside. She had to get away before he saw her. Whirling the walker around in its tracks she set off the other way, into her personal darkness. Towards the fire.

'Tiaan!' yelled Merryl.

She increased her speed, for his cry had given her away.

'Tiaan,' he yelled, pounding after her.

She could not move quickly in the gloom and Merryl caught her around the bend. 'Tiaan, what is it?'

'Those three are my enemies.'

He took her arm. 'You can't get out that way. Can't you smell the fumes?'

Just enough light came around the corner, now that her eyes had adjusted, to illuminate a dark, noxious cloud creeping along the floor. An odd tendril or two escaped upwards. One caught in the back of her throat and her lungs contracted.

'All right,' she said hoarsely. 'But don't tell them my back has been repaired. Please.'

'I'll say nothing,' said Merryl. 'I know nothing.'

At the corner she almost ran into a racing Minis. 'Tiaan? Is it truly you?' He stopped abruptly, staring at the walker. His eyes lifted to her face. 'Tiaan,' he whispered. 'What happened?'

Her back was throbbing. She couldn't deal with Minis. All she could do was keep him at bay with words. 'My back was broken when the construct crashed,' she said harshly. 'After your father attacked me without provocation.'

'I'm sorry. I tried to stop him . . .'

'Spare me your lies! I had enough of them in Tirthrax.' She ground the words out, then went past in silence. Tirior stared at her. Nish gaped. Tiaan did not acknowledge either of them.

In the open area, she said to Merryl, 'Is there any other way out?'

He pointed to the left, where another small tunnel

yawned. 'It may be possible that way. If not, we're trapped and will die here.'

'Is the way the construct came in completely blocked?'

'It seems so.'

'Then we have no choice. Shall we scout this passage out?'

They had gone only a hundred paces up the small tunnel when they encountered a rivulet of molten tar oozing along the floor.

'I was afraid of that,' said Merryl. 'It seems we're doomed to end our lives here, Tiaan.'

Tiaan said nothing. They went back to the construct.

Tirior examined the walker shrewdly. 'An ingenious device. Did you make it?'

'What's the matter with your machine?' said Tiaan, ignoring the question.

'The node has gone dead and taken all the fields with it.' Tirior was watching Tiaan, head tipped to one side, no doubt wondering how the walker could still move. It would not take her long to work it out.

'Merryl,' Tiaan said quietly. 'Order your people to take the Aachim, before they attack us.'

Tirior's hand darted for the pack she wore on her chest. Tiaan hurled the walker backwards, slamming painfully into the wall.

'Take them,' roared Merryl, throwing his handless arm across Tirior's throat and twisting her other arm up behind her back. The freed slaves did the same with Minis.

'Him as well,' Tiaan shouted, pointing to Nish.

'You misjudge us,' Tirior said softly, but under her breath she was muttering in an Aachim dialect Tiaan did not recognise.

Tiaan felt power flow from her controller and the walker's legs slowly splayed. Had Tirior not been exhausted from the mancery that had got her into Snizort, she might have succeeded.

'Stop her mouth!' Tiaan cried.

One of the slaves wound a strip of cloth three times around

Tirior's head and pulled it tight. Tiaan felt the flow ease. Her heart was beating irregularly and she felt faint. So close.

'You taught me the value of your word, Tirior.' Tiaan wrenched open the pack. Tirior had been reaching for a small glass tube, capped in gold, with a scintillating powder inside. Tiaan tossed it into the tar and pressed it down with one of the walker's feet. 'Bind them, please, Merryl.'

Cord was found in a storeroom and the three prisoners' hands bound behind their backs.

'I'm not your enemy, Tiaan,' said Nish. 'I was wrong about you before. I'm sorry.'

He seemed different to the Nish Tiaan had known. He was more sure of himself, less angry, and made no attempt to fight those who held him. But Tiaan could not forgive so easily. 'Every time I've met you I've regretted it, Nish,' she said wearily.

'We were looking for you, to bring you out of here.'

Tiaan activated the walker and moved away. 'I have a plan,' she whispered to Merryl.

'I thought you must.'

'I think, with my crystal, that I may be able to operate the construct. If you can direct me to the way out, it will carry us through the fumes. For a while, at least.'

'I know every tunnel,' he said.

'Lift me into the construct and I'll see what I can do. The tar around it will have to be cleared away.'

'I'll have it done.'

Taking the amplimet from the walker, Tiaan put it in her pocket, undid the straps and lifted herself on her arms. Merryl carried her across. 'I'm not too heavy, am I?'

He smiled. 'You're no burden at all.'

He boosted her up the side and she slid her legs in. As her feet struck the floor Tiaan's knees buckled. Her muscles might have been made from cloth. Pulling out the operator's seat she sat down hurriedly.

The layout was much the same as in her thapter. She pressed the small recessed button and a hexagonal tube sprang out. Flipping the cap open, she removed the crystal, which was pale blue and striated down the sides. She had never seen one like it. Slipping it into her pocket, she put the amplimet in its place. In her own construct, or thapter as she had called it after learning how to make it fly, she'd made a special device to reduce power.

Tiaan hoped that would not be necessary here, since she was drawing from such a distant node. In any case, she had nothing to build it with.

She pressed the hexagonal tube in and closed the cap. After a long moment, a faint whine came from below, and a subtle tremor. It was working!

It took hours to remove the great gouts of sticky tar, and the work was so exhausting that the slaves had to rest after every few strokes. The job had just been completed when Merryl cried, 'Tiaan, look out!'

She got the hatch down just in time, as an even bigger clot buried the construct completely. By the time that had been removed, the air inside was stale. A day had gone by since her escape from the patterner.

The black miasma, which had advanced and retreated a number of times, was now flowing steadily across the floor. It would be up to their knees within minutes.

'Better bring the prisoners on board,' she said to Merryl, who was anxiously watching the fumes. Tiaan popped the amplimet out and pocketed it, just in case. There was no room for trust; the whole world seemed to be against her.

The prisoners were brought in and taken below. Minis gazed sorrowfully at her, like a dog that had been kicked. Nish, who looked as though he hadn't slept in days, simply lay down, pillowed his head on his arms and went to sleep. Tirior showed no expression at all. She was the one to watch.

Everyone came aboard save the two who were mattocking away at the sticky tar on the right-hand side. When the black fog was at the level of their thighs, Tiaan called them in. Should a sudden surge overwhelm the construct now, it would be impossible to get out.

Merryl set guards on the Aachim and Nish. The remaining slaves went below, leaving just her and Merryl in the operator's compartment. It would be very cramped down there, with nine passengers. Tiaan reinserted the amplimet and took hold of the trumpet-shaped lever. The whine rose in pitch but the construct did not move.

'It's still stuck in the tar,' said Merryl. 'I don't think –'

'I'll try to work it free.'

He peered anxiously ahead. A billow of black mist was rolling towards them. Tiaan pulled down the hatch and fastened it. It became dark inside, except for the subtle glow from the plate in front of her. The front panel thinned to transparency. The outside was dimly lit by glowing globes that shone intermittently through the fog.

She wiggled the lever back and forth, ever so gently. The whine rose and fell. With a delicate shudder the construct pulled free and rose in the air until its base was at the level of the black fog. Tiaan edged it forwards.

'Straight ahead or to the left?' she said, after they'd been travelling a while.

'The way out into the main pit is straight ahead, but we may not be able to get through that way . . .' Merryl was looking at her expectantly. 'Is something the matter?'

She realised that she was frowning. 'I originally came here looking for Gilhaelith. He's a strange, unlikeable fellow, but he was good to me.' Even though he'd cared more for the amplimet than about her safety, Tiaan had to know that he was safe.

'He's an important man,' said Merryl. 'Surely the lyrinx will have taken him with them.'

'I was important to them, yet they panicked and left me behind. They may have abandoned him as well. Do you know where Gilhaelith was working?'

'In a tunnel excavated into the Great Seep.'

'A tunnel in liquid tar? How can that be?'

'They froze it first.'

'How?' said Tiaan curiously.

'One of their Arts.'

'If he was left behind, can he possibly still be alive?' she said to herself.

'Not if he's still in the seep.' He looked through the front. 'But, perhaps, in the tunnels near it . . . We *can* go that way. It's not much further.'

Merryl was a man of the same heart as Tiaan. She thanked him, silently. 'He treated me kindly. I have to know.'

'Then go straight on.'

They came to a high point in the tunnel where the heavy black mist had not reached. Merryl cracked the hatch open to let in fresh air, but it stank so badly that he quickly closed it again. The construct went down sharply, plunging into fumes which the globes could not penetrate. Tiaan had to creep along, and even then was continually bumping into the sticky, gritty walls.

They turned a sharp bend, then another that formed the other half of an 'S', and the black fog thinned. Ahead, two tunnels diverged at a shallow angle.

'Which way?' said Tiaan.

Merryl was staring blankly through the screen. 'I'm . . . not sure. The fog has confused me. Have we missed an intersection?'

'We could have missed fifty for all I could see.'

'Take the left. *I think.*'

After a few minutes, Tiaan felt the right-hand side scrape on the sandy wall. Shortly afterwards the other side did the same and the construct shuddered to a stop.

'It's the wrong way,' said Merryl. 'Better go back.'

'I hope we can,' Tiaan muttered.

After much jerking and heaving the construct began to move backwards. They had been heading down the other tunnel for some minutes when Tiaan saw a red glow in a cross-tunnel to their left.

'We're running out of options,' said Merryl. 'Can you go faster?'

She increased speed as much as she dared, following a

50

zigzag path away from the burning area until they hit a broad tunnel that ran straight. There were no fumes in it and they made good time. The walls and roof here were yellow sandstone, hardly tar stained at all. After ten minutes they came abruptly into blackened rock and then, where the tunnel opened out, into solid tar. The tunnel kept on.

'Is this where Gilhaelith was?' Tiaan did not like the feel of the place.

'He would have been some way ahead. We're close to the outer edge of the Great Seep – the solid edge. In a few spans it becomes soft and beyond that it's liquid tar for a league.'

'How did they tunnel it? And why?'

Merryl spoke to the huddled slaves in a language Tiaan did not know. A woman answered in the same tongue.

'They used devices powered by phynadrs,' said Merryl, 'to draw the heat out and freeze the tar hard. Why, I cannot say, only that it was mighty important to them. Matriarch Gyrull worked there every day, and a matriarch does not risk her life needlessly.'

They crept on. Objects were strewn here and there as if discarded in flight – rotting, tar-stained remnants of clothing, a small wooden chest. Further on was a distinctly human-looking body.

Tiaan caught her breath. Not Gilhaelith, surely? She drew the construct alongside, opened the hatch and looked down.

The body was small, female, and tar-impregnated. 'It has a . . . withered look,' Tiaan said. 'As if long dead.'

'Many people, and many animals, must have become stuck in the tar over the aeons, and been carried down into the depths. I saw a number of them over my time here, all perfectly preserved. You need shed no tear for her, Tiaan. She's been dead hundreds of years, at the very least.'

'I'll go on, just in case . . .' She edged the construct down the tunnel. 'I thought you said they tunnelled in a long way.'

'About a hundred spans, I heard.'

'We're only in twenty and I can see the end,' said Tiaan.

She lifted herself up on the side, the better to see. The end of the tunnel was but spans away, a smooth, shining black bulge dotted with fragments of wood and cloth. 'It's moving!'

Warm tar was creeping towards them like molasses squeezed through a hole. The tunnel had collapsed.

'If Gilhaelith was in there, he's dead.'

FIVE

Merryl gripped her shoulder. 'Was he special to you, Tiaan?'

'I wouldn't say that we were friends, for he had none. Gilhaelith was quite the strangest man I've ever met, and totally absorbed in himself. Yet he was good to me and I can't forget it. We'd better go, if we're to get out.'

Reversing the little construct, Tiaan turned it about and went back the way they had come. At the first intersection, Merryl said, 'Go left.'

She headed that way but was soon confronted by a baleful glow and another creeping fume.

'There's fire ahead, Tiaan. Try the other way.'

To the right they encountered a cave-in that completely blocked the tunnel. There was no hope of clearing it, for the fumes were knee high and rising. They turned back to the junction and took the middle path, their last hope.

'Fire,' Merryl said dully, after they had moved less than a hundred spans.

Tiaan kept going until it was certain there was no way past. 'What now?'

'Resign ourselves to death.'

It was hot here. Tiaan went back to the entrance to the tar tunnel. She could not resign herself to dying. Turning the construct again, she stared at the oozing face of the tar.

'Tell me about the Great Seep, Merryl.'

'It's a good league across, and hundreds of spans deep. Some say it's bottomless. Things, and creatures trapped in it, sink down and sometimes appear again, countless years later, with the wheeling of the slow currents in its depths.'

'If we remain here,' she said absently. 'We'll be dead within the hour.'

'I'd say so.'

'How long would the air in the construct last with the hatch down, and all of us inside?'

'I don't know. Two hours? Three? Four, possibly.'

'Then let's live those extra hours. Let's risk it.' Tiaan slammed the hatch, took a deep breath and moved the construct gently forwards until it met the convex face of the tar.

Merryl's eyes met hers. Tiaan's eyes were alive for the first time since he'd met her. 'What have we got to lose?'

The construct met resistance and stalled. Tiaan moved the controls, just a tickle. The skinned tar broke and the machine surged into treacly material that smeared across the screen. Everything went black.

'Are we even moving?' whispered Tiaan. 'I can't tell.'

Merryl looked through the rear screen. 'We're going about two spans a minute. The tar's coming over the top. I can't see anything now.'

She nudged the trumpet-shaped lever. There was no sense of motion. 'It's not fast enough. It'll take an hour to get to the end and we've still got to go up to the top of the seep. How far below ground are we?'

He shrugged. 'More than a hundred spans, but less than two hundred.'

'That's another hour, probably two. Can we make it before we breathe all our air?'

'I don't know.'

'I'll have to go faster.'

'Go too fast and it may tear the construct apart.'

'Too slowly and it won't matter,' she retorted.

The minutes ticked by. Occasionally they came up against an object that scraped along the skin of the construct. It was hot inside now.

'How hot is the tar in the Great Seep, Merryl?'

'I wouldn't know. It's warm on top, so it must be warmer inside.'

'Hot enough to cook us?'

'I couldn't say.'

'Do you think we're at the end of the tar tunnel yet?' Tiaan asked.

'Once the node failed, the walls of the tunnel would soon have gone liquid. We'd be in the swirl of the Great Seep right now.'

'We're too slow,' she fretted. 'And we're not going up. I've got to do something.'

She knew what to do but was reluctant to do it, since that would give away the secret of making thapters-constructs that could fly. But if they were going to die anyway . . .

'Could you have the prisoners blindfolded, please, Merryl? And ask the slaves to turn their backs. I've got to do something to the construct and I don't want anyone to see.'

He went down. Tiaan unpacked the set of pink diamonds – powerful hedrons – and the strands of black whiskers, fifty-four of each, weighing them in her hands. So much from so little.

'It's done,' called Merryl.

She lowered herself down the ladder by her hands and Merryl caught her at the bottom. Tiaan exercised her legs at every opportunity but it was going to take weeks before she could walk properly.

Opening a hatch in the floor at the front, she identified a black box among the tangle of parts inside, and prised the lid off. Inserting the diamond hedrons into their sockets, she fed the black threads up to the back of the amplimet cavity, checking everything carefully as she worked. There would be no time to do it again.

As soon as it was done, Merryl lifted her up the ladder. How quickly she had come to rely on him. Tiaan took hold of the controls. The amplimet meshed with her snugly now, not opposing her at all. It wanted to escape as much as she did. The whine rose in pitch as she pulled up on the flight knob but nothing seemed to happen. She could not tell if they were moving upwards.

'Is it working, Merryl?'

He thought for a moment. 'You know how, when you carry a bowl of water, it moves with your motion?'

'Yes! What a clever idea.'

He found a broad metal dish among the bits and pieces in one of the storage compartments, half filled it with water and sat it on the top of the binnacle. With a pointed instrument he scored marks around the dish, at the water level.

'That will show movement from side to side, or back and forth.'

'But not up, which is what I most need to know.' She wiped her brow. Sweat was running down her neck and her shirt was saturated. The air was getting stuffy, too.

'But if we had something springy . . .'

He was away half an hour of their precious time, before returning with thin strips of green material. 'I found a diaphragm in one of the drawers. It's a kind of rubber.'

Tying one strip from the ceiling, above the binnacle, Merryl knotted a small coin into the other end, one-handed. 'I've carried this copper nyd for twenty years,' he said with a hint of a smile, 'for luck – not that it's brought me any.' Merryl scored a line across the screen at the lowest edge of the coin and stood back. 'Try again.'

She moved the controller lever slightly. The water in the dish moved back a fraction. 'It works!' She gave him a triumphant grin, then a tentative hug. 'Let's try the other.' Taking hold of the flying knob, she pulled it up. The rubbery strip lengthened perceptibly before oscillating around its original position.

'How fast do you think we're rising?' she said.

'Haven't a clue.'

She pulled the knob up further until the machine began to shudder, then backed it off a little. 'If we're only rising at a few spans an hour . . . I suppose it'll be an easy death, if we run out of air.'

He did not answer.

Tiaan settled back in her seat. 'How did the enemy come to capture you, Merryl?'

'We lost an unimportant little battle near Gosport, way over on the east coast,' he said. 'We were fighting for a village you'd never have heard of. I don't remember its name. On the march we went through so many places that after a while no one could tell the difference.'

She wiped her dripping brow. 'Were you in the army a long time?'

'Only a few months. There was an emergency, and after a week of training we went to the front. I say "the front", though there wasn't one. The lyrinx prefer to fight in small bands, or even alone. Most of my friends died in ambushes and isolated skirmishes. Afterwards, no one knew where; no one survived to write their Histories. The cursed war!'

There was a bang on the roof of the construct, followed by a scraping down the back.

'What was that?' said Tiaan.

'Something in the seep. Perhaps a piece of wood, or a large bone.' Merryl was staring straight ahead, as if to pierce the black tar.

'What did you do before you went into the army, Merryl?'

'I was a translator, like my parents,' he said softly. 'But that's so long ago it doesn't seem like me at all. I can hardly imagine it now.'

They sat in silence, listening to the whine of the construct, the occasional *thunk* of some object or other striking the top of the machine, the creak and rattle of the metal skin. If we were going *really* slowly, she thought, the impacts wouldn't make any noise.

It grew hotter. Tiaan's clothes were sodden; Merryl's too. She could hear his hoarse breathing. Hers was the same. Surely they did not have much air left. Time seemed to be going very slowly.

'What about you, Tiaan? Tell me about yourself.'

She was equally reticent. 'There's not much to tell. I was chosen to become an artisan. I have a talent of thinking in pictures. I –'

Down below, someone groaned and began to thrash their

legs. Merryl swung himself down the ladder. 'They're not looking good,' he called.

She poked her head down until she could see. Three of the seven slaves were asleep, or unconscious. The others sprawled limply on the floor, eyes closed, lungs heaving. Tirior and Minis were in better shape, though they looked worse than she felt. Nish lay curled up on a pull-out bunk, halfway up the wall. He had worked his blindfold off but his eyes were shut.

'The air's really bad down there,' Merryl said as he returned to her side. 'They won't last much longer.'

She pulled the knob up until the machine began to shudder. The rubber strip elongated. Everything began to vibrate, including her teeth. The construct squealed as if its metal carapace were being wrenched one way and then the other.

'I don't like the sound of that,' she said.

'Doesn't matter much, either way.'

'No.'

A while later she said, 'How fast now?' forgetting that she'd asked that before.

'I couldn't say, Tiaan.'

It was too much of an effort to talk. She leaned back against the seat, panting. Her head drooped.

The hatch above their heads squealed and a ribbon of tar jetted in from one side, festooning her arm and shoulder with coiling black bands. She tried to brush it off but the hot stuff stuck to her fingers and burned. Tiaan yelped and with her free hand pulled the flight knob down until the shuddering stopped.

Merryl tightened the hatch and sat on the floor, resting his head back against the wall. Tiaan set the controls and scraped the tar off. She felt so very tired; her head nodded. She hauled herself up, hanging onto the binnacle. If she sat down, she would go to sleep, which would swiftly be followed by unconsciousness, and death for everyone.

Something struck the construct hard, sending a shiver through the bowl of water. The hatch scraped as if the machine were sliding along the underside of something large and hard.

Tiaan could not think clearly. She pushed the controller forwards, the squeal became a shriek of tormented metal then, to her horror, the hatch was prised up a finger's width and thick tar began to ribbon in.

The noise stopped. They were free of the obstruction. Tiaan tilted the front of the construct up. The bowl of water slid off the binnacle, pouring its contents down the ladder. Pulling the flight knob up as far as it would go, she prayed.

The machine shuddered, the tar boiled beneath it and with a roar the construct hurled itself vertically. A surge of hot tar coated the wall at her back. The sound was indescribable. Tiaan felt sure the machine was going to tear itself apart.

Then the shuddering ceased, so abruptly that she did not understand what had happened. Had they stopped? No, for the mechanism down below was still screaming. She'd done it. The construct was free, in the open air, and going up like a skyrocket.

Tiaan threw open the hatch and, gasping lungfuls of sweet, pure air, let the machine fly where it would. There were groans and cries as the passengers were flung from one side to the other, but they were alive, at least. She did not look down. Tiaan had strength only to cling to the side, her eyes watering in the gale that swirled in through the jagged hatchway.

It became bitterly cold and hard to breathe; she'd gone too high. Tiaan eased the flight knob down, wondering where to go, but the whine broke for a second. As she levelled out it broke again and smoke belched up on all sides. She put the front down, heading towards the ground. Had something vital been damaged in all that shaking and shuddering? If the mechanism failed at this height they would be smashed to jelly.

There were no more problems until, nearing the ground, she levelled out and the whine faded to nothing. An acrid smell drifted from behind the binnacle and a long black trail smoked in the air behind them. Perhaps she'd drawn too much power and the workings were burning out.

To her right stood the main encampment of the human armies, their command post perched on a flat-topped hill. A little closer, to her left, Tiaan glimpsed the seven-sided command area of the Aachim, next to thousands of motionless constructs. She wasn't going that way.

White fumes came up the steps from the lower level. Merryl cried out something she could not hear. There were yells and screams from below.

'Tiaan,' Merryl yelled. 'We're on fire! Put it down, *anywhere!*'

Better that humanity have the secret of flight than that the Aachim get it. She cut the power and turned right, skimming across the brown grass. The whine failed. The construct hit the ground, bounced like a stone on water, bounced again and skidded around in a circle, before thumping into a rock and toppling on its side.

Tiaan hit her head, hard enough to daze her. She hung onto the binnacle, gasping, as the people below scrambled for the ladder.

'Get out!' screamed Merryl.

Tiaan hit the release, snatched the amplimet and pulled herself out through the torn and tarry hatch, tumbling a short distance to the muddy ground. The underside of the construct must have been red hot – she could feel the heat from here because the brown grass began to smoulder, then burst into flame.

Two people emerged from the hatch, coughing so hard that they doubled over. They were freed slaves; Tiaan did not know their names. After them came Tirior, still bound and gagged, two more slaves, then Minis, dragging the fifth. Nish, whose hands were free, crawled out last. He untied Tirior and they hauled the others away from the fire. The burning grass was expanding away from the other side of the construct, which was now enveloped in flames and smoke. Where was Merryl?

White smoke puffed through the hatch. Tiaan thought she saw a shadow move inside. 'Merryl!' she yelled.

She dragged herself back to the hatch and sat up, stretching out her useless legs. The sixth slave lay unconscious in the hatchway. Merryl was behind her, pushing ineffectually.

Seizing the woman by the front of her shirt, Tiaan pulled her out and they fell together on the grass. Merryl flopped beside Tiaan, coughing so hard she could see specks of blood on his tongue.

'The grass is burning,' Tiaan said. 'We've got to get away from here.'

Tirior wrenched her gag off before carrying the unconscious slave to safety.

Merryl stood up, his eyes watering. 'I'm all right,' he said hoarsely. He picked Tiaan up and lurched away.

As they emerged from behind the construct, Tiaan saw a squad of soldiers racing down from the human command area. Behind them were uniformed officers, as well as shadowy figures in robes – the scrutators.

To her left, and closer, a small band of Aachim were sprinting towards her, Vithis at their head. Even from this distance she could see the angry set of his face. Tiaan let out an involuntary gasp.

'What's the matter?' said Merryl.

'That Aachim is my worst enemy.'

'Then he mustn't get you.'

He began to stagger the other way, towards the human lines. Tiaan looked over her shoulder. It would be a close thing. They went by Minis, who had freed his hands. He stared at Tiaan as she passed, his eyes tragic black holes.

'Minis!' roared Vithis, his robes flapping. 'You're alive!'

'Yes, Foster-father, I am.'

'Stop her!'

Minis, who looked as if he was about to cry, said, 'Foster-father, I will not,' and threw himself face-down on the grass.

Merryl kept going, lurching blindly from side to side. His red eyes were streaming. He looked around wildly then ran, not for the human camp but back towards Snizort.

'Merryl,' cried Tiaan, 'you're going the wrong way.'

He turned around, his eyes watering so badly that every-thing must have been a blur. Vithis was racing towards them but the scrutators were going to get there first.

In the confusion of the moment, Nish must have thought that Merryl was trying to carry Tiaan off. He roared, 'You're not taking her anywhere!' and launched himself through the air. His shoulder struck Merryl behind the knees. He went down, Tiaan flying from his arms.

It made all the difference. In a few strides Vithis was on them. Lifting Tiaan effortlessly in one arm, he drew his sword with the other hand. She struggled but he crushed her against his side, his arm squeezing the air from her lungs.

'Keep your distance!' he roared at the human soldiers. 'Tiaan stole what was mine and I will have it back.' More Aachim ran up to support him.

The soldiers skidded to a stop, swords drawn. Their line parted and a handful of black-robed figures pushed between them, including a tall, burly man and a short one with only one arm. His face was covered by a platinum mask.

'My name is Ghorr,' said the big man, 'Chief Scrutator. Give up the artisan, Lord Vithis.'

'I'll go to war against all humanity first,' hissed Vithis.

More Aachim were running up all the time. Already they outnumbered the humans. Behind them Tiaan was pleased to see that the construct was blazing head high. With a loud bang, pieces of metal spun through the air. The secret of flight – the diamond hedrons and carbon whiskers – would be burned to vapour. Only Malien knew, and Tiaan herself. But could she keep that secret from Vithis?

Ghorr raised a clenched fist, took one step forward, then stopped.

Tiaan trembled in Vithis's arms, but the scrutators could not find the courage to attack him. With a sneer of contempt, Vithis turned his back and headed for the Aachim camp.

SIX

Nish had made a terrible blunder and this time the whole world had been there to see it. Whatever had possessed him to think that the fellow was carrying Tiaan off? He pushed himself to his knees.

'Don't get up,' said Chief Scrutator Ghorr, pressing him down with a shiny boot. 'Lie in the dirt while we judge you, worm. Who are you, who has so betrayed humanity?'

Beside Ghorr stood Jal-Nish. Though he was greatly changed, and Nish had not seen him with the mask, he knew it was his father. What could be seen of Jal-Nish's face was white, but his one eye was blood red.

'The worm, surr,' ground out Jal-Nish, 'is my own son, Cryl-Nish Hlar. I have long thought that he was dead. Now I wish he had never been born.'

'So do I, Acting Scrutator Hlar. But since he *is* your son, and you *crave* elevation to the Council of Scrutators, I require you to prove that you are worthy. Devise a fitting punishment for the creature.' Ghorr's eyes showed his doubt.

Jal-Nish cast a wild glance at his son. Nish could not meet his eye; he was too ashamed. What would happen to him now? A *fitting* punishment. That could mean anything from the front ranks of the army to a death sentence. But blood was blood, after all. Surely his father would not –

'Cryl-Nish Hlar,' Jal-Nish said. 'You have failed as an artificer as you failed as a prober, a diplomat, and at every other task you've ever been set. You are a liar, a cheat and, as has now been proven before my very eyes, a vicious traitor. The tragedy we face today stems from your initial betrayal, with

Crafter Irisis, of Artisan Tiaan at your manufactory. Had you not conspired against Tiaan she would not have fled, *nor* fallen into the hands of the lyrinx, *nor* been ensnared by the Aachim. She would not have opened the gate that brought them here, with their invincible fleet of constructs. Had we still the use of her talent, and the precious amplimet, we might have gained the upper hand over the lyrinx. Alas, we've lost both, *and* the secret of flight, and now our alliance with the Aachim is sundered. And it's all down to you, *boy!*'

'I don't ask why you ensured that Artisan Tiaan, and this most precious of all secrets, should fall into Aachim hands. No doubt you've had your bloodstained pay already.'

'No, Father!' cried Nish. 'I never –'

'Be silent!' Jal-Nish thundered. 'The entire Council of Scrutators saw you betray us. Your guilt has been proven beyond doubt. Cryl-Nish Hlar, you are no longer my son. You will be erased, expunged, *obliterated* from the Histories of the Hlar family.'

'Father,' Nish whispered. 'You can't take my Histories from me.'

'I can and I will, before this day is over.'

'But – what am I to do?'

'You should suffer the ultimate penalty, as all traitors must. But,' Jal-Nish said inexorably, 'we are in sore need of labour to haul our clankers to the nearest node. Therefore, *Slave Nish*, you will be harnessed into a team of criminals and slaves. You will be teamed with the treacherous Slave Flydd, and every time he incurs a whipping, so will you. You will haul clankers without respite until your heart bursts, and then you will be buried in the road, face upwards, that the meanest citizens in the world will tread you down. They will walk over you, Slave Nish, until there's not a fragment of flesh or bone or sinew left. And ever after, an obelisk at that point shall name your crimes and their punishment. Such is the penalty for high treason.'

Even the chief scrutator looked shocked, though not, Nish thought, displeased.

Jal-Nish turned away, struggling to contain himself, but after a few steps he doubled over and vomited into the grass. Shortly he returned, pulling the mask back into place. A single tear glistened in the corner of his eye, then the iron control was back.

'It is done,' Jal-Nish said to the Council. 'Take Slave Nish to his doom!'

'You have proven your worth over the past year, *Scrutator* Jal-Nish,' Ghorr said softly. 'Should you save our clankers, *and* defeat the lyrinx in battle, a place on the Council will be yours. We have need of men such as you.' Taking Jal-Nish's arm, Ghorr led him up the hill.

A pair of white-faced soldiers stepped in beside Nish. 'I won't resist,' he said numbly, but they seized him anyway. One went through his pockets and removed everything of value. The other patted him down for weapons. Finding none, they lifted him between them and carried him away.

As Nish looked back, the crowd dispersed, except for two people. Tirior, who had been watching the proceedings from behind, walked slowly back to the Aachim lines. The other person was the one-handed man, Merryl, who had helped Tiaan. He stared after Nish, then began to trudge around the curve of the hill, away from the command post.

After a sleepless night in a solitary slave pen, Nish was hurled into the bloody slush of the battlefield. A clanker stood just a few steps away, its thick metal legs half-buried in mud. Wooden skids had been fitted underneath. To his left a group of people, slaves like him, were being harnessed together. They looked as despairing as he felt. Behind them were other slave teams, as well as teams of horses, oxen, donkeys and buffalo, soldiers and camp followers, women and even children. Every kind of beast had been harnessed to the impossible, heart-bursting task.

Nish was numb with horror. His own father had cursed him, had sentenced him to a bestial death. Even in this war, which had produced mountains of corpses, in which the whole fabric of human society had been torn apart, that was impossible to comprehend.

Crack! Pain flowered in Nish's ear. He put a filthy hand up and brought it back covered in blood. It felt as if something had bitten a piece out of his earlobe.

Crack! The other ear exploded with agony. Scrambling to his feet, Nish saw a grinning overseer coiling his whip, a good ten paces away.

'What the hell do you –?' Nish roared, driven careless by despair.

The whip lashed out again, catching him on the chest through the gape of his shirt. Muffling a cry, Nish looked around frantically. What was the brute trying to tell him?

He scrambled towards the head of the team, slipping and sliding in the muck, and every time he went to his knees the lash fell on his back or buttocks, or coiled around his waist to nip at his belly. The overseer was a monster, a sadist, and he, Slave Nish, the lowest worm in all of Santhenar, could do nothing about it.

Fumbling with the straps of the harness, Nish took several more lashes before he was fixed in place like a beast of burden. Go away! he prayed. Go and flog someone else.

Eventually the overseer did, the cries and wails of the whipped echoing down the line. Nish could feel no pity for them, though some of their groans were soul-wrenching. All that mattered was that the lash fall on another.

The man beside him at the head of the team, on his knees in the muck, was a scrawny old fellow whose back and meagre legs were crisscrossed with scars. He must have been a slave for a long time. It did not look as though he had much life in him.

'Just what I need,' Nish said to himself. 'Useless old coot will never pull his weight. He'll die in the muck and I'll be whipped for that too.'

The slave turned his emaciated, mud-coated head. Nish did not recognise him, nor even recall Jal-Nish's words, until the man spoke.

'How quickly they forget,' said Xervish Flydd, looking him in the eye.

'Scrutator! Surr!' Nish gasped. 'I'm sorry. I did not recognise –'

'You're just doing what you must, to survive,' said Flydd. 'Don't call me scrutator, Nish. That honour has been taken from me and, gossip tells me, given to your father. I'm Slave Flydd now. What brings you here?'

Nish told Flydd of his latest failing, in the smallest number of words he could. It hurt nearly as much as the lash. All his dreams were dead. He must face up to what he was, a worthless human being.

'We all make mistakes,' Flydd said out of the corner of his mouth. 'Get ready to pull.'

Nish looked around to see the overseer advancing, whip at the ready. The fellow caught Nish's eye, grinned and flicked the lash at him. It caught him on the nipple so painfully that Nish screamed. It felt as if his breast had been torn open.

'No talking!' rapped the overseer, lashing him again. '*Pull!* Pull until your hearts shudder and your bowels groan or, by the powers, I'll make you *suffer!*'

Nish threw his weight against the harness. Flydd did the same. The leather creaked; the rows of slaves behind them groaned. The whip cracked again and again, but the clanker did not budge.

'Pull!' roared the overseer.

Nish strained until his boots skidded in the mud, to no more effect than before. The overseer stormed back and forth, lashing and cursing them. Nish strained again until his heart felt about to explode in his chest. It made no difference. The clanker was irretrievably bogged.

If Nish had hoped for a respite, he was disappointed. While a bullock team was being brought up, they had to pull as hard as ever, and once it was harnessed in place the slave team was put beside the beasts. For every lash that fell on the haunches of the animals, the slaves felt three or four. All across the battlefield the scene was repeated: with soldiers, with other teams of slaves, with all the peasants and camp followers Jal-Nish had been able to round up, and with beasts of every description.

After hours of the most brutal labour Nish had ever experienced, the clanker began to creak and groan out of the mud wallow, though before it had gone a hundred paces it ended up in another, and many more lay ahead before it could be dragged to solid ground.

By that time it was well after dark. Each of the slaves was given a gourd full of sour water, a slab of black bread as hard as a brick and a mug of something which, with the most charitable will in the world, could only be described as slops. It had a sweet, off taste, as if it had begun to rot in the summer heat.

Nish took one sip and spat it into the grass. It was far worse than the food he had eaten in the refugee camp in Almadin in the spring. He was about to heave the mug of slops after it when Flydd said quietly, 'I'd advise you to eat every mouthful, and lick out the mug afterwards.'

'It's disgusting!'

'Aye, but you can't work without food. If you can't pull, the overseer will whip you into jelly and drag the clanker over you.'

'If this is my life, then the sooner it's over the better,' Nish muttered.

Flydd shrugged and sat down, jerking at the harness in a futile attempt to find a comfortable position. He ignored Nish, eating his slops slowly, as if savouring every morsel, and carefully wiping the mug out with lumps of bread.

'If you're not going to eat that, pass it over here.'

Wordlessly Nish handed him the mug. Had it been the finest food in the land, he could not have eaten a mouthful. His stomach was throbbing with despair.

'Better get some rest,' said Flydd. 'They'll be calling us out again in a few hours.'

'But it's dark.'

'It'll be light enough when they start to burn the bodies.'

A few hours later it started again, but this time it was worse. The battlefield was dotted with pyres, blazing piles of human and lyrinx dead. They provided enough light for the overseer to pick his targets, though not enough for him to be accurate. A blow aimed for Xervish Flydd's back came coiling around Nish's bent head, the hard tip of the lash catching him on the eyebrow with such force that he screamed.

'You stinking mongrel –' he raged, once the pain became bearable.

A dirty hand smacked him in the mouth, cutting off the abuse.

'Don't!' grated Flydd in his ear. 'Whatever they do, don't react in any way. Just pull, as hard as you can.'

Nish strained against the harness. 'The swine nearly took my eye out.'

'If you attack him, he'll take pleasure in removing the other eye, in a way you will *never* forget.'

'I want to die!'

'You won't be so lucky. We're put here to suffer, and while we can stagger, that's what we're going to do.'

'It doesn't seem to bother you.'

Flydd forced himself against the straps, grunting with the effort. 'I feel pain the same as any man, Nish. I've just learned not to show it.'

Nish supposed that must be true. The former scrutator was brutally scarred and he moved as though every bone in his body had been broken. There were rumours of his torment at the hands of the Council when he was a young man, for some unspecified crime.

'I can't take much more of this,' Nish groaned. 'It feels as if my leg bones are splintering with each step.'

'You'd be surprised how much the human body can endure,' said Flydd. 'You've got months of slavery ahead of you yet.'

'Then I'll kill myself.'

Flydd's fist came out of the dark, crashing into Nish's chin and knocking him backwards into the slush. The next pair of slaves went over him, tripped and fell down, pulling down the pair after that. The team ground to a halt.

The overseer came up the line, flogging indiscriminately. The slaves fell over themselves to get away. It took a good ten minutes before the tangle was sorted out and they were pulling in unison again. Nish took more lashes, though no more than his share.

'What did you do that for?' he muttered, feeling a split lip. Two teeth felt loose and one had a chip out of it.

'Do your duty like a man and don't whine about it!' snapped Flydd. 'I expected more of you, Nish.'

'But we're slaves,' cried Nish.

'Aye. Even so, we're doing vital work. The fate of humanity may rest on us getting these clankers to the field, and never forget it.'

Nish fell silent. Trust the scrutator (he could not stop thinking of Flydd that way) to keep his eye on the greater goal. Nish could not, and he felt bad about it. The survival of humanity hung by a thread and any little thing could make the difference, but it meant nothing to him. His own troubles were too overwhelming.

He tried to talk himself into it, telling himself what a self-ish, contemptible worm he was. Make something of your life, Nish! Do your very best, even if only as a slave.

It was impossible. He had fallen too far. Once he'd been part of a wealthy, powerful family. Now he'd lost everything, even his part in their Histories. Once he'd had an honourable trade; now he was beneath contempt. Once he'd had a father; now he had *nothing*. He *was* nothing.

They stopped just before dawn. Nish was so exhausted that he fell onto the mud and slept where he lay – blessed oblivion, though it did not last long.

He dreamed that he was sitting at a banquet table, dressed in robes woven with golden thread. A lovely young woman was at his left elbow, an even lovelier one at his right. He was speaking and the whole table hung on his words. Nish finished his speech to a roar of acclamation. As he bowed, he smelt the most delicious aromas as waiters hurried in, bearing huge platters of roast meats.

Nish woke salivating and the glorious smell was still there. He opened his eyes, realised where he was, and wept. He was covered in stinking, rotting mud. There was no dinner table; no audience. Worst of all, so horrible that he could not bear to think about it, the mouth-watering aroma came from the piles of burning dead. He was salivating over his own kind. He was a monster of depravity, no better than a cannibal.

'Ah, no,' he wailed, and flopped down in the mud again.

Flydd hauled him out, wiping his face with a callused hand. Nish, expecting to be smacked in the mouth again, pulled away.

'What is it?' said Flydd, watching the overseer over Nish's shoulder.

'I once had everything, and now I've lost it all. No, that's not true. I didn't lose it, I threw it away. I'm useless. And then, just then . . . my mouth was watering from the smell of cooked meat, and it was *human* meat.'

Flydd stared at him for a long time. 'Mine too. It's entirely natural. It doesn't make you any worse in my eyes.'

'You're a slave, surr. What you think doesn't matter.'

Flydd clenched his fist, but unclenched it. He sighed and, though plagued by his own self-doubt, put it aside. 'You've done plenty that's right, Nish. You got the best out of the seeker, little Ullii, where no one else could. You thought of the idea of air-floaters, without which the war might already be lost. You sailed a balloon all the way to Tirthrax, and found Tiaan there. You might have brought her and the crystal back, had you not faced people with far greater power than yourself. You killed the nylatl single-handed, and that was a feat worthy of half a page in the Histories. You saved the lives of thousands in the refugee camp. Had you not given warning in time, every person there might have fed the enemy.'

'How did you know about that?' said Nish.

'If a leaf falls in the forest when it should not, the scrutators hear about it.'

Nish must assume that the scrutator also knew about his disastrous attempt at diplomacy, and the unfortunate liaison, if it could be called that, with Yara's sister Mira.

'I have other failings,' Nish said, determined to scathe himself to the bone.

'Who does not? I have so many weaknesses that it makes me shudder to think about them. It doesn't stop me from trying, though. Don't take on the slave's mentality, Nish. Once you do, you might as well be dead.'

Nish glanced over his shoulder The overseer was not in sight, but a slave was squelching down the line with pannikins of water. Behind him, another bore a platter on which chunks of black bread looked as though they had been hacked up with an axe, and a filthy axe at that. 'There's one thing you haven't heard,' he said quietly.

'Oh?' said Flydd.

'After my latest failing, which put Tiaan into the hands of Vithis, I came before the Council of Scrutators. The head of the Council . . .'

'Chief Scrutator Ghorr,' Flydd prompted. He stared into space, lost in his own world, and Nish had to nudge him when the trusties held out the bread and water.

'Yes, Ghorr,' Nish said after they had gone. 'He demanded that my father prove his suitability to be a scrutator, by sentencing me. And Jal-Nish did.' Nish repeated the sentence, word by awful word. It was engraved in his mind, and would be until the day he died. 'My own father,' he said brokenly. 'He – he condemned me without a second's hesitation.' Nish related the whole terrible episode. 'I just can't comprehend it, surr.'

Flydd was staring at him, not breathing. 'And how did Ghorr react?'

'He seemed delighted.'

Flydd went so still that Nish wondered if he was alive. The

lump of coarse bread was held out in one hand, the gourd of water in the other. His scarred and knotted jaw looked as if it had been cast from bronze. Finally he gave a great shudder, turned to Nish and handed him the bread.

'Take this. I cannot eat.'

'But . . .' said Nish, 'yesterday you told me I must eat to survive.'

Flydd looked over his shoulder, then lowered his voice. 'What you've just told me makes my flesh crawl. There have always been people who would do anything, even sell their kin, to satisfy their lusts. I've met more than enough in my time. But for the chief of scrutators to encourage such a deed, to demand it as proof of worth to become a scrutator, shows that the Council is corrupt to the core.'

'I always thought the Council would do anything –' Nish began, but quickly censored himself.

'We did what was required for humanity to survive. I've done many things I'm not proud of, though, as scrutator, I would do them again. But this . . . How can the Council not see?'

'See what?' said Nish, gnawing at the hard bread, which had been milled so coarsely that many of the grains were whole. He spat out a particularly large grain, which turned out to be a pebble.

'That this deed, alone, makes Jal-Nish unworthy to be scrutator, and Ghorr to be chief. A man who puts ambition before anything else can *never* be trusted to act for the common good. And a man who demands such an act lacks the judgment to be a lowly prober, much less a scrutator. Ghorr must be brought down, and the Council with him.'

With a loud crack, the neck of the gourd shattered under the force of Flydd's grip, showering him with water. He put the ragged end to his mouth and drained it, then tossed the gourd into the mud.

With a rueful smile he spoke, quietly so the next pair of slaves would not hear: 'Well may you laugh, to hear a slave plot the downfall of the scrutators. But I swear to you that I will do it, whatever it takes. This monstrosity, this abomination of the Council, must be wiped from the earth.'

'Including my father?' Despite everything, Nish could not even think of revenge. All he felt was an empty bewilderment, that his father could have done such a thing to him.

'Especially Jal-Nish.'

SEVEN

In the panic after the node exploded, and the disabled air-floater crash-landed in the middle of the battlefield, everyone fled for their lives. No one noticed that little Ullii was not with them.

Ullii was so furious with Flydd and Irisis that she stayed behind. The scrutator had gained her cooperation by telling her that he'd found her long-lost twin brother, Myllii, but it had all been a lie. Flydd had no idea where Myllii was.

When the reverberations from the node had faded enough for her to open her lattice, the mental matrix by which she organised her unique view of the world, there were lyrinx everywhere. Huge lyrinx with bloodstained claws and shreds of flesh and skin between their teeth. Ullii stifled a gasp, jumped over the side and ran after Flydd. Better him than the clawers, as she thought of them, but the bright sun burst up, right into her eyes. Covering her face, she lurched back to the air-floater, but couldn't find her mask or goggles. In daylight she was helpless without one or the other. Ullii was groping under the tilted deck for them when she realised that she was completely alone.

'Wait!' she wailed, but her high, despairing cry did not carry. Despite Flydd lying to her, despite Irisis letting her down as well, in this nightmare of blood and violence Ullii could not do without them. '*Wait!*' she shouted in her high little voice.

It was impossible to hear anything above the battle cries of the lyrinx, the sound of weapons on armour, the hiss of spears and catapult balls, the screams of men and beasts in agony.

Her ears hurt; even after plugging them with lumps of wet clay she could still hear the racket.

Her burning eyes were streaming with tears and she could not leave the air-floater. Ullii searched for Irisis and Xervish Flydd. Since they both had a talent for the Secret Art, they should have appeared in the lattice. But Irisis and Flydd were far across the battlefield, and in the chaos Ullii could not pick them out. Thousands of lyrinx showed, and devices powered by the Secret Art. Only those capable of storing power were working now. Anything that relied on the field was dead.

Ullii felt abandoned – it had been happening all her life. What was she to do? She couldn't survive by herself. And what about the little intruder growing inside her? She felt protective towards the baby because she and Nish had made it together, but sometimes she hated it. One day it would abandon her, too.

The battlefield became so terrifying that Ullii had to shut down her lattice. She could not stand violence of any kind. The war was a nightmare brought to life and she did not know how to cope. Ullii did the only thing left to her. She crept into the smallest, darkest space she could find, a corner of the air-floater's tiny galley, curled up into a ball and closed down her senses one by one. The world vanished.

All day the battle raged around her. Several times the wrecked air-floater was struck by running lyrinx, hard enough to shake the flimsy structure. Once a minor battle raged inside as four soldiers pursued a wounded lyrinx and dispatched it. Men and lyrinx died to her left, then in the rear. Ullii was oblivious.

Thirst roused her in the cool of the evening. Uncoiling gracefully, she opened her crusted eyes. The galley was a mess. When the air-floater had flipped upside down, pans, pots, food and wine had been scattered everywhere. Ullii found a battered pot, tapped water from a barrel and gulped it down, though it had an unpleasant metallic taste. She found dried fruit, stale bread and a piece of mild cheese that had gone hard and cracked in the heat of the day. It suited her perfectly, for Ullii could not bear any kind of herb or spice, or other strong flavours, which were to her overpoweringly intense.

Sitting on the floor, she gnawed at the cheese while she used the lattice to sense what was going on around her. The fighting had paused; the battlefield was quiet apart from the piteous groans of the dying and the crackle of fires here and there. The smell of blood, excrement and raw flesh made her stomach heave.

Other fires lit up the human camps, as well as those of the Aachim, but not the lyrinx. They did not need camp fires. And in the distance Ullii could see, and feel, and sense with every one of her senses, the baleful incandescence of the exploded node. It was still molten, concealed by impenetrable fumes, and spurting and dribbling white-hot rock like a miniature volcano. The fields that had once been such a vital part of it had gone, though Ullii still sensed *something* there.

Once more she sought for Irisis and Xervish Flydd, but did not find them. There were too many people with uncanny talents, and too many devices employing the Secret Art. Her lattice glowed with them, like knotted stars in the heavens. Ullii did not look for Nish, though she longed for him. Having no Art, he did not appear in her lattice at all.

But one point stood out like a nova in the night sky, and she recognised it at once. It was the glowing knot of the amplimet, twinned to a smaller knot that signified Tiaan. After months of searching for them, Ullii knew those marks the instant they appeared

They were not far away, though she could not tell where. The lattice was twisted up on itself, blasted out of shape by the sub-ethyric explosion from the node. Everything was warped and confused.

Ullii did not feel safe in the air-floater but she had nowhere else to go. She had never felt so abandoned. *Nish*, she cried silently. *Where are you?* Ullii had last seen him as a prisoner of the Aachim, and he'd not seemed as pleased to see her as she'd been to find him. She suppressed that worry. Could he be at the camp surrounded by those shining metal constructs? Ullii dared not go to see; the Aachim leader was a harsh man, like the people who had tormented her in childhood.

She ate some more bread, then slept, the baby kicking in her belly like the feathery brush of a fish's tail. The night passed. The fighting stopped briefly before continuing, as brutal and bloody as ever. In the morning her sleep was interrupted by flashes brighter than the sun. One passed right across the air-floater, showing every rib, strut and wire of the collapsed gasbag, and her black glass goggles jammed under a bench.

Scrambling for them, Ullii stared up at the sky. The fleet of air-floaters was impossible to miss. Their crystals appeared faintly in her lattice, a perfect formation of three by four. Something else showed, too. The presence was also faint, denoting only a minor talent for the Secret Art, but it had a signature she would have known anywhere – a festering corruption of mind and body that made her belly cramp and her skin crawl. Ullii had not felt it since their escape from the mine at the manufactory, months ago. It was the man she feared most – Jal-Nish Hlar.

She tried to close down her senses again, but this time they would not obey her, for fear of what might happen when she was helpless. Scuttling into the galley, she closed the door and piled bags and barrels against it. Without a window, it was stiflingly hot – too hot for comfort – and though it was dim inside, for once that did not help.

She closed her eyes, but again that beam passed over the air-floater, and light streamed in through a tiny crack in the wall, so bright that she *felt* it. Ullii was not safe anywhere. As she put her hands over the goggles, the earth began to shake as if thousands of heavy feet were pounding it. The clawers were on the move. If they came this way, one of them would eat her in a few bone-snapping, brain-spurting gulps.

Clearing the door, Ullii crept out, peering fearfully through her goggles. Another blast of light seared from sky to ground. A great wail went up and she saw the enemy running for their lives, a horde of them heading directly for the air-floater. In their panic, they might crash right through the flimsy structure.

Not far away a clanker lay on its side, torn open from one end to the other. It offered better shelter, since the beasts would have to go round it. Slipping over the side, Ullii bent low to the ground and ran. The enemy pounded towards her. Halfway to the clanker she encountered a dead clawer lying in a depression. Ullii froze, staring at the great hulk, whose eyes seemed to be looking right at her.

It was almost her undoing. Ullii could not move, terrified that the creature would come to life and tear her in half. It didn't and, finding courage at the last instant, she leapt over it and scuttled the dozen steps to the side of the clanker. Pulling herself underneath its overhanging side, she closed her eyes and prayed.

The mob thundered past, rocking the clanker. The metal frame creaked and groaned. Ullii shuddered and curled into a smaller ball, knowing that the clawers could find her by smell if they wanted to.

The last went by, limping. She did not move. Not until the stampede faded into the distance did she dare to open her eyes.

The air-floaters still shone their beam one way and another. Ullii slipped inside the clanker, looking for water and food. She did not find any, only blood on the floor, the smell so sickly that she almost passed out.

She hid underneath in the small patch of shadow, following it around as the sun rose higher then sank towards the west. By the mid-afternoon it became clear that the enemy were abandoning Snizort, but Ullii did not know what to do. Experience had taught her that few people could be trusted. Nor could she live alone, in the wild. Food, clothing and shelter had always been provided for her and, by herself, she would not survive a week. She could not kill another animal for food, nor eat its bloody, pungent flesh if she did.

She would have to follow the clanker column and find a

way to live off it without being caught. Though Ullii was a creature of the night, used to moving silently and secretly, that thought filled her with terror. Stealing from the army was a capital crime. Should she be caught, they would kill her like a beast. But she had to eat.

Going back for water, she found the air-floater smashed to pieces. The gasbag, a good fifteen spans long, had disappeared. Searching in the mud she discovered a water barrel with a few handfuls of brown water in it, and drank the lot. There was nothing left of the food.

It was growing dark. She circled around one of the camps, and around again, silent as a ghost in the darkness. Many times she came on ruined clankers, but the smell of blood and death was so strong she could not bear to crawl inside. She was ravenous, and so desperate for a drink that, not long before dawn, Ullii approached a dead soldier. Holding her nose with one hand, she went through his pack.

She found nothing to eat or drink, but the next corpse had a stoppered skin of wine and a bag of flat honey biscuits. After wiping the mouth of the skin a dozen times, and suppressing a shudder, she put it to her lips.

The wine was so sour that it took her breath away, and the taste made her want to wash her mouth out. She took another sip, then a mouthful. It had been watered and was weak, but Ullii had not taken wine before, nor any kind of alcoholic drink.

Moving upwind of the corpse, she nibbled at one of the honey biscuits. It was delicious, though intensely sweet. She ate it all and took another sip of the wine, which now tasted even more sour.

Ullii wandered off, alternately nibbling to break the sourness of the wine, then drinking to rid her mouth of the excessive sweetness. In this way she circumnavigated the camp again. To her right she heard cursing and the distinctive sound of the whip. Groups of harnessed men were attempting to drag clankers out of a bog. She turned the other way and shortly came upon a ruined clanker, just as the sky was growing light. Her head felt strange. Ullii giggled, staggered and threw up.

The sun burst over the horizon, right into her eyes. Ullii stumbled around the clanker, found a hole in the side and crawled in. All around her echoed the roars of overseers and the groaning of slaves. There was only one consolation – the lyrinx had gone. In the core of her lattice she could see their columns, moving steadily away, abandoning Snizort and all they had made here.

Not quite all – they carried a number of strange objects with them, thick with the aura of the Secret Art. But they were shielded and Ullii could tell no more about them, even had she wanted to. She sought for the solace of sleep.

Ullii woke with a terrible headache, for she'd slept the day through, and the night. The sun was beating down on the clanker now, which creaked and squealed as the metal plates expanded and slipped over one another. Her mouth tasted foul; she was thirstier than ever but could not stomach the wine. She ate a few more honey biscuits, sniffed the contents of the skin and poured it onto the ground.

Not daring to go out in the daytime, Ullii lay panting in the clanker until sundown, growing weaker and weaker. Her headache was worse than before. She felt sure that she was dying.

The clanker cooled quickly once the sun set and Ullii, idly trailing her fingers along the upper side, discovered that it was covered in beads of moisture. She licked her fingers. Her tongue was so dry that it felt crackly. Following the trail of drops down the side she discovered a small pool of condensation, about a cupful, in a metal hollow. After drinking it dry, she felt strong enough to look for more.

Her senses were so acute that she could smell water, even among the fumes from the bodies that had been burned, and the putrid reek of those rotting where they had fallen. She found a gourd of water, drank her fill and went back to her hiding place, where sleep was her only escape from the

81

stench. The next morning she finished the water and went outside. Something had changed.

All was silent. The hauling teams had dragged the last of the undamaged clankers from the mire onto solid ground, and were now heading towards the nearest field. She was alone with the dead.

Ullii followed the column for days, sleeping in a tree or hollow by day, creeping at the coat-tails of the procession at night, and living on the few meagre scraps she could find. She did not know what else to do.

It was most unpleasant. Several times she saw the one-armed man in the platinum mask, and after that Jal-Nish's knot was always in her lattice, a shuddering horror. And even from half a league away, the smell of eighty thousand unwashed bodies was so strong than she had to plug her nose. The merest whiff made her gag, and it grew worse as time wore on. One night she found nothing edible at all, and was driven by hunger to creep to the front of the procession, where the noise and light were least, to see if she could steal anything.

It was the boldest deed little Ullii had ever attempted. Her whole life had been spent in fear of people and their punishments. Now she must steal or starve. She crept along the line of the leading column, keeping watch in her lattice for Jal-Nish. He was over the other side, thankfully. A gentle breeze drifted the stink of the army away from her. Ullii took out her noseplugs. Smell was her most powerful sense and she needed it here.

The column was still, the slaves taking a few hours' rest before the labour began again at dawn. She slipped closer, as quick as silk in the darkness. An errant breeze brought her an aroma from the camp ovens – fresh bread. Five hundred bakers had worked all night to feed the multitude their breakfast.

Salivating, Ullii scanned the area. The bakers' wagons and their portable ovens, were well lit and securely guarded, so there was no chance of stealing anything there. She moved up the line, looking for something she could snatch. It had to be done secretly. If they saw her she would never get away.

As she prowled, the wind changed, momentarily blowing from the head of the line. Even among the thousands of sweaty bodies, Ullii caught an elusive, familiar scent. Her eyes moistened. She raised her head, sniffing the air. There it was again. Her nipples stood up and Ullii felt an overwhelming flood of desire.

It was Nish! Her beloved Nish, who had looked after her so tenderly before. If only she could get to him, she would be safe at last.

EIGHT

Irisis screamed as the pair of lyrinx leapt through the door; she couldn't help herself. With a backwards flip that she had not known she could perform, she fled the other way, expecting to find Flangers dead.

He was working the sword furiously with his good arm, fighting for his life. The lyrinx was moving slowly now, the hole in its side pulsing purple blood, though one of its blows might still have disembowelled a man.

Flangers hacked at it but missed. It slashed with one hand, then the other, the blows tearing through the soldier's shirt as he wove backwards. He stumbled, slipped in purple blood and fell to one knee.

Irisis, still running, acted instinctively. Leaping high, she landed on the lyrinx's back, caught hold of its crest and brought her knee up hard against the base of its skull. The lyrinx reared up, shaking its head as it reached back with its left hand to tear her off.

As the blood-tipped claws came at her face, Irisis hung on with her knees and pummelled it about the side of the head. The blows seemed to daze it so she poked her fingers into its eyes.

Flangers came up off the floor like a ball from a catapult. The outstretched sword slid between Irisis's knees, found the gap in the plates and plunged into the creature's throat. Irisis, unable to untangle her legs in time, went all the way down with the falling beast. She hit the floor, rolled and came up holding her sword.

At the death of their comrade, the other two lyrinx

checked, though not for long. Irisis just stood there, her initiative exhausted. Flangers caught her hand, jerking her away.

'Through the door behind me.'

It was just a few steps away but she hadn't noticed it before. Irisis waved her sword around in a professional manner as Flangers jerked it open.

'Hurry!' he roared.

Irisis took one look over her shoulder and ran for the door. Flangers kicked it shut behind them. They fled across the oval space outside but, halfway, Irisis stopped to look back.

'Come on!' Flangers was limping badly.

She stayed where she was. 'There's something wrong. They're not coming after us.'

He felt his injured arm with his good hand. 'Perhaps they're sneaking round through one of the other doors, to take us from behind.'

Irisis tiptoed back to the door, beyond which she heard thuds and squeals. 'No, they're back at their bloody work, killing the little beasts. They don't want any of them taken alive. I wonder why?'

'I can't bear to think,' said Flangers. 'Hey, *no*!'

Irisis had opened the door and was peering inside. One of the lyrinx, not three steps away, broke off from its bloody work with the club. Its dark eyes, the size of lemons, were fixed on her. She trembled. In the past year she'd had a number of encounters with the great beasts. It could kill her with a blow, yet it fascinated her. Its size, its strength, the play of muscles down its armoured front, the flickering skin colours, now mauve, now purple and black – and something more.

'What are you doing?' she said, not expecting it to know her language.

'My duty,' it said clearly, in a rumble deeper than any human had ever spoken. The sound tickled her eardrums. 'Seek you to stop me, small one, I must end you the same way.' It hefted the bloody club.

No one had described Irisis as small before, but to a lyrinx the largest humans were puny creatures. The other creature called in a higher voice, almost a chirrup. The first brandished the club. Irisis ducked backwards, the door was kicked shut and something slammed against it.

'Whatever they're doing,' said Irisis, 'they're determined to finish it. I'd better have a look at your arm.'

'It's not too bad.' Flangers peeled back the shirt to reveal two raw gouges from wrist to shoulder. 'Painful, though.'

'I'll bet. What about the other wound?'

He looked abashed. 'Oh, it's all right.'

'Then why are you limping? Turn around, let me take a look at it.'

The seat of his trousers had been torn out, and four deep claw marks carved across his right buttock, two extending onto the left. 'That'll need attention . . .' she began.

'Don't see much point right now.'

'Hoy!' called a soldier's voice.

'Over here,' roared Flangers.

Young Ivar and the other soldiers came running, followed by Fyn-Mah and a dark-skinned man Irisis had never seen before – yes she had. It was Eiryn Muss, Flydd's spy, in another of his disguises. This one was masterly – he seemed to have altered his size and shape as well as his appearance. He was the same height, but lean, stringy, and his eyes were a glossy dark brown.

'What happened?' panted Fyn-Mah.

'We found their flesh-forming cages, at least five rooms of them,' said Irisis. 'All the creatures in the first three rooms were dead or dying. In the fourth we came upon a lyrinx, destroying the remainder. It attacked; nearly killed us too, and then another two appeared. Flangers managed to kill the first lyrinx and we got out the door. They didn't come after us – weren't interested. They're finishing off the rest of the flesh-formed.'

'They don't want us to get a live one,' said Fyn-Mah. 'All the more urgent that we do.'

'What are you doing here?' Irisis said to Muss, who reeked of tar smoke.

'Scrutators' business.' He looked frustrated. It was the first time she'd seen him show emotion.

'So are we. We need a hand.'

'In the struggle, some of the cages were broken open,' Irisis said to Fyn-Mah, 'and a few animals escaped. If we were to attack suddenly, we might overcome the lyrinx and catch one of the little beasts.'

'By the time we break down the door there'll be no taking them by surprise.'

'Especially since they've barricaded it,' said Flangers.

'But . . .' Fyn-Mah rubbed her fingers together, reflecting for a moment. 'If I were to blast the door off its hinges, using the Art . . . All right! I'll try it. Stand back.'

'The node is dead,' Irisis reminded her.

'Artefacts that store power will still work, though I'd have preferred not to waste one here. Put your hands over your ears.'

She pressed a bead into her right ear, another into the left. Taking something small and shiny from a buttoned pocket, Fyn-Mah rubbed it between her hands as if to warm it, closed her fingers loosely around it and held her hand high. The upraised arm shook, her face went red, and a blade of raw sound sheared out between her fingers. The air shimmered, marking its passage. The door burst into splinters. Fyn-Mah was tossed the other way, to land on her back.

The sound, even through Irisis's hands, was a nagging, rasping screech. She crouched down, put her head between her knees and pressed her hands over her ears. Beside her, Flangers grunted as if he'd been punched in the stomach.

Beyond the doorway, the cages had been piled against the far wall by the force of the blast. One lyrinx lay on the now empty floor, kicking feebly. A shard of wood the size of a pick handle had gone through its thigh, severing the artery, and it was bleeding to death. The one Irisis had spoken to had come to rest against the far wall, its neck broken.

Several flesh-formed creatures lay on the floor, dead. 'Go through all the cages,' said Fyn-Mah, stooped and shaking with aftersickness. 'If there's any beast left alive, we must have it.'

'Are you all right?' said Flangers.

'Go on. I'll be with you in a minute.'

They started on the grim task, keeping a careful watch on the wounded lyrinx. It tried to get up, its claws scraping at the soft sandstone underfoot, but was too weak. Finally it slumped on its side, unmoving, its yellow-brown eyes watching them.

It did not take long to search the cages, but they found nothing alive. Fyn-Mah appeared, shaking her head. 'They must have killed them all.' She knelt beside the dying creature; not too close. 'Are they all dead, lyrinx?'

'Yesss . . .' It was just a puff of breath. 'All dead.' Its head thumped against the floor.

'Some escaped their cages,' said Irisis. 'I don't think they could have got out of the room.'

The smoky smell had grown stronger, suggesting that the fire was moving this way. 'Search the room,' ordered Fyn-Mah. 'Quickly. Every minute we spend here lessens our chance of getting out of Snizort.'

'Here's something,' said the young soldier, on his knees beside a cupboard that had fallen on several others, leaving spaces between. 'A trail of blood goes in here.'

They dragged the cupboards out of the way. Underneath lay a flesh-formed creature, as dead as the others. Fyn-Mah stood frowning at it, took a notebook from her pocket and began to write swiftly.

She went around the room, describing and sketching the dead creatures while the search was completed. Looking bitterly disappointed, she disappeared into the adjoining room. The soldiers followed, leaving just Irisis and Flangers.

'Where's Muss?' said Irisis.

'He was right behind you –' Flangers scratched his head in bemusement. 'I wonder what he's up to?'

'It doesn't do to inquire into scrutators' affairs,' said Irisis. 'We'd better go.'

Flangers rubbed his wounded arm, staring at the floor. 'Take a look at this, Crafter.' He squatted down, further splitting his pants, and emitted the faintest of groans.

'What is it?'

His finger traced a bloody squiggle across the floor. 'This was made by something trying to hide. Give me a hand.'

They pulled the broken cupboards out of the way, inspecting each carefully, though it was not until the very last that they found anything. It was a furred creature about the size of Flangers's hand, the oddest little thing Irisis had ever seen. The fur was wet, bloody in patches and sticky in others. It scratched at Flangers as he picked it up, though its soft claws did not break the skin.

'It's newborn,' he said wonderingly. 'That must have been the mother and, as she lay dying, she gave birth.'

'Better than nothing, I suppose.' Irisis looked for something to keep it in. 'I'll tell Fyn-Mah. Flangers, what *are* you doing?'

He was crouched beside the dead mother, holding the little one to a teat. 'It'll need feeding, and there's nothing better than mother's milk.'

The man never ceased to surprise her. Leaving him to his domestic duties, she went into the next room. 'Fyn-Mah! we've found one – an infant.'

The perquisitor came running. 'Where?'

'Flangers is feeding it.' Irisis found a small, undamaged cage which she padded with handfuls of straw.

Fyn-Mah was standing over Flangers 'Come on, soldier!'

'One feed will make a big difference to its chances,' said Flangers.

'The time could make a big difference to our chances. Oh, all right, but only a few minutes. Where's Muss?'

'He just disappeared.'

Fyn-Mah did not look surprised. 'He's got other business to attend to.' With an anxious glance at the door, she hurried back to the adjoining room to resume her search.

Irisis sat the cage next to the dead mother. It made her

uncomfortable to see Flangers feeding the creature, but it fascinated her too. What an unusual man he was. 'Did you grow up on a farm?'

'No, I lived all my life in Thurkad, until I signed up.'

'Then how did you know . . .?'

'I'm just interested in things. Do you know –'

Fyn-Mah came flying through the door, followed by the soldiers. 'Come on!' She hurtled out.

Flangers slipped the little creature into his pocket. Irisis took the cage. 'What's the matter?'

Fyn-Mah was running on tiptoes. 'There are more lyrinx on the way.'

'How do you know?' Irisis panted. 'Where are they?'

'Shut up and run!'

She led the way, followed by Irisis and Flangers, then the soldiers. The young captain looked very uncomfortable to be bringing up the rear. They raced down the corridor, sticky tar rasping underfoot, turned the corner and saw half a dozen lyrinx ahead. Fyn-Mah spun on one slender foot and darted to her right, into a smaller, darker tunnel.

'I'm not sure this is the right way,' said Irisis.

Fyn-Mah glanced at the swinging cage as Irisis pounded beside her. 'Where is it?'

'Flangers has it in his pocket.' He was in the middle of the line of soldiers.

'Flangers! Up with me. Myrum, go back with Irisis.'

Flangers made his way up. Myrum, a stumpy chunk of scarred muscle, moved back. Irisis studied him as he joined her. Long black hair curtained a high, bald dome. The old soldier was missing one ear, most of his teeth and the tip of his nose, yet she had not seen him without a smile.

'What're you so happy about?' she said.

'Being alive,' Myrum said with zest.

'Enjoy it while it lasts.'

'I do – every minute.'

'Lead the way, Flangers,' said Fyn-Mah. 'And take good care of the little beast.'

He flashed her a grin, sketching a salute with his left hand, and moved ahead. Fyn-Mah came next and Irisis just behind, with a short gap to Myrum, the other four soldiers and the captain at the rear.

Fyn-Mah's eyes were fixed on Flangers's scored buttocks, which were round, tight and moved beautifully as he ran. Irisis found her own eyes drawn to the sight, and once there, it was hard to look anywhere else. She could not help wondering what it would be like to lie with him. She'd not slept with a soldier before. Her lovers had been men from the manufactory. She wondered if Fyn-Mah was drawn to him. Impossible to tell; the perquisitor never gave anything away.

Fyn-Mah was fleet, considering her small stature. Irisis's long legs could barely keep up with her. The soldiers were also labouring, but they wore chest armour and carried heavy packs. Behind them a sword clanged on something hard. A man cried out, then there was a thud, barely audible over the sound of their pounding feet.

One down, Irisis thought. Probably the captain who'd insisted on his orders in writing – fat lot of good it had done him. Why was this mission so important? Was this little creature what Fyn-Mah had hoped to find, or had she been looking for something else when she went off the other way? It was unlikely Irisis would ever find out. All quisitors, from lowly probers to exalted scrutators, were close-mouthed, but Perquisitor Fyn-Mah made an art form of it. And she had good reason not to trust Irisis.

Irisis caught a whiff of smoke – the throat-gripping reek of burning tar. When the node-drainer was destroyed, the incandescent blast would have liquefied rock.

A scream and there was one less pair of pounding boots behind her. Attacking from the rear, out of the dark, suited the lyrinx perfectly. There was nothing to be done about it. They had no spears to throw, no crossbows to fire, and they dared not stop to make a stand. The tunnel was too narrow. All they could do was run.

The third man fell without a sound, the sudden lack of

footsteps all they knew of his passing. 'That's three we've lost,' Irisis gasped. 'Slow down.'

A grunted cry. *Four!*

Fyn-Mah threw a glance over her shoulder. Her iron control was slipping; Irisis could see the panic in her eyes. 'We can't afford to.'

'We can't afford to lose anyone else,' said Irisis.

Fyn-Mah called out to Flangers, who wore neither pack nor armour and had been drawing ahead, despite his injury. 'Slow down, soldier.'

The two remaining soldiers closed the gap. Myrum was still grinning, though it was more forced. Young Ivar's eyes were ablaze with terror.

Myrum clapped him on the shoulder. 'Do your duty like a man, lad.'

Ivar nodded as he ran, his head jerking like a puppet. Myrum ushered him ahead, taking the last place in the line.

But he's not a man, thought Irisis. He's just a boy. What kind of monsters are we, that we demand such sacrifices of children? Yet, selfishly, she was glad that the lad was between her and the enemy. Those few extra moments of life were precious.

I'm sorry, Ivar. Myrum is going to be next, and then you. The old fellow will put up one hell of a struggle, maybe even kill one of the enemy, if he's lucky, but the next will get him. That's all his life was for. And then, just you, Ivar. You won't last a minute. Who'll mourn your insignificant life and brutal death? We won't, because we'll be following you. Everything we've done will have been for nothing.

'Where are you going?' panted Irisis. Fyn-Mah had called directions to Flangers whenever they came to a junction, but apart from that she'd said nothing at all.

'I left a *finder* in the air-floater. I'm tracking it back as best I can.'

Irisis had never heard of a finder. How could it show Fyn-Mah the way back through this labyrinth?

'Fyn-Mah!' she hissed. 'Why don't you blast them with another of those crystals?'

The perquisitor turned as she ran and Irisis saw torment in her eyes. 'I can't.'

'You don't have any more crystals?'

A long pause. 'I have one,' she said softly. 'I'm saving it for an emergency.'

'And this isn't?' Irisis said in a low voice. 'You could have saved those soldiers and you chose not to? You callous bitch!'

The whole left side of Fyn-Mah's face quivered. 'I have my orders, Crafter. If I use it now I won't have it later, and believe me, before we get out of here we're going to need it.'

Irisis lowered her voice. 'So the soldiers are expendable?'

'I don't like it, but yes, they are.'

'And me? Is that what I'm here for too?'

'You know it isn't. But, since you've asked, I'll sacrifice you, too, if I have to. What are any of our lives, before the fate of humanity?'

NINE

They ran until they could run no further, when Irisis realised that only Myrum was behind her. Ivar had fallen back and been killed without their even knowing it. Irisis brushed a tear from one eye. He had been just a boy doing his duty.

Myrum was scarlet in the face and labouring under his pack. 'I'd chuck that away, if I were you,' said Irisis.

'I can manage it,' he gasped. 'It's needed. We seem to have lost them.'

Iris doubted that. 'We must have run leagues, Fyn-Mah. Are you sure you're going the right way?'

The perquisitor avoided her eye, staring down the three passages ahead.

'In a straight line,' Irisis went on, 'we'd have gone right across Snizort and out the other side by now.'

Fyn-Mah checked the small object in her hand. 'We go right.'

'You're not leading us out at all!' Irisis said furiously. 'You're taking us further in.'

The perquisitor moved into the right-hand tunnel. 'We had to take the long way round,' she said unconvincingly. 'There's fire in a central core of tunnels surrounding the Great Seep.'

Irisis followed, keeping a careful watch over her shoulder. As she passed what seemed no more than a dark niche in the wall, something slipped out beside them. With a yelp she leapt out of the way, for it looked like a little wingless lyrinx. She had her sword out when it said, in Eiryn Muss's voice, 'This way!'

The disguise was a brilliant one – it might even have fooled a lyrinx, from a distance. Muss was truly a master. How did he create such wonders from the small pack on his back?

'I've found it,' he said to Fyn-Mah. 'The tunnel collapsed and they must've thought it was buried too deep to recover.' He still had that frustrated look.

'What's still here?' said Irisis. What were they up to now?

Muss did not answer, but led them past a T-junction down a tunnel littered with fallen rock. 'The floor drops sharply, just ahead.'

Several slabs of the tunnel had slid downwards, like slices off the end of a hollow loaf. Irisis made it down the half-span onto the first step, and a similar distance to the second, but the third slab had fallen so far that only a crescent-shaped hole, the size of a section through the side of a beer barrel, connected it to the space they stood in. There were smash marks on its upper lip, presumably where the lyrinx had tried to break in.

Irisis hesitated. It would be a tight squeeze. 'If we're halfway through and it slips again, it'll cut us in half.'

'I've been down there,' said Muss. 'It's as safe as anywhere in Snizort.'

'That's comforting!'

Flangers squeezed through head-first, grunting with the effort, his feet waving in the air. Abruptly he cried out and his legs whipped through. Fyn-Mah pulled back, snatching out her knife. Irisis drew her sword – not that it would be much use in such a confined space.

'You damn fool, Muss!' cried an enraged Flangers, following that with a stream of oaths Irisis had never heard before. 'Why didn't you tell me the drop was a span and a half? I nearly broke my neck.'

'I got down it without any trouble,' Muss said indifferently.

'Must be a bloody lizard! Pass me the lantern, Fyn-Mah, and come through carefully. I'll catch you.'

Being small, Fyn-Mah wriggled through without difficulty. Irisis followed. It was a tight fit for her and she felt sure she was going to fall on her head, but Flangers's upstretched hands caught hers and she slid into his arms.

He bore her weight without strain and set her on her feet. Taking up the lantern, he led the way down a series of tunnel slices like thigh-high steps.

'Aren't you going to give Muss a hand?' she said in his ear.

'He can bounce down on his pointy head for all I care.'

'You don't like our prober?'

'There's something a bit off about him,' Flangers said out of the corner of his mouth.

Irisis looked back but the spy was already standing at the base of the drop, as if he'd floated down. He brushed past, taking the lantern.

'He's a strange one,' she said quietly. 'His work is always flawless, but he hasn't a friend in the world, unless you count Flydd. He eats alone, even sleeps alone, if he sleeps at all.'

'Maybe being the perfect spy is all he needs,' said Flangers. 'It's a solitary profession.'

'It's just here!' called Muss. 'Get a move on.'

They crowded into a small, circular chamber whose roof was a perfect dome of sandstone. A squat object like an inverted sombrero stood knee-high on a pedestal in the centre of the room. It had a short brown stalk on which was mounted a yellow frilled brim. It was not alive – it had been created by the lyrinx in one of their patterners.

Fyn-Mah skidded to a stop. 'Myrum, defend the entrance. Muss, check that there's no other way in. Flangers, see if you can get that.'

'There isn't any other way in,' said Muss.

'What is it?' said Flangers.

'It's called a phynadr,' said Fyn-Mah. 'The enemy make them in all shapes and sizes, to draw power from the field. We're taking it back so we can see how it works.'

'The lyrinx tried to break in for it,' said Flangers, 'so it's likely they'll be waiting when we crawl out.'

'Then it it'll be time for you to do your duty, soldier,' said the perquisitor.

Flangers took hold of the object, which slipped through his fingers. 'Can't get a grip on it,' he muttered.

Irisis touched it with her fingers. The phynadr was superficially similar to the torgnadr, or node-drainer, she'd helped Flydd to destroy, though it had been leathery. This phynadr was soft, compressing under her touch but springing back into shape when she let it go.

Flangers put his arms around it and heaved, but his arms slid off. To their right, Fyn-Mah was sketching shapes in the air. Whatever magic it was, Irisis prayed that it would work quickly. She threw a glance over her shoulder.

Flangers whipped out his sword. 'Don't damage it,' yelled Fyn-Mah.

He slid the point of his sword under the flat base of the phynadr. The edges, tinged purple, seemed to recoil from the metal, revealing a white underside. Flangers pushed the sword all the way, levered, and the phynadr popped off, emitting a musky, molasses-sweet odour.

Irisis caught it as it toppled. It was rather heavier than it looked. The phynadr bent in the middle and the base pulled itself down hard, trying to reattach to the pedestal, but Flangers kept the blade underneath. Yellow jelly oozed from beneath the cap. Fyn-Mah pushed Irisis out of the way, drew a black bag over the phynadr and swiftly tied the top. Throwing it over her shoulder, she staggered under the weight, recovered and hurried back to the collapsed section.

'I'll go first,' she said at the vertical wall.

Flangers boosted her up. 'Keep a sharp lookout.'

'Don't worry.' She crawled through. 'It's safe.'

'It would be,' said Irisis. 'They want the phynadr more than us, so they'll be waiting around the corner.'

Flangers boosted Myrum, then Irisis. Muss gave Flangers a leg-up. 'Need a hand?' Flangers said.

'I'll be right,' said Muss.

'Come on!' Fyn-Mah called. 'It's not far now.'

A lyrinx roared near the T-junction. Myrum shouted a battle cry and ran for it. His sword clacked against a skin plate, something whistled through the air, then he was back-pedalling, attempting to defend himself against two lyrinx at once.

He cursed, slipping to one knee. Irisis was sure he was done for, but the old soldier sprang forward, fast and low, his sword sliding neatly between the belly plates of the leading lyrinx. It sagged to the left, crashing into the other beast, and they went down in a tangle of arms and legs. The soldier dispatched the second with a sword tip to the jugular.

'We go right,' said Fyn-Mah, leading the way with the bag slung over her shoulder.

'That was a neat piece of sword work,' Irisis said to Myrum.

'Just luck,' replied Myrum. 'I was sure I was dead.'

'Dare say you will be before we get out of here.'

'Dare say we both will.'

The tunnel now headed steeply down. It was dark, but the way ahead was illuminated by a reddish glow coming from Fyn-Mah's fist. The other crystal, presumably.

It was hard work running down the steep slope. Halfway to the bottom they passed from stone into solid tar. It was so sticky underfoot that with every step they were in danger of toppling. Myrum looked exhausted, Fyn-Mah was staggering under the weight of the bag, and Flangers winced with every step. The scabbed gouges across his buttocks were bleeding. Muss had disappeared again.

'Should we wait for the prober?' asked Irisis.

'He can take care of himself,' said Fyn-Mah, moving the bag onto her other shoulder.

'Do you want me to carry that?' Irisis offered.

Fyn-Mah shook her head.

They were still heading down steeply and the air was smoky. 'How far now?' said Irisis, worrying that Flangers would break down. She felt sure Fyn-Mah would leave him behind.

Fyn-Mah did not answer, which was worrying. They swung around a corkscrewing left-hand bend together and the floor, roof and walls disappeared. Irisis threw herself to the floor on the very brink of a chasm. Flangers landed on top of her. Fyn-

Mah held up her light. The details slowly emerged from featureless black.

A crevasse cut across their path. The solid tar, or rather brittle pitch as it was here, had recently been torn apart by some great force, leaving a gap of about eight spans to the other side of the tunnel. The far wall was a sheer face of pitch, as smooth and curved as fractured glass, apart from shards that hung down, or stuck up, here and there. The bottom could not be distinguished, though it must have been a long way below them. The crevasse extended beyond sight to left and right.

The gap had been rudely bridged by an upside-down arch of pitch, a solid, smooth black curve half a span thick but no wider than Irisis's hips. Lyrinx footprints tracked across it.

'What the hell has happened here?' said Flangers, picking himself up and rubbing his backside. His fingertips came up bloody.

'The exploding node must've wrenched the ground apart,' said Fyn-Mah.

'Or the Great Seep has drawn back into the earth,' Irisis muttered, 'cracking away the solid pitch around its edges. This bridge hasn't been here long.'

'And we could run into more lyrinx at any time.' Fyn-Mah edged out onto the span, holding up her glowing crystal.

Even as she spoke, a shadow appeared from the opening on the other side. An enormous male lyrinx spread its wings and opened its bucket-sized mouth in a grin of triumph.

Behind them, Myrurn's sword scraped as he drew it from the scabbard. Irisis looked over her shoulder. A lyrinx, no, two, were coming the other way. They were trapped.

'Let me go first,' said Flangers, drawing his sword. 'That's what I'm here for.'

'Stay back!' Fyn-Mah had one hand in her pocket. She gave Irisis a sideways glance, as if to say, Do you now question my judgment? 'When I give the word, cover your eyes.' She crept a little further along the bridge, which curved down then up, like a suspended rope.

The lyrinx stood at the other end, its eyes glittering in the light from the perquisitor's crystal. It had something in its left hand. Irisis could not see what, but her heart began to thump. This was no ordinary lyrinx. She could sense the power; the intensity. Many lyrinx had a talent for the Secret Art, though few used it for anything but flying. This creature was different. She sensed that it was a mancer every bit as powerful as the great human or Aachim mages, and the device in its hand felt potent.

Myrum sang out, 'Might need a bit of help, Crafter.'

She whirled. A pair of lyrinx were advancing from the tunnel, side by side. Drawing her sword, she stood shoulder to shoulder with Myrum. From the corner of her eye she could see Fyn-Mah on the bridge, only waist high to the mancer-lyrinx.

It let out a deep, roaring bellow that echoed strangely off the hard walls. The left hand slid out, palm upwards. Irisis felt a hot glow on her cheek, had the sense of an invisible cloud roiling outwards, and the floor softened under her. She instinctively lifted one foot, but when she put it down again, the surface had already hardened. The other foot did not move. She was stuck, like a fly to tar paper.

She jerked as hard as she could. It jarred the muscles of her leg but her boot remained firmly embedded in pitch. The two lyrinx were also stuck, though they probably had the strength to pull free.

Myrum cursed and began to hack at the pitch with his sword. She did the same, trying to watch the bridge and the enemy at the same time. Flangers, being closer to the source, was more deeply embedded, while Fyn-Mah was buried to the ankles. Lacking a sword, she had no way of freeing herself.

Flangers hacked the laces off his boots and pulled his feet out. Tearing off his socks, he ran out onto the bridge.

'Go back,' cried Fyn-Mah. 'You can't save me.'

'Then I'll die trying.' He hammered the brittle pitch around her boots with the point of his sword, sending chips flying everywhere.

'Take this and go! It's more important than I am.' She heaved the heavy bag to him.

He lashed it to his belt but kept hacking, the bag banging against his calves as he worked. 'There's nowhere to go, Perquisitor.'

'Take it!' she roared. 'It's an order, soldier.'

It was too late. The mancer-lyrinx was edging towards them, moving tentatively as if unsure whether the bridge would hold its weight. This small chasm was a dangerous place in which to fly, if it had to.

'Now would be a really good time to use whatever you were keeping for an emergency,' yelled Irisis, still prising at the pitch that held her boot fast.

Fyn-Mah just stood there, one hand holding up the glowing crystal.

Why didn't the mancer-lyrinx blast them? Irisis prised away. Her boot came free, along with a lump of pitch resembling a club foot. She smashed it off. Did the creature want to take them alive? That didn't make sense, since the other lyrinx had tried so hard to kill them. It had to be the phynadr.

The lyrinx edged closer, the bridge shivering under its weight. The beast gestured towards the bag. Irisis could see the knots in Fyn-Mah's jawline. She was terrified but defiant, and Irisis could not but admire her for it.

Behind Irisis there came a roar as one of the lyrinx freed itself and leapt, its foot trailing blood. Myrum, who was still stuck, slashed wildly at it. The lyrinx landed hard on the torn foot, lurched sideways but recovered to beat through Myrum's defences. Throwing its arms around him, it squeezed him against its chest plates. Ribs cracked as Myrum fell backwards, carrying it with him. The great mouth darted at the soldier's head. It reminded Irisis of the time she had been held beneath one of the lyrinx, and only Flydd's heroism had saved her.

She swung her sword against the back of the creature's armoured skull with every ounce of her strength. The armour cracked and the lyrinx's head was driven into the floor. It did not move, though the blow could only have stunned it.

Finding a gap between the skin plates of its side, she drove her sword through the ribs.

It took all her strength, and all of Myrum's, to get him out from under the fallen creature. He was so battered and bruised he could not stand up. The second lyrinx was still trying to free its feet from the pitch. She hacked Myrum's boots out.

On the bridge, the mancer-lyrinx was almost within reach of Fyn-Mah. The bridge shuddered. The creature reached out for her. Her eyes fixed on it, Fyn-Mah tossed the crystal towards the roof of the chasm and yelled, 'Cover your eyes!'

Irisis, watching the crystal arc up into the darkness, screwed her eyes shut. The explosion of light burned her eyelids and sent blood-red pulses through her brain. She opened her eyes, dazed and dazzled, to see the mancer-lyrinx topple head-first off the bridge. Its wings spread as it hurtled downwards, but they were insufficient to support it without the aid of the Art, and the exploding crystal had filled the ethyr with echoes, preventing it from drawing on a distant field. Only devices that stored power, like Fyn-Mah's crystals, could work here, and once that power had been used they were useless.

The bridge softened and began to droop beneath Fyn-Mah's feet. She pulled one foot from its boot and heaved at the other. Flangers scrambled down the curve to her

'Go back,' she screamed. 'Save the phynadr.'

Fyn-Mah was going to do her duty to the bitter end. You're a better woman than I'll ever be, Irisis thought.

The curve of the bridge steepened and thinned like molasses sagging between two spoons. Soon it must break, plunging Fyn-Mah into the abyss. Flangers kept moving towards her as the stretching strand of pitch pulled her away but, as he grasped her outstretched hand, the bridge snapped. Fyn-Mah fell, pulling Flangers with her. He threw his other arm around the pitch. They swung on the end of the still lengthening ribbon, then disappeared into the darkness. Irisis heard a thud as they struck the side of the chasm, a muffled cry, then nothing. Darkness, utter and complete, swallowed the world.

'Don't suppose you've got a flint striker in your pocket.' Myrum's voice came from not far away.

She felt it out and snapped it a couple of times so he could see the sparks. 'Here. What's happened to the other lyrinx.'

'Was still stuck, last I saw.' He lit a lantern. The creature lay on the floor, one foot at a strange angle as if it had broken its ankle. Its hands were pressed against its eye-sockets, its face covered in red-stained tears. 'Burned its eyes, I'd reckon. They don't like bright light.' He put his sword to the defenceless creature's throat.

Irisis turned away. It had to be done but she did not have to see it. 'Bring the lantern when you're finished. We'll have to recover the phynadr, and the little beast if we can, though I don't see how we're going to get out again.'

'I can smell fresh air,' said Myrum shortly. 'It must be coming from the other side.'

'No use if we can't get to it. Got any rope in that pack of yours?'

'As it happens, I have.' He produced a hank of thick cord, knotted one end around his burly torso, and the other around hers. 'Nice chest you've got here, Irisis.'

'This is as close as you 're ever getting to it,' she said with a cheerful grin.

He was philosophical. 'Ah well. I still have my dreams.'

'I hope you live to have many more.'

'What if you go down on the rope, and I hold you?'

'I'm heavier than I look.'

He eyed her up and down. 'Even so.'

'All right, but keep your thoughts on the rope.'

His gummy smile widened. 'Don't know as how you can dictate terms when I'm holding you up.'

Myrum lowered her over the edge, which turned out to be an overhang. Irisis held the lantern out in her right hand, though its smoky yellow glow barely penetrated the blackness. Heat wafted up past her and, as she swung back and forth, she caught a glimpse of something glowing in a crack, a long way down. It looked like lava, but wasn't. The tar was on fire and it would burn wickedly if she ended up anywhere near it.

Recalling that thud, she directed the lantern light along the nearer side of the crevasse. Here the wall consisted of a series of sheer miniature cliffs, broken by narrow platforms topped with jagged spires of pitch, some as sharp as broken glass. Irisis cringed at the thought of crashing into them.

It was hard to see, for the black surfaces reflected only an occasional glitter. Unable to get close enough to the wall because of the overhang, she began to swing back and forth on the rope.

'You all right?' called Myrum.

'Yes. Can't see much, though. Lower me down a few spans. Oh, and Myrum?'

'Yes?'

'Keep a sharp lookout behind you.'

He snorted. 'You've got the bloody lantern!'

'There should be another one.'

Her swing was now long enough to reach one of the spikes. She caught hold of it low down, where it was not so sharp, and pulled herself into a space between a cluster of spires.

'I'm standing!' she called, so he would not worry about the weight going off the rope. 'Let out a bit more.'

'Good-oh!'

Irisis edged as far as she could to her left, until she was brought up by a sheer drop that went all the way down to the fiery crack. If Fyn-Mah and Flangers had fallen that far, they were lost. She crept the other way, between spines, shards and spears of frozen pitch. Ahead, the surface formed an irregular series of steps, some almost as tall as she was. Holding out the lantern, she peered down.

Nothing that way either. She looked over the outer edge. A ribbon of solidified pitch was looped around one of the spires further down. It had to be from the bridge but she could not see anyone. Below her the crevasse wall curved out into another spike-studded mound, this one about fifteen paces by ten. Its edges fell away on three sides while the fourth was the sheer, unclimbable wall. Irisis leaned out, the lantern tilted, and a few drops of hot oil spilled. From below she heard a faint groan.

'Fyn-Mah? Flangers?'

No answer. 'I've found something,' she called up to Myrum. 'Lower me down a few spans, carefully.'

'Not much rope left,' he yelled.

'Give me all you have.'

She went down, swinging back and forth, pushing herself away from the razor shards with her feet. Several spikes broke off. How secure was any of this? The least shock might crumble the lot and send it into the abyss.

There was no rope left when her boots grounded on a shelf at the edge of the spiky mound and, in the light of the lantern, she saw Fyn-Mah wedged between two spires with her head at a strange angle. It looked as if she'd broken her neck.

'Fyn-Mah?' Irisis touched the perquisitor on the cheek.

The small woman's eyes opened, moving all the way up the crafter's elongated form to the rope around her chest. She moved her head back to the vertical. 'Didn't expect to see you,' she said in a faint, slurred voice.

'I came for the phynadr,' said Irisis coolly. 'To do my duty, of course.'

''Course,' Fyn-Mah echoed. 'Help me up. Stuck.' She tried to lift an arm but it flopped down.

'I thought your neck was broken.' Irisis held the lantern close. One pupil was larger than the other, which meant she had concussion.

'You'd be happy then.'

'I don't hate you –' Irisis began.

''Nother time, Crafter!' The last word trailed out and Fyn-Mah looked confused. 'Head hurts.'

Putting down the lantern, Irisis lifted the perquisitor to her feet. Her legs buckled. 'Where's Flangers?' said Irisis, holding her with one arm.

105

'Who?'

Irisis untied the rope, steadied the perquisitor and began knotting it around her chest.

'What – doing?' said Fyn-Mah, her voice slow and slurring more than before.

'Getting you out.'

Irisis checked the knots, then shouted up, 'Myrum! Fyn-Mah's alive. You're pulling her up now. Ready?'

'Ready.' The rope tightened and Fyn-Mah rose in the air, flopping like a rag doll. Her head went back to that unpleasant angle.

Irisis turned away, weaving through the razor-edged blades and spires. Shards crunched underfoot. 'Flangers?'

He lay at the rear of the mound, among a pile of shattered spikes, unconscious. There was a lump on the back of his head where he'd hit the floor, but that wasn't the worst injury. A long blade of pitch had gone through the outer side of his right thigh, sliding beside the bone almost all the way through before it broke off. There was a lot of blood, but not as much as if an artery had been severed. Flangers would live, though the wound was so wide and deep Irisis could have put three fingers into it. It would be a miracle if it did not become infected.

An even bigger miracle if she could get him across to the edge of the mound to the rope. Even if she could, she would have to stand him up while she tied the rope on. It wasn't long enough to reach to the floor.

She shook Flangers, gently, but he did not rouse. He must have taken a heavy blow. His breathing was steady, though, and his pupils not dilated, so he should recover. More importantly, the bag containing the phynadr was still tied to his belt. She felt it. It did not seem to be damaged. What about the little flesh-formed creature?

She went through his pockets, one by one. The creature was dead – he must have landed on it. She tossed it aside. They'd risked their lives, and five soldiers had lost theirs, for nothing.

Irisis lifted Flangers to a sitting position, regretting that she'd sent Fyn-Mah up first. Flangers was heavier than he appeared. It would be hard to get him as far as the rope.

Slapping him gently on the cheek, she called out, 'Flangers?'

He made no sound. She slapped a little harder and again he gave a muffled moan, deep in his throat. She eyed the wound. Perhaps if she hurt him . . .

Irisis cut off the ragged trouser leg and tore it into strips, which she laid beside him. She wiggled the shard in the wound. He groaned. It was tapered and should come out easily. Taking hold of it, she pulled firmly and it slipped free. The wound began to bleed profusely. She put two fingers in, feeling around for broken pieces, and drew a sliver of pitch out. There did not seem to be any other large fragments.

Flangers groaned and opened his eyes. 'Bloody hell're yer doin'?' he slurred. 'Get yer hand outta me leg.' A comical expression crossed his face, as if he had just realised what a stupid thing he'd said, and his eyes closed.

There came a faint, fluttering sound from out in the abyss. Irisis held up the lantern, but saw nothing. It must have been the rope scraping across the cliff face.

Lacking anything to sew him up with, she bound Flangers's leg with strips of cloth until the wound closed and the blood flow dropped to a trickle. Irisis tied another pad across the top.

'Flangers!' she said urgently. 'You've got to stand up.'

He didn't open his eyes. 'Can't.'

'It's your soldier's duty, Flangers.'

The soldier wept with pain as he struggled to get to his feet. Irisis crouched and gave him her shoulder, heaving him up with one arm around his muscled waist. They staggered between the spikes to the edge, swaying while she waved the lantern around, looking for the rope. It wasn't there.

'Myrum?' Her voice echoed shrilly.

There was a long pause before he answered. 'Yes?'

'I've got Flangers. He's badly injured. Where's the bloody rope?'

'It's coming. I've . . . had a few problems up here.'

Again that fluttering sound, a whispering echo back and forth in the crevasse. Sympathetic shudders fluttered down her spine.

'Hurry it up. I've got a nasty feeling about this place.'

The end appeared, wriggling like a brown snake in the lamplight. Setting down the lantern, Irisis pulled the rope as far as it would go and looped it around the soldier's chest. Flangers was just clinging to consciousness. His fingers dug into her shoulders and his knees flexed as he swayed, but the rest of him had shut down.

It was hard work tying a secure knot with his weight on her, but she managed it at last. 'It's done. Pull him up!'

The rope went taut. 'He's a heavy sod!' Myrum's voice echoed down.

'Get Fyn-Mah to help you.'

'She's passed out.'

The fluttering sounded again, closer, followed by a scraping sound like a fingernail on rock. Or a claw.

'Hurry up,' she shouted, unable to keep the fear out of her voice. 'That lyrinx is still alive.'

Flangers jerked up, stopped, jerked again. Blood running down his leg began to drip off the toe of his boot. She watched him pass through the circle of light, then directed the lantern around and below her, trying to pick the creature out. Maybe it wasn't the lyrinx. Worse creatures dwelt in the abysses of the world, creeping about their unknown and unpleasant business. All sorts of beasts had made their way to Santhenar when the Way between the Worlds was open, and at other times in the mythical past. Not all of them wanted to wage war, as the lyrinx did. But if they were disturbed, if they felt threatened . . .

TEN

'Stop it!' Irisis said aloud. 'Don't make things worse than they need to be. It's just the lyrinx.'

Just the lyrinx! There was no such thing as *just* a lyrinx, even if it was injured *and* unable to use the Secret Art. She scanned the gulf again, but finding a dark-skinned creature against the blackness was impossible. Her lantern began to flutter, making threatening shadows. She sloshed it back and forth: not much oil left.

Another scrape, much closer, followed by a deep rumbling purr. She still couldn't judge the direction, but it wasn't far away.

'Where are you?' she screamed. 'Show yourself!'

The echoes had a strident tone that frightened her. She was losing it. Stay calm – you've been in dangerous situations before and got out of them. You can do it again. It didn't help. Irisis was at her best when she could react swiftly to danger; she didn't like waiting. It allowed her to dwell on her inadequacies.

Well, *do* something. Take the initiative. Don't just stand there moaning.

Drawing her sword, Irisis swished it back and forth. It made a comforting sound as it sliced through the air. Pity she'd had so little training with it. If only she had a crossbow. Irisis had done most of her manufactory training with that weapon and was a fine shot, though of course she had to see her target. The lyrinx was not so handicapped. It could smell her well enough to strike in the dark.

'How's it going, Myrum?'

109

'Nearly done. He's a heavy bugger.'

She started to say, 'Hurry it up,' but broke off. Myrum was doing all he could, and he was injured too. Irisis paced back and forth on the platform. It was shaped like a stepped brain studded with spikes, which restricted her movement considerably. About to smash them down, she realised that they would also restrict the movement of the lyrinx, though it could probably take the risk of crushing them under its armour.

Irisis had not heard the fluttering for a while now, which was even more worrying. Why was the creature taking so long?

Lacking the Art to support itself, it would have fallen a long way. What she'd heard must have been its death throes. As she picked up the lantern to look down, the flickering light went out. Irisis clicked the flint striker, to no effect. The oil was gone.

Moodily, she tossed the lantern over the edge. It fell for several heartbeats before the glass smashed on something, and several more beats before crashing, rolling and banging all the way to the bottom.

'You all right, Crafter?' Myrum's voice echoed hollowly.

'Oil's run out. Where's the rope?'

'It's coming now.'

The darkness was not perfect. When she looked straight up, Irisis could see a feeble illumination. Myrum must have lit another lantern. Feeling her way to the brink, she peered over. Below her, a faint light appeared then vanished, like the reflection in a staring eye.

She looked away, and back. There it was again, shining steadily. Irisis felt in the air for the rope. She could hear it whispering down the sheer face above her.

Snap! That was a pitch-spine breaking off. She would know that sound anywhere. *Snap! Snap!* The lyrinx wasn't dead – it was coming for her.

Irisis reached up for the rope but couldn't find it. She waved arm and sword in the air. The tip of the sword met a

110

slight resistance. Her fingertips just caught the rope's end and she pulled it down.

Behind her a great shadow rose, one wing spread, the other folded. More spines snapped. She whirled. Forests of them went down as it crunched across the mound towards her. It was taking its time, watching her all the way, and still she could not see it.

Irisis felt the air swirl; smelled the hot breath of the creature. No time to tie on; she let go the rope and swung the sword in a low, vicious arc. The shadow, definitely a lyrinx, kept coming. Her sword struck it on its armoured thigh, wedging there.

'Crafter!' Myrum called urgently.

She had no time to answer. Jerking her blade free, Irisis took a step backwards and froze. She was standing on the brink. Could she lure it over? Unlikely. Lyrinx could see better in the dark than humans. She went sideways, fixing the location of the rope in her mind. It would be difficult to find again, if she lost it.

Irisis stumbled against a miniature pitch spike, too black to see. She hacked at the shadow, again connecting with its thigh plate. The lyrinx slashed back, though feebly. It must be badly injured. Irisis tried a higher swipe and this time the tip of the sword carved through softness. It had gone between two belly plates. Something gurgled; she hoped it was the creature's intestines.

The shadow slumped, panting. Irisis thrust the sword into its sheath, went backwards to the hanging rope and, by a miracle, found it. She pulled herself up, hand over hand, as far as she could go. Not far enough. Her arms didn't have the strength for rope-climbing and the swinging bag was pulling her down. It was all she could do to hold on.

The lyrinx sprang at her, missed, and its fingers brushed the rope. One hard pull and it would have her, and Myrum, over the side. Irisis twisted the rope around her left wrist a few times, hung on with her knees and slashed below her with the sword.

She missed. The lyrinx caught the rope end and began to pull, but very gently. First the phynadr, then her. She drew the length of the blade across the rope, below her knees. It parted and the lyrinx fell back, smashing a thicket of spikes. Irisis hauled herself up another arm's length but could go no further.

'Myrum,' she screamed. 'Pull me up, quick! The bloody lyrinx's right here.'

Silence. The rope jerked up a little way and stopped. The lyrinx lurched at her and missed, its eyes fixed on her as it gathered itself for another attempt. Irisis could only hold the sword pointed downwards, and pray.

Again it sprang, its claws whistling through the air just below the hanging bag. She pulled it up. One claw tore open the side of her boot, before ripping it off. She threw the other one at it, but missed.

'Myrum!' she wailed. 'Pull your heart out or I'm dead.'

The rope moved up again, as much as a couple of spans, before stopping. It was enough to get her out of the creature's reach, though Irisis began to fear that, with his broken ribs, Myrum was incapable of lifting her higher. What if he'd been slain and a lyrinx was now hauling her up? Her empty stomach contracted. *That* possibility had not occurred to her before.

Something winked in the dim light before whirring past her ear. The lyrinx had thrown a shard of pitch at her. Another spun to one side. They were poor projectiles, difficult to aim.

The rope began to creep up and Irisis dared to hope that she might make it after all. Then the fluttering began again and she heard a whooshing sound, as of a breath rapidly exhaled. What was it up to now?

With a deeper, gasping *whoosh* and a creaking flutter, the lyrinx lifted off. It moved out into the dim lantern light, its wings clubbing the air so violently that she was buffeted from side to side on the rope. How the beast had managed it she would never know, for one wing was torn in two places and its blood-covered head was the wrong shape, as if stoved in when it had fallen into the chasm. And since it could not use the Secret Art here, it must be flying on sheer indomitable will.

Struck with terrified admiration, she watched it drive through the air towards her, only courage keeping that heavy body aloft. Surely there had never been such a feat until now.

Her strength was fading. Even with both hands, she could barely hold on. There was no possibility of defending herself with the sword, so she sheathed it. Rising fumes whipped past her face, making her eyes water. Pulling up the frayed end of the rope, Irisis made a quick knot around her waist, one handed, in case she lost her grip when the beast attacked. It was staggering through the air, now rising, now falling, but always heading for her.

She looked up. No way to tell who, or what, was lifting her. The lyrinx rose above her, struggling to grip the air. Now it plunged, though *by* her rather than *at* her. It did not want to lose the prize.

Irisis tried to sway the rope out of the way. It moved but not far enough. The lyrinx caught her by the arm. She tore free, which must have upset the creature's delicate equilibrium for it veered off, flapping furiously.

Now it attacked from the other side. Strands of luminous saliva hung from its open mouth. It was tiring rapidly. She watched it come. If it was so easily disturbed, a more direct attack might just tip the balance.

It swooped. She doubled up her legs and shot them out at its head, as she'd done when a lyrinx attacked her at the manufactory last winter. The rope went the other way and her powerful kick ended up as no more than a tap on the jaw. Irisis lost her grip, fell and, caught by the knot around her waist, flipped upside down.

The lyrinx's teeth snapped together, it swung its left arm but just failed to snatch the bag from her belt. The rope slipped and she thought she was going to fall head first all the way down into that fiery crack, but it pulled tight. It held.

Irisis swung back and forth without the strength to heave herself upright. The lyrinx came again, a last desperate effort.

Ropes of clotted saliva oozed down its mighty chest. With a hoarse, despairing cry, it lunged for the bag that now hung by her shoulder.

'Help!' she wailed, staring at the flickering light just a few spans above. An unidentifiable figure swayed there, swinging something around its head like a cannonball in a sling. The object hurtled down, looking for all the world like a human head. I must be hallucinating, Irisis thought, as the object struck the lyrinx on its brow ridge. Red showered into its eyes.

The lyrinx gagged, the wings missed a beat, it slid sideways into the sheer black face, and fell out of sight.

The rope jerked and she was hauled up, still upside down. Her head cracked on the sheer fracture surface as she was dragged over the edge, then Irisis was dropped onto the pitchy floor.

'Myrum . . .' she gasped.

It was not Myrum, but Flangers, on his knees in a small pool of blood. He looked ghastly. A mutilated corpse lay not far away, strangely shortened, though she could barely see it through the tears of relief. Or perhaps it was the fumes. Fyn-Mah was sprawled on the path at the beginning of the broken bridge, unmoving.

'What happened, Flangers?'

"Nother lyrinx.' He sucked in a breath as though it was his last, glancing towards a hollow where the dead creature lay. 'Myrum thought he'd killed it.' Flangers hunched over, supporting himself with both arms, gasping. 'He hadn't. Tore his head off.'

'That was Myrum's *head* you threw at the lyrinx?'

'First thing I could reach. Poor fellow. A good soldier and a decent man.' Flangers lay on the floor without the strength to lift his head.

'Is Fyn-Mah dead too?'

'Don't know.'

Irisis crawled to the small woman and felt her throat. 'She's alive.' She peered over the edge. 'We'd better move. I wouldn't bet that lyrinx is dead.'

'Leave me,' said Flangers. 'Can't walk.'

'Then crawl – I'm not leaving you behind. That was a mighty heave, Flangers. Any idea how we get out of here?'

One finger pointed to the right.

She discerned a series of ledges between the pitch spears, which might have been close enough together to form a track, though it would be a dangerous one.

'I'll carry Fyn-Mah. Bring the bag and the rope.' Unknotting the phynadr bag, she handed it to him.

'Don't think I can.'

'Just try,' she said. 'I can't get it back without you.'

Once more the appeal to duty lifted Flangers beyond what any normal man could have achieved. What a hero he was. And what a waste that such courage should be directed to so bloody an end.

It buoyed her up as well, and Irisis found the strength to lift Fyn-Mah onto her shoulders. She set off, trying not to think about the path ahead. It was killing work. Several times she had to hoist the perquisitor onto a higher ledge, hoping she would not fall off while Irisis clambered up herself. After a desperate twenty minutes they reached the other side. The black mouth of the tunnel was just above them. She pulled herself up into it and smelled fresh air.

'It's not far now, Flangers.'

They lurched along like two bloody wrecks, turned a corner and emerged halfway up a deep but narrow mine pit. The sky was just growing light, though not enough to illuminate the pit. 'At last,' said Irisis, limping on bloody, pitch-stained feet. She turned the other way. 'Where's the airfloater?'

'This isn't the pit we came down,' said Flangers, who, astonishingly, appeared to have rallied a little. 'We're in the wrong place.'

Irisis put Fyn-Mah down on the ledge. 'Then we'll have to climb.'

Flangers was staring at the rim. 'I can see something moving up there.'

They stepped back into the tunnel entrance. Fyn-Mah said, more clearly than before, 'Go round base of pit . . . through tunnel . . . other side.'

'You're conscious!' Irisis wished she did not have to pick her up again.

The perquisitor did not answer. Hefting her, Irisis followed the path to the bottom of the pit, around the base and in through a tunnel that had not been visible in the black wall. They were underground for only a few minutes before emerging in a larger pit. The air-floater was waiting across the far side, right where they had left it, its four guards with their crossbows ready. Irisis pushed Fyn-Mah through the ropes, fell through herself and lay on the deck without the strength to rise. Two of the guards carried Flangers aboard.

Muss was already there, gazing up at the rim. He had assumed his old persona – the slim, middle-aged man she'd first met in Gosport – though he still looked frustrated and unhappy. So he didn't get what he went in for, Irisis thought. I wonder what it could be?

'Where were you when we needed you?' she snapped.

'On other duties,' he said, impassive again.

'Where are our mates?' cried a young soldier.

'Dead!' Fyn-Mah tried to sit up but sagged back against the wall of the cabin. 'Go up,' she whispered to Pilot Inouye. 'Out of crossbow range.'

The grapnels were pulled aboard. Inouye twisted a knob on the floater-gas generator and gas whistled up the pipe. The air-floater shot up out of the pit, rising above the hummocks and tar bogs of Snizort, and just in time. A detachment of some hundred soldiers had come through the broken eastern wall and were advancing towards the pit. They stopped and someone waved. Pilot Inouye turned to Fyn Mah. 'They're signalling. I think they want us to land.'

'Keep going!' said Fyn-Mah, forcing herself to her feet. She hung onto the rope mesh, swaying dangerously. 'I have other orders. Guards,' she said to the four men, 'ready your weapons. We cannot be taken.'

The soldiers looked uneasy, but complied. Irisis felt the hairs rise on the back of her neck. She took a crossbow for herself. The loyalty of these men had already been tested. Surely it would take little for them to mutiny – if Fyn-Mah was taken, they would be condemned with her.

On the ground, there was a flurry of activity at the front of the detachment. A black-robed figure waved its arms, a perquisitor Irisis did not recognise. A soldier put a speaking trumpet to his mouth.

'Land at once, whoever you are,' he boomed.

'Go higher!' hissed Fyn-Mah. Clinging death-like to the ropes, she shouted down. 'I may not. I'm on a special mission for Scrutator Xervish Flydd.'

The robed figure snatched the speaking trumpet. 'There is no Scrutator Flydd, only the condemned criminal, Slave Flydd.'

Fyn-Mah let out a muffled cry. She turned to Irisis and Flangers. 'What do I do now?'

'Follow your orders,' said Flangers unhelpfully.

'Muss?' she called.

Eiryn Muss was squatting on the deck, deeply immersed in his own thoughts, and did not answer. Whatever was bothering him, it was more important than their imminent demise.

'Land immediately, in the name of Acting Scrutator Jal-Nish Hlar!' shouted the figure on the ground.

'Perquisitor Fyn-Mah,' said Inouye, 'I must go down. I have a direct order from your superior.'

Fyn-Mah covered her face with her hands.

If the scrutator *had* fallen, what hope was there for any of them? 'You're risking everything on Flydd,' Irisis said. 'Do you think he can possibly rise again?'

Fyn-Mah groaned, then mastered herself. 'Scrutator Flydd ordered me to go on, no matter what happened to him, and so I must. No matter what the consequences.'

Irisis felt Death look up from his work on the battlefield, rub a testing thumb down the blade of his scythe, and smile grimly.

'The scrutators will torment us all,' cried Inouye, desperately defiant.

'I'm taking the air-floater,' Fyn-Mah gritted. 'If you won't cooperate, we'll throw you down to join your friends and Crafter Irisis will take over your controller.'

Irisis doubted that she *could* operate it, or that Fyn-Mah would be so ruthless, but the pilot did not know that.

Inouye licked her wind-chapped lips. The bond with the machine was intense, and pilots, like clanker operators, had been known to go insane after their craft was destroyed.

'They'll slay my man and my little children,' she said in a barely audible voice.

'Not if you're forced to it,' said Fyn-Mah in more gentle tones. 'Flangers, make a show.'

Flangers liked it no more than the pilot did, but he took Irisis's crossbow and pointed it at Inouye, in full view of those on the ground.

'This will ruin us all,' wept little Inouye. She obeyed and the air-floater lifted.

'Go north, with all speed,' said Fyn-Mah.

The soldiers on the ground fired their crossbows but the air-floater was out of range and the bolts fell harmlessly back. Someone ran to the broken wall, climbed it and began to signal frantically towards the command area.

'I feared this was going to happen,' said Fyn-Mah. 'With the scrutator lost, there's only one option left.' She groaned and slumped to the canvas deck.

Behind them, three black air-floaters rose from the mound next to the army command area, and followed.

'Or maybe none,' said Irisis, picking the perquisitor up and carrying her inside.

PART TWO
TEARS

ELEVEN

Gilhaelith was slipping ever deeper into the bottomless pit of tar and there was nothing he could do about it. He'd tried everything, but his geomancy was useless without some kind of a crystal to serve as a focus, and he had none. He'd even attempted to use one of his ever-troubling gallstones, but under the strain it had burst into jagged fragments that were causing him agony. Before they passed, should he live that long, he'd be wishing he were dead.

His only other resort had been mathemancy, that strange branch of the Secret Art Gilhaelith had developed long ago. It proved singularly useless. Mathemancy was a philosopher's Art, ill-suited to any kind of direct action, much less such immediate peril.

Gyrull, Matriarch of Snizort, had abducted him to scry out the remnants of a village lost in the Great Seep seven thousand years ago. Afterwards, she'd kept Gilhaelith beside her, refusing him the use of his globe and the other geomantic instruments he'd brought with him as his means of escape. But the tunnel into the Great Seep had failed, its shell of frozen tar had cracked and hot tar had been forced in. The lyrinx had fled with their relics, just in time. Gilhaelith had tried to follow but he'd not been quick enough.

He took the numbers again, raising a series of random integers to their fourth powers to see what pattern they offered. It was awesomely bad. He tried again, with an even worse result.

The tar now reached to his hips, its suction far too great for him to pull himself out. Ribbons of liquid tar, from a breach in

121

the roof, began to fold onto his head and shoulders, its bituminous reek burning his nose, throat and lungs.

And it was hot. Not burning hot, not enough to blister, but uncomfortable and getting worse. Eventually, if he survived long enough, he would simmer like a crab in a pot. Fortunately, he wouldn't survive. In a few minutes, when that great oozing clot came down on his head, he would suffocate.

A possibility slid into Gilhaelith's mind as if it had been whispered in his ear – to couple his two very different Arts. Geomancy was hopeless because he lacked a crystal to draw power and focus it. Mathemancy was not a tool for directing power at all. But what if . . . ?

If he could create a phantom mathemantical crystal, and use it to draw power and focus it, might *that* be the solution? It was a last resort – such a crystal must pull power directly into his head. A little too much would cook him from the inside, a gruesome, slow death. A lot too much and he would suffer the agonising fate of anthracism, human internal combustion, though that would not take long to kill him.

The very idea of such a crystal felt alien, and it reminded him of those links the amplimet had drawn throughout Snizort, including one to him. Could it be directing him for some purpose of its own? Too bad – without a crystal he was going to die.

He slipped further into the tar, which was now creeping up his groin. It felt hotter than before. Fortunately he'd worked out the mathemancy of crystals long ago, though to create one with numbers, purely in his mind, was another thing entirely. Still, he had always relished challenges.

Gilhaelith began to construct a crystal in layers, beginning at its base and building towards the apex. It was painfully slow – literally painful, he thought wryly. By the time tar had risen to his waist, the phantom crystal was only half done. His shoulders were covered with ribbony black epaulettes; it was dripping down his forehead, clotting over his eyes, and rubbing just smeared it everywhere.

As Gilhaelith built another layer, the tar seemed to dissolve beneath his feet and he slid down to his chest. A bucket-sized clot landed on his head, pushing him face-first into liquid tar, which was forced up his nostrils. Though he clawed it away, he could not clear his nose enough to breathe.

Turning his head sideways, he managed to get a breath through his mouth. Hurry! The layers went more quickly as he approached the tapering apex of the crystal. Only one layer to go. As he sucked another breath, the rest of the clot fell, burying him completely. And it was so hot. His feet were cooking.

But the crystal was done. Gilhaelith looked for power but found none – the field, which had been waxing and waning for days, was dying. The tunnel had failed because the phynadrs had not been able to maintain sufficient power to keep it frozen.

Yet for what he planned, only a little power was required. Gilhaelith sought in another direction and discovered a drifting loop of field, cut off from the rest. He drew power into the phantom crystal but there was not enough to energise it.

He had barely enough breath to try again. He found another loop, this one strong as the field waxed dangerously. The node was desperately overloaded and something had to give. But if it just lasted another minute . . .

His lungs were shuddering for air; fire burned behind his temple as the crystal powered up at last. Gilhaelith used a geomantic spell to drive heat from the tar surrounding him, into the seep itself.

He kept at it until the heat licked from his skull to his stomach, the first sign of anthracism. He had to let go. Would it be enough? As the spell faded, a most bitter cold enveloped him, as though he'd been frozen into a block of ice. Then, as the heat of the seep attacked that rigid, frigid shell of tar, it shattered into a thousand pieces.

The shards broke away from his body, leaving him in a cavity lined with fractured tar. The suction was gone; it was solid underfoot. The mosaic fell from his eyes and he could see. Gilhaelith took hold of the still-hard shell of the tunnel and, with a wriggle and a shake, pulled himself onto the floor.

He hurt all over and, behind his eyes, needles pushed relentlessly into the bone. He'd tried too hard and damaged something. He began to crawl blindly down the tunnel. That was where Matriarch Gyrull, who had come pounding back for him, found Gilhaelith. Tossing him over her shoulder, she clawed the last chilly remnants of tar from his nostrils and raced off.

The next few hours were a blur of belching fumes, pounding feet and panicky lyrinx. Gilhaelith saw nothing, for the pain was so all-enveloping he could not open his eyelids. And he was so cold – he could feel the shape of his stomach in ice.

He was carried through a myriad of tunnels, with Gyrull cursing and turning this way and that, and her growing escort hard put to restrain their terror. There was fire underground and they couldn't find a way out, though that wasn't their greatest fear. Gilhaelith had learned enough of their language to deduce that many of the escapeways had been cut off and they expected the unstable node to explode at any time.

They reached the base of a pit with steep sides. The lyrinx made a living tower which Gyrull climbed to get out, a box of relics strapped to her chest, and Gilhaelith, folded over in an elongated travesty of the foetal position, tucked under one arm. The gamy odour of her sweat was intense.

Before she reached the top, the phantom crystal picked up wild fluctuations from the field that seared his forebrain. Gyrull muttered something.

'What?' he croaked, but she did not answer. He could just see out of the crack of one eye. It was dark and he felt so very cold. Beyond the walls, the battle still raged – the groans of the maimed, the clash of weapons against armour, the thudding of catapult balls into walls, ground and tar seeps. Fire flickered in half a hundred places.

She climbed over the rim of the pit and set off without looking back to see if her fellows were following. Gilhaelith supposed they had sacrificed themselves to give their matriarch a chance, or to get the treasure away.

'The torgnadr is going to destroy itself,' she said, finally answering his question. 'How did the humans get in to attack it? They're more cunning than I imagined.'

In the distance, the ground surface domed and a fountain of fire tore through. He was in no state to see the danger. To Gilhaelith it just seemed extraordinarily beautiful.

The matriarch was running full pelt, considerably faster than a human could move. Several times she flexed her wings and leapt in the air, but each time landed hard and kept running. There was not enough in the field for her to fly with such a burden, for Gilhaelith was a big man.

He felt worse every minute. Either he'd burst something inside or the tar was poisoning him. He felt sure he was going to die. He would never solve the great puzzle and achieve a true understanding of the earth. His life had been wasted. And, to his surprise, Gilhaelith felt a creeping remorse for all he'd done, and all he'd neglected, in blind pursuit of that aim – most especially, Tiaan.

His stomach boiled and he threw up all over Gyrull's side and thigh. She wiped it off without breaking stride. Shortly, as she was climbing the southern wall, the sky erupted into a spindle of fire that he could see with his eyes closed. Pain crept, singing, along every nerve fibre. The fire died down, taking with it the last vestiges of the field, and Gilhaelith felt the snapping of that ethereal thread Tiaan's amplimet had drawn to him. His phantom crystal exploded into fragments with a hundred sparkle-like throbs. Now he truly was helpless. It did not matter. Nothing mattered – it was all over.

The new day dawned, as hot as the previous one, but the cold, which had bitten into him ever since he'd cast his freezing spell, grew steadily worse. He lost everything but the rocking motion. Like a pendulum running down, even that sense failed, until finally nothing was perceptible.

Gilhaelith roused twice, once to realise that Gyrull was still running, another time to discover that she had stopped and was speaking in low tones with several other lyrinx, though he still lacked strength to open his eyes. They seemed to be talking about the destruction of the node. What would such a thing look like? How could a node explode, all its contained energies vanishing into nothingness? Surely there had to be some residue?

He felt that there was something he should follow up, but was too lethargic to think.

Days and nights went by, full of running; hasty meetings in shadowed caves or gloomy woods; exhortations to hurry; and other urgent matters that were conducted out of earshot. Gilhaelith was dosed with potions and fed at intervals by a lyrinx who squeezed greasy pulp through its hands into his mouth. His senses were so numb that he could taste nothing, though he felt better afterwards.

On what he thought to be the fifth day after the escape, or possibly the sixth, Gilhaelith felt well enough to sit up. It was not long after dawn and the lyrinx had camped in a wooded valley by a meandering river. There were hundreds of them, with more appearing all the time. They must have felt in no danger now, for they were lying about in full view, chatting with voice and skin-speech, their bags and boxes of relics piled in the centre. It surprised him that they should be so casual, after the loss of Snizort.

The underground galleries had been on fire and the tar might burn for a hundred years, so whatever the result of the battle, they could not go back. That must have been a blow to the lyrinx, for Snizort had made a formidable beachhead on Lauralin from which to launch further attacks. On the other hand, the destruction of the node would have immobilised both constructs and clankers, so the lyrinx were in no danger once they escaped the immediate area. They could attack at night and do great damage, though it did not appear they were going to. He got the impression that the fliers planned to return to Meldorin.

In that case, why did Gyrull still want him? He could see her across the clearing, squatting under a tree, talking in a low voice to two other aged lyrinx. Their skin-speech lit up the shadows in lurid reds and yellows, which meant an important conversation.

He dozed during the morning, waking to see Gyrull giving orders to another small group, and later to a third. He learned nothing about what those orders were. His brain hurt whenever he tried to think. There was a strong field here, but he could not have blown a fly off the end of his nose with it.

A cry disturbed his chaotic thoughts. A lyrinx, one of the recent arrivals, was running around the clearing in circles, crashing into trees and other lyrinx, and making a shrill keening, as if in pain.

The matriarch sprang up. Several lyrinx tried to catch the distressed creature but its flailing arms knocked them out of the way. It began to claw at itself, tripped and fell just a few paces from Gilhaelith. He recognised it: one of the diggers who had excavated the lost village in the Great Seep.

The lyrinx was covered in red, swollen pustules and it began to claw furiously at itself, tearing its chest armour off in bloody chunks. The sensitive inner skin was exposed, not the usual pink, but red, pustular and oozing.

Within minutes the lyrinx had ripped most of its armour away, though that did not seem to improve matters. It began to scrape and scour at the living flesh, screaming in agony, until Gyrull motioned, *Enough!*

Another lyrinx came up behind it and slashed across the back of its unprotected neck, severing the spine. The suffering creature fell dead. They dug a deep hole, buried the lyrinx and left at once. The clearing was now a place of ill omen.

'What are you going to do with me?' Gilhaelith said to Gyrull a couple of days later. She was still carrying him, climbing a steep hill near the coast. He could smell the sea.

She worked her massive shoulders as if she were uncomfortable. The lyrinx often seemed to be, inside their armoured outer skin. 'You were not truthful with me, Tetrarch.'

'What do you mean?'

'When we were looking for the relics in the Great Seep, you

spent longer studying the node with your geomantic devices than you did searching for the lost village. You should have found it a week earlier, and we would have got everything away in safety. You're to blame for this situation.'

Gilhaelith was not going to deny it. 'What did you expect? You abducted me.'

'On the contrary, I saved your life. Vithis arrived at Nyriandiol just days later, with a great host of constructs. On learning of your perfidy, he would have slain you out of hand. Besides, you agreed to assist me –'

'Ah!' said Gilhaelith, 'but in the excitement at Booreah Ngurle the price was never fixed, therefore the contract is void.'

'Not so, Tetrarch, for I could see what was in your mind. You had nowhere to go, and both Aachim and scrutators were after you. It suited you well to be taken to Snizort under our protection, to spy on our work and further your own studies. Though never stated, you were happy with that price. The contract stands, and by your procrastination and deceptions, you've dishonoured it. I've not had my price from you, Tetrarch, but I will.'

Gilhaelith bowed his head. 'I can do nothing to stop you. What do you require of me?'

'I shall take you across the sea to Meldorin, and hold you until I find a need that you can satisfy. Once you've done that, I *may* release you.'

That also suited him. He couldn't save himself, so let the lyrinx do it for him. Once they'd taken him out of his enemies' reach, he'd find a way to get free. He had to, for his own sanity. Since Gyrull had first abducted him, he'd had no control over his life. To Gilhaelith that was like a never-healing sore.

As Gyrull lifted into the air from the top of the hill, with a host of lyrinx rising around her like moths from a meadow, Gilhaelith was trying to think of a way to win his freedom. Once on Meldorin, which was occupied by the lyrinx, he would be trapped. Even if he could get away from them, he did not have the skill in boat craft to make a seaworthy vessel. He would effectively be Gyrull's slave.

They were crossing the sea from a peninsula of Taltid where the gap was only three or four leagues. It would be about an hour's flight, since they were flying into a stiff westerly. Gyrull was at the head of a great wedge of lyrinx, the arms of the flight trailing back for the best part of a league. She was flying easily, despite Gilhaelith's weight, though from time to time her wings creaked as they were buffeted by a particularly strong gust. Ahead, Meldorin was already visible, a forested land clothing mountains that ran down to the coast. He saw little sign that humans had ever inhabited it, just the scar of an overgrown mountain road and what might have been the ruins of a port.

Gilhaelith's thoughts returned to the problem he had wrestled with earlier: what had happened at the node. As far as he knew, no node had ever exploded before, so all he had to go on was his experience as a master geomancer, and his intuition. Both told him that *something* could not be reduced to *nothing* – here had to be some consequence, other than the raw power of the explosion itself. But what could it be?

The traumatic escape had left his thoughts sluggish, memory fractured and logic in tatters. By the time they'd passed the midpoint of the journey, Gilhaelith had made no progress on the puzzle .

Then, as they were being battered by updraughts in the base of a cloud, it came to him – the answer that could set him free.

'Gyrull,' he cried, twisting around in her claws so he could see her face. 'I know what's happened at the node.'

The movement put her off-balance just as an unexpected gust jerked her upwards. Torn from her grasp, Gilhaelith fell towards the dark waters, far below.

TWELVE

Jal-Nish had taken charge of the clanker-hauling operation. Day and night his short stocky figure was everywhere, issuing orders and threats, and maintaining control of every aspect of the vast operation. The generals together could not have done in a week what he achieved in the first three days. The platinum mask reflected the light of the pyres by night, and the blinding sun by day. He was not seen to eat, drink or sleep in all that time.

Rumour of what he had done to his son spread, and when that mask appeared on their doorstep none dared refuse him. Eighty-two thousand soldiers, camp followers, peasants and slaves had been harnessed into teams. Neither women nor children, nor the wounded who could still walk, had been spared. Another eighteen thousand horses, buffalo and other beasts of burden had been assembled for the monumental task. Every usable clanker, more than five thousand of them, had to be dragged from the festering muck of the battlefield onto solid ground.

The haulers fell dead in their hundreds, hearts bursting under the strain. Many more collapsed, and those who could not get up quickly enough died where they lay, for Jal-Nish would not allow a moment's pause to get them out. He ordered the clankers, on their wooden skids, dragged over the fallen, as a bloody spur to the rest to do their duty. They did, and they kept dying.

Finally they'd heaved the clankers out of the putrid wallow, but that was only the beginning. They needed to move the machines more than six leagues to the field of the nearest node, and already man and beast were exhausted.

The agonising days went by. Nish's sunburnt, whip-torn back was covered in festering sores. Already lean from months of privation, after seven days of slavery he was so thin that he barely left a shadow. He could not sleep; could scarcely eat the slops they were fed on, which had a rotten stench and crawled with maggots, so desperate had the supply situation become. The army's supply wagons had been hauled by clankers, and half had been kept back, leagues to the east, in case the enemy overran the main camp, as they had. Most of the supplies here had been trampled into the mud. Without them, and with many more mouths to feed, everyone had been reduced to quarter rations. The slaves' portion came from that which even the guard dogs wouldn't eat.

Xervish Flydd looked unchanged. He'd been whipped even more than Nish, but was taking it better. He seemed, and it felt strange when Nish first had the thought, *at home* here. Not as though he belonged, but rather that he had adapted perfectly to his slavery. Flydd was a driven man. He was going to bring down the Council and nothing else mattered. Pain and privation he simply endured.

Tonight, through the smoke from five thousand camp fires, a blood-red moon, a few days past full, was rising over the eastern hills. Not a tree or bush remained and they were now burning grass and chunks of weathered tar. The army had stripped the land to its rocky bones.

Today had been the hardest. They were well out of the battlefield bog now, moving down the valley, and the overseer had driven them like the beasts they were, to make up lost time. Nish's boots were falling to pieces and would soon be gone. Slaving barefoot over this stony ground would cripple him, and the fate of crippled slaves was not something he liked to contemplate.

The whip master had allowed them a scant two hours' rest

this evening and it was nearly over. I can't go on, Nish thought, as he had many times, but each time, as the lash coiled around his belly and through the rags of his shirt, pain drove him to one last effort.

Flydd was slumped beside him, head between his knees, snoring. He took advantage of every opportunity to rest. The moon lifted itself clear of the horizon, showing mostly its dark, mottled face, said to be an ill omen. Nish did not believe in omens but its bloody visage made him shudder.

'Surr . . .' he began.

'Don't call me surr. I'm a slave, just like you.'

'Thanks for the reminder. Xervish?'

'What?'

'Where's Irisis?' Nish's thoughts had often turned to her over the past days.

'How would I know? A long way from here, I hope.'

'I hope she's safe.' And didn't hear about my disgrace. Nish couldn't bear for her to think ill of him.

Something scuttled across his field of view, slipping into the darkness further along the line of slaves. Nish felt no curiosity – that was a luxury no slave could afford. The figure flitted out again into the darkness. He yawned, closed his eyes . . .

A whip crack dragged Nish out of sleep. Instinctively he flinched, but it was just the overseer, practising on someone nearby. Nish dared not drift off again; sleeping slaves were a favourite target. He eyed the overseer, who kept raising something the size of a brick to his mouth. He liked to whip as he ate. As the man approached, Nish caught the aroma of freshly baked bread, a whole loaf. He would have killed the brute to get his hands on it. He thumped his clenched fist into the dirt.

'Easy,' said Flydd beside him. 'That'll only get you another lashing. Keep your head down.'

'I'll bet that bread was meant for us.'

'I dare say it was. Don't think about it.'

'I can't help it,' Nish muttered, drooling uncontrollably.

The little shadow flitted behind the massive bulk of the overseer.

'Did you see that?' said Nish.

'Someone's trying to steal the overseer's dinner. I wouldn't want to be the lad when he's caught.'

Nish shivered. The overseer stopped, sniffed the air, took the coiled whip from his shoulder and cracked it, reflectively, against a slave's belly. The man screamed. The overseer chuckled and tore at the bread. The hand holding the loaf fell to his side.

The shadow sprang, snatched the loaf and bolted. The big man cursed, swung the whip and caught the flying figure around the knees, sending it crashing to the ground. Within seconds the overseer was on the youth. A wail rang out; a very familiar cry.

'*That's Ullii!*' Nish hissed, pulling himself up with the harness. The other slaves began to grumble. 'What's she doing here?'

'Trying to survive.' Flydd was also on his feet, rubbing his scarred thigh.

'He'll kill her.'

'Or worse,' Flydd said grimly.

'What are we going to do?'

Flydd, still rubbing his left thigh, did not answer.

'Leave her alone, you vicious scum!' Nish bellowed.

The overseer whirled and, crushing Ullii under one brawny arm, strode to the head of the line, lashing indiscriminately. Something fell and was crushed underfoot – her goggles.

Ullii convulsed, almost succeeding in getting free. 'Nish!' she cried despairingly. 'Nish, help me.'

Her cry tore at him. All the slaves were on their feet now. Nish wrenched at his harness, which did not budge: no slave had escaped from this overseer.

'Stop it, you damn fool,' hissed Flydd. 'Get out of my way.'

Giving his thigh one last rub, Flydd threw out his right hand. Rays roared from his fingertips to strike the overseer in the belly, just missing the squirming figure of Ullii. The man was hurled backwards as if he'd been struck with a catapult

133

ball. Flydd moved one finger and the ray severed his harness, followed by Nish's, before fading out.

Ullii scrambled free and ran into Nish's arms. 'Nish, Nish!' she sobbed. 'Save me.'

'This is no time for a family reunion,' Flydd growled. 'Come on.'

He bent over the prone figure of the overseer, taking the whip and the man's belt, which he buckled around his bony hips. It held a sheath knife, a metal pannikin and a pouch that jingled. The loaf he broke into three chunks, handing Nish and Ullii a portion each.

The other slaves in their team began to cry out, holding up their chains and begging to be set free.

'You have an important duty here,' said Flydd sententiously. 'To haul clankers.' From the vicious cursing that followed, the slaves did not appreciate that duty as well as they might have. Flydd turned to Nish. 'Take one mouthful and save the rest. After me.'

Ignoring the wails and beseeching cries of the harnessed slaves, he bolted towards the south-east, where a cluster of low, rock-crowned hills broke the horizon. As Nish set Ullii down, she clutched his hand and they ran for their lives. Flydd, despite his age and a limp like a broken-legged crab, was at least fifty paces ahead, almost out of sight in the moonlight.

Ullii ran easily at Nish's side and they caught Flydd as the slope began to rise. He had slowed to a fast walk. 'What did you do back there?' said Nish.

'Later!' Flydd said, hobbling badly now.

He did not look well. Nish guessed it was aftersickness, which all mancers suffered after using their Art.

Flydd looked over his shoulder. Nish did too. There were lights everywhere along the line of the clankers, and someone was running with a torch back towards the officers' tents. More urgently, a group of figures with torches had formed lines at the head of the clankers and was moving in their direction. A bellow came to them on the wind.

'It's a search party,' said Flydd. 'The first of many. Jal-Nish will hunt me to the furthest corners of the world, but he's not going to get me.' He set off again.

'He'll hunt me just as hard,' said Nish. 'My father has betrayed me, Ullii. What am I to do?'

'My family cast me out to die,' said Ullii.

There was no answer to that. He squeezed her hand and followed, walking awkwardly, for the stitching on the side of his right boot had come undone and the sole was flapping. The other boot was nearly as decrepit.

'Why didn't you free the slaves, surr?' said Nish.

'Weren't you listening?' Flydd growled. 'Hauling clankers is vital work.'

'Isn't that a bit hypocritical?' panted Nish. 'After all –'

'I have *more* vital work,' Flydd said tersely, 'and no one else can do it. But feel free to go back, if your conscience troubles you.'

'It's more flexible than I'd thought,' Nish said hastily.

'So I've noticed,' Flydd said dryly. 'Besides, if I did set them free, they'd want to come with us, and then we'd never get away.' He broke into a pained, lurching trot. 'We'll go around this hill, not over it,' he continued. 'Else we might be seen in the moonlight.'

Beyond, to left and right, were more hills – not a range but a scatter of individual mounds that seemed to grow higher in the distance. All were topped with rocky crowns and a bristle of shrubbery or scrubby trees.

'Good land for running,' said Flydd, 'though not for hiding. They'll have the dogs on our trail before too long.'

'What are we going to do?' said Nish.

'I haven't the faintest idea.'

They followed a goat track that wound between the next pair of hills. The bushes were tall enough to conceal them, though the moon lit up the path, which was a blessing. The scrub was full of thorns and burrs, painful to negotiate in the dark.

By the time they reached the other side of the hill the moon was halfway up the sky. They stopped where a ledge of resistant rock stuck out over the slope like the edge of a plate hanging over a table.

'Let's take a breather,' grunted Flydd, sitting down.

'How did you do that?' said Nish, who was bursting with curiosity. 'If the node is dead, how can you do magic at all?'

'Mind your own business.'

Ullii crouched beside the scrutator. 'Does your leg hurt, Xervish?' She peeled away the torn flaps of fabric covering his left thigh. They were darkly stained in the moonlight. Ullii drew back, visibly distressed.

'More than somewhat,' Flydd replied. 'I'll just dress this, then –' A howl drifted to them on the wind, followed by a furious baying. He rose to his feet with an effort, muttering, 'I thought we'd have a longer lead.'

They hurried down the stony slope. The sole of Nish's boot was practically off but he couldn't stop to fix it. The path narrowed, the scrub closing overhead until it resembled a rabbit run.

Towards the bottom, Flydd, who was limping worse than ever, stopped. 'Ullii, can you smell water?'

'Of course,' she said.

'Lead the way, quick as you can.'

She went down on hands and knees, crept under a bush, turned left and scuttled along a path that had not been visible to Nish. He followed. Thorns tore at his clothing and caught in his hair. Ullii was out of sight, making so little sound that he could not tell which way she'd gone.

'Left!' growled Flydd in his ear, 'And make it snappy. Those aren't puppies behind us.'

'I can't see the path.'

Flydd muttered an imprecation, pushed past and stood up. Letting out a muffled gasp, he pressed his hand to his thigh.

'Are you all right?' said Nish.

'I'll have to be.'

They zigzagged down a steep decline where dry leaves and gravel slipped underfoot, over a bank between head-high tangles of berry bushes, and found themselves under some tall trees. The undergrowth disappeared and the ground became springy.

Ullii waited beside a leaning tree. 'The river is straight ahead, Xervish.'

'Can you swim, Ullii?' Flydd asked.

'No,' she said with a shudder.

'What about you, Artificer?'

Nish started. A long time had passed since anyone had called him by that title. 'I can, but not very well.'

'Useless fool!' Flydd said it without rancour. 'The rivers in Taltid aren't deep, or fast, but you can still drown in them. We have to go into the water or the dogs will have us. Ullii, come with me. Hang on to my shoulders, not my neck! Don't make any noise. Nish, you'll just have to do your best. No splashing.'

They went over the bank and Nish lost sight of them. Occasional shafts of moonlight touched the water. There came a splash, a faint cry, a curse, then the sound of paddling.

Nish followed gingerly. He had never been confident in water. To go into a river that he could not even see, in pitch darkness, took a deal of courage, though he'd done it once before and survived. Nish suppressed the embarrassing memories of the escape from Mira's house. Recollecting that the dogs were not far behind, and doubtless the overseer with his whip, he pushed forward.

The bank gave way, dropping him into the river with a mighty splash. Water went over his head and his foot caught on something – a fallen tree or branch. He kicked free, came up and looked around. The trees were taller here and the canopy closed. Not a glimmer of moonshine reached the water.

'Flydd?'

He could hear nothing over his own splashing and heavy breathing. Being prone to panic in deep water at the best of times, Nish was not game to stop paddling so he could listen.

He moved out into a current, which pulled him downstream. It was eerie. For all he could tell, the river might have been three spans wide, or a hundred, though Flydd had said there were no large rivers here.

Nish was beginning to feel more confident. He moved his arms in gentle circles, scissored his legs, and discovered he could keep his head above water without too much effort.

'Flydd?'

There was no answer. He'd surely go downriver as far as possible, so there would be more area to search. Nish floated along, calmly now. The water was cool enough to ease his throbbing wounds; it was the best he'd felt since his slavery began.

His feet grated on gravel – a shoal touched by light and moon-shadow. He pushed around the edge of it, heading for deeper water, then drifted towards the far bank.

A hand seized him by the collar. Nish thrashed, went under and water surged up his nose and down his windpipe. He was dragged choking and gasping onto the bank. He struck at his assailant, only to receive a blow that drove him into the mud. A big foot pressed him down; mud filled his mouth and eyes. He clawed at the bank.

'Don't move!' said a voice he had never heard before. 'Hoy, Plazzo! I've got one. Told you they'd come this way. Oh, boy, I can taste the reward money already.'

THIRTEEN

Someone grunted. The bushes rustled and footsteps came in their direction.

'Hey! Any sign of the others, Plazzo?' the fellow continued. '*Unggh!*'

A body fell into the water, making a loud splash. Nish was hauled up by the arms.

'What a useless fellow you are,' said Flydd amiably. 'Wipe the mud off your face – you're giving us a bad name.'

Nish blew the muck out of his nostrils and followed. 'There's another of them somewhere.'

'He's already floating downriver,' Flydd said laconically, tearing leaves into strips as he walked. It made a zipping sound, like cloth being ripped, and Nish smelt a pungent odour that resembled mustard oil.

'Where's Ullii?'

'She's here. Being *quiet.*'

They continued on a track winding through scrub. Ullii fell in beside Nish and took his hand. He made to pull away, knowing how badly he stank, but she clung to him.

'Where are we headed?' said Nish, feeling vaguely uncomfortable. The intimacy he'd had with her months ago at Tirthrax was long gone. Evidently her feelings were unchanged. He felt, as he had briefly when they'd met in the Aachim camp weeks ago, that she expected something of him. Nish could not work out what it was, and was too exhausted to think about it. He could have slept standing up.

'I'll tell you when we get there.' Flydd was still tearing leaves. Ullii was carrying them too – Nish could smell them on her.

'It's the red mustard bush,' Flydd said quietly, 'since I know you're going to ask. Ullii found it for me. Puts dogs off the scent, hopefully.'

'But not people?'

'I hardly think so.'

The sky had clouded over. Judging by an occasional glimpse of the moon, they now seemed to be heading north. Nish wondered why, but didn't ask.

Long before daybreak he smelt tar and knew they were passing Snizort again, further east. Flydd continued north, bypassing the now abandoned command hill, before turning onto a north-westerly heading across undulating country covered in crunchy, withered grass.

After several hours of weary trudging, it began to get light. The cloud had passed and it would be another clear, hot day. They climbed a rocky mound, not big enough to be called a hill. Nish sank into the shade afforded by a boulder shaped like a two-humped buffalo, closed his eyes and began to doze off. Flydd scanned the scene, keeping to the cover. 'I don't see anyone behind us.'

Nish grunted. He'd eaten his bread long ago and was so hungry he could have bitten off his arm.

'Better fix your boot,' said Flydd.

'With what?' Nish snapped.

Flydd tossed him the whip and knife. Nish unbraided several strips of leather, poked holes in the boot with the tip of the knife and began to weave the strips through.

Flydd picked shreds of cloth from around the tear in his left thigh, careful not to touch it with his dirty hands. The edges looked as though they'd been burned.

'What happened there?' said Nish.

Flydd waved the question away.

'Do you want me to bandage that?'

'Touch it with those filthy paws and I'm likely to get gangrene.'

Ullii squatted beside Flydd, staring anxiously at the wound. She was wearing a tent-like smock made from a piece of green cloth fastened at the throat, and baggy trousers. She knotted a mask out of a strip torn from the hem of the smock, and covered her eyes, nose and ears. Horizontal slits over her eyes allowed her to see, not that she needed to.

'You're hurting, Xervish,' Ullii said, eyes blinking behind the mask as the light grew.

'Somewhat, Ullii.' Flydd touched her affectionately on the shoulder. 'I'll attend to it as soon as we find water.'

She packed surplus cloth into her nostrils and snuggled up to him, which Nish found extraordinary. Ullii was so wary of people. Gazing up into Flydd's eyes, she said, 'I forgive you, Xervish.'

Nish had no idea what she was talking about. Ullii turned to him then, as if challenging him, and her stare was so intense that he had to look away. What did she want? More of the intimacy they'd shared at Tirthrax? It felt like half a life-time ago and, even though he cared about Ullii, Nish could not turn his feelings on like a tap.

She tossed her head, leapt up and stalked into the scrub. 'What was that about?' said Nish.

Flydd, bound up in his own troubles, answered the question he thought Nish had asked. 'A long time ago I promised to help find her twin brother, Myllii. They were separated when she was four and she hasn't heard from him since.'

'You mentioned him the other day,' said Nish.

'But I didn't tell you I'd lied to her in Snizort, at the node-drainer. Ullii was being uncooperative, so I told her Muss had found Myllii and was bringing him back. Unfortunately, she discovered that I'd lied.'

'Well, it's all over now.'

'I hope so,' said Flydd, 'though I've a feeling it isn't. Go and have a look around, will you?'

Nish was behind a tree on the other side of the mound when he caught a whiff of something burning, or at least extremely overheated. It was a strange smell, nothing like burning wood or leaves, or flesh of human or lyrinx. The odour was like roasted rock. He called Flydd over. Ullii came out of the bushes, scowling.

'What's that?' Nish said, sniffing.

Unusually, Ullii answered. 'Iron tears.'

Flydd gave her a keen glance. The rising sun carved him out in profile, a black cut-out in a bronze wall. 'You've been here before, haven't you, Ullii?'

She adjusted her mask over her eyes, moving a little closer to the scrutator. 'Came with Irisis ages ago, looking for the node-drainer.'

'Is it the *node*?' Nish couldn't see anything unusual.

'What's left of it,' said Flydd. 'Let's take a look, shall we?'

'Shouldn't we try to get away while we can?'

'I've got to check something first.' Flydd scanned the landscape. There was nothing to be seen, though ten thousand soldiers could have hidden in any of the valleys still in shadow, or behind any of the stone-crowned hills. 'We've time enough. They haven't found our trail yet. Over there.' He indicated the hill to their left.

They wound up the hill, which was no more than a grassy undulation. From the top, not two hundred paces away, a black hole in the ground emitted wisps of steam.

Ullii stopped abruptly, her small head darting this way and that.

'What is it?' said Flydd. 'What do you see, Ullii?'

'A *hole*,' she said.

'Of course there's a hole,' Nish muttered.

'Don't be a fool, boy! Ullii?'

'Hole in my lattice, Xervish,' said Ullii. 'A pair of holes.'

'*A pair*?' said Flydd. 'Are you afraid?'

'No,' said Ullii. 'They're empty now.'

Flydd's feet left pale trails in the dewy grass. Nish followed in silence, unable to make sense of it. Why was Flydd squandering their lead for the exploded remains of a node?

Shortly they began to encounter patches of burnt grass, each containing slaggy aggregations of melted rock which must have been blown out of the hole. The patches coalesced, the blobs of slag grew larger until the ground was knee-deep in them. The bigger ones were still hot enough to warm Nish's ankles as he wove between them.

The hole formed a perfect oval about forty spans wide by sixty long. Its rim was as sharp as cheese cut with a knife and crusted with exhalations of red, yellow and brown sulphur. Within, the land had subsided in a series of concentric oval rings, like a squashed spyglass. The outside ring, the highest, bore a hide of withered grass. On the next, the grass had been carbonised in place. The soil of the remaining rings was burnt bare. The centre of the hole was obscured by rising steam.

There were nine of these oval rings, each about the width of a span, the drop to the next being roughly the same distance. They formed a series of giant steps down to the centre, though the shimmering air obscured what lay below. The humidity was choking.

'You're not planning to go down *there*?' said Nish, eyeing the hole anxiously.

Flydd chuckled mirthlessly. 'Indeed we are.'

He lowered himself onto the first ring and held his arms up. Without hesitation Ullii slipped into them. Flydd could get her to do things that no one else could. The pair turned their backs and went to the edge.

Nish was reluctant to follow but Flydd was not a man for excuses. Going backwards over the first edge, he felt his chest tighten, his pulse quicken.

Flydd and Ullii were well below him as Nish climbed down to the next level. The sides of the oval rings, as smooth as polished stone, resembled a series of pistons one inside the other. At the ninth ring it was stifling, steamy. Waves of heat pulsed up from an oval trench five or six spans deep and, when the steam clouds parted, its base glowed red. Within the trench, a cylinder of rock rose from the centre, listing to one side. The once-smooth stone walls had run like toffee.

On its flat top, like a pair of teardrops on a pedestal, sat two shining globes of liquid metal, bright as quicksilver. They were shaped like drops of water, though each was the size of a soup bowl. A faint humming sound came from them. Ullii had taken her mask off and was staring at the globes as if entranced.

'My, oh my,' said Flydd. 'Can you hear the song of the tears?'

'What are they?' Nish sat near the edge, not too close, praying that Flydd was not going to go after them.

'The distilled tears of the node,' said Flydd.

'I don't understand.'

'No power is ever completely destroyed, Nish. There's always some residuum – and it's ever more complex, warped and strange. I wonder . . . Can this be an accident, or were they *created*?'

'Flydd?'

'According to myth, or rumour, the tears are the essence of the node, purified of all base elements by the blast that destroys it. They're believed to be made of the purest substance in the world, and desired by mancers more than any other. But no mancer has ever obtained so much as a speck of that matter, much less a complete tear. They represent the value of a continent.' Flydd gazed at the tears with greedy eyes.

'And you want them?' said Nish. 'Are they magic?'

'Empty,' Ullii interjected.

'Not at the moment,' said the scrutator. 'But their substance, which has been called nihilium, takes the print of the Art more readily than any other form of matter, and binds it *much* more tightly. Oh, I want them – to make sure no one else can have them.'

'How are you going to get across?'

Flydd gauged the distances. The oval trench was red hot, making it impossible to climb down and up the other side. The stone pedestal seemed cooler, though it still radiated such heat that they could not have gone within a couple of spans of it, even could they have reached that far. Besides, it was well out of reach, its top being three spans below them, and eight or nine out from where they stood.

'Even if we had a rope or a grappling iron we couldn't collect them,' Flydd muttered.

'And I dare say they're heavy?'

Flydd thought for a moment. 'If they have weight as we know it, they would be heavier than lead; they could have the weight of gold, or even platinum. But then again, they may weigh virtually nothing . . . Let's go up.' Flydd gave the tears one last, lingering look, then turned to the wall.

Nish boosted him up, then Ullii. Flydd reached down a hand to him.

'What are you going to do?' Nish wondered as they reached the top.

'I don't know. The time is all wrong.'

They repaired to the shade of a grove of trees some ten minutes' walk away. Flydd filled the overseer's pannikin from a tiny spring, kindled a smokeless fire under it with dry twigs, carefully washed his hands then lay back with his eyes closed.

'If the field is dead,' said Nish, 'how come you were able to make that blast back there, to save Ullii?' It had been preying on his mind ever since.

Flydd looked up irritably. 'Can you be quiet? I'm trying to think.'

Nish stared at the scrutator as if unable to make him out. Finally Flydd snapped. 'Damn and blast you, Nish! Go away.'

Nish rose abruptly but Flydd said, 'Oh, you might as well sit down. I've lost my train of thought anyway.' He peeled back his torn and bloody pants leg to reveal the jagged, blistered gash in his thigh. 'I had a charged crystal embedded in my leg a long time ago, for just such an emergency.'

'You had it all that time?' Nish exclaimed. 'Why didn't you use it to save yourself?'

'It was for emergencies.' snapped Flydd.

'And being enslaved didn't count?' Nish found that incomprehensible.

'My life wasn't in danger, apart from being *bored* to death by you. I wanted to remain with the army for as long as possible, so I'd know what Jal-Nish was up to. You do know that your father plans to lead an attack on the lyrinx? An unbelievable folly that can only end one way.'

'I've heard the slaves gossiping about it,' said Nish.

'Now I'm out of contact, and that's bad.'

'What about the crystal in your leg?'

'Once used, it can't be reused.'

'Why didn't you sew two crystals into yourself? Or twenty, for that matter?'

Flydd sprang up, his face thunderous. 'Don't you ever think before opening your mouth? Nothing comes without a price, Artificer, and putting powerful crystals inside you exacts a hefty one. Discharging one –' He shook his head.

It was a nasty tear, the length of Nish's little finger and burned at the edges. 'That must be painful,' Nish observed.

'You use words the way a blacksmith cuts flowers! Scrutators are trained to overcome pain, and I've had more practice than most, but this hurts like bloody blazes.' Tearing off the sleeve of his shirt, Flydd ripped it into strips and poked them under the boiling water. After a minute or two he fished them out, waved them in the air to cool them, then bound them around the injury.

'That'll do.' Turning away from the pit, Flydd began to limp towards a hill some half a league to the east.

'Where are we going?' said Nish.

'We can't recover the tears on our own. I've got to find help.'

It took the best part of an hour to reach the hill, which was mounded like a breast and topped with a cliffed nipple of gullied grey stone. Flydd panted his way up, emerging on a patch of flat rock some thirty paces across, bisected by a cleft from which a solitary tree sprouted. They sat in its meagre shade while he got his breath back.

'You'll have noticed that this hill is quite distinctive,' said the scrutator. 'Irisis and Fyn-Mah were to rendezvous here with the air-floater, if they got out of Snizort alive.'

'What were they doing there?'

'None of your business.'

'Did you know you were going to be taken prisoner?'

'Ghorr needed a scapegoat and there was nothing I could do about it without –' He broke off, staring back towards the node. 'But of course, if Irisis and Fyn-Mah did escape, they would have been here days ago. Spread out. Look for a sign.'

It took the best part of an hour to find it, an ornamental dagger partly embedded in the ground, as if dropped from a height. Rudely scratched on the blade was: *Yes, no, 3.*

'What can that mean?' said Nish.

'It means Fyn-Mah found what she went into Snizort to find, that she was hunted and had to flee, and that she's gone to the third place I mentioned previously.'

'That being?'

'None of your business.'

Nish sighed. In this mood, Flydd was impossible to deal with. 'Then we have to walk,' he remarked gloomily. Despite its dangers, air-floating was the most pleasant of all means of travelling. 'Is it far away?'

The reply was pure Flydd. 'Further than the people hunting us.'

They were climbing down the cleft when something winked in the sun to the south. 'That's an air floater!' hissed Nish. 'Could it be Irisis coming back for us?'

Flydd squinted at the object, which was moving low to the ground along a line of trees that marked the course of a creek. 'She wouldn't dare, in daylight.' The machine began to zigzag back and forth as if following something. 'What can they be doing?'

'Dogs!' whispered Ullii. She'd been so quiet since leaving the node crater that Nish had practically forgotten she was there.

'They've found our tracks,' said Flydd.

Nish hefted a knobbly stick. 'We'd better get ready to fight.'

'Stay down! We can't fight that many people.' A leathery tree grew horizontally out of the cleft before bending to, the vertical. Flydd pulled himself up into the curve and peered

147

around the trunk. Nish crouched between two rocks splotched with bright yellow lichen.

The air-floater lifted and ran directly towards the node crater. Flydd groaned, the tortured sound two trees make when rubbed together in a storm. 'Let's pray no one recognises what's down there.'

The machine settled. Nine figures went into the pit: seven people and two dogs. The pilot and one other person could be seen moving about on the air-floater. Nish twisted his fingers. together. After some minutes it lifted, moved over the depression, bucking in the updraught, and drifted down.

'That's a dangerous manoeuvre,' said Flydd. 'If the walls of the gasbag touch something hot, they're dead.'

Time passed. They could see nothing but the top of the airbag. 'What *are* they doing?' said Nish.

'A really good pilot could bring it down right over the pedestal. Someone could simply pick up the tears.'

'They're taking a long time,' Nish said later.

'Be quiet!'

The air-floater crept out of the crater and hovered in the updraught, its bow pointing at their hiding place. 'Whoever it is,' said Flydd in a curiously flat voice, 'they have the tears.'

The air-floater lurched, turned away and began to drift, low to the ground, towards the army camp in the distance.

'We'd better make sure,' Flydd said.

They scrambled down the gully. 'I dare say the tears are more important than we are,' said Nish hopefully.

'They are, but the scrutators won't give *us* up, Nish.'

They could see the smoke well before they reached the hole. It was yellow-brown with threads of black, and smelled like burning hair and meat.

'I can't see anything.' Flydd was peering over the edge. 'I'll have to climb down.'

'Do you mind if I stay here?' said Nish. The stench was making him sick.

'Good idea. Keep watch. You too, Ullii. Ullii?'

She was hanging back, holding her noseplugs in. 'This is a terrible place,' she whispered.

'You don't have to come near.' Flydd eased his injured leg over the side.

Nish watched him go down. A surge of greasy brown fumes obscured Flydd as he reached the fourth oval. He bent double, coughing. Nish moved away from the edge. When he returned, after the smoke had thinned, Flydd was not to be seen.

'Is he all right?' he said to Ullii.

She gagged and doubled over, unable to speak. Nish circumnavigated the depression, seeking a better vantage point, but did not find one. After five or ten minutes, Flydd began to labour up again.

Nish helped him out onto the ground. The skin below Flydd's eyes had gone the purple of a day-old bruise and it took him quite a while to focus.

'Are the tears gone?' said Nish.

'Yes.'

'Who could it have been?'

'Ghorr is my guess, though it could have been any of the scrutators. Can you tell, Ullii?'

'No,' she whispered 'Can't tell anything. Can't *see* anything.' In times of stress she sometimes lost her lattice.

'But whoever did take it,' said Flydd, 'they've made sure no one will ever know.'

'What do you mean?' said Nish.

'The trench at the bottom is clotted with bodies. Six soldiers and the air-floater's chart-maker. And the dogs. In an hour, the witnesses will be ash.'

'All but us,' said Nish. 'And the pilot.'

'He needs her to get back to camp, but as soon as the air-floater lands, she's dead. He'll call it a seizure.'

'And the soldiers?'

'He'll say I ambushed them and blasted the soldiers into nothingness with another crystal. No one will be able to prove otherwise.'

149

'If he knew we were watching, our lives could be measured in minutes,' said Nish.

'He knows we've been there,' said Flydd. 'The air-floater tracked us to the node. Once the tears are safely hidden, he'll come after us.'

'Then we'd better get moving. Which way, surr?'

'North.'

They set off, keeping to the lowest ground. Ullii whimpered and moved close to Nish for comfort, though he was too preoccupied to notice. After some minutes she flounced away and took Flydd's hand. Flydd put his arm around her as he walked. She was red in the face and struggling to keep up, which Nish found surprising. When he'd last been with Ullii, she'd climbed the slopes of Tirthrax more easily than he had.

'Was this an accident?' Flydd mused as they rested among a pile of boulders a couple of hours later, 'Or was it planned from the beginning?'

'What do you mean?' said Nish.

'What if the device Ghorr gave me was *designed* to be faulty, so as to destroy the node and create the tears?'

'How could that be, surr? You told me it was tested, independently.'

'I don't know. Scrutator Klarm would not be easily fooled, but neither can I believe that the destruction of the node, and the creation of the tears, was an accident. But if it *was* planned, why didn't the perpetrator come to the node straight away?'

'Maybe he was delayed by the battle,' said Nish. 'Or thought that the tears would form at the node-drainer.'

'I hadn't considered that,' Flydd said appreciatively. 'And perhaps, until today, it was too hot to get near, too steamy to see if the tears were there.'

'Then why not put a guard on it?'

'That would announce that there was something special in the crater. Whoever he is, he wouldn't want anyone to know about the tears.'

'Not even the other scrutators?'

'Especially not the other scrutators . . .' Flydd toyed with a piece of gravel, deep in thought. 'There's more here than the eye can see, Nish.'

'I don't understand,' said Nish.

'Neither do I, but it bothers me that someone knows far more about the Art than any of us. Why were the tears made?'

'To further one man's ambition.'

'Or one woman's. Four of the scrutators are women, remember? It doesn't do to make assumptions. But what ambition could – ?'

Breaking off, he began to pace, glancing from Nish to a silent Ullii, who sat by herself, arms crossed over her belly, rocking back and forth.

'What is it, surr?'

Flydd jerked his head. Nish rose and followed him. 'Surely you trust Ullii, surr?'

'She doesn't need to know.'

'Do I?'

'A half-baked mooncalf like you?' Flydd said fiercely. 'Certainly not, but you're all I've got. Breathe a syllable of what I'm about to tell you and you're a dead man.'

There wasn't a trace of levity in his tone. Nish swallowed.

'I'm wondering,' the scrutator went on, 'if this might not be an attempt upon a *higher power*.'

'I didn't know there was a higher power than the scrutators.'

Flydd hesitated, as if having second thoughts. 'It's worth my head to speak about this, and yours, but since we're both outlaws in peril of our lives, and I desperately need a sounding board, I'll make an exception. It's the best kept secret of all. The scrutators make out that they run the world, but the Numinator pulls their strings, and has since the Council was formed.'

'Clawers,' called Ullii. 'Coming fast!'

Her eyes were covered again, her face was turned to the north-west. Nish couldn't see anything, but Ullii did not make mistakes. In a few minutes three specks appeared, flying high, directly towards the fuming node crater, which was now a good two-thirds of a league from their hiding place.

'What can they want?' said Nish.

'They've worked out what really happened to the node,' said Flydd, climbing the jumbled boulders to get a better look. 'But they're too late.'

Two lyrinx flew down the fuming hole while a third circled, on watch. Within a minute, the two reappeared, rising high into the sky and flying in widening circles before heading in the direction of the human army.

'They won't find them,' said Flydd. 'The tears will be hidden by now. I wonder what they'll do?'

The lyrinx disappeared into the haze. 'Who is this Numinator?' said Nish.

'If anyone knows, they're not saying. Some scrutators think it stands for "The Numinous One", though anyone who styles himself as a divine power must be supremely arrogant. I can only say this: more than a century ago, soon after the war had become worldwide and the Council of Santhenar, as it then was, was struggling to form a united front against the enemy, the power calling itself the Numinator took command. There was a bitter struggle and many mancers died before the Numinator defeated them. The survivors became the Council of Scrutators. The Numinator, he or she, set down the rules by which the Council was to run the world, but afterwards took no part in day-to-day affairs. From time to time the scrutators have chafed under this regime, and even tried to rebel, but were always taught a brutal lesson.'

'And you were one of them?' asked Nish.

'That was long before my time. My crime was simply to inquire into matters that weren't my business. The scrutators taught me my lesson to avoid being punished themselves. They taught me well.'

Nish digested that. 'So you think the Council deliberately created these tears, so as to take on the Numinator?'

'Not the Council. One individual, who may want to control the Council, *first*.'

'But why now, when the war is going so badly, and division could be fatal?'

'I don't know. It may have been decades in the planning. And there's no saying that the person who created the tears is the one who ended up with them.'

'Are we going to find out?' said Nish.

'Don't be a bloody fool, boy. Look at me!' Xervish Flydd held out his arms. 'See the scars, the warped and twisted bones, the very flesh scraped away. I was a handsome man when I was young, Nish, but not after the scrutators had finished with me. I should have died then. They did their best to break me, but were ordered to let me live. I was to be a lesson to the other scrutators, not to pry into what wasn't their business. I've often wished they had killed me; I've not had a day without pain in thirty years. But here I am, a living example. Take heed, Nish. Some secrets are meant to be kept.'

Despite his words, Nish could see the resolve in Flydd's eyes – he was going to find out. And what then?

'So why the breeding factories? Why rewrite the Histories? Why—?'

'Good questions for which there are no answers.'

'But—'

'Come on!' Flydd said roughly. 'As soon as the tears are hidden, he'll be after us. He can't afford to let us live.'

FOURTEEN

Vithis took charge of Tiaan's amplimet and hedron, wrapping them in sheets of beaten platinum which he folded over carefully before putting the packet in his pocket with a shudder. He passed Tiaan to a young cheerful man, a deep-chested giant with blond curly hair, unusual for an Aachim.

'I'm Ghaenis,' he said to Tiaan as the group raced back to their own lines. 'Don't be afraid. You'll come to no harm while I'm looking after you.'

For some odd reason, she knew it was true. She had perfect confidence in Ghaenis, and she'd not felt that with any Aachim before, apart from Malien.

Vithis said no word to Tiaan in the half-hour it took to reach the Aachim war camp, running all the way. As soon as they arrived, Ghaenis set Tiaan down on a metal chair and drew Vithis aside. He began to put a case animatedly, with much arm-waving and gesturing towards the constructs.

Vithis listened with set face. Ghaenis's accent was difficult to follow and Tiaan learned only that it had to do with the amplimet. At the end, Vithis shook his head.

Ghaenis renewed the argument even more passionately but with the same good humour. One hand swept out in the direction of the stalled constructs. The other reached for Vithis as if begging a favour.

'I cannot permit it,' Vithis said tersely. 'It's too dangerous.'

Ghaenis kept on. Vithis paced up and down, head bowed, then finally he nodded. The young man listened carefully while Vithis gave a series of instructions, or warnings, then handed the platinum-wrapped packet to him.

Ghaenis gleefully shook the older man's hands, bowed low and, with a cheery wave to Tiaan, ran to a group of constructs and climbed into the leading one.

Tiaan went on with her exercises, surreptitiously clenching and unclenching her leg muscles. She needed to regain her strength. She had to be able to walk, and no one must know it. She was going to escape, somehow.

The camp was furious with activity. A dozen people vied for Vithis's attention, all urgently. He listened to their messages, frowned and called an attendant. 'Bring her!'

The fellow picked Tiaan up as if she were a child and followed Vithis halfway across the encampment to a large tent. From a good ten paces away, Vithis shouted, 'Come out!' in the Aachim tongue. Malien had taught Tiaan a little of the language in Tirthrax.

A young noblewoman emerged. She was small for an Aachim and, with her reddish hair and pale colouring, strikingly different from the other Aachim here. The attendant set Tiaan on the dusty ground.

'This is Tiaan Liise-Mar, the thief who stole our construct,' said Vithis in the common speech. 'Guard her with your life, *Thyssea*, or Clan Elienor will answer for it.'

The young woman bowed but, as the grim Aachim stalked away, she made an obscene gesture to his back, then gave Tiaan an impish grin.

Tiaan could not help smiling. 'Hello, Thyssea.' The name sounded strange on her tongue. 'Did I pronounce that right?'

'Well enough, for a human. It's Thyzzea.' She spoke the common speech fluently, though with a slight nasal intonation.

'I'm sorry. *Thyzzea*. I tried to say it as Vithis did.'

'Thyssea is an ... uncouth word. He was being deliberately insulting.'

'Why?' said Tiaan.

'Do you know that Clan Inthis is called First Clan?'

'Yes.' Tiaan put her hand over her eyes. She'd been underground for many weeks and, though it was late afternoon, the sun was painfully bright.

155

'Come into the shade.'

'I can't stand up,' said Tiaan. 'I broke my back.' She wasn't going to reveal that the lyrinx had repaired it – once her legs were strong enough to walk, it would give her a tiny advantage.

Though they were the same size, Thyzzea lifted Tiaan with little apparent effort, carried her beneath a scrubby tree which had red-tipped thorns growing out of the trunk, and sat her on the withered grass. 'Clan Elienor is, in the eyes of Inthis and some other clans, Last Clan.'

'Why is that?' Tiaan's curiosity was piqued. She was always more sympathetic to the underdog.

'We're different. Most Aachim are tall and dark, but our clan tends to be small and pale skinned, and many of us have red hair. Inthis reckons our blood was corrupted long ago, by a visitor from another world.'

'Was it?'

'I don't know. The elders guard our heritage closely. We're also disliked because we're not compliant enough. We often disagree with the decisions of the Ten Clans; or Eleven, now that Inthis has rejoined. We are seen as disloyal but, even worse, *individualist*. It's a great failing.' She smiled as she said it.

'You're not armed, Thyzzea. That seems odd, in a guard.'

'I'm not a guard. I am of noble blood, and my father's heir. Vithis hates my father, so forcing me to do guard duty is an insult to him and all Clan Elienor.'

Tiaan considered that. 'Is Elienor a small clan?'

'It was the smallest on Aachan. But, unlike other clans, we all made the decision to come through the gate, and most of us survived it. Of the twelve Aachim clans, we are now ninth in numbers. There are five thousand of us.'

'In Tirthrax I met an elderly woman called Malien,' said Tiaan, 'who had something of your looks. Her ancestors were Clan Elienor, she said, though the Aachim of Santhenar no longer hold to clan allegiances.'

Thyzzea frowned. 'A few of my clan were shipped here as prisoners, or slaves, in ancient times.'

'She's a famous hero. Malien is in one of the Great Tales.'

'Then I hope to travel to Tirthrax some day and meet her. We know little about how our kind have fared on Santhenar in the thousands of years they've been exiled here. Would you care for something to drink?'

'Yes, please. I'm really thirsty.'

'I'll carry you to our tent.'

Tiaan found herself liking the young Aachim, and that would be a problem when she tried to escape, though Thyzzea had not asked Tiaan for her parole.

The tent was the size of a cottage, with a large living area and small rooms opening off it. Rugs on the floor looked costly, though the space contained nothing but some metal chests and a small table, at which a red-haired youth stood, writing in a book.

'My little brother, Kalle,' said Thyzzea, holding Tiaan in her arms. 'Kalle, here is Tiaan, who opened the gate and made the construct fly.'

Tiaan felt embarrassed at being carried like an invalid. She resolved to exercise harder than ever.

Kalle dropped his pen, awe-struck. '*Tiaan!*' Remembering his manners, he put out his hand. The long Aachim fingers wrapped right around Tiaan's hand. 'It is a great honour to meet you.'

Kalle looked to be about thirteen, though it was difficult to tell the age of the Aachim. He was also her height, with pale, unfreckled skin, a lengthy, bladed nose, green eyes and hair the most brilliant deep red.

'How is it . . .?' he looked from Tiaan to his sister.

'Vithis ordered me to guard her,' said Thyzzea.

Kalle flushed the colour of his hair. 'But . . . Oh! Oh!' He could not look at Tiaan. 'We are dishonoured. What are you going to say to Father?'

'He hasn't come back from the battle . . .' Seeing the anxious look in her brother's eye, she amended hastily, 'yet.'

Kalle struggled to control himself. 'But he'll be all right, won't he?' His voice was shaky.

157

'Of course he will,' Thyzzea said in reassuring tones. 'You'd better get back to your studies.'

Kalle began to turn the pages of his book, but his eyes were fixed on the open flap of the tent.

Thyzzea picked up a basket in her free hand. 'Shall we sit under the tree again? It's cooler outside. This is a hot world.'

'For me too,' said Tiaan.

'You come from the other side of Lauralin, don't you? The city of Tiksi, on the west coast?'

'You know a lot about me,' said Tiaan.

'You saved us. You're in *our* Histories.'

'But . . .'

'Yes?' Thyzzea said politely.

'I don't wish to intrude on you. You must be anxious about your father.'

'I am,' she said, 'but that's a private matter and I've a duty to watch over you. Let's talk no more about it. In truth, you're a welcome distraction from worries I can do nothing about.'

'It still seems a bit . . . casual,' said Tiaan.

'What do you mean?'

'Sitting here, talking, while the war rages only a league away.' She waved one hand in the direction of the battlefield.

'The battle ended some hours ago and the enemy are retreating west.'

'Did we win, then?' Having been underground for so long, Tiaan had no idea how the struggle had gone.

'No, but nor did we lose.' Thyzzea explained about the unexpected destruction of the node, and the fleet of air-floaters turning the tide of battle at the critical moment. 'The enemy are withdrawing, as they must, because Snizort is on fire. But since there's no field, we can't move our constructs. Until that problem is solved, we young ones have little to do.'

'Why did Vithis leave me with you? I thought I would be imprisoned.'

'*You* made the gate that brought us to Santhenar, Tiaan. And you learned how to make the construct fly, a secret we've been searching for since the Way between the Worlds was

158

opened. Vithis may be our leader, but the other clans will not follow him into dishonour. You'll be treated with the respect you've earned, in our house.'

'Thank you,' said Tiaan, a little uncomfortable with such praise. 'But I don't understand. Am I a prisoner or a guest?'

Thyzzea looked embarrassed. 'The situation is an awkward one, Tiaan. You are Vithis's prisoner, but *my* guest.'

Tiaan found this difficult to take in. 'But why *you*? *I* mean no insult,' she said hastily, 'but surely, for such an important captive . . .?'

Thyzzea smiled. 'I'm skilled in all manner of arts – few of my age more so. Even were you not handicapped, you could not escape me. But that's not why I was chosen.'

'Why then?'

'To humiliate my father and degrade me. I'm firstborn, my father's heir, and he is the leader of Clan Elienor. That I should do guard duty for a prisoner who is not our own kind . . .' she coloured, '. . . and now it is *I* who mean no insult – demeans us both.'

'I don't understand.'

'Clan Inthis has always hated Clan Elienor and tried to do us down. Now Inthis has been reduced to two men, and Vithis is sterile, while Elienor has a higher place than before. It's bile to him.'

They returned to the tree, where Thyzzea unpacked the basket. 'I'm sorry there's no wine to offer you.' She handed Tiaan a mug of water. 'Our supplies are low.'

'I rarely drink wine,' said Tiaan. 'It makes my head spin.'

'We used to take it at every meal, on our own world, though that was the weak wine, not the strong. Strong wine is for adults, except on special occasions, and then only sparingly.'

'I thought you *were* an adult.'

Thyzzea unpacked hard bread, which was brown with a purple tinge, a variety of dried and smoked fruits of kinds that Tiaan did not recognise, a glass flask of red oil and a string of stubby sausages. With each item she apologised for the lack. Carving slices from the bread and the hard sausages, she drizzled them with red oil and handed the platter to Tiaan.

'In your years I would be about seventeen,' said Thyzzea. 'We mature slowly compared to old humankind. I am a woman, but not of adult age.'

Tiaan found it strange to be referred to as an old human. She just thought of herself as human, and the Aachim did not seem that different, though clearly they considered themselves to be a distinct human species. Perhaps that was connected to their obsession with their clans. 'Then we're not far apart. The day you came through the gate was my twenty-first birthday.' She took a piece of bread but laid it down again.

'I hope you find it edible,' Thyzzea said anxiously.

'I enjoyed the food Malien gave me in Tirthrax.' Tiaan tasted the sausage. It was heavily spiced, burning the tip of her tongue and making her eyes water. 'Delicious,' she said, taking a sip from her mug, 'though rather hotter than I'm used to.'

'I'm sorry,' said Thyzzea. 'If it's . . .'

'I'll just take a little at a time,' Tiaan said hoarsely.

Hearing a high-pitched whine from their left, Thyzzea stood up. 'It's a construct. The field must be working again.'

'I don't see how it could be,' said Tiaan though, lacking her amplimet, she had no way of telling. Shortly a construct floated by, whining furiously yet moving slowly, towing another seven with stout cables. The blond-haired giant stood at the controls, looking pleased with himself. He waved to Thyzzea and Tiaan as he passed.

'That's Ghaenis.' Thyzzea rose to watch him go by. She sighed, her breast heaved. 'Doesn't he look magnificent?'

'He carried me from the battlefield. He seemed like a decent fellow.'

'He's a brilliant young man, even cleverer than his mother. He's brave and honourable, and modest too. If anyone can get us out of here, it will be him.' Another sigh. 'But . . . of course,' she added, now speaking about herself, 'it can never be.'

'Why not?' said Tiaan.

'He's spoken for by the beautiful Rannilt. And even if he were not, his mother is Tirior of Clan Nataz, and she hates my father even more than Vithis does.'

Tiaan did not ask why. Deep currents ran between the clans.

Thyzzea wrinkled her brow. 'If one construct can go, why not the others?'

'Vithis gave Ghaenis my amplimet, and it's powerful enough to draw from a distant field.' Tiaan wondered how long it would take to move the thousands of constructs stranded here. Weeks, surely.

Thyzzea had gone pale. 'He's using the *amplimet*? Hasn't anyone told him? But of course, Clan Nataz have always desired it . . .'

'It'll be all right if he takes it slowly,' said Tiaan.

'You don't understand. We can't use –'

A few hundred paces away, the leading construct screeched to a stop and thumped down. The seven towed machines thudded after it, shaking the ground.

'He must have lost the field,' said Tiaan.

Ghaenis threw himself over the side and landed hard, rolling across the dry soil in little puffs of dust. He stood up, looking back at his construct as if he expected it to explode. A cloud passed in front of the sun and momentarily Tiaan felt icy cold.

'Something's wrong, Tiaan.' Thyzzea's eyes were huge.

'He'll be safe if he's lost the field.'

'You don't understand,' Thyzzea wailed 'He shouldn't have gone near it. We Aachim –'

'He begged Vithis for it,' said Tiaan.

'But Vithis has always been against using this deadly crystal.'

'Ghaenis was most persuasive –'

Scarlet rays streamed out of Ghaenis's torso. The air seemed to shimmer.

'Tiaan!' Thyzzea cried. 'You know the amplimet best – can't you do something?'

161

'I don't know what the matter is.' Yes, she did. The chill ran all the way down Tiaan's back. 'Power must still be flowing from the field.' She pulled herself up by the trunk of the tree, pricking her hands on the red thorns. 'It's hurting him. Carry me across, quickly.'

Before Thyzzea had taken a step, Tiaan could feel the power – and something else, a brittle, inanimate crystal rage. The treacherous amplimet had refused to be cut off, and it was directing all that power into Ghaenis.

'Can you stop it?' gasped Thyzzea, running as hard as she could.

'If I can get near enough.'

Ghaenis was staggering about with his hands tightly pressed to his ears. The Aachim from the other machines ran towards him, including a striking young woman, presumably Rannilt, whose wavy black hair streamed out half a span behind her.

'Ghaenis, love!' she cried. 'What's the matter?'

When Thyzzea and Tiaan were still a hundred paces away, Ghaenis collapsed. Steam or smoke wisped up from his mouth. He arched his back, drummed his heels on the ground then, to the horror of everyone there, burst into flame. Ghaenis screamed but once. Aachim raced up with buckets of precious water but it made no difference. He was burning from the inside out.

Thyzzea stopped dead. Ghaenis arched up in a semicircle, just his heels and outstretched hands touching the ground. His body was grotesquely swollen, his nostrils emitting rings of black smoke. Then he exploded. The legs and head fell back but the rest of Ghaenis was gone. It was the most hideous sight Tiaan had ever seen.

Thyzzea clutched Tiaan hard, making incoherent sounds in her throat. Rannilt screamed so shrilly that the flask of oil under the tree cracked. Two Aachim carried her away from the dreadful scene, still shrieking, and thankfully someone cast a cloak over the smouldering remains.

Thyzzea just stood there, choking. Tiaan wished she were

a thousand leagues away. 'Take me back, please. We can't do anything now.'

Thyzzea stumbled back to the tree, gasping for air. Putting Tiaan down, she fell to her knees and began to weep into her hands. Tiaan reached out, drawing Thyzzea to her and folding her arms around the younger woman. She said nothing. Words had no value whatsoever.

Finally Thyzzea disengaged herself and drew away. With a visible effort, she internalised her grief. The Aachim seemed able to do that – or perhaps they preferred not to show emotion in the presence of strangers. 'Rannilt will go out of her mind' she said hoarsely. 'Why, why did Vithis let him have the amplimet?'

Tiaan could not answer that. 'Once anthracism starts, there's no stopping it. But at least it was quick.'

'Ghaenis was a wonderful man. Everyone loved him. What will his mother –?'

Tirior, recognisable from a distance by the black curling hair, came flying across the dirt. Several Aachim tried to stop her from passing through the circle but she knocked them out of the way and pushed through. A great shuddering cry rent the air.

Vithis appeared from the other direction, robes flapping. No one hindered his passage. The crowd separated behind him, before moving away hastily. Vithis converged on Tirior, who was standing by the smoking remains. She turned, ground out something that Tiaan did not hear, then struck Vithis down with a vicious blow to the midriff.

Laying her cloak over the other cloak, she knelt by her son's remains, head bowed.

Vithis picked himself up and retrieved the amplimet from the construct, keeping the platinum sheet between it and his hand at all times. After wrapping it carefully, he stalked towards Tiaan's tree, waving an attendant across. 'Bring her!'

The attendant picked Tiaan up.

'Where are you taking Tiaan?' said Thyzzea with desperate dignity, determined to preserve her clan's honour no matter how far Vithis outmatched her.

Vithis did not deign to reply.

'I must insist on knowing,' she said stoutly.

'How dare you question me, child of an outcast clan!'

'You required me to take Tiaan into my house, and so I have. She has guest right.'

'The Eleven Clans do not recognise guest right for aliens.'

'Clan Elienor does,' Thyzzea said, 'and your actions are a deliberate insult to my father, our clan, and myself.' A red spot had appeared high on each cheek; one knee shook as she faced him. 'And to Tiaan, whom our Histories honour, despite your insulting behaviour.'

'You have not reached your majority and cannot offer guest right. How dare you lecture *me*!'

'My father put me in charge of his house when he went to battle. He gave me his seal and full authority to run his affairs.'

'Then let doom fall on his head! I shall tell you nothing. Attendant!'

As Tiaan was carried away, she was trying to work out what Vithis would do next. It was impossible to focus – she kept seeing Ghaenis's cheery face, and his gruesome death.

Now that his own efforts had failed so disastrously, Vithis would do whatever it took to force the secret of the thapter out of her. She had to resist him. Fortunately the construct, coated with tar, had burned hot. With luck the diamond hedrons and the carbon filaments connecting them to the amplimet had been consumed, and Vithis need never learn they had existed. Let him think the secret of flight lay in the amplimet and how Tiaan had used it. She could not resist torture but, after what Thyzzea had said, it seemed unlikely that the Aachim would permit that. On the other hand, after the death of Ghaenis, anything was possible.

Could she pretend not to understand the talent that enabled her to make the construct fly? Pretending stupidity was a dangerous course; they knew too much about her. But how else could she save herself?

They reached a tent guarded by four Aachim men. 'Let no one disturb us!' Vithis ordered.

The guards saluted and he went in. The attendant sat Tiaan in a metal chair and departed. Vithis walked round the room several times, pushing his fingers through his hair until it stood out like bristles. The hollows under his eyes had a yellow tinge.

He swallowed and turned to Tiaan. 'I have much to get done,' Vithis said softly, 'so let us get this over with as quickly as possible. How did you make the construct fly?'

Vithis, an exceptionally tall man, was standing so close that she had to tilt her head right back to look at him. A fly buzzed around the tent. The sun was going down but the heat and stillness remained oppressive.

'I don't know,' she lied. 'I've never understood how I used the amplimet, even after all the instruction the Aachim gave me. My talent just seemed to grow. Sometimes it was as if the crystal was instructing me.'

His face was as expressionless as metal; she could not judge his thoughts.

'You're lying,' he said without emphasis. 'You blindfolded everyone in the construct and did something to it to make it fly. What did you do?'

'Nothing,' Tiaan said as steadily as she could. She could not match his strength so she must give before him, then spring back. 'You can check Tirior's construct.'

'We will, once it's cool enough to get inside. If you didn't change it, how did you make it fly?'

'Any construct can be made to fly if you have an amplimet,' she lied.

'How?' he roared in her face. 'And why did you blindfold everyone?'

'I didn't want anyone to see the amplimet. Look what it's done to Ghaenis, after you gave it to him. It causes trouble everywhere I go, and everyone who sees it wants to take it from me. It's *mine*! Joeyn gave it to me with his dying breath. It's all I have left, since you forced Minis to break his promise to me. Since you killed little Haani.'

'I did not kill her!' he snapped, but it put him off balance. 'It was an accident and reparation has been paid. Neither

165

could Minis break his promise, since he did not have the right to make such a commitment to you.'

Tiaan had to reinforce his false impression of her character. She tried to make her emotions as flighty as a butterfly. 'I did everything for the love of Minis,' she said with a sweet, dreamy smile, like a smitten adolescent. Then she screeched, 'He promised me! He lied, and you forced him to it. *I hate you!*'

Vithis took a step backwards. 'Minis does not lie.' He grimaced as if he'd just swallowed something nasty.

'He lied to me!' she shrieked. *'Liar, liar, liar!'* You're overdoing it, she thought. Vithis is a clever, subtle man. Don't be too emotional.

'You show your true nature at last. The amplimet can never be yours, sad little creature that you are. You're unworthy of it.'

'No!' she shouted. 'It's mine.'

He shook her until she felt like vomiting fragments of red sausage all over him. 'You're no geomancer, Tiaan. You have a brilliant native talent, but not the intellect to control the amplimet.'

'I flew my thapter all the way from Tirthrax,' she muttered.

'The crystal would end up controlling you. For the last time, how did you make the construct fly?'

'I had to *work the balance* between the two crystals,' she said, making up a meaningless term. 'For flight, the balance between the amplimet and the smaller crystal, my hedron, must be just right. I set up a kind of . . . oscillation in the field, but it grew stronger and stronger, as if it was feeding on itself. It hurt *so much*! I thought it was going to anthracise me. Like you did to poor Ghaenis.'

He ignored the barb. 'But it didn't,' said Vithis. 'How did you overcome that?'

'The oscillation vanished and the field seemed to be pushing the other way, lifting the construct off the floor. Then . . . I can't explain it. I visualised the construct flying . . . something grew hot beneath the floor and up it went . . .'

'That's gibberish,' he said doubtfully. 'You're making it up.'

A drop of ice slid down her gullet. She *was* making it up,

and if he was sure of it he would crucify her. Careful, she thought. Be more convincing in your stupidity. 'That's what happened, I swear it!' she rushed out. 'I didn't understand. The feeling of the crystal was *soul-deep*.' She said it with wide-eyed, gullible sincerity.

'Soul-deep? What mumbo-jumbo is that?'

Someone was at the flap, beckoning. Vithis spoke briefly to the man, then returned. 'I have urgent business elsewhere. Before I go, answer me this. What did you mean, it *was as if the crystal was instructing you*?'

She seized on that. Back in the manufactory, one of the workers, a girl called Sannet, had heard voices all the time. It had been tiresome to work with her, for Sannet needed to consult her voices before undertaking the simplest task.

'I heard voices. In my head,' lied Tiaan, looking up at the Aachim stupidly.

He was disgusted. 'Have you always heard them?'

Could she reinforce his feeling that she was not completely sane? No, better to pretend that the amplimet had damaged her. 'Never!' Tiaan cried theatrically, 'Until I was given the amplimet by old Jocyn. He was my only friend.'

'I'm not surprised,' said Vithis.

'That very night I dreamed about Minis,' Tiaan went on. 'And afterwards. But . . . it wasn't until I used the amplimet in the ice cave that the voices began.'

'Is that so?' he said softly. 'And did you hear them all the time after that?'

'Only after I used the crystal, and then only for a day or two. In the months it took to travel from Kalissin to Tirthrax, I didn't hear voices at all. There were no nodes by the great inland sea; the crystal could draw no power there.'

'And after Tirthrax?'

'I've often heard the voices these last few months.'

'What do they tell you?' He sounded as if he believed her.

Tiaan did not relax. He was weighing everything she said, and if she made one inconsistent remark, one false step, he would have her.

FIFTEEN

Tiaan recalled something Vithis had said just after coming through the gate to Santhenar. Tirior had wanted the amplimet but *he'd* been afraid of it, saying that it was corrupt and dangerous. Could she play on that fear?

'I can't bear to be without the amplimet,' she said softly. 'I haven't suffered withdrawal since the gate was opened, but whenever someone else has my crystal, I feel the most indescribable longing for it.' She looked Vithis in the eye. 'Yet it frightens me. After Tirthrax, it was as if the amplimet wanted something. As if it were using me.'

The man who had come to the door was back, gesturing furiously. Vithis waved him away.

'*Using you?* How do you mean?'

'I felt that it was a *million* years old,' she said breathlessly. 'And all that time it had lain underground, drawing power from the node. Waiting, and planning what it would do when it got free.'

'What does it want to do?' Vithis spoke as if humouring her, but he was plucking uneasily at his chin.

Perhaps he was superstitious about such things. 'It's following a mineral . . . *instinct*, from times so long ago that the shape of the land was different. I dreamed that it was controlling me, though it didn't want *me*. It's looking for someone stronger, a great mancer *like you*.' She reached out to him.

He sprang backwards. 'Don't touch me! It's telling you to work on me now, isn't it?' His breath whistled in and out through his teeth.

'How could it be telling me anything?' she said with child-like innocence. 'I don't have it.'

'Wait here, if you please.'

How could she do otherwise? Again Tiaan reached towards him but he stepped back smartly and slipped out through the flap.

He returned some time later with a woman Tiaan had not met before. She was old, her dark skin weathered to the texture of bark, her hair as grey as aged thatch and her back bent.

'This little thing?' the old woman said, fixing Tiaan with cloudy eyes. She came up close but avoided touching her. Her voice was croaky, crackly. 'It hardly seems possible.'

'We've all seen her fly the construct, Urien, and we know she made the gate.'

Urien stared right into Tiaan's eyes. 'The crystal talks to you, child?'

Tiaan shivered and the old woman smiled to see it. Her gums had withered, exposing snaggly yellow teeth which looked as though they'd been stuck in clay by an inexpert hand.

'After I've used the amplimet,' said Tiaan, pretending awe, 'it whispers in my mind, the same way it talks to the node.'

'What!' cried Vithis and the old woman together.

'That was the reason Malien sent me away in the thapter –'

'Thapter?' scowled Urien.

'My flying construct,' said Tiaan. 'Malien had to send the amplimet away, even though she wanted the thapter for herself, because the amplimet was talking to the node. And then the Well of Echoes, trapped inside Tirthrax, began to thaw.'

Vithis's dark face went grey. 'Thaw?' he whispered, staring at her in dismay and a growing horror. Urien was more controlled, but for a moment Tiaan saw fear in her eyes and wondered just what it was that old Joeyn had given her with his dying breath.

'Malien was terrified that the Well would break free,' said

Tiaan, 'and with the amplimet there she couldn't hold the Well in place. Had she not sent the crystal away, the whole great mountain and city of Tirthrax might have been destroyed.'

The Aachim withdrew to the far side of the tent in agitation, then went outside and she heard no more. They were gone for ages. When they finally returned, Vithis looked sick.

'How was the amplimet talking to the node, child?' said the old woman.

'The tiny light in the centre blinked on and off, too quickly to count,' Tiaan replied truthfully. 'But as soon as I, or Malien, took the crystal out of its pouch the blinking stopped, as if to hide what it was doing.'

'What else can you tell us about it?'

'After I left Tirthrax, it wouldn't let me go where I wanted.'

Urien pounced. 'But you *did* get away.'

It was a dangerous moment; Tiaan didn't want them thinking too hard about the secret of flight. 'I took out the amplimet, put an ordinary hedron in its place and hovered away until I was beyond the influence of the node.'

'What else did the crystal do?' said the old woman.

'After fleeing your camp – where you shot at me without provocation! – I tried to take the thapter to Lybing, in Borgistry.'

'Why?' said Urien, ignoring the outburst.

'To do my duty and give it to the scrutators, but the amplimet wouldn't let me go that way. It took the thapter towards another powerful node, at Booreah Ngurle, but when we reached the mountain, and I turned for Nyriandiol, it wouldn't let me go there either. I was so furious that I resolved to smash the amplimet –'

'What happened then?' Vithis rushed out, and Tiaan was sure that he believed her.

'It cut off the field and the thapter fell into the forest. That's how my back was broken.' She didn't plan to mention that the lyrinx had repaired it.

'Do you have anything else to confess?' said Urien.

Tiaan did not like the implication, but explained about her

time at Nyriandiol and Snizort, and how the amplimet had seemed to be communicating with the nodes there as well.

'The ancient lore mentions such a thing,' Urien said quietly to Vithis. 'It may be at the heart of the mystery of the last amplimet we used – and the catastrophe it caused.'

'After the death of a clan, followed by aeons of cover-ups,' said Vithis, 'how can anyone tell?'

'You say the amplimet talks to you,' said Urien suddenly. 'What does it sound like?'

'What?' said Tiaan, who hadn't thought of that.

'You said it whispered to you!' Urien snapped.

'It sounds . . . a bit like you, but much older. It's a rustly, scratchy sound.' Tiaan made a hissing crackle. 'A bit like that. I can't do it very well.'

'What does the crystal tell you, Tiaan?'

Tiaan was ready for that question, for she'd spent the last two hours thinking of the answer. 'The node-master is coming. I must protect the amplimet for the node-master.'

'What node-master?' said Vithis, with a trace of eagerness.

'It didn't say. But . . .'

'Yes?' Urien and Vithis spoke together.

'I don't think he, or it, comes from this world.'

Vithis visibly steeled himself, then withdrew the platinum wrapped amplimet from a metal case and exposed it to view. 'Let's see if it wants to talk to you now, Tiaan.'

'Put it away,' cried Urien, shuddering. 'How dare you bring it here after what it's just done.'

'Do you think I want to?' he snapped. 'I've always coun-selled against it. But Urien, our supplies are nearly exhausted and without constructs we're helpless. Should the enemy return in force, they could finish us in a single day. The amplimet terrifies me, but it's our only way out. Take it, Tiaan.'

Tiaan could sense Ghaenis's death in it. 'I'm afraid.' She reached for the crystal, but stopped short of it. 'Everything seems so clear when it's talking to me, so perfect, but after-wards it fades like a dream.' Giving a little shiver of yearning, Tiaan put her memories of withdrawal into it, to make the action seem more real. 'All I want is to listen to it again.' She unfocussed her eyes, staring raptly at the wall of the tent.

Tirior slapped the tent flap out of the way and hurled herself in. Ghaenis's death had leached her chill beauty away, leaving her puffy faced, red eyed and aged by twenty years. Seeing the amplimet on Vithis's outstretched hand, a cold rage seized her. 'Have you learned nothing from my son's death?' she said furiously.

'Can *you* find us a way out of here?' said Vithis, taking a step away from her fury. He folded the platinum over the crystal but did not put it away.

Tirior's eyes followed it. 'There's no way out for Ghaenis!'

He could not meet her eyes. 'I'm sorry. He begged me for it, Tirior. I warned him of the peril – you know how I feel about it – but he would not relent. He said you'd taught him how to handle it.' His eyes burned like fire.

'How could I have?' she said, but now it was she who avoided his eye.

'I don't know, but either he lied or you're lying now.'

'You always return to the same tune, Vithis.'

'And Clan Nataz to the same obsession that brought us ruin in the past.'

What ruin? Tiaan thought. What history does this crystal have, or another just like it, that I know nothing about?

'At least my son didn't lack the courage!' Tirior flashed. 'If you were afraid to take the risk yourself, why not pass the amplimet to your foster-son?'

'He's all that's left of Clan Inthis,' he said, as if that explained everything.

'There's *nothing* left of Inthis but a callow, lovesick fool and an old man who's no man at all.'

'How dare you!' cried Vithis.

She spoke calmly, carefully, coldly. 'You're not sterile, Vithis, as you try to make out – you're impotent! You don't have the manhood, which explains your cowardice.'

'If I did not know that grief has turned your wits,' he replied, 'I would call you out for that. Clan Nataz has always lusted for this deadly crystal, as for the first in ancient times. And Inthis has always warned against it.'

'Enough,' said Urien. She did not raise her voice, but made a curious unfolding gesture with one hand, from Vithis towards Tirior.

Vithis, with a mighty effort, calmed himself and bowed his head towards Tirior. 'I am very sorry for your loss, Tirior. Ghaenis was a fine young man. He convinced me that he was strong enough, and reluctantly I allowed him to try. But tell me, Tirior, did you want the crystal for yourself, or for him to use?'

'I would never have risked my son.' Tirior's eyes flicked to the amplimet and Tiaan saw that, even after the death of Ghaenis, she still desired it.

'Let's get on,' said Urien.

Vithis reached for Tiaan with his free hand but was cautioned by the old woman. 'Best not to touch her while she's under the spell of the crystal. Tiaan, tell us about the node-master.'

'What are you talking about?' said Tirior.

Urien explained.

Tiaan tried to recall those images of Aachan she had seen in her first crystal dreams about Minis. 'Born on fire ..!' she put on a slurred, dream-like tone. 'Black star-flowers ... red rock creeping, creeping. A shadow in robes, against the flames. Dark hair and long, long fingers.'

Vithis and Tirior stared at one another. 'First Clan!' Vithis hissed. 'I was birthed by the very cracks of Mount Szath. *Born on fire.*'

'Or *borne* on fire,' said Tirior, 'which might be any of us. And the black unishhta flowers are the symbol of my clan.'

'Clan Nataz was at the heart of all the trouble with *our* amplimet, in ancient times,' said Vithis.

'Clan Shazmaor caused the trouble!' Tirior said coldly. 'Nataz saved Aachan at great cost to ourselves.'

'So *your* tales tell,' sniffed Vithis. 'Our Histories have always disputed it.'

She ignored that. 'Besides, if you *were* to be this node-master she speaks about, why has not Minis foretold it?'

'Who can say what his foretellings mean?' Vithis replied.

'You're too hard on the lad,' said Urien. 'Without him we wouldn't be here.'

'I don't count that in his favour,' Vithis said curtly.

'I do! And as for this business of the node-master, it could be that the little wretch has made it all up.'

How little regard Urien had for Tiaan's humanity, to speak that way in her own language. Unless they wanted her to know how they felt . . .

'It feels *so* right,' said Vithis. '*Can* she be lying, Urien?'

Urien turned away. 'I sense no falsehood. Come over here.' She drew them over towards the wall of the tent.

Tiaan, still staring into space, strained her ears to hear what they were talking about.

'This amplimet is even more deadly than we feared, Vithis,' said Urien in a low voice.

'It was I, remember, who cautioned Tirior about it in Tirthrax.'

'Had I taken it then,' Tirior said bitterly, 'we would not be in this situation now. I would never have allowed the crystal to come to the first stage of awakening.'

'It had already reached it,' said Urien. 'Had you taken it, your whole clan might now be dead. Destroy it, Vithis.'

'I can control it,' said Tirior. 'If I'd taken it, Ghaenis would still be alive.'

'Don't throw your dead in my face – I mourn my entire clan!' Vithis directed a smouldering glare at Tiaan. 'And I will do whatever is necessary to rebuild it.'

'First Clan is finished, Vithis,' said Tirior. 'You cannot rebuild it from two people. Two *males!*'

'A few First Clan women have partnered into other clans. They must come home. Duty to clan surmounts all other responsibilities.'

'You would break families, tear partners apart, to stay what is inevitable?' Tirior ground her teeth with rage. 'You'll create only clan war, and believe me, Clan Nataz is ready –'

'Even that, Tirior! I –'

'Enough,' snapped Urien, and they both fell silent. 'There's a higher duty than clan, and that is kind. We are all the Aachim left. I don't count the bastard breed of Santhenar, so corrupted by contact with humanity that they are scarcely Aachim at all. Our numbers dwindle each day this war goes on and, if we are to survive, we must put species first. Is that clear?' She fixed them with a glare that brooked no argument.

Tirior bowed her curly black head. Vithis nodded curtly.

'This amplimet is a great prize,' Urien said, 'but I cannot countenance using it. Remember the fate of poor Luthis?'

'The bitter tale is carved into my heart,' said Tirior, 'though the event was aeons ago.'

'We have no choice but to abandon our constructs,' said Urien. 'The risk of remaining here, defenceless, is too great. Tomorrow we'll march south to meet our brethren at the camp near Gospett.'

'Without our constructs, we'll starve,' Vithis announced after a weighty pause. 'This land has been stripped so bare it would not feed a grasshopper.'

'We can't recover them,' said Urien. 'Besides, we have five thousand more at Gospett, and elsewhere.'

'I can save these ones by using the amplimet,' Vithis insisted.

'No! In ancient times many Aachim died, corrupted inside by such crystals. Many more wished they could die. Luthis, as I recall the tale, lived another eighty years after the . . . incident with the amplimet, and suffered every minute.'

'Hear me out, Urien; we have to take the risk. But we don't have to risk ourselves,' he went on in a lower voice, just on the edge of Tiaan's hearing. 'Why not use *her*?' He tilted his head in Tiaan's direction. 'She's used it safely for months. And, watched carefully enough, we may learn more about this node-master she has spoken of, *if there is one.*'

'You think she's lying?'

'I think she's mad. She hears voices, Urien.'

'Only since she first came into contact with the crystal.'

'Even so. What do you say to my proposal?'

'I'll think about it overnight, Vithis, but I warn you: I'm against using this amplimet in any circumstances. And you know why.'

'I do. Until the morning then.' He came across to Tiaan. 'I may well have a use for you tomorrow. But for tonight, you will return to your guard dogs. Wait here.' He went out, calling for his attendant.

Sixteen

The black air-floaters rose swiftly from the mound next to the command area and sped towards them. Irisis watched them come, overpowered by those recurring feelings of doom.

Fyn-Mah was supporting herself on the door jamb, swaying with every bump and lurch. The perquisitor was uncompromisingly honest, yet if she obeyed the scrutators she must repudiate Flydd, her superior, whose orders she was following. But Flydd had failed and been condemned, so where did her duty lie? Neither the agony nor her injuries showed on her pallid face. Fyn-Mah was a native of Tiksi, and Tiksi folk kept their feelings to themselves, but by the set of her jaw and the quiver of her normally rod-like back, she was having a hard time of it.

So was Irisis. Flydd was now a condemned man, Slave Flydd, and all his plans were undone. Undoubtedly he was a wily old hound, but the scrutators were equally cunning. There was no possibility of rescuing him. Her face and figure were instantly recognisable, and she too faced a death sentence if Ghorr ever caught her.

Fyn-Mah thrust away from the door and stalked rearward. She'd made her decision. 'Faster!' she said hoarsely, seizing the crossbow from Flangers and brandishing it in Pilot Inouye's face.

'It won't go any faster,' the little woman wept. 'I'm doing all I can.'

'Then we'll be taken.' Fyn-Mah twanged the rope rail, gnawing at her lower lip. 'Flangers, how good are you with a javelard?'

'Among the best,' he said uneasily, seeing what was coming. He was slumped on the deck, hanging on desperately to the ropes, and the bandage around his thigh was completely red. Flangers should have collapsed long ago, but duty drove him on.

'There's a light one at the bow. See what you can do with it.'

'You're asking me to fire on my own?' he whispered.

'If they catch us, the scrutators will put us to a pointless death.'

'That's no excuse.' He was as honest in his way as she was in hers. 'I've always followed orders.'

'Then obey mine. If the war is left to the scrutators,' gritted Fyn-Mah, 'humanity will be defeated before the year is out.'

'They're my lawful superiors,' said Flangers. 'The war will be lost a lot quicker if we defy our officers as we see fit.'

She drew herself up, saying stiffly, 'As I understand it, I am your superior officer here. I represent Scrutator Flydd, who has ordered me to save myself, and what I carry, *no matter who should try to stop me.*' Taking a paper from her pocket, she handed it to him. 'Does this satisfy you?'

Flangers bowed his head. 'It satisfies the soldier but not the man.'

She seemed to take pity on him. 'No need to kill them,' Fyn-Mah said softly. 'Disabling the air-floaters will do as well. Aim for their rotors.'

Irisis helped Flangers to the bow and together they lifted the javelard out of its bracket. It was lightly built, like a large crossbow. They carried it to a bracket on the port side, halfway down. Flangers picked a wasps' nest out of the bracket and locked the javelard in. Irisis brought down an armload of stubby spears. He wound back the cranks and fitted a spear. His face was as grey as boiled mutton and he could not stand without clinging to the javelard.

'Can you hit the rotor from here?' said Irisis. 'It's an awfully long way.'

He wound the crank another notch, and another, sighting at the leading air-floater, whose large rotor was partly visible behind its cabin. 'I'd say we're just out of range, though it's hard to estimate in the air.'

The leading air-floater was furiously signalling them to go down. Flangers's eyes pleaded with Fyn-Mah. 'They're giving us a direct order, Perquisitor.'

She set her lips. 'Fire!'

Flangers wound the elevation crank, sighted on the first of the pursuing air-floaters, wound again. His hands were shaking. He wiped sweat from his brow and pulled the lever. *Click-thunngg.*

After a good few seconds the spear fell past the front of the leading air-floater.

Flangers seemed pleased, and Irisis could not blame him. 'Out of range,' he said. 'Only luck could hit the rotor from here.'

'Try again,' urged Fyn-Mah. 'Their shooters are getting ready, and they'll be experts. Inouye, slow up momentarily. As soon as Flangers fires, go full speed.'

The air-floater slowed, allowing their pursuers to gain fractionally. Irisis held Flangers up. He gave the elevation crank another quarter-turn and fired.

'Where did that go?' said Irisis to herself.

'I think that's Scrutator Klarm in command,' muttered Fyn-Mah, staring at the first machine through a spyglass. 'He's an honourable man, as scrutators go ' She bit off the heretical thought.

The spear, falling at a steep angle, plunged through the top of the balloon into the roof of the cabin. The impact must have created a spark for the floater gas exploded, sending fire in all directions. The air-floater turned upside down, spilling bodies into the air, and fell, trailing flame. The balloon of the machine beside it collapsed from the shockwave. The third machine veered away sharply, fired its javelard then raced back towards the command area.

Flangers cried out in horror. Irisis clung to the rail, her stomach churning. The fire had gone out and what was left of the first air-floater was spinning round and round, the rags of the airbag streaming out behind to break its fall. The second machine fell past, slamming into the ground hard enough to break bones. The first also struck and was dragged by the wind into a patch of trees.

Fyn-Mah's face had gone the colour of mud. Her lips were white, and she had trouble speaking. 'I've just killed a scrutator and broken my sacred oath.'

And condemned everyone on this air-floater. Irisis turned away. 'What do your orders say now, Perquisitor?'

Fyn-Mah turned to her. 'We run south with all possible speed and don't stop until we reach the uttermost pole. Or even then.' She covered her face and staggered into the cabin. Irisis heard retching.

Flangers lay sprawled on the canvas deck, arms up over his face. Stepping around him, Irisis went to the stern, where Inouye clung to the steering arm like a drowning sailor to an oar.

'Where are we going?' Irisis said, trying to be calm in the face of disaster.

Inouye was plucking at the hedron of her controller. 'The scrutators will expunge my family from the earth for this, even my little baby. I've brought doom on everyone I love.' Her voice broke and she hurled herself at the rail.

Irisis caught Inouye as she went over, dragged her back and carried the small woman to the cabin. Inouye began to wail and thrash about. Laying her in a hammock beside the silent Fyn-Mah, Irisis went out and bolted the door from the outside.

The air-floater was curving around in a circle. She wrenched it back on course, lashing the steering arm so the machine would continue due south. By the time she'd finished, the rotor had stopped. The air-floater would no more move without its pilot than a clanker could go with a dead operator.

Irisis could not use Inouye's controller, which was tailored just to her, without completely rebuilding it. She replaced it with her artisan's pliance, made from carnelian, layers of glass and silver filigree. Her pliance enabled her to see the field and tune a controller to it, and also to draw power. Nowhere near as much as a controller, of course, but air-floaters did not require much. Setting the pliance to channel power into the mechanism that drove the rotor, she left it to run by itself.

The four dark-faced soldiers stood together at the bow rail. They moved well out of her way as she approached, giving each other significant glances. Their muttered talk had broken off as she approached. They were afraid of her mysterious talent, and bitter that they'd been forced to become renegades.

None were from these parts, nor did Flangers know the country. That left only one person and Irisis had been avoiding him. She did not know how to deal with Eiryn Muss, a man who had reinvented himself so completely that there was no trace of his former self. He made her uncomfortable because she had no idea who he was or what he was thinking. He seemed impervious to everything in life, except the cloak he put on himself to become a different man each time he went out spying.

She found him around the other side, sitting on the canvas deck in the shade, studying a journal roll smaller than his little finger.

'Excuse me,' she said.

He looked up. 'You're wondering what to do and where to go.'

Irisis could not look at him without superimposing the fat, bald, leering halfwit from the manufactory, yet nothing about him, not even his voice, was the same. He did not fit. She preferred him as the halfwit.

'I'm lost,' she said. 'I have no idea what to do.' She wanted to throw up her intestines.

'Find a safe hiding place, then I'll try to contact the scrutator.'

'How?'

'That's what I do best,' he said simply, and his confidence calmed the roiling of her insides. 'Keep going south until we're out of sight of the battlefield. No, continue until after dark, then I'll give further instructions, if Fyn-Mah isn't capable.'

'She was told to leave Flydd a message,' Irisis recalled. Swinging around in a great circle, she drove the air-floater towards the hills north of the exploded node. 'In case he escapes.' Unlikely as that seemed.

That night they hid in a cluster of ovoid hills, like a nest full of eggs standing on end, in the forest south of Gospett. It was the best hiding place Muss could find close by. Without further word, he went into the cabin to change his clothes and appearance. Emerging scant minutes later as a bent old man, he walked into the trees.

Three days passed and nothing was heard from him. They spent the time on full alert. Though the air-floater was hidden at the bottom of a steep-sided valley between three of the egg-shaped hills, and concealed from all but a lyrinx or air-floater going directly overhead, they could never relax.

The air-floater was so cramped that privacy was impossible, but no one dared go far from it, in case of an emergency. The soldiers kept to the port side, muttering among themselves and giving everyone black looks. Fyn-Mah hardly spoke from one day to the next. She'd risked everything on her loyalty to Xervish Flydd. If he failed her, or if he was dead, she'd have betrayed her oath and her cause for nothing.

The little pilot had gone into a decline. Long periods of silence were followed by frenzied weeping and wailing for her family. Her only solace was her bond with the controller. She slept with it in her arms, rocking and humming to it as if it were a little baby. Without it, Inouye would have turned her face to the wall and withered away. Fyn-Mah, normally considerate of her inferiors, was incapable of comforting her.

Flangers also kept to himself, insofar as that was possible, fending Irisis off whenever she approached. However, on the third afternoon, as she was taking refuge from the heat by wading barefoot up a tiny rivulet, she came upon him sitting next to the water, head in hands. He must have heard her splashing but did not look up. There was a fresh bandage on his thigh and she was pleased to see that no blood showed through it. Flangers's sword and scabbard lay on a mossy ledge behind him, though she thought nothing of that. A good soldier always kept his weapons nearby.

She put a hand on his shoulder. 'This bloody, bloody war.'

Flangers did not look up. 'I'm just a simple soldier, used to obeying orders. But when the orders contradict each other, what's a man to do?'

'Follow your conscience.'

'It's pulled in two directions, Irisis. The scrutator is a good man and I'd have followed him anywhere. But Flydd has fallen, so how can his orders be legitimate? Or Fyn-Mah's, since her superiors have contradicted them? I *have* followed her orders, but at the expense of my oath, my duty, my honour. I'm forsworn, Irisis, a traitor in my own eyes. I killed the people in Scrutator Klarm's air-floater, betrayed those I'd sworn to protect. How can I live with that?'

'We must keep faith with our master,' said Irisis, 'and trust to Flydd's purpose, no matter how hard the road.'

'You don't understand,' he said quietly. 'You haven't been forced to choose. A soldier's oath is paramount. For six years I've laid down my life to defend those weaker than me. I did my duty and was decorated for it. I was a hero. Now I'm a vicious traitor who turned on his own and shot them down without warning.'

'You followed orders,' said Irisis uncomfortably.

'Can that excuse *any* act?'

'I don't know.' Irisis had never thought about it.

'I didn't have the courage to refuse Fyn-Mah, but I should have.'

Irisis could not find any words to say to him.

'All I ever wanted was to do my duty,' he went on. 'And afterwards, hard work, a good woman, children and friends to share my life. That's all lost. There's only one way out, and it's the coward's way, but at least it'll put an end to it. If you would leave me now, Irisis.'

He rose, reaching for his sword. Irisis was slow to realise what he intended until he had the scabbard in his hand and the sword half out.

'No!' she cried, barring his way.

Flangers was a gentle man, for all his trade. He did not thrust her out of the way, but said, 'Please go, Irisis. It's not a sight for –'

'Will you hear me first?'

'There's no point.' Slipping by her, he drew the sword with a silent, practised movement. In another movement he reversed it and put the tip to his belly.

Irisis hadn't expected him to be that quick. Surely there'd be some last words or, at least, a moment of reflection. Without thinking, she caught hold of the blade with both hands. The keen edges sliced into her palms and fingers.

He grew distressed at the sight of her blood. For a man of war, that struck her as strange. 'Let go, Irisis,' he said softly. 'This blade could take your fingers off in a second.'

'Then I'll have to live without them, for I won't let go. Put down your sword, Flangers. Hear me out.'

He measured her resolve, then, with a little shake of the head, his rigid body relaxed and he pulled the tip away from his belly. She went with him, not releasing the blade until he'd laid it on the ledge. She'd been down that road too.

Taking her wrists in his, he turned her hands palm upward. Blood was flowing freely from deep cuts across both palms and six fingers.

'Look what you've done to your beautiful hands! Why, Irisis?'

Truly an unusual soldier. 'Because we, and Xervish Flydd, can't do without you, Flangers.' She raised her head, never more beautiful, and looked him in the eye. 'And because you and I fought back to back in the tar pits of Snizort, and I care for you as a comrade-in-arms.'

'Then you'll understand that I must salve my honour in the only way left to me.'

'You won't relent?'

184

'I can't, Irisis. But first, let me see to your hands. You must be in pain.'

She said naught to that, but allowed him to lead her back to the air-floater, where he cleaned the cuts, smeared them with ointment and wrapped them in bandages of yellow cloth. When that was done, all with great gentleness and consideration, he put her hands in her lap. 'Now will you allow me to make my end?'

'Once you've paid your debt,' she said.

He frowned. 'What debt is that?'

'I risked my life, going down into the tar chasm to save yours. According to the customs of my people, and I think yours as well, you owe me a life. That is also a matter of honour.'

'And I pulled you out afterwards.' He was sweating.

'I might have climbed out anyway,' she lied, 'so you didn't save my life.'

'You're asking for *my* life in return?' said Flangers.

'It's the only coin you have.'

He thought the matter through, and finally bowed his head. 'It is, as you say, a matter of honour. My life is in your keeping, and no longer mine to take, until you should release me.'

She let out her breath. 'Thank you, Flangers. You won't regret it.'

'I'll regret it every minute my own honour goes unrequited,' he said, 'but I've given my word and won't go back on it.' He rose, turning towards the stern. 'But of course, should I ever save *your* life, the debt is paid, and mine will be in my keeping again. Honour must be satisfied.'

Irisis let him go, her troubles only postponed.

'Irisis, wake up.' Flangers was shaking her by the shoulder. 'There's something going on.'

'What?' she mumbled, still half in her dream, for it was the middle of the night.

'Shhh.' He hauled her out of her blankets. 'The soldiers are

185

set to mutiny. Take this.' Pressing a knife into her hand, he stood by the door of the cabin.

No time to look for her boots. She roused Fyn-Mah and Inouye. Inouye took a deep, quivering breath. Irisis slapped her bandaged hand over the pilot's mouth.

'Don't scream!' she hissed, 'Or we'll be slaughtered where we stand. Inouye, is there any way to get out of here without them knowing?'

Inouye gulped, her breaths coming hard on each other. 'Only by cutting through the ceiling canvas.'

Irisis climbed onto a shelf and pushed her knife through the fabric, which gave with a ripping sound, too loud for comfort.

'What are they doing, Flangers?' she whispered.

'Getting up the courage to attack. They're well trained. We can't hope to beat four of them.'

'I doubt if they'll attack women,' said Fyn-Mah. 'The prohibition against harming females of child-bearing age is a strong one. Besides, as perquisitor I have a certain legitimacy, even after what happened the other day. Whatever they do, they'll be blamed for it.'

'Desperate men with nowhere to turn might well slay us all,' said Irisis, 'and worry about legitimacy afterwards. Can you make a diversion while I cut through the roof?'

Fyn-Mah did something which, in the gloom, Irisis did not see. Suddenly a man's voice boomed through the wall. 'Kick the door in, Rulf. I'll take the traitor first –'

'Why are you shouting?' shrilled another, so loudly that it hurt her ears.

'I'm not –' He broke off.

'Sorcery!' whispered a third, as loud as steam hissing from a boiler.

Irisis slashed through the roof and pulled herself up. Flangers followed swiftly. The soldiers were milling about the door. A stocky man drew his sword with a squeal like a knife skating across metal. He hesitated for an instant, found courage and kicked the door off its flimsy hinges. The sound was like thunder in the still night.

The soldier sprang through, but came flying out again, juggling his sword, which was glowing red. He dropped it on the canvas deck. Smoke belched up and someone kicked it over the side.

'The next man to move gets a bolt in the eye,' said Flangers, showing his crossbow. 'Put down your weapons.'

The soldiers looked up. No one made any move for a long moment. Irisis held her breath. If he shot one, the others would be on him before he could reload. Four against one could only end one way.

'Who's going to be the first?' said Flangers, pointing his weapon at each in turn. 'You, big man?'

The dark-faced fellow still clutched his sword. 'I'm prepared to die for *my* duty,' he sneered, 'and I'm not afraid of a stinking traitor like you.'

Irisis could sense Flangers's pain, but he said nothing.

'But are you afraid of a perquisitor?' said Fyn-Mah from the doorway.

White smoke was coiling up from the bush where the red-hot sword had landed. As the leading soldier looked over the side, his weapon drooped.

'Run,' said Fyn-Mah softly. 'Tell the scrutators I forced you with the Art. It's close to the truth.'

He nodded, not looking at her, and slipped over the side. The others followed, disappearing into the forest.

'Inouye,' said the perquisitor, 'go to your station and be ready to take the air-floater up. Irisis, you and Flangers unfasten the tethers.'

'Where are we going?' said Irisis.

'To the next place on Flydd's list. I daren't stay here, in case they get their courage back.'

They spent more than a week travelling from hideout to hideout, sometimes staying only long enough to check if Eiryn Muss had left a message, though they did not see him in that time. On the ninth day after the mutiny, as they drifted over the latest rendezvous – a dead tree with a fire-scarred, hollow trunk, broken off about ten spans above the ground – a head appeared at the top. An arm waved.

Inouye hovered, Flangers let down the rope ladder and Muss scampered up. 'Go west,' he said.

'Did you find the scrutator?' cried Irisis.

'I learned where he is,' Muss said grimly. 'He was sent to slave in one of the clanker-hauling teams. Cryl-Nish Hlar was with him, condemned by his own father.'

'Nish?' Irisis found her voice had gone squeaky. 'He's alive?'

'For the moment.'

'You said *was*,' said Fyn-Mah. 'What's happened?'

'Flydd escaped six days ago and fled north, beyond the Snizort node, with Nish and Ullii.'

'We can assume he's received my message then,' said Irisis. 'We'd better get after him.'

'Unfortunately,' said Muss, 'they're pursued by all the might of the scrutators, including no less than three air-floaters. We can't risk it.'

'So what do we do?'

'Go to the rendezvous. Sit tight and wait.'

'Wonderful!' said Irisis, who hated enforced inaction in any form.

And there was another problem. The phynadr, which they had risked so much for, and lost more to recover, was withering daily. They kept it cool and damp in a wetted sack, but it wasn't enough. Within days, Irisis felt sure, it would be dead, and all their sacrifice would have been for nothing.

But at least Nish was alive. She'd thought she was over him long ago, but lately Irisis had been thinking about him all the time. She would have given anything to be with him now.

SEVENTEEN

Gilhaelith fell swiftly, feet first, so by the time Gyrull could react, he was a hundred spans below her, hurtling towards the Sea of Thurkad. At this speed it would be as hard as rock.

She folded her great wings into the shape of an arrow and dived after him, though at first she did not seem to be gaining. He looked up at her, then down at the sea. He could see whitecaps and the fluid streamlines of windblown spume.

She matched his speed, now more than matched it. Gyrull was gaining, but so was the sea. He knew what she was trying to do, but how could she do it in time?

She mouthed something at him, though the sound was whipped away by the wind. What did she want him to do? Slow down! Gilhaelith spread his legs and drew out his coat on either side. It flapped wildly, the wind trying to tear it out of his grasp, but braked his fall a little. Would it be enough?

As the water came hurtling up, Gyrull flung herself at him, the claws of her outstretched feet striking him hard in the sides. They went straight through his coat and shirt, his skin and flesh, and in between his ribs. Gilhaelith screamed in agony. It felt as if the claws had gone right into his lungs.

She roared out words of power as the huge wings cracked to slow her plummeting fall. Something tore in his side; it felt as if the strain was stripping the ribs from his living flesh. *Crack-crack*, another tear. The pain was excruciating. The angled wings broke the free fall into a dive, then into a steep glide. His fragile brain throbbed from the power she'd used to keep them aloft.

He guessed trajectories. They must still hit the sea, and

neither would survive it. Lyrinx were helpless in water, for their bodies were too heavy to float. Swimming was harder for them than flying, and panic soon pulled them under. Gilhaelith was a competent swimmer but could not survive these chilly waters to reach the shore, more than a league away.

Again his brain sang as she drew more power. The glide shallowed, the roaring waters rushed closer. She pounded her wings, digging into the salty air. Now they were just ten spans above the sea, now five, now three, two, one. His feet skimmed the water, the wings cracked harder and Gyrull lifted a fraction.

But the matriarch was very tired now. He could feel it in her movements, which were more sluggish than before, the slower beat of the wings, the droop of her neck. One claw slipped from between his ribs, leaving him dangling in the path of the swell. Driven by the wind, it was a good two spans high.

She tried to climb above it but only succeeded in dragging Gilhaelith through the crest. It broke over his head, drenching him. She let out a cry; her colours flashed and faded. He was sure she could not hold him. But Gyrull was not matriarch of a great and powerful race for nothing. Drawing on her last reserves of strength, she dug her claws further into his flesh, lifted him free of the water and slowly began to beat her way up.

The lyrinx surrounded her in a fluttering, spherical shell, offering their strength and shepherding her the last league to the shore of Meldorin. She hovered above a platform of yellow rock, a stone's throw from the water. Gyrull retracted her claws and Gilhaelith fell heavily, ruddy salt water streaming off him. Misty rain drifted down from the hills. It was as cool as Taltid had been sweltering.

Flashing dark browns and reds, colours he could not interpret, Gyrull settled beside him. He expected her to abuse him for his stupidity, but she bowed her head, displaying camouflage colours.

'I beg your indulgence, Tetrarch Gilhaelith,' she said hoarsely, inclining her head towards him. 'You startled me, but that is no excuse. The conveying code is a sacred one and I should not have dropped you under any circumstances. What was it you wished to say to me?'

Gilhaelith lay on the wet rock, so frightened and dazed that he failed to capitalise on the advantage. 'A matter of the greatest moment, and great urgency too. It concerns the Snizort node that exploded and died to nothing.'

She tipped her head to one side, studying him with eyes like liquid gold. Her breast was heaving. 'Go on, pray.'

He pressed his fingers against the throbbing punctures between his ribs, praying her claws were clean. 'My knowledge of geomancy, and my studies of many nodes, tell me that a node cannot simply explode and disappear.' He explained how he came to know that. 'There must be some residue left behind to balance what has been lost. That residue, in the wrong hands, could be perilous indeed.'

'Present your reasoning, if you please, Tetrarch.'

Before he was finished, he saw, from the look in her eyes and the patterning of her skin, that she had reached the same conclusion. He had forgotten what a frightening intellect she had. Indeed, because the lyrinx ate human flesh and mostly fought with their bare hands, it was easy to underestimate them, to think of them as savages. That could be a fatal mistake.

'This *residue*,' said Gyrull, 'could be a mighty power, in the hands of someone who knows how to use it.'

'That is my belief,' said Gilhaelith.

'And you want it for yourself, of course.'

'I don't,' he said untruthfully, 'for I've never sought power over others. Knowledge and understanding are my passions. I would, however, like the opportunity to learn from this residue.'

'Then why tell me?'

'As a token of good faith, to set against my debt.'

Again that sideways, birdlike glance. 'You hope I'll gain for you what you can't get by yourself. And when the debt is repaid, what do you ask of me, Tetrarch?'

'My freedom. And carriage to a place where I may continue my work.'

'We'll see about that after my searchers return.'

Calling her lieutenants together, Gyrull spoke rapidly in a low voice. For once she displayed no skin-speech at all, and the others little more than blushes of yellow or grey. After a few minutes, three of the strongest lifted off from the platform and headed back across the sea, in the direction of Snizort.

'They go to establish the truth of what you've told us,' she said. 'We'll rest for an hour, then take you to Oellyll.'

'What's Oellyll?' said Gilhaelith.

'A city of ours, the best part of a day's flight from here.'

He felt the familiar panicky tightness in his chest, the difficulty of getting enough air. Once she had him there, it was unlikely she would ever let him go. And, held like a pet in a cage, subject to Gyrull's whims, he must eventually go mad.

After flying through dense cloud that night and all the next day, they arrived at Oellyll on a dark and rainy evening. Gilhaelith had no idea where in Meldorin they were. He was carried blind-folded through caverns lined with cut slabs of carven stone, into a deeper underground that the lyrinx had excavated out of rock. It was warm here, which was pleasant, for he was still saturated with an inner chill.

He learned nothing about Oellyll that night, save that it was ventilated by great bellows up on the surface. Several times he passed through their blasts of air, so strong that they almost tore him from the lyrinx's grasp. He was left in a warm room on a low platform which passed for a bed. It had an open doorway. They had no fear of him escaping for he could not stand up.

He lay on the platform, closed his eyes and did not wake for twenty-four hours, not even while their healers attended his injuries.

Two more days Gilhaelith spent in his room, lying on the

platform without strength to raise his head. He had been badly hurt by immersion in the tar. His liver troubled him, his head still throbbed, his heart would race for no particular reason and he felt incredibly weak. Walking the few hundred steps to the privy was beyond him. And the movement of those gallstone fragments along his internal ducts proved more excruciating than his most dismal imaginings.

Making matters worse, the food they gave him was a murky sludge the colour of rotting leaves. Reaching over the side of the platform, Gilhaelith dipped a finger in the bowl. The stuff turned out to be vegetable in origin, but quite bland. He pushed it away. The only vegetables he cared for were strongly flavoured ones, such as onions, turnips and radishes. He'd lived on a diet of slugs, pickled organs and other delicacies most of his adult life, and his palate craved exotic and the intense tastes. But if this pulverised goop was all he was going to get, he'd better eat it. He extended bony fingers, scooped up a gob of the green-brown muck, and swallowed. The repulsive blandness reminded him of his miserable childhood and the repressed memories exploded.

An orphan who had been dragged screaming out of his mother's lifeless body, he'd been carried to a far-off land by his loyal nurse, travelling by night and hiding by day. Gilhaelith had never learned why, or who he was, and had long since decided that he did not want to know. It could only cause him more trouble.

He'd never fitted in. Gilhaelith shivered as the distant memories ebbed and flowed. He'd been plagued by illness and stomach upsets as an infant. As a child, learning had been difficult, and if not for the patience of his nurse he'd still be illiterate. Once he'd mastered reading, though, and especially numbers, the whole world had opened up to him.

Then came the greatest tragedy of his life. His nurse fell ill and died, and Gilhaelith ended up in an orphans' home, fed on tasteless gruel and little enough of it. He thrust the bowl away so roughly that mush slopped all over the floor. In the home his stomach had begun to trouble him again and it wasn't until he began to feed on slugs, grubs, fish organs and other exotica that it had settled down.

Gilhaelith had been out of harmony with the world and had to fight it every step of the way, though the world showed him only brutality or indifference. Always an outsider, his feeding habits made him an object of derision and disgust. He was ostracised and bullied, and the only way he could cope was with absolute self-control. Forced to master his feelings and emotions, he had gradually extended that control to everyone around him, and then to everything.

Once grown to manhood, that iron control had helped him to accumulate great wealth, which allowed him to retreat to a place he could control completely. He'd built Nyriandiol so as to be master of his own environment, though he'd discovered that, without perfect understanding of the world, he could *never* have complete control. Gilhaelith, a man determined to overcome all obstacles, had set out to do just that. And first he had to discover why the world was the way it was. His life's work was born.

He'd become a geomancer and, after a century and more of study, the greatest geomancer of all, but his goal seemed as far off as ever. He still felt threatened – some unpredictable event might still overturn his carefully constructed existence. Then it had: Tiaan had appeared, and her amplimet had opened up all sorts of previously inconceivable possibilities.

But Tiaan had upset his control mechanisms. At first, because of his attraction to her, he'd found that exhilarating. Soon, however, his carefully structured life had fallen into chaos, which he'd found increasingly difficult to handle. Vithis had come, and Klarm. His servants had begun to plot behind his back. Then Gyrull had abducted him and Gilhaelith's hard-won control began to falter. He'd felt like an orphan again. In Snizort he'd allowed his relationship with Tiaan to founder. Gilhaelith regretted it, both for the loss of her friendship, and the loss of an apprentice worthy of him, but at the time there'd been little choice.

Since being trapped in the tar his life had careered out of

control. His health grew worse each day, he felt ever more stressed and panicky, and there were signs of breakdown that he could not admit to himself. He'd never thought he could be so vulnerable. The panic exploded, choking him.

In an effort to calm himself, Gilhaelith began to recite a list of minerals and their properties. He'd previously found rote exercise to be soothing in times of stress. He'd listed all the properties of quartz and fluorspar and was about to begin on calcite when his mind went completely and unaccountably blank.

Calcite, he thought. Rhombohedral crystals, sometimes prismatic or . . . or . . . *Nothing!* He could not recall any of the dozens of properties on the list, not even the variety of its colours, only that calcite was mostly white.

He picked another mineral at random, barite. Nothing. Dolomite. Nothing. Sulphur. Nothing. Then, with a horror that could not be described, the entire catalogue of minerals faded from his mind. He'd known the list by heart for a hundred and thirty years, and in that time had never forgotten the smallest detail.

It's just exhaustion, he told himself. You're pushing too hard. Give yourself a chance to recover. He put the failure out of mind, or at least tried to, but the appalling thought kept returning. He hadn't been pushing at all – the recitation had been meant to be a comfort. And from there, only one conclusion was possible. During the escape from Snizort he must have damaged a part of his brain.

Gilhaelith did not try again; he was too afraid. In his long, long life there had been few problems he'd not been able to solve by intellect, geomancy or sheer will. He'd even found a solution to the vexation of human relations – he controlled everyone who came into his life. Those who could not be controlled he simply pushed away. Until Tiaan appeared, emotion had played no part in his existence, or so he liked to think. He was a man governed by pure reason, and if his intellect deserted him, what would he have left?

*

195

After a few more days' rest he was mobile again. Gilhaelith was tracing out the familiar journey to the privy for the third time in a few hours, hobbling like an old man, when a lyrinx fell in beside him.

'Would you come this way, please?' she said politely. 'The matriarch wishes to speak with you.'

Her tone gave no indication as to whether Gyrull was pleased or otherwise. He shuffled after her, unable to raise much interest either way. His illness preoccupied him all his waking hours. He had begun to wonder if he would ever recover.

Gyrull was standing at a stone table, an oval slab that rose from the floor on a tapered stalk carved out of the native shale. She was studying a collection of papers but put them aside as he entered.

'My people have come back from Snizort,' she said. 'You were right. There *was* a residue left behind by the failure of the node.'

'Did they recover it?'

'Unfortunately someone found it first.'

'Who was it?' said Gilhaelith. 'One of the scrutators?'

'It would appear so.'

His idea about the residue at the node-drainer had been an inspired guess. Now that it had been confirmed, Gilhaelith was furiously thinking through the implications. Could the residue have had anything to do with Tiaan's amplimet, its communication with the node and those strange threads it had drawn throughout Snizort? Or had so much power been taken from the node that it had been unable to sustain itself and had collapsed into nothingness – *nihilium*? Much depended on the answer. And how might it impinge on his life's work, to understand the workings of the world, and *control* them?

'This residue may give humanity additional confidence,' Gyrull added. 'But then, knowing they have it will benefit us, in a way . . .'

'How so?' said Gilhaelith.

'Despite their near-defeat at Snizort, the human army is pursuing our land forces towards the sea. We'll prepare a trap and wipe them out. What do you think of that, Tetrarch?'

'I would be sorry to see an army slain,' he said, 'whether human or lyrinx.'

'I regret the necessity, but we did not start this war, despite the propaganda of the scrutators. In the early days they rejected every peaceful overture we made. They regard us as abominations, even denying our right to exist. Now that we have the upper hand, and may soon win the war, I won't let the fate of their soldiers stand in the way.'

Gilhaelith was still thinking about the residue. 'So I was right about the node.'

'And I keep my bargains. I'll take you wherever you wish, within reason. I can't carry you far into Lauralin, nor to any place that would endanger my own life. Where do you wish to go?'

'I'm not sure,' he said. 'Because of . . .'

'Your betrayal of the scrutators,' she said helpfully. 'And the Aachim.'

He felt a momentary embarrassment. 'Quite. There are few places in Lauralin where I can live in safety now, unless I dwell in a cave as a hermit. I can't do that – my work is everything to me.' It had been and still was, though the earlier failure had shaken his confidence.

Gilhaelith realised that the matriarch was staring at him. 'I must have my geomantic instruments and be near a node,' he went on, 'preferably a powerful one. I'd prepared a refuge in the far south, but my health isn't good enough to go that far, without servants and loyal guards. Because of my, er, situation, suitable ones may be impossible to find. But . . .'

'Yes?' she said.

'Were you to give me a safe conduct, and a small number of your human prisoners to provide for my necessities, there's a place in Meldorin which would serve equally well. It's filled with ancient resonances and I could continue my work there.'

'You want me to provide you with servants?' she exclaimed.

'Now you're asking for more than the bargain. Should I agree, what can you offer in return?'

'My aid with problems you may encounter, of a geomantic nature,' said Gilhaelith.

'What makes you think I'm likely to encounter any?'

'I believe you will, as the war progresses. I imagine you may want to further develop your node-drainers, for example.'

'How can I trust a man who has betrayed his own kind in favour of an alien race?' Gyrull said reasonably.

'I'm descended from several human species, not just old humankind, so I don't consider I've betrayed anyone. Besides, you lyrinx are not as alien as you appear. And has not my word always been good?'

'Not always,' she said, 'since you make such a point of it. But it's enough, for the moment. You can't cause too much trouble in Meldorin, I think. Tell me – what is this place you want to go to, filled with *ancient resonances*?'

'It was called Alcifer, long ago.'

'Alcifer!' Slivers of yellow shone out on her flanks. 'Is that the limit of your needs, or do you demand yet more?'

Her reaction bothered him. 'It can't be more than a few days' flight from here. It was the great city built by Rulke the Charon –'

'Oh, I know all about Alcifer.' Gyrull began to laugh. Lyrinx rarely displayed amusement, but this became a great, side-splitting guffaw that showed all her hundreds of teeth and made her sides heave like the bellows upstairs. '*Alcifer!*'

'Is there some problem?' he said, anxious now. 'You did agree to do this for me . . .'

'I'm pleased to be able to repay you so easily,' she chuckled 'You could walk there from here. Oellyll is delved into the rock directly beneath Alcifer.'

EIGHTEEN

Ullii was sitting on a rock a pebble's throw away, staring at Nish, as she had done all morning. She expected something of him and he had disappointed her. What could she want? He liked Ullii and cared about her, but did she really expect him to pick up from where they'd left off, months ago, as though nothing had happened since? It seemed she did – her nature was single-minded, obsessional. Nish could not reciprocate, for his life had been turned inside out and he could not make sense of it. He wished Irisis were here – she understood such things instinctively.

'Let's get moving,' said Flydd.

Nish brushed away the few tracks they had left on the stony ground. Flydd rubbed crushed mustard-bush leaves over their boots and they set off to the north, taking advantage of the cover afforded by vegetation along dry creek beds. It was midday and a sweltering northerly blew in their faces. Nish, who came from a cold and drizzly land, had never experienced such heat. Green, iridescent flies hung about their eyes, noses and mouths, not to mention their wounds and whip marks, and no amount of arm-waving could get rid of them.

'I've swallowed enough flies to make a hearty meal,' he grumbled as they took a hasty break in the early afternoon. 'Where do they come from?' They were sitting under an arch of grey rock, its roof toothed like the mouth of a shark.

'Good eating for maggots, over on the battlefield,' Flydd grunted.

'Can't say the same for us.' Nish was chewing on the stem

of a piece of dry grass. It generated a little moisture, which only reminded him how hungry he was. And his boot was coming apart again. He looped another lace through it, knowing it would soon wear through like the others.

'Pull your belt in another notch.'

'If I do it'll cut me in half.'

'At least it'll be an end to your infernal griping.'

Nish didn't react – Flydd's carping was almost affectionate these days.

'I'm thirsty,' said Ullii plaintively.

'We'll get water down in that gully, Ullii,' Flydd said. 'It won't be long now.' He treated her far more gently than he did Nish. But then, Ullii never did anything wrong.

The baked earth crunched underfoot as they went out into the sun again. It seemed to grow hotter, and the flies more numerous, with every step. For some reason that Nish could not fathom, they swarmed around Ullii. The little seeker plodded on, not complaining, but in misery.

'Stop for a moment, Ullii.' Flydd tore the bottom off her green smock, knotted the corners into a bag and dropped it over her head. Ullii didn't need to see where she was going.

Several times they saw air-floaters behind them but all were moving around the army camps, or following the lines of clankers being dragged to the north-west. Late in the afternoon, however, one appeared close to the node crater, now two leagues distant. The machine circled it several times, floated upwards, then turned directly towards them.

They were scrambling along the rim of an undulating plateau which afforded a good view but little cover, just scattered mounds of orange boulders, sparse, scrubby undergrowth and occasional small trees twisted into bizarre shapes by the wind. Some distance to their left, a deep ravine cut through a corner of the plateau.

'I don't like it,' said Flydd. The air-floater seemed to be following every twist and turn of their path, as if they had left a trail on the ground. 'How can it track us from that height?'

'What if we were to slip into the ravine?' said Nish.

'Too easy to bottle us up.'

They watched the air-floater in silence. Ten minutes passed. 'It's still tracking us,' Nish said anxiously. 'Is there something you haven't been telling me, surr?'

'There are a thousand things I haven't told you!' Flydd exclaimed in vexation. Pulling his tattered trousers up, he felt along his right thigh. With his knife, he made a careful slit that matched the one on the left thigh, and felt inside. After some wincing he withdrew a bloody crystal half the length of his little finger.

Flydd bound the wound with his other sleeve. Limping across to the edge of the ravine, he peered over and tossed the crystal in, underarm. 'I don't know how they could track a charged crystal, but how else could they have followed us?'

'Perhaps they have another seeker,' said Nish, 'and she's sensing some aura it leaves behind.'

Flydd cast him a perceptive glance. 'I hope not. A seeker might locate *me*, in which case I've wasted my only weapon for nothing. We'll soon find out. Come on.'

Before it grew dark, from a hill only half a league away, they saw the air-floater drop out of the sky into the ravine. 'If they're tracking the crystal, that'll be the end of it,' said Flydd 'We'd better keep going, just in case.'

'I'm at my limit, surr' Nish felt quite light-headed from hunger. Nothing seemed real any more, and he could hardly think straight. 'My belly feels like a pickled walnut. And my boots are falling to pieces.'

'I thought you'd fixed them.'

'I did, but the leather is worn out.'

'Then you've got a long walk ahead on bleeding feet.'

'Thanks!'

'Sympathy won't get us out of this mess, only sheer bloody-minded toughness. How are you getting on, Ullii?' Flydd was always solicitous of her welfare, though Ullii was nearly as tough as the old monster himself. Life had taught her to endure.

Fortunately, the moment the sun had gone down, the flies disappeared. Ullii took off her head-covering and her mask. 'Hungry,' she said softly.

'Then we'd better find you something to eat,' said Flydd 'After all, you're eating for two.'

It was like having a bucket of cold water thrown in his face. Ullii was *pregnant*? How had that come about? It took Nish a long time to make the link to their lovemaking in the balloon after they had repelled the nylatl. It wasn't that it hadn't mattered to him. It had been a precious moment, but so much had happened since, it seemed like another life. Another him.

That day, he realised, probably marked his delayed transition from youth to adulthood. It seemed so far off; almost like a tale he'd heard about someone else.

'Are you saying that I'm a father?' Nish said, to Flydd rather than to Ullii.

'You will be, in a few months.'

'Why didn't anyone tell me?'

'I assumed you knew.'

'How could I know?' Nish exclaimed. 'I'm not a mind-reader.'

He perched on an angular rock, trying to come to terms with this dramatic, momentous development. He was going to be a father! Nish was so caught up in the whirlwind of emotions that he didn't even look at Ullii, who was watching him anxiously, desperately waiting for some gesture towards her. He gave none, for Nish was still running through the implications. And what would his mother say?

She would not be pleased. Ranii Mhel was a clever, ambitious woman who'd always tried to control her children's lives. Nish could only imagine what she would make of Ullii, who had no family, no money, no education or social graces. As far as Ranii was concerned, it would be the most disastrous match in the history of the world, and she would have no part of it. Ullii would be paid off and sent away with the baby, as far as a ship could take her. Nish would never see her, or his child, again.

202

And deep down, Nish understood why Ranii would do that. He and Ullii could have no future together, for he could never give her the total, cloying devotion she required. They would tear each other apart, or drive each other mad.

But how could he let her suffer so? Equally important, how could he go through life knowing that his child would never know its father? Plenty of children had lost fathers in the war, but few were abandoned by them. Not *his*! Children were infinitely precious. *I will not become my father!* he thought, and the decision was made.

Nish realised that Ullii was watching him out of the corner of her eye. She must feel exposed, vulnerable, afraid. She was looking for some kind of commitment from him and afraid he would not make one. Afraid that he would not want the child, or her.

On the contrary, Nish was pleased he was going to be a father. After all, everyone was brought up to cherish parenthood, in a world where there were never enough young to replace the people who had died because of the war.

'Oh, Ullii,' he exclaimed, reaching out for her. 'Why didn't you –?'

The blow came from nowhere, knocking him backwards. 'I don't want to have a baby,' Ullii said shrilly. 'And I don't want you!' She fled into the darkness. 'You abandoned me. You never cared about me. I hate you!'

'The balloon carried me away,' Nish cried. 'I couldn't get back.'

He began to run after her but Flydd caught him by the collar. 'It won't do any good. Leave her.'

'How can she blame me?' Nish said, bewildered. 'I was half the world away – I couldn't do anything about it.'

'She needed you but you didn't come back. To Ullii's mind, with her history, that constitutes rejection. And then, in the Aachim camp before the battle, you didn't seem very pleased to see her.'

'I was a prisoner,' said Nish. 'And . . . it's hard to show your feelings amongst a crowd of strangers.'

'It's hard to believe you even *like* her,' said Flydd. 'She's been reaching out to you and you've ignored her.'

'I –' Nish hesitated. 'I like Ullii a lot, but . . .'

'Just as I thought,' Flydd said coolly. 'You want the child but not the mother. Stay here.'

'What was I supposed to do?' said Nish.

'You were supposed to *think* before you made her pregnant. Some women just want the child and don't care about the father, but Ullii isn't one of them. When she gives, she gives her entire heart, and you've refused it. What is she to make of that, after *her* tragic life?'

'Can't you make her see sense?' said Nish.

'It would be easier to beat it into your numb cranium.'

'But it's my child too.'

'You took your time about it.' Flydd sighed. 'I'll see what I can do, though it has to be said my credibility with Ullii isn't high either.'

'But . . .' Nish was confused. How could she not want him? He was the father.

It was a long time before Flydd came back with Ullii, and Nish had plenty of time to fret about what had happened, and fail to understand it. Had she expected an instantaneous declaration of love and commitment? He wasn't like that; he had to think things through and become used to them. It didn't mean he cared any less.

They appeared out of the darkness, right beside him. Ullii could move as silently as a tracker. He could not see her face, so Nish had no idea what kind of mood she was in. Flydd, however, seemed pleased with himself.

'We found a tree in fruit,' he said, pressing a knobbly object, like a bush lemon, into Nish's hand. 'Try this. They're rather good.'

Nish broke the skin with his thumbnail. The fruit was soft in places, firm elsewhere, and with the creamy texture of avocado. He peeled the pointed half and bit into it. It had a rich, oily taste, immensely satisfying to a starving man, though a mucilaginous residue clung to the roof of his mouth afterwards. He put the other half in his pocket for later.

'Finish it off,' Flydd advised from the darkness. 'I gathered a shirtful.'

Ullii kept her distance and, with Flydd beside her, Nish found no opportunity to talk. They tramped through scrubby bushland then long dry grass before entering a patch of open forest. The moon was rising through the thorny branches surrounding a small clearing. It was nearly ten o'clock.

Flydd let out a stifled groan. 'We'll stop for a few hours' sleep. I can't go another ell.'

Nish was surprised the old man had managed to go this distance, with a wound in each leg and his back a mass of sores. Not daring a fire in case the air-floater was still searching from on high, they felt around on the ground for obstacles before lying down. At least, he and Flydd did. As Nish was working out what to say to Ullii, she disappeared. Perhaps she was curled up in the fork of a tree. There was no point looking, for she could have been anywhere. Tomorrow, he thought. As soon as it's light, we'll sort it all out.

Around midnight, Nish woke with a crick in the back of his neck. The moon cast long shadows across the clearing. He rolled onto his whipped back and had to bite back a groan. Through the trees, in the southern sky, a light flashed and was extinguished, like a silver dagger plunging through black velvet.

'Are you awake, Xervish?' he said softly, touching him on the arm.

'I saw it too.'

'What do you think –'

'I don't want to know,' Flydd murmured, 'but get ready to move.'

'What's the point, if they can find us wherever we go?'

Flydd did not bother to answer. 'Ullii?' he hissed. A small shape detached itself from the trees behind them. She went to Flydd, not to Nish. 'What can you see in your lattice?'

She was as still as the night. The tension in her was palpable. 'Nothing!' she muttered.

There was a long silence. 'I don't believe you, Ullii,' said Flydd.

She walked away into the trees. Nish turned to go after her.

'Leave her, Nish,' said Flydd. 'Something's very wrong. I can feel it.'

They stood together, staring at the field of stars. Nish caught another flash, though this one was the moon catching something high up.

'Was that a night-bird, do you think?' Nish knew it was not.

'It's an air-floater, searching for us, and it hasn't got this close by accident. They must be tracking *me*, and my only defence is at the bottom of that ravine. Why didn't I *think* before I threw it away?'

Shortly Nish heard the distinctive whirr of the air-floater's rotor and its silhouette appeared low down in the west.

'Shouldn't we run?' he said.

'It's too late – we can't outrun it. We must make our stand, Nish. Here we survive, or here we fall.'

Here we fall. The air-floater would carry armed, well-fed soldiers. Nish was no warrior and had no weapon. Flydd had only the overseer's knife and the partly unravelled whip. In the dim light Nish looked around for a stick, but all he could find was a sorry, worm-eaten item that would break at the first blow. Just slightly better than nothing, he thought, hefting it above his shoulder.

'I'm beginning to *feel* something,' Flydd said softly.

'What?'

'There's a weak field here. We must have moved into the influence of another node last evening, though I was too tired to realise it.'

'Does that help?'

'It just means I'm not completely defenceless.'

Ullii came drifting through the trees, again going to Flydd. Though it was a warm night, her teeth were chattering. What was the matter with her? She hadn't reacted that way the last time they'd seen an air-floater.

Flydd put an arm around her. 'You can see something in your lattice now, can't you Ullii?'

She pulled away, which was strange. In times of danger she sought out physical contact. 'See a crystal.'

'It's the one in the air-floater's controller, isn't it?'

'Yes,' she said, no more than a sigh.

'What else? Can you see any of the people in the air-floater?'

'No,' she muttered, in a way that meant, *Yes, but I'm not telling you*. When piqued, she took pleasure in nurturing her little secrets.

'Of course you can,' Flydd cajoled. 'Surely you can see the pilot? To use the controller, she must have some talent.'

'Hardly any –' Ullii began dismissively.

He drew her back to him. 'And of course, someone must be directing the air-floater, otherwise they would never have been able to track me. Someone with a considerable talent for the Secret Art. A querist, or perhaps a perquisitor. Maybe even a scrutator!'

She recoiled and tried to get away but Flydd held her firmly. 'Well, Ullii?'

'I can't tell,' she said, struggling furiously. 'I can't see into them. They're hidden.'

'What?' His head jerked up. 'Deliberately hidden? Shielded?'

'Yes.'

'Oh, this is bad. *Bad!*' Letting her go, Flydd walked across the clearing and back, staring up at the sky. The rotor sound had faded. He took Ullii under his wing again, and this time she did not resist. 'What else, Seeker? Is this person using some kind of device to hunt me down?'

'No.'

'Then how? Is there anyone else on the air-floater with the talent?'

She did not answer.

'There has to be,' said Flydd. 'Who is it? *Ullii!*'

The moon slid between the trees and a single moonbeam touched her face. She looked as if she had just seen her own corpse. Her face was silvery pale, her eyes wide and staring.

'Seeker,' she whispered.

'Another seeker?' Flydd cried.

'Yes . . .' The word trailed off to oblivion. She stared up at the empty sky.

Flydd took Nish by the arm and drew him across the clearing. 'We've got a problem and I don't know how to solve it.'

'If a seeker is watching you, you can never escape,' said Nish.

'Though I'm wondering if there might not be a way to confuse one. Or even use one against the other.'

'Could be dangerous,' said Nish, 'if Ullii begins to feel sympathetic to her counterpart.'

'Good point. Sometimes I'm glad I've brought you along, Nish.'

Faint praise, but better than nothing. 'How could you confuse a seeker?'

'I can't think.' Flydd went to the other side of the clearing and began tapping his knuckles against the side of a tree. 'If only I had that crystal.'

Ullii was still staring raptly upwards.

'There's no point in trying to find it, I suppose?' said Nish.

'They'd catch us before we got to the ravine.'

'What scrutator powers do you have that could influence the mind of another person?'

Flydd was still tapping. 'I – What's that?'

It was a subtle *ticker-tick-tick*. 'It's the rotor of the air-floater. They're coming back.'

It sounded as if it was heading right for them, though Nish could not see it.

'Take my knife,' said Flydd. 'I'll be busy with other things. I may have to hypnotise her.'

Thrusting the knife into his belt, Nish said, 'Isn't that a bit *lame*?'

'Mancery would be like cutting your toenails with an axe. It could break her mind. I'd get myself a big stick if I were you. Keep the knife for close-in work.'

Nish probed around in the gloom and came up with a better weapon than the wormy branch. The stick, heavy and gnarled on one end, made a fine cudgel, though he'd only get one blow against a swordsman. He moved into the shadows, trying to still his thudding heart.

'Ullii?' called Flydd. 'Come here. I need you for a minute.'

She was standing in the middle of the clearing, staring at the sky.

'Nish?' said Flydd, thinking he was near. 'This is what we're going to do –'

Leaves crackled underfoot and Nish did not catch the rest. He started back towards Flydd, who was an indistinct shape in strips of moonlight and shadow. 'Surr, I didn't hear what you said . . .' But now Flydd was moving his hands in front of Ullii. Nish caught whispers, soft and sibilant, but could not make out the words.

Suddenly Ullii began to scream. 'No! Get away.' She thrust both hands hard against Flydd's face. His head snapped back and he overbalanced. Wailing, Ullii ran into the trees. Nish hurried across and helped Flydd up.

'Someone must have tried that with her before,' said the scrutator. 'I suppose it was Chorrn, in Nennifer.'

'Or my father,' said Nish.

'As soon as I began, her defences went up.'

'What are we going to do, surr?'

Mistaking the question, Flydd replied, 'I'll have to try stronger measures.' His voice went strange, as if he was choking. 'Though it will be like betraying a friend. I –'

The rotor roared and the air-floater appeared above them, bathed in moonlight, a bladder like a gigantic ovoid football with a boat-shaped compartment suspended beneath it. Soldiers were ranged along the side. At the front a slim figure held an object resembling a stubby spyglass to one eye. The images of machine and men, black and white against the black sky, froze in Nish's inner eye like brushstrokes on paper.

The soldiers moved; it looked as though they were readying crossbows to shoot. With bare seconds to act, Nish did the only thing he could. He hurled his cudgel straight at the rotor.

'No!' hissed Flydd, but it was too late.

The whirling club went true, for once. It flew straight into the wooden rotor, which was not meshed at the back, and smashed it to splinters. Some scythed across the clearing, tearing leaves off the trees and sending up clouds of dust. Others went straight up, tearing through the fabric of the balloon. Floater gas hissed out. The air-floater lifted, hovering for a second before turning over and plunging towards the ground.

'You wretched fool!' cried Flydd. 'If there's a spark when that hits, it'll blow us halfway to Borgistry.'

The air-floater struck hard, hurling soldiers and crew everywhere. There were thuds, snaps, screams. The airbag collapsed. Someone called out in an unnaturally high voice. It was Flydd. What was the matter?

Nish tried to answer but his voice was just as shrill. He waited for the spark that would blow them to pieces, but it did not come.

'Flydd?' he whispered after a minute or two. His voice sounded normal again.

'Here' Flydd said. 'Quiet.'

Someone emerged from the wreckage. It was the slim figure who'd been looking through the spyglass, a young man dressed in white. Long hair streamed down his back like a waterfall of black ink. He disappeared into the shadows.

A pair of soldiers hacked themselves free. One helped out a third soldier, who fell down. A fourth crawled out from under the collapsed gasbag. The first two lunged at Flydd. The fourth soldier came for Nish, limping badly, though his sword cut the air in a professional manner.

The sword flicked out. Nish backpedalled frantically, feeling for his knife. He hit a tree, leapt sideways and almost spitted himself on the soldier's blade, which had anticipated his every move. He slipped on wet leaves and the point crunched into his ribs.

He hurled himself backwards, landing hard in the darkness behind a pair of close-growing trees. The soldier pushed forwards, feeling with the tip of his weapon to the right of where Nish lay. Nish held his breath. ·

The sword rustled in the leaves, left and right. Nish tensed. As the soldier moved, one leg was outlined in a sliver of moonbeam. Nish stabbed for the knee. The blade went in, the leg collapsed and the soldier went down.

Nish dared not go for the kill; the man still had the sword. He scuttled away, holding his ribs. Blood was trickling down his side though he felt no pain, so the injury couldn't be that bad.

Peering through the trees, he saw Flydd wrestling with a soldier. The other soldier lay on the ground. Ullii stood by the wreckage, staring into the forest behind the air-floater. The dark-haired man emerged, then froze, staring. She let out a faint cry; he ran at her.

A cloud drifted in front of the moon and Nish lost sight of them. Twigs crackled to his left. He turned slowly, so as not to give away his position. The rustling moved closer. He held his breath, afraid lest even that faint sound should give him away. Nish felt desperately frightened. A civilian with a knife could not hope to defeat a soldier with a sword.

A branch snapped, even closer, and he jumped. A drop of sweat made an itchy trail down his nose. He wasn't game to rub it. A shadow moved just a few steps away. Surely the soldier could smell him from here?

Nish's fist, clenched around the knife, shook. Just keep going, he prayed. He did not want to use the knife – he wanted out of here as fast as possible.

After an agonising wait, the shadow moved on and he lost it in the darkness, though a faint crunch of leaves told him that the soldier was not far away. Nish slid forward, one slow step after another, until he reached the edge of the clearing.

He could hear Ullii making a high-pitched keening sound. Where was she?

There, close by the air-floater, and she appeared to be struggling with the dark-haired man. Nish could only make him out because his clothes were white. Ullii's pale face seemed to be floating in mid-air.

Holding the knife out, Nish tiptoed across the clearing. The man seemed to be wrestling with Ullii, who began to make choking noises. Nish crept closer.

As the moon came out, he threw his arm around the young man's neck and pressed the knife to his back. 'Let her go! Don't move.'

The young man gave a frightened cry, reared backwards and the knife slid into him like a red-hot poker into a block of cheese. He let out a soft *sssss*, stood up straight and tall, and fell, thumping face-first into the ground.

Ullii threw herself on him, turned him over and tried to lift him. She got him as far as a sitting position before he slumped over again. A silver bracelet glinted on his wrist. A moonbeam caught his glazed eyes. He looked as if he had been dead for a week.

Ullii let out a scream of anguish that froze Nish's blood, and it went on and on. 'Myllii,' she wailed, kissing his face and hands. 'Myllii, come back.'

Nish could only stare at her, the fatal knife hanging from his hand. Myllii?

Flydd came running across, reeking of blood. 'What have you done *now*?'

'I thought he was trying to choke her,' Nish whispered. 'I tried to stop him but he reared back onto the knife. What is it, Xervish?'

'I hardly dare to think.' Flydd was shaking his head. He squatted beside the seeker, who was frantically trying to rouse the dead man. 'Ullii?'

She did not answer. Ullii began to rock the young man, making a moaning noise in her throat. Flydd conjured ghost light in the palm of his hand and held it out.

Ullii looked up and, momentarily, the two faces were illuminated side by side. Nish's scalp crawled. Apart from the young man's black hair, they were identical.

'Ullii and Myllii,' said Flydd in a voice as old as death. 'How often does that happen?'

'I don't understand,' Nish said.

'Twins identical in all respects but their sex,' said Flydd. 'They were separated when she was four, Nish, and the trauma drove Ullii to become the sensitive creature that she is. You've just killed her long-lost brother, Myllii. She's been searching for him all her life.'

Nineteen

Tiaan leaned back in the chair and closed her eyes, afraid that she'd not convinced the Aachim. She was a novice at intrigue, while they were experts – especially the cold-eyed Urien.

She was woken by someone at the flap of the tent. It was Thyzzea, with her brother. 'Are you to be my guard again?' said Tiaan, taking comfort from a friendly face. Don't trust, she told herself. Thyzzea is Aachim, too. You have no allies here.

'I am. Vithis is determined to grind my family into the dust.' Thyzzea coloured, as if realising her words could be taken as an insult.

Tiaan politely ignored it. 'What would happen if I escaped?' she asked as Kalle picked her up.

'You would not.' Thyzzea seemed to find the idea amusing.

'I don't suppose so. But, just say I did?'

'Since we are at war, my family and clan would have failed in their duty. We could lose everything, if Vithis so chose.'

It confronted Tiaan with an unexpected problem. No matter how much she told herself not to like Thyzzea, she did. So how could she escape, if Thyzzea and her family would be punished for it?

Kalle carried her through the dark; Tiaan smelt cooking before they reached Thyzzea's tent. A middle-aged woman stood outside, in the light of a glowing globe half-covered in black moths. She was searing meats and vegetables on a metal plate, then stirring them into a bubbling pot. She looked up with the same smile as Thyzzea, though hers was tentative, fretful. She was smaller than her daughter and her hair was red-brown.

'Welcome, Tiaan Liise-Mar,' she said. 'I'm Zea.' Switching the ladle to her left hand, she held out the right. 'What a terrible day. When I think about poor Ghaenis – such a world this is.' Seeing the despairing look on her daughter's face, Zea said, 'Come inside, child. Put it out of mind, just for the moment.'

Tiaan shook hands. 'Are you Thyzzea's mother?'

'And bound to regret it.' Her quiet amusement was reflected in Thyzzea's face. They had the capacity to submerge their pain, these Aachim. 'I'm joking, of course. Thyzzea is a daughter entirely without faults.'

Thyzzea rolled her eyes, but shortly the despair was back. The grief was more than she could cover up.

Tiaan liked Zea instantly. Like her daughter, she seemed so *normal*. The other Aachim Tiaan had met were remote and wrapped up in their own affairs. 'Dinner smells good,' she said, unable to remember when she'd last had a full meal.

'I hope it isn't too hot for you.' Zea exchanged glances with her daughter.

'After being interrogated by Urien and Vithis, it won't seem hot at all.'

Again that exchange of glances. 'Urien,' said Zea with a little shiver.

Shortly they were sitting in the tent, in surprisingly comfortable metal chairs, with bowls on their laps. Tiaan was about to take the first sip when the flap opened and a man came wearily in. He was of modest stature, trim and well proportioned, but with the same dark-red hair as his son. He looked exhausted, his clothes were torn and muddy, and the front of his shirt was stained with purple blood.

Zea ran to embrace him, her eyes moist. Thyzzea followed, and Kalle clasped his father's hands. The man's gaze swept across the room to Tiaan; he checked for an instant then came on.

215

'Hello, I'm Tiaan,' she said, placing her bowl on the floor and putting out her hand. 'I'm sorry – I can't stand up.'

He flinched, shot a glance at Zea, then took Tiaan's hand. 'Tiaan, of the flying construct. My name is Yrael. We are your jailers, I presume?'

'I'm afraid so. I'm sorry for the trouble –'

He gave her a genuine smile. The folk of Clan Elienor recovered quickly. 'Guest right is yours while-ever you are under our roof.'

'But . . .'

'First Clan will do what they can to bring us down, whether you're here or not. Let's say no more about it. How is the water, Zea?'

'Running low, but there's enough for a hero of the battle-field to wash his face and hands.'

She followed him into the other room, her arm linked through his. Water splashed in a metal bowl and shortly he returned, dressed in clean clothes. He took a bowl, filled it, and they sat in silence while they ate.

After the meal, Zea opened a flask of wine and poured them each a small portion.

'This is our *strong* wine,' said Thyzzea, sniffing delicately at her goblet. 'For special times and honoured guests.'

Tiaan raised her glass and said, 'To the good fortune of Clan Elienor, wherever it may be.'

'To Clan Elienor,' they echoed, after which Kalle went to his room and his studies.

'If you will excuse me,' said Yrael to Tiaan, 'I must speak to Zea about the war.'

'Would you like to carry me outside?'

'I've nothing to say that an honoured guest may not hear.'

'What is the news?' said Zea. 'There are a thousand rumours, though if there's truth in any of them I've not sorted it out.'

'The lyrinx have gone, apart from the last few still creeping out of hidden tunnels delved deep inside Snizort. Who knows how they survived the cataclysm? The human armies have begun to drag their clankers north-west to the nearest field, using teams of animals, soldiers and slaves. Rumour has it that Scrutator Flydd, with whom we negotiated recently, is now one of the slaves. The old humans fall on each other like dogs.' Glancing at Tiaan, he looked abashed. 'I'm sorry. That was ill-mannered of me.'

'How long will it take for them to haul away all their rattletrap clankers?' asked Zea.

'Many days, though they'll be long gone before we move any of our constructs.'

'Do you think they might help us?'

'Not after Vithis snatched Tiaan from under the scrutators' noses.'

'I had not heard that,' said Zea.

'Did you hear about Ghaenis?' asked Yrael.

'Tiaan and I were there,' Thyzzea cut in. 'It was horrible, Father.'

'Yet I'm told Vithis still presses to use the amplimet,' said Zea. 'What will come of it?'

'Such a dangerous device. Some of the clans,' he named several on his fingertips, 'consider that the crystal should be destroyed, unused. I confess that I think so too.'

'And others want to use it whatever the cost,' said Zea. 'Especially Clan Nataz.'

'That's so. Dissatisfaction is building with Vithis's leadership, particularly among Clans Nataz and Dargau, who have been intriguing for the amplimet since the moment they knew of its existence. Tirior has done everything she could to stymie Vithis's plans, so as to create an opportunity to seize it. Nataz is not displeased at Clan Inthis's fall.' He turned to Tiaan as if feeling a need to explain. 'When we came to Santhenar, we should have met your leaders at once, and parleyed for land. There's plenty here for all and we had much to offer humanity. What could the scrutators have done but agree? They could not send us back.'

'Vithis could not humble himself,' said Zea, her eyes contracted to steely points. 'Embittered by misfortunes of his own making, he must seize first and make demands.'

'But he hasn't taken any land,' said Tiaan.

'He will once he gets what he really wants,' said Zea. 'Your flying construct. *His* obsession has cost us dearly and the clans are close to rebellion. Abandoning all our long-laid plans, he brought us to this bloody battlefield in pursuit of your flier.' She laid a hand on her husband's arm. 'Be sure your heroism and sacrifice is appreciated . . . What is it, Yrael?'

Yrael began to flush in waves of deep red until his face seemed to be on fire. He rose abruptly, to pace the room with jerky steps, head bent. After half a dozen turns he sat down again, meeting Zea's eyes.

'We're not heroes!' he said harshly. 'We weren't allowed to be.'

'What are you saying, Yrael?'

'The clan leaders would not allow us to fight beside our old human allies. They pulled us back time and again. When our allies looked desperately for our aid, it was not there, and they died for it. We are deeply shamed.'

Zea stared at him, her hands over her mouth. 'But you're the leader of Clan Elienor . . .'

'Not on the battlefield. Our clan was commanded by Vithis and *I* had no say in the matter.'

'But this is terrible, to have so let down our allies when they needed us. The old humans must be calling us cowards.'

'With reason,' Yrael said heavily.

'So we've lost thousands of young lives, and more injured, for nothing! And our supplies are running low, we'll surely have to abandon our constructs. Once that happens, we'll be beggars in a hostile land.' Zea's voice rose. 'So why are we here, Yrael?'

'That's what I keep asking myself.' Yrael sat with head bowed. 'We'll have to plunder to survive and the whole of Santhenar will rise up against us.'

Zea made an effort to be the one in control. 'This is a big world and there's land aplenty. In the last year of the war humanity have lost more people than all our population put together. If we deal honourably with them, surely they will embrace us.'

'I doubt that,' said Yrael, 'though I agree it's our best course.'

'Clan Dargau urge war against humanity,' said Zea. 'To strike hard, seize what we need and be ready to hold it.'

'Dargau have always been warmongers.' Yrael contemplated his untouched goblet. 'Though when it comes to the sticking point they prefer to risk the lives of other clans.'

'Rumour tells that the enemy have fled,' said Zea. 'Is that so, Yrael?'

'They've withdrawn but I doubt that they're far away. We're terribly vulnerable, should they attack again.'

He looked afraid and it spread to the others, but Zea said, 'If it comes to that, we'll fight – even if we must fight barehanded. We won't go meekly to our deaths. In the meantime, we must attend to our dead.'

'We begin recovering the bodies in the morning. Luxor is designing a memorial and we'll work together on a protection for it.'

Tiaan could only admire them. Even in such peril, they were driven to honour their fallen. 'Urien warned Vithis against using the amplimet,' she said into the silence. 'But he says there's no other way to save the constructs.'

'He may be right,' Yrael agreed, 'though after today, who would dare?'

'Urien suggested that they force *me*,' said Tiaan.

'Such dishonour!' said Zea.

'And folly,' added Yrael. 'In ancient times an amplimet almost destroyed our civilisation and undermined our very world.'

'What happened?' asked Tiaan.

'I don't know. It occurred before our clan was founded, and the whole truth has never been revealed,' said Yrael. 'It's said that not even Urien, Matah of Aachim-kind and Keeper of the Secrets, knows all. Some chroniclers say that the Charon found our world because we had used that crystal, and their invasion led to thousands of years of slavery. You should be *very* afraid of the amplimet, Tiaan.'

Kalle came hurtling in. 'Vithis is coming for Tiaan.'

Thyzzea covered her face with her hands.

Tiaan was back in Vithis's tent. It must have been long after midnight. The interrogation had been going on for some time, and the differences between him and Urien were more acute than ever. Urien had rejected his proposal to use the amplimet, whereupon Vithis tried another tack – to employ it to uncover the secret of flight.

'With flight,' said Vithis, pacing back and forth, 'we can recover all that we've lost.'

'Except the lives!' Urien countered. 'I forbid it, Vithis. We must cut our losses, abandon the stranded constructs and go.'

'Flight is the only thing that can save us. I won't give it up.'

'Tiaan doesn't know how to explain what she does,' said Urien. 'We can't indulge you any longer, Vithis.'

'I'm not walking away from a fleet of constructs, carrying my goods on my back like a homeless vagabond.'

'You don't have any choice.'

'I want to put Tiaan at the controller of a construct,' said Vithis. 'If she truly needs no more than the amplimet, she can make it fly. And if not, she can tow the other constructs to safety.'

'You'll only succeed in destroying her, and probably your-self as well.'

'She's been using it for months, so she doesn't have our vul-nerability.'

'It can develop over time,' Urien said ominously.

Tiaan looked from one to the other, fearful of the conse-quences no matter who prevailed.

'Those who fear the crystal can walk to Gospett,' snapped Vithis. 'I got us into this situation and I will get us out, with our fleet intact. And if I don't, you may elect a new leader. Just give me the chance, Urien.'

Urien stared at him, unblinking, for a very long time. 'Very well,' she said. 'But you may make one attempt only.'

'I'll begin right away,' Vithis said.

Tiaan, afraid as she had never been afraid before, was carried to the nearest construct and strapped into the seat. The night was as black as the pits of Snizort.

Vithis, holding the amplimet between a folded sheet of platinum, slid it into its cavity. 'Tiaan, find a suitable field and make this construct fly.'

She was going to be exposed as a liar. What was she to do? Tiaan took a deep breath then drew just enough power to lift the construct off the ground. She pretended to strain for more as she drew upwards on the flight knob. The construct did not move, of course, and then the field slipped from her mind. She couldn't concentrate for fear of the amplimet taking charge, as it had done to Ghaenis.

'What are you doing?' said Vithis sharply, as if suspecting her of sabotage.

'This is how I made my thapter fly,' Tiaan lied. She wiped her face and tried again. 'It's not working,' she said in a small voice.

'Try harder!'

'Don't push her,' snapped Urien. 'That kind of talent must be coaxed.'

'I'm sorry.' Vithis bowed to the Matah. 'Zeal overcame my good sense for the moment.'

After pretending to make several more attempts, Tiaan said, 'I can't seem to work the balance correctly. The field isn't oscillating at all.'

'You're not trying,' said Vithis. 'You made Tirior's construct fly in a few minutes.'

'That was different,' Tiaan said, white-faced. 'We were all going to die. My talent just flowed.'

'If you're keeping the secret from us,' Vithis said fiercely, 'I'll make sure you regret it.'

'Threats aren't the answer,' said Urien. 'If she goes the way of Ghaenis, we've got nothing.'

He regained control of himself. 'Will you try again, Tiaan?' Vithis said softly.

Urien had shown Tiaan the way out, though she had to make it convincing. She drew power hard, as much as she could bear safely, then a little more. To her relief, the construct's mechanism spun up to a roar. *Could* she make the field oscillate, to convince them?

She fed power into the field, drew hard, then fed it back even harder. The roar from below rose to a screech, died to nothing and rose again. Suddenly the construct whirled like a top, throwing the Aachim against the side, though Tiaan had not moved the controller.

Vithis let out a muffled curse, Urien a cry of fear. Tiaan could feel her hair standing up, smell the ends beginning to smoulder. Her cheeks grew hot; her vision blurry. She rubbed her eyes. She could just make out Vithis and he wasn't convinced. She had to make him believe, and it had to be done quickly. She could not withstand him much longer.

She forced more power through the controller, then back into the field, then out, then back again, until the field began to go *whoomph-whoomph, whoomph-whoomph* like a fire driven by a bellows. Even with her eyes open, she could see its patterns beating all around her.

So could Urien, for she cried out in alarm, 'Enough, Vithis. This isn't right.'

'Keep on, Tiaan,' he grated.

The mechanism let out a metallic screech and began to thump itself to pieces. A burning pain flared up Tiaan's middle. She tried to cut off the field but power kept flowing – the amplimet had taken over. She'd gone too far.

She opened her mouth to scream but only steam came out. The burning intensified. Even her eyes felt hot. Tiaan had no idea what to do about it. She could no longer think straight.

Vithis was staring at her in horror. He cried out a warning but his words emerged as a dry croaking, like a frog caught in a forest fire.

Urien slammed her fist down on the release. The amplimet shot out of its cavity and she fumbled it out of the air in age-twisted fingers, grimacing as though it had burned her. Still holding it, she uttered three words in a guttural tongue. Tiaan's pain eased. Urien hastily wrapped the crystal in the platinum sheet and thrust it into her pocket.

Tiaan fell off her seat, hanging by the belt. As she swooned, Urien's crackling voice came to her.

'You're a bigger fool than I thought, Vithis. Are you satisfied now?'

He was staring at Tiaan as if he expected her to explode in his face. He looked as if he were going to be sick.

Tiaan came to as she was being carried to the healers' tents Vithis and Urien were still arguing.

'You will abandon the search for flight, as of now,' Urien said coldly, 'or I will dismiss Inthis from the Register of the Eleven Clans.'

'Inthis has always been First Clan!' he cried. 'And it was re-chosen just one year –'

'Only because you manipulated the votes,' came Tirior's voice from the other side. 'Inthis is not fit, Urien. Do you know what Vithis really did to my son?'

'Go on,' said Urien in a deadly voice.

'He made it a matter of honour for Ghaenis to use the amplimet, knowing that he was too noble to refuse. Vithis killed him –'

'He begged me for it,' said Vithis, rigidly controlled.

'You didn't have to agree.'

'He convinced me that he had the best chance of anyone, because you had taught him how it was to be used.'

'Tirior?' Urien said sharply. 'Is that so?'

'Ghaenis and I had spoken about it,' Tirior said reluctantly.

'I knew it,' said Vithis. 'You put him up to it and now blame me to ease your own guilt.'

'That's a lie! Dismiss him and his clan, Urien. Put them below Clan Elienor.'

'You hypocrite!' Vithis cried furiously. 'And all this after you took Minis, the *sole survivor* of Inthis First Clan, into

Snizort in defiance of my direct order that he remain in our main camp.'

'So that's what this is all about,' said Tirior. 'Your shabby revenge.'

'Explain your actions, Tirior,' Urien said sharply.

'Minis begged me, over and over, to take him with me. I rightly refused but he kept pestering me, and finally used his rank to countermand my order. There are witnesses, not of my clan.'

'I've spoken to them,' said Vithis. 'They say you preyed on his weakness for Tiaan. You took Minis into Snizort hoping he would die there, and Clan Inthis with him. Clan Nataz has always chafed at its inferior status and you'd take any risk to raise it above its station.'

'*I* brought Minis safely out of Snizort,' said Tirior. 'You killed my son and heir.'

'*Tiaan* brought Minis out. She saved your life, and his.'

'Enough!' said Urien. 'The clan leaders will determine the rights and wrongs, later. Put your grievances aside. We must find a way out of here.'

'We must, but who dares risk the fate of my son?' said Tirior.

They were walking across uneven ground. Tiaan kept her eyes firmly closed, though brightness on her eyelids indicated that it was morning. It was hard to concentrate on what they were saying, for she hurt inside as if scalding water had been poured down her throat.

'Urien could use it,' said an unknown voice.

The person who was carrying Tiaan stopped dead. Someone let out a shocked cry. Another said, 'How dare you insult the Matah of all the Aachim?'

'I'm sorry,' said the unknown voice. 'I allowed myself to be carried away.'

'No need to apologise,' said Urien. 'The Matah has a duty to her people, as much as they to her. And here is my reply. I might use the amplimet once or twice, and get away with it, but not even I could employ it every day for weeks, as would be required to save our constructs.'

'What if we took it in turns?' said Vithis. 'If our strongest, all volunteers, could just use it for a few hours each, we could save some of our constructs.'

'Yes, show us the way, Vithis,' Tirior said venomously.

The silence was finally broken by Urien. 'Well, Vithis?'

'How can I do that and leave my clan undefended?' he said.

'Inthis Last Clan,' sneered Tirior. 'Cowards all!'

'There will be no volunteers,' said Urien, 'for most would die as horribly as Ghaenis did. And there are greater risks . . .'

'Not here!' cried Tirior.

'We must talk about the *other problem*,' said Urien.

'What problem?' said a dreary voice that Tiaan recognised as Luxor, chief of Clan Izmak.

'The amplimet communicated with the nodes at Snizort, Booreah Ngurle and Tirthrax, where it went close to unbinding the trapped Well of Echoes.'

'So it *is* like the one that nearly brought down our world in ancient times,' said Luxor heavily. 'I feared as much. It would be better to destroy the amplimet and walk away from our constructs. Even if we abandoned all these here, we still have five thousand near Gospett, and elsewhere. Nothing on Santhenar can match them.'

'The old humans would take apart the abandoned ones,' said Vithis, 'and soon learn to make their own. Where would we be then? And there's another matter. The lyrinx have not gone very far. If they attack in the night, they could wipe us out. We can't risk it.'

'What are we to do?'

'How is Tiaan?' asked Urien.

Tiaan felt the cool hands of a healer on her brow. 'She'll recover,' said an unknown voice, 'though she'll be in much pain when she comes round. You'll get nothing out of her today or tomorrow.'

'Give her the best treatment we have,' Vithis ordered. 'Don't spare our most precious medicines. Tiaan must be ready by dawn the day after tomorrow. She must use the amplimet to tow our constructs to safety.'

'I forbid it,' said another unknown voice. It seemed that other Aachim had joined them on their long walk. 'Even if Tiaan were an enemy, this would be a dishonourable act. But she's a hero who saved us from extinction. This is sheer infamy!'

Two more voices, both unknown, objected just as strenuously.

'What do you say, Urien?' said Vithis. Do you still forbid it?'

She did not answer at once. There was silence for several minutes, broken only by the tramping of many feet. 'I have agonised about this all evening and night. I've weighed the arguments. Every choice represents a hazard.'

'And your decision?' said Vithis.

'You may use Tiaan to try and save our constructs, but for no other purpose, and it must be done with great care.'

'I will not put my name to it,' cried Luxor.

'Overruled,' said Urien. 'My position on this amplimet is well known – I hate and fear it – but Vithis has convinced me that we have no choice. We must wield this perilous crystal for our very survival.'

'Then our Syndic must be told of these matters,' said the second unknown voice, 'and given the opportunity to debate –'

'There's no time,' said Urien. 'Vithis, your leadership is suspended. In this emergency, I've no choice but to rule by decree. We will use Tiaan and deal with the consequences afterwards.'

'How dare you subvert the very founding principles of our Syndic?' cried a new voice, high in outrage.

'The Matah is above the clans, and even the leader,' Urien reminded them. 'In an emergency that threatens our survival, it is my duty.'

That only raised more outrage, until Urien declared in a voice that brooked no disobedience, 'It is done in the name of the Matah. Let anyone challenge it at peril of their life *and their clan.*'

Silence fell, long and pregnant. Tiaan could hear her heart thumping.

'What if the crystal comes to the *second* stage of awakening and takes control of her?' said Luxor. 'Should it break out to fulfil its destiny, we won't be able to stop it.'

'From what she's told us,' said Urien, 'the amplimet is far from ready. We'll salvage all the constructs we can, for as long as her body can take it.'

'We will rue this dishonourable day for as long as our Histories last,' said Luxor.

'How will we write this into our Histories?' said another objector. 'How will we explain it to our children, and their children?'

'History is as it is written,' said Urien. 'It will be recorded thus: Tiaan begged to be allowed to aid us in our extremity, out of her great love for our kind, and recognising that Aachim are the superior species.'

'You would put a lie into the Histories?' said Luxor incredulously.

'Once it's in the Histories, it is truth.'

'Not if everyone knows otherwise.'

'All other Aachim will be kept away from her. How will they know?'

'*I* know,' muttered Luxor. 'I will make it known.'

'Then you have your own dilemma. Let it be done.'

'What if –?' Luxor began. 'What if the worst comes to pass and the crystal reaches the *third* stage – full awakening? Would you risk *this* world, too?'

'We'll stop well short of the node,' said Vithis. 'The amplimet won't be able to get close enough to draw real power.'

'And if it takes over Tiaan?'

'Archers will be standing by in the towed constructs,' said Urien. 'And mancers, alert for any sign that the crystal is overpowering her. If they detect such signs, the archers will be ordered to shoot to kill.'

Even Vithis let out a muffled cry at that. Perhaps he was

remembering that Tiaan had saved Minis from a fiery death in Snizort. It was all Tiaan could do to remain silent as they reached the healers' tent and carried her within.

'It's a shabby way to treat someone who saved all our lives,' said Luxor.

'If she knew what a fully woken amplimet would do to her,' said Urien, 'she'd thank us on bended knees.'

TWENTY

There was shouting in the night, not far from Thyzzea's tent. Recognising Minis's voice, Tiaan looked out the window flap.

'How dare you abuse her so!' Minis roared, struggling against a number of guards.

Shortly Vithis came running and, after a low-voiced argument, Minis went away with him. Tiaan was pleased to see him go. Whether sincere or not, Minis could do nothing for her.

She was woken before dawn by Thyzzea, who handed her a steaming mug. 'You must be quick, Tiaan. Vithis will soon be here. I brought you clothes, since yours are . . . in need of cleaning.' That was a politeness. Tiaan's clothes were no better than tar-stained rags. 'Do you need help to dress?'

'Thank you,' said Tiaan, 'but I'm used to doing it.'

Once Thyzzea had gone, she eased her legs out of bed. Her thigh and calf muscles ached but she had more coordination than before; more strength too. She was able to stand up and take a couple of halting steps, and it felt like a personal triumph.

The red drink practically needed to be eaten with a spoon. It was sweet, with a slightly bitter under-taste that she came to appreciate by the time she had finished, for without it the beverage would have been cloyingly rich.

The clothes fitted well enough. She was dressed and sitting at the table, eating bread and hot sausage, when Vithis burst through the flap of the tent.

'Time to go to work. Bring her, *Guard*.'

Thyzzea put her head through the door of her parents' room, said something and picked Tiaan up. Vithis set off with great strides, so that Thyzzea had to trot to keep up.

'What do you want of me?' Tiaan asked Vithis as they crossed between row after row of silent constructs. She knew, but wanted to hear him say it.

'You're going to operate my construct with the amplimet, and tow the other machines to the nearest field. Thyzzea will guard you, and if you attempt to escape, her family will suffer the prescribed penalty.'

At the furthest end of the row, Vithis stopped at a construct that was somewhat larger than most others. Its hatch was open. Aachim ran back and forth, packing gear into it and into a number of other constructs. Each was connected to the first by stout ropes, around which were looped finer cables that ran underneath.

Vithis climbed in. Thyzzea followed, struggling under Tiaan's awkward weight. Vithis handed Tiaan the package, wrapped in platinum, which she unfolded to reveal the amplimet. Again she felt that blind terror, but fought it down. The amplimet offered the only hope of escape for her, too.

'This machine is linked to six others,' said Vithis. 'Once you draw power, they will take enough to rise off the ground and maintain direction, though not to drive themselves. Do nothing hastily. Don't attempt to escape. I'll be with you the whole time, and I have two guards in the following construct, armed with crossbows.'

Tiaan was not planning to escape just yet. First she must be able to walk, even *run*.

Vithis climbed onto the rear platform, looking back. 'All is ready. Begin, very slowly.'

The nearest node lay not too many leagues to the south. Though small and nondescript, weak and wavering, she could use it. Locking onto its field, she drew power smoothly. The construct rumbled and rose up to hip height. She looked over her shoulder at Vithis, who was shivering with tension. Small wonder.

'All is well,' he said. 'Head directly towards the node. Take it steadily or you'll break the cables.'

She eased the lever and the construct crept forward until the slack of the first tether was taken up. The machine shook as the weight of the second construct came on the line. A dull ache tickled across the top of her skull. Tiaan rubbed the spot with her fingers and drew more power.

So it went until all six constructs were underway. After that it was routine, though the work was draining. She headed south towards the node, the construct moving across undulating plains at slightly more than walking pace, in the general direction of Gospett. There was no sign of life. The once plentiful game had been slaughtered to feed the armies.

'Go round in a circle and stop,' called Vithis some hours later. The constructs behind him were signalling. 'They can see the field.'

They were in a circular valley with a rim of low hills on all sides. White quartzite outcropped in lines across the slope, and along the crest. A dry creek, its bed filled with white pebbles, meandered across the floor of the valley. Its path was marked by trees with slate-blue pendulous leaves and hanging purple fruits like curly beans.

'Set up camp here and dig a pit in the creek bed. We'll find good water there.'

Vithis gave orders for the layout of the camp and his people ran to carry them out. The constructs were unhooked, disgorging about a hundred Aachim. The cables were reloaded into Tiaan's construct. The others moved under their own power, making a defensive ring around the camp.

'Head back to the Snizort camp, Tiaan,' said Vithis, smiling. She'd not thought him capable of it. 'Make all the speed you can.' He came down from the turret to stand beside her, leaving a wide gap between them.

Tiaan glanced up at his stern profile and, despite the way he'd treated her, for the first time she felt a trace of empathy. Vithis had lost everything. She could not truly understand his loss, but she could *feel* it, and it reminded her of something

231

that had been troubling her for a long time. She opened her mouth to speak, but closed it, afraid he would blame her again.

But surely, in spite of everything he'd done to her, it would be wrong not to tell him. She flipped back and forth as they floated along then, when they were halfway back, it just burst out of her.

'I heard them!' Tiaan said suddenly.

'What?' He roused from his thoughts.

'When the gate opened, in Tirthrax . . .'

He spun around, staring at her. 'Yes? *Yes?*'

'I heard a host of people crying out in agony.'

He put his hands on her cheeks, probing her eyes with his own. 'What did you hear?'

'They were lost,' she said softly, closing her eyes and immersing herself in the horror of it. 'Lost in the void. It was terrible.'

'You heard,' he said. 'Ah, my clan, my clan!' He began to weep, but dashed the tears away. 'Before I do anything else, my dead must be honoured. I will find them and bring their bodies back, no matter how far I have to go or how long it takes.' He sprang out through the hatch.

When she looked back he was standing in the shooter's turret, legs spread, grim face fixed on the horizon. His cloak streamed out in the wind, lifting his hair, which had changed from black to silver since his coming to Santhenar. Tiaan wished she had not spoken.

Vithis worked Tiaan without respite. For the next trip, ten constructs were linked to hers, and on the one after that, fourteen, and they travelled more quickly. It took the most intense concentration to draw enough power, and keep it flowing smoothly. The amplimet could handle it, though Tiaan was not sure how much more *she* could take. The inside of her skull felt as if hot channels had been bored through it.

Once, using her talent had been pure pleasure and the highest fulfilment she could imagine. No more – now there was just pain and a feeling of being driven beyond her strength. She wasn't a human being, or even a slave. She was just a tool to be used and discarded when it was worn out.

They stopped for lunch in the mid-afternoon, while twenty constructs were linked to her machine. On the trip after that, the number was thirty. By the time she had hauled all those to the field, it was long after dark.

There was no break, apart from dinner eaten while they waited for another thirty to be linked up. They kept going all through the night, pulling thirty each time, Vithis driving her mercilessly. Dawn revealed another thirty, ready to be linked up, but Tiaan could do no more.

'My brain is burning.' Unfastening her belt, she slid off the chair onto the metal floor.

Thyzzea and one of the soldiers carried Tiaan out, laying her on the brittle grass. A healer was brought, then Urien appeared and laid her hands on Tiaan's head.

'No harm has been done,' said Urien, 'but you must take better care of her, Vithis.'

'We've moved only a hundred and forty constructs,' said Vithis. 'At this rate it'll take six weeks.'

'That's a hundred and forty more than was thought possible yesterday, and if you work her to death you'll get no more.'

'In two weeks our supplies will run out, Urien!'

'Surely you understand the risk you're taking?'

'All right!' he said. 'But there's got to be a way.'

Tiaan lay in a daze, watching as Vithis held a heated conference with Urien, Tirior, and other Aachim she did not know.

A buzzing started in her ears, and hot flushes began to radiate out from the centre of her head. Tiaan heard sounds like speech but could no longer make out the words. She turned over, shielding her face from the sun.

Thyzzea helped Tiaan to a seat in the shade and the symptoms gradually faded. She was sitting there, sipping at a cool drink, when Vithis and Urien approached.

'How are you feeling?' said Urien.

Tiaan told her. 'You're killing me, just as you killed Ghaenis.'

'We've got to move the constructs faster,' said Vithis. 'Should the lyrinx come back we'll be defenceless.'

'We've faced this problem before,' said Urien. 'There may be a way. Your sickness is not from the *amount* of power you're drawing, Tiaan, but the *source*.'

'I don't understand,' said Tiaan.

'You're taking all that power from one small field and the draw is too concentrated; that's why it's damaging you. But if you were to draw from a number of fields at once, spreading the load evenly, you could take as much, or even more, without harm.'

'I've tried it before. As soon as I turn to the new field, I lose track of the old.'

Urien rose, drawing Vithis out of earshot. They had another long, heated argument before heading their separate ways.

'What was that about?' Tiaan asked Thyzzea after they had gone.

'It has to do with forbidden knowledge, and the danger of giving it to you.'

'What forbidden knowledge?'

'I don't know.'

'Suppose that it works,' said Tiaan, 'and the constructs are saved. What then?'

'Better to ask my father that,' said Thyzzea, looking worried. 'But . . .'

'Yes?'

'How could they ever let you go?'

TWENTY-ONE

Ullii had gone, fleeing into the night. Nish began to run after her but Flydd took hold of his collar. 'You'll only make it worse, if that's possible. She'll come back when she has to – *I hope.*'

'I have to explain,' Nish said desperately. 'I've got to tell her I'm sorry. It was an accident, surr. She'll think I don't care.'

'You'll never find her,' said Flydd. 'No one is better at hiding than Ullii.'

'What if she doesn't come back? What about my child?'

'You'd better pray she does, for all our sakes. And that when she does, you know what to say to her.'

What *could* he say? *I'm sorry I killed your long-lost brother, Ullii. I didn't mean to.* It was pointless.

They searched the clearing, using Flydd's ghost light. Both of his opponents were dead, as was the soldier by the air-floater. The one Nish had wounded in the leg had fled, leaving only a few specks of blood on the leaf litter. There were three more bodies in the wrecked air-floater, two soldiers and the pilot, a young woman who looked unharmed but was already growing cold. She had a broken neck.

Nish stood by her, his guts crawling with horror. She had been younger than he was. The young soldier, too. 'How could everything have gone so wrong?' he said softly. 'I tried so hard.'

'I *told* you I wanted to capture the air-floater,' said Flydd, glaring at Nish like an executioner choosing his next victim.

'I didn't hear your orders, surr. I was coming across to ask you what you'd said—'

'Couldn't you have *thought* before you threw your cudgel at the rotor?'

'There was no time. The air-floater was coming down fast, surr, and I knew we couldn't deal with that many soldiers. If they'd landed, they'd have had us. I reacted instinctively.'

'Surely it was obvious that I planned to escape in it?'

'No surr, it wasn't. I'm sorry.'

'I was going to rendezvous with Irisis and Fyn-Mah, then stop your wretched father before he attacks the lyrinx and destroys another army. Now its fate is out of my hands. All I can do is run like the whipped cur I am.'

Nish hung his head. What a miserable, useless worm he was. He wanted to crawl under a rock and die. The wound in his side was painful but had stopped bleeding, so, not wanting to draw any more attention to himself, he didn't mention it.

'Why so few in the air-floater?' said Flydd to himself.

'Perhaps the others got out on the other side of the forest.'

Flydd took no notice. 'Who was directing them? This search must have been led by a querist, at the very least, but there's no sign of one. Unless this seeker was doing it, shielded from us and under their control.'

Nish was sure he knew what Flydd was thinking: that he, Nish, was the most worthless fool who had ever drawn breath. That his father had been right – he was a walking disaster.

'I'll keep going north,' said Flydd. 'Not that I can do anything there, except sweat blood about the war. At least with Myllii dead they won't be able to track me.'

'Do you want me to come too?' Nish asked in a low voice. The way Flydd was talking, Nish was afraid of being left behind.

'*Want?*' said Flydd. 'Of course I don't want you – though I suppose I've got to have you.' He gave Nish a furious glare, then relented. 'Come on, lad, put it behind you. You clearly didn't know I planned to take the air-floater, and maybe you were right. Six soldiers probably were beyond me. In other circumstances you'd be a hero.'

'But I killed Myllii, surr.'

236

'A tragic accident that could have happened to anyone. Besides, he reared back onto the knife after you told him to hold still, so you can hardly be blamed for it.'

'I thought he was attacking Ullii,' said Nish. 'I was trying to save her, and now he's dead – an innocent man.'

'You were doing your best, so let's say no more, eh? Besides, it remains to be seen whether he *was* innocent.'

'What do you mean?'

'Was he embracing his sister, or holding her for the soldiers? Did he put his arms around her because he loved her, or because Ghorr ordered him to find her? But enough of this speculation – fit yourself out and gather what food you can, and make it snappy.'

They replaced their rags with clothes from the victims, the least bloodstained garments they could find. Nish's were too big, but he found a pair of boots that were roughly his size, and a hat. In ten minutes they were ready. Pilfered packs contained spare clothing, food for a couple of weeks, water bottles and all the other gear that soldiers carried. Nish had a shiny new sword, unused by the look of it. Flydd had taken the hedron from the air-floater's controller, as well as the chart-maker's spyglass, which had survived the crash.

'Not sure what use this will be,' he said, tossing the crystal in his hand. 'But you never know. Let's go. This place will be swarming with scrutators in a few hours.'

'Are we going to the rendezvous?'

'There's no point. By the time we walked all that way, Irisis would be long gone. You can't hide an air-floater in country like this.'

'Where are we going?'

'Into the wilderness.' Flydd smiled grimly, as if at some private joke.

'What about Ullii?' Nish's voice squeaked. 'We can't leave her.'

'There's no way of knowing where she is. If she wants to find us she will, though that's hardly likely now.'

He said it without rancour, but Nish cringed.

*

237

It was another sweltering day. They walked all that morning, taking advantage of the cover along creeks, mostly dry, and ridges, whenever they ran in the right direction, which was not often. They saw no sign of Ullii.

In the afternoon, Nish began to flag. The wound in his ribs grew increasingly painful but he could not stop to attend to it. He was continually falling behind and Flydd kept yelling at him to keep up. The scrutator had not mentioned Myllii's death again but Nish ached with guilt.

Flydd seemed to be making for a hill knobbed with round red boulders, one of many in this endless landscape of undulating plains and gentle mounded hills. Nish up-ended his water bottle but the few drops it contained barely wet his tongue. They had crossed half a dozen watercourses in the afternoon, all dry. He sat on a rock, staring at the ground. It was hard to find the will to go on. Every moment of the day he'd regretted his follies; he'd looked everywhere for Ullii but she was gone and his child with her. Why couldn't he have *thought* before he brought down the air-floater, or held the knife to Myllii's back? Why hadn't he realised Ullii was pregnant? Why, why, why?

The scrutator appeared. 'What's the matter? We can't stop out in the open.'

Nish struggled to his feet. Pain spread from the wound up into his shoulder, and down his hip to the outside of his leg. His feet hurt, too, for the boots were too small and had already rubbed the skin off his toes and heels.

He fell several times on the way up the hill, which was steeper than it had appeared. Flydd, well ahead, did not notice. The next time Nish looked up, the old man had vanished.

Nish slipped on rubble. As he picked himself up, he spied another air-floater on the horizon. They couldn't see him from so far away, but he lay still until it drifted out of sight to the south. He had to crawl the rest of the way up the hill – his feet hurt too much to walk.

He eased between two boulders and saw Flydd sitting in

the shade, eating another of those knobbly fruits, licking the skin with the gusto of a child with a piece of honeycomb. The green pulp had oozed all down his front and he hadn't noticed. 'I just saw an air-floater,' Nish croaked.

'It's been there a while. We should be safe from it, unless they've picked Ullii up to track me.'

The cold was spreading across Nish's chest now, but his forehead was dripping with perspiration.

'Is something the matter?' said Flydd.

Nish managed a limp wave with one hand. 'S'orright,' he slurred, holding his side. 'Just a flesh wound.'

'Where?' Flydd unfastened his shirt. 'How did you get this?'

'Soldier in the forest. Stuck me in the ribs. Not serious.' Nish tried to lie down.

Now Flydd was furious. 'I'll be the judge of that. You're a fool, Nish. Why didn't you tell me?'

Nish groaned as the scrutator probed the wound with fingers that seemed deliberately rough.

'This should have been treated last night. Now it's infected. You need a swift boot up the arse!' Flydd proceeded to give Nish one, knocking him down on his face. He leapt up with the empty water bottles and disappeared.

Nish closed his eyes. He deserved no less.

It was dark by the time the scrutator returned. Nish woke from a feverish sleep to find Flydd looming over him.

'I didn't want to risk a fire,' he said, the anger gone, 'but we've got to have hot water. That wound must be cleaned out.'

'I didn't think it was that bad,' said Nish, who felt cold all over. 'It didn't bleed much.'

'You've been lucky, but if the infection sets in you'll die of it. And that might not be such a bad thing,' Flydd said cheerfully. 'At least you won't be able to cock up anything else.' At the look on Nish's face, he added, 'I'm joking.'

The scrutator kindled a small fire well under the overhang of a boulder and climbed up to check that it could not be seen from above. 'This'll have to do. I'd have to be really unlucky for that to be spotted. But lately, I *have* been really unlucky.'

When the water was boiling, Flydd cleaned the wound with rags soaked in scalding water, before making a poultice of herbs beaten into the pulp of one of the knobbly fruits and binding it over the gash. Subsequently he stewed meat and vegetables for dinner.

Though famished, Nish was unable to take more than a few spoonfuls. The scrutator ate the rest, pulled his coat around him and closed his eyes. Nish did too, and slept, until his dreams forced him to wake.

Seven people had died last night and he was responsible for five of them. He hadn't meant to kill anybody, but they were dead nonetheless. It was not an attractive thought. The soldiers might have killed him without a qualm, but he could not feel the same way about their deaths. Myllii had been harmless. Worse still, the pilot of the air-floater had been a female, as most pilots were. He had killed a *woman*. In a world where the falling population was a disaster, to kill a woman of child-bearing age was the worst crime in the register. He let out a small, squeaking choke.

Flydd rolled over in his coat. 'What is it now?'

'I killed the pilot. A *woman*. What am I to do, Scrutator?'

'Find a way to atone for it. And you can start by not disturbing my sleep.' Flydd rolled back the other way, snapping the collar about his ears.

Nish kept seeing her face – she had been a pretty little thing. It became a night of horrors. Each time he dozed off he dreamed about the dead, but now all were women with babies in their bellies – his children. Each time, the dreams jerked him awake. Nish stared into the night but their faces were painted on the darkness. And *Myllii*. For all that it had been an accident, he had killed Ullii's brother and nothing could undo that. It must destroy everything that had ever been between him and Ullii. If only she would come back and he could, at least, explain.

*

Flydd's poultice proved efficacious, for Nish's wound was better in the morning. It was just as well, as Flydd's left thigh, the one torn open and burned by his first crystal, had become infected. Nish spent the best part of an hour cleaning and dressing it in the foggy dawn, with the scrutator stoically enduring the pain.

There was no sign of Ullii. They continued north and west in silence. It was like being a slave all over again, only that Nish was pushing himself to the limit of his endurance. He'd hoped that exhausting mind and body might keep the nightmares at bay, but even in his most agonising moments, when the blisters on his feet had burst and he drove himself on raw, weeping flesh, the dead faces were there.

They began before dawn each morning and walked long into the evening. In this flat country they must have been making four or five leagues every exhausting day. Flydd matched Nish stride for stride for the next few days, despite the infection. Nish lost track of time, so long had the days been, and so full of torment.

The scrutator now took them on a westward path, towards the sea, not wanting to get too far from Jal-Nish's army. Outlandish though it was, he still intended to try and stop him. Flydd never gave up, no matter how hopeless things became, and that was a lesson to Nish.

However, when they had wandered more than forty leagues and seen not a soul, one day Flydd began to fall behind. Around dusk, Nish turned to say something to him, only to discover that the scrutator was just a dot on the horizon.

Nish sat down to wait for him, but resting was too pleasant. There was no pain in it. He drove himself back to the ailing figure.

'What's the matter?'

'My leg,' Flydd gritted. 'I can barely lift it.' In a few hours his left thigh had swollen to twice the size of the right, and the wound had become an inflamed, weeping sore.

The dust cloud was moving in a south-westerly direction.

The spyglass resolved it into a large column of soldiers, set to pass a league or two north of him. He made signals with his coat until his eyes were raw, and eventually a small group broke away from the column, heading in his direction.

Nish watched the riders with a feeling of mounting terror. If the army belonged to the scrutators they would torture him publicly, to serve as a lesson to others. For malefactors in every profession or trade, an ironic and appropriate death had been prescribed, and each victim's fate was subsequently written into the Histories, so that all would know that justice had taken its merciless course.

Nish could not forget poor Ky-Ara, the clanker operator who had gone mad with grief at the loss of his machine. He had killed another operator then run renegade with the man's clanker. Flydd had ordered the clanker dismantled before Ky-Ara's eyes and every part of it fed into the furnaces. Ky-Ara had been forced to destroy the controller hedron himself, but instead had called so much power into the crystal that it had burned him from the inside out.

Nish was used to death, in all its forms and horrible finality. He hoped he could face his with dignity intact; he had to, though it would not redeem him. The Histories would describe his folly and inglorious end for as long as they endured. He would be a cautionary tale for the children of the next twenty generations. The only consolation would be that he had done his best.

A horseman trailing a blue banner galloped towards the foot of the hill. Three others followed. Nish waved the coat and trudged down to meet them.

'Did you put out the fire?' Flydd rasped as Nish passed by.

'It's an army. I signalled them and riders will be here shortly.'

'If you're wrong you won't have to worry about the scrutators. I'll kill you myself!'

Nish avoided Flydd's eye and kept going. At the base of the hill he stood on a fallen tree trunk, waving as the soldier with the banner raced up. Nish vaguely recognised the fellow, a pitch-black, good-looking man with a halo of frizzy hair and a nose as hooked as a parrot's beak. What was the name? Tchlrrr, of course. He'd accompanied Nish on that humiliating embassy from General Troist to the Aachim. Nish felt his face grow hot at the thought of it.

Tchlrrr grounded his pole. Two soldiers trotted forward, followed by an officer in a cockaded hat, and another pair of soldiers. The uniforms were familiar.

'Who are you?' called the first soldier. 'Why did you signal us?'

Nish took a deep breath. 'I'm Cryl-Nish Hlar. My travelling companion is Scrutator Xervish Flydd, and he is sorely wounded. Without the service of a healer he may die.'

'C-Cryl-Nish Hlar!' stammered the officer in the middle. 'I've often w-wondered what happened to you. Come down.'

Nish practically fell off his rock. The officer was Prandie, one of the lieutenants of General Troist. Nish had saved Troist's twin daughters, Liliwen and Meriwen, from ruffians near Nilkerrand, a hundred and fifty leagues to the north, and subsequently rescued them from a collapsing underground ruin. The army must be Troist's, which meant that, for the moment, he was safe.

'Lieutenant Prandie,' he said. 'I'm so very glad to see you.'

TWENTY-TWO

No questions were asked. The soldiers rigged a litter between their horses to convey a weak but querulous Flydd back to the main force. Nish rode behind Tchlrrr, keeping well out of the scrutator's way, and within the hour they had joined the column. Flydd was placed in a wagon pulled by one of the clankers, and Troist's personal healer called to attend him. Healing was a mancer's Art these days and had advanced rapidly during the war, so Nish had hopes that she could save him.

Nish was taken into another clanker, where he lay on the floor and tried to sleep, though that was hardly possible with the bone-jarring shudder of the machine, and the squeals, rattles and groans of its metal plates against each other. Clankers lived up to their name. However, he did doze, to be shaken awake in the late afternoon. Finding good water, the convoy had stopped for the night.

'General Troist wishes to see you, surr,' said an aide.

Nish got out the rear hatch and looked around, rubbing his eyes and feeling more than a little anxious. Shortly General Troist appeared, a stocky, capable man. His sandy curls were longer than before, and tousled as though he'd been running his hands through them all day. His blue eyes were bloodshot, his uniform the worse for wear, but the soldiers saluted him smartly. Troist drove his troops hard, but not as hard as himself, and he took care of the least of his men before attending to his own needs. They loved him for it.

'It's good to see you again, Cryl-Nish,' Troist said. 'Come this way.'

Nish followed, sweating. True, he had saved Troist and Yara's daughters, twice, but there had also been that unpleasant scene at Morgadis with Yara's sister, Mira, and the fiasco of his embassy to the Aachim camp. Every success was matched by a failure. And no doubt Troist already knew of Flydd's fall, if not Nish's own.

They went up the line to Troist's command clanker, a great twelve-legged mechanical monstrosity the size of a small house, with a catapult and two javelards mounted on the shooter's platform. Nish had never seen one like it. Troist offered him a seat, an oval of slotted metal with an embroidered cover depicting a vase of bluebells, cheerfully but amateurishly sewn. The work of his daughters, no doubt. Troist was a methodical general, but a sentimental father.

'What are you doing here, Cryl-Nish?' Troist asked, holding out a leather flask of ale.

Nish took a careful sip, not sure what to say. The general knew his duty and, if that required him to give Nish up, he must do so whatever his personal feelings. 'I was sure you'd know all about it,' he said obliquely.

Troist frowned. 'Know what? Tell me straight, Cryl-Nish, I don't have time for foolery.'

So he hadn't heard. Nish saw a chance to save himself, and Flydd, if he could just put things the right way. 'The great battle at Snizort, weeks ago.'

'I knew there was going to be one, but I've not heard how it went. There's been no news from the south in a month, so I brought my army this way to find out.'

'No news at all?' said Nish. The scrutators prided themselves on their communications; it enabled them to control the world.

'The lyrinx locate our messengers from the air. They've also worked out how to track our skeets and kill them. It's next to impossible to get messages through to garrisons along the Sea of Thurkad. Were you at the battle for Snizort?'

'Yes,' said Nish, 'though not as a soldier. I was held prisoner by Vithis the Aachim.'

'You two have come a long way on foot, with such injuries.' Troist was studying Nish as if he suspected something had gone unsaid.

Nish wasn't sure how to proceed. If the general discovered what had really happened, he might clap Nish in the brig and deliver him up to the scrutators. But if Nish lied . . .

He took a deep breath. 'I must be completely honest with you, surr, no matter what it may cost me. The Snizort node exploded, destroying the field, and after that the battle went terribly wrong, for neither our clankers nor the Aachim's constructs could move.'

'I knew something was amiss,' said Troist, rubbing his lower belly, for he suffered with his bowels. 'Tell me all that has happened.'

Nish related the tale of the desperate battle at Snizort, the failure of the node and the consequent slaughter, the scrutators saving what remained of the army with their airborne mirrors, the underground fire and the abandonment of Snizort by the lyrinx. He hesitated, then told the rest, including Flydd's slavery and his own condemnation by his father, the escape, his folly which had caused the death of Myllii and the loss of Ullii, and his father's mad quest to attack the lyrinx. 'That's all, surr,' he said finally, 'save for a secret to do with the node—'

'I don't want to know any mancers' secrets, lad,' said the general. 'Go on.'

'I've been condemned by my own father, surr, and Scrutator Flydd by the entire Council. We fled for our lives, and now you have us . . .' Nish could think of no defence, nothing at all. 'You must send me back in chains, I suppose.'

'I have no orders concerning you, Cryl-Nish, and must rely on my judgment. In the past you served me well. I haven't forgotten that.'

Nish blushed to think of his flight from Mira's house with his trousers about his ankles. 'But there was an incident at Morgadis . . .'

'A misunderstanding on your part, Mira tells me. She was mortified that you fled her home in terror of your life, but I'll

246

leave her to explain when next you meet. She's suffered terribly, my wife's sister, and can be emotional . . .' He grimaced. To Troist, such feelings were a private business. 'To matters that do concern me. You say that the surviving army is being led into greater peril.'

'My father, Jal-Nish . . . I don't know how to say it, General Troist, but his injuries have transformed him. He's a bitter man, full of hate and rage. He even condemned me—'

'You told me already.' Troist turned away, his mouth hooked down. 'How any father could do that to a son – the man is surely a monster. And you say Ghorr required it of Jal-Nish, to prove his worth? How can that be? Duty is everything to me, yet such deeds shake my faith in our leaders.'

'After the battle, the lyrinx withdrew south-west from Snizort, towards the Sea of Thurkad,' said Nish. 'My father plans to hunt them down, once he's dragged our clankers to the nearest field, and surely he's done that by now.'

'Where would that be?' Unrolling a canvas chart, Troist spread it on a table.

Nish heard shouting outside, then the rear hatch was jerked up and Flydd appeared in the opening, swaying on his feet. His face was grey-green, his lips blue and he was clearly in great pain. It had not improved his temper. A young woman in a healer's cap clutched at his arm but he pushed her away.

'I'm Scrutator Xervish Flydd!' he rapped. 'You are General Troist?'

'I am,' said Troist, leaping to the hatch. 'Are you sure you're—'

'Surr, I implore you,' cried the healer, tugging at Flydd's sleeve. He fixed her with a glare of such ferocity that she drew back, twisting her fingers together. 'This is most unwise. You risk—'

'You've done your work, now leave me be!' snapped Flydd. 'The fate of the world hangs upon my stopping Jal-Nish. Your coming is timely, General Troist.' He tried to pull himself up but let out a gasp and fell against the sill of the hatch.

Troist and the healer lifted him in and guided him to a seat. Behind Flydd's back Troist beckoned the healer, a sturdy young woman in her mid-twenties, blonde of hair and blue of eye, with worry lines etched across a broad forehead. She sat in the shadows, looking troubled.

'You didn't think so a few hours ago,' Nish said quietly.

'And I'll make you suffer for disobeying my order,' Flydd snapped. 'Out of the way, boy! The men have work to do.'

Nish moved back next to the healer, feeling empty inside.

'I value Cryl-Nish Hlar's counsel, surr,' Troist said evenly. 'He has served me well on more than one occasion.'

'And failed you disastrously on others, no doubt,' said the scrutator curtly. 'To business.'

'If you would take the rear seat for the moment, surr,' said Troist. 'Cryl-Nih was briefing me on the situation at Snizort and I value his account.'

Nish sat up, astonished. It was unheard of for anyone, even a general, to defy a scrutator. Of course, Flydd was now ex-scrutator, but it would be prudent to avoid offending him. What kind of a man was Troist, to stand up for someone who was of no further benefit to him?

'More than you fear the just wrath of the scrutators?' Flydd said menacingly. He was unused to defiance and did not like it.

'I *do* fear the just wrath of the scrutators, surr,' said Troist, 'as any sane man would. I even fear the wrath of those who are *no longer* scrutators, should I meet one of them.' His eyes held Flydd's and, though Flydd played the game of staring him down the general did not look away.

'Is there no secret you haven't blabbed, boy?' cried Flydd.

Nish made allowances. The scrutator was in pain and not himself.

'I believe the lad felt he was doing his duty,' Troist put in. 'If you please, surr.' He indicated the seat up the back. 'Cryl-Nish, would you go on?'

Flydd sank onto the bench, wincing. He delivered the healer such a black look that she shrank into the corner.

Nish collected his thoughts. 'The constructs were being hauled north-west to a node. About here, I'd guess.' He pointed. 'The lyrinx fled this way.' He traced a line on the map with his fingertip, south-west towards the narrowest section of the Sea of Thurkad. 'But that was weeks ago. They could be anywhere by now.'

'Only the boldest of men would engage the enemy so close to the sea,' said Troist. 'Reinforcements could fly from Meldorin in less than an hour.'

'Jal-Nish thinks his forces will have the advantage of a demoralised and weakened enemy,' said Flydd. 'He doesn't know the lyrinx as I do. They abandoned Snizort because they'd got what they wanted, and they'll be waiting for him.'

'I don't know that country well,' said Troist, 'but something nags at me, Scrutator. Why has the Council given Jal-Nish command? He's junior to them all.'

'The scrutators are afraid to lead,' said Flydd, 'for none are battle tacticians and they value their own skins too highly. Yet they can't bear to give up control to the generals, so Jal-Nish is the only choice. He's a dangerous man, General Troist, for he truly believes he's better than them all.'

'What does he want?'

'Not gold. Nor knowledge, nor the company of beautiful women. Jal-Nish Hlar desires only one thing – to take over the Council and impose his twisted will on the entire world. He's a driven man.'

Someone rapped on the rear hatch. The healer threw it up and a young aide whispered something in Flydd's ear. Flydd nodded and made to climb out, but a man concealed by cloak and hood pushed forward. He and Flydd spoke in low voices for several minutes, and Nish caught only one phrase. 'At the node?' the man hissed in surprise, before turning away.

'General Troist?' said Flydd.

'Yes?' Troist was puzzled by the interaction.

'That was my personal prober, Eiryn Muss, who's just had urgent news by skeet.'

Nish gaped, for even under his cape the man had not

resembled the fat halfwit from the manufactory. 'How did he know you were here?'

'Muss's talent for spying, and finding, verges on the miraculous—' said Flydd. He gnawed at a fingernail before going on. 'Sometimes, *beyond* the miraculous. His news: Jal-Nish's army left the node some days back, heading for Gumby Marth, a valley east of the coastal town of Gnulp Landing, here. It's preparing to do battle in a few days with a small force of lyrinx, maybe seven thousand. It's a trap, of course.'

'How can you be sure?' said Troist.

'Muss could find no evidence that the rest of the lyrinx have withdrawn across the sea, apart from a small number of fliers, so they must be hidden, to draw Jal-Nish in. And they would number an additional twelve thousand, or more.'

'And Jal-Nish's army?'

'Forty thousand men.'

'A man so bold, so forceful and aggressive, might even beat such a force of lyrinx,' said Troist thoughtfully.

'Not on a battlefield of their choosing. If he fights, we'll lose the entire army and a month later the enemy will be dining on the fat burghers of Lybing.'

'How can you be sure?'

'I was there when Jal-Nish addressed the Council, and I know him better than he knows himself. His tactics rest on the enemy being a demoralised rabble, but the lyrinx are leading them into a trap. More than twenty thousand of them got away from Snizort, and that many alone would be the equal of his army. To be sure, Jal-Nish has five thousand clankers, but the country near Gnulp is rugged and rocky, with great swamps to either side. Our machines will be little use there. But that's not my main worry.'

'What is?' said Troist.

'As you said, the lyrinx can swiftly bring in reinforcements from Meldorin, by flying and by boat. Whatever position we occupied, they could surround us. The army would be annihilated; humanity could not recover from such a loss.'

Troist walked six paces to the empty operator's seat, head

bowed beneath the low roof. He turned back. 'What do you have in mind? My force might make the difference, if I could get there in time.'

'Or it might be lost as well,' Flydd said. 'I'd prefer to avoid battle, if that's possible.'

'What's your plan, surr?'

'To wrest control of the army from Jal-Nish and retreat back east to safety.'

And then take on the scrutators, Nish guessed.

'How are you going to do that?'

'I won't know until I get there.'

'If you're planning a mancers' duel . . .' Troist frowned. 'How can you be sure you'll win? He has a reputation for cunning.'

'As do I, General.'

'Of course,' Troist said hastily. 'And yet—'

'If you don't think I'm up to it, say so!' snapped Flydd.

'Certainly I do . . . Er, when you're in health . . .'

'Then I'll just have to get better in a hurry, won't I?'

'What if the enemy attacks before you're ready? If the main army of the west is lost at Gumby Marth, mine cannot long survive,' said Troist. 'Scrutator Flydd, there's no time to wait. We must risk all to save all. We must march to the rescue straight away.'

Troist glanced at Flydd, who was rubbing the bandage on his left thigh. A dark bloodstain, spiralling like a coiled snake, showed through it.

'I suppose we must,' said Flydd.

'Is that an order from the scrutator?'

'It is.'

'Then I will obey it, since I have no *official* reason to suppose you are scrutator no longer.'

Troist's army had grown both in men and in efficiency since Nish had left it, long months ago. It now numbered thirteen thousand men and more than nine hundred clankers. A powerful force, and seasoned in a number of battles, though seven thousand of the enemy would be its match.

251

That night, after a dinner that sat uncomfortably in Nish's shrunken belly, they stood around the chart table to make plans. Yellow globes glowed to either side.

The general was measuring distances on his map with a pair of silver dividers. 'Presently we're here, around twenty leagues north-west of Snizort, and only a few leagues from the sea. Gumby Marth is some forty leagues south. In good conditions, my clankers can manage ten leagues in daylight, so it'll take us four or five days to get there.'

'Too long.' Flydd lay back in his chair. He was too weak to sit upright for any time, but would not go to his bed. 'What if we travelled through the night?' He already knew the answer, but wanted to hear the general say it, or make excuses.

'We have to sleep sometime, surr, and that's as good as impossible in moving clankers. Travelling part of the night, we might do another league or two, where the country permits us, of course.'

'Of course,' Flydd said sardonically. 'And it does, most of the way from here to the Landing, I believe. It's open plains and gentle hills, easy going for men and clankers alike. The last five or ten leagues are rugged, forested too, but that could be to our advantage.'

'Unfortunately . . .' Troist hesitated.

Flydd smiled, as if he had been expecting it. 'Yes?'

'We don't have enough clankers to transport thirteen thousand men.'

'Do the numbers.'

'What?' said Troist. 'Oh! We have roughly nine hundred clankers. If each carried ten soldiers, which is their limit, that's only two-thirds of my force.'

'How many are mounted?'

'Another eight hundred and fifty, more or less.'

'The riders should be able to keep up with the clankers.'

'If their mounts don't go lame.'

'Any that go lame, we'll eat,' said Flydd. 'The horses, that is. So all we have to do is cram another soldier inside, and two up on top with the shooter, and we can do it.'

'In theory,' said Troist, 'though it'll put a big strain on the mechanisms and the operators, not to mention the soldiers.'

'Not as big a strain as facing the lyrinx all by yourself, soldier, after they've annihilated Jal-Nish's army.'

'If they come upon us instead of Jal-Nish's army, they'll destroy us.'

'I may be able to prevent them finding us,' said Flydd, 'with help from your military mancer I propose to attempt a form of cloaking.'

'Cloakers haven't been a great success with clankers, surr, with all due respect.'

'This spell is greatly improved,' said Flydd. 'I learned of it in Nennifer just a few months ago. I think it'll prove satisfactory, for a short time at least.'

'If you say so, surr,' said Troist, 'then I suppose it could be done.' He looked dubious.

Troist was an ambitious man, but an honourable one. He did not want to drive his men or his machines beyond their breaking point, as a headlong march was likely to do. And perhaps he lacked confidence in his ability to fight a full-scale battle. Troist had been a junior officer when the bulk of his army was destroyed by the lyrinx attack on Nilkerrand, and all the senior officers killed. He had built this army from the surviving rabble, scattered across a hundred leagues of country. Troist had done a brilliant job and his soldiers would have followed him anywhere, but he surely worried about his limitations. His skirmishes with the enemy had involved no more than a few hundred soldiers; here he must manage thirteen thousand. If he achieved the impossible, it would make him. Should he fail, he and his army, and Flydd and Nish, would end up in the bellies of the enemy.

Flydd seemed to be weighing the general up. Finally he nodded to himself, 'Then let it be done.'

The fretting healer, who had been sitting in the shadows behind Flydd since dinner, said, 'Surr, such a journey is likely to kill you.'

Flydd swung around in the metal seat. 'What business is that of yours?'

The healer was shocked. 'Surr—'

'What are you doing here anyway, Spying on my secret councils?'

'I—'

'I told her to sit there, Scrutator!' Troist said coldly. 'And I'll thank you not to harass my healers, or anyone else under my command.'

'How dare you tell me what I may or may not do!' cried Flydd. 'I could break you to a common soldier for such insolence.'

Troist stood up. Though a compact man, he had to bend his head under the low roof. 'Then break me you must, *Scrutator* Flydd, for I will defend my healer, as I would any soldier in my army, to the last breath.'

Flydd hauled himself out of the seat, glowering at the general; Troist stood his ground. Nish trembled for what might happen.

Suddenly Flydd let out a great, booming laugh. 'I like you, General Troist. You're my kind of man.' He put out his twisted hand.

After a momentary hesitation, Troist took it, though it was some time before the wary look left his eyes. 'I'll see to the orders,' he said. 'We move in thirty minutes.'

Nish wasn't sure whether to be glad or sorry. He hoped he'd done the right thing this time, but what if it all went wrong and the lyrinx attacked Troist's army instead of Jal-Nish's much larger one? That worry was soon dwarfed by another that had been growing ever since the possibility had first been raised. What would happen when he met his father again? Just the thought made his heart race and his palms sweat.

TWENTY-THREE

Someone was screaming, a long, drawn-out wail of anguish that rasped at Ullii's nerves. Having lost her earmuffs and earplugs long ago, she could do no more than push a finger in each ear. It made no difference – the dreadful wailing penetrated her entire body. It came out of the ground up her legs; down from the sky through her skull; it was everywhere. She ran into the night and the sound followed her.

Ullii burst through thickets, heedless of the brambles tearing through her clothes and scoring her baby-soft skin. She crashed over crumbling embankments, through sandpaper shrubbery and into a boggy wallow where buffalo came down to a creek to drink. She splattered through the muck but the ghastly sound went with her, as if a ghost had thrust its head inside hers and was screaming into her brain.

Ullii slipped in the mud, fell into cool water and, as she went under, the sound cut off. The relief was so miraculous that she lay on the bottom, thinking that she might stay there forever. She felt no urge to breathe; there was no reason to live. Her beloved Myllii was gone, snatched away the instant she'd found him. Killed, murdered by Nish, her lover. He'd done it deliberately, to hurt her. He must have, or he would have come after her and told her how sorry he was. But he wasn't sorry. He didn't care about Myllii, or the baby, or her.

Flydd and Irisis, once her friends, were nearly as bad. They'd lied to her, used her, and when they didn't want her any longer, they'd simply abandoned her.

Her body's will to live drove Ullii to the surface. She stood up in the shallow water and breathed. The screaming had stopped but the pain was still there, and it was unendurable. Reaching inside herself, Ullii flicked the switch that severed her consciousness. Blessed oblivion.

An hour later she was still standing there, seeing nothing, hearing nothing, feeling nothing.

A memory woke in her and Ullii realised that she was standing in waist-deep water, tears streaming down her cheeks. Her beloved Myllii lay in his blood in the clearing, alone and abandoned.

Ullii had no idea where she was. In that fit of madness and grief she might have run in any direction. She searched the lattice for her brother's knot, which had appeared so miraculously last night, but it was not there. Myllii was dead; his knot had vanished forever and she was lost.

The sense of abandonment grew stronger. Myllii, Myllii, lying on the hard ground all alone. Was there a way to find him? He'd left no trace in the lattice, nor had the other dead at the air-floater. Not even the unfortunate little pilot made a mark now, for death wiped all knots away.

But the air-floater was powered by a controller, and it must still have a working crystal. She sought for it but found nothing – Flydd had taken the crystal with him and he was beyond range. Deeper, further, she sought; there had to be some trace left. At last she picked up a tiny smudge of aura, a chip broken off the controller crystal in the crash. It gave her the direction. Ullii turned that way and started running.

It was only an hour off dawn when she got there. The declining moon slanted across the clearing to light up the canvas of the air-floater from behind. The collapsed airbag was a crumpled rag outlined by black struts and wires. The little pilot lay with her head over the side, her neck bent at an unnatural angle.

Ullii only had eyes for the slim shape lying in the moon-shadow: beloved Myllii. She did not run. Ullii was afraid to approach him too quickly.

Stopping on the far side of the clearing, she stared at her

brother. Unlike the pilot and the soldiers, who all looked dead, he just appeared to be sleeping. She felt, as her sensitive eyes strained to pierce the blackness, that she saw his chest rise and fall. She tried to make out his features but they blurred into the dark.

She allowed herself to hope that it had just been a horrible nightmare. She did not want to wake him in case it turned out to be real. How could he be dead? Nish was a kind, gentle man who had done so much for her. He would not harm Myllii. It had to be a dreadful mistake, a dream that she had woken from. Or was it? She felt so confused.

Ullii took a slow, fluid step, careful to make no sound. Any noise might wake her brother and everything would turn out wrong. A warm breeze soughed through the treetops, curling round the clearing and tickling the back of her neck, lifting the hair of her nape just as it lifted the dry leaves on the floor of the clearing, sending them whirling like fairy dancers in a circle. It made her smile. Myllii would have loved to see it – he had always been fond of music and dancing.

She took another step, and her brother's prone form seemed to shift, as if moving to a more comfortable position, before settling back into sleep with a little sigh. The gesture was so familiar that it made her heart ache. Tears sprang to Ullii's eyes and suddenly she had to take him in her arms.

Her small feet made barely a sound as she ran. From halfway across the clearing, Ullii called her brother's name. Again he seemed to move, then suddenly went still, and with every step she took Myllii grew more rigid. The silver bracelet on his wrist was a manacle fixing him to the earth.

'Myllii!' she cried, but he no longer seemed to be breathing.

She crossed the short distance that separated them and threw herself at him. 'Myllii!'

He did not move. Myllii was as unyielding as a log. Ullii pushed her arms under his back. A bubble burst in his throat and the remaining air sighed out of his lungs. The ground was damp beneath him. His whole back was wet, and when she withdrew her hands and held them up, his congealed blood was black in the moonlight.

'Myllii,' she wailed, picking him up in her arms, holding his body tightly as she rocked back and forth, back and forth . . .

A faint *ticker-tick-tick* roused her this time. It was an air-floater, not far away. Ullii sat up, not so much listening as watching its knot in her lattice. It was roving back and forth across the country south of here, coming steadily closer as if searching. It had come after the wrecked air-floater, and something far more precious – Myllii the seeker.

The machine turned, flying directly towards the clearing. They were coming to take Myllii away. They must not get him. She tried to lift her brother, but he was heavier than he appeared. Ullii had him halfway to her shoulder when a sharp pain in her lower belly reminded her of the baby.

Taking Myllii under the arms, she tried to drag him, but had only gone three steps when the air-floater was overhead. It was bigger than the crashed one, and she could tell that there were scrutators aboard, though in her distress Ullii could not identify them.

'It's down there!' roared a barbed voice. 'Stay well up, Pilot. Captain, your troops must be ready for anything.'

If the scrutators caught her, they would use her in place of Myllii. She had to let her brother go. Gently laying the body down, she crouched beside him for a moment, saying her farewell. Her eye caught a gleam from the bracelet and she tried to unfasten it, as a token of him, but the clasp would not budge. No time to work on it; they were coming. Ullii scuttled into the trees.

The air-floater remained hovering above the clearing while soldiers came down on ropes. They were big, heavily armed, and Ullii was repulsed by the smell of their unwashed bodies. The first three assumed positions at the points of a triangle, crossbows thrust out, while the remainder came to ground inside the triangle. They formed more points and expanded outwards.

Lanterns were unshuttered and directed at the forest. The troops, heavily armoured and helmeted, looked like savage demons. Ullii could not bear to look at them – nor away from them.

'Search it,' said the captain, pointing to the wreckage of the air-floater. He shouted orders.

Powerful lanterns illuminated the wreckage. Two soldiers headed for it while others moved towards the edges of the clearing. Ullii crept away and, climbing a slender tree, little more than a sapling, took refuge in its canopy. It was so small they would never look for an enemy there. She had to stay close; she could not leave her brother.

The soldiers had set up their lanterns on poles and some began to quarter the clearing while others moved into the forest.

'Here's one,' someone called, bending over the still form of her brother. 'Hey! It's the black-haired seeker. He's dead.'

Dead! As the word echoed through her skull, Ullii almost fell out of the tree. Myllii was dead; she could no longer deny it. The leaves rustled and a man cried out, 'There's someone in the forest!'

The grimly efficient soldiers searched everywhere. They found more bodies: one of the soldiers from the first air-floater, then the dead in the wreckage. Ullii clung desperately to the trunk, fighting down an impulse to scream.

Finally the clearing was secured and the captain called up to the hovering air-floater, 'It's safe. There's no one about. It was just the wind.'

Someone shouted back, 'They're coming down. Stand to attention.'

Ropes whirred through pulleys and a big man in robes was lowered in a suspended chair.

Ullii choked, recognising him now. It was Chief Scrutator Ghorr, and he made a barbed, tangled knot in her lattice. She remembered Ghorr from the visit to Nennifer months ago. He had shown nothing but contempt for her. 'Scurry away, little mouse,' he'd said sneeringly. But subsequently Ullii had done what had never been done in the history of the world. She had used her lattice to get Irisis out of her cell without breaking the spell on the lock or setting off the alarm, and Ghorr's rage had shaken the foundations of Nennifer. Ullii was more afraid of him now, for she knew he wanted that secret even if he had to tear it out of her living body.

The air-floater swung in a gust, causing the rope to sway back and forth like a pendulum. The rotor roared as the terrified pilot tried to regain position but, before she could, Ghorr was dragged through the spiny upper branches, tearing his silken shirt to shreds. Bunches of hard leaves slapped him in the face, releasing a pungent oil that brought tears to his eyes.

'What the devil are you doing, Pilot?' he bellowed. 'Put me down, quick smart, or you'll go to the breeding factory!'

Soldiers ran back and forth, anxiously holding up their lanterns. Ghorr cleared the trees, though his shirt remained hanging from the spines. The pulley-man lowered him precipitously, whereupon two burly men ran to catch him as he swung across the clearing, cursing in a voice as much alarmed as furious.

Ghorr shook them off and wiped away the mortifying tears. His chest proved unexpectedly flabby, while the great belly was held in by a tightly-laced corset. One of the soldiers sniggered. Ghorr spun around furiously but could not identify the miscreant.

'My cloak!' he snapped.

It was tossed down at once. Pulling it around him he stalked off, wounded in dignity, to examine the crashed air-floater.

Two other scrutators came down in the hanging chair, the black-bearded, snake-eyed Fusshte and a cold, dumpy old woman whose name Ullii could not recall, though she remembered her knot in the lattice. She was just as hard and corrupt as the men.

The three scrutators gathered around the air-floater, inspected the dead then came to stand by Myllii. Lanterns flared brightly. One of the soldiers turned the body over.

'Stabbed in the back,' Ullii heard. 'See the knife wound here – it went straight into his heart.'

Ghorr gestured for silence while he held his hands out, parallel to the ground, muttering under his breath as he strained to perform some mancery. Fusshte's black eyes glittered in the lantern light.

'Flydd was here,' said Ghorr after a long interval.

'And he murdered the seeker so they could get away,' murmured Fusshte.

'He may have ordered it,' said the woman, 'but he did not do it. And since Ullii would not have killed her brother, it can only have been that black-hearted villain, Cryl-Nish Hlar.'

Ullii wept silently. It was as if the knife had been twisted in her own heart. Nish must really hate her. But why? She'd done everything he'd asked of her.

'After so much trauma, Ullii would have fled,' said Ghorr.

'The body's growing stiff,' said Fusshte. 'They're long gone, and without our seeker we'll never find them. We should have killed Flydd while we had him.'

'We'll wait for daylight,' said Ghorr. 'It won't be long now. Then we'll look for tracks. Since we've lost our seeker, we must find Ullii. I'll use her to hunt down Flydd and Cryl-Nish Hlar, and this time they must be executed on the spot.'

'What about the air-floater?' asked Fusshte.

'The artificers say it can be repaired, though it'll need a new rotor and controller crystal. We'll send a team back to fix the damage.'

'And the dead?'

'Burn them.'

Ullii clung desperately to her tree as the bodies were dragged into the centre of the clearing like worthless pieces of rubbish. Ghorr crouched by Myllii for a moment, though Ullii could not see what he was doing. He stood up, gestured, and the soldiers piled faggots, branches and logs on top. It was all happening too quickly. She couldn't cope. She hadn't said goodbye to Myllii, taken care of his body, washed him or brushed his hair. It was agony to watch, but neither could she cover her eyes.

A burning brand was thrust into the centre. The dry wood blazed up and within minutes the pyre was a mass of flame from one end to the other. The stench of burning flesh made her insides shudder.

The sun rose through the smoke. When the light was strong enough, the soldiers and the two scrutators crisscrossed the forest before picking up Flydd and Nish's tracks, heading north. The vile Fusshte was following another trail, which meandered like an ant walking across a piece of paper. It was the path Ullii had taken in her initial flight, though she did not recognise it. She had no memory of that time, nor ever would have.

The air-floater went after the two scrutators and disappeared from sight. Ullii dared not move, though she was now faint with thirst and hunger. The baby kicked feebly. Some hours later, Fusshte reappeared, tracking back. He began going through the forest in a series of parallel lines, methodically inspecting the ground and the trees. She felt sure he was going to discover her.

Fusshte came closer, studying marks on the bark of a nearby tree, claw gouges from some climbing animal. He turned to the northern sky, cocking his head as if listening for the return of the air-floater. Hearing nothing, he kept to his tracks, this time passing right by her sapling. Ullii prayed that she had left no marks on the bark.

Fortunately the ground was stony here. Ullii did not breathe as he went by, and Fusshte must have thought the sapling too small to bear her, for he did not look up. Soon he disappeared.

The day wore on. The fire died to ash and embers, though a stench of burnt flesh and hair lingered. Ullii remained where she was. Near dusk, the air-floater landed in the clearing. The three scrutators conferred on the ground for some little while, climbed in and it took off, heading south, as the sun plunged below the smoky horizon.

After an hour, when they were far away, Ullii judged it was safe to come down. The moon had not yet risen but the starlight was more than enough for her eyes. The pyre no longer smoked. The fire had burned itself out.

She circled around the oval patch of ash, marked here and there with elongated humps, the ash-grey residue of the bodies. Something caught her attention, tangled around a white stick a few steps away from the pyre. It was a clump of long black hair, a few dozen strands torn from Myllii's head as they'd dragged him across.

Ullii reached out with a fingertip. The strands were as silky soft as her own hair. As she touched it, the place in her lattice that had once held his knot flared and faded. She shivered, then carefully freed the lock of hair and tied it around her throat.

Returning to the pyre, Ullii went to the place where her twin had been laid, staring at the dimly lit ridge of ash. She could not believe that Myllii was gone – that this was all there was of him.

Stepping into the warm ash, she began to sweep it away from around the ridge with her fingertips. The ash slipped through her fingers but there wasn't a grain in it. Where Myllii's head and body had been, the fire had burned so hot that even the bones had gone.

She flung the ash this way and that, crying for her brother. Then, on a rock not far away, the silver bracelet glinted in the starlight. It must have been pulled from his wrist as they dragged Myllii across. She picked it up, holding it in her cupped hands, and caught the scent of her brother on it. It was all there was left of him.

Cradling the bracelet to her breast, she wept her heart out. There was no longer any doubt that he was dead. Myllii was gone forever and she was all alone in the world.

The moon came up. Ullii was still sitting by the pile of ash, nursing the bracelet, utterly bereft. As the light slanted down into the clearing, her thoughts became increasingly bitter.

263

Nish must have murdered Myllii to show how much he hated her. Everything he'd done since making her pregnant in the balloon had been designed to hurt her. Nish was a cruel man and must be punished.

The baby kicked, sending a sharp pain through her over-stretched bladder. Ullii looked into her lattice and, for the first time, saw the infant's tiny knot. It was beautifully regular and symmetrical, the way Nish's might have looked, if he'd had a talent. Wonderingly, she traced the curves, in and out, over and under, around and back, until she knew them perfectly.

The baby kicked again, and the knot trembled. The child was distressed, for Ullii had not eaten or drunk for a day. Food and drink were not even on her horizon. She was thinking that, though he obviously hated her, Nish had wanted the child.

The contradiction confused her. She stroked the bracelet, breathing in the fading scent of her brother. It was the only thing linking her to Myllii now. Wanting to fix that link, she slipped the bracelet over her hand and snapped down the catch. At first it was loose on her slender wrist, but then the links slithered together and it became so tight she could not slide her little finger underneath.

The baby kicked her bladder, three times in a row, and this time it really hurt. She touched the bracelet for comfort but saw an image of the three scrutators – Ghorr, Fusshte and the evil old woman – standing over her as if she were lying on a table. Ghorr turned to Fusshte, whispering in his ear, then they laughed.

Ullii cried out in horror and the baby began to kick furiously, doubling her over until she was on her hands and knees on the ground. She rolled onto her back, her hands on her belly, which seemed to calm the baby. Lying still, she changed her lattice so the child's knot filled her mind, mentally caressing the surfaces, which were as soft, as silky as her brother's hair. Myllii's face came to her, but as a child, and Ullii lost herself in memories of the time they had been little twins together, the pale and the dark, so perfectly matched.

The complement of each other. When they had been perfectly happy.

She could hear their childish chatter, their happy cries, but a sharp throb low down drove the memories away. 'Myllii,' she gasped, clasping the bracelet in panic, but again came that flash of the scrutators.

Come to us, little seeker, mouthed Ghorr. *We've work for you.*

'Leave me alone,' she said aloud. 'My baby needs me.'

Baby? Ghorr said to the others. *She can't have a baby – it'll ruin her precious talent.*

She must have dreamed that, for the next instant they were gone, as if she'd only imagined it; then gone completely, her memories of the moment wiped clean.

Myllii wasn't there either, but that awful screaming rang in her ears again. She reached out to the baby's knot, for the screaming seemed to be coming from there. An agonising pain, far worse than the baby's kicks, sheared through her belly. She wrapped her arms around her stomach, trying to protect the baby, but the pain grew until it was like barbed hooks tearing through her.

Ullii made a supreme effort to reach beyond the pain but the barbs ripped through her flesh and she felt a great convulsion inside her, a shearing agony, as if the baby's sharp fingernails were tearing desperately at the walls of her womb. Something burst inside her, then water gushed out between her legs, carrying the baby with it.

'No!' Ullii screamed, falling to her knees and clawing at the ground, but it was too late.

The baby, a little boy no longer than her hand, lay in a puddle, kicking feebly. She picked him up, staring at him in wonder. He was pink and healthy, and so beautiful that she felt a flush of love, but as she nursed him in her hands, the cord stopped pulsing and her stomach contracted again and again to expel the afterbirth. Ullii lifted the baby to her breast.

'Yllii. Your name is Yllii,' she said, as if that could protect him.

She desperately wanted him to live, for it was the only

happy link left between her and Nish, the only good memory of their time together, and she loved him so.

Yllii gave one feeble suck, a little sigh, but his head fell away from the nipple and blood from his mouth trickled down her breast. Ullii tried to blow the breath back into the infant but the pink colour faded steadily from his face. The baby breathed no more. Yllii was dead – her grief for her brother must have killed it, and it was all Nish's fault. He'd taken away everything good in her life.

Ullii felt a terrible, aching loss, but that was replaced by the most bitter fury at what Nish had done to her. A rage that could only be assuaged when he had suffered the way she, and Myllii, and little Yllii had.

TWENTY-FOUR

Ullii dug a hole through the remains of the pyre, lined it with ash taken from the place where Myllii had lain, so that it made a grey blanket over the dry earth, then placed the tiny body of her baby inside. It was blue now, and even in the moonlight she could tell that he was not at peace. His fists were clenched, his toes curled, his eyes wide and his mouth blood-dark.

My poor little Yllii, she thought. You never did anything wrong. Why did you have to die? Ullii covered the tiny eyes and arranged the clump of Myllii's hair over the top, protectively. She tried to put the bracelet in too, but it would not come off. It was locked to her wrist. There was not a trace of Myllii's scent left on it; it had no sense of him at all. She filled in the hole and covered it with stones so that nothing could dig her baby up, continuing until the place was covered by a flat-topped cairn as high as her waist. Then, finally, Ullii broke down. Turning her face away, she began to walk blindly.

She woke with an ache in her belly that was more than hunger. Ullii had not eaten in days, but that was not the worst of it. Her empty womb was throbbing. She had failed in her duty to protect her child.

Ah, but who made you do it? The voice was a whisper in her head, a rich burr that reminded her of Mancer Flammas, who had let her live in his dungeon for five years, and never once harmed her. His kindly indifference meant more to Ullii now than the professed friendship of Irisis and Flydd, or the supposed love of Nish. Their words had been empty, and in the end they had betrayed and abandoned her. Only Flammas had never let her down.

You were out of your mind with grief, came the voice again. Never having heard voices before, she assumed it was Flammas talking to her. *You can't be blamed for protecting yourself. You loved your baby, despite the father.*

I did love Yllii. I would have done anything for him. He was the only good thing that ever came from Nish.

Cryl-Nish is the very devil himself. He is evil incarnate, just like his father, and if you don't stop him he'll destroy the whole world.

'No!' she cried aloud, remembering Nish's many little kindnesses back at the manufactory, on the journey in the balloon, and fleeing from Tirthrax.

Cryl-Nish just lives to destroy everything good.

'What about that time in the balloon, when he saved me from the nylatl, and then I saved him? When we made our love in the balloon afterwards? He was the kindest, gentlest lover in the world.'

He wasn't in danger at all. He just did it to get his way with you. He used you from the very beginning.

Ullii knew that wasn't true, for she'd seen the look of terror on Nish's face as he clung, weaponless, to the ladder with the nylatl crouched over him. It had roused her protective instincts and she'd attacked the creature so furiously that it had scuttled away. But on the very first few times they'd met, Nish had manipulated her so she would cooperate in the search for Tiaan and the amplimet. He'd done it kindly, thoughtfully, but also because it was the only way to get what he wanted.

You see, said the voice that was so like Mancer Flammas, *that's how clever he is. Cryl-Nish doesn't have to be a monster – he knows that you catch more wasps with syrup than with gall. Everything he's done since you met, every single thing, has been to get what he wants from you. He's even wickeder than his father. Everyone thinks he's just a bumbling fool, and it's the perfect disguise. It even fooled you.*

'No!' she cried. 'Not Nish.' She put her hands over her ears. 'It's not true.'

The voice came through just as loud and clear. *It is true, and you know it.*

'Why would he do this to me?'

He wants to take over the world and corrupt it in his own image. And only you can stop him.

'I can't do anything.'

You must. He's fooled everyone except you. You have to save the world, Ullii. No one else can.

'Why should I?'

Because you're good, and it's your duty.

'I don't care about duty.'

But you must take retribution for Cryl-Nish's wickedness, or little Yllii will never rest in his grave.

She began to cry. 'Go away. Don't torment me.'

The only way out is to do as I say. Stop Cryl-Nish, and then Yllii will be at peace, and so will you. You can have peace forever, if you wish it.

'But what am I to do?'

First you must eat and get back your strength.

'There's nothing to eat. They took the food in the airfloater.'

Look over there, at the edge of the forest! See the ears sticking up? It's a hare, and you've been still so long it's forgotten you're here. Bend down, slowly. Pick up that egg-shaped stone.

'I can't kill a living animal,' she whispered.

If you don't, you'll starve and your baby will go unavenged. Pick up the stone.

Ullii bent her knees, ever so slowly, until she could reach the stone. The bracelet slipped on her wrist and for a moment she could not remember what she was doing, or why. She shook herself, it locked again, she recalled, and her fingers closed around the stone. Warm from the sun, it felt smooth, hard and heavy.

The voice was there again. *Draw back your arm, slowly.*

'I've never thrown a rock in my life. I won't even hit it.' That was a comfort.

Just do as I say. Don't aim at the hare, for it will dart away.

See that little tussock just to the left? Aim for the very centre of that, then throw with all your strength.

Ullii sighted on the tussock.

That's good. Now throw hard!

She hurled the stone. It went cleanly from her hand, exactly where she had aimed. The hare was slow to move, then darted to its right, directly into the path of the stone, and fell dead.

Animals did not show in her lattice, as a rule, but as the hare expired, Ullii felt a flare of pain. She ran across to the small creature, hating herself and regretting its death. She picked it up, stroking its fur. It was still warm, the eyes still bright. She had no idea what to do with it. She rarely ate meat, and then only the smallest amounts.

'What do you want me to do?' She had no knife to skin it, no flint and tinder with which to kindle a fire.

Tear off the skin with your teeth. Drink the blood before it congeals, then eat the meat and the organs.

The very idea made her want to vomit.

This is your first test, Ullii, and if you fail it, you won't succeed in anything and Yllii will lie in torment for eternity.

'But it was a living creature.'

Is it wrong for the lion to kill the lamb when her cubs are hungry? Of course not. Eat it, that you may survive, that poor Yllii may be revenged, and the world saved.

Ullii put her sharp teeth to the creature's throat and began to tear at the fur.

She did not hear the voice for days after that. Ullii wandered across the plains, sheltering from the sun in the day, moving at night. She learned to hunt and kill small animals with her bare hands, or with sticks, stones, pits or snares, drinking their blood and eating their flesh raw. She did not think at all, for thinking led to all sorts of mad thoughts that she could not bear, and grief that overwhelmed her. She simply became an animal.

Then, one morning, maybe a week later, she was snapped back to full consciousness.

Wake, said the voice, and this time there was an inexorability about it that made her afraid. The voice had grown more powerful, and bleaker. It no longer sounded like Flammas. It reminded her of the evil scrutator, the dumpy old woman. *It's time!*

'Time for what?' Ullii shuddered, but now she was afraid to disobey.

Time to begin your retribution. Time to set the world to rights.

'I don't understand.'

Look in your lattice Look for the knot of Chief Scrutator Ghorr.

She searched the lattice and found it at the very limit, a long way to the south. 'I can see it.'

Call him to you.

'I don't know how.'

Change his knot. You can do that.

'I don't dare. He'll attack me.'

He's looking for you. Change it so he knows where you are, and he will come.

'I'm afraid. He's a cruel man.'

Ah, but now you can give him what he wants, he'll do anything for you.

'What does he want?'

He wants Scrutator Flydd, Cryl-Nish Hlar and Irisis Stirm, and you can find them. You must, for they've all betrayed you.

'I don't know where they are.'

You can find them.

'Flydd and Irisis aren't in my lattice any more. Nish never has been.'

Ghorr will help you find them. Wherever Flydd is, there Nish will be. Call Ghorr to you.

Ullii reached into her lattice, traced out Ghorr's jagged, angry knot and began to tug at the ends. As soon as she did, a feeling of dread crept over her, a cold shivering of the flesh. He was a wicked man, even worse than Jal-Nish. Just looking closely at his knot made her shudder with terror.

He's not the worst. Cryl-Nish is the worst, for he pretends to be good.

Yes, she thought. Nish is worse, and I'll use these evil people to punish him. She plucked at the knot again, and all at once felt an alertness searching for her.

Withdraw.

She drew back, shivering, though the day was warm.

Reach out again, carefully. Don't alarm him and he won't strike at you like an enemy; just make him know that you're here.

Ullii reached out, touched the knot and turned it around, and as she did so she felt Ghorr thinking, *Aaahhhhhh! There she is.*

Withdraw and shut down the lattice. Go out into the open. See where that great tree has fallen and the wind has piled scrub and dead glass against it? Burn it.

'I've nothing to light it with.'

I will show you how.

The voice had her collect dry grass and crush it between two stones until it was a bone-dry powder. Then it led Ullii around the fallen tree, picking up sticks and putting them down again until she found two different kinds of wood, one hard, the other softer, that were just right. She rubbed the hard stick back and forth across the softer one, pressing firmly, with a steady motion that she could keep up for a long time.

Eventually Ullii was rewarded by smoking wood-dust that set the grass powder ablaze. Lighting a handful of twigs, she thrust it into her prepared nest of kindling, and within minutes the timber was roaring. She stood back and waited for Ghorr's air-floater to find her. The voice in her head had gone. Ullii felt that she had taken command of her life at last.

The air-floater landed just before dusk, well away from the fire, which had consumed the centre of the vast trunk and was now creeping along the length of it. Ghorr got out. Ullii remained standing in front of the blaze, in full view. Her gut tightened as he headed towards her, robes flapping, followed by Fusshte and the dumpy old woman with the balding head.

Ghorr could have picked Ullii up in one hand; he was her master in every respect. And yet, halfway to the fire, his stride faltered and he stopped, staring at her.

Ullii did not meet his gaze. She did not have the strength for that kind of contest, yet she knew the balance had changed between them. She might be little and weak, but she had called him, and he had come. It made all the difference. Furthermore, she knew he was remembering those strange things she had done in Nennifer, that no one else on Santhenar could have explained, much less duplicated.

'I knew I'd find you,' Ghorr said.

'I summoned you.'

He smiled at her use of that word. 'Did you really? Why?'

She caught her breath. 'My brother, Myllii, is *dead*.' The word sent a spasm through her bowel. 'Nish killed him. My baby is dead and that's Nish's fault too. He is evil and must be punished. I will find him for you.'

Chief Scrutator Ghorr's eyes narrowed. 'What about Ex-Scrutator Xervish Flydd, the greatest enemy of them all?'

'He lied to me, betrayed and abandoned me.'

'Will you find him for me?'

'I will find him,' said Ullii. 'Wherever he goes. There is nowhere on Santhenar that he can hide.'

'And Crafter Irisis Stirm?' He bared his hyena teeth.

After a considerable pause, for Irisis had not betrayed her as badly as the others had, she whispered, 'Her too.'

Ghorr raised his hands to the sky and roared in exultation. She had to stop her ears until he was done.

'I'll put it about that you're dead,' Ghorr said after some reflection. 'That way Flydd won't try to hide from your talent. Is that acceptable?'

'No one cares whether I live or die,' she said softly, sadly.

Ullii stood watching him, hating him almost as much as the others, but that did not matter. Nothing mattered but that she find the three who had tormented her, and bring them to justice.

'Well done, Scrutator T'Lisp,' Ghorr purred to the old

woman. 'I never would have believed it possible, even with your talent, but you've excelled yourself.'

T'Lisp smiled and caressed a bracelet on her arm, identical to the one that now strangled Ullii's wrist. She said nothing at all.

'It was a stroke of genius, trapping her with Myllii's bracelet,'

Ghorr went on. 'She didn't realise for a second.'

Ullii looked from one to the other, her guts crawling with horror as she understood what they'd done. They'd set the snare and she'd put her head right in it. From the instant she'd slipped on the bracelet she'd been under their control, just as they must have controlled Myllii before. It hadn't been Flammas in her head at all, but wicked Scrutator T'Lisp. Ullii hadn't taken charge of her life; she'd simply done their bidding.

'Oh yes,' said Ghorr, sneering at her distress, her futile struggle to wrench the bracelet off. 'You're mine, Ullii, just as your brother was, and there's nothing you can do about it.'

TWENTY-FIVE

The race to Gumby Marth had been plagued by breakdowns and mechanical problems that could not be allowed to delay the army. Where these could not be fixed at once, the affected clankers and their cargo of soldiers were left behind with an artificer, to catch up when they could. Troist fought furiously with the scrutator about it, for the general did not care to leave the least of his soldiers behind, but if they were to save Jal-Nish's army it had to be done. He had abandoned the idea of travelling at night, instead rousing the army before dawn so they could begin at first light, but still they were behind schedule.

Flydd spent most of his waking hours closeted in another twelve-legged clanker with the army's chief mancer, who went by the absurd name of Nutrid. He was an elongated stick of a man, quite meagre apart from an improbably round, quivering belly, like a jelly moulded in a bowl. His head was the shape of a hatchet, his eyes huge and glassy, and his fluted, constantly pursed lips had the look of an insect's proboscis.

Nish never spoke to Nutrid, nor even went close to his clanker. Mancers were particularly irritable when at work and Flydd's natural irascibility was growing as he recovered. Nish did glean, however, that the two mancers were trying to modify a cloaking spell to conceal the entire clanker fleet from sight and hearing, for the last day of travel. Camp gossip told him that Nutrid was dubious. Such spells had had limited success previously, and had never been attempted for an army as big as this one. The strain on the mancers, not to mention the field, would be prodigious.

Twice on the first day of travel, and three times on the second, the entire column had to be stopped so the two mancers could test their makeshift spell. During the first three stops, nothing happened, though Flydd was so exhausted afterwards he had to lie down.

On the fourth attempt, as Nish was climbing out of Troist's clanker, the air turned a shimmering green and every anthill within two hundred paces of the column exploded, deluging the army with red clay and little green ants. Nish was still picking them out of his hair an hour later – and so, unfortunately, was the cook from his cauldrons. Lunch reeked so pungently of crushed ants that not even the hardiest soldiers could force it down.

The mancers tried again at sunset, as camp was being set up for the evening. Nish was taking his turn on watch when a burst of purple flame set fire to a row of canvas privies, sending the occupants hopping, trousers about their ankles, in fear of their lives. Unfortunately the chief cook was one of them and took it personally. He locked himself in his supply clanker and not even Troist could coax him out in time to supervise the preparation of dinner. That task fell to the under-cook, a good assistant but a disorganised supervisor, and the food he served three hours late was worse than lunch had been. A grim Troist, whose belly was giving him more trouble than usual, ordered the chief cook to his post at once, and the troublesome mancers to get it right or desist forthwith, before the soldiers mutinied.

On the following morning, the fourth, a loud bang from Nutrid's clanker was followed by puffs of orange smoke and the two mancers hurling themselves out of the rear hatch.

'Another failure, surr?' called Nish, keeping a safe distance away. He couldn't resist getting a little of his own back. Whenever Nutrid and Flydd went to work, the wags among the soldiers had begun to snigger behind their hands.

'Nothing that compares to your gross and repeated incompetence,' Flydd said coldly, beating out acrid yellow fumes issuing from the seat of his pants. 'Now clear out!'

The fleet stopped in the middle of the fifth day, a good few leagues from their destination, to give Nutrid and Flydd one last chance to master their cloaking spell. The sky was clear and Troist was afraid of being spotted by flying spies.

Nish went for a walk across a plain covered in long grass, and studded with orange anthills twice the height of his head. He was thinking and fretting about Ullii when a hot breath of air stirred the hair on the back of his head. That was odd, for the cool breeze in his face was blowing from the sea.

He turned, frowning, to see an air lens form all around the fleet. The whole camp seemed to rise off the ground, and then the ground with it, as if the light had been bent upwards. A mirrored wall appeared, there came a shrill whistle, rising to a whip crack, Nish blinked and the fleet was gone. The plain seemed to be empty but for the anthills and the gently waving grass.

He paced back, a hollow core of fear in his belly. The army could not have vanished just like that, spell or no. But everyone had heard stories about squadrons of clankers overloading a node and disappearing into nothingness. Could Flydd and Nutrid – ridiculous name! – have taken too much from the node? From a hundred paces he could see nothing but grass and the depressions where the clankers had stood. They were simply gone. He raced back. Fifty paces away the air began to shimmer and he ran right over Flydd, who was lying flat on his back in the grass, observing the effectiveness of the cloaker. As Nish sprawled on the ground, looking up, the fleet appeared out of nowhere.

'I knew we could do it,' Flydd said cheerfully. 'Now we'll give the enemy something to put in their dispatches.'

It was mid-afternoon and they were going slowly over rough ground, in open forest that ran most of the way to their destination. After much tinkering the cloaker was working well, though Flydd was concerned about its massive drain on the field, not to mention Nutrid's ability to maintain the spell while Flydd was recuperating. The cloaker required constant attention and maintenance, and was a strain on everyone who lay within its umbrella, especially the clanker operators and Flydd himself. He was far from recovered and, after an hour supporting the cloaker spell, had to lie down for four hours.

The inside of the clanker was dark but for a conjured ghost light at Flydd's right shoulder. He was deep in a small, thick volume bound in maroon calf, its title inlaid in platinum leaf.

'What's that you're reading?' asked Nish. 'Yet another tome on the Secret Art?'

Over the past days, able to walk only with great discomfort, Flydd had gone through every volume in Nutrid's small library. He was in a fine humour, now that the spell was working.

Wordlessly, the scrutator lifted the volume. *The Great Tales, 23: The Tale of the Mirror.* No chronicler's name was listed.

'Reading a story!' Nish said with mock sarcasm. 'You really are relaxed.'

'Every human should know the Great Tales,' Flydd said pompously. 'They are the very foundation of the Histories.'

'You're old enough to be in them!'

'Choose your words with care, Nish,' growled the scrutator. 'I'm no older than I look.'

'Two hundred and fifty?' Nish ducked out of the way as Flydd swatted at him.

'I'm sixty-four. A good, round age. An important number too, if you care for such things.'

'Only sixty-four?' Nish said seriously. 'I thought you mancers could extend your life forever.'

'This one has been hard enough; don't inflict another on me.'

'But didn't some of the great mancers live for a thousand years?' Nish bit his tongue, in case Flydd took offence. Perhaps he felt himself to be a great mancer.

Flydd chuckled at Nish's embarrassment. 'Only two, to my knowledge. Extending one's life is a hazardous process, and more mancers have died in the attempt than have survived it. Mendark, the long-time magister of Thurkad, did it many times but he was a very great mancer, the like of whom we will not see again. And in the end he died, as we all must. Yggur was also long lived, but in his case it was natural longevity: no one knows why. All those who extended their lives, male or female, were motivated by greed. They wanted what only the other human species – Aachim, Faellem and Charon – had a right to. I've many failings, Nish, but greed isn't one of them.' He pointedly took up his book.

'What part are you up to?'

Flydd sighed, but laid the book aside. 'I *was* reading the final section of the tale, where Rulke the Charon opened a gate between the worlds and tried to bring the remnant of his people to Santhenar.'

'I . . . don't recall that,' said Nish.

'I thought you knew the Great Tales well?' Flydd's continuous eyebrow formed a knot in the middle of his forehead.

'I thought I did.'

'Well, to cut this story to its basics, just a hundred Charon survived the void and the taking of Aachan, many thousands of years ago. The Hundred, they were called, but for some reason they could not reproduce on that world. It seemed as though they would live forever, but theirs was an increasingly bitter, lonely existence, as one by one they became infertile. The Charon were on a one-way road to extinction.

'To save them, Rulke brought the handful of fertile ones through the gate to Santhenar. But Faelamor, the leader of the Faellem, who had always feared the Charon, opened a gate into the void and brought forth several thranx, intelligent winged creatures akin to lyrinx . . . I think the lyrinx may have flesh-formed themselves to resemble thranx, actually.' He reflected on that for a moment, before continuing. 'While Rulke struggled with Faelamor's illusions the thranx slew the Charon, every fertile one. From that moment, Rulke's species

279

was doomed. Noble Rulke was killed soon after, and the remainder of the Hundred went back to the void to die.'

'I'm surprised you don't know that part of the story,' Flydd concluded. 'It is, to my mind, the greatest tragedy in all the Histories, and the most poignant tale. Not even the fall of Tar Gaarn can compare to it.'

'I've heard many of the tales told, though not by a master chronicler or teller.'

'There aren't many left, since the College of the Histories at Chanthed was sacked by the lyrinx. Most of the masters and students were eaten, and deservedly so, for their scandalous lack of talent.' He smiled – a joke! Flydd was almost back to his normal, crotchety self. 'I prefer to read the Tales as set down by the masters of old. They're closer to the truth—' He broke off, as if censoring a thought.

'I didn't know there was a College of the Histories,' said Nish.

Flydd raised the left side of that famous eyebrow. 'What did they teach you, lad? The college was there for thousands of years. Ah, but it was sacked before you were born – the beginning of the end for all Meldorin. After that it was only a matter of time until the whole of Meldorin was lost, even ancient Thurkad. The city fought bravely and long, a noble failure that might have made another Great Tale, were there any master chroniclers to tell it.'

'But there *are* master chroniclers,' said Nish. 'My mother studied under one for a while.'

'Crass amateurs compared to those of olden times, such as Llian of Chanthed, who made the twenty-third Great Tale. This one!' Flydd lifted the book and began turning the pages.

'Llian the Liar!' cried Nish, recalling his school lessons. 'The biggest cheat in all the Histories. His tale was a fraud. The scrutators had it rewritten a long time ago. My father told me so . . .' He trailed off. 'What's the matter?'

'I can't talk about what the scrutators may or may not have done, Nish. You know that.'

'You said they were corrupt and you were going to bring them down.'

'And I plan to, but I still can't betray my oath of secrecy.'

'But you told me about the Num—'

Flydd shoved a gnarled fist into Nish's mouth. 'Don't ever mention that name!'

'Why not?'

'I can't think how I was indiscreet enough to tell you,' muttered Flydd. 'The infection must have turned my wits. All I can say is, learn to think for yourself.'

He took up the book again. The pages turned steadily. Nish had a thousand questions, but he did not suppose that Flydd would answer them. How had the Council of Scrutators come to hold more power than the generals and the leaders of nations? Why had they censored the Histories?

They went without a break until just before sunset, when the leading clankers stopped on the sloping top of a square hill. Higher hills could be seen in all directions, clothed in forest.

The rear hatch was jerked open. Troist stood there with a rolled map under one arm. Climbing in, he spread it on the table in front of Flydd.

'My scouts report that Jal-Nish's army is camped in the valley of Gumby Marth, two-thirds of a league away across those rugged ridges to the north.' He indicated the location on his map.

Nish's stomach cramped at the thought of meeting his father again.

'That's not all, is it, General?' said Flydd.

'The scouts report that there's not a single lyrinx to be found, and no one has the faintest idea where they've got to.'

'Maybe they don't want to fight after all,' said Nish.

'I smell a trap,' Flydd replied, bending over the map. 'It's rugged country between here and there.'

'More than rugged, the scouts tell me,' said Troist. 'It's impassable to clankers and mounted men alike. Foot soldiers could struggle through, though the upper parts of the valley are bounded by cliffs with few paths down, and none are safe. We can't go that way. We'll have to march west, this way, for several leagues, to find a way into the valley. We'll begin at first light, Scrutator. With luck we should reach the army by this time tomorrow.'

'Let's hope we're in time,' said Flydd. 'Make ready for war, General, then see everyone gets a good night's rest. For some, maybe most of us, it could be our last. Especially if . . .'

'What is it?' said Troist. 'You don't mean to tell me . . .'

'I don't think we can maintain the cloaker much longer. And going after a superior enemy without it will be suicide.'

TWENTY-SIX

When the camp had been set up, the lines of sentries had gone to their watches and all was cloaked and quiet, everyone turned gratefully to their tents. No one could remember when they'd last had a full night's sleep. Soon the clearing echoed to the gentle snores of thousands. Even Flydd was abed.

Nish was not. His father was down in Gumby Marth at the head of the army, and Nish had been brooding about him for weeks. Jal-Nish was the great obstacle in his life and Nish was dreading meeting him again, as surely he would tomorrow.

It was still hot in the clanker, and Flydd was snoring like a hog. Nish felt claustrophobic and oppressed. An insomniac at the best of times, he soon gave up hope of getting a wink of sleep, for his thoughts were racing. Putting a cloak under his arm, he slipped out of the rear hatch. Walking helped him to think and he had a lot of thinking to do. It was pleasantly cool outside though it might grow chilly later on.

He paced along the lines of clankers, keeping inside the envelope of the cloaker. What did Jal-Nish hope to achieve, bringing the army into country like this? The enemy could be anywhere. He must have some plan – his father always did – but Nish could not imagine what.

Nish saw few people, for the soldiers were in their tents sleeping, or trying to, while the sentries were well out from the camp. Flydd had worked the cloaker so that wisps of glamour clung to everyone as they moved. If the enemy came upon a sentry, even half a league from the camp, he would see just a foggy blur.

Reaching the end of the lines of clankers, Nish kept going. Being a private person, he'd found the past days, surrounded by thousands of people day and night, especially confining. He longed for a little solitude, even if only for a few minutes.

Pushing through the cloaker envelope, he felt a moment of unreality when everything inverted, another when he looked back and the entire army was gone. Enveloped in his own little wisp of cloaker, he walked across the few hundred spans of open grassland to the surrounding forest. It had already been checked for signs of the enemy but there had been none.

Just before he reached the edge, something fluttered overhead. It was just an owl, but Nish had a premonition of utter, bloody disaster. Hunching down against the bole of a tree, he tried to shrug it off. Surely it was just a fancy to do with meeting his father again. He'd thought he was free of Jal-Nish a long time ago – Nish remembered talking to Minis about it last spring, when Minis had been so admiring of him.

What a joke that now seemed. He was just as trapped as Minis, and Jal-Nish was less than an hour away, across the rugged ridges beyond the forest. Nish's guts churned. He looked back to the lines of clankers but saw not a glimmer of candlelight. The cloaker was still working, at least. He slipped into the forest, needing to walk, and soon realised that he must have passed through the inner line of sentries without being noticed.

The moon was a few days off full but the forest was dense here, the shadows deep beneath the trees. Nish had learned to move quietly of late. His feet made just the faintest crackle on fallen leaves. Hitting upon a winding path through the trees, probably a deer or bear trail, he ghosted along the edge where there was less danger of being seen.

On the other side of the patch of forest he emerged into an open area of short grass and grey rock, covered with an array of pinnacles roughly the size of termite mounds. Gleaming whitely in the moonlight, it looked like a field of standing stones, but why had they been assembled here, of all places? He scanned the sky; not a cloud. The night was absolutely still. Curious, Nish gathered the cloak about him and, keeping his head low, slid like a shadow across the grass.

Reaching the first pinnacle, he ducked behind it. It wasn't a standing stone at all, but a long vertical blade of limestone formed by the elements. Its top has been etched by rain into a series of steeples with fluted, razor-sharp edges. Nish wandered along the shadowed side, feeling the smooth rock with his fingers.

He had just passed around the edge when he heard the faint but distinctive creak of a crossbow being wound back. As Nish threw himself into the shadows, a bolt smashed right through the blade of stone above his head. He scampered the other way, using all the cover he could, then ran for his life. The guard must be jumpy, to fire without knowing what he was shooting at. The glamour still covered Nish but his shadow had given him away.

There was shouting behind him, and answers to left and right, but Nish did not call out his name. It occurred to him, rather belatedly, that he should not have left the camp. He would get a severe dressing down from Flydd and Troist if he revealed himself, to say nothing of the risk of being shot by an over-anxious sentry. Better to wait until the guards had settled down, then sneak back in. On second thought, Troist's well-drilled guards would stay alert all watch. He decided to circle around and approach the camp from the other side.

He concentrated on moving with absolute stealth and, as he progressed, silence settled around him. He was past the last line of guards. Beyond the pinnacle field he encountered another patch of forest, after which Nish found himself crossing a rugged expanse of grey limestone etched into mounds and sinkholes, grey ridges only a few spans high and canyons little deeper. Shortly that developed into another pinnacle field, much more extensive than the first.

He'd gone further than he'd planned. Beyond, Nish knew from Troist's map, a steep escarpment ramped down to the broad oval box-valley of Gumby Marth, where Jal-Nish's army was camped. On the far side, white peaks rose up equally steep and sharp, while the upper end of the valley was defended by a sheer limestone cliff.

He tried to work out his position. Gumby Marth narrowed to a rocky neck halfway down, there falling sharply away before broadening out in the direction of Gnulp Landing. The lyrinx could not come through the neck without being seen. They might fly in, but lyrinx in the air were vulnerable to archers and spear-throwers, unless they came at night, and Jal-Nish would be sure to have his watch-fires burning.

On the other hand, if they held the neck of Gumby Marth they could bottle up Jal-Nish's army and starve them out. Why had his father brought his army into such a perilous battleground? Surely he was planning a trap of his own. He must have some secret weapon or strategy, but what could it be?

The precipice could be no more than ten minutes away. So near, and if Nish went to the edge he would see the camp fires and, in this moonlight, even the tents and clankers, far below. And, Nish rationalised, if Troist did catch him sneaking into camp, having information about Jal-Nish's forces might get him out of trouble. I'll do it, he thought. I'll just slip across to the edge, have a quick look and go back.

The moon told him that it was after nine o'clock. He could be back in his hammock by ten. Edging through the rows of pinnacles, he found himself in a narrow defile where the light did not penetrate. It was so dark that it was eerie. As he felt his way along, imagining what might be lurking in those thousands of narrow walkways, his heart began to pound. Nish's outstretched hand touched an edge so sharp that it slid through the skin. He drew back, muffling a yelp. As he licked his fingers, the hairs on the back of his neck came erect.

Nish looked around. It felt as if someone was watching him, though that did not make sense. The passage between the pinnacles was barely wide enough for his shoulders. He crept back, hands outstretched like a sleepwalker, but encountered only rock. If someone had been following him, they were gone. He could not be seen from above – nothing heavier than a sparrow could have perched on those razor-topped edges.

Shrugging the unease away, he kept going and eventually found a way through the maze to the other side. Only as he emerged onto an expanse of white rock, almost glowing in the bright moonlight, did the feeling of being watched dissipate. Making it to the edge unscathed, he looked down on the oval of Gumby Marth, hundreds of spans below. Countless watch-fires blazed on this side, up to his right, marking out the rectangular pattern of the army camp. The shapes of the tents were clearly visible, as well as the camouflaged outlines of the clankers. Nish was looking along the length of the cliff when his eye caught a dark, fluttering shape, halfway down.

A lyrinx, spying on Jal-Nish's army! Did that mean the attack was imminent? Now what was he supposed to do? Nish's initial impulse was to go back though, if the enemy were about to attack, the warning would come too late. Troist's army was still a day's march away.

He leaned out as far as he dared, caught another brief glimpse of that moving form, then lost it. It seemed too big to be a man, and the wrong shape. It had to be the enemy, and his duty was horribly clear – he must climb down the cliff, if he could without killing himself, and take the warning to his father.

At that thought, Nish's heart began to pound like a thresh-ing machine. Was there any other way? Even if he screamed out a warning at the top of his voice, it would not carry as far as the camp. No; he had to go down.

The escarpment consisted of a series of cliffs broken by rock outcrops only marginally less steep. After some search-ing along the edge, he discovered what appeared to be a goat track heading down, though in the moonlight he would be easily spotted against the pale rock.

Taking off the black cloak, he tied it around his waist and set off, hanging on with hands, feet and knees. It was a long, difficult climb, dangerous, too, for the moonlight played tricks. Once he was about to step on what seemed solid rock, only to realise that there was nothing underneath his foot but empty air.

After a good interval of heart-in-the-mouth scrambling, Nish was creeping down a precipitous defile, anxiously watching a small cloud that had covered the moon, and hoping he could get to the bottom before it shone out again. As he reached the base of a knob of white rock shaped like a brain impaled on a stick, a guard stepped out in front of him and levelled his spear. The man was huge: as high and wide as a door, with a cape that stretched out behind him in the updraught.

Nish was not armed. Not intending to leave the camp, he'd left his weapon in the clanker. The soldier jerked his spear and Nish thought it was going right through his belly.

'I'm not a spy!' he gasped.

'Hands in the air!'

Nish complied and the moon shone full on his face. There was a long pause, then an astonished cry: 'Well, blow me if it isn't Cryl-Nish Hlar, and hardly changed! What the blazes are you doing here?'

The soldier's face was in shadow. Nish had no idea who he was, though the nasal tones were vaguely familiar, and the man had an Einunar accent.

'Should I know you?' he said hesitantly.

'You certainly should.' The soldier emitted a booming bellow of a laugh. 'We used to play together when we were little, Cry-Nish.'

The soldier came out of the shadow. He had a big square head, dark curly hair and a grin that crinkled one corner of his mouth. Nish stared at him. Memory stirred. 'Xabbier? Xabbier Frou?'

'At your service.' He put out a hand the size of a lobster.

Nish clasped it in both of his, remembering Xabbier fondly: a big, rough but kindly boy, always breaking things and being punished for it, which he'd shrugged off with that endearing grin. He'd more than once rescued Nish from schoolyard bullies who'd picked on him because of his father's reputation. 'How did you get here? I haven't seen you since I was . . . nine or ten, I suppose. It's good to see you, Xabbier.'

'And you, Cryl-Nish. I worked with my father for a while, lawyering, and hated every moment of it. One day I walked out and joined the army. It's a bloody life, but better than being a poxy notary. I ended up in a unit that your father took to the manufactory near Tiksi, and after that I came west on one of the air-floaters.'

'And now you're a guard for *my* father.' Try as he might to repress it, there was the faintest hint of scorn, that Xabbier should have ended up a common soldier.

Xabbier was not easily slighted. He gave Nish a cheerful clap on the back that almost drove shards of backbone into his lungs. 'I'm a lieutenant now, and will be made captain if we survive the coming battle.' He frowned at that thought, then grinned. 'Which of course we must. I like to take my turn at sentry duty. Prefer the air out here to the fug in the command tents.'

Not to mention the company of my father, Nish thought.

Xabbier scanned the slope, up and down. Nish stood beside him, thinking about his childhood. They had been friends until Xabbier's mother had died in childbirth and his father moved to another town.

Seeing nothing, the soldier turned back to Nish. 'What are you doing here, Cryl-Nish, creeping about like a spy? You're not a spy, are you?' Xabbier gave Nish a troubled look. 'I know what your father did to you, and there's not a man in this army agrees with him. I won't speak a word against him, out of respect for you, but my men obey him out of sheer terror.' He shook his head.

'I was at the top of the cliff, looking over, and I saw a moving shadow halfway down. I thought it was the enemy, spying on the army . . .' It occurred to Nish that a man as large as Xabbier, with a cape blowing out behind him like a wing, might easily have been mistaken for a lyrinx in this light.

'Where?' said Xabbier. 'And when was that?'

'That way.' Nish pointed to the right. 'Nearly an hour ago.'

Xabbier relaxed. 'It was probably me, but I'll take a look,

just in case.' He fingered a coiled horn hanging from his belt, but let it be.

They did not find anything. 'It must have been me you saw,' said Xabbier. He glanced at Nish. 'I was glad to hear you'd escaped with the scrutator. He's a good man, but . . . But Nish, why are you here?'

Nish chose his words carefully. Though Troist's army had come to aid this one, he did not have leave to reveal that secret. 'I can see what you're thinking, Xabbier. I'm held to be a traitor and now I've been found spying . . .' Though Xabbier's manner was friendly, Nish knew the soldier would not shirk his duty, if it came to it. 'Ever since my father took command, I've been afraid he was leading the army into a trap. I had to find out.' Though that was the truth as far as it went, to Nish's ears it sounded unconvincing.

Two meaty hands took him by the shoulders, and Xabbier turned Nish so that the moon lit his face again. 'I'm troubled, Cryl-Nish. I should turn you in – my life is forfeit if I don't. Yet I still feel I know you, and I don't believe you'd lie to me. And the people's scrutator, Xervish Flydd, is said to hold you in high regard. Even the slaves on the hauling teams spoke about it. In our army, no man is held in greater respect than Xervish Flydd.'

'Even though he's an outlaw and a non-citizen, cast down from the Council of Scrutators and condemned?'

'Even so,' said Xabbier. 'Should Scrutator Flydd appear at our head tomorrow, every man in this army would follow him. And you're his man, Cryl-Nish, so I'll risk my life on you and let you go. Don't let me down.'

'Thank you, Xabbier,' Nish said. 'If I can do anything for you—'

'You can tell me your story, one day. And when the war's over, I'll tell it to my children. I've often heard tales about you, these past six months, and wondered how you were getting on. I was heartbroken when we left all those years ago. After my mother died, losing my best friend was more than I could bear.'

'I'm sorry,' said Nish. He'd made new friends quickly, as children did at that age. 'It's funny how things turn out, Xabbier. I've done everything possible to keep out of the army. I was sure I'd be sent to the front-lines and be eaten in the first hour. Yet in the last six months I've lived a more dangerous life than most soldiers would.'

'You'd better go, Cryl-Nish.'

Just then the shrubbery rustled a few spans away and another sentry appeared. 'It's been a long watch, Xabbier. I'll be glad – who the blazes is this?'

Xabbier swore under his breath and his grip tightened on Nish's arm. Nish cursed too. There was no way Xabbier could let him go now.

'Look who I found,' said Xabbier. 'Cryl-Nish Hlar, no less.'

'Jal-Nish *will* be pleased,' the other soldier purred. 'Let's hope he shows his appreciation. I'll take him down if you like.'

No! Nish thought, for the soldier was motivated either by greed or malice.

'I'll do it,' Xabbier said curtly. 'My watch is over and you've got an hour to go. Come with me, Cryl-Nish.'

He led Nish down the steep track, shortly encountering a sentry coming up to relieve him. They spoke for a minute or two and Xabbier continued.

Nish wasn't ready to meet his father, and could never be. What can I say to him? he thought despairingly. And what would Jal-Nish do to him this time?

'You're troubled, Cryl-Nish,' said Xabbier as they reached the bottom and turned towards the camp.

'You know what my father is like. Imagine—'

'I can't imagine.' Xabbier put an arm across Nish's shoulders. 'But my thoughts, my hopes, go with you. I'm sorry, Cryl-Nish. If I could have prevented this I would have, but once you were seen there was no choice.'

'I understand duty,' Nish said hollowly.

'I'll take you up to his tent.'

As the lieutenant led him up the slope of Gumby Marth,

through row after row of tents, Nish fought a desperate urge to run. That would be the act of a coward. Besides, he'd never get away from Xabbier.

Xabbier ushered him through a dozen guards surrounding a tent the size of a cottage, lifted the flap and stepped through into an anteroom. Light shone from an open flap ahead. Jal-Nish was alone, his back to them, bent over a table covered in retorts, alembics and a variety of other types of alchymical apparatus. Nish's mouth went dry. He had never been able to stand up to his father.

Xabbier cleared his throat. Jal-Nish turned and his head jerked up as he saw his son standing before him. The loose mask shifted on his face, revealing part of the scarred and writhen flesh beneath. Jal-Nish tossed his head and the shining platinum face-cover settled back in place.

'Well, Lieutenant?' he said to Xabbier.

'I found him on my watch, surr, halfway down the escarpment. He thought he saw—'

'He can tell me himself. Leave us, Lieutenant. Wait outside for my orders. Don't allow anyone in!'

Once Xabbier had gone, Jal-Nish drew the tent flaps closed with his one hand. Returning to Nish, he stood chest to chest. 'I heard you escaped with Flydd. He's behind this, I suppose?'

Nish had been expecting that question. 'Flydd's dead,' he lied.

'Dead? How?'

'An injury he took in the escape turned bad and he got blood poisoning. There was nothing I could do to save him.'

'A pity,' Jal-Nish said indifferently. 'I wanted to see him suffer, first. And you, Cryl-Nish – what do you want?'

Panicky and unable to think clearly, Nish said the first thing that came into his head. 'I want to be free of *you*, Father. Forever!'

'What?' Jal-Nish looked disconcerted.

'You've ruined my life. Since I was three years old I've slaved to please you, but not once did you praise me or show you cared in any way. Not once did you comfort me, when I was little and had those awful nightmares . . .'

Jal-Nish opened his mouth, beneath the mask. 'I—'

'I haven't finished!' Nish said desperately, and, to his surprise, Jal-Nish allowed him to go on.

'Say it, whatever it is,' he said, smiling malevolently.

'I know I've done stupid things, but I've suffered for them. I've also done brave deeds, and clever ones, and not had a word of acknowledgment from you. That used to hurt me more than you can ever know, but it no longer matters. Do you know why? Because I no longer care! You mean nothing to me. I used to pity Tiaan because she had no father. Now I envy her, because no father at all would be better than one like you.'

Oddly, considering his heartless denunciation of his son, this rejection seemed to strike Jal-Nish to the core, but Nish ploughed on.

'I don't know what you wanted from life, or whether you're happy now, but I know one thing. As a father, you were a miserable failure and I'm happy to go to my death if it means I'll never see you again.'

Jal-Nish lurched backwards into the table and overbalanced. As he fell, the back of his head caught on the edge of the table, flipping the platinum helm off.

Jal-Nish looked up and Nish almost vomited. He well remembered the ruin of his father's face after the lyrinx attack, but that was nothing to what he saw now. The claws had torn three jagged gouges from ear to mouth, under which the flesh had grown back in ugly lumps and depressions. The scars were purple and blistered with pus-filled boils that even after three-quarters of a year had not healed. His left eye was a purple socket filled with bulging veins the size of earthworms, his once proud nose a crusted hole that could have accommodated a lemon. The mouth, a twisted ruin that would no longer close, leaked stringy green saliva with every breath.

Jal-Nish rose, but did not bother with the helmet. He approached his son. Nish tried to back away but Jal-Nish's hand caught his jaw in a crushing grip.

'I too had a father, Cryl-Nish, and if you think I'm a bad one, he's the reason for it. He taught me all I know. He hated me because my mother died giving birth to me. He loathed me because I was clever and he was not. He *despised* me because I was handsome and he was a hideous little weasel. You remember that, Nish? I was handsome, wasn't I?' His lips contorted in the most nauseating travesty of a smile Nish had ever seen.

Nish swallowed bile, wanting to look away but held fast by fingers as strong as steel. 'You were, Father. I envied you your looks and, yes, your easy charm.'

'He tormented me, Cryl-Nish. Every day for fourteen years he beat me black and blue. Before I was a grown man, I'd suffered more horrors than the soldiers in this army have in all their service. He was a small-minded man who wanted to be great, and failed, and ever after forced me into the mould he could not fill. I hated him and all he stood for, yet he's twenty years in his grave and still I have to drive myself higher, though every success only causes more pain. It would not have been enough for him, so it cannot satisfy me. I must be great.'

'But you *are* great,' Nish muttered. 'A scrutator, no less. One of the mighty who control the world.'

'It can never be enough until there's nothing left to achieve, because I must have it all.'

'And then?'

Jal-Nish gave another of those ghastly smiles and green crusts flaked off his lower lip. 'There'll come a time when I've finally beaten him. That's what keeps me going, even in this hideous state.' He thrust his face at Nish and Nish recoiled. 'You can't bear to look at me, though it was you who made me this way. I begged you to let me die, Cryl-Nish – remember? After the lyrinx tore me apart I pleaded for death, but you would not give it me. You had to save my life, so I could *suffer* ever after.'

'I couldn't let you die,' whispered Nish, recalling that horror up on the icy plateau. 'Despite everything, I couldn't . . .'

'You made me this way,' Jal-Nish thrust one finger into the yellow-green cavity where his nose had been. 'You and that cur Irisis.'

'But there must be a way, with the Secret Art, to restore you to what you once were.'

'Do you think I haven't sought for it? There is no way. Even with the alchymical power I now have, I can't repair what you did to me.'

'Then what good is seeking more power?'

'Revenge!' hissed Jal-Nish. 'It's the one pleasure I have left.'

'But, Mother—' Nish began, looking anywhere but at that ghastly face.

Jal-Nish caught his son by the shirt and pulled him close. He was ferociously strong. 'Your mother has cast me aside. She always looked down on me; now she can't stand the sight of me. Though I'm scrutator and will soon be elevated to the Council, I'm no more use to her.'

'No!' Nish whispered. 'Not Mother.'

'All my life, women have betrayed me. My mother died, abandoning me to the monster. My wife has repudiated me. Irisis humiliated me and performed this butchery on me, from which I've not had a moment without pain since. Tiaan, by her treachery, has torn down everything I worked so hard for. Let me tell you this, Cryl-Nish! When I'm Chief of the Council of Scrutators I'll put them in their place. Women will go where they belong – to the breeding factories.'

'You're a monster,' cried Nish.

Jal-Nish gave him a pus-smeared smile. 'And who created me?'

'I'll hear no more of this.' Nish backed away. 'I'm leaving, Father. I repudiate you. You'll never see me again.'

'You're not going anywhere, Son. Now that you've come back, I see something in you I can use. You're mine and ever will be, and just to make sure—'

Nish leapt for the flap of the tent but Jal-Nish hauled him back. Hypnotised by that face, Nish could not defy him.

Jal-Nish dragged a small rosewood chest out from

underneath the table. The timber had a sweet, spicy fragrance. Turning the key, he lifted the lid. 'Bend over the chest!'

Nish looked in. The inside of the chest was as black as the void, and a familiar humming set his teeth on edge. Jal-Nish flipped back a swatch of ebony velvet and the light from beneath was so dazzling that Nish stumbled backwards.

His father took hold of Nish's right hand and pulled it down into the box. It struck something both hot and cold, hard yet yielding, metal yet liquid. Nish cried out and tried to pull away but his hand would not move. Jal-Nish took Nish's left hand, forced it into the box and he felt the same sensations there.

Nish's hands clenched around, or within, those uncanny objects, while surges of force boiled through him. His vision inverted: black became white; colours turned into their opposites. He saw the bones of his father's arm through the flesh. He saw right through the walls of the tent, the iron scales of nearby clankers, the rocks of the cliff face. He saw the world under Jal-Nish's rule: cities burning; people crowded into workhouses worse than the one in the refugee camp, fetters on their ankles; the guards lashing them with whips. He saw everything, and *nothing*.

Jal-Nish was no longer holding him down. He was standing at the table, holding high a flask that contained a red, fuming liquid and reciting some kind of rhyming spell. Nish tried to get away but his hands were stuck fast.

His father began another rhyme – a series of alchymical spells, Nish assumed. He recognised his name and several other repeated words: *servant, slave, mine*. Jal-Nish must be casting a spell of control or domination, but Nish, lacking any talent for the Art, could not tell more than that.

His hands grew increasingly painful. Nish resisted until his overstrained mind rebelled and he collapsed face-first into the chest.

Jal-Nish cursed under his breath, pressed Nish's hands more firmly into the globes and began the spell again. The sensation faded. Nish found himself on his knees, bent over the chest. He pulled his hands free. The objects rippled like balls of quicksilver then went solid again, and he understood what they were: the distilled tears created by the destruction of the Snizort node. Jal-Nish had been the man in the air-floater, the one who had taken the tears and left that pit full of smouldering corpses.

'Damnation!' cried Jal-Nish, beginning the spell for the third time. 'Why isn't it taking?' He poured liquids from one flask to a second, then a third. Yellow clouds belched up around him. 'Ah, that's better. Drink this!'

He threw Nish over onto his back and forced the contents of a small glass phial down his throat. It burned all the way.

'What have you done to me?' whispered Nish. His throat had the texture of sandpaper.

'I have *woken* you, Cryl-Nish!'

'What do you mean? Woken me *to what*?'

'Not the Art, if that's what you're hoping. You don't have the talent, nor can you acquire it – yet another way that you're less of a man than me.'

'Then what?' Nish screamed, the sound tearing at his tender throat.

'You'll see horrors no one has ever seen before. You'll hear what has previously been unheard. And you'll feel – well, I leave that to you to discover. The gift of the tears is not pre-dictable. But you'll know what it is like to suffer. You will know what it is like to be your father, as you stand beside me for the rest of your life.'

'I have no father,' Nish mumbled.

'You had that opportunity, but you made the wrong choice; you held me to this existence and now I hold you to me. You were right, Son.' The lips writhed as Jal-Nish fought to form the words that had once come so easily to him. 'No father *would* be better than the one I've become. But I *am* your father, and ever will be, and nothing you say or do can change that. Be sure that you'll spend your life ruing it for, once the spell sets, you'll have no choice in the matter. You'll serve me all your remaining days.'

Nish rose, holding his hands up before his face. They burned like icy fire, yet they were unmarked. The pit of his stomach tingled and he felt that a long-dormant bud inside him had opened. He shuddered to think what the tears had done to him.

'You're a monster, Father. The outside simply reflects what is within you, and I'll bring you down if it takes me all my life.'

'You won't, Cryl-Nish, because you're a blunderer, a failure and a fool. You're not my equal in any respect, and never can be. I often wonder how I came to have a son as unworthy as you, if, indeed, you *are* my son!' He bellowed the last words so that the whole camp might have heard. 'Lieutenant!'

Xabbier appeared smartly, and from the look in his eyes he'd heard all that had gone on. 'Yes, Scrutator Hlar?'

'Take Cryl-Nish to the punishment cells and lock him in. No one must go near him for four hours, until . . .'

'Yes?' said Xabbier.

'Never mind. Lock him up tight until the morning, Lieutenant.'

Jal-Nish saluted Nish with the platinum mask. An aura, shaped like a horde of jackals, streamed and snapped around him. Shuddering, Nish allowed himself to be led away. The mask snapped back over his father's head.

PART THREE

TESSERACT

TWENTY-SEVEN

Those Aachim not engaged in moving constructs, or travelling to the southern camp inside them, were busy on a great memorial to their dead. The bodies had been recovered and buried as soon as the battle was over. In the summer heat they had to be, though it grieved the Aachim deeply to lay their fallen in alien soil.

Tiaan saw little of the construction, apart from a day on which she spent hours hauling stone with the construct, but it showed the importance they placed on the memorial.

She now lived in fear of the amplimet. Though essential for her survival, as much as for the Aachim's, Ghaenis's fate had shown her how capricious it was. It might allow her another day, a week, a month, but eventually it would strike her down. If it chose to replace her with a more powerful servant, all it had to do was let the power flow after she'd tried to cut it off.

The Aachim had experimented with a number of node-sharing devices before settling on a silver helm, like three-quarters of a globe, whose inside and outside were polished to mirror smoothness. The outside was studded with rubies and garnets which had been set in swirling patterns into perforations in the silver. The inside was plain metal, through which the tips of some of the crystals could be seen, scattered like stars in the evening sky.

Tirior placed the helm on Tiaan's head but it proved too large, for Aachim had bigger heads than old humans. A leather headband was fitted and adjusted until the helm sat perfectly.

Subsequently the crystals were *charged*, not with the amplimet but via a device the like of which Tiaan had never seen before: a plain cube of black metal whose sides were about the length of Tiaan's forearm. The inside was as black as a pit. The helm was placed within, pushed towards the back wall, and promptly vanished.

It was not, as far as Tiaan could tell, an illusion or stage magician's trick. The helm, though solid metal, was no longer in the box. After a few minutes, a ruby flash came from within. Tirior reached in, her arm now disappearing to the shoulder, and withdrew the helm. The rubies and garnets were lit up, though the glow faded as the helm was brought into the light.

The instant Tirior placed the helm on Tiaan's head, the headache and the dull feelings vanished. Someone handed her the wrapped amplimet. As she unfolded the platinum sheet, thread-like silvery rays streamed out from the crystal in all directions and she saw something impossible: five other cubes were attached to the black box in ways that could not exist. It was a four-dimensional cube: a tesseract.

'I feel dizzy.' Tiaan closed her eyes. Artisans had gone mad trying to see into the fourth dimension. She swayed in the chair and Thyzzea steadied her.

'Is that better?' said Urien, standing over her.

Tiaan rubbed her eyes but the strange image was gone, the black box just a simple box again. 'I . . . think so. It'll take time to get used to it. Just give me a few minutes.'

Thyzzea gave her a mug of water and Tiaan drank it in one gulp. Even sitting down, her knees felt shaky. 'I'm ready to try.'

Back in the construct, the amplimet was installed in its socket. Tiaan put the helm on her head and again, just for a few seconds, saw the creeping, impossible shapes of the fourth dimension. As she turned her head, fields swirled and ebbed all over the place, and all were brilliantly clear. It unnerved her – there was too much to take in.

'Time is precious, Artisan,' said Vithis from behind.

She drew power from the nearest field, attempting to hold its image while she attempted a second. Power flowed from both, and both fields stayed in her mind. She looked for a third and took power from it as well, then a fourth and fifth. It was like a miracle.

'It's ready,' Tiaan said.

Tirior gave the signal and the construct crept forwards. Before the rope became taut, the construct following them began to move, then the one after that. Tiaan could see the distortions they made in the field, and now they did not have to be towed. Enough power flowed down the cables for them to propel themselves.

Looking back to the shooter's turret, Tiaan could see the raw emotion on Vithis's face. It was going to work after all.

Progress was slow at first. With so many machines attached by lines to the leading construct, a moment's inattention could damage dozens of them. Nonetheless, by midnight she'd done four trips. Another two hundred and forty constructs had been transported safely to the new field. On each return trip she ferried back supplies brought from the main camp at Gospett.

A day later the work had become routine. The best part of three hundred constructs could be moved in a day. Of the eleven thousand that had come through the gate, about six thousand had come to Snizort, though five hundred had been damaged in battle and must be abandoned. Vithis did this with great reluctance – the Aachim did not care for their constructs to be examined by allies or foes – but could do no more than break the controlling mechanisms to disable them.

Tiaan was too worn out to sit up, much less eat, and the operation would take at least seventeen more days, even if all went perfectly. Despite the helm, she did not see how she was going to survive it.

Vithis kept Minis away, for which Tiaan was thankful. He was a problem that had no solution.

The following morning, Thyzzea replaced Vithis in the

construct and for ten days all went well. On the morning of the eleventh, Tiaan woke so weak that she could hardly get out of bed. She felt eroded inside. The channelled power seemed to be eating away at her, as it had in Kalissin. She had lost all the weight gained in Nyriandiol, and more.

It made no difference to Vithis. She was carried to the construct and strapped into her seat. Other straps held her upright when she was too weary to do that for herself. Another three hundred constructs were hauled to safety that day, and so it went on, day after, day, until only three hundred or so remained. Most of these belonged to Clan Elienor, left to the last as always.

Despite her exhaustion, Tiaan had forced herself to practise walking in her room every night. After a week she could manage a hundred steps unaided. After two weeks it was a thousand.

Vithis had not mentioned flight again, which bothered her. If he'd dispatched one of the first constructs back to Tirthrax then, travelling day and night, it could have reached there days ago. Malien would reveal the secret and Tiaan would be dispensable. Worse than that: it would be dangerous to allow her to live.

It was time to put her plan into effect. Tiaan had learned much about the Art over the past weeks. Normally, in any of the Secret Arts, power was used as sparingly as possible. That was, she mused, like an archer only being allowed to shoot one arrow a week. After drawing on multiple fields for sixteen hours a day, Tiaan had more experience than most mancers would have gained in a lifetime.

Unfortunately, she lacked the background and knowledge to make sense of it. She had tried to fit it into the geomantic framework Gilhaelith had begun to teach her in Nyriandiol, but he had not taken her far enough. That did not matter here, where there were any number of Aachim mancers to guide her, and healers to pick her up when she fell. But on her own it would be a different matter.

She had to act now, ready or not. Once the last construct

was moved, they would make sure she never had contact with the amplimet again.

Tiaan was woken by a commotion outside. The hanging door was thrust open and someone tall entered, carrying a lantern.

'Tiaan!' he whispered urgently.

It was Minis, and she was wearing only a flimsy sleeping gown. Her heart began to crash around in her chest. Tiaan pulled the covers up to her neck.

'What do you want, Minis?' she said coldly.

He fell to his knees. 'To say how much I have wronged you, and to beg for your forgiveness. No more.'

She turned her face to the wall of the tent. 'You led me on. You made promises and refused to keep them. From the very beginning you used me, Minis. Everything you said to me was a lie. The Aachim must have been building constructs for a decade before you contacted me, so innocently. So *accidentally!*'

He reached for her. She thrust both hands under the covers and he stopped dead.

'I *did* break my promise, Tiaan, and I've never stopped regretting it. But I was used as much as you were.'

'It's all just words, Minis,' she said, not looking at him. She dared not, for despite all her vows, all her fury, he still moved her. 'Life has taught me that words can mean nothing, or *anything!* I put my faith in actions, and by yours are you revealed, as are all the Aachim.'

'Please believe me, Tiaan. Don't judge me by the deceits of others. I never lied to you.'

'Prove it!' she hissed, but before Minis could respond she heard Vithis roaring his name. Minis went through the flap without another word.

Tiaan pulled on her clothes and readied herself for her last day. Thyzzea would accompany her, as usual, but there had been no let-up in the Aachim's vigilance. The construct behind her always carried two guards armed with crossbows, as well as a mancer monitoring everything she did with the field, and they never took their eyes off her.

The day went badly, for Tiaan could not stop thinking about what must happen tomorrow. Halfway though the first trip she lost the fields and the construct thumped into the ground so hard that it jarred her teeth. Behind her, all the others did the same.

'What's the matter?' Thyzzea asked anxiously.

'I can't see it,' Tiaan gasped. 'My brain feels like porridge.'

'What's porridge?'

'Never mind.'

Vithis came running from one of the towed constructs and sprang onto the side of her machine. So he *was* still watching her. 'Is there a problem?'

'I've lost the fields.'

'Minis is behind this, isn't he?'

She did not answer.

'I'll make sure he doesn't bother you again!' Vithis sprang down.

The delay was only a short one, but twice more she lost the fields, and on the second trip three constructs crashed into each other and were damaged so badly that they had to be left behind. Vithis was livid, and with all the delays they did not complete the return journey until sunrise the following day. There were still more than two hundred constructs to move.

Tiaan was so exhausted that she kept sagging against her restraints. Thyzzea carried her back to their tent, where Tiaan lay on her mattress, unable to sleep. Weird images kept flashing through her mind, objects she knew belonged in higher-dimensional space, though she was incapable of comprehending them. Finally, as dinner was being served outside, she drifted into sleep.

She woke to find Vithis sitting by her side. Tiaan started and moved away under the covers.

'Don't be afraid,' he said. 'I'm not that kind of man.'

'I know what kind of man you are. What do you want?'

'Have you remembered anything else about my lost people?'

She thought before answering. Her memories were clear

now, though she was not sure what they meant. 'I heard cries. Some seemed to be death cries.' She looked him in the eyes. 'I'm sorry,' she said, and was. Her weakness was that she empathised with his grief, despite the way he'd used her. 'There were cries of agony, as if people were being turned inside out.' He flinched. She went on slowly. 'And people wailing that they were lost. Others calling to one another, as if they were trying to collect together.'

'Lost in the void,' he said, 'but not dead. I'm not sure if that's better or worse.'

'I don't know anything about the void.'

'It's a different kind of reality to ours. Nothing is stable; everything is in flux. Things are possible in the void that cannot be done in the material worlds. The lyrinx flew everywhere there, preying on other creatures and being preyed upon in turn.'

'No wonder they wanted to escape.'

'The void is filled with vicious creatures, and the struggle for existence is more violent than anywhere. No beast can relax for an instant. They must adapt constantly or go to extinction.'

'Your people are clever,' said Tiaan, 'and they have their constructs. They might do well there.'

'It's true that we of Clan Inthis are not easily bowed by adversity. And the void is filled with raw energies, like the fields surrounding nodes on this world, and my own. The constructs might draw on those fields, providing my people with protection and shelter, at least for a while. But even so, I fear they're all gone now, and the hopes of First Clan with them. How could they adapt to the savagery of the void in time?'

The interrogation resumed that night Vithis was there, as well as Tirior, Urien and Luxor. They went over her story repeatedly, trying to learn more about the voices Tiaan heard after she used the amplimet, and the secret of flight that still eluded them.

The night was almost as exhausting as the previous day. It took all her effort to maintain that air of being slightly mad and rather stupid, while having a natural genius for reading the field and working with crystals. She could feel the sweat trickling down her back by the time they finally withdrew to a far corner of the tent.

'I'm not sure I believe her,' said Tirior, still speaking in the common tongue – they must want her to know what they were saying about her, and be afraid.

'We'll soon know the truth,' Urien replied. 'About flight, at any rate.'

'What are you up to?' asked Tirior.

'The day she came here, three weeks ago, I dispatched three constructs to Tirthrax. I instructed them to ask Malien how the flying construct came to be built.'

'I knew nothing of this,' Vithis said darkly.

'I sent word to my own people, near Gospett,' said Urien, 'with a captured messenger skeet. If all went well, their constructs could have reached Tirthrax ten days ago. I asked them to send word back the instant they came within flying distance. I hope to hear the truth any day.'

The old woman looked across and caught Tiaan's eye. Urien wanted her to know that she had little time left.

TWENTY-EIGHT

Outside, the moon now seemed dazzlingly bright. Nish stumbled past the guards, barely able to see, for his throbbing eyes were dripping. Just what had the tears and the potion done to him? And why all that talk about him serving Jal-Nish? Had his father meant to corrupt him, to make Nish more like himself? *Had he?* No, Father – whatever you've done to me, I'll fight it with all the will I have. I'll never become like you.

Someone took him by the arm. 'What's the matter?' Xabbier hissed.

Nish swayed on his feet. 'My father—' Better not say anything about the tears. Nish shook his head, but that only made things worse. Coloured auras streamed up from among the soldiers, and in the background he could still hear the faint whine of the tears. 'He's poured a potion down my throat and bespelled me. I don't feel well, Xabbier.'

'Come this way.' Xabbier led him through the rows of tents to one whose flap was folded back, but did not enter. 'Open your mouth.'

'What?'

Xabbier thrust two fingers down Nish's throat and Nish brought up the contents of his stomach. When he'd done heaving, which took quite a while, the soldier wiped Nish's face and led him inside.

Xabbier lit a lantern. 'That's got rid of the bulk of it, though surely not all. I don't know much about the Art, Cryl-Nish, but this I do know. You must fight the spell with all the strength you have. Don't give in or it'll take you.'

Nish shielded his eyes from the light. He tried to speak but could only manage a dry rasp. Xabbier held a pannikin of water to his lips, then fed him a slab of bread torn into pieces. After wolfing it down, Nish felt better. His vision inverted again but came back to normal. His belly throbbed. He rubbed it and a bubbling belch rumbled up. The sick feeling faded but did not entirely disappear.

He sat up suddenly, seized by an urge so powerful that it burned him. 'Father's calling. I must go to him.'

Nish scrambled to his feet but Xabbier stood in his way, as solid as a tree trunk. The mighty arms went around Nish, binding him immovably. He struggled, for the urge to run to his father's side was overwhelming. Nish knew what Jal-Nish was; he saw the evil more clearly than ever, but he had to go to him. The compulsion was impossible to resist.

He struggled until he was worn out, and once broke free, slipping by the big man like a ferret. Xabbier threw out a foot and sent Nish sprawling, then sat on him. Nish kicked and beat his fists on the ground, clawed at the earth floor, snarled and tried to bite his friend. Xabbier held his nose until, finally, the compulsion snapped. He felt a desperate grief for his father, but the urge to go to him had passed.

Xabbier let Nish up, watching him warily as he wiped dribble off his chin with his sleeve. 'I suppose . . . You'd better take me to the cells, before he punishes you, too . . .'

Xabbier turned away, crouching down with bent head, as though thinking, but he held on to Nish's wrist just in case. He reached a decision. There was a knot in his jaw, a furious light in his eye. 'I heard everything he said to you, Cryl-Nish, and what he did. It makes me sick to my stomach to think about it. I can't let him have you.'

'What?' said Nish dazedly. Nothing made sense any more.

'I'm taking you away from here.'

'But he'll destroy you. He'll flay you alive.'

'We might all die tomorrow or the next day. I can't go to my doom knowing I've betrayed a friend. I've closed my eyes to too much of his evil already.'

'But Xabbier—'

'My mind's made up. Come on.'

Nish said no more. Xabbier led him through the camp and the sentries by the darkest ways, back to the escarpment and finally up a different track from before. Halfway to the rim, Xabbier stopped.

'Wait here and don't make a sound. I'll find the guard for this section and distract him while you slip past. Go that way.' He pointed to Nish's right.

They embraced. 'Thank you, Xabbier. I'll never forget this,' said Nish. 'Good luck.'

'And you,' said the lieutenant, 'wherever your path takes you. I hope we meet again in happier circumstances. And remember, he'll try again, Nish, and again. You'll have to fight him every time. You must not give in, no matter how easy it seems.'

He turned away. Nish watched Xabbier until he disappeared, then began to labour up the faint path, agonising about his friend. When Jal-Nish found out, he would crucify Xabbier.

After many rest stops, for his muscles were like putty, Nish made it to the top and headed into the maze of limestone pinnacles. Once more he felt that prickling feeling of being watched, or followed, though he saw no one. Nish continued, stumbling now. The touch of the tears had drained him to the marrow of his bones, but the interview with his father had left him an emotional pincushion.

At the thought, he felt another burning spasm and a return of the compulsion. Nish's skin tingled. It was hard to fight it on his own, and when he had, he had to rest for a moment.

Flat on his back on a broken shelf of limestone, Nish rubbed his eyes. They were still watering; the moon still seemed unusually bright. It was midnight. He covered his eyes, which felt better until that unnerving feeling of being watched recurred. Nish peered through his fingers. Though the pinnacle in front of him lay in shadow, he could see every surface detail. More than that, he could see inside it. And it seemed to have *bones*.

311

Nish blinked but the bone shapes were still there. They weren't human bones, nor the skeleton of any wild animal he knew; they were too massive, and the wrong shape. Rising into the upper arch of the pinnacle he could just make out robust, hollow wing bones, yet the cranium was colossal, with hundreds of large teeth, and the jaw gaped open.

I'm hallucinating, Nish thought as he slid off the shelf. It must be the touch of the tears. He shook his head and kept moving, looking steadfastly ahead. As he edged around a corner into another corridor, his eye fell on the limestone face to his left, where he saw the same kind of bones. There could be no doubt – it was the skeleton of a lyrinx.

Could this place be an ancient lyrinx graveyard, all limed over? But how could it have turned to rock so quickly? Then, and the realisation felt like a fist inside his chest, Nish saw a grey shadow within the skeleton contract and expand, contract and expand. It was the great heart of the beast. No skeleton this – there was a live creature inside!

Tearing his gaze away, Nish began to walk faster. Now he saw bones everywhere, twisted up in strange positions inside the pinnacles, and there could be only one explanation – the enemy had *stone-formed* themselves. There were thousands of them, probably tens of thousands, if even a quarter of the pinnacles contained the beasts, and they could be across the valley on the far escarpment as well.

Could it be another vision arising from the touch of the tears? He did not think so, for everything else was diamond clear. He inspected the pinnacle on his right. The claws of its stone-formed occupant were extended towards him, and they seemed to twitch.

He wanted to scream and run. Closing his eyes, Nish concentrated on showing no reaction. Could it know he'd seen it? And if it did, how quickly could it react? The lyrinx might take hours to break out of its lithic state. Alternatively, it might come out in an instant.

No terror Nish had previously felt was the equal of this. He was alone in the midst of a mighty enemy force, an ambush, and his arrogant father had walked right into it. If so many lyrinx fell on Jal-Nish's army in the night without warning, as surely they planned to, they would annihilate it.

What colossal magic it must have taken to stone-form tens of thousands of lyrinx so effectively. Nish could not imagine such power. His gaze wandered to the top of the spire of stone. It wore, where the grey rock was outlined against the sky, a faint yellow nimbus. The other pinnacles looked the same.

Nish hurried on. His mouth was dry; his fingers, hanging at his sides, were locked into claws. He dared not look back, for fear that some great beast would shatter its stone refuge and come lunging out of the darkness. He could practically feel its breath on the nape of his neck.

Should he go on to Flydd and Troist, or carry the warning back to Xabbier? Never had he held such responsibility. If he chose wrongly, thousands would die.

Somewhere behind him, a piece of rock snapped. Nish let out a muffled cry, thinking they were coming after him. He closed his eyes and hastened into the next tunnel of darkness, which was worse. Even with his eyes closed, he could see lyrinx skeletons everywhere. They had the faintest luminosity and were blurred, as if shivering.

Or were they preparing to break out, en masse, and attack his father's army in darkness? The box valley would become a slaughterhouse whose streams would carry more blood than water.

Jal-Nish's army was alert, the watch-fires bright, so the enemy could not take them by complete surprise. But there were too many lyrinx for the army to fight alone. They would have no chance unless he warned Troist, and he had to do it right away. Troist's army would have to do a forced march through the night, cloaked, to reach the neck of the valley in time. He could only hope that the enemy would take ages to break free from their stone-formed state and assemble into battle formation.

It took all Nish's courage to keep walking and look neither right nor left. The cracking sound was not repeated. It might have been the stone contracting in the cool of night. He concentrated on taking one step after another, doing nothing suspicious. How good were lyrinx senses in this stone frozen state? Could they sense what was going on outside, or were their brains as petrified as their bodies?

Ahead, the open ground was brilliantly lit by the moon. He could not move across unseen if there were winged sentries on high, and dared not take the time to go around. Should he run, or creep like a spy?

The lyrinx had poorer eyesight than humans in daylight, but better at night. Nish walked out into the brightness, trudging like a lookout at the end of a long patrol, and his weariness was not feigned. Above, he thought he heard the whisper of air across leathery wings. He stopped, mid-stride, looked around and kept going. That was hard. A diving lyrinx would kill him before he realised it was there.

Again that whisper. He kept going, gaining the shelter of the next pinnacle without further incident. This one was just rock; no inner bones. Stepping into the shadow, he looked up. Was that something in the tree; a shadow of wings? No, just a shape made by the branches. The sound must have been an owl.

There was nothing to be seen, no matter how carefully he looked, but something was different. Though Nish had no talent for the Art, he could feel a subtle strain and a distortion of the darkness, which he imagined was a drain in the ethyr.

There was still quite a way to go. Ahead lay the open area, sparsely studded with rock pinnacles. Beyond that was a strip of forest, the cleared expanse with the first set of pinnacles, and, further on, the other wood beyond which Troist's army lay hidden under its cloaking spell. He prayed that it still held.

Each step seemed to take an hour, but he made it across into the forest, and through it to the next pinnacle field. As he stepped into the rustling grass on the other side, something sharp jabbed him in the back.

'Don't move, spy, or you're dead.'

Nish went very still. 'I'm not a spy,' he said in a low voice. 'I'm Cryl-Nish Hlar and I've been on a secret mission for the scrutator.'

The spear point went through his clothes, breaking the skin above his right buttock. 'Is that so?' the soldier hissed. 'Then explain why Scrutator Flydd has got the whole camp looking for you.'

'I . . . don't know.' For once Nish could not think of a single excuse. 'I think you'd better take me to him, soldier.'

'I'm going to. If you try to escape, my friend, you'll get this right up your liver.'

By the time they found Flydd, who was with General Troist, Nish had half a dozen throbbing gouges in his back, low down, and one in each buttock. He made a mental note to return the favour, if he ever got the opportunity.

'Where the bloody hell did you get to?' the scrutator said furiously as Nish was prodded into the clanker.

'I found him sneaking through the forest, surr,' said the soldier, giving Nish another jab in the bum for good measure. 'He's been spying—'

'I have vital news, surr,' Nish interrupted. 'It can't wait for anything.'

'Thank you, soldier,' Flydd interrupted. 'That will be all.'

Nish waited until the man had gone, then moved gingerly into the centre of the clanker.

'Well?' snapped Flydd.

'I've just escaped from my father.'

'What?' cried Flydd and Troist together.

'You bloody fool!' Flydd went on. 'This is the end, Nish. If you've given us away, I'll hang you with your own intestines—'

'I didn't mean to go anywhere. I was all knotted up inside, and couldn't sleep, so I went for a walk and—'

'This had better be good, Artificer,' growled Troist.

'It's important, surr,' cried Nish. 'The fate of an army hangs on my news.'

'And the fate of a man on my whim,' Flydd said darkly. 'Spill it, Nish, and be quick about it.'

Nish explained how he'd come to leave the camp and end up near the escarpment, what he'd seen there and how he'd fallen into Jal-Nish's hands, and then, what his father had said and done to him. Flydd and Troist exchanged glances and Nish knew they believed him. 'But surr,' Nish dropped his voice, 'there's something I must speak to you privately about.'

'I'm sure it's nothing that General Troist can't hear.'

Nish hesitated. 'I . . . believe it is, surr.' He looked anxiously from one man to the other. 'It has to do with a remarkable form of the Secret Art, if you take my meaning.'

'I've a hundred things to do before the morrow,' said the general. 'Not to mention getting a few minutes' sleep. I'll leave you for the moment.' He went out.

'Get on with it!' Flydd snarled. 'And don't ever do such a stupid thing again or you'll suffer more than a spear point in the bum.'

Nish moved close, speaking softly. 'My father has the tears of the node, surr. Both of them.'

'So it was Jal-Nish,' Flydd breathed. 'He killed them all: the soldiers, the dogs and the poor pilot, to make sure no one would ever know. And no one would have. As the node cooled, the walls would have collapsed and buried any remains. Tell me, what was Jal-Nish like?'

'Cold; bitter; implacable. I could make no impression on him, but one thing was clear—'

'Yes?' Flydd rapped.

'He wants to be chief scrutator, and to revenge himself on his enemies, particularly Irisis.'

'And me.'

'No, surr.'

'Why not?' cried Flydd as though it was a mortal insult.

'I told him you were dead, surr. Of blood poisoning.'

'You what?'

'Dead, surr. As a maggot!' Nish took a wry pleasure in putting it that way.

'Why?' snapped Flydd. 'Who gave you leave to lie to a scrutator?'

'It seemed like a good idea at the time, surr.'

'Did it now?' Flydd considered. 'Perhaps it was. So Jal-Nish has the tears. What for, I wonder? He cannot be allowed to command the scrutators. They have more power at their disposal than anyone realises, even without these glorious, perilous tears. Tell me everything he said.'

Nish related what had happened. 'And at the end, he thrust my hands into the tears, and I felt the most extraordinary sensations. Everything that was black became white, each colour took on the hue of its opposite. I saw right through to the bones of my father's arm and he said, "I have woken you, Cryl-Nish!"'

'Go on.'

'He said, "You'll see horrors no one has ever seen before. You'll hear what has previously been unheard. And you'll feel – well, I leave that to you to discover. The gift of the tears is not predictable. But you'll know what it is like to suffer. You will know what it is like to be your father, as you stand beside me for the rest of your life."'

Flydd took a step backwards, regarding him uncertainly. 'And then he just let you go?'

'No – he was behind me, casting some kind of spell. His table contained all sorts of alchymical apparatus – stills, retorts—'

'I should have thought of that,' muttered Flydd.

'What is it, surr?'

'His particular Art is alchymical in nature, and what better way to enhance it than through the tears, which represent nature's purification and distillation of the essence of a node. They would fit his Art like a glove. It's worse than I thought. The tears could make him too powerful. What did he do then?'

'He cast his spell, to corrupt me and make me his servant, but it didn't take.'

'Not even with the power of the tears?' said Flydd, astonished. 'Why ever not?'

'I've no idea, but he seemed disconcerted. He had to do it three times.'

'He's not yet mastered the tears, evidently. And then?'

'He forced an alchymical potion down my throat . . . What is it, surr?' Flydd was looking at him suspiciously.

'And then?'

'Father ordered Xabbier to take me to the brig and hold me in solitary confinement until the morning, so the spell would have time to set. But Xabbier had heard all he'd said and done to me. He forced me to vomit up the potion right away.'

'He did?' Flydd said gladly. 'I'd like to meet this friend of yours.'

'I hope he's still alive. When Jal-Nish finds out . . .' Nish related how Xabbier had helped him to escape.

'I see. Is that all?' Flydd seemed to be regarding him ambiguously.

'Not quite.'

'I can't imagine anything worse.'

'I was coming back, through a great field of limestone pinnacles,' Nish began, 'which lie near the edge of the escarpment. The tears must have changed me, somehow, for I realised that I could see right into the stone. But it was not stone inside.'

Flydd was staring at Nish as though seeing *him* in a new light. 'What did you see, Nish?'

'I saw the skeletons of lyrinx, and their beating hearts. Uncounted thousands of them lie hidden within stone pinnacles above the southern escarpment, near the army camp and, for all I know, as many on the eastern and northern sides. The beasts must have been stone-formed, surr. It's an ambush and, if we don't warn him, Jal-Nish's army will be annihilated to the last man.'

Flydd threw his arms around Nish, hugging him to his scarred and scrawny chest. As abruptly he let go. 'Would that *I* had a son, and you were he.'

Nish's hands fell by his sides; he was astounded, and so proud that his eyes flooded with tears. He wasn't a complete failure after all.

Before he could say anything Flydd ran to the hatch, bellowing, 'Troist, quickly!'

The general threw himself in. 'What is it, surr?'

'The enemy are between us and Jal-Nish's army. They've stone-formed themselves into limestone pinnacles above the main camp. It's a trap. Break camp; we must leave immediately and march through the night to Gumby Marth.'

'How many were there?' said Troist.

'I couldn't be sure,' said Nish. 'Tens of thousands, like as not.'

'Why this way?' said Troist. 'Why not fly in an army at night, from across the sea?'

'Most lyrinx aren't fliers,' said Flydd. 'They wouldn't have enough of them to attack an army this size. And even a short flight would weaken them. This way they can appear out of nowhere, without warning. And remember the fliers we saw near the exploded node, Nish? They may have guessed Jal-Nish has the, er . . . secret weapon, and know they have to ambush the army to succeed. I'd better check the cloaker. The original spell wasn't designed for this big a force, or an enemy so near, and it would take a dozen mancers working together to make it so.'

'It was still holding the last time I spoke to Nutrid,' said Troist.

'It could feather around the edges without him knowing. Besides, the enemy's stone-forming must take much from the field. If it's drawn down too far, the cloaker won't conceal us.'

'We'll march at once.' Troist threw up the rear hatch, snapped orders to a messenger waiting outside and turned to the chart on the table. 'What if we head west, this way, and cross into Gumby Marth below the neck? When the enemy attack, they'll hold it, so as to trap Jal-Nish's forces inside. If we keep the escapeway open, the army will have a chance.'

'How far is it?'

Troist was busy with his dividers. 'It's four leagues before we can get into the valley, then another two back to the neck. A brutal forced march and the clankers will be slower than the men.'

'Can we do it by mid-morning?' said Flydd.

'We have to find a way through rugged country in the dark. I don't know how long it'll take.'

'Try very hard, General. If we're too late, there won't be any point.'

'We'll do our best, surr, though we won't be in prime condition when we get there.'

'Just as long as we do get there. And we'll have to send someone to warn Jal-Nish. Someone he'll believe.'

Nish's skin crawled, but he knew duty when it faced him. 'I – I'd better go, surr.'

'I need you here,' said Flydd.

'Do you think I *want* to go? It's a tricky passage through the pinnacles in the dark, and the path down the escarpment is not easily found. We can't risk the messenger getting lost. The enemy could be breaking out already.'

'If they are, you're dead, Nish.'

'And so is everyone else.'

'I won't risk it,' said Flydd. 'Jal-Nish could be calling you back.'

'I don't think so. When he did it before, it made my skin tingle.'

'He's cunning, Nish. He might change the compulsion each time. And once he sees you again, you'll be powerless to escape him.'

'Then you'll have to free me, surr.'

'I still don't like it.'

'I've got to warn them, surr. I – I've a lot to atone for.'

Flydd stared at Nish for a second, then nodded. 'Yes, go!' He gave him his hand. 'I hope we meet again.'

'So do I,' said Troist. 'I really do. Take this.' He handed Nish a piece of rolled flatbread stuffed with spiced ground meat, and a skin of sour beer, the weak kind soldiers were given on the march when the water was not fit to drink. 'I'll send someone with you to the edge of the watch.'

'I'd appreciate that, surr.' Nish munched on the roll. 'My backside isn't feeling so hot.'

He felt better with food in his belly. The beer did not

improve matters, however, so after a couple of swigs he slung it over his shoulder for later. The guard, a small man whose breath whistled in his nose, said no word all the way through the forest and into the pinnacles beyond. At their furthest edge he left Nish silently.

Nish stayed where he was for a moment, still thinking about his father and the spell. What if Jal-Nish caught him and Flydd could not set him free? His father would bind him with the spell and Nish would be forced to serve him, committing all kinds of atrocities, to the end of his days. He might even become corrupt and grow to enjoy that servitude, even to take pleasure in the suffering he inflicted. Better that he hurl himself over the precipice and leave Jal-Nish, and his army, to their fate.

But that wasn't an option either. He'd taken this task upon himself and could not set it aside. Nish took a deep breath, squared his shoulders and moved on.

He made it through the next patch of forest and into the main series of pinnacles without incident, but had not gone a dozen steps before he realised that something was different. He hesitated, then kept going. He had to act normally, in case the enemy could tell he was there.

What had changed, though? He hadn't yet lost the *sight*. He could still see the robust, odd-shaped skeletons, the bodies bent in strange shapes to accommodate themselves to the form of the rock. Occasionally he saw a heart pulse, or a claw flex.

It was hard not to look over his shoulder. It was very hard not to run, to pant, to gasp. He was less than halfway through the maze, which was now more difficult to negotiate, the moon being low. Shadows covered all but the tops of the pinnacles.

What was different? He strained his ears, as if to detect the racing heartbeats as the lyrinx prepared to break out. There was no sound. Not a sigh of wind in the trees; not a rustle in the grass; not the scuttle of animal feet on the rocks.

No sound at all. Wild creatures could tell the danger better than he could. He walked a little faster. Then, as he squeezed between two knife-edged blades of stone, Nish heard it.

Crack-crack-crack. That was not rock contracting in the night. It was rock being shattered from the inside as a stone-formed beast came back to life and prepared to break out.

TWENTY-NINE

Nish gasped. His head whipped from side to side. He saw nothing, but from ahead, came that crack-crack again. In his mind's eye, enhanced by the tears, rock cracked off the monstrous armoured bodies; leathery wings slowly unfurled into the night. The lyrinx were coming.

He began to run, but had not reached the end of the corridor of limestone pinnacles when something pushed up in front of him like a statue rising from the sea. Chunks of stone fell like hail. Great thewed arms rose slowly into position; wings twice the height of Nish snapped taut. The head creaked around.

It was moving sluggishly, as if the stone-forming spell was not completely undone. Nish did the only thing he could think of. He dived between its spread legs, hit the ground hard and scrabbled out of the way.

The creature gave a drawn-out roar, tried to turn in that narrow space, and stuck. Nish came to his feet, looking back to gauge his peril. The lyrinx was caught at the hips. Raising one mighty fist – slow, *slow* – it smote the pinnacle to its left. The limestone snapped off halfway. Nish fled.

The crashing continued behind him, which at least told him where his enemy was. It was more unnerving when it stopped, for then there was only the pounding of his feet and the thumping in his chest. Until the footsteps began.

The lyrinx was after him. In the open it could run much faster than he could but, within this maze of pointed rocks and bladed pinnacles, Nish might just have the advantage. He could hear it crashing against the stone, snapping off the fragile tips. Its armour gave it an advantage there.

He turned left, found he was in a dead end and had to backtrack. Panic began to seize him. This wasn't the way he'd come earlier, and the low moon only illuminated the tips of the pinnacles. If he wasn't out of here before it set, he'd never find the way.

Nish went right but that led to another dead end. Letting out an inarticulate cry, he retraced his steps, then edged down a corridor of stone so narrow that he had to turn sideways to negotiate it. With luck it would hold the enemy back.

It did not. Fully flesh again, his hunter rose up on its wings and flapped across the spires directly towards him. Where could he go? A long straight lane, too wide to hide in, ran ahead and behind. Nish stumbled down it, gasping for breath. Spotting a crevice between a pair of low spires, he thrust himself into it.

The lyrinx turned this way and that, trying to see where he had gone. It climbed, flapping noisily, then used the Art to hover for a few seconds. Its head turned as it picked up the sound of his breathing. The creature glided towards him then dropped, attempting to trap him in his hiding place, to crush him. Nish threw himself deeper into the crack. The lyrinx came down hard into the darkness. Rock cracked all around Nish and he was sure he was going to die.

The lyrinx gave a muffled *Ugh!* and began to flail at the rock, hurling shards in all directions. Wetness flicked against Nish's cheek. The claws of one thrashing foot gouged scars across the soft limestone. He protected his eyes with his hands. The great feet gained a purchase and the thighs flexed, hurling the beast back into the air.

For a second it was outlined against the moon, then it plummeted into the next row of pinnacles, smashing them to fragments as its frantic wings beat back and forth. A spike of stone hung from the low part of its belly where it had impaled itself. The blade had gone in between the cracks in its armour.

Nish couldn't tell if it was badly wounded, and didn't wait to find out. He bolted along the corridor in front of him until he could no longer hear it. Then – *crack, crack* – ahead of him, and now to every side, more lyrinx were freeing themselves. Had some master mancer among them decreed that it was time for the ambush, or were they coming to get him? He staggered on. There was not far to go now – he was almost through. Ahead, a last row of pinnacles guarded the rim of the escarpment like a row of sentries.

They were cracking open as he went by them, the lyrinx moving sluggishly as they strained against the fading spell. One threw out a claw and almost hooked it through his collar. A great fist, still partly stone-formed and as hard as rock, caught Nish in the chest, knocking him off his feet. He struck the ground on his back, the breath knocked out of him, and waited for his doom.

The lyrinx was slow to move. The blow must have been accidental. He did not give it the chance for another, but scuttled by it on hands and knees, came to his feet and ran.

Nish sprinted across the platform of white limestone and reached the cliff edge. Where was the precipitous way down? He ran back and forth. The cracking grew louder. Ah, there! As he gained the path, Nish looked back.

The moon, just tipping the western horizon, shone across the field of stone, illuminating a hundred thousand spikes, spires, pinnacles and blades of limestone. It was beautiful, for the tips and edges were as translucent as milk. In many of them he could see the bones of the stone-formed creatures.

A single clap of thunder reverberated across the valley, and before his eyes the spires began to burst open in waves that spread from one end of the pinnacle field to the other. Lyrinx thrust their heads high, moving as sluggishly as chickens just hatched from eggs. The moonlight caught their eyes, dozens of them, hundreds, thousands upon thousands, and still they emerged, stone into flesh.

The first lyrinx lifted, flapping ponderously, evidently still weighed down by the spell. Nish felt an internal sucking, which his charged senses knew was due to the creatures drawing on the field to keep them aloft. Within a minute, dozens were lurching into the sky.

'Soldiers, wake!' Nish roared, bolting down the perilous goat track, screaming so loudly that it tore at the flesh of his throat. He gave no further thought to Jal-Nish. 'Wake, wake! Ambush! The enemy are upon us. The lyrinx are coming down from the heights. Soldiers, wake. Xabbier, *Xabbier*!'

Nish never knew how he got down, and later, looking at the cliff in daylight, could not believe that he had. The previous time it had taken nearly an hour; this journey he completed in a scant ten minutes, leaping off boulders, skidding down loose gravel in miniature landslides, scarcely looking where he put his feet, giving his fate up to instinct. And, perhaps because his senses had been so enhanced by the tears, he had made it unscathed, apart from a badly wrenched knee where a stone rolled underfoot when he was nearly down.

He was still roaring hysterically when he reached the bottom. The camp was alive, the highly disciplined soldiers running to their formations, the watch-fires stirred to blazing brilliance. The great war machine had been alerted just in time and was grinding into battle position.

'Soldiers! Wake!' Nish kept shouting long after there was any necessity for it. 'Xabbier! Lieutenant Xabbier!'

A soldier caught him by the arm. 'Come this way please, surr.'

He ran, pulling Nish after him. Nish's mind was ablaze with that image of the enemy streaming into the sky. He could still see the skeletons through their flesh.

The soldier stopped by a blazing pyre. Xabbier stood there, tall and broad as a door, rapping out orders. He sent his troops off and turned to Nish.

'Cryl-Nish, that was you brought the alarm?'

'Yes,' Nish said hoarsely. It felt as though he'd screamed his throat out.

Xabbier took Nish's two hands in his, squeezing hard. 'Never was a warning more welcome.' He looked up at the sky, now full of wheeling lyrinx, touched by the setting moon.

Nish tried to estimate the number. More than ten thousand, surely, and still they cracked out of the pinnacles. There could be twenty thousand of them, even thirty. Not all would be fliers, of course, but those who weren't could come down the cliffs more quickly than he had. Cold fear dripped down Nish's back. And if there were more on the other side of the valley . . .

'We'll talk afterwards,' said Xabbier. '*If there* is *one!* Are you armed, Cryl-Nish?'

'No, I didn't think to bring a weapon. Stupid, isn't it?'

Xabbier sprang through the rear hatch of a clanker and tossed out a metal helm, a set of chest and back armour made of hardened leather, and a long dagger in a sheath. Nish buckled the helm under his chin – it fitted well enough. Taking off the forgotten skin of beer, he put the armour over his shoulders, settling it in place. It was made for a bigger man than he, but protected his body, shoulders and upper arms without encumbering him too greatly.

The lieutenant passed Nish a short, dark sword. 'This has a virtue set on the blade and may even penetrate the armour of a lyrinx, if you strike a lucky blow.'

Nish buckled it on. 'I'm not much of a hand with a sword, Xabbier, but I can shoot a crossbow well enough.'

'I've none in my squad, unfortunately. Ready?'

Nish took a hefty swig from the skin of beer. It no longer tasted sour; it was just what the situation required. He downed half and held it out to Xabbier.

The lieutenant shook his head, then said, 'Why not? It'll probably be my last.' He squeezed a stream into his mouth, grimacing at the taste. 'Ugh! I hope *that's* not my last memory of beer. Bring it. Fighting lyrinx is thirsty work.' He looked up at the sky. 'How many are they?'

'Ten thousand, at least,' Nish replied. The wheeling creatures now darkened the sky. 'Maybe twenty or thirty, counting the ones climbing down the cliffs.'

'So many? Why didn't they attack head-on?'

'Perhaps they're afraid Jal-Nish has a secret weapon. Or they've some weakness we don't know about.'

'I hope so. Come this way.'

Xabbier's position was high enough for the fires to outline the shape of the surrounding valley and reflect off the streams. The camp lay at the upper part of the valley, which was a tilted bowl about a league across, mostly pasture land with patches of trees here and there. A pair of streams divided the width of the valley into thirds, though the camp lay in the southern third. Each stream was ten or fifteen paces across and, though not deep, was fast enough to cause trouble for a man weighed down with armour and weapons. The jagged escarpments to east, south and north formed the steep sides of the bowl, the tilted western side the valley entrance. The rocky neck midway down the valley could not be seen in the dark. They might escape that way if the enemy failed to defend it, though that seemed unlikely.

The lieutenant led Nish to the troop he commanded, called out his name and gave final orders. The soldiers assumed defensive positions behind their clankers.

'Who the blazes picked this place?' said Nish. 'If the lyrinx come up the valley, as surely they must, we'll be trapped.'

'Your father chose it,' said Xabbier, 'against the advice of his generals.'

'Why?'

'He failed to communicate his strategy to his officers.'

'Where's my father's tent?' Nish had no idea where Xabbier had taken him on his previous visit.

'Further up, near the northern rim,' Xabbier pointed. 'Keep well away from there, and should we win—'

'Don't worry. I'll be out of here so fast that you'll see nothing but smoke.'

'Better keep away from the command tents, too. They're below your father's tent.'

'I forgot to mention,' said Nish, 'that Troist is coming around to hold the mouth of the valley open.'

'Who the hell is Troist?' Xabbier moved his sword in and out of its sheath.

'General Troist. He's come down from Almadin with an

army of thirteen thousand soldiers and nine hundred clankers.'

Xabbier threw his arms around Nish and crushed him to his chest. 'Thirteen thousand, you say?'

'Yes,' said Nish. 'I served under him earlier in the year. He's a good man and a fine leader, though he's not fought a battle like this one.'

'None of us have, Cryl-Nish. How did he come to be nearby?'

'Flydd and I brought him here.'

'The *scrutator* is with him? Even better news. We must talk more of this later.' Xabbier called his messengers, a pair of tall soldiers who looked like twins. 'Run to the command tents. General Troist of Almadin is coming to our relief with thirteen thousand, and nine hundred clankers. He'll try to hold the valley neck. How long will they be, Cryl-Nish?'

'They were going to do a forced march from their camp, south of here. They left an hour ago, maybe more. How long would that take?'

'The country's rough that way,' said Xabbier. 'They'll be lucky to reach the neck of Gumby Marth before noon. I hope we can hold on that long.'

The messengers ran off, separately. Xabbier, one eye to the sky, marshalled the hundred and twenty soldiers under his command into a ring around the fires. All across the battlefield, other shadows were doing the same.

'It's a tactic we devised for night fighting,' Troist explained. 'The enemy see better in the dark than we do, but they don't like bright light. This way we have a tiny advantage.'

But we also have our backs to the fire, Nish thought, and they're much bigger than us. If we're forced to retreat, there's nowhere to go.

The last rays of the moon failed. The wheeling lyrinx disappeared against the black sky. 'That's what they're waiting for,' muttered Xabbier. 'It won't be long now.'

'Jal-Nish will have his commanders spread out through the camp, of course,' said Nish, 'so the enemy can't attack them all at the same time.'

Xabbier frowned. 'That's normal practice these days, but Scrutator Jal-Nish has gone back to the old way – a central command area, heavily defended by troops and clankers. He doesn't like to delegate.'

'But surely . . .' Nish began. 'What use are such defences when the enemy can just drop out of the darkness on top of them? The officers will be slaughtered in the first attack.'

'The generals tried to tell him that, but he insisted his secret plan would overcome the enemy, and deprive them of their best and strongest.'

'Father loves to be mysterious,' said Nish. 'He has to prove that he's cleverer than everyone else. What can his plan be?'

'I don't know, Cryl-Nish, but I pray it's a good one.'

Something to do with the tears, no doubt. Jal-Nish must be planning a great display of the Secret Art, to win the battle and prove himself to the scrutators at the same time. Nish's father was a competent mancer rather than a brilliant one but, with the tears enhancing his alchymy, who knew what he might be capable of?

It was another step in his campaign to gain admittance to the Council of Scrutators. Once there, he'd try to oust Ghorr and impose his twisted will on the world.

THIRTY

'They're coming!' someone bellowed.

Nish scrambled up onto the shooter's platform of the nearest clanker, trying to get a picture of what was happening. There were lyrinx everywhere, falling from the sky so thickly that they could not be counted. They seemed to come out of nowhere, and thousands more were swarming down the escarpments.

And, Nish saw, they fell most thickly further up the valley, above the officers' tents. It was the tactic they'd used in the battle for Nilkerrand, wiping out the commanding officers in a few minutes, then routing the leaderless army. Troist had gained his command that way.

There's too many, Nish thought despairingly. Unless Jal-Nish used his magic immediately, this was going to be a massacre. Another wedge of lyrinx were falling further down the valley, to bottle them in. They would try to drive them into the fires. Any who escaped would be forced into the streams or up against the escarpments. When Troist finally arrived, he would enter a valley of the dead, and the enemy would finish the story with him. Better that he hadn't brought Troist here at all, than bring him into this.

'Don't lose hope, Cryl-Nish,' said Xabbier as if reading his thoughts. 'We're a tough force—'

Suddenly the lyrinx were everywhere, landing in the darkness all around them, bounding down the lower slopes of the escarpments and running up the valley from the west.

Nish drew his sword, shrugged the armour into place and prepared to fight and die. The beasts roared their drawn-out battle howls, each with a vibrating whip crack at the end, then charged.

There came a shriek from further up the slope. Nish's hair bristled, for no human throat could have made that sound, nor lyrinx either. The enemy froze where they stood, then every head turned towards the source, as if on wires.

Nish stood up on his toes on the platform, but was not high enough to see. The sound went on and on. It was coming from the direction of the command tents, and his father's tent, where the lyrinx clustered as thickly as bats in a fruit tree.

A violet light appeared in the centre of the command area and began to swell like a balloon. The lyrinx surrounding it rose in the air and hovered, as if resting on the surface of a transparent dome. The violet surface developed spines like those of a sea urchin, and they slowly extended out and up, pushed by a metallic silver sphere whose surface roiled like the surface of the tears.

Nish felt the heat-cold again, and again that charging up of his unknown inner senses. Here and there, a violet spine touched one of the hovering lyrinx, which fell from the sky in flames. They did not seem able to move out of the way.

So Jal-Nish did have a secret weapon – his Art was bolstered with the tears. Nish prayed he would succeed; and prayed he would fail, too. His father was an evil man and the more power he gained, the worse he would become. But if he failed, it must be the end for everyone here.

It didn't look as though he was going to fail. More lyrinx fell, impaled on the thousands of violet spines that now bristled upwards and outwards like spikes on a helmet. The enemy seemed to be drawn to the spines like moths to a lantern.

That drawn-out, inhuman shriek came again. The roiling dome swelled prodigiously and more spines formed, until they might have numbered as many as all the lyrinx on the battlefield.

'I don't know how he's doing it,' said Xabbier, 'but he's luring them in.'

332

'He's going to beat them,' Nish said to the shooter, a rangy, balding redhead who was standing up behind his javelard, gaping.

All at once the shriek was cut off. The dome set and the violet needles froze. A great black lyrinx spiralled down into the firelight above the command tents and hovered there, its head thrust down, wings beating slowly.

'What's going on?' Xabbier called from below.

'I'm not sure,' Nish yelled back. 'Got a spyglass?'

Xabbier snapped an order and shortly a stubby brass ocular was passed up. Climbing to the top of the javelard frame, Nish focussed the glass.

'It's an enormous, black, golden-crested lyrinx, hovering above the dome just out of javelard range. It must be a mancer of surpassing power – I can feel it drawing down the field from here.'

'What's it up to? Quick, Nish! These lyrinx aren't going to stay quiet for long.'

'It's fighting against Jal-Nish's Art. It seems to be holding him for the moment. It must be incredibly powerful – I've never heard of a lyrinx that could fly and do great magic at the same time.'

The struggle went on. No one said a word. The dome swelled, contracted then swelled again. The violet rays pushed up thickly towards the mancer-lyrinx, almost touching him. Nish held his breath. So very close – there could only be a span between life and death for the mighty creature.

He felt a psychic sucking as the field was drawn down. Then the mancer skin-spoke, his whole body inverting in an instant from coal-black to brilliant white, and back to black. Triumph, or despair? Nish couldn't tell. The violet spines crept up again until they almost reached his armoured chest.

Father's going to do it, Nish thought. He'll defeat the creature and the battle will be over before it's begun. The thought did not fill him with joy. After such a victory Jal-Nish would be unstoppable. It could change the world, if the tears really were that powerful.

Once more the mancer-lyrinx flashed black-white-black. This time the spikes were pushed down a fraction. Nish felt weary from watching the struggle.

Again he experienced that psychic sucking, as if the field had been drawn swirling through a plughole. Nish's skin prickled. Suddenly Jal-Nish's roiling dome shrank, shrank again, and the violet spines thinned almost to nothing. The golden-crested lyrinx drifted down, and through the spyglass Nish could see its hands making patterns in the air. The dome was crushed down, down towards the tears from which it came.

'The lyrinx appears to have your father's measure after all,' Xabbier said quietly. He had climbed up unnoticed and now stood beside the red-haired shooter.

'I'm afraid so—'

The atmosphere seemed to charge up. Discharges wavered in the air from every metal object and the violet spikes shot up as if it had all been a ruse. One almost skewered the mancer-lyrinx, who twisted out of its way, moving his hands furiously in denial. Black-white, black-white, black-white, *black*!

With a tearing shriek, the dome split along its circumference. The air thrummed and a white disc of light roared up vertically, bright as the sun, sharp as a razor.

The great lyrinx somersaulted in the air, avoiding the scything blade. Some were not so lucky. Nish saw a hovering lyrinx cut clean in two, the parts continuing to float for a few seconds before falling out of the sky. Other lyrinx lost wings, limbs, heads.

The golden-crested lyrinx raised its arms, then plunged them down, pointing directly at the centre of the dome. The thrumming grew louder, more urgent, before cracking as the white disc shattered and vanished like smoke.

Nish felt another drain on the field and now, under the mancer-lyrinx's overwhelming power, the dome was crushed down and down, until it was no bigger than a wagon, a barrel, a melon. He lost sight of it. No – it swelled momentarily and again that bladed disc of white light roared out, but this time it was forced horizontally, low to the ground. Though it had no effect on the hovering lyrinx, it made a deadly scythe through the tents, the generals and their elite guard, extended out a hundred and fifty spans, faded then vanished.

The roiling dome imploded in a crash of thunder that reverberated off the cliff walls. Nish had to block his ears. It was over and Jal-Nish had lost ruinously. Smoke belched into the sky. Whatever happened next, as hundreds of lyrinx fell on the survivors at the command tents, Nish did not see it.

'It's the end!' he said softly to Xabbier. 'No one could survive such an onslaught, not even with the tears.'

'Then let's make a good account of ourselves before we die,' said Xabbier.

Nish had no time to dwell on his father's fate, for at that instant the lyrinx charged. As he drew his sword, the inner sight that had been with him ever since he'd touched the tears, and had allowed him to see the stone-formed lyrinx, faded away. He was glad to see it go. It had felt wrong – like wearing another man's underwear.

Someone screamed, the sound drawn into a viscous gurgling as the soldier's throat was torn out. The man two to the right of Nish went flying backwards into the fire. A lyrinx lunged at Xabbier – a small, wingless one; it must have climbed down the escarpment. Xabbier's sword flashed in and out, drawing purple blood at its chin. It reared backwards then sprang, arms whirling like flails. Xabbier avoided those blows but the backhander came out of nowhere, slamming into the side of his head and knocking him to one knee.

Nish lunged. His sword went into one of the plates of the creature's side but did no damage. He wrenched it out and cut at the beast's upper arm. The blade skated off the armour. It ignored him, slashing at the lieutenant's head. Xabbier managed to get the flat of his sword up but the blow tore the blade out of his hand and sent it flying into the fire.

Xabbier groped for his knife. The lyrinx reached out with

both hands, intending to tear his head off, though it seemed sluggish compared to those Nish had met previously.

Gathering his strength, he raised the sword with both hands and plunged it into the creature's back. It went right through a back plate and into its heart. The lyrinx reared up on the impaling sword, jerked around and fell dead at Nish's feet.

He slumped to his knees. From start to finish the struggle hadn't taken a minute. He'd struck but three blows, yet he was exhausted.

Xabbier pulled Nish's sword free and handed it to him, hilt-first. The blade ran with gore. Xabbier's own was in the fire. He replaced it with the dead soldier's and they fought on.

An hour or two later, the sun creaked up onto the bloody battlefield. Nish had no idea how he'd survived. Xabbier was also alive but most of his troops lay dead. It was much the same story across the valley. There seemed to be more dead and wounded soldiers than living ones.

Army discipline had disappeared long ago. They no longer fought in any kind of formation – it was just man against beast. Nish had taken a number of wounds, though none was serious. He could not even feel them, he was so keyed up. He had killed another lyrinx, this time face to face, and the creature had bled all over him.

Someone called his name, over and again, though it was the fifth time before it registered. 'What?' Nish said dully.

His arm was shaken until he roused from his stupor. He stood staring at the body of a lyrinx, belly carved open and entrails hanging out. Nish had no idea if he had killed it or not. Dead soldiers lay to left and right, men he had fought beside in the darkness, had exchanged the odd word with, without ever seeing their faces. Some no longer had faces.

'Come *on*, I said.' It was Xabbier, quite as bloody as Nish, though he seemed to be coping better. But then, he was a professional soldier.

'Hoy!' the lieutenant roared across the battlefield. 'To me.

To me!' He waved his sword above his head and a handful of soldiers ran, or limped, to him. They too began roaring to attract the attention of other stragglers.

Xabbier led them onto the higher ground to the south, where they could get a view of the scene. Gumby Marth had been a pretty place, its green sward dotted with patches of forest and bisected by silver streams, the encircling cliffs topped with limestone pinnacles like palisades. Had he really come down there in darkness, twice?

Further down, the upper valley narrowed at the cliff-bound neck, where the river ran deep over pale rocks. If they survived, the next battle would be there. He looked hopefully down the valley but there was no sign of relief.

Skirmishes were still going on all over the battlefield, which had spread across the upper third of the valley. This high, the streams were not deep enough to trouble the lyrinx. The air reeked of blood, smoke and burnt meat.

Xabbier appointed guards, then called Nish and a nearby soldier to him.

'As far as I can tell, we've lost two-thirds of our number, dead or too badly wounded to walk. That still leaves thirteen thousand, if we can rally them. I see no flags, no pennants, no signallers, so our senior officers must be dead. But we've survived the night, and done better than I could have hoped when the attack began. We've killed almost as many of them as they have of us, and I don't think that's ever happened before.'

'They seem somehow . . . sluggish,' said Nish. 'They're slow and awkward, and less coordinated than before.'

'I've noticed that too,' said Xabbier. 'Could it be a residue of your father's magic?'

'Or an after-effect of being stone-formed?' said Nish.

'Whatever the reason, it's all that's saved us. Now that the sun's up, things should go better. We can bring our catapults and javelards to bear on them. All we need are people to give the orders.'

'There's no senior officers left alive,' said the third soldier, a grey-haired, scarred man of about forty-five. 'And not many sergeants, either.'

'You've seen experience, haven't you, soldier?' said Xabbier.

'Lemuir, surr. I've been in the army for twenty years. Was a sergeant once, in charge of a squad of clankers, but broken to private for insubord—'

'You'll do. You're sergeant again, Lemuir. Here's a hat.' He plucked a bloody sergeant's cap from a dead soldier. 'Run to the clankers and get them moving, in formation. Shepherd our troops this way. We'll try and move down this side of the valley, towards the neck. If that's not held against us, we'll keep going to the sea, then on to Gnulp Landing. The town is walled; we can take refuge there.'

'And with luck,' Nish added, 'we'll come upon General Troist by noon.' If noon isn't too late.

Lemuir saluted and ran off.

'Cryl-Nish, you're promoted to lieutenant. Find yourself a hat. Go across the stream and round up the soldiers over there. Send them to me On the way back, see if there's anyone alive up at the command post. Any soldier that looks up to command, give them a hat. I'll do the same, and between us we just might make it. We've got a chance, but only if we take advantage of it now.'

Sheathing his sword, Nish limped off.

THIRTY-ONE

It took an hour, and several more skirmishes, before he reached the first stream. The lyrinx *were* more sluggish than before; he killed another on the way, though this one had been badly wounded and could barely stand. Nish had rallied well over a thousand soldiers and sent them back to Xabbier. He'd capped nine others, with orders to spread across the battlefield and send everyone who could walk to Xabbier's command post.

The stream barely came up to his hips, though the cold water bit into wounds Nish did not know he had. On the far bank he looked back. The valley spread out like a map below him and he could see threads of soldiers moving across it, as well as the larger force Xabbier had already gathered. Unfortunately the enemy could see them just as clearly. Several bands of lyrinx were also heading that way. Fortunately there were none in the air. That could mean they were too sluggish to fly. It might also mean the field was too weak to support them.

A clanker crossed his path, moving slowly. Nish waved his lieutenant's hat and the machine turned towards him. There was enough in the field to drive it, at least. He pulled the rear hatch up and yelled inside. 'Find all the clankers you can and lead them across to the southern side. We're making a stand further down the valley.'

'Got no shooter,' the operator stated mournfully. Without one, a clanker was little use on the battlefield, and terribly vulnerable.

Nish made a quick decision. 'You have now.' He climbed

atop, settled in the seat and loaded the catapult and javelard. 'That way.'

Should have thought of this earlier, he realised. Soon he had been around a dozen clankers, ordering them to contact every machine they came to, and escort the surviving troops to Xabbier. With his lieutenant's hat, no one questioned him. All they needed was someone to tell them what to do.

'How's the field?' he yelled down through the hatch on the way back. The clanker was creeping across the stream, its feet slipping on the pebbly bottom.

'Weak, but it'll do,' the operator said.

'Head up towards the scrutator's tent, in case there are any officers left alive. You know where that is?' Nish couldn't imagine that any officers had survived, but that wasn't what he was looking for. He'd come to find out the fate of his father and retrieve the priceless tears. They must not be allowed to fall into enemy hands.

'Know where it *was*,' the operator muttered, turning up the slope.

This part of the battlefield was empty now, though there were torn and trampled tents everywhere, and each of the night's bonfires wore a halo of dead. In places they lay so thickly that it was difficult to avoid running over them. Nish often heard the cries of wounded soldiers but steeled himself to ignore them. If he stopped for the barely living he would soon join the dead.

'It was here,' said the operator. 'But it ain't here now.'

'Are you sure?'

'I'm sure. Scrutator's tent was two up from the row of command tents. That's them there.'

The command area was a horrific sight. That bladed disc of white light had cut through everything it encountered – tents, clankers, horses and men – half a span above the ground. Right in front of him, half a dozen officers lay together, sheared off between waist and chest. He recognised several of them. The majority, from their uniforms, were generals and other senior officers. The sight made his empty belly heave.

He continued up the slope. A square of yellowed grass, stained with alchymical droppings, marked the site of Jal-Nish's tent, though not a shred of canvas or rope remained. His father's strategy must have been to lure the strongest of the enemy to him, then to destroy them with his Art, fantastically boosted by the tears of the node. It would have been a master stroke, had he succeeded. Jal-Nish would have gained his own page in the Histories, and perhaps Ghorr's hat as well.

But the black, golden-crested lyrinx had turned the spell back on him, crushing it down, and finally Jal-Nish had done the lyrinx's work for them, scything through most of his commanders in one bloody second. He might still get that page in the Histories but it would be known as Jal-Nish's folly.

The yellow grass was littered with smashed glass, remnants of Jal-Nish's alchymical equipment. Orange fumes still rose from a small patch stained red by some corrosive fluid.

A crumpled mass of canvas and poles lay a bit further on. Something big had gone through the tent and dragged it away. 'Hold on,' Nish called to his operator. 'I've got to take a look.'

He jumped down, jarring the knee he'd hurt coming down the cliff, and limped to the wreckage. There was nothing inside the canvas but the remains of Jal-Nish's table and a torn map. The chest that had held the tears lay ten spans on, smashed to fragments. He went back and forth across the area a dozen times but found no trace of the tears. Presumably the golden-crested lyrinx had them, in which case they would be safe over the sea by now. Nish kept searching among the bodies for his father's. There were corpses strewn everywhere, and signs that the enemy had fed here – bodies partly eaten, dismembered limbs, loose heads.

And then, something glinting in the dirt: his father's platinum mask, crumpled as if a lyrinx had stamped on it. He turned it over with the toe of his boot, not wanting to touch it. The inside was stained with blood, though that did not mean Jal-Nish was dead.

He kept searching, and finally he found it – a long black

boot, mirror-polished under its covering of dust. Jal-Nish took pride in his attire and Nish would have known the boot anywhere, with its intricate tooling down the sides and the carefully built-up heels to make him seem taller than he was. It was his father's, and there was a foot inside it, bitten off halfway down the shin.

Jal-Nish was dead and eaten. It was all over. Nish studied the remnant, feeling no horror, no sorrow, no relief. He felt nothing at all, and surely that was wrong, no matter what a monster his father had been.

'Enemy!' called the operator.

Nish looked over his shoulder but saw no immediate danger. He headed back to the command area and checked every body there. None of the officers, nor any of their guards, had survived. The army's war chests had been broken open in the battle, leaving gold and silver scattered across the sward. He did not touch it.

Trudging around a neatly bisected clanker, Nish ran straight into a lyrinx that was just as surprised to see him. He grabbed for his sword.

Nish had developed a technique for dealing with these strangely sluggish lyrinx. They seemed to lack the dexterity of those he'd encountered on previous occasions, taking a long time to regain their balance after striking. He would go forwards, almost within reach, and feint with his sword, left then right. The lyrinx would swing wild blows at him with one arm, then the other. If off-balance to its left, he would lunge from the right. If to its right, he would attack from the left. If off-balance forwards, he would dive straight at it, the most risky attack of all, come up inside the sweep of its arms and thrust through the groin plates, or into the belly.

He'd nearly died three times, and once the creature had trapped him in its arms and was attempting to bite his head off before he got the sword in far enough. But so far he'd always been the victor.

This time it didn't work. As he went forwards the lyrinx brought a knee up into Nish's belly, sending him flying. He landed hard, rolled and tried to draw his sword but the scabbard tangled between his weary legs. He hopped out of the way as the lyrinx lunged.

The sword came free; Nish slashed at the join just below the creature's armoured kneecap, but missed. The lyrinx tried to kick the sword out of his hand. Nish brought it up just in time and the tip speared into the creature's instep, grating on bone.

He wrenched it out, feeling faint. No matter how often he did it, he would never get used to the feeling of his sword hacking through the enemy's flesh. It was horrible.

The lyrinx screamed, put its foot on the ground and collapsed, leaving its belly and throat exposed. Nish should have slain the creature, but did not have the stomach for it. He collected an armload of javelard spears from a clanker that had been neatly cut in half, staggered back to his machine with them and climbed aboard.

'There's no one alive in the command area,' he said. 'Head up towards the cliffs.'

He'd seen soldiers hiding up there earlier though, if they were there now, they weren't coming out. There might well be thirteen thousand left alive but Xabbier would be lucky to round up three-quarters of them. And who could blame the others, after their second massacre in a month?

He spent another two hours scouring the battlefield, sending men and clankers across to Xabbier, appointing sergeants from any soldiers who had battle experience, and giving them their orders. He encountered lyrinx, though not many, for they had moved further down the valley, following the mass of the army. Nish used his javelard three times, killing two more of the creatures, and fired the catapult many times without doing any damage. It was only accurate in the hands of an expert.

Despite his earlier vow, he did stop for those wounded who had some chance of recovery. The seriously injured he had to leave where they lay, despite their piteous groans. He'd just lifted a cruelly wounded man, speared through the groin, when another called out to him. This fellow had his stomach torn open and was bound to die.

'I'm sorry,' Nish said, crouching beside him and giving him the last of the beer. 'I've no room left inside.'

'I'm dying anyway,' said the soldier, clutching at his wrist. 'Please, end it for me.'

Nish looked into the fellow's eyes and knew what had to be done but, despite his father, he could not do it. No matter how good the justification, killing the man to put him out of his misery was beyond him. He was sick to his heart of all the violence.

'I'm sorry,' he said, and had to walk away. For the rest of the day he could see the pain in the soldier's eyes, and the bewilderment.

The clanker was bursting with wounded by the time he finally reached Xabbier's staging post, having replenished his missiles from wrecked machines several times on the way. They were creeping along now, at little more than walking pace.

'What's the matter, Operator?' Nish called. He did not know the fellow's name. 'Can't you go any faster?'

'There's not much left in the field,' said the operator mournfully. Nish had yet to meet a cheerful one – the bond with the machine was so intense that all human interactions palled by comparison. 'It's been going down all morning. It's only a small node hereabouts and we've nearly drained it dry.'

Not surprising, given the number of clankers that had drawn on it, and lyrinx too, not to mention that great struggle between the golden-crested lyrinx and Jal-Nish. And if our clankers can barely move, he thought, Troist's won't be doing any better. But at least the enemy won't be able to attack us from the air.

A great mass of soldiers had gathered on a grassy mound, with smaller detachments grouped above and below. Rows of clankers defended them, some hundreds, but it was a pitiful remnant of the great army of yesterday.

The enemy had drawn off, for the moment. An army of

lyrinx had collected under the trees near the closest stream, watching the scene. Nish had his operator drive the clanker up to Xabbier's flag.

'I've done all I can.' He climbed down. 'I've sent across about four thousand men and a few hundred clankers.'

'And I've gathered another six thousand,' said Xabbier, 'but that's not a quarter of those who were alive last night.'

'There are thousands of undamaged clankers with no operator to drive them,' said Nish, 'I saw a lot of soldiers further down the valley, across the second stream, though they were too far away to call back. There's no one left alive in the middle of the valley. At least, no one with a chance of living.' He saw that dying soldier's eyes again. 'There are so many injured, just dying there in the sun. And to go past and be able to do nothing for them . . .'

'It's cruel,' said Xabbier. 'But what can we do? If we stay to comfort them, more will die.'

'And all for the folly of one man, my father! How can I ever make up for it?' Nish knew he had to – the night, and the morning, had changed him forever, and he felt a need to atone for his father's crimes as well as his own blunders.

'You've already begun to,' said Xabbier, 'by what you've done last night and today.'

'It can never be enough,' said Nish. 'I can't bring the dead back to life.'

'Don't take on more than your due,' said Xabbier. 'Your father committed this terrible folly all by himself.' He looked burdened. 'I don't know what to do now. What do you think, Cryl-Nish?'

Why ask me? Nish thought. You're the soldier. But Xabbier hadn't commanded such a force in a rout either. 'We're low on spears,' Nish began, 'so I'd send a few clankers round the battlefield to pick up used ones. Then make our way down to the neck, fast as we can. The enemy have suffered terrible casualties, more than they must have expected, and their morale may be faltering.'

'Doesn't look that way,' said Xabbier.

'Well, in bright sunlight they're slightly handicapped, but if we're not out of the valley come nightfall, there's not a man will be living in the morning.'

'That was my plan too,' said Xabbier. 'And we can expect Troist's army before too long.' He sent the clankers off, then conferred with his sergeants. He gave orders and the signallers relayed them to the troops.

'We can hope for it,' Nish muttered.

The clankers returned, distributed the spears, and the army and escorting clankers set off. Before too long the bright sunshine was replaced by dark clouds sweeping in from the distant Sea of Thurkad. Raindrops pattered on the top of the clanker. Nish wiped his face, gloomily. Rain would disadvantage them and aid the enemy.

Soon they ran into heavy fighting. The army was quickly broken into struggling bands of soldiers and the leaders fell like flies. Nish had no idea what was going on, so he ducked through a line of fighting men and climbed a knoll. The soldiers were spread out all across this side of the valley and no one seemed to be leading them. He went back and forth in the clanker, issuing fruitless orders while he searched everywhere for Xabbier. There was no sign of him. He must have fallen in the assault.

Nish felt panic rising; this was going to be another massacre and at the end there wouldn't be a soldier left standing. He had to do something, hopeless though it was. He would try to rally the soldiers and get them down to the neck.

'Down there!' he ordered his operator. 'Take me to the front.'

The fighting was fierce; within minutes Nish had used all his spears. Rotating the javelard out of the way, he settled behind the catapult, wound it back a few extra notches and took aim at a band of lyrinx running towards him.

Nish pulled the release lever. The cords snapped, shaking the clanker, and the catapult ball rolled gently off the side.

'What's that?' cried the operator, peering fearfully up through the hatch. His 'crown of thorns' – a headband of wire and crystals that allowed him to control the clanker – hung askew over one ear.

'Catapult's broken,' Nish said. 'Keep going.'

Nish couldn't see the clankers with the extra spears, and could not go back for more without leaving his troops leaderless. His clanker was damaged and moving at less than walking pace so, ordering it back for spears, he slipped off the side, pulling out his bloodstained sword. He had learned more about sword play this morning than he had in the years of intermittent training at the manufactory. Every muscle throbbed, every bone ached, but he was inured to it now.

He fought his way down Gumby Marth, rallying the scattered bands of soldiers into a fighting force, and praying that when he topped the rise he would see Troist's army stretching before him. All he saw was more enemy and, despite the debilitating effects of stone-forming, in one-on-one combat they won more often than they lost.

At last he reached the opening of the neck with a dozen other soldiers. The survivors of the army were now close behind, at least, and their sergeants had them in hand. Here the valley was only a few hundred paces wide and cliffs hemmed them in on either side. A rocky ramp occupied the middle, over which the river, as it now was, roared in a series of cascades. There was room for the clankers and soldiers to pass down between the river and the cliff, though the broken country restricted movement to a few narrow passages, each guarded by lyrinx. At least the army had the advantage of height, though several lyrinx had climbed the cliffs and could hurl rocks down at them.

The slope dropped away steeply for the length of a bowshot, then flattened out as Gumby Marth broadened again. Down there, patches of trees, and folds in the land, made ideal places for an enemy ambush. In the distance he could just make out the Sea of Thurkad, there close to its narrowest as it rushed towards the Karama Malama, the chilly Sea of Mists.

He scanned the lower valley, searching for the nine hundred clankers and thirteen thousand soldiers of Troist's army. All he saw were lyrinx, thousands of them, holding the neck of the valley against him.

THIRTY-TWO

It occurred to Tiaan that Minis might have come the other night in search of absolution. He wanted to please everybody and to have everyone like him. Minis jumped every time he heard his foster-father's voice.

She walked around and around her room, treading softly so she would not be heard. Her legs were now strong enough for an escape attempt, though she hadn't worked out how. Every Aachim kept an eye on her. Thyzzea and her family watched Tiaan especially closely, since her flight would mean their punishment.

To flee, she must have command of a construct, and that meant getting Vithis out of the way. Could she play on his obsession with his clan? If some of them *had* survived the gate, he would surely drop everything else to find them.

A plan began to germinate. She spent half the night working it out.

Thyzzea was woken in the early hours of the morning by moans from Tiaan's room. She slipped in through the open flap. 'What's the matter?' she said softly.

Tiaan jerked up in bed, the bedclothes falling all around her. 'I saw them!' she said, staring into an infinite distance.

The girl took her hand. 'Who did you see, Tiaan?'

'They were crying out, as in torment,' Tiaan whispered.

'What are you talking about?'

'It's my fault they were lost.' A tear ran down Tiaan's face. Her eyes closed and she sank onto the pillow, fast asleep.

349

Thyzzea went out. 'Just a bad dream,' she said to her mother.

Twice more that night the Aachim were disturbed by similar dreams, though Tiaan seemed not to be aware of them. However, when Thyzzea came to wake her at dawn, Tiaan would not rouse.

Thyzzea shook her by the shoulder. 'Tiaan, wake. Vithis will be here soon.'

Tiaan hid her face and began to wail and groan. 'All my fault. All my fault.'

Abruptly Thyzzea was thrust out of the way. '*What* is your fault, Artisan?' grated Vithis.

Tiaan groaned, tossed her head from side to side and squeezed a tear out from under one eyelid. The Aachim's hand caught her shoulder.

'I saw them,' she whispered. 'Just as I saw Minis, after I first used the crystal. I saw lost Inthis—'

'My clan!' He screwed up his face in anguish. 'What did you see?'

In a single movement he heaved her out of bed and held her high. Tiaan almost gave it away then, for her borrowed nightgown was revealing. She had to force herself not to react, as if she was still asleep.

'They were crying out for help.' Opening her eyes wide like a sleepwalker, Tiaan looked wildly about. Her voice rose to a shrill cry. 'I saw them, standing by a broken construct.'

'Lord Vithis,' said Zea, who had come in quietly. 'This is not seemly.'

Vithis put Tiaan down. 'You saw Inthis? Where, Tiaan?'

'There was a man who looked like you,' she improvised. Last night, after working her plan out, Tiaan had dreamed it, over and over. Her dreams were especially intense after using the amplimet and now she could hardly distinguish what was dream and what was fiction.

'Like me?'

'Not as tall, and younger. There was no grey in his hair but

350

he had your face.' An easy guess. Family resemblances were strong among the Aachim.

'My cousin, Nythis! Did you see anyone else?'

The desperate hope in his eyes almost undid her. How could she work such a shabby deception on him? Though Vithis had used her, that did not make it right to give him hope where there was none. But if she did not, she was doomed.

'I did see others,' she said faintly, 'though not so clearly as the man. There were three children . . . No, four, and two young women, both tall and black haired. Or were there three? It's fading.' She used the commonest images of Aachim. Hope must do the rest, and make them into his lost loved ones.

'Gia and Mien, surely,' he said with an exhalation of breath. 'Is that all, Artisan? Just those few?'

She screwed up her eyes as if trying to see what was far away. 'Other constructs lay in the distance – some were broken, others whole. There may have been more people; I couldn't see clearly.'

'Where, Artisan?' He reached for her, as though to shake her, but thought better of it.

An image from the dream came to her. 'It was no place I've ever seen before.'

'What did it look like?' he gritted.

Tiaan had not thought her plan through that far but another memory, or dream, sprang into her mind. 'All the land was white. White as snow, though I don't think it was snow.'

'Ice?' said Vithis.

'It could have been ice . . . There were no trees, no animals. The sky was so dark it was almost purple.'

'A purple sky? There are such places in the void,' said Vithis. 'But it is endless. They might be anywhere.'

He twisted his long fingers, then turned to Thyzzea, who stood in the doorway behind her mother. 'Call Urien; and find Larniz the Mapmaker, at once.'

Thyzzea glanced at Zea, who nodded. She hurried away.

'What else, Artisan?' said Vithis. 'You haven't given me enough.'

Tiaan didn't want to make up anything else. It would be too easy to be trapped by an inconsistency. She couldn't remember much about the time when the gate had opened, though she recalled the *feelings* very well; the cries, the torment, the loss. Wait; there *had* been something, just before Vithis had taken control of the gate. Clan Inthis, panicking, had ignored his pleas to stay back. A host of constructs had roared up the spiralling path to the gate, and she recalled that their smooth metal had a bluish tint. None of the constructs she had seen since had that colour. They were all black.

Tiaan hesitated. If she was wrong, it would ruin all the work she'd done so far. She gave a little shudder, opened her eyes and looked Vithis full in the face.

'What do you remember, Artisan?'

'The constructs were different to these ones. The metal was blue.'

His smoky brown eyes lit up. 'Are you sure? Only Clan Inthis knows the secret of working the blue metal.'

'They were blue,' she said. 'All of them. That's all I remember.' She closed her eyes again, as exhausted as if she had not slept at all.

Thyzzea came running in. 'I've sent word to find the map-maker, Lord Vithis.'

'Where's Urien? I need her counsel.'

'She has ridden to the main camp near Gospett.'

He scowled. 'I knew nothing of this. When did she go?'

'Last night. She planned to take a construct from Gospett and meet those returning from Tirthrax. Word came yesterday afternoon that they were on their way, I'm told.'

Tiaan went rigid under the covers. She could only hope the seed she had planted in Vithis would germinate before Urien got back.

'Why did she conceal this from me?' he said fretfully. 'How far away are they?'

'Near a place called Saludith, south-east of here, Lord Vithis,' said Thyzzea. 'Two days, if they travel hard.'

'I can't wait that long. If Tiaan truly *has* seen my people, alive, they're in terrible danger. Where's Larniz?'

'I'm here! How may I help you, Lord Vithis?' The speaker was an extremely burly man, thick of arm and leg, with a bald head and a short, dense beard quite as black as coal.

'The artisan has had a vision – at least, I hope it's a vision, and not an hallucination – about lost First Clan. She saw people in blue metal constructs, in a barren land that was all white, with a purple sky. Not covered in snow, but possibly ice. That's all you saw, Tiaan?'

'Yes,' she said faintly.

'Where could they be, Mapmaker?'

'If not for the sky I would have said somewhere on this world, in the frigid south, or the doubtless equally frozen north. But a purple sky? Can it be the void?'

'Surely you know your trade, Mapmaker!' Vithis said imperiously.

'None of us has ever ventured into the void, Lord Vithis.'

'Then consult the archives!'

'Such records would be from the ancient past. We don't have them.'

'Why not?'

'Our libraries had to be left behind on Aachan, including most of what we know about the void.'

'So you can't tell where this place is,' Vithis said furiously.

'My construct is packed with maps and charts, but none are of the void.'

'What if we had ended up there?'

'We would have died, with or without my maps. Others may have the information you are seeking, but I do not.'

'Do you know anything about seeking out the lost, Mapmaker?'

'I am not a mancer, Lord Vithis.'

'You're dismissed. I'll go after Urien. If anyone can find them, she can.' He turned to the door.

Larniz followed him out, calling, 'Lord Vithis?'

'What is it?' Vithis cried. 'I can't wait for any man.'

'It may be more fruitful to mind-search the artisan—'

Vithis returned. 'You're right. I must not favour one approach over another. Once I come back, we will attempt a *dream-forcing*. Larniz, run and find Minis for me. I'll put her under his personal guard. I can't trust treacherous Clan Elienor if I'm not here to watch over them. Tiaan must complete the recovery of the constructs. When that's done,' he gave Larniz a meaningful look, 'we shall see.'

Shortly, Minis appeared and formally took custody of Tiaan. They went straight to work. The day was hard, and the work slower than before, so by the time exhaustion put an end to it in the mid-afternoon, Tiaan had only done two trips. Eighty-nine constructs still remained to be moved. Another day's grace though, by the end of it, Vithis and Urien would be back.

Minis had stood in the shooter's turret all day, with another Aachim, and there had been no chance to talk to him alone, much less implement Tiaan's plan. She had to gain his cooperation. There was no possibility of escaping without it.

On the way home Minis got in beside her, but did not speak. Vithis must have ordered him to keep his distance.

'What does dream-forcing mean?' Tiaan asked when they were approaching the camp, now shrunken to barely a few hundred tents. Everyone was gone but the last of Clan Elienor, Minis and a few of Vithis's guards. In the distance she could see a towering pavilion, the temporary monument erected to the Aachim dead.

'It's a form of truth-reading, whereby knowledge, or secrets, hidden deep in the subconscious mind can be drawn to the surface . . .'

'Is it painful?' she asked, imagining what it would be like to have Vithis rummaging through her mind, not to mention having all the lies she'd told him exposed.

'Not physically . . .' He trailed off, looking over the side at the withered grass.

'But what?' she persisted.

'It reveals everything, including what has been mercifully forgotten. Nothing can be held back. Dream-forcing is always traumatic, for it can reveal truths hidden even from oneself. Especially from oneself,' he said softly. 'It's rarely used – it hurts the forcer just as much, and can drive them insane.'

Can *anyone* do it?'

'Only a handful of us, for it requires a powerful comprehension of the Art. Foster-father is able to dream-force, though, in your case, he would not.'

She relaxed. 'Why not?'

'He desperately wants to know the fate of our clan, so dream-forcing you would be particularly hazardous for him. I expect Urien will do it, when she returns tomorrow, but take no comfort from that. She's a hard woman.'

Tiaan pressed her hands to her head, which was still ringing from the day's exertions. All the more urgent that she go on with her plan. Minis must come to her tonight. He lifted her onto the side, looking around for the guard, but the man had already gone. Minis sprang down, reached up his arms and she slid into them. He turned in the direction of Thyzzea's tent. Tiaan had to distract him. She'd have no chance to subvert him there.

As they passed the large tent house he shared with his foster-father, she made a gagging sound and sagged in his arms. 'Minis, my head is spinning.'

'It's not far now.'

'Could I have a drink of water, please?' she said hoarsely, plucking fretfully at his sleeve. He carried her to his tent, settling her in a round chair just inside the door.

'I'll call the healer. I—'

'No need,' she said hastily. 'It's from using the amplimet. It happens every night.'

He frowned. 'I've never seen you like this before.'

'It usually comes on after I finish work. I'll be all right in a while.'

He fetched her a container of water. She drank the lot and

355

laid her head on the edge of the chair. 'The light hurts my eyes. I need to lie down somewhere dark for a few minutes.'

Again that troubled look. 'You . . . could go in my chamber.'

'Please,' she said.

He picked her up, torn between anxiety and longing. Tiaan hooked one arm around his neck. She felt bad about using him but there was no alternative.

Minis laid her on the bed, and the look in his eyes burned her. She turned away, too exhausted to deal with him. The work took so much out of her. Sleep, and the crystal dreams that came with it, were the only remedy, but that was not what she had in mind.

The room was plain, being just a walled section of a tent, though the fabric was woven like a costly tapestry. The only furnishings were an intricately patterned rug on the floor and two carved wooden chests. Both were of the finest quality and beautifully decorated, and the lids of both were up. The larger held folded clothes and other personal items. The smaller contained half a dozen books bound with covers of chased metal, a crystal seeing-globe and several mechanical devices whose purpose was not readily apparent. Another book lay on the chair beside the bed. It was also beautiful but, being in the Aachim script, she could not read it. What must his home have been like; his foster-father's mansion?

She felt a pang for their art, craft and civilisation, lost in the volcanic fury Aachan had become . . .

Tiaan woke to discover that it was dark outside. She'd slept after all and her headache was gone. Better get on with it. She looked out. Minis sat at a folding table, writing in a journal. A candle cast a pool of yellow light in front of him. He looked young and, for the first time, carefree. Her heart lurched, but she fought it.

'Minis?'

He came at once.

'Thank you,' she said. 'I feel better now.'

He smiled, though it faded at once, as if he'd caught

himself imagining what he had no right to. 'I'll take you home.'

'Could I . . . have something to eat? I'm famished.'

'Of course. I was about to have my dinner.'

He brought her a platter on which sat a spherical knob of the spicy red sausage she'd grown accustomed to eating, as well as sticks of cheese, bread, pickled vegetables and wine. It was all very fine but she did not take much. Tiaan had never felt so nervous, not even on that fateful day when the Aachim had come through the gate and she had first seen Minis in the flesh. How different it could have been. This cosy domestic scene could have been real. And, Tiaan was shocked to realise, a part of her still wanted it.

Ashamed of her fickleness, she reminded herself of little Haani's pointless death, the crushed chest, the thin arms and legs hanging lifeless. Tiaan rubbed the worn leather bracelet on her left wrist, the birthday present from Haani. Her twenty-first birthday felt a thousand years ago.

You were in on it from the beginning, Minis. Or, if not, you did not have the courage, when you realised what the clan leaders were doing, to refuse to be a part of it. Either way you failed me.

She was not sure how to go about her plan. Tiaan was, by nature, neither cold nor calculating, but now she had to be. She looked up. Minis's eyes were on her and it sent a shiver up her spine. She poured a dribble of wine into her cup, filled his and sipped, holding the cup in both hands. The wine was so beautiful it was hard not to keep drinking, but that would be fatal. Time passed. She filled his cup again, his third. Enough to loosen his inhibitions.

His big eyes were moist. 'Tiaan, I'm so sorry. I've been the biggest fool of all time.'

'Yes, you have!'

'I – you don't know what it's been like for me. Both my parents were killed when I was five.'

Was this an excuse? 'How did it happen?'

'A volcano threatened our vineyards; they were studying it

357

when it erupted and buried them in red-hot ash. They were burned alive.'

She shuddered. 'What a horrible way to die.'

'I lost everything that day,' he said bitterly. 'Vithis took me in, even though he hated my parents and their values. He's of the old Aachim: the arrogant, unloving kind. Whatever they liked, he hated; whatever they praised, he derided. Whatever they believed, he denounced as lies, charlatanism and folly.'

'What about your foretellings?'

'Especially my foretellings! Each time my talent showed itself, he mocked me and told me that I was unworthy, even *unmanly*. And that's the worst of it. Though he sneers at my foretellings, he's superstitious and takes them to heart. He wants to believe, but can't because he doesn't believe in *me*! It's tearing me apart, Tiaan.' He bent his head to the table, though not in time to conceal the tears on his long lashes.

'Is that why you feel you have to please him?' she said.

The question appeared to surprise him. 'He's my foster-father, Tiaan. He's my only relative, and I'm all he has. We're bound together.'

'So when he asked you to use your empathic talent to reach across the void, you agreed.' She was guessing about that.

'There was no hope for us on our own world. I was proud to be chosen for such an important task.'

'How did you come to contact me?' She stretched out her hand, hoping he had been drawn to *her*, out of all the people in the world. 'Were you looking for someone like me?'

'It could have been anyone.' He was still staring at the tabletop.

She snatched her hand back, hurt and insulted.

Not noticing, he went on, 'We called out across the void, to anyone, on any world, who had the ability to hear.'

'You were not the only one to call?'

'Many Aachim who had *seeing* talents, or empathic ones, were set to the task. I called for four of our years, more than two of yours. Others for much longer.' He looked up and met her smouldering eyes. 'But I was the only one who ever got an answer. I saw you.'

That pleased her, though it did not make up for the previous insult. 'How did you call? Did you use some kind of crystal, like my – the amplimet?'

'Another way entirely.' His mouth set. 'I cannot tell you about that.'

'And yet you harassed me to tell you everything about my work, and talents, and our use of crystals,' Tiaan said coldly. 'Not only did you use me, you demanded everything of me and gave nothing back.'

'I was trying to save my people.' He could not meet her eyes now. 'Would you not have done the same? Besides, I didn't know you then.'

'You did the same, *after* you protested your love for me!'

'We . . . had to understand how your talent worked, and your amplimet, else how could we teach you what you needed to know?'

'From the result, you did not teach me very well.'

'Perhaps you didn't tell us all you should have.'

Again the blame was put on her. 'Why should I tell my enemies anything!' she snapped. Tiaan felt achingly weary and she was getting nowhere. She had to take charge. 'You claimed you loved me, but that was a lie. They told you what to say to me.'

'No!' he cried. 'That's not true.'

Tiaan quivered with fury. 'You can't lie to me, Minis. I've a perfect memory of our conversations. When I was trapped in that sphere of ice, near the manufactory, Tirior tried to get me to use geomancy. Even then I thought that she was keeping something from me. She took you aside and told you what to say. You protested, and Luxor looked shocked, but Tirior persisted. Finally you came back and told me that you loved me. That was your first betrayal, Minis.

'Once she saw that I cared for you, Tirior cynically used me. And, fool that I was, I believed you. I would have done anything to help the one I loved. But my feelings were incidental – once you gained my aid, I was as expendable as little Haani. You would have sacrificed a thousand of me to get what you wanted.'

'You are cruel, Tiaan.' Minis was grey about the lips. 'The child's death was an accident that I bitterly regret, but I can't bring her back. I did love you, *and I still do.*'

Tiaan looked into his eyes. 'You'll have the chance to prove it, tomorrow.'

'I'll prove it now. Do you still have the ring you made for me?'

The ring she'd crafted lovingly with her own hands, woven from the gold and silver old Joeyn had given her as he lay dying in the mine. 'The ring you rejected? Yes, I have it.' It hung on a leather thong around her neck. She drew it out.

'Give it to me.'

After a hesitation, she untied the knot and passed the ring to him. His eyes met hers. He held the ring between the fingers of both hands and took a deep breath. 'Tiaan, I swear by this ring, the most sacred object to me, that I will do all in my power to save you.'

'Tomorrow!'

'Tomorrow,' he said.

Was he trying to convince her, or himself? She held out her hand and he laid the ring on her palm. She put it back on the thong and unwrapped the amplimet. He sprang up in alarm but before he could stop her she had spoken.

'And I swear, by this amplimet, that if you fail me again you'll rue it all your remaining days.'

She looked up. He'd gone stiff and staring and she knew she'd done the wrong thing, but it could not be undone.

'Never, never swear upon an amplimet,' he whispered.

'It's too late. I've done it.'

'Yes, you've done it now.'

THIRTY-THREE

Nish's tattered army was now below the junction of the two streams, which here formed a river some twelve spans across, too deep and fast flowing to cross. At the neck it narrowed in a rocky cleft, rushing over a chain of rapids down the steep part of the slope before forming a series of wide meanders below it, where Gumby Marth broadened. 'How deep is the river down below?' he asked the soldier at his side.

'We forded it on the way in,' said Sergeant Lemuir. 'It was hard going – chest deep for the most part. The clanker operators weren't pleased.'

'I can imagine.' Clankers could move even when half full of water, as long as the operator's head was clear, but it must have been an alarming experience.

There were troops on the other side of the river too, in scattered groups, and doubtless enemy as well, although the bulk of lyrinx seemed to be on this side.

'What are we going to do, Lieutenant?' said Lemuir.

A professional soldier was asking his advice? But as far as they were concerned, he *was* their lieutenant. A good five thousand troops were staring expectantly at him, with the rest forming up behind them, escorted by seven or eight hundred clankers and a scattering of men on horseback. He'd asked about Xabbier but no one knew what had become of him, or any other officer. It was past noon and there was no sign of Troist, either. Privately, Nish no longer believed that any relief would arrive, but he wasn't going to say that aloud. What was he to do? It was one thing to give orders to a few dozen soldiers, another entirely to command an army. But, if they expected him to lead them, he'd better get started.

'Lad,' Nish said to a young signaller, 'call all the sergeants to me. Does anyone know the land further down the valley?'

'I do,' a tattered youth said.

'If we can get past the enemy, what next?'

'It's easy marching downriver to the sea, and then only a couple of days south along the coast to Gnulp Landing.'

Nish climbed the side slope to get a better view down the valley. Lemuir followed.

'What do you think, Sergeant?'

Lemuir gnawed at a bloodstained fingernail. 'Looks to be nine thousand holding the neck. More than us.'

'And a good few behind, sheltering under the cliffs and trees,' said Nish. 'They can afford to wait till dusk, but we can't.'

'Never heard of an attack on a superior force of lyrinx succeeding.' Lemuir tore off an arc of fingernail, chewed pensively on it a moment, then spat it onto the grey rock.

'Nor I,' said Nish. 'We could wait. Troist might yet turn up.'

'We'd have seen him coming up the valley by now.'

Nish had the same fear. 'He'll come over the ridge further down, where he can cross with the clankers.'

'Not in time. The lyrinx aren't going to wait, surr. They're getting ready to attack.'

Down the slope, the gathered lyrinx were moving, and behind them others were coming out of the trees. 'It's always better to attack,' said Nish. The decision had come easily after all. 'And they're fighting uphill.'

It wasn't much of an advantage, the enemy being so much bigger and stronger, but it was all they had. Nish ran down to his assembled sergeants and explained his plan, and the way he'd been successful in attacking the sluggish lyrinx.

'This has got to succeed,' he concluded. 'If they can keep us up here until dark, we're done for. General Troist can't take the neck against such a force. With the field so weak, his clankers might not be able to move uphill. But ours can still go down the slope. We must attack now, and *know* we'll win. Anything less is our doom. And we *can* win!'

'How?' said a squat sergeant with a bushy beard and a pair of oozing lyrinx scalps hanging from his shoulders, one green-crested, the other red. 'My men are as brave as any, but this has been a day without hope.'

'I've told you how I fight them,' said Nish. 'I'm not a trained soldier, and I've killed six of the enemy today, with sword alone.'

'That's not much help,' grunted the sergeant.

'They don't like fighting in the heat and brightness of midday, so now's our best chance.'

'It's going to rain again.' The sergeant looked pointedly up at the sky.

'The sun's out further down the valley. The cloud's breaking up. And, running downhill, our clankers can go through them even with the weak field . . .'

The sergeant shook his head. 'To beat such fierce fighters we'd need an entirely new battle plan, and all the luck in the world.'

'The enemy have another weakness,' said Nish, improvising desperately. 'They've lost twice as many as they'd have expected, so their morale must be low. Also, they're not used to losing and tend to panic after a sudden reversal. Let's form a flying wedge of clankers, cavalry, and our biggest, stoutest fighters, and charge them.'

'Never been done,' said the sergeant. 'Besides, it's too narrow for the clankers to manoeuvre down there. It'd be suicide.'

'So is standing here doing nothing.'

'Look, surr, we need a proper plan. I can't inspire my men if I don't believe in it myself.'

Nish had an idea. 'The lyrinx don't like to break off an attack when they're winning. What if we were to attack with, say, a third of our army, then turn and flee as if in panic. If they follow us out of the neck, we hit them hard with the rest.'

'That's not much of a plan,' the sergeant said, rubbing his stubble.

'I haven't finished yet. In our counterattack, we drive five hundred clankers at full speed right into the middle of their formation, then attack out in all directions, driving some of them up against the cliffs and others into the river. In the deep water, they'll panic and be swept down the rapids and it'll alarm the rest. Once their front line turns around to defend themselves, the remainder of our force attacks them from the other side. They won't have been pressed like that before, and if we're strong enough, we might break through.'

The sergeant considered Nish for a long moment. 'Your father was one for reckless plans, though I never saw him in the front lines. He always took good care of his own life.'

'My father is dead,' said Nish, 'and eaten by the enemy. I'm not reckless, Sergeant. In fact I'm terrified, but I'll be out in front, leading us – to victory or to death.'

The sergeant seemed to be weighing Nish's youth, stature, parentage. The other sergeants and soldiers held their breath. The sergeant asked a question of Lemuir, though Nish did not catch it. The man turned back to Nish and now, Nish knew, he was weighing his reputation, and what he'd done last night and today. The whole army knew of those deeds.

The sergeant grinned and thrust out a hand. 'We'll do it, surr. Death or glory!'

The whole army sighed as Nish clasped the callused hand. He addressed the sergeants. 'Then let's get to it. I want an advance guard, a third of our number. Not your best fighters, but the fleetest and wiliest of them, for they've got to put on a good act. They'll attack, accompanied by a hundred and fifty clankers, but the machines will be driven as though there's barely enough power. The rest of the army is to hang back, breaking lines and generally looking afraid.'

'We won't have to put on an act,' Lemuir said dryly.

'When the attack is almost to the enemy lines, the clankers will grind to a stop, as if there's not power to drive them. The shooters will scream out in panic. The soldiers will fight for another minute, then everyone will turn and flee as a rabble. The lyrinx will, I hope, follow them. If they do take the bait, we attack when they're right out of the neck and hit them with most of our remaining clankers and our biggest, toughest fighters. The fleeing advance guard will run to the rear, rearm and reform. Sergeants of the advance guard, ready your troops.' A number of the sergeants ran off.

'You,' Nish said to a lanky, long-legged messenger, mounted on a stubby roan, 'run down to the clankers. Make sure the remaining operators and their troops know to act panicky, but if the attack succeeds, they are to form into a wedge behind my clanker. We'll drive straight at the lyrinx with all but fifty clankers and half our troops. Sergeants, put your best and biggest along the wings, the others behind.' He issued detailed orders for that attack then, 'Should we break through, we'll make for the river and ford it at the meanders. Get ready!'

The remaining sergeants and signallers turned away. The advance formation came together quickly. They were a disciplined force but Nish was pleased to see they were acting as if on the verge of mutiny. Overacting, he thought, but the enemy could hardly tell that from their lines. He estimated the enemy numbers again. They might have been as many as ten thousand now. He'd lost well over a thousand in the earlier fighting, for he had less than nine thousand men and nine hundred clankers. So few.

Nish's ultimate plan depended on the strength of the field, or rather its weakness. It required a lot of power for the lyrinx to fly. If he could get his soldiers across the river they would have the advantage, given the lyrinx fear of water. But if there was enough in the field they'd fly across the river, attack again and his army must be defeated.

'They're ready, surr,' said a signaller beside him.

Nish checked. 'Go!'

The advance guard charged. He held his breath, for the enemy completely blocked the neck and were so numerous that his troops might simply be annihilated. A hail of bolts and javelard spears fell on the lyrinx but made very little difference. They held the line until Nish's soldiers were within spear-throwing distance. Many lyrinx fell, but more of his troops.

'Turn now,' he groaned aloud, seeing what deaths he'd sent his men to. They kept on.

The clankers creaked to a halt, their shooters crying wildly to each other as if in panic. What if they were, and it spread? The operators lurched their machines around. The soldiers screamed, threw their weapons away and fled. Nish's nails dug holes in his palms. It was all too convincing.

Would it work or not? Everything depended on what the lyrinx did. Nothing, it seemed; then, all at once, the enemy bounded after the fleeing soldiers, taking some down with their own spears. Lyrinx were faster than men. The slaughter was sickening and there was nothing he could do about it – they were a sacrifice to save the rest.

The soldiers scattered; the clankers ground away in all directions, troops hanging off the sides. 'Your orders, surr,' Nish's signaller said urgently.

'Not yet.' Let the lyrinx come up just a bit further. The wait was agonising, the deaths horrible, but finally the enemy were clear of the neck. 'Charge!' Nish roared, waving his sword in the air.

Running to one of the leading clankers, he clambered up the side, settling into the seat in front of the shooter. The clankers moved; the soldiers too. 'Is this as fast as we can go?' he called through the hatch.

'We'll pick up speed down the slope,' came the voice of the operator, 'but there's not much in the field and it's getting weaker all the time.' His teeth chattered. If he lost the field, he'd lose his clanker too.

Running full tilt downhill, they converged rapidly on the enemy. The shooter fired his catapult, the ball whizzing over Nish's head, and suddenly it was on. The other shooters were firing balls and spears. Gaps appeared in the enemy lines. The catapult ratchet went furiously. Nish, swaying with the bumps and lurches, heaved his shooter another ball. He wished he could fire the javelard but the clanker was an early make, not designed to use both at the same time.

With only fifty paces to go, a rain of missiles came at them – used javelard spears, balls of rock and any other object the enemy could lay their hands on. A heavy spear took the shooter on the clanker beside Nish's right off his platform. The enemy also used catapults but none were in evidence here. Such large weapons could not have been stone-formed.

For the first time in his life, Nish felt no fear for himself. He'd passed beyond such emotions, though he did feel a terrible, knotted pain for his troops, who were being slain and maimed all around, and even for the enemy. Perhaps the touch of the tears had heightened his senses. It was brutal and senseless, and all he could do was try to save as many of his men as he could.

He could see the expressions on the enemy's faces now, they were so close. Nish could almost read their flickering skin-speech. They were uneasy at his unprecedented mode of attack. Good!

The flying wedge of clankers and men struck the enemy lines with shattering violence. Nish's clanker drove right over a slowly moving lyrinx, which must have been injured. Another beast leapt for the shooter's platform, beheading Nish's catapult operator with a single blow.

Whirling the javelard around, Nish discharged the spear. It went straight though the beast, lifting it over the side. The clanker kept going. He pushed the dead shooter out of the way and flopped into the sticky seat, trying not to think about it. He had an army to manage and it was impossible to take it all in.

The front of the wedge, a couple of hundred clankers and three times as many men, had burst right through the front ranks of lyrinx and now formed into a circle three ranks of clankers deep, firing furiously into the enemy. After half a dozen salvoes that left the ground littered with enemy dead, the soldiers moved out behind their shield wall, trying to split the lyrinx ranks apart. Nish fired the catapult and struggled to load another heavy ball, turning the weapon around to fire over his soldiers' heads. In this situation he could not miss.

Further uphill, the survivors of the advance guard had rejoined the rest of his troops, armed themselves, and were attacking with the strength of desperation, taking what advantage they could from their uphill position. Nish could not tell how the battle was going. Even from his elevated seat it was just a blur of violence that went on and on, but, under attack from front and rear, the leading ranks of the lyrinx must be feeling the strain. To his right a squad of lyrinx were forced into the river, where they panicked and could not save themselves. A ripple of ash-grey skin colours passed through the enemy. Drowning was a terror that death in battle could never be.

He fired until all his rock balls were gone, and all but one of his spears. Almost every shot went true, exacting sickening slaughter. How could they not, where the enemy ranks were so tightly packed? A shiver went through the lines of the lyrinx. Their jagged red-and-black skin patterns indicated distress, which flicked in an instant to camouflage colours as their front line broke.

It was far from over, but it was the first sign that his tactics were working. Nish signalled twenty clankers to secure the gap, and the rest fought on. After another vicious ten minutes, the tide seemed to be turning. The uphill section of his army was less than a hundred paces away, and their line still held.

Nish rallied his troops again and again, bolstering the weak places in the circle and expanding it to wedge the enemy forces apart. The lyrinx, now fighting in five or six bands all showing black-and-red distress patterns, split at the rear. Nish's uphill and downhill armies flowed together. They had broken through and the way to the ford was clear.

His troops and clankers streamed through the gap. 'To the ford!' he signalled to the second wave. Then, to the survivors of his flying wedge, 'Form a rearguard, clankers last of all; we'll hold them off. Shooters, replenish your spears.'

They leapt off their machines and gathered up the fallen spears. Nish remained on his platform, watching the enemy. The lyrinx had drawn away to the side of the valley, shocked at the defeat and near to panic. Their leaders were trying desperately to rally them, so Nish fired a ball at a small group of officers and was pleased to see them scatter. His troops were vulnerable to a counterattack from the rear.

The army raced through the narrow passages of the neck and down the hill. He signalled his flying wedge into a defensive line, trying not to think of the injured, whose piteous cries could be heard above the thudding of the clankers. Again, anyone who could not walk had to be left behind to die, and there were hundreds of them. It was cruel. Tears poured down Nish's face at the thought of abandoning men who had fought so bravely, and who were in such agony, but nothing could be done. Any man who stopped to attend the injured would be slain by the enemy.

A band of lyrinx to their left had rallied and were getting ready to attack. Nish checked over his shoulder. The main body of the army was halfway to the ford. A soldier came running towards him, staggering under the weight of an armload of spears. 'Thought these might come in handy,' he said laconically.

'Thanks, soldier. Now run.'

The wings of the rearguard clankers were already in position. 'Fly!' Nish shouted to the foot soldiers of his rearguard. 'Wait at the ford for us to defend your backs.'

He gave them a minute or two to get away, firing salvoes at the enemy to help keep them at bay. 'Move out!' he signalled, and the clanker rearguard turned as one.

The eight metal feet of his machine thudded against the ground, crushing stones and pebbles into powder. The clanker crashed down the steep slope, screeching across rock outcrops, slipping on wet clay and skidding from side to side. The operator over-corrected, skidded the other way then gained control.

Now Nish noticed an irregularity in the beat of the feet, *thud-thud, thud-thud*, which grew worse as they went on.

'What's the matter?' he yelled.

'I don't know,' wailed the operator.

THIRTY-FOUR

The operator was cracking under the strain. Nish had to be the strong one, the one who never gave up, for his operator's sake, for the sake of all the survivors.

'Stay calm,' he yelled, firing his javelard. 'We'll be all right. General Troist can't be far away now.'

Nish had never seen the operator's face, just a pointed nose, dark hair thinning at the crown and no chin at all. It sounded as if the field was about to fail. He looked back; the battered lyrinx were close behind and gaining. How quickly they'd overcome their fear.

The open land on the far side of the river was empty, though in the distance he saw other groups of soldiers and clankers. More were coming out of the trees, and from other hiding places, now that they saw some hope. On the whole, Nish couldn't blame them. He did not see any enemy over there, thankfully.

'Pull up,' he ordered as the clankers approached a cut in the bank that marked the ford. The army hadn't gone across yet. Standing up on the shooter's platform, hanging on with one hand as the machine bounced and lurched across the uneven ground, Nish signalled to his clankers to form a defensive fan. Once that was in place, and it was pitifully thin, he signed to the main body of the army, 'Go across.'

The soldiers, accompanied by the leading clankers, began to move into the water. Further up the hill, the lyrinx were regrouping. Nish considered his one remaining spear and shivered. 'Hoy?' he yelled to the blood-covered shooter on the next clanker. 'Got any missiles left?'

The man shook his head. Nor did the one after, nor the one after that. Nish signalled the clankers that had crossed the river to fan out and ready their javelards, in case the enemy broke through his line. It would take fifteen minutes to get the remainder of the army across and his small rearguard would be lucky to survive that long.

Springing down, he scoured the ground for missiles. The pebbles were too small, though closer to the river there were flat stones the size of oranges. He gathered a couple of basketfuls and packed stones into the leather bucket of the catapult. The other shooters did the same. There was no telling where they would fly, but it was better than that desperate feeling of being defenceless.

Nish monitored the soldiers' progress. More must have come out of hiding than he'd thought. Four and a half thousand had crossed, he estimated, and there were four or five thousand to go. Not many clankers, though – less than six hundred. He'd lost three hundred in that desperate twenty minutes above the neck. Last night there had been five thousand. What a rich haul of precious iron for the people who dwelt near here, if any had survived the lyrinx raids.

The lyrinx, at least a thousand strong, charged.

'Clankers, hold formation,' he yelled, though they could not have heard him.

'Don't fire until I give the word!' Nish could not even hear his own voice and already the shooters were firing spasmodically, wasting their precious missiles. Leaping down, he ran around the front of the fan, waving his arms. 'Don't fire yet! Pass it along the line.'

He hobbled all the way to make sure they had the message. Nish was exhausted before he got there. There was nothing in his belly – nothing driving him but sheer will. The enemy were coming on fast and a good number were heading straight for him; they had learned that lesson early in their struggles with humanity.

Nish reached for his sword but his groping hand closed on an empty scabbard. It had been in the way when he'd been sitting behind the catapult, so he'd laid it on the shooter's platform.

He looked over his shoulder. The enemy were only a hundred paces away – less than ten seconds. *'Fire!'*

The shooters fired a stuttering volley that tore a ragged hole through the enemy line, but it was quickly filled. A dozen lyrinx were still heading towards him. With luck the shooters might fire another salvo before the lyrinx struck, but most would survive it. He leapt for the handholds on the side of the nearest machine, but his bad knee folded up and he fell.

The ground was shaking underfoot. No time for another attempt; the enemy would drag him down and tear him to pieces. Nish hurled himself between the second and third pairs of metal legs, tearing off his fingernails in his desperation to evade those flailing claws. He almost made it.

The lyrinx caught him by the boot. Nish kicked furiously, trying to pull his foot out, but the lyrinx squeezed his ankle so hard that its claws went through the leather. It heaved. He grabbed hold of a rod underneath the machine and clung on with all his might, but it was no use. The lyrinx was much stronger. It heaved again, breaking his grip, and jerked him out. This was it. He was dead.

Nish twisted as he came out, so he could see his enemy. It was a small one, and the green crest meant that it was female. Females were often larger than the males, so this one might not be fully grown, though its teeth were as sharp as any. He thrashed helplessly as she drew him towards her.

The lyrinx stumbled backwards and kept falling, a red spot blossoming on the right side of her forehead. Her grip did not relax in death and Nish had to prise the fingers off. His ankle turned when he tried to stand up but he eventually managed to drag himself onto the shooter's platform. Lyrinx lay dead all around and it took him a moment to work out what had happened. A host of soldiers had turned back from the water to defend them, laying down a withering fire with crossbows.

'Thanks,' he said to the big man, blood all over his head and shoulders, who was reloading a crossbow. 'I'll do the same for you some day.'

'You already have,' the man croaked, turning his way. It was Xabbier. 'There's another bow and a few bolts in the basket.'

Nish loaded the crossbow, wound the crank back and fired. 'Where have you been? I looked everywhere for you.'

'Inside, unconscious,' his friend said. Xabbier bent his head to reveal three bloody furrows across the top of his head, where the scalp was torn to the bone. 'Going to have trouble with haircuts for the rest of my life.'

'How are we doing?' Nish scanned the melee but his eyes were having trouble focussing.

'You've done brilliantly, Cryl-Nish. Most of the troops are across.'

'But we've only got nine thousand left.' The scale of the disaster left Nish speechless.

'You've saved *nine thousand* lives, Cryl-Nish. Not many men can say that. And more have survived across the river. It could have been much worse.'

'It will be for this rearguard,' said Nish. 'If the enemy rally again, as they seem to be. What are we going to do? I can't think straight.'

'Make an orderly retreat towards the river. Give the order.'

'But you're the officer here.'

'You've done well today, Lieutenant.' Xabbier saluted him.

A simple thing, but Nish felt such a swell of pride that he almost burst. He *had* done well, all on his own. He stood up, holding onto the frame of the catapult, and waved a flag. 'To the crossing!' he yelled down the hatch.

The clanker turned clumsily, the legs on one side beating faster than the others. This was a newer machine and both weapons could be used at once. Xabbier rotated the catapult so that it faced the rear, aimed and fired. Nish loaded the javelard with the last spear.

At first it looked as though they were going to make it, but the lyrinx began to gain on them, hurling whatever missiles they could find – sticks, stones, dead bodies. A good-sized log came whirling through the air, right at Nish. He ducked and it went over his head, smashing the catapult into a tangle of ropes and timber.

'Xabbier?' called Nish.

No answer – he was somewhere under the wreckage. A lyrinx leapt onto the back of the clanker. Nish took up the crossbow, swaying on his feet as the machine crashed into a depression and, metal feet thrashing, climbed out again. He fired, the clanker lurched and the bolt went wide.

Scrambling backwards, Nish frantically wound the crank, knowing he was not going to be ready in time. The lyrinx threw itself at him. He tried to get around the side of the wrecked catapult but there wasn't room.

Snap, right behind him. The lyrinx went down with a bolt in the throat. Xabbier, firing from underneath the broken timbers, had saved his life yet again. Nish helped him out and they heaved the quivering body off the side. Half the rear-guard were across. Nish's clanker was racing for the ford now but they weren't going to make it. A formation of lyrinx, hundreds strong, were streaming along the river bank to cut them off.

Nish loaded his bow with the next-to-last bolt, and waited He might as well make it count. He stood shoulder to shoulder with his friend – head to chest, really – but Nish felt Xabbier's equal in every respect.

The enemy were closing fast. He sought out a target, fired, felt in the basket for the last bolt, and waited. The lyrinx were also choosing their moment, determined to snatch one small victory from the afternoon's rout.

A trumpet call echoed across the river – a familiar call. Nish shaded his eyes, staring into the distance. Over the hill came a clanker, then another, then a dozen. From the first machine, a vast, twelve-legged monstrosity, fluttered a familiar pennant that brought tears to his eyes. It was Troist's army at last.

'Hey!' he roared, knowing that they could not hear him but

still having to yell out his joy anyway. 'Troist! Troist! Here!'

The clankers, hundreds of them now, altered course towards the ford. The leading machine fired its catapult. The ball soared across the river to land in the middle of the lyrinx with red carnage, and suddenly they'd had enough. The enemy dispersed in seconds, skin-changing to camouflage colours as they ran. It was over. The last of the rearguard was crossing the river. They'd done it.

'Go across, Operator,' Nish ordered wearily. He desperately wanted to lie down and never get up, but he had to be on his feet to the end, to give his report to General Troist and the scrutator.

His clanker ground its way into the river. The water rose higher and higher, the operator cursing softly as it crept up his chest. But the other clankers had made it and so would he.

Ragged bursts of cheering rose up from the soldiers bunched on the far side of the river as Nish's squadron splashed across, last of all, and again as the clanker pulled up before Troist's wedge of machines, water pouring out through its overlapping armour plates. The soldiers formed a great circle, twenty or thirty deep all around, and then they began to cheer and beat their swords against their shields. It became a ground-shaking chant: 'Cryl-Nish Hlar, Cryl-Nish Hlar!'

Nish climbed down and had a struggle to stay upright. He was shaking uncontrollably; his ankle would scarcely bear his weight and his wrenched knee throbbed. He bore twenty or thirty wounds and was purple and black with the dried blood of the enemy.

Xabbier by his side, each supporting the other, they made their way to the party that had come down from the first clanker. He recognised Troist, the scrutator, Tchlrrr and Lieutenant Prandie.

They stopped, several steps apart. Nish opened his mouth but nothing came out. The sound of chanting was deafening. If only Irisis were here to see it.

'I'm sorry to have come so late,' said Troist. 'When the field faded, it slowed us tremendously. Once the cloaker failed, we came under attack from the forest. We beat the enemy off, though it cost us dear. And then we came upon a stream too deep to cross and had to ford the river, which is why we're on the wrong side. I hope—' He scanned the battered remnant of the once great army, and a terrible sadness showed on his face. 'Is this all?'

'The damage was done in the night, surr,' said Xabbier. 'Before you could have hoped to reach us.'

'Even so,' said Troist, 'it's a bitter day. But not as bitter as it could have been. We must recognise that.' The general raised his sword high. The chanting ceased.

Xabbier pulled his hat off. 'Lieutenants Xabbier Frou and Cryl-Nish Hlar, at your service, surr.' His other hand deftly whipped off Nish's battered cap. 'Lieutenant Hlar will give the report.' He thumped Nish on the back.

Nish swallowed. He could not think of anything to say, and his mouth was too dry for speech. Tchlrrr passed him a skin of water and Nish took a mouthful, which tasted of leather.

'I – I got through in time, surr,' Nish said to Troist. 'Though I was lucky to make it. The enemy were already coming out of the stone as I entered the labyrinth. The army had a few minutes' warning – not enough, for there were near thirty thousand lyrinx. They went straight for the command tents and everyone there was killed.'

'Everyone?' said Flydd, meaningfully.

'Scrutator Jal-Nish Hlar lured the enemy's strongest to them. He attacked with the . . . with a special aspect of the Art, surr, if you take my meaning. The enemy was too strong.' Nish described the initial success of Jal-Nish's Art and, and, after it was countered by the great mancer-lyrinx, its disastrous failure.

'We'll talk privately about that later,' Flydd said in a low voice.

'Subsequently, everyone in the command area was slain, including my father. They . . . *ate* him.' In the past day there had not been time to think about that, nor was there now.

'We fought them all night and all morning,' Nish went on. 'We did the best we could; better than you might expect with such numbers against us. We've slain twenty-five thousand lyrinx, surr, but the cost has been terrible – nearly thirty thousand of us. Nine or ten thousand survived to cross the river, but only six hundred clankers. There are survivors on this side too. I don't know how many. That's all, surr.'

'That's not all, General Troist, surr,' said Xabbier. 'Lieutenant Hlar rallied the troops a dozen times; he killed at least ten of the enemy with sword and bow, and no one knows how many with the javelard. While I was unconscious, and no other officer remained alive, he led our forces on a frontal attack against a superior force of lyrinx, and broke them, and that's not been done in the history of the war. Had it not been for Cryl-Nish Hlar, not a man of Jal-Nish's army would have survived.'

There was a long silence, then General Troist stepped forward. 'Well met, Cryl-Nish. I heard part of the tale from the vanguard of your army, before we came over the hill. You can give me your report later, after we've made a secure camp and attended to the needy. But for the moment, I wish to recognise what you've done today.'

He signalled behind him and an aide came forward, bearing a black sword with a silver hilt and a single white jewel in the pommel. Troist took the sword, balanced it on his palms and in the same movement went to one knee, holding it out before him.

'Cryl-Nish Hlar, take this sword in recognition of your valour, and as a token of your commission as a lieutenant in my army.'

Nish just stood there, staring dumbly at the beautiful weapon. 'I don't understand . . .'

'He's confirming your field commission, you bloody fool,' said the scrutator, standing one step behind the general. 'Take the damn thing. Wave it in the air or something.'

Nish went to one knee and took the sword, which was unusually heavy for its size. 'I don't know what words I'm supposed to say,' he said in a hoarse voice, 'Thank you for arriving in time. And for the honour, surr. I hope I prove worthy of it.'

'The honour is mine,' said Troist. 'Were there more like you, Cryl-Nish, we would have won the war long ago. Rise up, Lieutenant Hlar. Salute your men.'

Nish stood, saluted the general in the correct manner, with sword in hand, then raised it high in the air and carved a salute, north and south, east and west, to the soldiers he'd fought beside all day. And to the ones who had not survived.

Letting out a roar that hurt his ears, they began to chant, 'Cryl-Nish Hlar! Cryl-Nish Hlar!' and beat their weapons on their shields, and did not stop until they had roared themselves hoarse.

It would have been the greatest day of Nish's life, had it not been for the thought of all their dead. And his.

THIRTY-FIVE

Later that afternoon, Flydd drew Nish aside, questioning him about the fate of his father, and how Jal-Nish had used the tears. When Nish had finished, the scrutator said, 'We'd better ride up there'

Nish had been expecting that. Flydd would have to see for himself, and try to find the tears, or discover what had happened to them.

'Now?' Nish said.

'Later. There are still too many lyrinx about. Get some sleep. We'll go in the night.'

Flydd woke him at midnight. It was cloudy and drizzling as they mounted and headed out, without a solitary guard. Flydd said it was better that way. They crossed the ford and he led them carefully up the valley, with lengthy stops where he sat his horse, sniffing the air and listening to the night.

'I believe they've gone,' Flydd said. 'The enemy don't linger around battlefields filled with their dead, and this one has cost them dear. Come on.'

It was not far off dawn when they reached the cliff-bound upper end of Gumby Marth, where the command area had been. They hunched under an overhang of limestone, out of the wind, to await the light. It was cool enough for the breeze to carry little taint. Nish hoped they would be well gone before the heat of the day ripened the dead.

'You must be feeling rather grim,' Flydd said.

'In truth, I don't know what to feel. I'm glad Father's out of his misery, and I suppose it's better this way, for everyone. He was an evil man, and becoming more wicked every day. Had he lived . . . And yet, despite all he did to me, he was still my father and now I have none.'

'It's a loss for any man. I still remember the day I heard the news about mine . . .' Flydd sighed, rummaged in his saddlebags and brought out a large silver flask, which he offered to Nish.

Nish took a healthy swig and promptly choked. 'That's strong!' His eyes began to water.

'A stiffener!' Flydd leaned back against the stone. 'It'll set your belly right for the job.'

He raised the flask to his lips but, despite his words, did not drink. It was just growing light. The grey cliffs separated from the grey sky, the lower valley from the horizon, the rocks from the dry grass. The brown earth from the humps and mounds made by the dead.

Wisps of fog hung in hollows and along the course of the streams. The scene was grey, dank and utterly, utterly dismal. Nish wanted to weep. 'So many dead, and all for the folly of one man, one scrutator. My father!'

'It took more than one man's folly to create this disaster,' said Flydd. 'You might as well ask how the Council came to have such power, yet lack the ability to use it wisely? Or how they delegated it to such a flawed man?'

'Or gave it to one so corrupt as Ghorr in the first place?' said Nish.

'He was a good man once,' Flydd reflected, 'but too ambitious. When his time was up, Ghorr couldn't let go, and perhaps it suited the power behind the Council—'

'When I mentioned that the other day, you put your fist in my mouth.'

'Clankers have ears, Nish. As I was saying, Ghorr refused to step down. He had the statutes of the Council changed to allow permanent tenure and that, I believe, was the first step on his path to corruption. The Council became unaccountable, even to itself. Others followed Ghorr's path and, once they grew old, many took the path of renewal, or rejuvenation – making their bodies young again. It's an evil I've sworn never to undertake.

'Not all survived it, but those who did soon had such power, such knowledge and experience that no one could better them. Instead of working for the security of the realm and the good of all, they became obsessed with maintaining control over everything. Power became more important than winning the war – indeed, the scrutators needed the war. It was their excuse to tighten the screws ever more, and in our terror of the enemy we allowed them to do so. Once that happened, Santhenar was on the road to ruin.

'It was only recently that I realised where we'd gone wrong, but by then it was much too late. The lyrinx had entrenched themselves and were outbreeding us. The war was no longer winnable.'

'What?' Nish leapt to his feet. 'You're joking.'

'I wish I were. Short of some brilliant breakthrough, it's already been lost. That's a secret that must never be revealed, Nish – the effect on morale would be disastrous; yet another reason to keep everyone in the dark. But the more you clamp down, the more people look for ways around it. Take your friend Mira, for example.'

'You know Mira?'

'I know she communicates, by skeet, with a network of like-minded people all over Lauralin.'

'Does the Council see them as enemies?'

'No, or they would have been eliminated by now, for all that they include many important and powerful people. But they are watched, very carefully, and if they make one wrong move it will be the end of them.'

'Not Mira, surely,' said Nish. 'She's already lost a husband and all three sons to the war.'

'She's safe for the moment. The Council have finally realised that, in seeking to control everything, they lost control of the war. Unfortunately, they're not capable of doing anything about it.'

'Are you saying that we're doomed? That we might as well give up?'

'There are always things that can be done, if you have the wit and will for it, and the arrival of the Aachim has changed the balance. We've a better chance than we had before they came, but there's greater danger, and more uncertainty. I know only this: if we are to have any chance at all, this millstone of stinking corruption, the Council of Scrutators, must be eradicated. Ah, here comes the sun. Let's go.'

Hundreds of scavenging beasts had come out of the hills, and they did not look up from their grisly business as Nish and Flydd went by. Thus far they'd made little impact on the dead; there were simply too many.

Nish led Flydd to the former command area. He hardly needed to explain – the evidence of Jal-Nish's folly was clear enough, in the cleanly truncated bodies of the officers, the amputated limbs, the tents and even clankers shorn neatly in two by that bladed disc of white light. Many of the bodies had been fed on by the lyrinx, and since then by the scavengers that slunk around Nish and Flydd in circles, not daring to take them on, but not planning to be driven from their feast either.

'Here's General Tham,' said Flydd. 'And Grism beside him. Both good men we'll find impossible to replace.' The scrutator shook his head in incomprehension. 'Such unbelievable stupidity. He destroyed the entire command structure of the army, wiped them out in a second. Why did he assemble them all in one place? What can he have hoped to achieve?'

'I suppose he wanted to make a display of his cleverness,' said Nish, answering the first question. 'Father was ever like that.'

Flydd squatted by the war chests and began to pick up the coins. 'We'd better take this back. Disaster or no, armies on the march burn gold and silver. Do you recall where Jal-Nish's tent was?'

Nish pointed up the hill and told Flydd what to look for. 'There's not much to be seen. I'll leave it to you, if you don't mind.' He did not want to go near. Nish especially did not want to see that booted foot again. He busied himself collecting the coins.

Flydd walked around and around, holding his hands out parallel to the ground. Stopping at the shredded tent, he pressed his palms against the surface of the broken table, then squatted by the splinters of the box that had held the tears. Picking up a splinter he ran his gnarled fingers up and down it, sniffed, closed his eyes, spun around and tossed the splinter whirling into the air. It fluttered to the ground. He picked it up, sighted each way along it, then grunted.

'The tears are gone,' he said over his shoulder.

They were the last thing on Nish's mind, for he was quite preoccupied with his memories. He poured a double handful of gold into the chest. 'Where?'

'I can't tell, nor who took them, though my guess would be that lyrinx with the golden crest. If so, they're safely across the sea by now, where even the scrutators can't get them. Hello – what's this?'

He picked up the bloodstained platinum mask. 'I'll take this with me.' He looked around. 'You mentioned your father's boot and foot.'

Nish felt ill just thinking about it. 'It was just over there, beyond the tent poles. I should bury it.'

'It's not here now. The scavengers—' Flydd looked around. 'Hoy!'

A hyena-like creature had the booted foot in its mouth and was slinking up the hill, ears lowered. Flydd bent, picked up a stone and threw it, awkwardly but accurately, at the creeping beast, striking it in the ribs. The hyena let out a howl and dropped the foot. Flydd ran after it but before he got there the hyena took it up by the shank. It tossed its head and the boot went flying off.

Flydd reached for another stone but the scavenger was off, creeping into the bushes below the escarpment, and they saw no more of it. The scrutator retrieved the boot, inspected it carefully and let it drop.

'It's his, all right. The man is dead, the tears gone beyond our reach, and perhaps it's better that way. It's hard to imagine the lyrinx doing any greater harm with them than the scrutators would have.'

'They matter, then?'

'Oh, they matter. Why don't you sit down in the shade – you look exhausted. I just want to check again, to make sure.' Flydd collected a handful of splinters from the tears' box and began to pace up and down, tossing them in the air one by one. 'Hello?' he said sharply.

Nish looked up, too tired to be curious. 'What's the matter?'

'Eiryn Muss has been here.'

'Does that matter?'

'The other day I sent him posthaste to Gnulp, and this isn't on the way. Why did he come *here*?'

Nish didn't have the energy. He found a tree that fitted the shape of his back, leaned against it and closed his eyes . . .

Flydd said little on the way back, and Nish kept his silence. There was too much to think about, not least his own future. The moment when Jal-Nish had forced Nish's hands down into the tears had been a life-changing experience. Until then he had been a prisoner of events, and preoccupied with himself. But on touching the tears he'd had an insight into what the world would be like under Jal-Nish, and it was not pretty. Now, Nish realised, he must begin to shape events to his own ends, ends that were against everything the scrutators represented. In that he stood alongside Flydd.

How was he to do it? For all his heroism on the battlefield, Nish could not see himself as a soldier. Even were he to rise high, he would spend his life prosecuting the war. But this war, he knew already, would not be won on the field of battle.

'Xervish?' he said tentatively.

'What?' Flydd replied absently. 'What is it, Nish?'

Nish looked down at his boots, not knowing how to put it. 'I know I've been a damn fool more often than not. I've done enough stupid things to condemn me for a lifetime, and made some disastrous blunders . . .'

'Indeed you have,' said Flydd. There was a gleam in his eye and a hint of a smile on his whiskery lips. 'I can't think when I last met such a callow, feckless fool as you. I'm sure I never have.'

'But . . . even so, I think I've displayed a few positive qualities as well—'

'I dare say,' the scrutator said carelessly, 'though it doesn't do to dwell overmuch on such things, lest you be thought bigheaded.'

'What I meant was—'

'If you want something, lad, then spit it out. Name the reward you require and it shall be yours. Is it coin, or high honour, or a brace of comely—?'

'I want to serve you, surr,' Nish burst out.

'I don't need a manservant. I may be decrepit but I'm still capable of wiping—'

'You know what I mean, Xervish.'

'I have no idea what you're on about. Speak plainly, Nish, or not at all.'

Nish's mouth snapped closed. Was Flydd just being perverse, or was he trying to tell Nish something? To have confidence in himself? He pulled his horse away, cantered around in a circle and pulled up beside him again. Taking a deep breath, he said, 'I want to help you, surr. To bring down the Council of Scrutators and create a new order that truly serves the people of Santhenar. And then, to defeat the enemy.'

Flydd pulled up his nag. The sun shone on his cheek, outlining every gouge and scar, every hump and hollow from the scrutators' torment. 'Anything else you want to achieve this afternoon?'

'That's all, surr.'

Flydd considered him for a long time. 'You realise that what you have just uttered is treason of the direst complexion. Should the Council take you, and surely they will, they'll make you suffer far longer, and more horribly, than ever they made me.'

Nish knew it, and dreaded it. And, to be realistic, they probably would take him. They had the resources of a world to fight their enemies. All Nish had was his wits.

'If we lack the courage to oppose tyranny, surr, we don't deserve freedom.'

The scrutator regarded him, head to one side. 'Well spoken, lad. Had you made this offer at any time before your deeds of yesterday, I would have refused you. Willingness is not enough. But you've gone through the furnace and come out again, reforged. We'll oppose these vicious tyrants and overthrow them or, more likely, die in the attempt.'

He held out his hand. Nish took it. Flydd groped for the silver flask in his saddlebags and tossed it to Nish.

Popping the cap, Nish raised the flask high. 'To victory!' he said, over-dramatically. He took a healthy swig and almost fell off his horse.

Flydd snatched the flask, which was spilling its precious contents everywhere. 'And to the scrutators' chief torturer – may we spend little time in her company.' Draining the flask, he kicked his horse into a gallop.

That was not the end of the fighting, though it was not on the same scale as before. The lyrinx attacked every night, shooting from a distance with captured javelards and catapults. The troops became used to building defensive camps, with their clankers on the outside and rows of bonfires all around. It kept them alive, but they took losses, and every day their supplies dwindled.

'We can't last much longer,' said Troist, on the third night after the battle. Travel had been painfully slow, for the field was still depleted and they had not reached a better one. They were camped just half a day's march from Gnulp Landing, once a rich fishing and trading city, but these days an outpost brutally exposed to enemy raids.

'How many are we now?' asked Nish. More soldiers had joined them on the way, survivors from the other side of the river, who had lost everything.

'Twelve thousand of my army,' said Troist, 'plus another eleven thousand of Jal-Nish's, though many are injured. I dare say more stragglers will come in. Were we able to go back we might find most of them. And we have the best part of two thousand clankers, though some are in poor condition. A sizeable force, though considering . . .' He looked away into the night.

Considering Jal-Nish started with forty thousand soldiers, Nish thought. And only weeks before that, when the battle for Snizort began, sixty thousand. A disaster indeed, no matter how much damage had been done to the enemy.

'But we've only a week's supplies,' said the scrutator, 'and even that will require a good bit of eking.'

'What are your orders, surr?' said Troist. 'If you require us to stand and fight, we'll do it, though in the end we must all die.'

'The loss of one army is going to be disastrous for morale,' said Flydd. 'To lose two would be catastrophic. We must survive to fight again, and show our people that we can still win.'

'We did far better than expected against so many,' said Nish. 'These lyrinx were not much more formidable than men. Previously, one lyrinx was the equal of two or three of our troops. Why the difference? Is it because they were stoneformed?'

'I don't know,' said Flydd.

'And your orders, surr?' Troist persisted.

'I see no choice but to head for Gnulp and beg them to take us in,' said the scrutator.

'My thought too,' Troist replied, 'but even if they do, it only postpones the problem.'

'Why wouldn't they?' asked Nish. 'Where would they be without the army to protect them?'

'The master of the city might ask what good an army is if it can't even protect itself? He might say it's bringing trouble that they didn't have before.'

'Either we die outside the gates,' said Troist, 'or within.'

'I'll go to Gnulp,' said Flydd, 'and meet with the master in the morning. Be sure you're camped by the gates at dawn, General. It'll make it harder to refuse us. Nish, come with me.'

They rode for several hours on a road illuminated by the moon, stopping just around the corner from the city gates. They could smell the salt sea and hear waves bursting over the breakwaters.

'I hope you've got some kind of plan,' said Nish.

'For once, I haven't. Let's climb the hill and get an idea of the layout.'

'Don't you know this place?' Nish was surprised. 'I thought you'd been everywhere in the world.'

'I've been many places, but Gnulp Landing isn't one of them.'

They rode up a winding path to the crest of a steep hill armoured with flat, slanting black outcrops like the serrations down the spine of a chacalot, the water-dwelling reptile that even the lyrinx feared. At the top stood a ruined watch-tower, its black stones coated with lichen that shone like silver mancing glyphs in the moonlight.

'Don't they keep the watch here?' said Nish.

'Look up,' said the scrutator.

In the light and shadow of the moon, the city was bleakly menacing. A double wall ran around it, thick and high, inside which stood three guard towers, tall enough to defend the wall but not close enough to be attacked readily from it. The defences were massive and designed with lyrinx in mind. Every flat surface was covered in long metal spikes, protection against attack from the air.

The harbour was formed by two breakwaters curving into the racing waters of the Sea of Thurkad. Inside that oval, wharves and jetties had been built out from the shore, and all were occupied. Nish counted a hundred and fifty ships at anchor.

'How have they survived so long, so close to the enemy?' he wondered.

'By exploiting the lyrinx's fear of water. The city is easily defended from the shore, and the air, and the lyrinx are not going to attack from the water side. Perhaps they've decided that there are easier targets. Wait here – I think I'll go in alone, after all.'

The master of the city took them in grudgingly. Twenty-three thousand men would be a tremendous strain on his stores but he dared not incur the wrath of the scrutators, much less a man leading such a powerful army.

Despite the overcrowded barracks and indifferent food, Nish enjoyed the first few days in Gnulp Landing. It was a relief not to have the grinding squeal of the clankers in his ears; not to wear armour and weapons day and night. He even managed to put Ullii and Myllii, and all the dead, out of his mind for a while. He'd used his initiative, pushed himself to the very limit of his abilities, and had succeeded. He felt good about himself for once.

The lyrinx attacked on the second night and the following nights, and every day the master of the city grew colder.

'I curse the day I opened the gates to you, Scrutator Flydd,' he said on the fifth morning. 'Your soldiers are eating their heads off and my precious stores are dwindling. Were I not an honourable man, I would put you out tomorrow.'

His dark eyes had the lustre of a toad's; Nish imagined him spitting poison at them.

'But of course, you *are* an honourable man,' Flydd said smoothly, 'and the Council of Scrutators appreciates that. Be certain of their generosity to those who demonstrate their loyalty.' His eyes flicked sideways at Nish. Never trust a man who makes a point of his honour, he seemed to be saying.

Nish did not trust the master an ell. A man who counted the cost of everything and valued nothing that he could not price, Nish had met many like him in his days as a merchant's scribe. The master couldn't work out how Flydd fitted into the scheme of things. He must have heard about his fall, yet here he was at the head of an army, which obeyed him as if he were its rightful commander. But should the Council confirm Flydd's dismissal, as in time they must, the master would put them out of the gates in an instant.

'The scrutators begrudge every copper grint,' said the master. 'I'm feeding your troops out of my own pocket, Scrutator, and it's not bottomless. Another week will bankrupt me, and we have a hard winter ahead of us. After today, you'll get nothing until I see *your* gold.'

'You'll get your due,' said Flydd with another significant glance at Nish. He rose. 'And now I must attend to another pressing problem. We'll talk further on this matter.'

'We will indeed,' hissed the master.

'Bloody old hypocrite,' Flydd said when the door had closed behind them. 'It's not his food we're eating, nor is he paying for it, though he's already doubled the price of meat and grain from his storehouses. He's gouging every grint out of the people and blaming us.'

'What are you going to do?'

'Go down to the waterfront. I've an idea.'

Nish waited outside while Flydd spoke to one sea captain, then another. After the second visit the scrutator emerged, smiling. 'I think it may work after all.'

'What?'

'I'm going to hire an armada to get us out of here.'

'There's twenty thousand of us! More.'

'I'm sending the clankers back east to Lybing, packed with soldiers and the injured. If we can put a hundred on each boat, the hundred and fifty boats in port will be enough to carry the remainder.'

'Some are only fishing boats.'

'And others are traders that can sail all the way to Crandor and the North Seas. It's the only way, Nish.'

'Where do you plan to go?'

'Into the Karama Malama, then south-east to Hardlar. The lyrinx seldom strike that far south. From there we'll march north to Borgistry.'

'The Karama Malama is a dangerous sea, isn't it?'

'It can be, in the stormy season.'

'Isn't that right now?'

'Er, yes. But it's not as dangerous as staying here.'

'I dare say the master will be pleased.'

'He'll be furious, which will please me.'

'Furious? Why?'

'He wants our gold more than he wants rid of us, and nothing could give me more pleasure than to deprive him of it. The sea captains think the same. They've all been robbed by him, at one time or another.'

'So they'll be happy to take us?'

'Delighted, though they'll charge the best part of Jal-Nish's war chest to do so. They know desperate men when they see them.'

'When are we going?'

'We load in the morning, as soon as it's light. It'll take two days. Better get ready. You're in charge.'

'Me?'

'Yes, you.'

THIRTY-SIX

As if they knew what was being planned, the lyrinx attacked from the air that night, dropping rocks on the storehouses and granaries near the port. The defenders were ready, driving the enemy off with a hail of arrows. The next time they attacked, half an hour later, the lyrinx kept higher. The missiles had further to fall and did greater damage, but not a single lyrinx fell.

Nish was at the docks well before dawn, with his list of squads and the vessels they were to embark upon. No one was to move before Flydd gave the word. The clankers, bearing their load of soldiers and injured men, were going to leave at dawn and head east. Twenty leagues inland they would be out of danger, now that Snizort was no more.

A windstorm had come up in the night, with spitting rain and wild gusts that would have made it difficult for the lyrinx to stay aloft. Nish hoped it would abate during the day; it would mean hard sailing for the small vessels and there was little shelter in the narrow waterway.

A messenger came running in. 'Go!' he said, and that was all.

Nish felt a vibration in his head, nearly two thousand clankers drawing on the field at once. The vaguely dizzy, sick feeling faded though it did not pass completely. He supposed it had something to do with touching the tears, all those days ago, and it reminded Nish of his father. For all that the man had become a monster, Nish grieved for his loss. Still, it was for the best. Jal-Nish's suffering was over now.

All day he spent at the waterfront with his lists and

schedules, making sure the squads were loaded onto the right vessels. Not until a good half of them had embarked, around two in the afternoon, did any word come from the scrutator. It was the same messenger, and he said the same word again, 'Go!'

Eighty captains opened their sealed orders, their vessels weighed anchor and sailed into the gale, which had intensified during the day. It was blowing directly from the north. Had it been southerly they could not have gone at all, for there was no room for tacking in the narrow sea.

The remaining vessels continued loading all night in driving rain, and an hour after dawn the work was complete. The gangplanks were drawn up. Flydd should have been here hours ago but there was no sign of him.

Nish stood at the rail, hood angled to keep out the worst of the rain, though inevitably much found a way in. Water trickled down his neck. Where was Flydd?

Two hours after dawn the messenger appeared, gave the message a third time, 'Go!' and climbed aboard the neighbouring ship. Nish signalled to the remaining vessels, all save his own. One by one they weighed anchor, pulled themselves out through the breakwater, heeled over in the wind and disappeared south.

Nish watched them go, uneasy. The sea was covered with whitecaps and the air full of blown spume; the gale looked like turning into a full-blown storm. He'd travelled by ship on several occasions and had been seasick each time, but never had he sailed in conditions like this. Next to suffocation in a lightless pit, drowning was the death he feared most.

Fingering his black sword in its sheath, he wondered what to do. Should he try to find out what had happened to the scrutator? He paced another hour; two; three. Flydd did not come. Nish was tempted to go looking for him, though Flydd had given strict orders to remain here. Surely Flydd had gone to see the master, and perhaps the master had not been pleased about the loss of all that coin.

Succumbing to a mad impulse, Nish said to the captain, 'Don't go without me. There's double the gold in it for you,' and raced down the gangplank.

It was a good fifteen minutes' run to the master's mansion and his knee and ankle were troubling him long before he got there. The great brass doors were closed and the door warden would hardly open them for a junior officer in an army that had been eating its head off at the master's expense. On the other hand, the fellow on morning duty now might not have seen him before, so if he could pull it off . . .

Nish was not sure he dared. How could one man beat the master of a city and all his guards? But he had cast his lot with the scrutator; he could not fail now.

Drawing his sword, Nish rapped three times on the door with the silver hilt. Wrapping the cloak around his uniform, he pulled his hood over his face. The door was opened a crack.

'Perquisitor Mun-Mun Hlar to see the master, without delay!' he snapped, taking the name of his oldest brother.

'The master is still in his bed,' said the door warden. 'Come back in the afternoon.'

Nish caught him by his frilly shirt-front and jerked him forwards. 'I'm *Perquisitor* Hlar,' he snarled. 'I've come all the way from the Council of Scrutators with an urgent message for the master. I demand admittance, *at once*!' He put the blade of his sword against the lackey's neck.

The man collapsed like a punctured bladder. 'At once,' he said, bobbing and puffing. 'Follow me, Perquisitor, surr.'

Nish accompanied him up the steps, prodding the door warden every so often to remind him that perquisitors were ruthless fellows. For everyone's sake, he must not falter now. Flydd had a plan but Nish did not know what it was. If this lout got in the way, too bad for him.

Outside the master's doors, inlaid with rosewood and gilt, the door warden hesitated, then raised his hand to knock.

Nish whacked him over the buttocks with the flat of the sword. 'Just open it. I'll announce myself.'

Giving him a terrified glance, the door warden lifted the latch and went in. Nish followed, treading on his heels. Easing the door shut with his foot, he bolted it. He could not risk anyone coming to investigate.

Raising his fist, he struck the door warden on the back of the head in the way he'd been taught in his defence training, long ago. The man crumpled to the floor. Nish went around a couple of corners into a bedchamber the size of a small mansion, with tables, chairs and divans enough to furnish a house. At the further end, by a crackling fire, stood an eight-post bed the size of a clanker.

The master was sitting up in bed, facing the other way, reading a set of dispatches. A red wallet lay on the covers. Even from halfway down the room Nish recognised it as a Council of Scrutators message wallet. Flydd's secret had been exposed.

Scampering to the wall, he fleeted along until he was behind the head of the bed and drew his sword. Nish took a deep breath, slid around the bedpost and put his sword to the master's throat. 'Where is the scrutator?' he hissed.

The master looked up calmly. 'I'm not going to tell you, Cryl-Nish Hlar. Your father is dead and you are an outcast condemned by the scrutators. Put down your sword.'

Nish had expected the master to be a blustering coward who would do anything to save his own neck. For a second, the defiance threw him. Well, damn him; the fate of the world might rest on Nish getting the scrutator out alive. The master was a villain; let him take his chances.

He flicked the sword at the master's face. The man threw up his arms and Nish slashed the tip of the sword across his wrist, severing an artery. Blood spurted right across the bed. The master gasped then caught the wrist in his other hand and pressed hard with his thumb. The flow dropped to a trickle, and stopped.

The violence sickened Nish but there was no alternative. He pressed his blade to the man's throat. 'You may survive that, but not the jugular. Well?'

The master was a quick thinker and a pragmatic man. 'He's downstairs, in my cells. I have the keys here.' With his elbow he indicated a hook on the wall. 'I'll take you.'

'At once,' said Nish, snatching the keys. 'And remember, I'm a condemned criminal with nothing to lose. I don't care if you live or die. Nor, I suspect, do the scrutators, since your profits come at the expense of theirs.'

They went down the master's personal staircase and along to the cells, a row of small rooms with solid wooden doors. 'Take the keys,' said Nish. 'Open the door.'

'My wrist . . .' grimaced the master.

'If you're quick you won't bleed to death.' Nish put his sword to the man's throat again.

The master let go his wrist and grabbed the ring of keys. Blood spurted, though not as far as before. He forced a key into the lock, tried to turn it but let go and grabbed hold of his wrist. Blood dripped from his fingers.

Nish turned the key one way. Nothing happened. He turned it the other and the lock clicked. He kicked the door open, still covering the master with his sword, though the man was now crouched on the floor, trying to stem the flow. His thumb kept slipping on his red wrist.

'Come out, you bloody old fool,' Nish said 'There's not much time.'

The scrutator came out into the light. He looked as if he had been beaten, though he was not cowed. 'What the blazes are you doing here? I gave you your orders.'

'A situation arose that they didn't cover. Do you know the way out?'

'Haven't a clue,' said Flydd.

Nish prodded the master with his sword. 'Show us to the stables. Better hurry; you're looking faint. You must have lost quite a lot of blood.'

There was a puddle on the floor next to him. The master nodded and stumbled down the corridor. By the time they had negotiated several more flights of stairs and long passages, he was weaving from side to side.

'I don't think he's got much left in him,' said Flydd.

'Blood or courage?'

'Either.'

'How far?' Nish said to the master.

'Just around the corner,' he whispered.

They emerged in the stables. 'Can you ride bareback, Nish?' Flydd said.

'If I have to.'

They mounted two sleepy horses. The master collapsed into the straw. Nish urged his horse towards the stable doors, stopping on the way to kick the side of a manger where a stableboy lay sleeping. 'Open the doors!' Nish roared.

The boy ran to comply. 'Your master lies back there, bleeding.' Nish pointed with his sword. 'Attend to him before he dies.'

He kicked his horse into the rainy night. Flydd followed. Five minutes later, by the time the alert had been raised, they were weighing anchor.

The wind was blowing even harder now, a fierce gale. 'Are you sure it's safe to go out?' Nish said as they headed for the entrance. The Sea of Thurkad was a mess of white. Waves could no longer be seen, just white, driven foam.

'Been out in worse,' said the captain. 'Not by much, mind you, but for double the payment, we'll dare it.'

Flydd's head jerked around and he gave Nish a hard stare. Nish smiled blandly back. 'I thought your life was worth it. Was I right, or was I wrong?'

'For all you knew,' hissed Flydd, 'being taken prisoner might have been part of my plan.'

'You just can't admit you've been bested.'

After a long pause, Flydd said, 'I thought I was done for. You're a tough sod, Nish.'

'I was taught by the best.'

'Don't let it become a habit.'

The vessel passed between the arms of the breakwater. The blast heeled them over till the gunwale practically touched the water. The captain brought the ship around, the current caught her, the wind kicked her in the stern and she roared down the channel under just a rag of sail.

'If the wind comes up any further,' the captain said, 'even that'll be too much, and we'll have to sail on bare poles.'

'At least we're in no danger from the lyrinx,' said Nish.

'There's nothing can harm us tonight, save wind and rocks.'

'How far till we reach the Sea of Mists?'

'About twenty leagues. Four or five hours at the rate we're going. But there are a few things to worry about before we get there.'

'Like what?'

'The Pinch,' said Flydd, dashing spray out of his eyes. It burst over the bows with every plunge of the boat, smacking them in the faces.

'What's that?'

'Ahead, the sea narrows till you could practically shoot an arrow from one side to the other. The current is fast there, as fast as you've ever gone. It requires a strong hand on the tiller and the right kind of wind, or none at all, to get through. You don't recover from your mistakes in the Pinch.'

'How do you come back?' Nish wondered.

'They all ask that,' chuckled the captain mirthlessly. 'They pull us through. Windmills and cables. No boat can sail against this current.'

'Pull you through? I'd like to see that.'

'You'd fill your breeches,' said the captain. 'Now get out of my way. I've got work to do.'

Nish went to the rail but it was too dangerous to stand there. He leaned against the wall of the captain's cabin, where there was a modicum of shelter from the wind and rain, quietly going over the past hours. He'd surprised himself, dominating the master in that violent, ruthless way. It wasn't like him at all. More like his father, in fact. And most shocking of all, he realised now that he'd enjoyed it.

The wind screamed, the spray flew, the iron cliffs raced past. Nish never understood how the captain could see to navigate his way between them, but somehow he did. The Pinch was a league long and they roared through it in ten minutes. The crescent of the waning moon came out through racing clouds; the cliffs disappeared; the current slackened. They were out of the Sea of Thurkad into the Karama Malama, where the waves were mast high. The little vessel rolled like a cradle in the wind.

Nish groped his way below, into the reeking dark, and found an empty hammock, though he could not sleep. The ship's timbers, strained to the limit, shrieked and groaned. The hammock swayed through the same arc as the rolling vessel, before jerking back the other way. The landlubber soldiers were already spewing their guts into the bilge. Soon Nish was doing the same. The smell was abominable.

Morning came, but he was too seasick to notice it. Hours later he staggered up on deck, where Flydd and the captain were talking anxiously. 'What's the matter?' asked Nish.

'We want to go east,' said Flydd, 'but the wind's driving us south and west, and there's nothing we can do about it.'

'What lies to the west?'

'Just wild sea for a hundred leagues—'

'And the Reefs of Karints,' said the captain.

'Where are all the other ships?'

'Safely in the port of Hardlar, I hope.'

'So we're all alone.'

No one answered. Flydd jerked his thumb in the direction of the hold. Nish went below, where he discovered that a soldier had thrown up green bile in his hammock. Nish turned the hammock over, his stomach groaning as loudly as the ship's timbers, and crawled into it.

Finally, in the middle of the day, in spite of the reek of vomit, he slept. He slept all through that day and woke after midnight, not that he could tell, then slept again. It had been weeks since he'd had a full night's rest.

He was woken by cries and an almighty crash that spun him full circle in his hammock. The other occupants of the hold were not as lucky. He heard thuds and groans. Another crash, not so loud, made everyone cry out. Nish fell out of the hammock onto someone, who groaned. Picking the man up, Nish stood on shaky legs and made for the ladder.

Crash, crash, crash. It sounded as if the ship were beating itself to death. He made the deck, which was tilted at the angle of a slippery-dip. They had run full tilt onto a rocky reef in the night, and it was all that was keeping the ship from going to the bottom.

Huge waves broke in a curving line from one side of the reef to the other. Each breaker lifted the ship and drove it further onto the spine of the rocks, wedging the timbers apart. After each wave, the vessel was lower in the water.

On the seaward side, the sailors had managed to launch a boat. Half a dozen jumped in, took the oars and clawed at the water. The boat moved out into the wind and was driven away. Nish soon lost sight of it in the towering waves.

He peered over the side. Men were struggling in the water and being crushed between the boat and the reef. 'Scrutator!' he yelled.

No answer. 'Scrutator? Flydd?'

He put his head down into the hold and screamed Flydd's name. No answer from there either. Nish was about to go down when he saw him, clinging to the shrouds at the stern. Nish ran that way. 'What's the matter?'

'The reef seemed to come up out of the water,' said the scrutator. 'Got a prize bang on the head. I'm all right.'

'Where are we?'

'Middle of bloody nowhere.'

'Any chance of the other boats rescuing us?'

'They wouldn't know where to look.'

'Hadn't we better try and get the people in the hold out?'

'They'll have a better death down there,' said the scrutator, watching an enormous wave moving towards them. 'Look at the sea pounding at the reef. It'll tear us to pieces.'

'I'll just go down for my sword.' It was his most precious possession. 'I won't be a—'

The stern was tossed up on the wave, lifting them into the

air, then the whole vessel was thrust sideways. When they came down, there was nothing under them but water.

It was nearly as perishing as the sea at Tiksi. Nish, a poor swimmer and prone to panic, thrashed at the water. Something thumped him in the ear. 'Stop, you fool,' screamed the scrutator. 'Hang onto this.'

It was a plank or rib torn from the boat. Nish threw his arms around it. The scrutator turned on his side and kicked. The next wave pulled them out, away from the rocks. Flydd paddled furiously towards a streak of white and caught a current, which carried them through a gap in the reef.

The water was desperately cold – so cold that, no matter how hard Nish fought it, the will to survive began to slip away. Flydd tied him to the beam and kept slapping his face till he roused.

Nish endured as best he could. The rest of the night, long or short, was a daze. Near dawn, he realised that the pounding was not his heart, but surf breaking on a shore. The waves carried them in and dumped them, tearing Nish away from the plank. The water rolled him over and over, before depositing him halfway up a gritty beach.

Flydd got him up, and Nish had enough strength to crawl up out of the surf zone and flop down in the sand. That was all he could do.

THIRTY-SEVEN

'You say you love me, Minis, but after what you've done, I need more than oaths. If you do love me, prove it with action, not with words!'

Hope flared in his brown eyes and she felt guilty. There was no hope for him.

'I *will*,' said Minis, 'as long as you don't ask me to betray Foster-father, or my own kind.'

Yet again he equivocated – anything that helped her could be seen as a betrayal of the Aachim. 'What's going to happen to me once Urien comes back?'

'Vithis will release you, I suppose.'

Clearly he'd not thought about it. 'He'll never release me, Minis. I must remain a prisoner of the Aachim all my life, and be watched night and day lest I smuggle out a message. Or . . .?' She left it hanging.

'Foster-father is an honourable man.'

'Vithis is *not* an honourable man; he's shown that many times. Besides, he doesn't have to kill me with his own hands. All he need do is indicate that I'm a problem, and plenty of Aachim would dispose of me, just to gain his favour. To your kind, we old humans are little better than vermin, for all that I saved your lives.'

'It's not so,' he whispered.

'Once Urien returns, I'll be under a death sentence. No one will be able to save me then. But *you* can save me now.'

'At the price of betraying Foster-father,' he said bitterly. 'I will be ruined in his eyes.'

'He'll get over it. You're all he has. You must stand up to him, Minis. He'll think more of you for it.'

'You don't know him.'

'You say you love me, you've sworn to save me, but you qualify it every time. Prove your love – help me to escape. If you do I'll give myself to you, soul and body. Fail me and you collude in my death sentence.'

Minis could not meet her eyes. He marched up and down the tent, casting glances just shy of her direction. 'You do not, you *cannot* know what you are asking.'

She allowed him no respite. 'All I'm asking for,' Tiaan said sweetly, 'is my life.'

'At the price of my honour.'

'How will your honour withstand my execution?' she snapped.

'Please, Tiaan. It hurts to hear you speak that way.'

'How else should I speak to a man who professes love but won't lift a finger to save my *life*. You're pathetic, Minis. You're not a man at all – you're a snivelling child.'

'That's not true, Tiaan,' he wept. 'I do love you.'

'Then save me.'

His face became dark, congested. The veins in his neck throbbed. 'Ah, Foster-father, what am I to do?'

'Run away with me. *Now!*'

'I can't get you out of the camp. Every construct must have a pass, and every person in it.'

'But surely, as Vithis's son . . .?'

'He doesn't trust me with you. But maybe, in a few days' time—'

'Tomorrow will be our last day, as you know very well. The camp is nearly empty. There are only eighty-nine constructs to go. After tomorrow we'll be in the main camp and they won't let me near one. You can't put it off, Minis. Once Vithis comes back, it'll be too late.'

'But what can *I* do?' he wailed.

Tiaan wanted to hit him. *It's my life! Doesn't that mean anything to you?* She closed her eyes, thinking desperately. She'd tried everything with Minis, but he was too cowed by Vithis. There was only one option left, though it went utterly against her nature. She'd have to really hurt him.

'*Nothing!*' she said with all the sarcasm she could muster. It was not strong enough. She had to shake him to his toes. 'You can't save me because you don't have the balls, Minis. You're a boy trying to fit into your foster-father's pants, but you don't have what it takes to fill them. No wonder Vithis holds you in such contempt.'

He reeled. 'You are cruel, Tiaan.'

She stared him down. The time for words was over.

'I . . . may be able to do something,' he said. 'Tomorrow, when you're towing the last of the constructs. I'll try then.'

'Try what?' She did not allow herself to hope – Minis had let her down too many times.

'We'll stop midway. I'll find a way to distract the guards. I'll unfasten the tether, as if to check something. We'll have to be quick, but we can do it.'

Tiaan hadn't thought that she would ever convince him. 'You're sure?'

'Yes. My mind is made up.'

'Oh, Minis.' Pushing herself up in bed, she reached out to him.

He threw his arms around her and wept, which made her feel even more guilty.

'I'm sorry for doubting you, Minis,' she said. 'I was so afraid.' Tiaan looked up at him and, acting purely on impulse, pressed her lips to his.

She'd not kissed a man before and did not expect anything of it. The kiss was like touching an electric eel. It sensitised her whole body and, when they parted, her lips felt swollen to three times their normal size. She saw the desire in his eyes and for an instant Tiaan was tempted, but only ill could come of that.

'Take me home, please,' she said. 'First the proof.'

Tiaan was woken at dawn by an Aachim she did not recognise. 'Where's Minis?' she said.

'He has other business to attend to.'

Tiaan took that as a sign that Minis had taken the coward's way out after all. By the time the sun rose she was getting ready to haul the chain of sixty constructs to safety, the second-last trip. The crystals of her helm had been freshly charged in the black tesseract. The Aachim guard carried her to the construct, lifted her in and after that never moved from her side. Minis must have betrayed her plan.

Two hours later, the sixty constructs had been delivered safely to the southern camp and the Aachim there were all smiles. The rescue, which few had ever believed possible, was almost complete. Only twenty-nine machines to go. She returned to Snizort. The tents had been packed and the remaining Aachim, all but her two guards being from Clan Elienor, were waiting in their constructs. The war camp had disappeared, the only evidence of it the flattened grass, the humps of the infilled latrine trenches and, in the distance, the memorial pavilion beside the battlefield.

It was past lunchtime. As the constructs were being cabled up, Minis appeared.

'I'll take the last set,' he said to Tiaan's guard. 'It'll give you the chance to ready your own gear.' The fellow nodded and sprang down.

Tiaan sat in the machine, eating bread and sausage. 'I've nothing to say to you, Minis,' she said as he climbed up.

'I've found a way to save you. It's all planned.'

She was unable to believe, unable to trust. 'How?'

'We'll take the constructs halfway, then stop as if there's a problem. I'll call to the first construct to check the cable. As soon as he unfastens it, we'll flee.'

Tiaan had had time to anticipate all the problems. 'It's not much of a plan. If the constructs fire before we're out of range, we won't have a chance.' They didn't need the field for that, their catapults and spear-throwers being mechanically operated. But she hadn't come up with anything better, and once she towed the last set of constructs to the southern field it would be too late.

He stared into her eyes, quivering with emotion. 'You must trust me, Tiaan. I'm prepared to renounce my birthright for you.'

The declaration failed to comfort her as he'd hoped. It was too late for Minis. Whatever he did, she would find fault with it. I've become a monster, she thought. There's no way back now.

'Very well,' she said. 'We'll do it.'

The cable was attached to the first construct, and from it to the two lines of the others. 'Wait one moment,' said Minis.

'What is it?'

'You'll see.'

The Aachim were calling to one another and two of them began walking, five or six paces apart, in the direction of the distant pavilion. Both wore helms not unlike the one Tiaan used, and the woman on the right held out a rod-like object, which she pointed towards the pavilion. The man on her left did the same.

Someone behind them called a series of Aachim words that she did not recognise, followed by one she did. '*Now!*'

A blue ray shot out from the woman's rod and a green ray from the man's. Where they intersected, above the pavilion, the air shimmered. There came a distant sound of thunder and a glimmering dome formed, swelling until it covered a good part of the battlefield where the Aachim had fought. Coloured lines writhed across it, like tamed lightning.

'It's beautiful,' said Tiaan, 'but what is it?'

'Let me see.' Minis lifted the helm off her head and put it on his own. 'Ah, what a marvel they've built!' He passed the helm back to her. 'It's a kind of protection – to keep out intruders and scavengers until we find a way to retrieve our dead, and our constructs. Now we can go.'

The protection had vanished as soon as the helm was taken off Tiaan's head. She put it on, took one last look at the shimmering luminescence of the dome, and reached for the controls.

Tiaan eased her machine into motion, uncomfortable

about placing her life in Minis's unreliable hands. What if this passion wore off, or he got cold feet again? She must be prepared to act on her own, the instant an opportunity came.

Within minutes her head was throbbing, for she wasn't able to give her full attention to the task. Tiaan rubbed her temples and allowed the fields to fade from her mind. The relief was almost painful. In spite of the helm and the techniques she'd been taught, holding five fields at once was a killing strain.

'What is it?' Minis said, looking anxious as the note of the construct faded.

'It's hurting today.' That was true enough. 'It seems harder than before. Maybe the helm didn't charge fully this morning.'

They drifted to a stop. Heads appeared at the hatch of the next construct. The two armed guards in the turret were on alert, their crossbows at the ready. 'Give me the helm,' he said. 'I'll charge it again.'

She was reluctant to let it go. 'Why don't you bring the tesseract here?'

'All right.'

He signalled for the tesseract, placed the helm inside for the required time, then withdrew it.

Tiaan put it on her head. 'That's better,' she said, though it felt the same as before. 'Is this the time, Minis?'

'Not yet,' he mumbled, not meeting her eyes. He was sweating so profusely that the whole front of his shirt was wet –another bad sign. He simply couldn't find the courage to defy his own people.

The whine resumed and the construct rose in the air. Behind her she heard the other machines doing the same. They went another half-league or so. Time was running out. She must save herself and she had to do it now.

Tiaan caused the flow of power to rise and fall rapidly, making the constructs jerk wildly. Behind them, someone roared out a warning in the Aachim tongue.

'Stop!' cried Minis.

She pretended to, while making the construct jolt harder. A

loud crash came from behind. Two machines further back in the line had collided at high speed. 'What is it?' Tiaan said, cutting off the field, though she knew full well what had happened.

'I don't know. I'll have to see what the matter is.'

'This is our chance, Minis.'

'Just a bit further.' He flushed; again he could not meet her eyes.

It was over. He was too weak. She had to get him out of the construct, then make her break, as fast as she could.

'You'd better see how long it'll take to fix that.' She jerked a thumb at the two constructs, locked together by the impact. As soon as his feet touched the ground, she would do it. If she ducked down, they might not get a clean shot. It was a slim hope, but it was all she had.

He began to climb down but the guards shouted and pointed at Tiaan. They weren't going to leave her by herself in the construct for a second. She cursed as Minis came back and carried her down to the ground. Another chance gone.

The Aachim were already gathering around the two constructs, assessing the damage. It did not look severe, though it was going to take time to prise them apart.

'Could you put me down in the shade,' said Tiaan. 'It's hot out here; I feel a little faint.'

Minis saw no harm in that, since he believed she was unable to walk. He sat her under a spindly tree about fifteen paces from her construct, and went down the line to the site of the accident.

Tiaan flexed her leg muscles. It would be difficult to escape from here, for she was in full view of the guards in the leading construct, but if they gave her the slightest chance she was ready.

The Aachim had brought up metal bars and half a dozen of their strongest were attempting to pry the two constructs apart. The others, after watching for a while, went back to their own machines and began spreading cloths on the ground for lunch. Thyzzea and her family were among them.

The two guards came down from their turret. It would have been sweltering up there, for it was a baking hot day with not a breath of wind. No one was looking her way. Since they knew she could not walk, there was no chance of her escaping from where she was. Tiaan was about to get up when one of the guards checked over his shoulder. Seeing nothing to bother him, he went down to watch the prising operation.

Tiaan saw Thyzzea moving in and out between the constructs, coming to carry Tiaan down to share lunch with the family. She had to go now!

Thyzzea disappeared between the constructs and Tiaan stood up. Her throat was dry, her palms damp. She dared not run – the movement would attract attention. She simply walked casually to her construct and ducked behind it, out of sight.

There was no outcry. She climbed the side, her hands slipping on the metal rungs, which were almost too hot to hold, then went over the top and in.

Tiaan put on her belt, but as she eased the helm over her head it clinked against the metal hatch, a noise that would carry a long way. She looked over her shoulder. Minis's head whipped around but he did not give the alarm. Perhaps he hadn't seen her. She felt sick. It was now or not at all.

Thyzzea came out from between the lines of constructs, looking for Tiaan, and saw her in the construct. She looked distressed, but loyalty to her family and her kind came first.

'Hoy!' she roared.

One of the guards sprang up and, following her outflung arm, sighted with the crossbow. He lowered it again. Unable to get a clear shot at Tiaan from the ground, he was running towards the leading construct and his shooter's turret.

'Tiaan, wait for me,' cried Minis, throwing out his arms like a lover betrayed, as if he'd planned to save her after all. Had he? She'd never know and could not stop to find out. If she did, she'd be taken or killed.

Pressing the helm tightly on her head, Tiaan drew power

and directed it all into her machine. The whine rose to a shriek and the construct surged forward.

'Look out!' she heard someone cry. There was a momentary resistance as the cable went taut. She applied more power but it did not pull free as she'd expected. The construct shuddered, then the amplimet took over, sucking a torrent of power from the field. She tried to stop it but it was out of control. *Never swear on the amplimet!* The construct took off, the cable thrummed then snapped just behind her, the free end whipping back the other way.

Over the roar of the mechanism she heard an agonised cry. Turning in a shallow curve, Tiaan looked back. The flailing cable had caught Minis about the waist and hip, snatching him off his feet. It whirled him sideways across the rock-strewn ground, thumping him into one boulder, then another.

Tiaan gasped and popped the crystal to slow the machine. Minis lay unmoving, blood drenching him from the hip down. Even from here she could see the bone sticking out of his leg. Had she killed him? What was she to do?

Aachim were running everywhere, shouting. Thyzzea and her father reached Minis, lifted him to a sitting position, then hastily laid him down again. Thyzzea stood up and shouted something at her, a cry of rage and betrayal. She, Tiaan, had repaid their kindness by maiming Minis, and Clan Elienor would be condemned for it.

If Minis was not dead already, he was surely dying. Soldiers raced towards her. A crossbow bolt sang off the hatch just a hand's breadth from her ear. From the corner of her eye she saw Aachim scrambling into the weapons turrets. If she was to save herself, she must run for her life and leave Minis lying on the bloody ground.

The thought of Vithis's rage was terrifying. There was only one thing to do. She slammed the amplimet into its cavity. Pulling so much power from the nodes that her hair smoked, Tiaan fled south towards the wilderness.

THIRTY-EIGHT

The Aachim fired. One or two missiles struck the racing construct but the others fell behind, then Tiaan was out of range. They could not pursue her – they were leagues from the nearest field and would have to send a runner to the southern camp, which must take hours. But once the Aachim knew what she had done, whether Minis lived or died, they would hunt her to the corners of the globe.

How had it gone so wrong, so quickly? Perhaps she'd judged Minis too harshly. How could she have expected him to help her by betraying his own people? And, having forced him to, the flaws in her own character had been exposed. She was worse than he was. She was the most contemptible speck of ordure in all Lauralin.

This was the worst day of all. Her beloved grandmother had taught her to face her problems, and Tiaan had always tried to do that. Now she had run away. Tormented and tormenting herself, she headed south across the plains. After crossing the Westway that ran south-west towards Gnulp Landing, and northeast in the direction of Clews Top and The Elbow, and then the River Zort, she turned west. The original Aachim camp was near Gospett and she must avoid it too. The town itself had been practically emptied of its population, to drag the clanker fleet to the node.

This land, within raiding distance from lyrinx-infested Meldorin, seemed unoccupied. She saw no sign of human habitation all day. Late in the afternoon she passed into forest. The field was strong here, so Tiaan travelled as fast as she could, racing through the trees until it was too dark to see.

The amplimet was no longer drawing power of its own accord. She stopped the construct and slumped in the seat, staring into the blackness. She could not bear to think about what she had become.

Her brain swarmed with crystal dreams, so guilt-inducing that she forced herself to wake from them. It was overcast: no stars, no moon, nor any way of telling the time. The spaces between the trees were as black as the tar pits.

Even when awake, she kept slipping in and out of those dreams, just as she had that time at the manufactory, before her calluna-induced madness. Perhaps it really *was* crystal fever this time.

Tiaan could not find it in herself to care. Madness would be an escape; a refuge. She almost found herself looking forward to it. Until she sensed something.

What was it? Pulling herself up onto the top of the construct, she stared around her. Something was definitely different, though she could see nothing, hear nothing. She slid down, put on the helm and checked the field. It looked the same as before. Or did it?

When she studied it closely, Tiaan noticed tiny distortions here and there. It took a while for her to work out what they were, for she was not used to seeing the field that way. Without the helm she would never have noticed it.

Something was drawing on the field. She enlarged the image in her mind and checked it carefully. There were tiny fluctuations, like nibbles out of its myriad frilled edges, and they marked the drainage of power. People were following her in constructs. A runner must have reached the main camp.

Tiaan did not think they could find her in the dark, while she was not drawing on the field. Closing the hatch, she lay on the floor and tried to sleep. It did not come, but as she watched the ebb and flow of the field, she noticed more of those distortions. The field had nibbles out of it everywhere, which meant lots of constructs. Hundreds, maybe thousands of them. She recalled Vithis using an aura-tracker at Nyriandiol. He was following with everything the Aachim had, and he could track the amplimet's aura wherever she took it. That many constructs could even surround the great forest. There was nowhere to hide. Why had she stopped here? She should have kept to the plains, where she could move in darkness, and continued all night.

Tiaan fought down panic. She tried to recall a map of the Gospett area but it would not come to mind. She could, however, visualise a chart of Western Lauralin. The Sea of Thurkad lay about ten leagues to her west, and was narrow there. Dare she go that way? Crossing seas while depending on the field was hazardous; everyone knew that. And on the other side, Meldorin Island was infested with lyrinx. Surely not even Vithis would dare hunt her there?

To her north lay open plains all the way to Almadin. Northeast was the enormous Worm Wood, and the rugged lands around the Great Chain of Lakes, with its rift valleys and volcanic ranges, including Booreah Ngurle. But there were Aachim in the north already and Vithis could signal them at night. They would cut her off before she could find a hiding place.

Open country also lay to the east, the impoverished state of Nihilnor that ran to the ranges encircling Mirrilladell. In that land's myriad lakes, vast swamps and endless forests she might lose herself forever, if she was prepared to sink the construct into the depths and adopt a peasant life in the middle of nowhere. Though what would be the point of that? Besides, Mirrilladell was too far away. As soon as she stopped to sleep, as eventually she must, they would have her.

South lay the Karama Malama, the treacherous Sea of Mists, almost as big as the linked seas of Milmillamel and Tallallamel, down which she'd sailed for weeks on her journey to Tirthrax and Minis. Only death by drowning lay that way, once she passed out of range of the node.

So west it would have to be, to Meldorin and the lyrinx, the instant it was light enough to move.

*

Daylight stole like a ghost through the trees. She'd hoped for fog or mist but it had been a warm night and the air was clear and still. Bringing the construct to life, she edged it forwards, took bearings from the flush of dawn in the east, and turned west.

The forest was dense here and it was slow going. Sometimes she found herself in places too tight to get through and had to back the machine out again, sweating all the while in case her enemies came upon her.

She had been travelling for some hours when Tiaan detected a much stronger influence on the field. Though she could not tell which direction they were coming from, they had to be close by.

The forest was thinner here. She travelled faster, winding between the white-trunked pines and up a gentle incline where the rocks were black and the soil red. According to her mental map, she should only be a few leagues from the shores of the Sea of Thurkad. Of course, her mental map might be wrong. Once Tiaan would have known but she couldn't tell any more.

The slope became steeper; the upper parts of the hill forming a series of cliffs a span or two high, broken by ramp-like inclines. She took the nearest of these, whirring across the tussocky grass and up again, through a moist patch of forest dotted with tree ferns.

On the top of the hill, which was like a rocky pimple rising above the trees, she turned the construct through a circle. Tiaan saw nothing but a series of scalloped ridges covered in forest. Behind her the rocks outcropped in a stack like roughly piled books, several times her height. She cut off the field. All was quiet.

Tiaan got out and began to climb the stack but her knee folded and she tumbled down again, taking a gouge out of her wrist. Her legs lacked the strength to push her up. She had to drag herself all the way.

She checked the horizons. To south, east and north she could see only trees, but in the west she spotted water. The

Sea of Thurkad lay no more than a couple of leagues away. Tiaan prayed there was no obstacle in her path, for constructs could rise no more than hip-high and even the smallest cliff would defeat them.

The sun was hot on her bare head and her knees felt shaky. She took a sip from the flask at her hip, regretted that she had nothing to eat, and sat down. Had she stood a moment longer, she would have seen movement in the trees beyond the foot of the hill.

She leaned forward, rubbing her aching calves. It still felt strange to have feeling in her legs, and she often had nightmares that she was paralysed again. She kneaded the muscles until they hurt.

Something cracked in the distance. She sat up straight. It had sounded like a breaking branch, or a dislodged stone. Peering over the edge, Tiaan saw constructs everywhere. A line of them were creeping up the hill, taking one of the few clear paths to the top. Further down she saw others, waiting to block off any escape.

Sliding off the side of the stack, she lowered herself as far as her arms could reach, feeling around with her toes for a foothold. Her fingers lost their grip. She fell, landed on the edge of a lower ledge, which broke off, and crashed onto the slope below. It moved under her and she slid all the way to the bottom on her backside, ending up next to her construct in a deluge of gravel.

She made it into the machine as the first construct came over the crest. Tiaan whirled hers around and headed in the other direction. Too late; the Aachim were coming that way as well.

The only advantage she had, and it was a tiny one, was that she could take more power than they could. Tiaan spun the machine, buckling her belt with her free hand and pulling it tight. She would need it. All the paths were guarded – there was no way out unless she went over the edge.

Once again, she had nothing to lose. She kept spinning until the construct was at the centre of a whirling cloud of dust, leaves and torn-up grass. When she could see nothing at all, Tiaan took a random direction and gave the construct all the power she could bear. If she had no idea which way she was going, it must take them by surprise.

The construct roared out of the dust, straight for the largest tree on the edge of the hill. The leading machine fired a missile shaped like a javelard spear. She saw it out of the corner of her eye but the shooter had misjudged her speed – it missed by a span. The construct rocketed towards the tree. Let them think she was out of control. At the last instant she swung left and went off the edge, where the hill dropped away sharply below the little cliff.

Her stomach slid into her throat. The drop was steeper than she remembered – a good two spans. When she struck the slope it could smash in the bottom of the construct.

She eased back the controller, then, just before the construct hit, drew power hard. The machine slowed as if it had landed in a cushion of dough. The rear struck first with a shower of sparks and the sound of rending metal, tipping the front down. Tiaan thought it was going to tumble end over end, but the base slid and bounced down the tussocky slope, slowing so sharply that her head struck the binnacle. The machine slammed into a patch of tree ferns, shearing them off, before slewing sideways, the front heading towards a rock, the rear for a tree.

She fought the controls, managed to straighten it up and slid between the obstacles. Ahead was a staggered line of constructs; she could see half a dozen. They were tracking her with springfired javelards which, in the hands of skilled operators, were deadly accurate at this distance. The Aachim were skilled at everything they did. With their long life spans, they had the time to master any craft they desired.

The javelard spears looked designed to attack armoured soldiers and lyrinx, though they might not be able to penetrate the tough metal of the construct.

The two directly in front of her fired together. She ducked. A club-headed missile, similar to the kind that had killed little

Haani, thumped into the open hatch cover behind her head, shattering its shaft and embedding splinters in the back of her neck. The other missile, which must have been metal-tipped, screamed off the side of the machine.

Before they could reload, she shot between them, keeping low. Another missile thudded against the side. She heard cries and the whine of construct mechanisms as she fled into the forest.

Because she could draw power from several fields at once, her construct was faster than theirs. Had she been out on the open plain, she would have left them far behind. However, she was no match for their operators in manoeuvring her large machine through the trees.

With every twist, every turn, they were gaining. The leading constructs were only a couple of hundred paces behind, within firing distance. Club-spears whirred overhead; one thumped into the back of the machine. They would be lucky to hit her at that distance, but once they came closer they could pick her off, or lob a catapult ball into the compartment, smashing everything to bits and pulverising her.

Ahead was a large clearing studded with spreading trees. Swerving around a clump of bushes, Tiaan shot across golden grass towards the dubious shelter of the forest on the other side. When she was only halfway across the clearing, another line of constructs appeared. At their head, slightly out in front, was a larger one she recognised. Vithis stood tall, smoking with rage. She could see his expression from three hundred paces away.

There was nowhere to go. They were behind her and to either side. If she turned, they could hit her with dozens of weapons at once.

It's between me and you, Vithis. I've got nothing to lose. Let's see if you have. She turned the construct so it was heading directly for him, pressed the helm tightly onto her head and drew power from five fields at once.

The machine leapt. The golden grass fled by. Missiles flashed overhead; others struck the sides. She pulled her head

418

below the level of the sides, gritted her teeth and hung on.

Time seemed to slow to nothing. The distance between the two constructs shrank. Vithis's arm moved, as if in slow motion.

He seemed to be shouting at the other constructs, though she could hear only the roaring of the wind in her ears. There was nothing in the world but the two of them, and neither was going to give way. She wondered what the impact would look like from outside. At least it would be quick.

His teeth were bared, the look in his eyes maniacal. He was not going to give way. Minis must be dead. *Dead!*

She gave the construct more power. The distance closed swiftly. She braced herself for the impact that was going to reduce her to a splatter on the wall.

At the last conceivable instant, the other construct translocated sideways. Had she not accelerated, Tiaan would have missed it completely and been away, but the flared side of her machine struck Vithis's a glancing blow, thrusting it side-on into a tree so that Vithis was tossed out. Had she killed him too? Her own construct careered the other way, out of control. She fought the levers, narrowly avoiding the trunk of a giant tree, darted between two others almost as big, and went flying into another clearing as large as the first.

Straightening up, she dared to look over her shoulder. There was no one behind her. Taking her bearings from the angle of the sun, she headed west as fast as the trees would allow her. Surely it could not be far to the sea now. She prayed that it was beyond the next patch of forest, for she could not do that again. She was limp with relief, though her heart was going like a threshing machine.

She managed to make it into the forest before any of the constructs emerged from the other side, but Tiaan took no comfort from that. They knew which direction she'd gone, and would be heading to high points, to flash signals to other squads. Within the hour they could have spotters on every peak.

Tiaan slowed, trying to slide smoothly between the trees.

Her arm had developed a twitch and she almost went head-on into one. She was coming down from the rush too soon. The chase was nowhere near over.

The Sea of Thurkad could not be more than a league away – ten or fifteen minutes' travel at this speed. But a lot could happen in ten minutes. She kept on, trying to master herself. She was still trying to control her twitching arm when the construct shot out of forest into scrub somewhat higher than her head. The bushes had small leaves tipped with sharp points or hard grey needles. She roared along a bare strip of sand that ran up the side of an elongated ridge. As she rose over the top, Tiaan saw a series of parallel ridges, forming waving lines from south to north – sand dunes – and caught a whiff of the salt sea.

She could not see it from the top of the dune. The scrub cut off her view in every direction, and her passage too, unless she forced a way though it, which must make such a racket that the Aachim would hear her from half a league distant. Tiaan went back to the edge of the forest, turned north, then changed her mind and headed south.

The forest thinned in this direction. She climbed another long, shallow dune and from the top saw across the band of scrub land to the sea, and Meldorin beyond that. There were no constructs in sight. Tiaan allowed herself to hope. Temporary refuge was only five minutes away, if she could find a clear passage there.

And then she saw one – a series of scalloped blow-outs along the dunes, where the wind had torn away the scrub to reveal bare yellow sand which ran almost all the way to the water. A barrier of scrub blocked the last few hundred paces. She would have to crash through, trusting to speed and sur-prise to reach the coast before the Aachim could cut her off, and pray it did no fatal damage to the machine.

Taking a deep breath, she checked in all directions. Nothing. Tiaan moved on, steadily but slowly, so as to keep the whine of the construct as low as possible. She took advan-tage of every scrap of concealment, always travelling below the ridge of the dune and, where possible, on the shadowed side.

Before the scrub barrier she stopped, rinsed her dry mouth with what remained in her flask, wiped sweaty palms down her legs and cut off the flow of power. Silence fell, broken only by the creaking of metal as it came to rest, a gentle sighing of the breeze in the scrub and, more distantly, one bird chirruping to another. This was it. She gauged the density of the scrub. The trunks were thinner than her wrist, but wiry. They could still do damage.

Tiaan accelerated to a moderate pace, about the speed of a trotting horse. Too slow and resistance would bring her to a dead stop, too fast and she would not be able to avoid a large obstacle, like a trunk big enough to smash in the front of the construct.

The construct hit the wall of scrub, tearing through the bushes and sending a rain of branches and leaves into her face. She flipped the hatch down and continued. The racket was unbelievable; like being under a metal dome in a hailstorm. She could see nothing out the front but a hurricane of leaves and swirling bark. The construct struck something hard, evidently the trunk of a small tree. She heard the snap, then it went sliding by. Surely there could not be far to go now.

The machine burst through and there was nothing in front of her but bare sand, a dune that rose steadily, obscuring her view of the sea. Tiaan popped the hatch, wiped leaves out of the binnacle and dried her sweaty hands. So close. She looked around carefully. Still nothing. She eased the construct ahead, still at trotting pace, in case there was a cliff beyond the crest.

Topping the dune, she saw a long gentle slope running down to a rocky shore. The wind blew strongly here and the sea was flecked with whitecaps. To her right the shore ran straight for half a league, just sand and dark patches of jumbled rock. To her left a black headland loomed, too steep and rocky for the construct to climb. She saw no sign of the enemy. It scarcely seemed possible, but Tiaan did not question her good fortune.

She kept going at a steady pace towards the shore. Scanning the rock masses for the safest passage to the water, she saw nothing odd about the curved black rocks to her left, nor those on her right. She saw nothing amiss until a net rose up from the sand and the construct drove straight into it.

It gave before her then began to pull taut. The webs of another net whipped against the back and over the top, enclosing the construct. Tiaan panicked, but instinct moved the controls. The construct lurched forwards but the ropes snapped tight, slowing her machine until it was barely moving. Now it was not moving at all. Now they began to pull it backwards.

Tiaan shot a glance over her shoulder. The huge nets were attached to three constructs on her left, two on her right. She could draw more power than they could, but not five times as much. Poured directly into this machine, it would either destroy it, or her.

She took as much as she dared. Her backwards progress halted. She inched forward a few spans, stalled, and was dragged back. Now the net began to tighten as they reeled it in from the ends. As soon as she was immobilised, they would swarm all over her.

What if she turned and went for the join of the net? Unfortunately, its two leaves overlapped above her. Whichever way she went, it would hold her. And it was too strong to break; thus far she had not torn a single strand.

There was one last hope, though she had only seconds to do it. With the helm, and the skills the Aachim had taught her, she could draw power more precisely than ever before. If she could locate the spot from which the other machines were drawing power, she might be able to snatch that power from under their noses. It would only stop them for a few seconds, but it might just be enough. The problem was, how to tell *which* machine was drawing power from *which* part of the field.

Maybe it didn't matter. She could distinguish these five from the many distant constructs. Tiaan identified all the sources and locked onto the first, the second, then each of the others. She did not draw power yet, but allowed the Aachim to pull her backwards. Let them think she was weakening. This must be hurting them, too.

Tiaan sensed an irregularity in one of the power draws. The field there was fluttering. She pounced, taking all the power she could. The tension on the right-hand side of the rope eased and her construct jerked forward. Sensing another flutter, she drew power from there as well. Another jerk, and there came a rending noise behind her and the net gave. It was now tangled around one of the three constructs. Back to her right it was still fixed, though one construct had lost power and was being dragged sideways. The other could not hold her by itself.

Tiaan was now approaching the water. A long way to her right, hordes of machines were racing along the water's edge, flinging clouds of sand and mist into the air. She took power jerkily, trying to break free of the other two constructs. One rolled onto its side, jammed against a rock ledge and the ropes broke. The other was still attached and, no matter how she tried, Tiaan could not get rid of it. If she didn't, they would have her. She could now see hundreds of constructs. They were coming from her left as well, through the scrub near the black headland.

Her only chance was straight ahead. Tiaan gave it everything she had. Her construct leapt across the sand and onto the water, dragging the other machine. It struck a boulder in the surf, was hurled high and came crashing down, nose first, to plunge beneath the water.

The sea hissed like a kettle, boiled over and, as the cold water came in contact with the hot innards of the construct, it exploded in all directions. Pieces of flaming construct hurtled skywards and, to her horror, several bodies.

The net came away. Her construct soared like a skipping stone, came down hard and bounced, spinning sideways. Tiaan hung on grimly as the whirling force tried to throw her out. The machine hit the water on its base and skipped again.

Constructs were converging on her from all directions. Hundreds more – how had she not seen them? – had formed into a curving barrier further across the sea. There was just one small gap, to the south. She darted through and raced south down the Sea of Thurkad.

She was not going to make it across, for the seaward constructs were tracking her all the way. She could not get through them to the dubious security of Meldorin. Even if she did, its shore here was edged with impassable cliffs.

That first impact with the water must have damaged something, for Tiaan's construct now had no more speed than her pursuers. She curved back towards the Lauralin shore. Ahead, the Karama Malama, hung with banners of mist, was an endless expanse of slate grey. Just a narrow, scrubby peninsula now separated her from it.

She rounded the tip, looking east and west. More constructs were coming along the south-facing shore and down out of the scrub. There were thousands of them. She could only go one way. She turned due south, out into the centre of the Sea of Mists. Let them follow her there, if they dared.

The Aachim did follow, a great host of them, for an hour and more. At the end of that time they began to fall back, one by one, as the separation from the node became too great to sustain their motion. Soon there were only two left, then one. Finally the last construct turned back. She was alone with her bleeding conscience on the empty sea.

Tiaan looked for another node, not knowing if there was one. Some seas were barren of them. If she could not find a node, any sudden failure of the fading field would sink her. Tiaan was no longer sure that she cared, but she did find another. It was nearly as distant as the first, with barely enough power in it to move the construct. She took some from each and continued.

THIRTY-NINE

A week or more after his arrival in Oellyll, when Gilhaelith was trudging the tunnels in a vain attempt to regain his strength, he heard a number of lyrinx engaged in furious argument up ahead. He eased forward and peered around the corner. He was looking into an excavated chamber shaped like a cloverleaf, its roof supported by columns of fused stone. Two lyrinx stood at the far side, in one of the lobes of the room, before a crowd of twenty or more.

'This is our future on Santhenar,' urged one of the two out the front, 'and we must take it.' She was small with transparent, unarmoured skin and magnificent wings that quivered as she spoke, casting rainbow reflections around the room. 'Now that we *know*, we cannot stay like this,' she said passionately.

Know what? Gilhaelith thought, sliding across the tunnel into a shadowed aperture where he could see but not be seen.

'Neither can we re-order the grains of time, Liett,' said the other, a muscular female, twice the size of the first. Her skin armour was scarred and battered as if from a lifetime of fighting, though she was not old. 'No amount of flesh-forming can change what we are.'

'You fool – of course we can change! We must.'

'How dare you speak that way to me! You can't even take your place in battle – you have no *armour*.'

'I don't need armour,' Liett said furiously, 'and I'm just as good as you are. My work has saved many lives, and taken many of the enemy's.'

'You can't even skin-speak.' The big female's armour flickered a display of brilliant reds and yellows – a sneer at

425

Liett's lack. 'You should have been drowned at birth.'

'How dare you!' Liett shook her wings at the other. 'Your kind came from the monstrosities we had to flesh-form in the womb, to survive in the pitiless void.'

'I am true lyrinx,' said the muscular female, 'and this is my nature.'

'You're has-beens. You're wrong for this world and must submit to *amendment*.'

Amendment? Gilhaelith peered around the corner. Were they planning to flesh-form themselves anew, to better suit Santhenar?

The other lyrinx rose onto her toe claws, towering over Liett and extending finger claws as long and sharp as daggers. 'You speak blasphemy! Take it back or suffer the consequences.'

Liett lowered her wings, though not in submission. 'I'm sorry, Inyll. I put it badly. Let me explain. I once thought as you do, but Matriarch has opened my eyes. We've become creatures designed for just one thing – perpetual war! We're prisoners in our own armour.'

Inyll tore the soft shale underfoot with her toe claws. 'War is our existence.'

'But don't you yearn for peace, and the chance to live our lives without fear?'

'What do I want with peace? I am a warrior from a line of warriors. The line of battle is my life.'

'But surely for your children –?'

'My children yearn to do their duty, not change their nature to suit some *selfish* whim.' Inyll used the word as if it was obscene, which it was. To the lyrinx, placing oneself ahead of the group was the greatest evil of all.

'Ah,' said Liett, 'but we must change for the best of all reasons – to ensure our survival.'

'We're winning the war as we are. There's no need to change.'

'In so winning, we could be sowing the seeds of our ruin. I've been among humans, Inyll,' said Liett softly, carefully, 'and I used to hate and despise them too. I wanted to kill them all. But now I envy them, for the meanest of humans has something that we lost so long ago we cannot even remember it. Where is our culture? Where are our arts and sciences? We have none. In the void we rid ourselves of everything not essential to survival. In doing so, we cast away all that made us unique. We became machines.'

Liett raised her voice, threw out her arms and addressed the group. 'Listen to me, my people. Unless you want to go back to the void, our future lies on this world. We must transform ourselves so that we can embrace it. Creatures like me, which you see as deformed, *half-born*, are the future of the lyrinx. Yet even we must renew –'

'I'll hear no more of this . . . this *sedition*!' Inyll cracked her wings and threw herself at Liett who, lacking armour, was at a severe disadvantage. She was brave, though. She bared her claws and stood up to her opponent, ducking one blow that could have taken her head off and just managing to sidestep another.

'Enough!' roared Gyrull, who had been standing behind a pillar, out of sight of Gilhaelith. 'Inyll?'

The larger female drew back, bowing with ill grace.

'Liett, my daughter,' said Gyrull sternly.

Liett bowed to her mother, and to Inyll, flashing dark looks from beneath her heavy brows. Possessed of an aggressive nature and a powerful sense of her own rightness, she found it difficult to defer to anyone.

'I have fostered this debate,' said Gyrull to the group, 'for it is clear to me, as matriarch, that we *must* change. In the void we gave up our culture, our humanity and, yea, our very identity, in our desperation to survive. It was necessary, but we have come to lament it. Think about what has been said here today. We'll meet again tomorrow.'

'To change now would be to warp our very souls,' said Inyll. 'I can't do it and I won't.' She stalked out, head held high, saying over her shoulder, 'Don't try to convince me, for I will never relent.'

The remainder of the lyrinx followed, arguing among themselves, leaving just Liett and her mother in the cloverleaf chamber.

Liett started after them but the matriarch laid a hand on her shoulder. 'Leave it for a while, my child.'

'But I'm right!' said Liett in a passion. 'Why won't they listen?'

'Their attitudes have been frozen by thousands of years of adversity, and all that time your kind has never been good enough. Until now, *reverts*, half-borns such as you and Ryll, have been a blight on our line.'

'But *they're* just designed for battle,' said Liett. 'It leaves nothing for any other kind of life. We're handicapped, Mother. We may win the war – it looks as though we will – only to find that humanity has transformed its whole society again, and come up with a weapon we can find no defence against. Humans are infinitely flexible, so we must be the same.'

'Or else,' the matriarch said provocatively, 'we must wipe every living human from the face of the world.'

'I used to think that way,' said Liett, 'but after working with their females in the patterners in Snizort, I came to see them as people, not just food animals. We must embrace the future *before* the war is over, Mother, and we reverts are the best equipped to do it.'

'You may be right, though it will take much to convince Inyll and her many followers.'

'Why don't you talk to them? They would follow you any-where.'

'My time is coming to an end and I can't lead them where I cannot go myself. A new young leader is required for a bold new direction.'

'You could order them to obey.'

'Liett, Liett,' said Gyrull. 'You have much to learn, and many to sway, if you're to be chosen matriarch after me.'

'But I've worked so hard, at every task you've given me. I've done well –'

'At *most*. I recall a number of reprimands.'

428

Liett bit her lip.

Gyrull continued. 'You are intelligent, my daughter, a brilliant flesh-former and patterner, and your mancing talent is of the highest order. You have many of the qualities necessary to lead our people into the future, different qualities from those that I required. But Liett, you're too impetuous. You can't direct people to obey as though you know better than everyone else – even if you do. You must learn to persuade, to cajole, to *lead*.' She turned and saw Gilhaelith in the shadows of the tunnel.

'Begone, Tetrarch! You have no place here. Liett, would you escort Gilhaelith back to his quarters? We'll talk more about this tonight.'

Gilhaelith returned to his room, thoughtfully. By the sound of it, the lyrinx were on the verge of a momentous transformation. If they did find the courage to make the leap, how would that change the balance? And could it have anything to do with what they'd found in the Great Seep?

He wondered if mathemancy might give him a clue. He began to calculate a series of fourth powers, a preparatory exercise before beginning the divination, but as soon as he finished the first calculation, the number resonated wrongly. This horror was far greater than his previous failure, for Gilhaelith prided himself on his utter mastery of numbers. He never made a mistake. Never! He did the calculation again. Worst yet – he got a different answer and it was also wrong.

Gilhaelith sank to his knees and pounded the floor in anguish, though cold resolve overpowered the impulse. This could not be happening; not to *him*. It was just another problem and he'd solve it as he'd solved every other difficulty in his adult life, with sheer, unconquerable will.

Standing up to his full height, he took a series of deep breaths, ignoring the persistent gripe in his belly. I can do it. *I must!* Selecting a different number, 127, he raised it through its powers – 16,129; 2,048,383; 260,144,614. No, that couldn't be right. The last digit had to be odd, not even. About to try again, he discovered that the calculation had faded from his mind. Worse, though it was a simple operation, he'd forgotten how to repeat it. *He was lost!*

What if his other abilities were failing as well? If he could not complete his great work soon, he never would, and would die having achieved nothing. Achievement was all he'd ever had. Without it his existence had been meaningless.

Gilhaelith spent the next three days on his stretcher, refusing all food, just lying there with his eyes closed, raging against his fate and searching feverishly for a way out of it. He could not be beaten this easily. He had to know what was wrong with him.

After much labour he devised a series of tests to probe the workings of his mind. The results were conclusive. In escaping from the tar, the phantom crystal he'd created had drawn too much power and literally cooked one tiny segment of his brain. Small parts of his intellect had been lost forever, though other aspects might, with diligent mental exercise, be recovered. But that was not the real problem.

The explosion of the node had burst the phantom crystal into fragments that remained within his subconscious, doing more damage. Each time he used power, part of it leaked from the fragments and made the damage worse. Eventually it would progress beyond the point of recovery.

There was only one solution. As soon as his health recovered sufficiently, he'd have to use his Arts to locate and unmake every fragment. Not the tiniest shard could be missed. If he could do that, he would at least have the chance to retain most of his remaining intellect.

There was one more problem. Using his Arts in that way would require drawing a lot of power, and that risked destroying the faculties he was trying to save.

The following morning, when Gilhaelith went for his walk, he discovered a sentinel, or zygnadr, sitting in the corridor outside his room. It was a weird, twisted object that looked grown though not alive, and was nothing like the mushroom-shaped sentinels he'd seen in Snizort. This one, knee-high, was shaped like a ball wrenched into a spiral. Its surface looked vaguely organic, like the patterners in Snizort, and bore traces of a crablike shell and segmented legs. As he passed, what appeared to be compound eyes rotated on stubby stalks to follow his movement. It did not hinder him so he kept going.

He turned randomly right and left until he reached an area he was not familiar with. Oellyll comprised a maze of shafts containing lifts operated by ropes, declines that spiralled down in loops and whorls of varying diameters, and tunnels that ran in seemingly random directions. Often they followed particular layers in the rock. Some were broad thoroughfares, others barely shoulder width, or so low that they could only be navigated on hands and knees.

After half an hour of trudging, punctuated by several rest stops, he entered a decline that sloped gently down, lit at intervals by lanterns. Seeing no one to forbid him he headed along it.

Partway down, he encountered a great shear zone where the upper rocks had ground over the lower. Below it the strata were crammed with fossils of every kind: the remains of little, creeping creatures; bones large and small; shells; rat-like skulls as well as feathery leaves like the fronds of ferns. Few of the fossils resembled animals that Gilhaelith had seen before, and some were oddities indeed.

He crouched next to the lantern, studying the remains. Until now, he'd paid little attention to such relics of the past, and perhaps, for a geomancer, that had been a mistake. Gilhaelith stood up, rubbing an ache in the middle of his back, then trudged down to the next lantern. The fossils here were similar, though each kind bore subtle and curious differences to the ones above. At the lantern after that, which illuminated a lower layer of rock, they were subtly different again, and so it went all the way down.

One particular fossil, a creature like a crab curled into a twisted ball, was especially common. It had big compound eyes on short stalks, and it was his fancy that they followed him as he moved.

Gilhaelith turned away then spun back. It had just been his imagination, though the creature was shaped rather like the sentinel outside his room. The zygnadr must have been modelled on this ancient fossil. According to the Principle of Similarity, one of the primary laws of the Art, every specimen of this fossil could be linked to the zygnadr, in which case the whole of Oellyll might be spying on him. Was there nowhere he could go, in light or in darkness, where they could not monitor what he was doing? But then, did it matter any more?

Gilhaelith's stomach spasmed. His life had been out of his control for so long that it was killing him.

Gilhaelith was sitting in a large dining hall, picking at the unpalatable green sludge in his bowl and brooding about his decline into helplessness. Gyrull had promised to loan him a dozen human prisoners, some of them skilled crafters of metal, wood and stone, as soon as he was well enough to go to Alcifer. The others would cook, clean and assist him with the rehabilitation of a suitable workplace. The matriarch had returned his geomantic globe and other devices, though it would be weeks before he had the strength to use them. His physical recovery had proved painful, slow and incomplete.

The matriarch had allowed him to go wherever in Oellyll he wished, which suggested that she did not plan to release him. He'd set out to learn all he could about the city and was pleased to discover that the lyrinx did no flesh-forming here. Gilhaelith had few fears, but those creeping monstrosities inspired a particular horror.

There was a commotion outside and a band of travel-stained lyrinx burst in, led by a small, wingless male. Gyrull, who was studying a parchment, set it down with a glad cry. Liett, eating gruel from a wooden bowl the size of a bucket, dropped it on the floor. Her iridescent wings snapped out, two spans on either side, then she bounded across the room and threw herself at the wingless male. The impact knocked him to the floor, whereupon she sat on his chest and began pummelling him with her fists. He tried to catch hold of her wrists but she was too quick for him.

The other lyrinx were laughing, an extraordinary sight. What was going on? Even Gyrull was beaming.

'Thlapp!' she said at last.

Liett got up, helping the young male to his feet and linking her arm sinuously along his. He was smiling too.

'Welcome, Ryll!' said Gyrull. 'We were afraid you'd been killed in the siege.'

'There were times,' Ryll said, 'when we were struggling to cross the sea in a boat no bigger than a human outhouse, that I wished I had been. But we survived even the dreadful waters.'

He came to her with lowered head, a sign of deference, but she lifted his chin, speaking warmly to him in a dialect Gilhaelith did not recognise. Ryll's skin showed a cheerful, flickering pattern of yellows and blues. Finally he bowed and went out, Liett still attached to his arm.

Later that day Gyrull came to Gilhaelith's room with the young male close behind her.

'This is Ryll,' she said, 'one of my most skilled young patterners.'

'I know you,' said Gilhaelith, trying to recall where he'd seen Ryll's face before.

'I fetched you to Tiaan, in the patterning room in Snizort,' Ryll answered coldly. 'She thought you cared for her, but all you wanted was her crystal.'

Gilhaelith shrugged. He wasn't going to explain himself to an alien. 'You speak as though she's your *friend*.' The emphasis made that into an absurdity.

'Tiaan acted more than honourably to me,' said Ryll, 'and I deeply regretted having to use her to aid the war. In other circumstances we *would* have been friends.'

'What happened to her?' said Gilhaelith.

In Nyriandiol, he'd begun to care about her in a way that

had disturbed him, for it had meant losing control of a part of his life. To care at all was truly unusual – normally his feelings for other people were no more than efficiency required. People got in the way, made unreasonable demands, and therefore had to be controlled at all times. Abandoning Tiaan had been the easiest solution to his uncomfortable loss of control, but now he regretted it. He'd lost the chance to have an apprentice who would have complemented him perfectly. He'd also lost – what? The possibility of a friend? The chance of intimacy, both intellectual and – though he shied violently away from the recurring thought – physical.

'I don't know,' Ryll replied. 'I was sent to the battle –'

'A shameful mix-up,' said Gyrull with set face. 'Fortunately Tiaan escaped in a construct, though she is now held prisoner by the Aachim. But enough of her. From now on, Tetrarch, Ryll will take care of your needs, when he has time free from his other duties. No one else will attend you, so make no claims on them. And once you go up to Alcifer, take this warning to heart. Savage creatures from the void dwell in the forests of Meldorin – the vicious lorrsk, among others. They keep clear of our boundaries, but put one foot over them and you're game for their table.'

Outside, Gyrull said quietly to Ryll, 'Keep a close eye on the tetrarch and don't trust him the length of a claw. He's a dishonourable man who would betray his birth-mother if it served his purpose. Question everything he says and does. On second thoughts, you've enough to do. I'll tune the zygnadrs to him, night and day.'

'I don't like Gilhaelith,' said Ryll. 'He'll cause us all grief one day. Were it up to me, I would bite his head off.'

'He served us tolerably well in Snizort and may do so again. I've an idea I'd like you to think about, and Gilhaelith's own studies may assist it.'

Ryll grimaced. 'I will do my duty, of course. What is it?'

'It arose from the work you were doing with the torgnadr, and Tiaan, in Snizort. This will be a new kind of device – I call it a flisnadr, that is, a power patterner – and we'll need it to put an end to the war. The enemy are creating a myriad of new devices to take the place of the people they no longer have, and each must draw power from the field. If we could find a way to *control* that power, rather than just draining it away with torgnadrs, their devices could be made to act against them. Should we succeed they'll have to surrender, or die.

'I've had the eleventh level cleared for this work and you will be in charge. No one will be allowed in save those working with you, and especially not the tetrarch.'

'May I have Liett to assist me?' Ryll asked, a trifle over-eagerly.

The matriarch sighed, then considered, her skin colours flickering a silvery mauve. 'I'm minded to say no, because of the trouble there's been between you in the past.'

Ryll opened his mouth but closed it again without speaking.

'But then,' she went on, 'together you seem to be worth more than separately. Yes, take my daughter. And whatever you require, you have only to ask. Come, this is what I want you to do . . .'

FORTY

Gilhaelith trudged up a steep ramp towards the lower levels of Alcifer. He was alone, for Gyrull had simply indicated the way and left him, and he'd lost hope of being given the servants he'd asked for.

His helplessness was corrosive. He had not fully recovered and no longer expected to. His stomach throbbed constantly, and walking for as little as half an hour exhausted him. By himself he'd be hard pressed to carry up his geomantic instruments. Even if he managed that, how could he live without servants? It would take all the hours of the day just to find food and prepare it, if there was any to be gathered so close to Oellyll. But he had to go on. Giving in had never been an option for Gilhaelith.

Heart palpitating from the effort, he turned off the ramp at a great black door that marked the gate between Oellyll and Alcifer. Another of those crab-like sentinels stood beside it. He pushed past without incident and approached the door, which was made of a black metal that shone in the lantern light as though it had a hundred coats of lacquer. As he reached out, the door swung open silently. He froze, then peered through, carefully. The floor was thick with untracked dust, so the lyrinx had never been this way.

It was so dark that he could not see what lay beyond – palace or rat hole. He raised the lantern. Faint gleams appeared here and there, reflections off distant surfaces whose shapes shifted as he moved. He stepped into Alcifer and the darkness seemed to suck the light from his lantern. The floor shivered underfoot. He scuffed the dust away with a boot toe to reveal solid stone, yet it was quivering ever so slightly.

Go back! came an errant thought. *You should not be here.* He shrugged off the unease. Alcifer was a ruin abandoned an aeon ago. Nothing here could harm him, save the decaying stone and mortar falling on his head.

Hours he walked through haunted, magical halls where the dust lay so thick that his boots made no sound. Hours more he sat on seat or rail, staring into the darkness as he tried to gain a feeling for the building. He was searching for the perfect place to work but a palace such as this confused the mind as it tricked the eye. He could not take it in.

My mind is definitely failing, he thought. *Before my illness I could have visualised the entirety of this palace, like rows and columns in a catalogue. Am I reaching my end sooner than I'd thought? Please, not this way, with my work so far from completion. If my mind is going, let me not fade dismally away. Rather would I die in a cataclysm of my own making, as long as in doing so I can approach my goal.*

He stood up, staring around him in the darkness and shivering like the very stones. In all the years he'd worked on his study of the world, there was one experiment he'd not been game to attempt. Though it held the best promise of all, it was deadly perilous. Should he try it? If it succeeded, he might use it to find and remove all the fragments of the phantom crystal at once and even, faint hope that it was, repair some of the damage to his brain. He'd either crash through to his goal, or crash to his doom. More likely the latter, but what did he have to lose? Better to die violently than live this way, feeling his faculties slowly fading, knowing he'd either lose his intellect and go mad, or end up a vegetable that the lyrinx wouldn't deign to dine on.

'I'll do it!' he said aloud. 'I'll dare the great experiment and curse the consequences.'

First, the place to work. Ignoring the dark, magnificent surroundings, he dragged himself up a last set of stairs to a vast hall covered ankle-deep in ash, through which occasional black tiles were exposed. The frescoed walls were stained brown from flowing rainwater, for the roof had collapsed long ago. Gilhaelith picked his way through the mess towards a tall pair of doors, wedged ajar by a leaning pine that had grown between them. He squeezed through the gap and out.

A broad boulevard, knee-deep in crusted ash, littered with boulders and fallen masonry, and overgrown with great trees whose roots had lifted the paving stones, ran away from him up a round hill. Despite the debris, its noble proportions were evident. The open space across the boulevard had once been a park, it seemed, for the trees there were vast and gnarled with age. A partly collapsed pavilion stood among them, to its right a marble fountain choked with debris, the stone dissolving from the volcano's acid rain. On Gilhaelith's left was an edifice of black stone, apparently the twin of the one he'd just come out of, though this building had an intact roof of some green metal that glinted here and there.

It was a bright, sunny day but Alcifer felt cold and brooding in a way that other ancient places did not. As if something – the city itself? – was waiting for a master who would never return, to complete a purpose that had been overtaken by time and treachery. The tilted paving stones in the street shivered underfoot, such was the power leashed here.

But there was no longer any point to Alcifer, Gilhaelith mused as he mentally reviewed its Histories. Originally built during the chaos of the Clysm, the city was said to have been one vast machine designed to open the Way between the Worlds, but had never been put to use. Soon after its completion, Rulke had been captured by his enemies and cast into the Nightland, a nowhere place that had contained him for a thousand years. During his imprisonment he'd designed a better artefact than Alcifer, reworked it until it was perfect, and on his escape had built it in Fiz Gorgo and Carcharon – his construct.

The constructs of the Aachim were based upon his model, though the original had never been equalled. Rulke's had been a vehicle that could fly, a means of attack and defence, and a device to open the Way between the Worlds.

After his death, Alcifer had slumbered under its covering of forest and volcanic ash for another hundred years, until the lyrinx were attracted to its extraordinary node-within-a-node that now energised both Alcifer and Oellyll. He could sense it from here: a pair of spheres one inside the other, each swelling and contracting to its own rhythm. Their potent fields also expanded and shrank in a complex dance that never repeated itself.

Gilhaelith crossed the boulevard to the fountain and sat on a carved soapstone bench covered in crumbs of volcanic ash. How could such a node have formed? Had it anything to do with the dormant volcano to the north, or could it have been transformed by that pinching-off of force that had created the rolled-up dimensions of the Nightland? He felt awed in the presence of power so much greater than any he'd dealt with before.

The lyrinx had no fear of the place, nor of any hidden purpose it may have had long ago. They had cleared some of its boulevards, built ventilation bellows powered by the field, and begun to delve their own city beneath Alcifer.

Getting up and brushing the ash from his pants, he paced along the boulevard towards the hill, wonder growing with every step. Alcifer was vast, but even under the volcanic detritus and forest growth he could see that every structure, from the smallest to the greatest, formed part of one harmonious whole. A single mind had shaped each part of it, a single principle guided his hand – Pitlis the Aachim, the greatest architect who had ever lived, and the biggest fool. Rulke had seduced him with the creation of Alcifer, used it to uncover the defensive secrets of Gar Gaarn, the Aachim's greatest city, and destroyed it.

Gilhaelith spent days trudging the debris-strewn city, trying to understand it so as to find the perfect place to work. His great experiment could not be done anywhere – location was critical. Some places would assist the task not at all, while others would hinder it or even make it impossible. Yet somewhere there would be the perfect locale. It need not be vast or grand. The simplest of pavilions in a park might suffice, but he would not know until he found it, and had tested it with mathemancy, assuming he was still capable of it. One day a talent would be there, the next it would be gone. And every attempt at using mancery caused jagging pain in one part of his head or another, indicating that the phantom fragments were still doing damage.

After five days he was more confused about Alcifer than when he'd entered the city. The genius of Pitlis's design, and Rulke's building, would take half a lifetime to unravel. It humbled him and made his own achievements seem puny.

The city consisted of arrays of buildings, great and small, set along seven intersecting boulevards. Every side street was curved, the intersections being circles or ovals. There were vistas only along the boulevards. Off them, every corner revealed a new surprise, some vast and ornate, others simple – a mossy cul-de-sac with a fountain, a set of elegant steps, a pond or a piece of statuary. Although many of the buildings had been ruined by time, the bones of the city endured, for they had been fused to the living rock with an Art no human could duplicate.

Despairing of ever gaining a mental picture of the whole of Alcifer, he begged Gyrull to take him aloft, so he could view it from the air. She agreed readily, though he was carried up by Liett, the small lyrinx with the transparent, soft skin, now covered with a paste to prevent it from burning in the sun. Despite her size she lifted him easily, flying in circles over Alcifer for two hours while he tried to impress the city's patterns on his mind. It still wasn't enough, though on the way down he spotted a white building shaped like a five-pointed star that he planned to take a closer look at from the ground.

That afternoon he went back on foot, accompanied by a male lyrinx who spoke not a single word the entire time. In the centre of the city, at the intersection of the seven boulevards, stood the white palace, and it proved to be unlike any building he had ever seen. It consisted of a core covered by a glass dome – no, not a dome, a soaring shell – with five arms, or wings, each identical, spinning out from it. The arms were roofed with a series of curving shells made of white stone so polished that they had once dazzled the eye. Even now, weather-stained as they were, the building was breathtakingly beautiful.

Gilhaelith went up the broad steps and pushed at the left-most of the four bronze doors; it grated open. The shivering of the stone grew as he paced down the hall. In the very centre, where the five buildings fused, he entered an enormous, airy and bright chamber, for the covering shell consisted of a single piece of glass. Red water stains ran down the walls, rubble lay here and there, and dust everywhere, but otherwise its magnificence was unmarred.

Just off the centre of the chamber stood a circular bench, many spans across, made of volcanic glass. The rest of the space was empty. Gilhaelith had a keen eye for beauty, though this place held more than that. Without even taking the numbers he knew it was exactly what he'd been looking for.

'Pulke know the ways of power,' he said aloud. 'He built this palace here because the resonances were perfect, and so they will be for me.' Gilhaelith turned to the silent lyrinx. 'I'll work here. Would you bring up my servants now?'

The creature turned away without answering, leaving Gilhaelith to wonder if Gyrull would allow him any assistants. He no longer expected her to.

Somewhat to his surprise the lyrinx returned the following morning with twelve slaves. They were a rough-looking lot, to be expected after years of servitude. Before they so much as picked up a crate, Gilhaelith had to ensure their loyalty, and it would not be easy. They must see him as a traitor, and the only way to overcome that was with naked self-interest, backed up by inflexible control.

'My name is Gilhaelith,' he said to the assembled group from the top step of the white palace. 'Gyrull has given you to me. I'm not a harsh master, but I demand instant and total obedience. In return, if you serve me faithfully until my work is done, I'll see you freed and take you home to your loved ones.'

'Seems to me your word is worth no more than any other stinking turncoat's,' said their spokesman, Tyal, a hungry-looking fellow with a starkly white complexion. His hands were covered in wiry yellow hairs, the hair on his head was carrot-coloured and his beard was red.

'How long have you been held prisoner by the lyrinx?' Gilhaelith said pleasantly.

'Nine years,' said Tyal.

'And in that time, how many prisoners have they freed?'

'None,' he replied grudgingly.

'And how many escaped from the lyrinx?'

'Couple dozen got away in the early days,' said a short, greatly scarred woman from the back of the group. 'Course, the lyrinx et them all. Weren't many escapes after that, and *they* got et as well. Every one of 'em, right in front of us.'

He let them think about that for a full minute. 'So, Tyal,' said Gilhaelith, giving him the cold stare that had quelled hundreds of minions over the years, 'it seems your only chance of seeing your loved ones again is through me. If you can't trust me, go back and take your chances with the lyrinx.' He held Tyal's gaze a moment longer before turning to the others. 'But to those who stay, and do as I require, I promise you'll get your freedom. What is it to be?'

They all stayed, of course. Any hope was better than none. He smiled thinly. 'Bring my instruments inside. Treat them like eggs.'

After days of work the glass-roofed chamber had been cleaned to Gilhaelith's exacting standards and his instruments arranged correctly. He took the omens with a series of fourth powers, an effort that left him drained and shaking. In the end, unable to do the calculations mentally, he'd had to call for pencil and paper. It was another small failure, though the number patterns were, for the most part, harmonious; not perfect but good enough. Dismissing the servants to their quarters he stood in the geometrical centre of the room, by the great bench, revelling. After months of chaos that had been torment to him, his life was ordered again. He would soon control everything in his small domain. Gilhaelith had little hope that he could reverse the slow decay of his mental faculties, but his health might recover enough for him to complete his work and die fulfilled.

He'd last worked on his great project back in Nyriandiol in the spring. It was late summer now and today he would make a new start. As he paced beneath the glass roof, under bleak, rainy skies, he mused on what he'd learned since being taken from Nyriandiol, trying to place it into a pattern he could make sense of.

Firstly, the variety of nodes and fields was greater than he'd ever imagined. He'd always thought that there had to be an underlying pattern – that nodes weren't just random concentrations of power – but he'd never been able to work out what it might be. If only he could, he knew it would form an important part of the puzzle.

Secondly, Tiaan's amplimet was, inexplicably, *awake* and able to communicate in some fashion with nodes. In Snizort it had drawn a network of filaments throughout the city and pulses had flowed along them. That implied some kind of purpose, if not necessarily intelligence, which was incomprehensible. It was, after all, just a lump of crystal. It had also drawn a filament to him and he must beware the amplimet in future.

Gilhaelith shrugged away the fear. He had always been supremely self-confident and his recent problems had not completely undermined that. He was still a great geomancer. Should the crystal reappear, *he* would control it, not it him! And, perhaps, if he could reproduce those filaments, he could learn to control a node as well.

Thirdly, he'd gleaned that the lyrinx, on the closed-off eleventh level of Oellyll, were working on a new and powerful artefact. The war was escalating into a magical weapons race between humans, Aachim and lyrinx, with every new development requiring more power. Eventually it must drain the nodes past the point of no return. What then? Inexplicable things had already happened when nodes had been stripped of their fields. A whole squadron of clankers had once vanished into nothingness. Another time, the fragments of a hundred machines, and the people inside them, had been strewn across forty leagues of countryside, and for weeks after there had been green sunsets. What if that kind of catastrophe occurred worldwide? He could not allow it to happen.

Fourthly, a node could be completely destroyed, though that left a residue of unknown nature but disturbing potential. The residue from the Snizort node was now in the hands of the scrutators, assuming that Gyrull had told the truth. What would they do with it? And had the amplimet anything to do with the node's destruction?

Fifthly, there was some undiscovered potential about Alcifer, and it was more than just the remarkable node here. Whatever lay sleeping, it might just prove to be the last part of the puzzle.

Gilhaelith felt sure there was a way of putting these disparate discoveries together, to reach the understanding that he so craved, but his exhausted brain rebelled. Where the mind failed, it was his policy to put the hands to work. The great and perilous experiment required him to recreate his geomantic globe, incorporating all he'd learned about the world so far.

The pattern of nodes and fields was just the surface expression of tensions between the great forces that moved and shaped the world. If he could model them on his geomantic globe, he might uncover these ultimate forces. *As the small is to the great*, he thought – another of the key principles of the Art. But of course, his globe would have to be perfect, and he already knew of errors in it. There was much work to be done.

He turned to the globe, a glass-surfaced sphere half a span across, slowly rotating on its cushion of air above an ebony pedestal. It was so bitterly cold that moisture from the air formed wisps of vapour, drawn out to streaky clouds by its motion. Beneath the glass, so detailed that it looked like Santhenar seen from the surface of the moon, was his model of the world. The light reflected from its restless oceans, its glittering ice caps, and even the minute threads that represented great rivers.

With a gesture, Gilhaelith attempted to still the globe, as he'd done so many times before. It was the most trivial of magics, but nothing happened. He tried again, with the same result. Panicky fear clutched at his heart and momentarily he found it difficult to breathe. What had he done wrong? He couldn't think. The process, once intuitive, was lost to him.

He laboriously reconstructed it using pure logic and tried once more. It worked this time. Points of light sparkled here and there on the glass – representations of the most powerful nodes. Taking up a hand lens the size of a frying-pan, he inspected the surface. It had not been harmed by its long journey, but he frowned and plucked at his lower lip. Though he'd made the globe from the best maps in the world, he now knew Meldorin was inaccurate in some important details. Therefore other lands could also contain errors, while those parts of the globe known only from ancient adventurers' maps might be completely wrong.

No wonder he'd never been able to discover how the world worked. Two-thirds of his globe was based on charts that could have been made up, and he couldn't see how to remedy that. No, there was one possibility, though it would put him in such deep debt that he might never escape it. But then, if the globe worked, it offered another way out of here.

'What progress do you have to report?' Gyrull asked Ryll a few days later.

'The work goes slowly,' he replied. 'A flisnadr is much more difficult to pattern than our torgnadrs, and we only made a handful of them in years of labour. The human slaves we use in the patterners are not strong enough – they keep dying, ruining all our work. And also,' Ryll looked around, in case they were being overheard by other lyrinx, 'I'm unhappy about . . . the *morality* of it.' He used the word uncomfortably, as if, applied to the enemy, it was a new concept for him.

'You surprise me,' Gyrull said ambiguously. 'I begin to wonder if you've also been corrupted by association with the human, Tiaan.'

'She made me realise that humankind are not so different. And then, what you discovered in the Great Seep . . .'

'It's always on my mind.' She scratched a scaly armpit. 'The war will be over within a year. We must prepare for the peace now, though –'

'Not all of us want to change,' he said perceptively. 'We've had too much of it, and it's uncomfortable. The way we are is a refuge. Take that away, what do we have left? And yet . . .'

'Go on,' she said.

'It's not enough to be the greatest and most successful martial species of all, for in our hearts our people know that they're destroying a great and glorious culture, and replacing it with a desert. We know because we've lost our own civilisation, and the best among us lament it. Our ordinary folk just have a feeling that their victories are hollow, their very lives and purposes meaningless. For thousands of years they've been warriors but, once the victory comes, we won't need warriors any more. What will they do then? They don't know anything else. They don't *want* anything else.

'So now,' he went on, 'some of us are asking what this war was for. It is no longer mere survival – it's now existence.'

'Indeed, though that's a debate for another time. Let's talk about your patterning. I've the impression that you're thinking along new lines.'

'It was Liett's idea,' he said over-generously. 'To link a dozen patterners, each with its human inside. Each contributing, in its own way, to the flisnadr we're trying to create.'

'I don't see how it can work,' said Gyrull.

Pink speckles flushed his chest and throat, as if he took her words as a criticism, but he quickly skin-changed to the brilliant blue of resolution. 'We also have doubts, but first let me tell you about the advantages. If Liett's idea works it will give us a stronger and more robust flisnadr. A weak human must result in a feeble device, if she survives at all, and many don't. This way, we need not pattern any human to their limit, which gives us a better chance of success.'

Gyrull was pleased by the idea, and the forceful way he presented it, though she foresaw difficulties with his plan. 'How can the individual patterners be linked, and how are the different efforts coordinated? It's never been done before.'

'In the past year,' said Ryll, 'we've done many things that had never been done before. I – I have an idea,' he said, now hesitantly. 'I'm not sure you're going to like it.'

'Allow me to decide that for myself!' she said peremptorily.

Again the blue of resolution and she smiled to see it. Ryll was developing well.

'Do you recall the behaviour of Tiaan's amplimet in Snizort, just before the end?' said Ryll. 'It appeared to be com-municating, via threads of *force*, with the node.'

'I do. Continue!'

'I thought we might . . . I don't know . . .'

'Use the amplimet, and perhaps Tiaan too, to link the pat-terners together?'

'Yes,' he said quietly. 'It's against our creed, but . .'

'We've used her and her crystal before. It was not an unqualified success.'

'The torgnadrs we made by patterning Tiaan never reached their potential,' Ryll agreed. 'What happened to them?'

'One failed in Snizort and had to be destroyed. The other burned in the fires.' Gyrull rubbed her chin. 'I think I know what the problem was, and how to solve it, but Tiaan is far away. Do you propose to make a foray after her?'

'Not if there's any other way,' he said. 'And there may be. Remember how she came to Snizort, even though crippled, to find the tetrarch? Tiaan's weakness is excessive compassion; she cares about people even when they don't reciprocate. She even felt for *me*, an alien and her enemy. If we were to make it known that the tetrarch was here, I believe she'd find a way to come after him.'

'She might,' mused Gyrull, 'if she gets the opportunity, but we can't rely on it. And this amplimet is a perilous device – we may not be able to control it. We must have an alternative plan.' She strode up and down, her armour flashing in waves of colour – mauves to reds to purples – as she thought. 'We might link the patterners another way. The tetrarch's geomantic globe offers certain possibilities. It might, if carefully formed, and *used at a certain place within Alcifer*, be made to serve.'

'How so?' said Ryll curiously.

'Alcifer's original purpose was never fulfilled. The city sleeps, but it is still powerful.'

'I don't understand.'

'How could you – you don't know the place. Leave it to me. I've been spying on the tetrarch. He's begun to rebuild his geomantic globe and already realises it has a number of flaws.'

'How do you know?'

'I studied it carefully in Snizort, and I've been feeding him information since then, to make him aware of errors in it. He will come to me for assistance – he has no other option. Were I to provide him with certain knowledge, and he to mould the globe according to it, if taken to a particular place in Alcifer it might just be what you need.'

'I don't know what you're talking about,' said Ryll.

'No matter – I was just thinking aloud. We'll go over it later. In the meantime, I'll assist you in the design of the new patterners, so they can be linked. Once that's done you must begin patterning the flisnadr, but don't take it beyond the juvenile stage. Leave it in stasis until the geomantic globe is ready. I'll spread a rumour in Lauralin that the tetrarch has fled to Alcifer. If Tiaan does come, we'll be waiting for her. If she doesn't, I'll send a force to snatch her from the Aachim. Between her amplimet and Gilhaelith's globe, we'll create a perfect flisnadr. And then let the humans beware!' she concluded fiercely.

'I – I would like to put one condition,' he said, diffident at first but finishing forcefully.

Gyrull looked taken aback, but replied, 'One who would lead must learn how to be strong. What is your condition?'

'I would have Tiaan treated with due respect, and given her freedom afterwards.'

She inclined her head, watching him with her penetrating eyes. 'I applaud your nobility of spirit, though to be freed by us will rouse suspicion in the eyes of her own people. And what of Gilhaelith? Do you feel compassion for him too?'

'He's a danger to the whole world,' said Ryll.

'Yes, he's a brilliant, blind fool. He cannot see what others will do with his work, if it succeeds. It would give them power undreamed of, power that, if misused, could sterilise Santhenar for all forms of life. We must prevent that, or turn it to our own purposes. So, Ryll, what are we going to do about Gilhaelith?'

'Once we've no further use for him, he can go to the slaughtering pens.'

FORTY-ONE

Irisis was sitting by herself, slicing onions as she watched the sun go down from the mouth of the cave they'd been living in for well over a month. The ragged slot was etched into a pebblestone cliff on the seaward edge of a barren island in the Sea of Thurkad, half a league off the coast of Lauralin. It was the safest refuge Muss had been able to find – hidden from all but a direct pass by Ghorr's remaining air-floaters, which was unlikely here; and, being surrounded by water, it was even less likely to be visited by the enemy. It was, however, exposed to the chilly south-westerlies, which intensified every day as the season turned. Winter was still months off, but every morning it felt a little closer.

Squatting by the smoky camp fire, she tossed dried beans into the cooking pot. They had been eating bean-and-onion soup for a week and not even her cooking could make it interesting. Irisis had no herbs, spices or oil left. Just beans, onions and water, three times a day, washed down with ginger tea. She'd dug some ginger root that morning in the moist bank of the only rivulet on the island.

There was nothing to do and Irisis was bored out of her mind. Fyn-Mah had withdrawn completely, Pilot Inouye didn't let out a peep and Flangers had taken to going on long walks by himself along the clifftops, which did nothing for Irisis's peace of mind. She would not have been surprised to find him at the bottom one day. Flangers's destruction of the air-floater, and inability to honourably account for it, was corroding his very soul. And Irisis could not talk to Muss about her fears, on the rare occasions he was around. Muss required nothing of anyone, nor gave back any human warmth.

Irisis sometimes felt that she understood the lyrinx better than she did Muss. He gave his reports to Fyn-Mah, fully and completely, and advice when specifically requested, but not a sentence more. Muss recreated himself for each spying role, revealing nothing of the inner man. She had no idea what his hopes or dreams were, or even if he had any. But in any case, having procured a tiny skiff from somewhere, Muss was away most of the time, doing who knew what. It could have been Flydd's work or Muss's own. There was no way of telling.

She'd already taken the controller to pieces twice, rebuilding it to improve the way it drew power. She'd also disassembled the floater-gas generator but, not understanding how it created gas from water, had put it back together the way it had been. Irisis had, however, made one innovation vital to their morale. They could not use any kind of flame on the air-floater, but the floater-gas generator became hot when in use and she'd worked out how to heat water with it, for tea.

At midnight, when everyone else was asleep, she heard the snap of a sail in the wind. Muss had been away five days this time. She was sitting by the fire, making jewellery out of silver wire, as she did every night. Once each new work was complete, she took it apart and used the silver and crystals in a new arrangement. Irisis made jewellery because she had to. She could not sit idly, as Fyn-Mah seemed able to do. Irisis did not like to think too much, for her unpleasant foreboding was growing, day by day. Things were going to get worse before they got better, but they would not get better for her. She had committed enough crimes against the scrutators to be executed a dozen times.

The keel of the skiff grated on pebbles as Muss brought it in to shore. Shortly he appeared, face pinched from the cold wind.

'I had news of Flydd and Nish,' said Muss, 'but they've disappeared again.' Shaking his head, he squatted down to warm his hands by the fire. A cold wind came off the water, coiling around into the mouth of the cave and lifting sand into their eyes, not to mention into the stew pot.

'Have you eaten?' Irisis asked.

'Not since breakfast time.'

'Did you bring any supplies?' she said hopefully.

'No. What we have will do me.'

She cursed him under her breath. Muss must have been through many towns on his long trip.

He took a bowl of bean-and-onion stew while she made a warming cup to wash it down. He kneaded his back with his fingers. 'A long sail, a hard paddle, and a day and night's walk before that,' he said without expression.

Irisis chopped a knob of ginger into small pieces. Scraping it into another pot, she filled it with water and sat it on the fire. When it began to boil she stirred it with the blade of her knife and filled two mugs, passing one to the spy.

He sipped the scalding liquid. 'Jal-Nish got his army, and the clankers, to a usable node west of Gospett. They tracked the retreating lyrinx towards Gnulp Landing, some twenty leagues south of here, planning to lure them into a trap, but the enemy disappeared.'

'Where to?'

'It was assumed they'd escaped across the sea to Meldorin.'

'But they hadn't?'

'Some thirty thousand lyrinx were enchanted into a field of limestone pinnacles above the valley of Gumby Marth, where the army lay hidden. It was a perfect ambush.'

Her blood ran cold. 'What happened?'

Muss's face showed nothing. 'Three things saved them from annihilation, and all down to your friend Nish.' He explained how Nish had led Troist's army to the relief of Jal-Nish's forces, sounded an alert about the stone-formed lyrinx at the last moment, and led the breakout that had saved the survivors.

Irisis's eyes were glowing by the time he finished. 'I always knew Nish was destined for great things. Where are they now?'

'The army took ship from Gnulp Landing, in two merchant fleets, and both landed safely at Hardlar, near the mouth of the

River Libbens in Nihilnor. Flydd and Nish were delayed, sailed into a storm and did not reach Hardlar. The Council of Scrutators has put a price of a thousand gold tells on Flydd's head, but only if he can be taken alive.'

A thousand gold tells was an immense fortune. 'Why alive?' said Irisis.

'The list of allegations is too long to enumerate, but they add up to treachery of the blackest kind. The scrutators don't like to delegate their justice.'

'I see Jal Nish's hand in this.' Irisis shivered. She had never experienced such utter loathing as he had directed at her, the last few times they'd met. He would not rest until he had destroyed her.

'Not any more. Unfortunately, or fortunately, depending on your point of view, Jal-Nish was killed in the battle, *and* eaten.'

She stood up, spilling her tea. 'You're sure of that?'

'I've seen the battlefield. He tried to work a great magic against the lyrinx as they attacked. The survivors said he'd lured the enemy into battle for that purpose, to prove his mastery to the Council, but the enemy turned his magic against him and cut his own officers down. It doesn't do to underestimate the lyrinx. The army was routed. About ten thousand got to Gnulp, of the forty that set out from Snizort to pursue the enemy.' He gave the dreadful numbers without regret or compassion.

Thirty thousand dead. Irisis warmed her hands on the mug, then rubbed it over the back of her neck. The chill faded. 'It's hard to believe Jal-Nish is no more. You've no idea how much I wished for it.'

'Anything can happen in battle,' said Muss. 'Though the official story is different.'

'Oh?'

'Xervish Flydd has been accused of murdering him.'

'Can that be possible?'

'No. He was with General Troist, leagues away, when the ambush took place, but the scrutators can make any lie into truth.'

453

'And any truth into a lie,' said Irisis, thinking about the Histories. 'Do you have any idea where Flydd might be?'

'His ship sailed into the Karama Malama, was driven south by a gale, and there disappeared. He could be anywhere between Fleen Haven and Karints, and there's a hundred leagues of water in between.'

'Or he could be dead,' said Irisis. Nish too. Tears pricked at the corners of her eyes.

'He probably is. I learned yesterday that their ship was wrecked on a reef. A skeet brought the news. A lifeboat got away with the captain and a handful of sailors. Neither Flydd nor Nish was on it. The captain did not think anyone could have survived.' Muss still showed no emotion, though he'd served Flydd for many years.

This time the chill slid all the way down her backbone. Flydd dead? For all their sakes it must not be. And Nish? Yet they were mortal men – they could die, or be killed, as easily as anyone else.

Fyn-Mah shot up in her sleeping pouch, rubbing her eyes. 'Where did this happen?' Her voice went shrill.

'In the middle of the Karama Malama,' said Muss. 'The ship struck a reef.'

'There are a thousand islands in that part of the Sea of Mists,' said Fyn-Mah hopefully.

She'd served Flydd just as long, but it mattered to her. Irisis wondered if, secretly and hopelessly, she loved him.

'And Flydd is a strong swimmer,' Fyn-Mah went on. 'There's a chance he's survived.'

'A slim one,' said Muss. 'A man would soon die of cold in those waters, even at this time of year.'

'Nish isn't a strong swimmer,' said Irisis.

'Then he's dead. And Ghorr has sent a fleet to make sure.'

'We must find them first,' said Fyn-Mah.

'That's a task beyond our powers,' said Muss.

Fyn-Mah began to say something, looked across to where Flangers and Inouye lay sleeping, and said, 'Come outside.'

Irisis followed her and Muss in her bare feet across the

454

round pebbles. It felt as if she were walking on eggs.

'The scrutator is a particularly thorough man,' Fyn-Mah said obliquely. 'Since he first fled the manufactory after being suspended from the Council, he's tried to anticipate every kind of eventuality.'

'I don't see how he could have anticipated this one,' said Irisis.

'Of course not. But he took steps to ensure that, if lost in desperate circumstances, or held prisoner in a secret place, he might be found.'

Irisis's heart began to pound. 'What kind of steps?'

'We learned a lot from Ullii. About the traces that the Secret Art leaves in its surroundings. And we've learned about nodes, and flows of power, and crystals too.'

I'm surrounded by people who can never get to the point, thought Irisis. Clenching her toes around a pebble, she tried to be patient, though it was not in her nature.

'In short,' Fyn-Mah went on, 'the scrutator had a lodestone implanted in his buttock in case he ended up where there was no field, or his other powers were stripped from him.'

'I wouldn't have thought his bum was big enough to hide one,' Irisis muttered.

'You'd know!' Fyn-Mah said spitefully. 'But the stone was quite small.'

'How is that possible?' For all her work with such materials, Irisis couldn't imagine how it could work.

'In ancient times, a mancer called Golias the Mad made a device that had never been made before or since – a farspeaker – a way of speaking across the distances of the world. The secret of the device is long lost, but when Flydd was using Ullii to locate Tiaan and her amplimet, it gave him an idea for tracing the faint emanations emitted by certain objects. Xervish Flydd is cleverer than you know. He was, for some years, scrutator supervising all the mancers and artisans in Nennifer, and they've invented hundreds of devices powered by the Art.'

'I didn't know that,' said Irisis. 'How will you look for it?'

'I carry the complementary crystal, which is tuned to Flydd's lodestone. If he *is* still alive, we should be able to find it.'

'What if he's dead?'

'The stone requires the warmth of the human body to operate. If he's dead, we'll find no trace of it.'

They went back to the cave and the firelight. From a lined wooden box no bigger than a needle case, Fyn-Mah took a grass-green translucent crystal, the length of a needle and not much thicker. After warming it in her fingers, she set it aside. Filling a beaten gold bowl with water until it reached the very top, she added more, drop by drop, until the surface rose minutely above the sides. With a pair of tweezers, she lowered the crystal to the surface and let it go. It floated.

'Don't move. Don't even breathe in this direction,' Fyn-Mah said softly. 'I must now give it power.'

She made a fist of one hand, wrapped the other around it and closed her eyes. Muss sat watching, motionless. Irisis felt her scalp prickle.

A tendril of steam rose from the water. Outside, the wind rushed by the entrance, shaking the bushes and making the firelight dance on the walls of the cave. The crystal sparked on one end then slowly moved, as if embedded in treacle. It rotated almost a half-turn, went back a little way, turned a quarter-turn, back again, then stopped.

'He's alive?' cried Irisis.

'Flydd lives,' said Fyn-Mah. 'Now all we have to do is find him.'

'It's pointing a little west of south, into the Karama Malama.'

'That would seem to cover a large area,' said Irisis.

Fyn-Mah stood looking down at the quivering needle and a tear formed in one dark eye.

'The scrutators have a fleet looking for him,' Muss reminded her. 'And air-floaters.'

Fyn-Mah pulled her coat around her. 'Then we'd better get moving.'

FORTY-TWO

Before dawn broke, the air-floater was cruising low over the Karama Malama, which lived up to its name. It was a cold, windy day, the slaty sea reflecting a leaden sky. Patches of mist drifted over the surface. The air-floater bucked and rolled so much that Irisis felt seasick.

'You might as well get some rest,' said Fyn-Mah. 'The reefs and islands of the central sea lie well south of here. It'll take all day and part of the night to reach there.'

Irisis nodded but remained where she was, too hyped up to sleep. The day passed slowly. Long after dark they settled on a cobble beach on the lee side of a rocky island, to await the dawn.

Irisis shivered in her coat all night, and the following morning too. They had been going back and forth for hours and had passed over dozens of islands, though few were more than lichen-covered rocks in that dismal sea. There had been no sign of human life.

'Any luck?' she said to Fyn-Mah, who was crouched over her basin again.

The perquisitor scowled. 'It's too gusty. The crystal shakes as if it were sitting on a jelly.'

'What if we were to set down?'

'Wouldn't help much, in this wind. Water's troublesome at the best of times. The crystal is meant to be floated on quicksilver, but I don't have any.' They kept working, aware that time was ebbing. Not long before dusk, the pilot struck the alarm gong. They ran out.

'Boats!' said Inouye, pointing.

Fyn-Mah scanned the sea with her spyglass. 'A fleet, to the east. And flying the Council flag.'

Signal mirrors flashed. 'Looks like they've seen us,' said Irisis.

Fyn-Mah went back to her shivering bowl and crystal, but as dark fell she gave it away. 'It's shaking worse than ever now. We'll never find him.'

'It won't be easy for Ghorr, either,' said Irisis.

'He's got a whole fleet, and Arts for seeking and finding.'

Nonetheless, they continued. Giving up was not an option.

'Islands ahead,' Flangers called, around eight in the evening.

'Where are we?' Fyn-Mah was staring at the floating crystal, illuminated by a single candle.

Irisis pointed to the place on the chart. 'It shows half a dozen small islands, plus dozens of islets, no more than wave-washed rocks.'

'Go low, and slow. We'll all keep watch. Yell if you see anything.'

Irisis spent hours at the rail. They were flying so low that occasional breakers dashed spray in their faces. An icy wind cut straight through her summer coat. There was just enough light for her to distinguish sea and land.

'What's down there?' she said to Muss. 'I can't see a single light. Not even a camp fire.'

'Most of these islands are uninhabited. There are no trees, therefore no wood. There's nothing to eat but fish and sea-weed.'

'No wood.' Irisis wrapped her arms around herself. 'If they are down there, they'll be freezing as well as starving.'

'Well,' said Muss, coming up from the stern, 'at least we know where Flydd isn't. And we might assume he's not on one of the islands to the east, since the fleet has come from there.'

'How many more islands are there to search?'

'About eight hundred, though if the crystal is accurate we can rule out most.'

'Even so, it'll take days,' said Irisis. 'Or weeks. They'll shoot us out of the air first. It's hopeless.'

'There is one thing,' said Muss.

'What's that?'

'I know where we can buy a flask of quicksilver.'

They turned south-west to Jibstorn, a town on the Highpath that ran from Tyrkir, the capital city of Oolo, through the edge of Candalume Forest, then south into frigid lands unknown even to Muss The trip took all night and part of the following day, for the field was weak here.

Jibstorn was a grim, grey place, a town of smoking chimneys and grimy walls, where the waste of ten thousand humans and five times as many animals flowed down a ditch in the centre of the street. In the five-month winter, which was already on the doorstep, the noisome effluent froze in the drains, diverting fresh muck all across the road.

'I'll just put on a disguise,' said Muss as Inouye set the air-floater down at the waterfront, scattering a noisy flock of seagulls and a gaggle of red-nosed, staring children. 'You can never be too careful.'

He slipped into the cabin and closed the door. Irisis, who'd always been curious as to how he did it, went around the other side where there was a small tear in the canvas. She put her eye to it, feeling like a voyeur.

She caught just a blur of movement. Muss did not change his clothes or make up his face – he simply morphed, clothes and all, from the old shape to the new. His garments changed at the same time. She turned away in case he realised she was there. Muss wasn't a lowly prober at all – he had to be a morphmancer and didn't want anyone to know it. And clearly he was a master of the Art who didn't suffer any appreciable aftersickness. She wondered if Flydd knew.

Muss came out dressed as a rustic trader, a red-faced, bald-headed man with spindly legs and a sagging belly. The change was masterly – she could even smell the sourness of stale beer on his breath. She did not meet his eye. Irisis was afraid to, in case she gave herself away.

Fyn-Mah went with Muss to find his contact and buy the quicksilver. Irisis and Flangers bought supplies in the markets. Jibstorn turned out to be a putrescent, sour town where the scrutators held no sway. The people were unfriendly and the merchants out-and-out thieves.

'At least the quality's good,' said Irisis, eyeing a haunch of venison. After a fortnight on bean-and-onion stew she could have eaten it raw.

'It'd want to be, at these prices!'

Irisis fingered silver out of her wallet. 'It's the scrutator's coin, not mine, and if he were here he'd have the best.'

They bought supplies for a fortnight and, by the time all had been delivered to the air-floater, Fyn-Mah and Muss were back. Fyn-Mah was smiling, a rare sight.

Inside the air-floater, she cleaned her bowl and filled it with quicksilver. The surface made a perfect mirror and the crystal sat neatly on top of it. As she drew power, the crystal rotated smoothly until it was pointing back the way they had come. She tapped the side of the bowl. The mirror shivered but the crystal did not budge.

'That's better.' Fyn-Mah checked the direction against the lodestone in its case and made a mark on her chart. 'Tell Inouye to go with all speed; we're a long way behind.'

And maybe too late already, Irisis thought.

The return trip proved to be a slow one. They flew into a headwind all the way and sometimes it seemed to be blowing them backwards. By nightfall they weren't even halfway.

Irisis began to pace the sagging canvas deck; she couldn't help it. There was a knot under her breastbone. After giving both friends up for dead, and having Flydd, at least, miraculously reappear, her emotions had been wrung dry. The scrutators' fleet must have reached the main group of islands this morning. They could have searched dozens by now. Could have found them.

What would Ghorr do to Flydd? She didn't think he would

be executed on the spot, for the scrutators liked to make public examples. He would be taken back to Gospett, or some other suitably large centre, for trial and punishment. And once in their hands there would be no escape; no way to rescue him, either. Nor Nish, if he'd survived.

She went into the cabin. Fyn-Mah stood by the window hole, an aperture normally covered by a piece of canvas, watching the crystal. Fumes of quicksilver were deadly in a confined space, so everyone had to sleep outside in the bitter wind.

'Any change?' said Irisis.

'No.'

'What if they've already been taken? Is there any way to tell?'

'No.'

'So by following the crystal, we could be heading into a trap.'

'Yes.'

Irisis tried to meet her eyes but Fyn-Mah looked away. She was in one of her moods and nothing would be gained by talking to her. Irisis went to her sleeping pouch, in a hammock strung on the port deck, and swayed there all night. Every movement swung her out over the rail. If the rope broke she would go flying over the side to her death. Her feet were freezing and sleep would not come. Further back, Flangers tossed in his hammock, no more at peace than she was. On the starboard side, Muss was snoring gently. Nothing affected his repose.

The sun rose to reveal the same bleak sky and slaty, misty sea. To their left, the narrow peninsula of Karints stretched into the unfathomable distance. Ahead were hundreds of islands and thousands of reefs, the bane of many a mariner. Irisis stamped her feet in a vain attempt to get warm.

'Hoy!' shouted Fyn-Mah. 'You're shaking the bowl.'

Irisis took up the perquisitor's spyglass and scanned the horizon.

'Anything?' Flangers appeared beside her, rubbing blue fingers.

'No.'

'Cup of hot ginger tea?'

'Thanks,' she said. 'That'd be lovely.'

They warmed their fingers on the wooden bowls, feeling no need to talk. It was not until the middle of the day that she saw the first sail, dead ahead.

'That's a bad sign,' said Muss. 'Either the scrutators are heading directly for him, or . . .'

'Or they already have him,' Fyn-Mah finished bleakly. 'If we hadn't spent a day and a half getting the quicksilver –'

'We might still be looking,' said Flangers.

In half an hour Ghorr's fleet was spread out across a great arc of sea. The air-floater, following the crystal, was still heading directly towards the first ship.

'What's ahead?' asked Fyn-Mah.

'A scatter of islands, in that bank of mist,' Irisis replied without consulting the map.

'The ship's going to get there first. Pilot!' she shouted. 'Can't you go any faster?'

Inouye did not answer, though the sound of the rotor rose slightly. It didn't seem to make any difference.

'The headwind's too strong,' said Irisis. 'The harder we go the more it resists us.'

'Go lower,' said Muss. 'The wind won't be as strong near the sea.'

They angled down. The sails disappeared back over the horizon and the race continued. The mist clung about a handful of low, round islands, scattered like potatoes hurled from a bucket. There were about twenty of them, most just uninhabitable wet brown rock.

'How long has it been since the shipwreck?' asked Fyn-Mah.

'Nine days.'

Fyn-Mah shivered. 'I wouldn't last two days down there. I'm going back to the watch bowl. Keep an eye out for smoke.'

'They'd have the fire out now,' said Irisis. 'If they had one.'

'From sea level they wouldn't be able to see the fleet.'

'But they could see us,' said Irisis. 'We're still not going fast enough.'

'Go right down,' the perquisitor said to Inouye. 'Just skim the waves.'

Inouye turned her head, and her eyes seemed to take up half her small face. 'If a gust drops us into the water, it'll tear the cabin off.'

'As low as is safe.' Fyn-Mah went back to the scrying basin.

Irisis followed her into the cabin. 'Can you tell which island it is?'

'No.'

Irisis couldn't stand the inactivity. She went back and stood next to the pilot. They did seem to be making more headway at this altitude. Shortly Flangers appeared, relaying a minute change of course. Inouye moved the steering arm slightly and checked the heading against her lodestone.

'Which island are we heading for?' Irisis asked. This low, they could see nothing but mist.

'A group of three in a line,' Inouye said softly, ducking her head to avoid Irisis's eye. She moved to her left, opening the space between them.

What was it about the little pilot? She was agonisingly shy and kept everyone at a distance. And doubtless she's afraid of me, Irisis decided. I've got powerful friends; I can choose. She has to do what she's told. It's taken her away from friends, family, man and children, and she'll probably never see them again. They may have been killed simply because Inouye had obeyed Fyn-Mah's orders, and she could do nothing about it.

'How many children do you have?' Irisis said.

'Two!' Inouye whispered.

'How old are they?'

'Sann is three and a half. Mya will be two . . . next week.' She looked away, gripping the steering arm so hard that her hand shook.

Irisis did not know what to say.

The sails appeared on the horizon, two ships close together. 'Do they have him?' said Irisis.

No one answered. It was impossible to tell.

'Go up a trifle, Inouye,' Irisis went on. 'Flangers, run back to Fyn-Mah.'

The first island grew swiftly. It was shaped like a bean with a bite out of it. Beyond it lay another, like a grey dishrag crumpled on a floor; then the third, an oval plate piled high in the middle. The two ships were passing the third island.

'They're gone past without stopping,' said Muss. 'Curve round towards the second island and the crystal will tell us which one it is.'

'It'll be the middle one, of course,' said Irisis.

So it proved to be. By the time they approached the island, which was at best a third of a league across, the vessels had dropped anchor outside the reefs and were launching boats through a gap for the shore. Other sails converged on them, though Irisis judged they would be too late to play any part in this drama.

'We've still got the advantage,' said Fyn-Mah, abandoning the scrying bowl. 'We can search the island from the air before they get to shore.'

'I doubt if we can do it before *they* reach us!' Irisis pointed.

A pair of air-floaters had appeared in the north-east quarter, rising from a group of islands a few leagues away. Signal mirrors flashed between ships and air-floaters, which turned in their direction.

Fyn-Mah snatched her spyglass out of Flangers's hand and began to sweep it back and forth across the second island. 'I can't see anyone. But Flydd's got to be there.'

'Perhaps the crystal is picking up some other kind of signal, or even a node,' Irisis speculated.

'*Don't!*' the perquisitor said savagely.

They soared over the dishrag hump in the middle of the island, a ragged hill some hundred spans high. The exposed rock was bare of anything taller than moss, though the sheltered gullies on the leeward side contained scrub.

'That's where they'll be,' said Flangers. 'Somewhere in that gully. Look out for smoke.'

They went over the top and drifted down the valley. The scrub was grey and wind-twisted. There was nothing so grand as a tree, the tallest plants being bushy and only a couple of spans high.

'Two boats have landed,' Muss called. 'The third is coming round the point. If Flydd and Nish *are* here, they'd better show themselves quickly.'

'They could be hiding from us,' Flangers observed, 'thinking that we're part of Ghorr's force. Irisis, why don't you stand at the front – he'll recognise you.'

She did so, letting her yellow hair stream out in the wind. They went all the way down the gully to the shore. Nothing. Irisis had to climb down, for her nose and cheeks had gone numb. She warmed them with her palms.

'Turn around,' cried Fyn-Mah. 'Go back up.'

'Have you seen something?' Irisis called.

'No,' she said in a strangled voice.

They returned to the summit, drifting just a few spans above the ground. 'Where else could they be?' Fyn-Mah had bitten through her lower lip.

'Why don't you check the bloody crystal!' Irisis snapped.

Fyn-Mah ran back to the cabin. Irisis followed, but even from the door she could see that the needle was jerking back and forth. 'Perhaps we're directly above them.'

The perquisitor hadn't thought of that. 'I'll see what I can do. Keep a lookout.'

Irisis gazed down at the pair of boats, which were empty. Soldiers were already storming up the ridge. A third of the way up, a pair of big men were staggering under the weight of a javelard. Behind and below the air-floater, the third boat was riding the surf to shore. The two enemy air-floaters were closing rapidly and a third now appeared, well back. Signals were exchanged between them with flags.

Irisis had the feeling that they were looking in the wrong place. A couple of smaller gullies ran down from the summit on this side, and others back in the direction of the ships. 'Check the other gullies,' she rapped to Inouye.

The pilot was trembling like a rush in a gale. Irisis pitied Inouye. For herself, she had been in so many desperate situations that this one had no impact at all. She just felt empty.

The third boat had landed on the south-western side of the island and the troops were unloading another javelard, fitting a spear and winding back the cranks. Inouye ran the air-floater down the second gully and up the third, but they saw no sign of any living thing. 'Where can they be?' said Fyn-Mah, dashing from stern to bow, then back along the other side. Most of the island was bare rock.

'Run north around the shoreline, a few spans high,' said Flangers. 'There may be a cave.'

Inouye turned away from the boat. Its javelard fired but the spear fell short.

'Quick!' cried Flangers. 'It'll have the range next time.'

They sped down the coast, which was rocky as far as Irisis could see. There was no sign of a cave, or even a large crevice beneath the rocks.

They rounded the northern curve of the island. The two ships were anchored offshore on the eastern side, half a league away, and the soldiers two-thirds of the way up the hill. The air-floaters were coming fast, with the advantage of the wind. Inouye brought the machine up a few spans and turned, giving them a view all the way around the island. The third boat, having disgorged its troops, was rowing furiously towards them, parallel to the shore. A soldier stood at the bow, ready with a crossbow.

'They're not here,' said Irisis dully.

'They've got to be. Keep going.' Fyn-Mah had gained control of herself. Her arms were folded across her chest and she wore her customary impassive expression.

'We've got to turn away,' wailed Inouye. 'We're practically within range.'

'Flydd's our only hope, Pilot,' said Fyn-Mah. 'If we can't find him, the whole world is dead.'

Inouye wiped a tear from her eye, though it might have been the wind in her face. Gripping the controller hard, she clenched her jaw. The rotor screamed, the air-floater shuddered as if it had been struck from behind, then leapt forwards. The pilot's pale hair streamed out behind her. Irisis hoped she was not drawing more power than her body could handle.

They shot down the eastern shoreline, between the offshore ships and the soldiers on the ridge. A javelard was fired from the leading ship, the missile arcing towards their position of just a few moments ago. The other ship readied its weapons. As they reached the rocky point, where a wave-carved platform extended a hundred spans offshore, Muss cried, 'I saw something. Go round, Pilot.'

Inouye threw the steering arm out at right-angles, flinging the machine into such a tight turn that Irisis's stomach lurched. They hurtled back the other way. To their left, some way inland, an oval outcrop rose above the surrounding rockscape. Its surface was mottled with red and yellow lichens and patches of green moss. In the crevices behind it, scrubby bushes stuck up like bristles on a brush.

'Up there,' yelled Muss. 'I saw something behind that rocky dome. Go lower.'

The spy certainly had keen eyes. Irisis was clear-sighted compared to most people, but had seen nothing.

The machine curved towards the dome. Seized by a sudden panic that Flydd would think they were the enemy, she climbed onto the railing at the front, hanging onto the airbag's guy ropes, and roared, 'Flydd! Nish! Where the blazes are you? Come out or we'll leave you behind.'

The machine was hurled the other way, so hard that Irisis was left hanging by one hand. She yelped and snatched at the rail. *Crash.* It sounded as though a javelard spear had come through the wooden keel up into the cabin. Looking back, she saw that it had. The point stuck out through the cabin door. Flangers broke it off and kicked it over the side.

She threw herself to the deck and almost went over again as the air-floater turned even more sharply. Another spear whistled through the air, just missing the airbag. Whatever else Inouye was, she was a brilliant pilot. Then, as she clutched the lowest rail, Irisis saw, as clear as anything, Nish stand up on the round rock. Her eyes misted over.

'It's Nish!' she screamed. 'Go down.'

'I don't dare,' said Inouye. The soldiers up the hill were within easy range. The pilot turned; turned again. Her cheeks were blotched, her eyes glassy.

She's taking too much power, Irisis thought. She's going to burn her mind out. Without thinking, or even knowing what she was doing, Irisis ran to Inouye's side and wrapped the chain of her pliance around the controller, putting crystal to crystal.

Laying an arm across the pilot's shoulder, she sought for the node. Inouye's whole body was shuddering with the strain. Irisis took some of the load through herself, into her pliance and thence into the controller. To her amazement, it seemed to be working. The colour came back into the pilot's cheeks. The rotor spun more quickly.

'Flangers!' Irisis screamed. 'See if you can do something about the soldiers with the javelard. Quick, they're nearly ready to fire.'

Flangers was already behind the loaded weapon, tracking the soldiers as the air-floater ducked and dived. He fired.

'Missed!' He cursed under his breath and reached down to reload.

Muss was on the other side, holding a crossbow inexpertly. Come on! Irisis thought, I could do better than that. He fired, though with no result.

Fyn-Mah pushed through behind Irisis, shaping the air with her fingers. Tossing them high, she clapped her hands together with a crack like a dry stick breaking. A series of puffs crystallised in the air between her and the enemy javelard, one after another. The last puff burst around the weapon and the soldier behind it. He went head-first over a smooth rock and came to rest with his legs waving in the air. The javelard fell over but another soldier wrestled it up onto its stand and began to aim it.

'Go down, *now*!' snapped the perquisitor, pale with the strain.

'He'll put a spear right through the airbag. He can't miss.'

'The spear is jammed in the javelard,' said Muss calmly. 'Hurry, before they free it.'

Inouye threw the machine about so sharply that Irisis fell to her knees. It seemed to skip across the air, bounced and fell. The keel slammed into the rock. Struts creaked and groaned.

Irisis looked around frantically. 'Flydd, Nish?'

'Here,' came Nish's voice from the other side. 'You nearly took my bloody head off.'

Leaving her pliance wrapped around the controller, she leapt over the rail. Inouye shrieked but Irisis could not be in two places at once. 'Come on. Get in! Where's Flydd? Is he . . .? Is he . . .?'

'He's down there.' Nish pointed to the crevice. 'He's hurt his ankle.'

She skidded down the steep side of the rock, ploughing red lichen off with her boot-heels. 'Xervish? Are you all right?'

'Of course I'm all right,' he said querulously. 'Why wouldn't I be?'

'Well, you're taking your bloody time. This isn't a picnic.'

He was leaning on the stone and looked more emaciated than ever, if that was possible.

'What's the matter with you?' she snapped.

'I've been running for the past hour and I've hurt my ankle.'

'You look like an old bag of bones,' she muttered.

'And you're as fat as a pig! Hey, what do you think you're doing?'

She hoisted him over her shoulders and scrabbled up. He was heavier than he looked.

'Come on!' Fyn-Mah was screaming.

Her boots slipped on moss. Nish gave her his hand and heaved, which got them up the steep part. Irisis ran across the top, looking over her shoulder. The soldiers were struggling to free the jammed spear. The two air-floaters were approaching rapidly. The third was still hanging back. Must be scrutators in it, Irisis thought, the gutless swine.

Flangers fired his javelard, its spear smashing through the cabin of the leading machine. It kept coming. He slammed another spear in place, winding back the cranks like a sweat-drenched, red-faced demon.

They reached the side. Irisis's knees were so wobbly that she dropped the scrutator onto the deck.

'Bloody cheek!' he roared.

She tried to throw her leg over the rope rail but it wouldn't go. She tried again, then Nish's hand slid under her thigh and heaved her on top of Flydd.

'Go!' screamed Fyn-Mah, as Nish vaulted the rail. She pulled Irisis off Flydd. 'Are you all right, surr?' she said tenderly, helping him into the cabin.

She does care for him, Irisis thought as she got up. That's going to change a few things.

The front of the air-floater tilted and the machine shot up at a steep angle. Nish fell backwards, slid all the way down the deck and slammed his head into the stern post below the rotor. He sighed and lay still.

'Nish?' Irisis shrieked, hanging onto the ropes as she went down the canted deck.

He did not answer. The naked blades of the rotor were whirring just above his nose, for the wire guard did not run underneath. Stay unconscious, she prayed, falling to her knees in front of him. If he sat up, the rotor would puree his head.

'What's the matter now?' yelled Fyn-Mah from inside.

'Bloody fool's knocked himself out.'

Inouye levelled out. Irisis, ever so carefully, eased Nish out from under the rotor and carried him into the cabin. Fyn-Mah was decanting the deadly quicksilver into its flask. She stoppered it. The machine tilted up again.

Laying Nish on the rear part of the floor where he'd be as protected as possible, Irisis kissed him on the forehead, then

470

went out and slid down the steeply sloping deck to the pilot, who was choking and shuddering as she clung to the controller arm.

Abruptly Inouye doubled over, clutching her belly. Steam wisped from her mouth. Irisis threw her arms around the little woman and tried to take power through herself. Her entrails grew boiling hot. If she failed it would anthracise them both.

PART FOUR
GLOBE

FORTY-THREE

Inouye began to jerk as if she were having a fit. Droplets of sweat burst out all over her, saturating her clothes in a few seconds. Irisis grew hot all over. Her eyes clouded until she could see nothing but floating specks of blue light.

The pilot slid from her grasp and power struck Irisis like a sledgehammer, knocking her to her knees. She fought against it, catching Inouye's hand with her free hand. If she let go the controller would fail, for it was tuned to Inouye alone.

As the air-floater turned, she saw the soldiers at the javelard halfway up the hill. They had freed the bent spear and were inserting a good one. The lever went back, the spear hurtled towards them. She threw her weight against the steering arm, having difficulty keeping her balance. The air-floater did not move quickly enough. The heavy spear whistled over her head, smashing through the back end of the cabin and out the front. *Nish!* Nish was inside.

'Shoot them!' Her voice cracked.

Flangers was cranking a crossbow. 'No spears left. Not many bolts, either.'

The pair of air-floaters were approaching. Both were armed with javelards and soldiers bearing crossbows, though they were not yet in range.

Another spear shot by, passing close to the top of the airbag. Where had *that* come from? Her erratic movements had taken the air-floater offshore and it had come within range of one of the ships' more powerful javelards. Irisis felt a flurry of panic but bit down on it. She would get everyone to safety or kill them all in the attempt.

'I need some help here,' she gasped as Inouye's weight pulled her hand off the controller.

The air-floater kept turning. Irisis, realising that it would take them towards the air-floaters, pulled the steering arm the other way with her boot. That brought them past the soldiers on the hill and, as they drifted west, she saw the soldiers from the third landing boat climbing the ridge ahead of them. There was nowhere to go.

A bony hand fell on her shoulder. 'Turn north-east towards the air-floaters,' said Flydd, taking the steering arm. He fired Flangers's crossbow one-handed, to no effect. 'We may be able to do something.'

'I can't imagine what,' Irisis muttered, but did as she was told.

As they passed over the water, she cast a glance over her shoulder. Flangers was pouring the flask of quicksilver through a sieve while the perquisitor did something underneath with her hands. Irisis could feel the cold from here. Pellets of frozen quicksilver, far heavier than lead, rattled into a bucket. Fyn-Mah gave the scrutator such a look of hopeless longing that Irisis was touched. Flydd did not notice.

With a gloved hand, Flangers scooped a handful of pellets into a silk bag. He placed the bag in the cup of the javelard, binding it loosely with thread.

'Get a move on,' roared Flydd.

Flangers swung the javelard around, tracking the air-floater to their left. It was doing the same, and fired first. The spear was aimed high, and looked as though it was going to fall short, but a gust drifted the air-floater into its path and it cut through the airbag just above its base, emerged a couple of spans away and fell past them.

Irisis gave the floater-gas generator as much power as she dared. Floater gas whistled up the pipe, though it seemed to be coming out the rents in the airbag just as quickly. Try as she might, she could not keep the machine level.

'Can you patch it?' she called over her shoulder.

'Fire, dammit,' said Flydd.

Flangers fired. A scrap of silk drifted in the air, then the soldiers on the leading air-floater screamed and threw their arms in the air. A scatter of holes appeared in the airbag, tore into a huge gash and the airbag began to collapse. The air-floater went nose-down.

'Again!' said Flydd.

While Flangers charged the javelard with another bag of quicksilver pellets, Muss climbed to the roof of the cabin. He hauled up Flydd, who was carrying a repair patch – a square of canvas coated in sticky tar.

'Keep it steady,' said the scrutator, wincing as his weight went onto his twisted ankle. He held the canvas in place while Muss pressed it against the lower tear in the balloon and smoothed it down, taking care to eliminate any wrinkles.

Flangers fired at the second air-floater, but this time the silk did not break and the bag of pellets tore harmlessly through the wall of the cabin.

'I've pellets left for one more attempt,' Flangers called.

Flydd, struggling with the other piece of tarred canvas, snapped, 'Get on with it. The quicksilver won't stay frozen forever.'

Irisis turned north into the wind, trying to keep her distance from the air-floater. That proved impossible for it had the wind on its starboard quarter. She also had to keep the machine steady and hold Inouye up. Power kept flowing through the controller, so something must be clinging on in the pilot's subconscious.

The second tear proved harder to fix, for it was well above Flydd and Muss's reach. They had to press the canvas patch on with poles. One side went on cleanly but as they smoothed the patch across, the canvas wrinkled. There was no way to fix it without setting down.

Flangers fired. Several people at the front of the enemy craft, including the pilot, went down. As it fell, the controller arm was jerked to one side and the air-floater veered towards them. Irisis turned away as sharply as she dared, prompting a flurry of oaths from the roof of the cabin, but still the enemy shooter had a perfect, side-on shot.

The spear whizzed by the cabin, clanging off the housing of the floater-gas generator. Irisis held her breath. One spark and they would light up the sky for ten leagues. Nothing happened, but the whistle of the generator died away.

The pilotless air-floater fell in looping corkscrews towards the sea. The shooter abandoned his weapon to stand at the rail, staring down fearfully. The first craft had already hit the water and now lay on its side, its airbag deflated. The nearest ship was moving towards it, and the dark-clad figures thrashing in the water. The third air-floater signalled with flags but made no attempt to come after them. Definitely scrutators on board, Irisis thought sourly.

'The floater-gas generator's busted,' said Flydd, climbing down. He was now limping badly. He looked around, marking the positions of the fleet, which was spread out to the south and east of them.

Irisis let Inouye slide to the deck, for she could no longer hold her up. The machine slowed dramatically – Inouye's subconscious had finally given out. Flangers and Fyn-Mah carried her inside, and Irisis ran in after them to check on Nish. He was asleep and unharmed. She returned to her post, took out the controller's crystal, put her pliance in its place and set it to channel to the rotor what power she could. The air-floater limped on, slowly losing height as floater gas trickled out from beneath the wrinkled patch.

'Which way?' she said to Flydd. 'With the fleet between us and land, I don't dare head south or west. If they've got other air-floaters, or we're forced to land, they'll have us. We can't go back towards Snizort, either.'

The afternoon sun angled across one cheek. If Flydd had been gaunt before, now he was nothing more than bone and sinew over which the skin was stretched drum-tight. As he clenched his jaw, knots formed under the skin.

'Go north-west,' he decided at last.

'Towards Meldorin?' Irisis said incredulously. 'But the lyrinx control it.'

'We're outlaws. There's nowhere on Lauralin to hide; nowhere the scrutators won't track us down. So we must go to the one place where they don't dare, and take our chances with the lyrinx. Which reminds me – how did you get on in Snizort?'

That adventure was so long ago Irisis could hardly recall what he was talking about. 'It began well, surr . . .'

'Oh?' he said sharply.

This wasn't the way she'd imagined their reunion. They'd been friends for a long time now; she'd been so glad to see him and imagined he would feel the same. Evidently she'd invested too much in the moment – Flydd was scrutator first and human being second. 'We managed to take one of the flesh-formed creatures alive – a newborn infant.'

'But?' said Flydd.

'The lyrinx attacked us on the way out and it was killed. They'd slain all the adults before they left. They nearly killed us too. We lost all six of our guards, and Fyn-Mah and Flangers were badly hurt. Only Muss was unharmed, but he was never around when the fighting was on.'

'I don't allow him to fight, except to save his life,' said Flydd. 'He's too valuable to me. And the other?'

'The other, surr?'

'The phynadr, dammit. I saw Muss before the battle of Gumby Marth and he said you had it.'

'I did . . .'

'What happened?'

'It didn't thrive, surr. We did everything we could.' She took him into a corner of the cabin and retrieved the bag from under a bench.

He opened it. The phynadr had collapsed into a slimy mess with a strong, meaty smell, like buffalo broth. 'What a waste,' said Flydd, tossing it over the side.

She just stared at him. Was that all? Didn't he even care? Suddenly she felt furiously angry. 'Thank you for trying so hard, Irisis,' she said sarcastically. 'Next time you get lost, you miserable old fleabag, you can rescue yourself.'

'Hey,' he said. 'I didn't mean –'

She had already stalked away.

Nish was still sleeping peacefully, his knees doubled up, one hand under his cheek. It made him look very young. Irisis stood looking down at him, reflecting. She knew now that she wanted this man, but would he want her? Either way, she was glad that her brief affair with Flydd had ended before they came west. She tucked a blanket around Nish and left him to recover.

The air-floater had caught a breeze and was moving more quickly now. In an hour they had left the enemy behind and were drifting across an empty, mist-covered sea.

'Can't we go any faster?' said Flydd, coming up beside her. 'If I stuck my head out the back and blew, we'd move quicker than this.'

'Off you go, then,' Irisis said coolly.

He did not reply. He looked terrible.

She felt contrite. How could she know what he had been through? 'What's the matter, Xervish?'

'I'm sorry,' he said. 'I didn't mean to sound ungrateful, earlier. This past week and a half . . .'

'You look as though you haven't eaten since I last saw you.'

'Close enough.' He stared up at the balloon. 'The bag's still losing floater gas. At this rate, we'll be lucky to make it to land.'

'How's Inouye?'

'Who?'

'The pilot.'

'I've never seen anyone go so close to anthracism and survive.'

'Can she come up and take over?'

'Only if you want to kill her,' said Flydd.

'Then you'd better hang onto this.' She gave him the controller arm.

'Hey!' he cried. 'I can't operate one of these.'

The alarm in his voice amused her. 'In that case you'd better start blowing.' She went down to the cabin.

Inouye lay on the canvas bench, her eyes as red as tomatoes. Her lips were like crumpled paper and her fingernails had gone black. Her skin was completely white, as if all the blood had withdrawn from beneath.

'I thought you were going to die,' Irisis said, taking the small woman's hand.

'I want to,' said Inouye in a whisper like the rustling of papers. 'The one thing I have left is to die.'

'You saved us all, and the scrutator. You've done more than your duty.'

'I couldn't save my family.' Inouye turned her face to the wall.

'I don't think the Council would harm them.'

'I'll never see my children again!'

How could Irisis answer that? She stroked Inouye's limp hair, then returned to the pilot's position and coaxed a little more speed from the rotor, at the cost of exhausting herself. Without training, or a controller tailored to her, piloting was a debilitating business. Fortunately the tailwind had picked up, though Meldorin was not in sight and from here must be a day's flight away – if the floater gas lasted that long. She leaned back against the cabin wall and closed her eyes, feeling as if she'd not slept in a week. There would be none tonight.

Flangers and Muss had rigged up a rope ladder between the bottom of the airbag and the rail, and run a line around the floater-gas generator, which had a huge dent in one side. Flangers was hammering out the crusted pins that held it to its mountings.

'Gently,' Irisis called. 'Don't make a spark –'

'There's no iron in it,' said Flangers.

'What about your hammer and punch?'

He looked down, grinning sheepishly. Morons! she thought.

'We're still losing altitude,' Irisis said to Fyn-Mah, who was standing in the doorway of the cabin with the map flapping in her hands. 'Better find a place to land. The gas won't keep us up much longer.'

'Turn due north. There are reefs and islets not far from here.'

'Doesn't sound very promising.' Irisis turned onto the new heading and an hour later, when she could barely stand up, saw surf breaking on submerged obstacles. 'I don't see any *dry* land.'

Fyn-Mah was now on the cabin roof with her spyglass. 'There, to the left.'

Irisis rotored that way, shortly encountering a platform of black rock fringed with olive-green seaweed. The surface was only half a span above the water, crisscrossed with water-filled gutters and rockpools, and none of it was dry.

'Is this the best we can do?' she said, dismayed. The wind was jerking the air-floater this way and that and she wasn't experienced enough to control it. She aimed for a flat slab of rock but overshot. The machine set down with a crash, right in one of the gutters. Water dribbled in through the canvas floor.

'Up!' yelled Flydd as a wave foamed towards them. 'The next wave –'

'I know, I know.'

The air-floater would not rise, of course, for the floater-gas generator was no longer connected. She spun the rotor hard, grinding the keel along the gutter and bouncing it up onto the next slab. Grapnels were flung out, pulled tight and the machine came to rest canted over on its side. Irisis let go the controller and lay down on the sloping deck. She simply could not stand up.

'What happens when the tide comes in?' asked Flangers.

'The Karama Malama isn't big enough to have tides,' said Eiryn Muss.

'Let's get the damn thing fixed and get out of here,' Flydd said tersely. 'I've spent enough time in this bloody sea.'

'You'll have to do it,' Irisis said. 'I'm utterly worn out.'

'It can't be that difficult,' said Flydd.

Flangers shot him an unreadable glance. He and Muss tightened the grapnel ropes to bring the deck horizontal, then brought the floater-gas generator down to the front deck and began to take it apart.

'Does anyone know how these things operate?' Irisis heard Flydd say.

'I imagine Irisis could work it out,' said Flangers.

'She's exhausted. Pull it apart, see what you can find. And don't break anything.'

'Which way does this screw?'

'It doesn't screw at all, you clot,' said Flydd cheerfully. 'You –'

Irisis was amazed to realise that they were enjoying themselves. Good-natured though the banter was, it irritated her. Men! She slipped over the side. Being a genius with her hands, she couldn't bear to listen as they squabbled about how to get the case open.

She trudged across to the far edge of the rock platform, the brown pea-sized bladders of seaweed popping underfoot. There was nothing to see but water. Irisis sat down on the wet rock, but even that was tiring. She lay on her back, feeling the cold water seeping through her coat but too drained to do anything about it. Irisis was hurt that Flydd hadn't recognised all they'd done to find him; she felt unappreciated. She could have fixed the device, weary though she was, but let Flydd have his go. When he failed, he must realise how much he needed her.

She put up with their incompetence for another ten minutes, then looked up to see dark clouds gathering behind them. A wave broke next to her and she scrambled to her feet. They were dreadfully exposed here – the mildest of storms would drive head-high breakers right across the platform. A strong wind would simply blow them away. It had gone on long enough. Irisis wobbled across to the air-floater.

'Get out of the way, you dills! Can't you see, it goes like this.' She twisted the housing one way, then partway back.

The mechanism clicked and she tugged gently on each end. The two parts slid open.

She laid the internal workings on the canvas, turned it over and said, 'There's the problem. The crystal that draws power into the mechanism was smashed by the impact. I'll pop in another one and we'll be on our way.'

It didn't turn out to be that simple, of course. There were no replacement crystals.

'We had a spare,' said Inouye in that dreary, husk-like voice, 'but one of the other air-floaters had a problem on the way from Nennifer, and we had to give it to them.'

'Don't you have any other crystals?' asked Flydd.

'Only in the spare controller for the rotor. But it wouldn't fit.'

'What about my scrying crystal?' said Fyn-Mah.

'It wouldn't do at all,' said Irisis without looking up. 'I'll have to cut down the spare controller crystal. And that won't be easy without suitable tools.'

After an hour of careful labour, during which time the storm clouds came ever closer, she managed to obtain a suitably shaped sliver of crystal, which she tested with her pliance. 'It's far from ideal, but it's the best I can do.'

Flangers had pounded the dent out of the housing on the rock platform, keeping well away from the airbag in case of sparks. Irisis inserted the crystal and put the case together. Flangers and Muss climbed the ladder, hefting the device onto its frame. They filled the barrel with seawater. By the time all that had been done the airbag was as flabby as an old bladder.

Irisis held her breath as she worked the controller. The floater-gas generator shuddered and gave a cheerful whistling hiss.

By this time the sea had come up and waves were breaking over the platform, foaming all the way across and swinging the keel on its mooring ropes. The wind had risen, jerking the airbag this way and that. It took a long time before the air-floater began to lift; when it did, it reached a height of a few hundred spans and would rise no higher.

They crept north-west, crossing the southern coast of Meldorin after noon the following day. She'd expected to see lyrinx everywhere but, apart from a sea eagle wheeling in the distance, the sky was empty. Some way off to their left she saw a town or port, abandoned long ago, with trees growing in the middle of the streets. They crept on. Directly ahead, a range of mountains towered above them. The air-floater would never rise that high.

'Go east around it,' said Flydd, who had a rolled map in one hand.

'We've got to set down,' Irisis said, rubbing her swollen eyes. 'I can't go any longer without sleep.'

'I'm not keen on stopping just here. I believe there's a lyrinx town not far away.'

'There'll be no light tonight.' Irisis cocked an eye at the dense overcast. 'It'll be just as dangerous floating in the dark, if we can't get higher than this.'

'We'll have to take that risk. Keep going as long as you can.'

It was completely dark before they had passed by the eastern end of the range and turned back onto their north-westerly tack.

'What's ahead of us?' said Irisis.

'Grassland, then forest, swamp, more forest, more grassland and, finally, desert.'

'And the lyrinx control the lot?'

'Most of it,' said Flydd. 'Not being keen on water, they keep clear of the bog country.'

'Even so, I don't see how we're better off than we were before.'

'There are creatures in Meldorin that even the lyrinx are afraid of.'

'Very comforting. So where *are* we going?'

'I'll tell you, *if* we get there.'

She shivered and drew her coat around her. There had been snow on the mountains and she could feel it on the wind.

The dark became so intense that finally they were forced

to land, creeping down with the rotor off while Flangers stood at the front, and Muss at the rear, with lanterns held out on poles to watch for trees and other obstacles. Normally they were forbidden on air-floaters because of the danger of explosion. Irisis held her breath all the way but they made it safely to the ground, hammered in wooden pegs and tethered the machine.

'If there are lyrinx about, we've just told them exactly where we are,' said Fyn-Mah.

FORTY-FOUR

'Can't be helped.' Flydd paced up and down, cracking his knuckles and muttering under his breath.

'I'll make the camp fire,' said Irisis. 'I'm starving.'

'Can't risk fire here, in case there are enemy patrols on high. Have something from the stew pot.'

'Cold bean-and-onion soup? We've been eating that for weeks.'

'The youth of today!' he muttered. 'When I was on the clanker-hauling team, I would have given my right foot for a bowl of bean-and-onion soup. Fetch me some, would you?'

'Get it yourself!' Irisis felt like hitting him. They'd passed half a dozen isolated peaks where they could have hidden for the night, built a roaring fire and cooked a decent meal from the supplies they'd bought in Jibstorn. Not even a brazier was permitted on the air-floater, lest it set off the floater gas. Irisis could think of nothing but the haunch of venison in the larder.

He was unfazed. 'Shall I wait on you with a bowl?'

'No thanks, I'm going to sleep. Why don't you pull the airbag down and patch those gashes properly?'

'Good idea.' He strolled down to the galley as if nothing had happened.

They warmed a flat iron against the floater-gas generator. Flangers ran it over the patches until the tar softened enough for the patch to be eased off, re-tarred and replaced smoothly. A larger patch was placed over that, just to be sure. Irisis set the floater-gas generator running and went to the cabin. She lay on the floor next to Nish, listening to his steady breathing, and suddenly, out of nowhere, realised that she loved him.

This changed everything – she could no longer be fatalistic about their probable fate. She had something to live for. And everything to fear.

The night passed uneventfully. Nish was still asleep in the morning, which bothered her. It was almost two days since he'd hit his head. However, he was breathing normally and nothing seemed broken so she left him to it.

The airbag was so full that the machine was straining at its ropes. They did not wait for breakfast, just went up as fast as they could and kept going, north by north-west.

In the mid-morning they passed over a city, also abandoned and partly overgrown. 'Garching,' said Flydd. 'It was held to be a beautiful place, in its time. A garden city at the foot of the mountains.' He scanned it with the spyglass, frowning.

'What is it?' said Irisis, who was standing beside him, Inouye having recovered enough to take the controller.

'Oh, I was just thinking of the past. Garching features in one of the Great Tales, you know. I was wondering if such times will ever come again. If, indeed, there'll be any more Great Tales. Or anyone to hear the old ones.'

'I don't imagine the ancient days were quite as wonderful as they're made out.'

'I'm sure they weren't but, except for the dark days of the Clysm, they weren't as desperate as our time, either. I'm afraid, Irisis. Afraid this is the end, not just for us, but for every human on Santhenar.'

Again Irisis felt that chill. She had never heard him talk like this before.

'Surely the scrutators can't be *that* bad?'

'They're worse than you can imagine! I hadn't realised it before – I was too busy with my provincial concerns to see the true picture. But since this last phase of the war began it's become all too clear. The Council of Scrutators, for all their control, for all their spy networks, for all their power, are not only corrupt, but incompetent. They're fossils and must be swept away.'

A shiver of dread started at the soles of her feet and ran up the backs of her legs, all the way to her scalp. 'That's treason, Xervish, punishable by the most gruesome death that human ingenuity can come up with.' Irisis had fought the scrutators, opposed them in many ways, escaped from their bastion of Nennifer, but those crimes were nothing to what he was proposing. It was worse than treason – it was sedition, the worst crime of all, and it would mean not only his death and hers, but the execution of her family, her friends, and every single person of her family's line. The House of Stirm would be expunged from the earth.

'I never thought I'd say it,' Flydd said, 'but the age of scrutators is over.'

'But who would order the world?' Despite everything she'd experienced, Irisis was no revolutionary. She believed in the system they had, faulty though it was.

'I don't know. The trouble with tyrants is that so few *are* benevolent. Power corrupts, and most of those who seek it are already corrupt. That's the insoluble problem – replacing the Council without making things worse.'

'What about you, surr?'

'I don't want it, Irisis.'

'I've heard it said that the only man suitable for high office is the one who refuses to accept it.'

'An appropriate paradox . . .'

He broke off and Irisis did not question him further. It was all too disturbing.

Around the middle of the day they saw trees in the distance, and sunlight shining on water. 'Orist,' said Eiryn Muss.

A land of lakes, mires and swamp forests, it stretched northwest beyond sight. 'Where are we going, Muss?' asked Irisis.

'I don't know,' said the perfect spy, which was also worrying.

Sometime later, Irisis saw, away to her left in the west, a rugged coastline, and beyond it, what she took to be the Western Ocean.

'I presume we're not going across the ocean?' she said to Flydd. 'I hope not, since the patches are leaking again.' They had been losing altitude steadily, despite the floater-gas generator.

'We're not.' Flydd folded his arms across his skinny chest.

'Hadn't we better look for a refuge for the night?'

'I already have a place in mind,' he said.

'I didn't know you'd spent time on Meldorin before.'

'No reason why you should.'

'I wish you'd tell me what's going on!' For the past few weeks she had felt in control of her life, but as soon as Flydd reappeared, that had all been overturned. She didn't like it.

'I will, when I know myself.'

He turned away. She followed him down the back, where the pilot sagged in a canvas chair, listlessly holding the controller. 'How are you feeling, Inouye?'

'Better, though my fingers hurt.' Inouye inspected her blackened nails.

'You'll probably lose your fingernails,' said Flydd, 'though they'll grow back.'

'It doesn't matter,' she said. 'I have no man to admire them.'

'If it is in my power,' said the scrutator, 'you will be reunited with your family. You have my promise on that.'

'Oh!' A flush crept up Inouye's cheeks. She clenched one fist around the controller knob, concealing the other in her pocket. 'What may I do for you, surr?'

'I'd like to get there before dark. Can you go a little faster?' He checked the map against the country below. 'And somewhat to the left.'

The rotor spun up and the air-floater edged onto its new heading. Irisis watched the lakes and bogs go by. If Flydd did not want to tell her what he was up to, no force could make him. She supposed he had his reasons.

Nish came up beside her, rubbing his eyes.

She wanted to throw her arms around him and squeeze him against her, but Irisis restrained herself to an affectionate pat on the shoulder. She could wait. 'How's your head?'

'Better. What happened? I don't remember going to sleep. Have I slept all day?'

She laughed with relief. 'You fell down and smacked your head against the stern post, just after we rescued you.'

He glanced that way. 'How could that happen?' Nish went pale. 'The rotor –'

'The air-floater was going up steeply. You slid backwards under it and whacked into the post.'

'I knocked myself out?'

'You've been asleep for two and a half days.'

He ran a hand through his thick hair and winced. 'That explains the hollow in my belly.'

'Can I get you something to eat? It's only stew, I'm afraid, and days old.'

'Stew!' he exclaimed.

She mistook his meaning. 'I'm sorry, but bloody old Flydd –'

'Where is it? Quick!' He took her by the hand.

'Down here. Look, we've a little galley.' She led the way out of the cabin to a tiny room behind it, so small that she could touch all four walls with her outstretched arms. 'And we can't cook anything here, of course, because of the floater gas, so it's cold I'm afraid . . .'

Nish pushed past her, snatched a ladle off its hook and took a scoop out of the pot. Slurping down a mouthful, he gasped, 'That's goood!'

'You've got soup all over your face,' said Irisis, wiping his cheek with her hand. They'd not spent time together since he'd left the manufactory in the balloon, last winter. She'd missed him terribly.

'I'm so hungry I could go into the pot head-first, and not come out until I'd licked it shiny clean.'

'It's not that good,' she said.

'Do you know what our last meal on the island was?'

'Fish? Mussels? Bird's eggs?'

'There weren't any edible shellfish and I don't recommend

barnacles. In nine days we didn't catch a single fish. There's nothing to eat down there – no snakes, no lizards, no eggs. Not even an earthworm.'

'How did you survive?'

'Seaweed and belt soup.'

'What's belt soup?'

'We cut my belt into strips and boiled it for about ten hours. It still tasted like boiled leather. Next we were going to eat Flydd's stinking old boots, and if you think I was looking forward to that –'

'I get the picture,' she said hastily. And it explained why Flydd had been so irritable, if he'd been close to starvation.

Irisis watched Nish while he ate, thinking how changed he was from the young man she'd seen off in the balloon, and even from the Nish she'd encountered briefly at the Aachim camp, before the battle of Snizort.

'It's so good to see you, Nish. So good.' Impulsively, she embraced him.

He set down the ladle before it dribbled down her back, and wiped his mouth. 'And you, Irisis. I feel as though I've lived an entire life since I left the manufactory. And, from what the scrutator told me, you've been just as busy.' Nish pulled away, inspecting her. 'You look . . .'

'What?' she prompted after a long pause. 'Old? Haggard? Ugly?'

'You look the same, though . . . There seems to be more of you –'

'Well, thank you very much,' she said in mock outrage. 'Actually –'

'I meant as a person. You look more confident, even stronger than you were, and . . . at peace with yourself.'

'If you only knew!' she exclaimed. 'And yet, in a way, I *have* found peace. Life has never been more insecure, I'm an outlaw under sentence of death, the scrutators will probably execute me in some hideous way, and yet – Oh, Nish!' She threw her arms around him again. 'I've got my long-lost talent back. I'm not a fraud any more. I feel almost *happy*.'

'You never were a fraud to me, Irisis.'

'But I was in my own eyes.' After a moment's reflection she said, 'So how are you? You've changed, Nish. You're not the man who left us, last winter.'

'The *boy*,' he said scornfully. 'I was no man. Yes, I have changed. I've seen enough adventure for a dozen lifetimes.'

'It's done you good.' She looked him up and down. 'You're a handsome man now. I like your beard.'

'It's better than scraping the skin off my face every morning.' He eyed her. 'I do believe you look more magnificent than ever. You seem to have bloomed.'

'I had a new lover for a while, Nish, no less than the scrutator himself, though it's over now.' She hadn't told Flydd yet. She hoped he'd take it well.

'I thought there was something between you, back when Flydd came to negotiate with Vithis. What else have you been up to?'

'Oh, I've had a few adventures too. A couple of run-ins with your father. A spell down in the tar pits of Snizort. You know the sort of thing.'

He leaned on the wall, companionably, 'It's a wonder we didn't run into each other. Why don't you tell me about it?'

'I'd rather hear your story, Nish, if you don't mind.'

He was happy to relate it, sitting on the port side, towards the stern, out of the wind, with Irisis facing him. She listened in silence until he mentioned Ullii being pregnant with his child.

'You didn't know!' she said incredulously.

'No one told me, and she was wearing a smock like a tent. How was I to tell? Nonetheless, I let her down, and now I'm paying for it.'

He went on with his story: the attack in the clearing, how his folly had brought down the air-floater, the ghastly death of Myllii, Ullii fleeing and not being seen again, and all the anguish that had caused him.

She knew he was telling the whole truth. Irisis took his hand, glad she'd held off from saying how she really felt – he was in no state to hear it. Her suit was going to be longer than she'd expected, and she'd have to be more careful. Not Ullii! she thought. No woman could be more wrong for him. Surely it could never come to pass?

She bit down on the jealousy. 'How you must have suffered.'

'It cost me dear – not least the child I'll never know. That's the hardest thing of all.'

'There's been no word of Ullii?'

'It's as if she vanished off the face of Lauralin. And she *hates* me, Irisis, though it was just a terrible accident. It was dark; I thought he was attacking her. He just reared back onto the knife and it went right into him.' He choked.

She drew him to her, folding her long arms around his compact, muscled body. 'You don't have to justify yourself to me,' she said softly.

'But I do have to live with it. Ah, Irisis, how I've missed you.'

'Do you want to tell me the rest of the story?'

'Maybe later. Where are we, anyway?'

'Heading up the western side of Meldorin Island.'

'Meldorin!' he cried, looking over the side as if to see lyrinx everywhere. 'Where are we going?'

'No idea. Bloody Flydd is acting all mysterious, as usual.'

The sun went down into the ocean to their left, and the evening light faded swiftly, though before it grew completely dark they beheld the walls of a great fortress in the distance. Black it was, even blacker than the shadowy forest that surrounded it, a forbidding wall of stone encircling a yard, and an inner fortress with horned towers.

'Is that our destination?' Nish asked Flydd, who was walking by.

'It is.' Flydd cast him an unreadable glance. 'Dragged yourself out of bed at last, I see.'

Nish didn't rise to the bait. He was used to Flydd's ways by now, and the tone had been almost affectionate. 'It's not a lyrinx fortress?'

'It belongs to an older power.' Flydd continued down to Inouye. 'Go over the outer wall, Inouye, and come down in the yard by the horned tower. See it there?'

'I see it.' Her voice was like a single page falling to the ground.

The air-floater passed over the wall. No guards could be seen, so Inouye settled the machine in the bleak yard. It came to rest without a bump. The rotor slowly spun down, the floater-gas generator fell silent.

Again that shiver up Irisis's spine.

'I don't like this place. Where are we?'

'We're in the one place in Meldorin that the scrutators will never find us. Not even the lyrinx dare come here. This is the ancient Aachim fortress of Fiz Gorgo.'

Somewhere within the fortress an alarm clanged, like a broken bell.

FORTY-FIVE

'Fiz Gorgo!' cried Nish. 'Wasn't that the fortress of the great mancer Yggur, back in the time of the *Tale of the Mirror*?'

'It was,' said Flydd, and Irisis could hear him cracking his knuckles anxiously.

'Who controls it now?'

'We're about to find out. Climb up on top of the cabin, Nish, and tear open that patch on the airbag.'

'What?' he cried.

'Just do it, and be quick,' Flydd hissed, 'or the enemy will breakfast on your kidneys.'

Irisis wondered if the scrutator had gone mad. So, evidently, did Nish, but he did what he was told, then sprang down again. Floater gas sighed from the gash and slowly the balloon sagged until, in a few minutes, the structure of its wire ribs could be seen. Gravel crunched under the keel as the cabin tilted onto its side.

Nish began to climb over the rail. 'Stay where you are,' Flydd said quietly.

They waited. All was silent. No bird sang, no cricket chirped. Not a single leaf rustled.

Irisis's nape prickled. 'Someone's watching us,' she said under her breath, without knowing how she knew it.

'Be quiet.'

Her eyes were drawn up the tower, all the way to the horns on each extremity. No, not there. She followed the rough stone down to a point a little more than halfway from the ground. A balcony projected straight out, a shaped slab of stone without roof or rail. Someone stood there, or something, but she could not see what it was.

A lamp or glowing globe on the wall came on, outlining the figure from behind. It was very tall, and man-shaped, but concealed by a greatcoat that swept to the floor. The figure stepped to the edge.

'Begone, whoever you are, back to where you came from. Visitors are not welcome here.' It was human, a man with a mellow, carrying voice that bore more than an underlying hint of steel. This man was master and no argument, Irisis sensed, would sway him.

'I am Xervish Flydd, surr,' the scrutator called up, respectfully. 'Scrutator for Einunar –'

'Then you've a long journey home, Scrutator Flydd. Begin it at once. You are not welcome in Fiz Gorgo.'

'I would, surr, but as you can see, our air-floater floats no more and cannot be repaired today. I beg your indulgence until the morning.'

The man shifted his weight. 'I am bereft of indulgence and every other form of human weakness,' he said coldly. 'Take your abominable machine and begone!'

'It can't be moved, surr, within twenty-four hours. We'll go if we must, but the machine must stay where it lies. If you would care to inspect it . . .'

The figure whirled, the light went out and a door slammed.

'Don't say a word, unless he speaks directly to you,' Flydd said over his shoulder. 'If he does, confine your answers to yes or no. Venture no explanations.'

Before them, up a few steps from the base of the tower, stood a set of doors so vast that the cabin of the air-floater could have fitted between. The doors opened silently and a blinding light shone through them, revealing that the yard was paved in black stone. There was no living thing in sight. Not a single weed grew inside the walls.

The man appeared, greatcoat flapping. Illuminated from behind, he looked twice the size of any normal man. He strode through the door and came down the broad steps to the air-floater.

'Get out!'

They scrambled over the side, to congregate at the base of the steps. As he turned to inspect the machine, the light fell full on him. He was no giant, but tall and well proportioned – broad in the chest, slim hipped and with long, muscular legs. He had a long, weathered face, frost-grey eyes and dark hair, worn long, that was streaked with silver at the temples. He wore a grey shirt, grey trousers and pale grey boots. His great-coat was as black as the flagstones.

Climbing onto the sloping deck, he inspected the structure, the controller, the torn airbag and, last of all, the floater-gas generator. As he climbed down, Irisis noted that he moved stiffly, as if an old injury troubled him.

'Very well,' he said. 'You may stay until the morning. At first light you will repair your contraption and remove yourselves.' He went up the steps, turning before he went through the entrance. 'Bring that device to me.' He pointed to the floater-gas generator.

'At once,' said Flydd, motioning to Irisis and Flangers. 'Would you like to see the controller too?'

'I am familiar with its type,' said the man, and disappeared through the doorway.

They gathered their gear. 'You'd better bring the contents of the larder,' said Flydd. 'He doesn't seem a very hospitable fellow.'

Muss collected the food, including the great haunch of venison. Nish and Flangers carried the floater-gas generator, and little Inouye came behind with her controller. It was her lover, her friend, her family, and the bond with it was the only thing that kept her going.

Irisis picked up her bag and followed. Fiz Gorgo was a grim place, strongly built but undecorated. There were no tapestries on the walls, no rugs in the hall. What furniture it had was of the plainest construction. The hall was high and wide, the rooms large, square and barren of ornament save for time-worn patterns etched into the stone. And it was quite as cold as the manufactory where she had spent her working life.

Halfway down the long hall, the man stood by an open door. 'You may stay here. There is a stove. Water may be drawn from the small cistern out by your infernal contraption. Good evening!' He nodded formally.

They filed past, Irisis last, which gave her the chance to gain a better look at the fellow. He appeared to be in hale middle age.

He caught her gaze and turned, inspecting her from head to toe. Irisis was a tall woman but he was almost a head taller. She looked him boldly in the eye as she went past and knew that his gaze lingered. There was a strange, almost wistful look in his eye. Then he was gone.

Flydd chuckled. 'You'll do no good with that one.'

'I have no intention of *doing good*, as you so charmingly put it,' she said frostily.

'Who is he?' said Muss, who had been silent for a long time.

'Oh, come now,' said Flydd. 'You're telling me that you, my best spy, don't know?'

Muss looked vexed. 'I've not done any work across the sea.'

'Surely you know your Histories, man?'

'But . . .'

Nish spoke from behind. 'He, surely, is Lord Yggur, a great mancer who comes into several tales, including the *Tale of the Mirror*. I thought he was dead long ago.'

'So did everyone,' said Flydd. 'He disappeared at the end of that tale, some two hundred years ago, and has not been seen since. Everyone thought he was dead. Well, almost everyone.'

'Why did he come back to this miserable place?' said Irisis. 'He might have dwelt anywhere on Santhenar.'

'I dare say he likes it here,' Flydd remarked. 'But who knows where he has been? For all we know he could have travelled seven times around the known world, and the unknown. In his day, he had the best –'

'A day long past,' said Nish. 'As I recall it, his courage failed him in the *Tale of the Mirror*.'

'I'd watch my tongue if I were you,' Flydd said coldly. 'He may be listening to our every word. Besides, he was a great man once, and deserves your respect.'

Nish glanced around uncomfortably.

Irisis packed kindling into the stove, shrugging Fiz Gorgo and Lord Yggur away. 'I've been looking forward to this dinner for a long time.'

She had been thinking and dreaming about food for weeks. Among her many skills Irisis was a brilliant cook, and in times past she'd cooked for herself, and friends, when she could no longer bear the muck provided by the manufactory. Since leaving there last spring she'd had few meals worth thinking about, and most of those had been with Flydd in Gospett. In the past month the food had been horrible, and there had been little enough of it. In Jibstorn she had spent a fortune buying the best of everything. Tonight was going to be a meal to remember.

'How much longer are you planning to torment us?' said Nish, several hours later. The smells arising from the stove were glorious. Even Flangers, deeply withdrawn since she'd forced him to remit his life to her, had a gleam in his eye.

Irisis smiled inwardly. Food always served, if there'd been lack of it for long enough. 'Not long now. Why don't you set up the trestle?'

By the time that was done, dinner was ready. She gave one of her sauces a gentle stir. A shadow drifted down the hall, hesitated for a second outside the door, then went on. A minute later it came past again, glanced across to the stove and continued. Irisis pretended not to notice.

She served up the platters, and no one seemed to notice that an extra one contained some of the choicest portions. While everyone was sitting down, she took up the platter and slipped out the door. Irisis could not have said why, only that she was curious about the master of Fiz Gorgo.

It did not take long to find him, for Yggur sat at a big table in a room at the far end of the hall. He was reading and did not look up as she approached. The floater-gas generator sat on the table beside him, in pieces. There was a faint smell of liquorice in the air, and several slices of peeled root on a dish.

Irisis stood in front of the table, feeling more than a little foolish.

'What do you want?' he growled, still with his head in the book.

'I thought you might be hungry, Lord Yggur.'

At the sound of her voice his head snapped up and the book fell shut. 'Ah, the artisan,' he said. 'I am no lord, and outside this place I don't go by the name Yggur. The past is dead and I prefer it to stay that way.'

'You called me artisan. How do you know me, surr?'

'"He may be listening to our every word,"' he quoted. 'I know everything that goes on in my own realm. I presume your scrutator has sent you to cozen me?'

Irisis blushed, which she found embarrassing. 'Since you've overheard everything we said, surr, you would know I'm going against his direct orders. It's just that, well, you were so kind as to provide us with a roof for the night, and I wished to repay you in what small way I could.'

His lips twitched and Irisis felt as though he could read her mind, the bad as well as the good. In truth, she had no idea why she had done it, though it was not attraction to Yggur. She'd chosen her man and had no interest in any other.

'Very well. Put it on the table. Your own dinner will be getting cold.'

She bowed and turned to the door, feeling his eyes boring into her back and resisting the urge to run away. A disturbing man. And then, sitting down at the trestle with the others, she ate the entire glorious meal without tasting a thing.

They slept the sleep of the truly exhausted that night, and not even Flydd noticed when Yggur slipped into their chamber in the pre-dawn hours. Conjuring ghost light with his fingers, he inspected each in turn. His gaze lingered longest on three: the scrutator, Nish and Irisis. As he turned to go, Yggur almost stumbled over the little pilot, who lay by herself in her sleeping pouch, tossing and groaning. Bending down, he placed the glowing light to her temples, left and right. She rolled over onto her side and slept soundly, and Yggur withdrew.

They went to the machine at dawn and began to repair the tear in the airbag. 'Work slowly,' said Flydd. 'We don't want to leave today.'

Though they dawdled as much as they reasonably could, the airbag was repaired before midday. Inouye installed her controller and Flydd sent Nish to find Yggur and recover the floater-gas generator.

Nish went to the room at the end of the corridor where Yggur sat at the table, writing. The reassembled generator was at his right hand.

'Take it,' said Yggur, his nib looping across the page.

Nish reached out, rather gingerly, and lifted the heavy generator in both hands.

As he turned to go Yggur said, 'You are Cryl-Nish Hlar, weapons artificer, son of Jal-Nish Hlar. Your life is now at a crossroads. Women have been your weakness and you believe that lack of courage is mine.'

Nish flushed. 'I'm sorry, surr. Last night I was tired and hungry and afraid. Sometimes I speak without thinking.'

'Honest, at least,' Yggur said grudgingly. 'Put the generator down for a moment. Cryl-Nish, why have you come here?'

Nish sat it on the table and rubbed his aching arms. 'Scrutator Flydd brought us, surr. I don't know his reasons, though he's looking for help and can't find it anywhere else.'

'Not surprising, since he's a renegade who has been cast out and condemned.'

'The scrutators are fools, surr, who cannot –'

The black brows knitted. 'Who are you to judge the mighty, lowly artificer that you are?' Yggur thundered.

Once Nish would have slunk away, but he stood fast. 'I have eyes to see, surr. And, since you've been listening to our talk, you'll know that I've seen many great deeds done, and terrible ones too, on both sides of the world. My late father –'

'Do you tell me that Jal-Nish Hlar is dead?'

'He was killed at the great battle near Gnulp Landing, a few weeks ago. Killed and eaten by the lyrinx.'

'I'm out of touch, living here,' said Yggur. 'News travels slowly to Meldorin, if at all.'

'I'm a dutiful son, surr. I mourn my father, though he was an evil man who was prepared to do anything to gain a position as scrutator on the Council, including sentencing his youngest son to a miserable death as a slave.'

Yggur sat up at that. 'Oh?'

Nish briefly related that tale.

'A severe punishment for a father to inflict on a son, even for so great a blunder.' Yggur weighed Nish up. 'And yet, such qualities as your father had may be required to win this interminable war.'

'With respect, surr, I disagree. My father was corrupt, I'm sorry to say, and many on the Council, including Ghorr, are just as depraved. They could have won the war long ago, but it gave them the excuse to maintain their own power.'

'Tell me more, Artificer.'

Perhaps Yggur was more interested in the outside world than he pretended. He questioned Nish for the best part of an hour, more incisively than any interrogation by Flydd, Vithis or even his own father. All the more surprising that Yggur hid himself away from the world.

Finally Flydd came looking for Nish. Yggur dismissed him and Flydd accompanied him back to the machine; they carried the floater-gas generator between them. Nish felt quite drained.

'You seemed to be having a merry chat,' said Flydd, after an uncomfortable pause. 'I thought I told you to say as little as possible.'

'If you can stay quiet when he questions you, you're a better man than I am,' Nish snapped. He added hastily, 'Which of course you are.'

'Indeed I am,' chuckled Flydd, and left it at that.

The generator was fitted and its barrel filled with water to which a little salt had been added. Flydd cocked a glance at the sky. 'We'll break for lunch. I don't want to finish it too early.'

'Not much chance of that,' said Irisis. 'It'll take a good ten hours to fill the airbag from empty.'

'Even so.'

They were sitting around, taking a leisurely meal in the watery sun, when Yggur strode down the steps. 'Better get moving,' he said. 'You're to be out of here by nightfall.'

'I don't see how we can be,' said Flydd. 'It'll take –'

'That's your lookout.' Yggur strode off, the wings of his coat flying out behind him. 'And once you're gone, you won't mention me by name.'

'What are we going to do?' said Irisis after he had gone.

'I have no idea.'

As soon as Inouye drew power into the floater-gas generator, it let out a shrieking whistle and began to hiss loudly.

'I don't like the way that sounds,' said Irisis but, on checking, found it to be working perfectly. She frowned at the mechanism. 'In fact –'

'What?' Flydd called.

'It seems to be working *better* than before. He must have done something to it.'

'Damn him!' Flydd paced furiously across the yard.

The bag was full an hour before dark. 'Get the blasted gear aboard,' Flydd said. It was not only that Fiz Gorgo had been his last hope. Even more vexing, Yggur had contrived to speak alone with Nish, Irisis, Muss, Fyn-Mah, Flangers and even little Inouye, but had refused to talk to Flydd. He felt neglected and insulted.

'I've got to do something,' he said. 'This is our last chance.'

'What if . . .?' Irisis began. 'No, that wouldn't work.'

'What?' he snapped.

'What if *I* were to speak to him again?' she said softly.

'What could you possibly say? He's more than a thousand

years old. He's seen everything and heard everything.'

'If he's spent the last two hundred years here by himself . . . there may be things he hasn't seen for a quite a while.'

'What do you mean?'

'You know,' she said.

'Oh, very well. There's nothing *I* wouldn't do to get him on
my side, so if you can seduce him –'

'I didn't mean *that*,' she said coldly. 'What do you take me
for?'

Flydd looked embarrassed. 'Someone who's not quite as
corrupt as a scrutator, obviously.'

'I'll take that as an apology, but don't expect to be warming
my bed again.'

'I had a feeling it was over,' he said. 'I suppose it's Nish, is
it?'

'I have no idea what you're talking about,' she dissembled.

'I'm sure! I'll go with you,' said Flydd. 'I've an idea. And if
we ever get out of here, you'll repeat nothing of what you hear
inside.'

'I understand.' She hadn't the faintest idea what he was
talking about.

Yggur was not in his room but, as they crisscrossed the
halls of the ground floor, Irisis heard the mancer's bootsteps
on the stair of the front tower.

Yggur thrust his head over the edge. 'No need to say goodbye, or to thank me. Just go.'

'I must talk to you first,' said Flydd. 'The scrutators are
losing the war and I –'

'There's always a war being lost somewhere,' Yggur said
indifferently.

'You must help us!' cried Flydd. 'The very fate of humanity –'

'I don't care for your war, Scrutator Flydd, nor for you. You
come to my door a beggar, sabotage your flying machine so I
can't get rid of you, then presume to tell me that I have to
help you. I've nothing more to say to you.'

'But surely, for the war . . .'

'I live in harmony with my neighbours, including lyrinx. Go and make peace with yours.'

'The enemy don't want peace.'

'Small wonder, the way your Council has treated them these past hundred and fifty years. I may not know what's going on at the present, but I'm well informed about the origins of this war and I want no part of it. Good day.' Yggur turned and went back up.

Flydd cursed under his breath. He looked old, meagre and bitter, and, Irisis thought, did not like the comparison with a hale, confident Yggur.

'Let me try,' Irisis muttered. 'Go down, Xervish.'

Before he could say anything she began to run up the stairs. 'Yggur, surr! If you please?'

Yggur climbed to the next landing, sighed audibly and turned to wait for her.

Irisis knew she was an enchanting sight, with her generous bosom bouncing, her yellow hair streaming out behind her and her cheeks flushed prettily. She had no idea what she was going to say, but he would listen. Only a dead man could have turned her away.

'Yes?' he said coolly. Maybe he was made of stone after all. After living more than a thousand years, perhaps such passions were quite extinct in him.

She stopped at the far edge of the landing, three paces from him. Her chest was still heaving. Irisis caught her breath. 'Xervish Flydd is a good man, surr. An honest man.'

'He's a scrutator and the very name means stinking corruption. I should have burned him out of the sky.'

'The scrutators cast him out,' she said desperately. 'They condemned him to slavery.'

'He must have been too rotten even for them.'

'He's always treated me –'

'He's your lover, isn't he? Stinking old hypocrite.'

'Not for months,' she said softly. 'And Flydd isn't old; barely sixty.'

'And you're what? Twenty? Twenty-one? He's a filthy old pervert.'

Irisis might have mentioned Yggur's own liaison with a much younger Maigraith, but that would not have been helpful. She changed tack. 'I've read the Histories, surr.'

'Everyone has read the Histories. The world is obsessed with them, much to its detriment.'

'I know the *Tale of the Mirror*, surr. The true tale; my uncle had a private copy hidden away.'

'Oh?'

'And I know your story. How you were betrayed by the Council of Santhenar a thousand years ago.' She reached up and put a hand on his arm. He looked down sharply but did not shake it off. 'In times long past, you were tormented by Rulke the Charon and driven into madness. You wandered the world for hundreds of years, neither ageing nor using your powers, before making the ancient Aachim fortress of Fiz Gorgo your own, and plotting your revenge. You found Maigraith, the love of your thousand-year life. And I know you're a noble man, surr. You destroyed Rulke's deadly construct, which threatened the Three Worlds, even though in doing so it left Maigraith trapped in Aachan. You did that because you loved our world more than anything.'

'I did it because it was the only way to save her,' he said, staring into nothingness.

She went on as if he had never spoken. 'And then, after she miraculously returned, you abandoned all claim on her and on your empire, rather than plunge the world into war.'

'Not so,' he murmured, still trapped in the past. 'She would not have me. She'd had the best, Rulke himself, and after him I came a distant second. I abandoned my empire because without her it meant nothing. I came home to Fiz Gorgo to die, but I endure, scarcely changed, while she is but a memory. A dream.'

'Then surely it's time to move on.'

He scanned her from her feet to her face. 'You're a beautiful woman, Irisis, but you don't move me. Make your point, whatever it is, then go.'

She lowered her voice, so Flydd would not hear. 'Did you see how scarred and battered Flydd is, how the very flesh was gouged from his broken bones? The scrutators did that to him thirty years ago, because he dared inquire too deeply into the doings of their master.'

That caught his attention. 'What master?' he said sharply.

She left that question hanging and continued. 'And recently they cast him out and condemned him to a cruel death as a slave on the clanker-hauling teams.'

'Which I'm sure he deserved.'

'They ordered him to destroy the lyrinx node-drainer at Snizort, gave him a flawed device to do the job, then blamed him for its failure. It destroyed the node and all its fields with it, and a good part of Snizort.'

'What?' he cried. 'I've heard none of this.'

'The clankers and constructs stalled on the battlefield and the lyrinx overran them. Flydd was blamed for the disaster, though he did everything possible to avoid the battle.'

'A node was *destroyed*?' Yggur said incredulously, pushing past her down the steps and stalking towards the scrutator. 'Is this true, Flydd?'

'It made the most colossal explosion you can imagine,' said Flydd, his eyes alight. 'We were in an air-floater, five hundred spans above the ground, and the blast went up past us as high as a small thunderhead.'

Yggur stared down at him. 'And afterwards? Did anyone go to the node and look in, to see what had come of it?'

'I did, and Nish, and Ullii the seeker, who is no longer with us.'

'What did you see?' cried Yggur.

'Two metal tears, each larger than a grapefruit, and as shiny as quicksilver. I could not get to them –'

Yggur let out a sigh. 'So it *can* happen! What became of the tears?'

'Scrutator Jal-Nish Hlar took them, though we did not discover it was him for many weeks. He left the bodies of his guards in the pit, so that no one would ever know. He had the tears with him before the battle of Gumby Marth, near Gnulp Landing, for he forced Nish to touch them, and Nish was changed by it. It gave him a special sight afterwards, for half a day, though Nish has never had a talent for the Art.'

'Is that so?' said Yggur. 'Go on.'

'Jal-Nish used the tears to enhance his alchymical Art, but a mancer-lyrinx broke the spell. Jal-Nish was slain and eaten, and the tears disappeared. It is believed that the lyrinx took them.'

'I see,' said Yggur. 'Tell me, what were your doings thirty years ago, scrutator, that the Council did such mischief to you?'

'Surely your spies have told you?'

'I no longer have spies. The only news I hear from across the water comes from traders and wandering vagabonds as disreputable as yourselves, and it's usually months old.'

'I pried into forbidden secrets,' said Flydd. 'That's why they punished me.'

'For uncovering the scrutators' master?'

'Where did you hear that?' cried Flydd. 'It puts the lie to –'

'I told him, surr,' said Irisis

'That secret was not yours to reveal,' Flydd said furiously.

'Then you shouldn't have told me about it in your cups,' she retorted.

'Well, Flydd?' said Yggur.

Flydd shook his head. 'I cannot speak of the secrets of the scrutators, surr, even to you. I am sworn and do not lightly break my oath.'

'I don't break sworn word for any reason,' Yggur said scornfully. 'I won't trouble your conscience further, for I can see what a fragile thing it is. Come down, Artisan. Have you given your sworn word to say nothing? Your sacred oath?'

'I said I wouldn't tell,' she said weakly.

'Oath or no oath?'

'No oath.'

'Then, since you boast about how well you know the *Tale of the Mirror*, and my part in it, you know that you *will* tell me.

509

Not even your scrutator can resist me, though I won't force him to break his oath to his corrupt masters.'

Flydd stood staring at her, gnarled hands by his sides. Just give the word, she thought, and I'll resist him with all the strength in my body. But Flydd said nothing. Perhaps he wanted her to reveal what he could not.

'The only thing I know,' said Irisis, 'and that was mentioned several times in . . . *extremis* . . .'

'An excess of wine!' said Yggur. 'What price your oath now, Scrutator? Two cups? Three?'

'. . . it was a reference to the Numinator,' Irisis finished.

'The Numinator?' Yggur said, puzzled.

'The person who gives the scrutators their orders, surr. The one for whom they have shaped our world.'

'Ahh!' He let his breath out. 'I've often wondered how such a collection of fools and incompetents came to gain such power; and how they maintained it for so long. Who is this Numinator?'

'That's all I know, surr,' said Irisis.

'It's enough. You've bought your master a refuge.'

'No man is *my* master,' said Irisis.

'Whatever you say. Well, Flydd, you may stay for a few days. We'll speak more about these matters tonight. Are you happy, now that you've gained what you wanted?'

'Time will tell if it was worth the price,' said Flydd.

FORTY-SIX

Ghorr's air-floater carried Ullii back to the main camp. She
did not say a word the whole way – she was overcome by
a crawling horror of him and the scrutators, and her own folly.
They'd trapped her with the bracelet and now controlled her
utterly.

Ullii tried to retreat to her inner refuge by cutting off all
her senses, as she'd often done in the past, but Ghorr just
dragged her out again. She could find no comfort in her lattice, either, for it seemed to be fading. What had once been
brilliantly clear was hardly there, and when she tried to make
the lattice anew, her mind's eye was empty. It was one blow
too many. She collapsed and lay on her sickbed for a week,
raving with a brain fever.

As soon as she began to recover, Ghorr dragged her out of
bed. Flydd and Nish had disappeared and she had to find
them. Ullii looked for her lattice and it was back, though not
as strong or clear as before. For days she sought in vain; Flydd
was beyond its reach.

The search went on and, many troubled days later, high in
the air-floater, she detected a faint trace of him at the battlefield of Gumby Marth. By the time Ghorr had assembled a
force strong enough to brave that lyrinx-infested place, Flydd
was gone again. Subsequently the news came that his ship
had been lost and Flydd drowned. Ghorr refused to believe it
and ordered a search of the entire Karama Malama, by ship
and air-floater.

Three air-floaters, and a fleet of commandeered ships,
criss-crossed the Sea of Mists for days until she found him

again, but before Flydd could be taken he was rescued by a stolen air-floater in which Ullii recognised the knots of Fyn-Mah and Irisis. They flew out of range and, though Ullii lost the individuals, she was able to track the air-floater's crystals into Meldorin before they vanished yet again.

Ghorr held a furious conference with his fellow scrutators before heading to Lybing, the capital of wealthy Borgistry, in his remaining air-floater. There a number of the scrutators disembarked to continue prosecuting the western war. Ghorr's air-floater took to the air again, heading north across the Great Chain of Lakes, then east past the Ramparts of Tacnah, forbidding gateway to the Great Mountains. The country began to make distinctive patterns in Ullii's lattice, for they were reversing the route by which she'd come west with Flydd and Irisis last spring. Dread grew in her as she recognised their destination. They were heading for the scrutators' hidden bastion of Nennifer, between the Great Mountains and the arid depressions that lay to the north.

Nennifer, the most frightening place in all Lauralin, appeared before them. It lay on a narrow rim of plateau with the mountains rearing up, thousands of spans high, to the east, west and south. The northern side of Nennifer was truncated by a monumental cliff, a thousand spans high, at the base of which lay an oval of sunken land, the Desolation Sink, as desiccated and lifeless as the Dry Sea itself.

'Why are we going to Nennifer?' she whispered. The very stones it was built from were imbued with the odour of the scrutators, and it was full of wicked, cruel people.

Ghorr gave his vulpine, snaggle-toothed smile. 'I have plans.'

'Nish and Flydd are gone,' said Ullii. She no longer knew what to do about them.

'They killed your brother and must be punished. You'll find them, Ullii, and we'll do the rest. Nennifer is where we design the weapons of tomorrow. Two hundred and twenty-three mancers work night and day, utterly devoted to inventing new devices of terror. Four hundred and seventy artisans make controllers for these weapons, and find ways to draw on the fields ever more efficiently. A thousand artificers, and three thousand smiths and other workers, build and test these devices. Five hundred and thirty-five draughters create the plans and patterns that will be used by our manufactories, across the breadth of Santhenar, to make innumerable copies. We have made many breakthroughs since you left us so . . . precipitously.' Ghorr chuckled at his meagre wit. Ullii and Irisis had escaped through a tunnel that discharged over the precipice into the Desolation Sink.

'Our workers are already designing the mighty craft that will take us back to Meldorin,' he went on, 'in a force so powerful that the lyrinx will flee in terror. Then you will find our enemies again, Ullii, wherever they've hidden. We'll take them with overwhelming force and destroy this burr in my side for good.

'In the meantime,' he continued, 'there's another way for you to help me.'

They were alone in his room. Ullii felt trapped in every possible way. Why had she listened to the voices? Why had she imagined she could use this monster to gain her revenge? She was not strong or clever, but weak and insignificant. All she'd done was put herself back in prison, and this time she had no friends to take care of her.

'Yes?' she whispered, for even had she the strongest will in the world, the bracelet on her wrist would not allow her to say no.

'Tell me how you magicked Irisis out of her cell last spring, without opening the lock or setting off my alarm. And how you translated Flydd's air-floater, in an instant, from a thousand spans above Nennifer to the end of the tunnel where you and Irisis were hiding.'

That had been her own precious little secret that not even Flydd had understood. Her lattice was her own creation, the world she retreated to when the physical world failed her. It was the one place no one else could go. Was even that to be taken from her?

'Don't know!' she said mulishly, keeping her eyes firmly on the floor.

His hand went under her chin, jerking her upright. He looked like a mature, handsome man but up close his skin was shiny and pinkly smooth, like baby skin on top of scar tissue. The feel of it, the softness clinging to those underlying ropy ridges of flesh, made her shudder with disgust. He tried to appear in his prime but Ullii's lattice told her what lay beneath the surface. He was old and rotten inside.

'Don't play games, Ullii. Do you want me as a friend, or as an enemy? It would not be wise to incur my enmity.'

She had often had this nightmare, after the first visit to Nennifer, and still she'd given herself up to Ghorr. Why, why had she put on the bracelet? Why hadn't she tested it first? Because it had been so cunningly designed to trap her that it did not even show in her lattice. The scrutators were too clever for her, as they had been too clever for Myllii.

'I have cunning mancers here, Seeker,' he resumed when she did not reply. 'Men and women who know how the mind works, even a mind as special as yours. And they know how to break it! They can go deep into your mind, Ullii. They can learn everything about you. They can make lattices of their own – *or take yours from you.*'

'Make another one,' she muttered, trying to look away. Though she tried to deny it, her greatest fear was losing her precious lattice and being unable to make another.

'They won't let you. So, Ullii, are you going to tell me how you managed it? How did you free Irisis?'

If she told him, surely he would leave her alone. 'I held the magicked lock in place and turned the lattice around it,' she said simply.

He stared at her. 'That's nonsense.' But, after chewing over it for a minute, he reconsidered. 'You *turned* the lattice? Did you translate the air-floater the same way?'

'No. I just moved its knot, and Xervish's, in my lattice.'

'Astounding! If I hadn't seen it happen I would not have believed it. You can't tell me any more, can you? You simply don't know what you did. But I'll have the secret out of you, and then there won't be anything I can't do.'

His eyes dissected her, then he swept out. And Ullii knew he *would* get the secret out of her, if he had to take her apart to do so. He was the most evil man in the world. Worse than Flydd. worse than Nish. And she was going to find them for him, so he could destroy them. She could not do otherwise – there was no way she could fight Ghorr.

And once she did find them, it would be her turn to suffer.

FORTY-SEVEN

Dirty, ragged and weary to the point of exhaustion, Tiaan approached the hidden city of Tirthrax. Three weeks had passed since her escape from the Aachim nets on the shore of the Sea of Thurkad. She had no idea why she'd come back, only that there had been nowhere else to go. But surely, after the crimes she'd committed, Malien would turn her over to the Aachim. Vithis could be here already.

She was so overcome by guilt that Tiaan gave only passing thought to her reason for fleeing Tirthrax previously – the amplimet's communication with the great node here, and the thawing of the perilous Well of Echoes, which had been frozen in place long ago. Despite her fears, the amplimet had given her no trouble on her long journey. It was hardly glowing now, and did not change as she neared Tirthrax. She wondered if it wanted to come back. Or if she'd exhausted it.

It was a hard climb up the slopes of the mountain, and many times Tiaan thought she would have to complete it on foot, for the construct was now a battered, limping thing. Each morning, when she unlocked the hatch and set off again, it was slower and more erratic. There was any amount of power this close to Tirthrax, far more than the amplimet could draw, but the construct could no longer use it.

Yet, despite everything, she'd made it. She crept up the ragged track, carved out by the great glacier, to the lip of the broken hole in the side of the mountain. It looked the same as when she'd left here at the beginning of spring. Tiaan stopped outside. Tirthrax was a place of bitter memories. Here, little Haani had died and her body had been sent to the Well. Here,

Tiaan had made the fateful gate. Here, Minis had rejected her.

That's all in the past, she told herself. Go on. She inched the construct up and over the top. The vast cavern, just part of one level of the grand city, yawned before her. Tiaan stopped abruptly.

Malien stood in the middle of that open space, arms folded across her chest, watching her with those cool green eyes. Though an old woman, Malien was as strong as anyone Tiaan had ever met. She was kindly by nature, yet could be hard as stone when she had to be. How would Malien treat her now?

'I've been expecting you,' Malien said evenly. 'Take the construct down to the very end of this level and leave it there.'

Tiaan did so. Whatever Malien ordered, she would do. Whatever punishment Malien imposed, she would suffer it without complaint, though it could not make up for the harm she'd done Minis, or Malien's own Clan Elienor.

She stopped near a spiralling staircase, withdrew the amplimet and climbed down. Her breath steamed in the frigid air and she felt a trifle light-headed. The city was high up and the air thin.

Malien indicated a small table to one side, set with a cloth, two plates, knives and forks. A round loaf, freshly baked, sat on a wooden carving board. A variety of meats, cheeses and pre-served vegetables had been arranged on a platter. 'Sit down.'

Tiaan sat. Malien carved slices of bread, sprinkled them with golden oil from a glass jug, and handed the platter to Tiaan. She took two slices, Malien one. Tiaan selected a fra-grant cheese. Malien poured wine into silver goblets, handing one to her. They ate.

'Why have you come back?' said Malien when Tiaan's plate was empty. Her voice was without expression. Tiaan could not tell if she was pleased, indifferent or enraged.

'I had nowhere else to go. And you said – you once said to call on you, if I needed help.' Tiaan's palms were sweaty.

Malien inclined her head in acknowledgment. She regarded Tiaan steadily. 'Your back is better, I see.'

'You heard about that?'

'Urien sent messengers here. They told me you'd broken it, though that doesn't seem to be the truth.'

She thinks I'm a liar. 'It was the truth. I broke my back when the amplimet made the thapter crash near Nyriandiol, but in Snizort the lyrinx flesh-formed it together.' Tiaan shivered at that memory.

'Why would they do that?' Malien asked.

'They were using me in a patterner, to pattern a great torgnadr, or node-drainer. My affliction hindered the patterning, so they fixed it.'

'I see.'

'You can look if you like,' Tiaan said hastily. 'The scars are still there.'

'I can tell truth from lies, Tiaan. How is it now?'

'It still troubles me, especially at the end of a long day.'

'But better than the alternative, I dare say,' Malien said with a wintry smile.

Tiaan did not need to reply. She would never forget those months of paralysed helplessness in Nyriandiol and Snizort. 'You look different, Malien.'

'How so?'

'Not so – younger,' she corrected hastily. 'There seems a little more red in your hair, and your face isn't as lined . . .'

Malien picked up the metal platter, brushed away the crumbs and examined her face in it. 'I was just serving out my time when you first came here, but I have a purpose now. That can rejuvenate us, for a little while.'

'What purpose?' Tiaan said curiously.

'Keeping you out of trouble, for one thing.' Malien changed the subject. 'You escaped from Vithis?'

'I had no choice. When Urien's messengers returned from speaking to you, he would have had me killed.'

Malien laid down her slice of bread. 'Why do you think that?'

'To prevent me telling anyone else about the secret of flight.'

'But he doesn't have the secret. No one knows, save you and me.'

Tiaan's mouth fell open, 'But surely . . .? You did not tell them?'

'Why should I?'

'They are Aachim.'

'We were sundered from them thousands of years ago, and no matter how we may yearn to go back, Santhenar is our home now. We are our own people, Tiaan. We broke the clans in ages past and will never return to that futile struggle for supremacy. Besides, our Histories tell us to beware of Inthis First Clan, and especially of men like Vithis. He sounds too much like Tensor, and Pitlis before him, for my liking. Both were great men, but also great in folly that brought ruin upon our kind. I would never put such a treasure into his hands.'

'He may be on his way here now. I . . . I hurt Minis during my escape – I may have killed him. I dared not stop to find out. And others certainly died. And then . . .' Tiaan felt so ashamed that she could not meet Malien's eye. She'd taken the easy way out and regretted every moment since.

'Yes?' Malien said mildly.

'The people of Clan Elienor were good to me while I was under their guard. And I escaped, knowing they would be punished severely.'

'Was your parole asked for, or given?'

'No.'

'Then your conscience is clear. Indeed, after they get over their initial dismay, Clan Elienor may feel a certain admiration for you, for outwitting them.'

'But Minis . . .'

Malien sighed. 'Disaster follows you everywhere you go, and that's something I must think about. You'd better tell me about it. Start from the day you left here.'

That took all afternoon, several pots of tea, another meal and, late that night, a tot or two of liqueur from Malien's private stock. At the end of it, she said, 'For such a gentle young woman, you certainly have a talent for mayhem.'

'If Vithis had not held me against my will . . . If he hadn't been planning to—'

'You don't need to explain.' Malien leaned back, pressing her fingers against her lips.

'There's one more thing.'

'Go on.'

'I did a foolish thing, Malien. Minis swore on the ring I made him – this ring – that he would do everything in his power to save me. And . . .'

'What?'

'I didn't believe him. He's so weak. I tried to reinforce his vow for him. I – I swore by the amplimet—' Malien started. 'I swore by the amplimet that if he failed me, he'd rue it all his remaining days.'

'That was . . . not wise, Tiaan.'

Tiaan could see that she was disturbed. 'And surely, if he's alive, he does rue it.'

'He may. So Vithis will track the amplimet and eventually discover that you came here. I won't be able to hold him back.'

'I'd better get going,' said Tiaan. 'I was expecting that. And, of course, the Well of Echoes—'

'It's stable now. I had a painful struggle after you left, before I tamed it, and more than once I thought it was going to defeat me. But what the amplimet did once, it may do again, and more quickly. It may have grown stronger too. Tell me, did it communicate with any other nodes?'

'Yes, at Nyriandiol and Snizort. But not since the Snizort node exploded.'

'I heard about that,' said Malien, shaking her head. 'Was it a unique problem with that node, or might all nodes be at risk? I must take advice on the matter.'

'Is it safe for me to stay till the morning?' Tiaan said wistfully. 'I so long to sleep in a bed and not be afraid of what's out in the dark, hunting me. I've not felt secure since I left here.'

'You may sleep in perfect ease. In the morning we'll leave Tirthrax for somewhere safer.'

'You're coming with me?' Tiaan could not keep the joy out of her voice.

'Someone has to look after you,' Malien said dryly. 'Go up.

Your old room is ready and I've laid out clean clothes for you.'

'How did you know I was coming?'

'Vithis sent a skeet, ordering me to hold you if you came back. And indeed, where else could you have gone?'

'Where are we going?'

'To my own people, though I'm uncertain of the welcome either you or I will get there. Bathe and rest in security. I'll keep watch, if that comforts you. We're going to Stassor in the morning.'

Tiaan took out the amplimet, the other crystal, the helmet and the tesseract, and did as she was bade.

Malien woke Tiaan only minutes before dawn. To Tiaan's surprise, she was ushered into a different construct, which Malien had repaired during Tiaan's absence. Tiaan reached for the controls, discovered they were completely unfamiliar, and drew back. Malien motioned Tiaan into the seat beside her, took hold of a padded yoke and the machine lifted smoothly into the air.

'It flies!' Tiaan exclaimed.

'What we did together last winter rekindled my longstanding interest in the secret of flight. I feel quite rejuvenated.'

'Where did you find another amplimet?'

'I didn't. I use the Art in an entirely different way, if you recall. I've done so all my life. I found my own path to controlling a thapter.'

Tiaan was stunned. 'How long have you had this one working?'

'Three months, more or less, though I've tinkered with it nearly every day, improving it in various ways. Learning how to make your thapter fly was the hard part. Once we'd discovered that secret, making another was easy.'

'You once said you only had a minor talent for such work.'

'I dissembled. I've a very considerable talent, although for most of my life I've avoided using it.'

'Why, Malien?'

'You don't know your Histories well, do you?'

'Not of your time.'

'When I was young . . . well, younger, at any rate, I was partner to Tensor, a brilliant man but one whose obsession led the world to the abyss. The war, and the invasion by the lyrinx that led to it, arose out of his folly. Because he was obsessed with devices, I swore not to use my talent, and for more than two hundred years I have not.'

'And now?'

'Times change, and so must we, to suit them. Not using my talent for the cause I believe in would be just as great a folly.'

'Does Urien know about your thapter?'

'No. I had warning of her messengers, so I made sure it looked innocuous. Even had they gone inside, they could not have flown it. It's designed to be controlled by my mind, and mine alone.'

'What if I were to put in my amplimet?' said Tiaan forlornly. She'd thought, after coming to Tirthrax, that she might obtain another set of carbon whiskers and diamond crystals, and make her construct fly.

'I wouldn't want to risk my life that way. Should it become necessary, I'll make changes so you can fly it.'

Passing through the entrance, which was hung with blue icicles as long as Tiaan was tall, Malien turned the thapter over the great Tirthrax glacier and followed it, winding up into the high mountains, until the air grew so thin that Tiaan's every breath was an effort. Malien did not seem to be troubled, but she had lived in the mountains all her life. It grew bitterly cold, even with the hatch closed.

'Go below,' the Aachim said. 'Pull out the bunk at the rear. It's warmer there.'

Tiaan did so. It lay directly above the mechanism that drove the thapter but, even so, wrapped in blankets, Tiaan was cold. She lay down and closed her eyes, fretting. All the Tirthrax Aachim had gone to Stassor the year before last, to a great meeting about the war. Only Malien had remained in Tirthrax. Though she was venerated as a hero from the

Histories, her own people did not trust her. She had not been welcome at their meet, so how could Tiaan be?

Stassor lay within the great mountain chain that ran down the eastern side of Lauralin, from beyond Tiksi in the south, all the way to the north-easternmost tip of the continent at Taranta. In a straight line, Stassor was about two hundred and forty leagues from Tirthrax, but they could not travel in a straight line.

First they had to cross the Great Mountains, which were so high that not even Malien could breathe at their summits. She had to travel a winding course along glacier-filled valleys, with bare ridges as sharp as flakes of flint towering above them on either side, and then across the high plateau, the most inhospitable environment in the world. That rugged land was perpetually sheathed in ice. Nothing grew there. Nothing could have lived there, unless it had crept out of the void through some dark aperture when the Way between the Worlds was open, and delved deep into the underlying rock to suck at the warmth, and brood.

Malien dawdled, as if no more anxious to reach Stassor than Tiaan was. She ventured up every icy valley to its vantage point, sometimes only travelling for an hour or two before stopping to spend the rest of the day at some spectacular lookout, wrapped in her blankets and silently taking in the scene. It felt like a farewell journey, a final visit to everything that was beautiful and unspoiled.

The trip took twenty-one days, though only after fifteen had passed did Tiaan shake free from the helpless terror that had controlled her life since Gilhaelith had been taken from Booreah Ngurle many months ago. For the first time she felt safe. Who would not, with Malien looking after them? No one could have tracked them across this wasteland. No construct could cross the Great Mountains. They were impassable on foot, by any land conveyance and even by air-floaters, since the lowest passes were higher than such machines could rise.

Malien did not question Tiaan about the intervening

months, though she did show an unexpected interest in Gilhaelith. 'Where did he come from, do you think?'

'Somewhere on Meldorin. He would not talk about his past, more than I've told you.'

'An interesting man,' said Malien. 'And not entirely old human, surely. I wonder what his lineage is?'

'What do you mean?' said Tiaan.

'To have lived so long, surely he must have blood of the longer-lived species in him – Aachim or Faellem, or even Charon.'

Tiaan had not thought about that. 'But mancers can lengthen their own lives.'

'More lose their lives in the attempt than survive it, so it's attempted less often than you might imagine. And even at its best it rarely returns them to their youth. A hale middle age is the most that can be expected. For the unfortunate, however, it means death, or worse.'

'What could be worse?'

'Ending up as a monstrosity with your body parts in the wrong places, begging for release and being unable to find it.'

'Well, Gilhaelith's dead, so it doesn't matter,' said Tiaan after a long silence. He was another painful memory. It reminded her of the one man who hadn't let her down: Merryl, last seen trudging around the side of the hill near Snizort. Had he just exchanged one form of slavery for another?

'How do you know?' said Malien.

Tiaan came back to the present. 'I don't suppose I do . . .'

'The matriarch of Snizort went to great lengths to abduct Gilhaelith. Surely, when she fled the tar pits, she took him with her.'

'And yet they left me behind.'

'That could have been confusion when Snizort was attacked.'

'Or because the torgnadrs they patterned on me turned out to be useless!'

FORTY-EIGHT

Tiaan did not know what to expect of Stassor, except that it would be striking, beautiful and different, for each of the Aachim cities was unique. Tirthrax, carved out of the mountain's heart, bore no resemblance to the towers, pavilions and kidney-shaped dwellings she had seen in paintings of Aachan. Different again was Shazmak, their abandoned city on an island in the middle of the gorge of the River Garr, in the mountains of Meldorin. Tiaan had seen images of it in Tirthrax. Shazmak was a place of breathtakingly slender towers and pinnacles connected by swooping and coiled aerial walkways that looked as though they were made of glass. The city appeared so delicate that it might have been broken by a tap with a hammer, yet it had endured the galoo for a thousand years. And still, in the end, it proved no match for treachery. The city's betrayer had been one of its own.

She was thinking these gloomy thoughts as they descended a long black slope streaked with ice, at the base of which lay an ice-filled basin bounded by crevasses. A glacier flowed out of its downhill lip. In the distance, partly concealed by a razor-topped ridge, Tiaan saw an isolated steep-sided mountain with four individual peaks, inside which nestled a field of ice. She surreptitiously checked the amplimet but it wasn't glowing at all. That didn't comfort her. Tiaan was beginning to feel that it was waiting for something; lurking; even preying.

As they approached the mountain with four peaks, Tiaan realised that the material between them was not ice at all, rather a vast silvery cube that reflected first one peak and then another, so that the whole top of the mountain appeared to shift before their eyes.

'Behold Stassor,' said Malien. 'The greatest of our cities, now.'

'It's nothing like I expected,' Tiaan murmured. 'It's so plain, so simple! Do the Aachim no longer care about their art and craft? In Tirthrax, every surface was decorated, every space shaped to perfection.'

'Time moves on and so must we. We yearn for simplicity now. Stassor is a new city built on the foundations of the old, but it has a beauty of its own. You'll see.'

'Tirthrax was hidden inside a mountain, yet Stassor stands on the highest peak around, for all the world to see. Do your people feel more secure these days?'

'Who could threaten us here? Not even a construct could climb these rugged passes, and what army could lay siege to Stassor? This entire land,' said Malien, a sweep of her arm indicating the white-tipped ranges on every side, 'is our land, and no one may cross its borders without our knowing.

'Besides, we no longer care to hide from the world. For thousands of years we looked back to Aachan, but our future is bound to Santhenar now. From the breaking of the Forbidding, two centuries ago, we began to take down old Stassor and build it anew, to celebrate our coming out. Do you not see its beauty now?'

The thapter had curved across a vast valley steeped in snow and up the other side, towards the four-peaked mountain. Tiaan caught her breath. With every movement the ice-coloured cube shimmered with colour – now like oil on water, now like the iridescence of a beetle's wing-case, now like the light of the sun fading from the sky. There were colours and patterns within its depths, too, and they resembled the shifting lines of sand on a wave-swept beach, or the flickering flames of a camp fire, or the play of colours in precious opal.

The thapter lifted sharply on an updraught. Tiaan's stomach lurched but Malien steadied the machine expertly and directed it towards the base of the great building, where a pattern of smaller cubes appeared to indicate an entrance.

She brought the thapter to ground on a paved rectangle outside the smaller cubes. 'Best if we show ourselves as friendly,' said Malien. 'My people have not seen a flying machine before. At least, not since Rulke was slain, and his was a weapon of war. Tiaan, I ask only one thing – that you say nothing about my part in the creation of this thapter.'

'Of course,' said Tiaan, 'but why?'

'My people may well suspect that I made it, but it would be better if they did not know. That way—' She broke off as shadows appeared behind the smaller cubes. 'Later.'

Tiaan reached for the pack containing the amplimet and her other possessions. 'Leave everything,' said Malien. 'They will be brought, after inspection.'

Were the Aachim just being careful or were they, for all their brilliance, insecure? Tiaan was reluctant to leave anything behind, least of all the perilous amplimet, but there was no alternative. She climbed down onto the platform, which was made of compressed ice. It was bitterly, bone-achingly cold outside, far worse than Tirthrax, and the air so thin that just placing one foot in front of another was exhausting.

As they approached the entrance, a dark line divided it vertically into two halves, which separated into four individual cubes on either side, and each of those into four more, a pattern which Malien described as cubular. The myriad glassy cubes seemed to float through the air, leaving an opening which exhaled a breath of warmth. Tiny crystals of ice whirled and tumbled and twinkled in the sunlight. Gilhaelith would have been enchanted, Tiaan thought. The tetrarch had an obsession with numbers.

'Come,' said Malien, and they entered.

'I'm afraid.'

'Just so Karan and Llian must have felt as they entered the forbidden city of Shazmak. But they were met there by Rael, my son, and treated with all the hospitality due to visitors, even unwelcome ones such as I.'

'What happened to him?' asked Tiaan, not recalling that part of the tale.

'Alas, he drowned, nobly helping Karan and Llian to escape their fate. I still think about him every day. *You* need have no fear, Tiaan.' Her eyes glittered and she turned away.

'I would like to talk to you about that tale, sometime,' said Tiaan.

'I would be happy to. Have you read it?'

'The original is a forbidden book. There is a new *Tale of the Mirror*, but it was rewritten by the scrutators before my birth.'

Malien stopped in mid-step. '*Rewritten*? The greatest of the Great Tales retold by a gaggle of spies and torturers? How did this come about?'

'I don't know.'

'Llian of Chanthed, who wrote the Great Tale, must lie uneasy in his grave,' said Malien.

'He's now known as Llian the Liar, the chronicler who debauched the Histories.'

'The Histories have indeed been debauched,' Malien said coldly. 'We must speak further about this. Ah, our hosts are coming.'

'Did you know Llian?' said Tiaan.

'As well as I knew any human man! The Histories were his life and his world. Nothing could have compelled him to tell them falsely.'

'But . . .'

'Later.'

Malien strode forward, holding out her hand to a stocky man of middle years, whose black hair was marked by twin streaks of white sweeping back over his ears. Half a dozen other Aachim stood behind him, three men and three women, all dressed in robes that reflected the light like metallic silk.

'Harjax,' Malien said cheerfully. 'I heard of your elevation. You will make a fine autarch.'

He took her hand, without enthusiasm. 'Thank you, Matah Malien. Why have you come, and how did you get here?'

'Come, Harjax, you've been observing us for ages. Tiaan Liise-Mar here, an artisan from the other side of the world, has uncovered the secret of flight which has eluded all the mancers of this world, and Aachan, since the death of Rulke. In a short time she converted this construct, abandoned by Vithis in Tirthrax, into a machine that flies.'

'She may have assisted,' Harjax said, 'but the mind behind this discovery was yours, Matah, as your hand was at the controls when it set down. What are you up to?'

'The secret of flight will benefit us all, Harjax.'

'Have you brought this thapter as a gift, then?'

'I had in mind to see what progress you'd made before—'

'You think you know better than everyone else,' he said with a sorrowful air, though it seemed just a veneer of manners or custom. These Aachim were angry folk. 'You show us no more loyalty than you did in the past.'

'Stassor is more magnificent than ever,' she observed calmly. 'You've done well for yourselves, without me, as you've made clear many times.'

'For good reason. You don't cleave to your own, Malien.'

'I *am* Matah,' she reminded him, 'an honour specifically created to free the recipient from such burdens, and permit her to think outside the cube, as it were. Anyway, flight has been discovered, for good or for ill, and you must plan what to do with it.' She glanced at Tiaan. 'Must we quarrel in the yard, forgetting all courtesy to our guest, or will you offer Tiaan her due?'

All this time, the Aachim had given Tiaan not a single glance, but now he turned dark eyes on her, of such singular penetration that Tiaan could not meet his gaze.

'The last time an outsider was admitted to our precincts, it brought about the downfall of a city – beloved Shazmak.'

'And the death of my son,' Malien said pointedly. 'He's gone forever, yet Shazmak endures. We can go back if we choose.'

'To a land infested with lyrinx!'

'They cannot thrive in the high mountains. They are no threat to us, now we have the secret of flight.'

'But they *are* a threat to the order of this world and we must consider what to do about it. Come inside.'

They followed the seven Aachim down a broad hall into a

rectangular room that appeared to be made of glass, though unlike any glass Tiaan had ever seen. The walls glowed like oiled opal, the patterns forever changing.

'The Council of Stassor was called the year before last,' said Malien. 'What choices have you made?'

'The situation changes rapidly,' Harjax said, uncomfortable with her directness.

'Meaning you cannot come to a decision. I'm glad you didn't invite me. I could have died of old age before you did anything.'

Harjax grimaced, for to speak so plainly bordered on insult. He indicated a small table around which were distributed a number of oddly shaped chairs, each like a bean opened in the middle and the ends folded out. They sat and refreshments were brought in. Tiaan's chair proved surprisingly comfortable. She took nothing to eat, feeling out of place and unwelcome, but sipped at a mug of clear liquid as thin and clear as water, though more refreshing.

'But when we do reach our decision,' said Harjax, 'it will be the right one. Look what happened before, when we allowed unfettered power to a leader who was not worthy of it.'

'Tensor was a fool, and no one knows that better than I,' said Malien, leaning back. 'I rue every hour that I let him have his way. But that's ancient history. The world that existed when you began your council last year has been forever altered. Should you ever reach your *right decision*, it will already be irrelevant. And our fellow Aachim, from Aachan—'

'We've met with Vithis's emissaries,' said Harjax. 'We found much to talk about. Much to agree upon.'

'I found much to fear and more to dread,' said Malien. 'Not least the way they abused Tiaan. They forced her to use the amplimet all day and every day for weeks.'

Harjax squirmed in his seat. 'To what purpose?'

'To save their fleet of constructs, stalled by the destruction of the node.'

'A justifiable end, I would say. And after all,' he gave Tiaan a sideways glance, 'it's not as though she's . . .'

'*One of us!* Have the decency to speak your prejudice plainly.'

'It's not as if old humans are our equals.'

'In some respects they're our superiors, but that's not the point. We're all human.'

'That's heresy!'

'And the cause of all our problems. I've spent my life trying to bring the peoples of this world together, and little has come of it.'

'Aye, and at the expense of your own kind,' growled Harjax. 'You might have taken back the Mirror of Aachan, yet you did not. You made alliance with old humans, forfeiting our own interests. And look what that led to.'

Malien looked pointedly around the magnificent room. 'Peace and prosperity for us, while old humans are being crushed on the anvil of war.'

'They are not our kind, Matah.'

'We sprang from them in the distant past.'

'That's a lie!' he cried, and the polite veneer was stripped away. 'Old humans are degenerate, not ancestral. Vithis's Aachim are our kind and we must support them!'

'They are the *old* kind, full of hate, prejudice and rivalry.' Malien spoke more reasonably than before, as if to throw up the contrast between them. 'They still adhere to *clans*, Harjax, and they see themselves as better than us. They come to take, not to share. To rule, not to meet as equals. They will grind old humans into the muck and then . . .'

'Yes?' he said coldly.

'We'll be next. We abandoned the clans before the Clysm, and we're the better for it. Vithis will bring back rivalry and revenge. He wants to make us *tribes* again, with himself as the chief. He's a barbarian dressed up as a civilised man.'

'I agree,' said an aged man who hitherto had done nothing but sip from a greatly elongated mug. 'Vithis is like Tensor reincarnated, only without the nobility. These Aachim are almost as primitive as old humans. We should be leading them.'

'Thus, the nub of our problem.' The new speaker was a

man who seemed little older than Tiaan herself, a dark, handsome fellow with a square jaw and a nose like the prow of a ship. 'We cannot agree on anything. We'll still be arguing when the last old human is eaten. Only when it is too late will we understand what we have lost. Old humans have made this world safe for us, and we owe them our support.'

'Thank you, Bilfis. What would *you* do, Sulleye?' said Malien to the smallest of the women beside her.

'Old humans have wrought havoc on this world. To build their clankers, and the other powered devices they rely on utterly, they've razed mountains and fed whole forests into their reeking furnaces. These constructs reduce us to their level. They're an abomination we will long regret. We must abandon all such devices, including the nodes, and go back to the ways of the past.'

'How would we maintain Stassor, or any of our cities, without the Art?' said Harjax.

'By intelligence and hard work,' she snapped.

'The lyrinx would overrun this world all the sooner.'

'They rely on the Art more than you think,' said Bilfis. 'Without it they cannot fly, in which case their wings are a hindrance rather than an advantage.'

'Nor could they flesh-form,' said Tiaan.

Every Aachim stared at her, as if a servant had just spoken up in a king's council.

'Just so,' said Malien, smiling at their discomfiture. 'Neither could they use their spying devices. All they would have is their strength and native wit, which is less advantage than you might suppose, without a civilisation to support it.'

Harjax jerked his head at an aide, who took Tiaan by the elbow. 'Would you come with me, please?'

Tiaan shot up in her chair, thinking they meant to do her mischief, but Malien laid a hand on hers. 'Don't be afraid, Tiaan. My people only wish to discuss matters privately. You won't be harmed.'

Tiaan went with the aide, uneasily. Though she trusted Malien, she'd also heard such assurances before.

FORTY-NINE

Nish was standing by the air-floater early the following morning, when Yggur appeared at the front doors. 'Come with me, Cryl-Nish.' He strode across the yard.

Nish had to trot to catch up to him, which he found undignified. He followed the mancer up a set of stone stairs onto the outer wall, which was gravelled and as wide as a road, and down to a corner with a stone guard post, not presently manned, though Nish had seen guards there yesterday.

Yggur turned to face him. 'Tell me about these *tears* your father found.'

That endless night, and the hideous scene in Jal-Nish's tent, came crashing back as vividly as if Nish were there still. It unreeled from beginning to end and he could not stop it: Jal-Nish without the mask, the rage against the world. His father thrusting Nish's hands into the box, *inside the tears*, and that extra dimension it had temporarily brought to his sight, his other senses, even his emotions. And finally, Jal-Nish's alchymical compulsion.

Nish opened his mouth but found himself too short of breath to speak. He swayed on his feet, even now feeling the urge to go to his father. The compulsion was painfully strong.

Yggur reached out and steadied him. 'What secret are you hiding for your master?'

The compulsion faded. 'I have no master,' Nish said shakily.

'Another one!' Yggur gave a grim smile. 'It's no wonder the world falls into ruin.'

'I'm not hiding anything, surr. I—' Nish's knees buckled

and he slipped through the mancer's fingers, to lie sprawled on the floor.

Yggur crouched beside him. 'What is it, lad? I touched a spell of sorts just then, didn't I?'

'My father put it on me.'

'Why, Artificer? Here, let me help you up. Calm yourself – take your time.'

The memories, or the spell, faded. Nish explained about his part, and Irisis's, in condemning his father to life in a ruined body, and all the rest of it. 'Jal-Nish has hated Irisis ever since, and despised me, and I can't blame him. No man should have had to suffer what he's suffered. I should have let him die.'

'Sometimes there are no right choices,' said Yggur. 'What was it like, when he put your hands into the tears?'

'It's . . . impossible to describe. They were hot yet cold, hard yet yielding, metal yet liquid. They were far more than that, but I can't find the words for it. And then—'

'Yes?'

'Briefly, the touch of the tears heightened my senses. I think it was the tears, rather than the potion he forced me to drink. The moon became dazzlingly bright, and I could see through things that were solid. I saw the lyrinx twisted up and cramped into the rock pinnacles, stone-formed to ambush my father's army.'

'Briefly, you say?'

'By the following day it had faded, although the tears did change me.'

'In what way?'

'I—' Nish gave a shamefaced grimace. 'I used to be obsessed with myself; with achievement, success and being recognised for it. But after touching the tears, I saw things so much more clearly. I saw what the world would be like under tyrants like my father. What it *will* be like if the scrutators remain in power.'

'The tears did not change you in *that* way, lad,' Yggur said softly. 'You simply grew up.'

'I have to fight this tyranny, whatever it costs me, but I'm terribly, terribly afraid. I'm not a brave man, Lord Yggur.'

'Your companions tell a different story. About this spell – I wonder why it did not take?'

'Perhaps he'd not yet mastered the tears.'

'Let me see.' Yggur put his hands to Nish's temples and closed his eyes. 'Ah, I see it. It's made with a strange, alchymical kind of Art that I don't know much about.'

'It's still there?' cried Nish. 'Inside me?'

'Just a trace, fortunately. Had you not brought up the bulk of the potion, you'd have become his slave.'

Thanks to Xabbier's quick thinking. Nish wondered where he was now. 'Not for long. I'd have been killed with him.'

'But you weren't. And unless the spell is removed, a trace will remain there until you die.'

'But—' said Nish. 'What if someone else compels me?'

'They could not, unless they had the tears.'

That wasn't comforting. 'Can't you remove it?'

'Not without the tears.'

Day after day, Yggur sat at the big table in his workshop, reading or writing in his journals as though nothing had happened. Nish could see how frustrated the scrutator was. After five days of inaction, Flydd went to see Yggur, taking Irisis and Nish with him.

A map of the known world was spread out on the huge table and Yggur was measuring distances on it with a pair of black calipers. He did not look up.

'We've got to get moving,' Flydd said abruptly. 'The lyrinx mature quickly. If we don't strike them now, by spring they'll have another army and they'll be unstoppable.'

'I have no grievance with the lyrinx,' said Yggur, making a note in his journal.

'But you agreed to help us,' Flydd spluttered.

'I agreed to give you a refuge for a few days, Scrutator. That doesn't make us bedfellows.'

'But I thought—'

'You aroused my curiosity about the Numinator and the tears, but what I'm doing about that is my own affair. I'm not going to fight your wars for you.'

'You're up to something!' Flydd said furiously. To have power, as Yggur undoubtedly did, and not want to use it, was incomprehensible.

Yggur simply raised his hands in the air. 'Then leave. I didn't ask you to come here, consuming my supplies and disturbing my peace.'

'You don't care about the fate of your own kind.'

'If I were threatened by the lyrinx, would you have come to my aid?'

'That's different,' said Flydd.

'I see. Why don't you go to the Aachim?'

'Our alliance was not a fruitful one,' Flydd said uncomfortably.

'Meaning you've made enemies of your friends and now look to me to fix it for you.'

'Vithis is an unreasonable man, even by your standards,' snapped Flydd. 'Besides, he's withdrawn to the Foshorn, near the southern corner of the Dry Sea—'

'I know where the Foshorn is,' said Yggur. 'I've been there.'

'The Aachim have driven out the people that dwelt there and closed the borders. Vithis isn't going to help us.'

'Then you'll have to abandon Lauralin. Go north across the tropic ocean. You may find a haven in that hemisphere.'

'The lyrinx breed like maggots,' said Flydd. 'In a few generations they'd overrun Lauralin and come after us. Win or lose, the battle must be fought now.'

'You will lose,' said Yggur with such studied indifference that Nish wondered if he was testing their resolve before committing himself.

'When you're the last human left alive, you'll regret that you did nothing for your fellows.'

'I'm immune to emotional blackmail.' Nodding stiffly, Yggur went around the table and out.

'Arrogant swine!' said Flydd as they were walking back to

their rooms. 'To have such power, yet refuse to use it.'

'How do you know he still has power?' Nish wondered.

'I don't suppose I do,' Flydd said slowly. 'I just assumed . . . Perhaps I was wrong. Perhaps he hides here because his power is failing.'

'But he does live in harmony with the lyrinx,' said Irisis. 'Why should he turn on them on our say-so? It's up to us,' she sighed. 'I suppose it always was.'

'But what can we *do*?' cried Nish. 'We're exiles cowering in our hidey-hole a hundred leagues from Lauralin. We've got no army, no coin, just a handful of weapons and a decrepit airfloater. We've no friends, no influence, and face instant death if we return to Lauralin. How can we hope to overthrow the scrutators? How can we do anything at all?'

No one spoke. They seemed shocked by the outburst, though Nish had only put into words what they'd all been thinking: they were deluding themselves.

'I expected Yggur to take over,' said Flydd. 'I was steeling myself for a fight to maintain our objectives. The last thing I expected was a complete lack of interest.'

'Then we'll have to find a way to gain his support,' said Irisis.

Flydd went out, head bowed, looking very careworn.

For a long time after that, the scrutator did nothing but sit by the fire, reading Yggur's volumes of the Histories or, more often, just staring into the flames. The pain of his ancient torments troubled him more than usual, and Irisis often noted him sipping from a flask of poppy syrup, though not even that could bring him the oblivion he so desperately sought.

'It's been my life's work to protect the people and the civilisations of our world,' he said one bitter night. 'To stop – if not to reverse – the long decline that's been going on ever since the Forbidding. In that time we've had failure upon failure, defeat upon defeat, and I'm forced to the realisation that I simply can't do it. No one can reverse the damage caused by the reign of the scrutators. It's too late.'

'It's not like you to despair, Xervish,' said Irisis.

'It's the only thing left to do. Ah, but it's a tragedy. The loss of Thurkad, the destruction of the College of the Histories. A hundred cities are gone; whole nations and cultures have disappeared. The past was a glorious place, Irisis, where men and women were free. The scrutators have turned the present into a slave pen. What can the future hold but a slaughterhouse for us all, until humanity is no more?'

He began to weep, silently and terribly, and Irisis could not bear to see it.

Another week went by, more painful than the previous one. In Yggur's absence, for he kept to his rooms, they debated the problem over and again. Whatever scheme was proposed, and there were many, the group always reached the same conclusion: there was no way a handful of people, in hiding so far from Lauralin, could affect the war.

Irisis came back from a walk to Old Hripton, a fishing town a few leagues away along the bay, to find Flydd sitting on his bed, head in hands. She ducked out again before he could see her and went looking for Nish. Flydd had always been so strong, and had always known what to do. It hurt to see him laid so low.

'Where the masters fail,' Irisis said to Nish, 'the peasants must take charge. It's up to you and me, Nish.'

'I don't follow you.'

'Come outside, where we can talk.' She led him into a chilly corner of the yard. 'Do you get the impression that Yggur knows more than he's letting on?'

'It's just rivalry. No mancer can bear to be told what to do. And they've always got to go one better.'

'That's not what I meant. I think Yggur, despite his gruff manner, does feel some sympathy for our cause. But he's been burned in the past and that's why he's withdrawn.'

'Doesn't help us much,' said Nish glumly.

'He was one of the greatest mancers of all time.'

'A thousand years ago.'

'He played a great part in the *Tale of the Mirror*, too. We've got to convince him to help us.'

'Good luck!' said Nish.

'I've an idea. I'm going to see him.'

'What are you going to say?'

'I won't know until I say it.'

Nish followed her inside and down the corridor. She rapped on Yggur's door, which was firmly closed. There was no answer. She rapped louder.

'Go away!' he roared.

Irisis took hold of the handle. 'Coming?'

Nish, who was hanging back, shook his head. 'I've felt enough of the wrath of mancers for one lifetime. I'll see you later.'

'You coward,' she said amiably. She opened the door and slipped inside.

Yggur was down the far end, working at a bench littered with objects familiar and unfamiliar. 'Go away, I said.'

Irisis kept coming. 'I know you want to help us. You're a hard man, Yggur, but not a mean one. You'll happily turn the screws on Flydd, out of mancer's rivalry—'

'It's not rivalry, Irisis. I'm not that petty.' He smiled ruefully. 'Well, hardly ever. It's not the man, but his office. The Council is notoriously corrupt. I'm sorry, but I just can't bring myself to trust a scrutator.'

'He's not like them.'

'How do you know?'

'I'm a good judge of character—'

'Clouded by feelings for your lover.'

'He hasn't been my lover for months, but I admire him as a man and a friend. Trust me.'

'Hmn.'

'You're an honourable man, Yggur, and I don't believe you'd refuse us if you could help.'

'Don't you?' he said, trying to stare her down. She held his gaze, defiant as always. 'Remarkable. Very well – I'll share what I have with you.'

'May I call Xervish Flydd?'

'With you alone,' he growled. 'Come here. You understand devices. Tell me what you think of this.'

It looked like a glass onion the size of a grapefruit. She could see layer upon layer inside, each different, each made of glass etched or painted in colours and patterns, or bonded with geometric shapes in gold, silver and copper foil. A faint luminescence at the core was irregularly eclipsed as the layers revolved and rotated independently of one another.

'It's beautifully made,' said Irisis. 'I've never seen such craftsmanship. Where did you get it?'

'I've had it for hundreds of years, and before that it must have been through many hands. The man who . . . sold it to me claimed it was made by Golias the Mad, though I can't verify that.'

'Didn't Golias invent the farspeaker?' she asked.

Yggur gave her a keen glance. 'Indeed, though its secret died with him.'

She touched a finger to the glass. 'What does it do?'

'I haven't learned that, despite diligent study. I was hoping you might be able to help me.'

'Me? But I know little of the Art.' As Irisis picked up the sphere, the internal layers spun.

'I believe it requires a different kind of understanding – a capacity for thinking *across* the Arts, if you will.'

'I've heard Flydd talk about Golias's farspeaker,' said Irisis. 'Could it not speak from one side of the world to the other?'

'So the ancients have it, though all his devices failed on his death and no one has been able to reproduce them.'

Yggur took the globe from her hand, replacing it on the bench. 'Now *this is* entirely my own work.' Reaching up to a high shelf, he brought down an object even more incomprehensible than the first.

Made of metal, and rather heavy, it was shaped like a legless beetle the length of a man's finger. Its iridescent top was convex. Though flat underneath, it was so well made that the joins in the metal could scarcely be seen.

'What is it?' she said.

Yggur touched it at what, if it *had* been a beetle, would have been the rear. It emitted a high-pitched whistle and slowly rose off the table, to hover a hand-span above it.

'Just a toy.' They watched it rocking in the air for a moment, whereupon Yggur touched it in the same place and it sank down, rather more quickly, to thump into the surface. He was panting from the strain.

'You're trying to make a flying machine,' exclaimed Irisis.

He took a while to get his breath back. 'Not as a weapon of war, merely for the intellectual challenge. I saw Rulke's original construct. I studied it as closely as I could, from a distance, and I destroyed it. For two hundred and seven years I've been trying to recover his secret, and this is all I've achieved.'

'No one else did better, until the Aachim came.'

'And they made the real thing – eleven thousand constructs.'

'But they had the original to model it on,' said Irisis. 'At least, what was left of it. And they haven't made them fly, only hover. No one but Tiaan has done more.'

'Even so, I call this little thing a failure . . .'

'But?' said Irisis 'That's not the end of it, is it?'

He gnawed at his lower lip; then, as if reversing a long-held policy in a moment of weakness he was bound to regret, said: 'I've a mind to take a trip in your air-floater, to the battlefield at Snizort. Hundreds of wrecked constructs lie there, I'm told. No doubt they've been disabled, but I may learn a thing or two. Of course, I'll need a skilled artificer to go with me . . .'

He looked uncertain, as if not used to asking favours. The great mancer was vulnerable too. 'Will Nish come, do you think?'

'I'll make sure he does.'

'Tell him to bring his artificer's tools.'

'He has none. He escaped Snizort with just the rags on his back.'

Yggur frowned. 'Instruct him to go to my lower tool room and select what he needs. We may have to take a construct apart. What about you, Irisis?'

'I'll be there, if the scrutator will release me.'

'You said you had no master,' Yggur reminded her.

She turned away. 'I meant it in a different way.'

'Ah, how you use words.'

Flangers went with them too, and Inouye to pilot the air-floater. She was as meek and quiet as ever, though once or twice, when she moved the controller arm and the machine responded more precisely than before, Nish thought he detected the faintest of smiles. Yggur had worked his magic there as well, to Flydd's irritation. Flydd did not come. He had planned to refuse but Yggur hadn't invited him. The other passenger was Eiryn Muss, whom Flydd was sending back to Lauralin, where he could be useful.

'How long to Snizort, Inouye?' Yggur said as they floated up from the yard and turned south-east.

'Depends on the wind, surr. If it's strong behind us, we might be there in fifteen hours. If against us, it could take two days.'

He studied the sky. 'Hard to tell what it's like up there. There's not a cloud to be seen.'

The trip was uneventful, the winds light and variable but generally assisting them They flew all afternoon and most of the night, arriving over the battlefield around five in the morning. Dawn was still some way off and there was no moon; the stars barely illuminated the hummocky ground.

'The smell . . .' said Inouye faintly.

Eleven weeks had gone by, and the maggots and scavengers had reduced the unburnt bodies to bone, sinew and hide, yet still the battlefield stank of its dead. The Aachim had buried their dead deep, but the other remains lay where they'd fallen. The stench brought it all back to Nish: the knee-deep, bloody mud, the futility of war. He put his hands over his nose and breathed shallowly. It helped, if only a little.

Yggur laid one big hand on his shoulder. 'The sooner we begin, the sooner we can leave this place.' He checked something concealed in his fingers. 'Settle down over there, Inouye, by those pointed rocks. Stay at your post while we're gone; you never know what we may encounter here. Flangers, keep the watch. Cryl-Nish and Irisis, bring your tools.' He shrugged a pack onto his back.

The air-floater set down, the crusted ground crunching under the keel. Eiryn Muss slipped between the ropes and was gone without a goodbye. They followed Yggur over the side. An early autumn frost crackled underfoot. He moved purposefully towards a hump about fifty paces distant, which turned out to be a wrecked clanker. The oily smell reminded Nish of his time as an artificer.

The mancer muttered to himself and a light glowed in his hand. He strode off to another hump. This one was a construct, tilted on its side with solidified mud holding it in place.

'Keep watch,' said Yggur curtly.

For what? Nish thought. A thousand lyrinx could be out there and we wouldn't see them.

Yggur made ghost fire in his palm and held it up to the base of the construct while he walked around the machine. 'It's so like the original. Why, I wonder?'

'Perhaps they felt it was perfect as it was,' said Irisis.

"The Aachim's work is their art and they seldom make two objects exactly the same way. Rulke was their most bitter enemy, so to copy his creation must have been bile to them. Why did they not remake it in their own image?'

'Perhaps they were afraid to,' said Nish. 'If they did not understand . . .'

'Yes,' said Yggur. 'They've not been able to solve the secret of flight, which can only mean one thing – they didn't understand what they were doing. They copied his work blindly, afraid to make changes in case they modified something vital. We've found their weakness.'

He went round it several times, studying everything, then prised open the hatch and climbed inside. A few seconds later he was out again, gagging.

'There's a rotting corpse in there. We'll have to find another.'

'And burned underneath,' added Nish, 'doubtless destroying what we came for.'

Yggur leapt down and set off across the rutted field, breathing heavily. They followed him in silence. Dawn was dabbing patches of colour on the eastern sky by the time they found another construct. This one was a wreck, the metal skin torn open and curled back on itself, the hatch completely gone and even the underside smashed in.

'I doubt I'll find what I'm looking for here,' said Yggur, but he inspected it as carefully as the first. He did not spend much time in this one either.

'There was a fire.' He wiped sooty hands on his cloak. 'It looks like the drive mechanism burst open. What's not burned has melted. Even the bones inside are charcoal.' Standing up on the shooter's platform, he scanned the surroundings. 'There's another. We'll have to be careful. The lyrinx may still keep an eye on this place.'

That clanker was also ruined, and the one after. 'This could take days,' Nish said gloomily.

'Why don't we go up in the air-floater?' said Irisis. 'I've seen this place enough times from the air to be able to find you a construct.'

'It'll tell everyone within five leagues that we're here,' said Yggur, 'but I suppose we've got no choice.'

They floated over the walls of Snizort. 'The Aachim constructs were concentrated to the west and north-west,' said Irisis. 'Over there.' She pointed west. 'I can see hundreds of them, close together.'

The humps were clearly visible, and in the middle they saw a magnificent pavilion of golden sandstone, its carven dome standing on seven columns. In the distance a creek, dry save for a few small pools, meandered between the hills.

'That structure wasn't there before,' said Irisis.

'It'll be a memorial to the Aachim dead,' said Yggur. 'So much death! On a dark night the ghosts will be thick as mist.'

Nish snorted. 'I don't believe in ghosts.'

'Nor did I, until I took pilgrimage to places where I'd sent armies to their deaths. My Second Army in Bannador; the thousand of my finest who fell in Elludore Forest. I wept for their lost souls, Nish. As will you, should you ever revisit Gumby Marth, or any other place where men's lives were in your keeping.' He went down the back to speak to Inouye.

'Cheerful company, isn't he,' said Irisis, though she couldn't help thinking of the mancer she'd obliterated on the aqueduct at the manufactory. What hopes had she had? What dreams? What fears all too brutally realised?

'Bloody mancers!'

They strolled after him.

'Down there, I think, Inouye,' said Yggur.

The pilot moved the steering arm and released a little floater gas. The machine had just begun to sink when she turned around. 'Something's there, Lord Yggur.'

He did not correct her. Yggur seemed to be sniffing the air, his head questing this way and that. 'I sense it, too. It's . . . a kind of defence, or *protection*.'

'Against what?' said Nish.

'I can't say, but it's likely to cause us some trouble.'

'Can't you break it?'

'Only a fool would break a magical defence without understanding what it was for, or who put it there.'

'What's that?' hissed Irisis.

'Where?'

'Way over to the west, by that loop of the creek. See the smoke?' She reached out blindly for the spyglass.

Nish put it in her hand. 'Can you see what it is?'

'A camp fire. A big one, and wagons pulled by clankers, though they're the oddest clankers I've ever seen.'

'What's odd about them?' asked Yggur sharply.

'They're clankers below, but above they look like shacks.'

'Nothing to do with the scrutators, then,' said Nish. 'Appearances are everything to them.'

'And rightly so,' Yggur observed, taking the spyglass. 'The outside is a mirror to what lies within.'

'My father was the most fastidious of men,' Nish countered, 'yet inside he festered.'

The air-floater was closer now and he could see the contraptions unaided. There were three, each with a six-wheeled wagon connected behind. A host of people had emerged, staring up at them. Some were loading crossbows, others manning javelards.

'Scavengers,' said Yggur.

'Where'd they get the clankers from?' said Nish.

'There are wrecked ones everywhere, and not just on this battlefield. The human maggots are always the first to get there.'

'How can they use them without trained operators?'

'A question Irisis would do well to ponder,' said Yggur. 'But there are many with talents who remain outside the law.'

'I meant, how do they get away with it?' said Nish.

'The scrutators' writ no longer holds in this land, so the scavengers can do what they like. It's marvellous what human ingenuity can achieve when survival is at stake.'

'Is that where the protection spell comes from?' asked Irisis.

'I doubt it,' said Yggur. 'It's too strong, and doesn't have the right flavour, but we'll keep well away from their camp, just in case. Go down to the other side of the battlefield, Inouye. Stay low so they can't see where we're heading.'

They descended to within a few spans of the ground, Yggur staring over the side, gripping the rope rail with both hands.

'I'm losing the field,' Inouye sang out. She was drawing from a distant one, of course, since the Snizort node was completely dead. The rotor slowed until it was barely ticking over.

'Try another.'

She did so. 'Nothing.' Inouye looked anxious but determined. A threat to her controller was a threat to her and she would fight to protect it.

'What's the matter?' said Yggur.

'The field's still there but I can't draw from it.'

'Can it be the protection?' Irisis wondered.

'It must be,' said Yggur. 'Let it drift, Inouye, and I'll make sure.'

A breeze carried them further west. Shortly the rotor began to tick again and soon spun up to full speed.

'Set down,' said Yggur. 'There, on that little mound. And keep a sharp lookout. If anyone comes, go up fast.'

'What if it's lyrinx?' said Flangers, checking that the crank of his crossbow turned smoothly.

'Use your initiative. Irisis, Nish, come with me.'

They slipped through the ropes, dropping to the ground before the keel touched, and turned towards a group of damaged constructs that lay close together. Before they'd gone a hundred paces, Yggur, who was a little way ahead, stopped abruptly. He put his hands up, feeling the air in front of him.

'Is it the protection?' said Irisis.

'Yes. It's a defensive shell designed to keep out living things.'

'What for?' said Nish.

'The Aachim greatly revere their dead. It would distress them to leave the bodies here, in alien ground. Some day, as soon as they can manage it, they'll come back and remove the remains. Until that time they've protected them from scavengers and looters, and those who simply want to pry into what's none of their business. And also, I think, they'd want to keep people from studying their abandoned constructs. The ones outside the protection, you'll recall, were all ruined.'

'How is the protection made, and maintained without the field?' said Irisis.

'The Aachim have used sentinel devices, self-powered, for thousands of years. They may have linked dozens together to create this. Or it may be a more potent spell. It's a mighty work, however they've managed it.' Yggur was walking sideways, hands still in the air. They followed in silence. He seemed to be feeling, or *sensing,* for something.

After a good while he stopped, moving his hands slowly in circles. His lips moved. 'Ah!' he said softly, pulling outwards as if peeling open the flap of a tent. 'Come through. Be quick. It's a strain to do this.'

It looked odd, for the barrier, whatever it was, was completely invisible. It felt odder going through, a tingling of the skin that extended into Nish's ears and up his nose, only to disappear once he was through, though the soles of his feet itched for a long time afterwards.

Inside looked exactly the same as outside. The sun was just as bright. He could hear birds calling, and the gentle tick of the rotor, and the same breeze ruffled his hair. Yet it was totally different. Nish felt enclosed. And also, that he was in a sacred place.

Yggur strode past, not awed at all, heading for a pair of constructs, seemingly undamaged, some way further in. 'Come on. Those scavengers might come to investigate and I don't want to be trapped in here.'

There were no bodies inside either machine. Yggur wasted no time. 'Nish, pull the base of this one apart and see if you can get the driving mechanism out in one piece. Irisis, we'll work in the cabin, to discover whatever we can about how it's controlled. We'll have to be quick.'

The metal was cold but Nish had experienced far worse. And having spent so much time with Minis and the Aachim, he was quite familiar with constructs, even if he'd never taken one apart by himself.

By the time the sun was halfway up the sky, he had removed the base plate and was struggling with the mechanism inside, a complicated structure of reciprocating metal parts set in a black metal casing the size of a small barrel. As he sat back, trying to work out how to remove it, he heard the hum of the rotor. The air-floater shot up and turned away.

'Keep down!' hissed Yggur from above. 'If they see us, they'll hang around until we come out.'

'Who?' said Nish, who couldn't see very far from his vantage point.

'The scavengers.'

FIFTY

Lying still, Nish felt the ground shake in that familiar *thump-thump*. A clanker went slowly by, greatly modified from its original purpose. The shooter's platform had been enclosed with pieces of metal in all shapes and sizes, and then roofed over with leaves of cast-iron armour from wrecked clankers. The roof bristled with metal spikes and the machine had a javelard at front and rear. Everything was rusted, makeshift and appallingly ugly.

Metal screeched and squealed as it shuddered to a stop. Three men leapt out, wild-haired, dirty creatures dressed in rags and pieces of armour. All were armed with swords and knives, and two had crossbows strapped to their backs.

One bent down, pointing. 'They've found our keel marks,' Yggur said quietly. 'Now they'll follow our tracks, coming this way but not going back.'

'Better hope we didn't leave tracks all the way,' said Nish.

The scavengers prowled around the curve of the barrier for the best part of an hour before returning to their machine and thumping off.

'Get working, Nish,' Yggur called. 'You too, Irisis. I'll keep lookout. I don't think they've gone very far.'

When the sun was as high as it was going to get, Irisis slid down the curved side of the construct. Yggur passed a sack to her, which she placed carefully on the ground in the shade, and sat beside it.

'What's that?' said Nish.

'All the controller workings.' Irisis picked at a broken fingernail.

'Do you know how to use them?'

'They've been disabled, but I expect we can work it out,' said Yggur. 'How are you going, Nish?'

'I've freed the driving mechanism,' he replied,, 'but it's too heavy to lift by myself. Even with three of us, I don't see how we're going to carry it to the other side of the barrier.'

'Let's get it out first.' Yggur moved under the construct, which was tilted at an angle, having come down onto a boulder when the field failed. He began to pull. 'Irisis, get that stick over there. Put it underneath the mechanism and, as we pull it free, let it slide gently to the ground.'

They did that, accompanied by much grunting and heaving, not to mention the near loss of Nish's toes when the mechanism slipped at the last moment; but finally it lay on the stony soil, undamaged.

'Wait here,' said Yggur, heading for the invisible barrier a few hundred paces distant. He passed through, looking up for signs of the air-floater, and disappeared among the sparse shrubbery.

Several minutes went by. 'I hope it hasn't gone too far,' said Nish.

'Or worse,' Irisis replied darkly.

Thump-thump.

'The scavengers are coming back,' she added.

'Afraid so.'

'What are we going to do?'

'Haven't a clue.'

Neither spoke for several minutes. The clanker contraption reappeared, tracking along the outside of the barrier. The same three men got out.

'I've just had an uncomfortable thought,' said Nish.

'What's that?'

'This protection keeps out living things, but the wind blows straight through it.'

'I'm not sure what you're saying,' said Irisis.

'What if they can fire their weapons through?'

A big, hairy man climbed on top, peering in their direction with a rusty spyglass. The pair on the ground squatted down.

'We're in trouble,' said Nish. 'Don't move.'

'You're the one who's breathing so loudly,' Irisis retorted with her famous calm.

'I hope Yggur sealed the protection when he went out.'

The spyglass tracked across to where they huddled in the shadow under the construct, passed on, then came back. The hairy man shouted instructions, though Nish could not distinguish them.

Shortly a woman emerged from the rear hatch of the clanker, pulling a child by the arm. The child, a girl of ten or twelve with tangled black hair, resisted. The man roared at the woman, pointing at the tilted construct. The woman screeched back, clipped the struggling girl over the ear and dragged her to the barrier by her hair.

The girl shook the woman off, turned towards the hairy man, who was still roaring, and gave him a two-fingered sign. She poked her tongue out at the woman and received another clip over the ear.

Pressing her grubby hands to the barrier, she stared through it. As her gaze passed across him, again the soles of Nish's feet tingled.

'That's done it,' said Irisis. 'She must have a native seeker's talent.'

'Doesn't explain how she found me,' said Nish. 'Since, as you frequently point out, I've got no talent at all.'

'You make up for it in other ways, Nish.'

The girl pointed at them, shouting excitedly.

'Look out!' cried Irisis as the hairy man swung his javelard in their direction.

No time to run. All Nish could do was flatten himself against the ground and pray that he made an indistinct target. The spear slammed into the base of the construct next to him. Irisis cried out.

'Are you all right?' said Nish.

'Just dirt in my eye. Run! Next time he'll put it right through one of us.'

They scrambled out, clawing their way around the other

side, where he would not be able to see them. Another missile whizzed by Nish's backside as he went.

'He's bloody fast to reload,' Nish said, panting.

'Now what do we do?'

'Wait for them to go away?'

'Have you got any water?'

'No. Have you?'

'No. It could be a thirsty wait.'

'At least the company's good,' said Nish.

'I've been wondering when you'd notice,' she said, pretending to be piqued.

'You know what I'm like—'

'Slow!'

'I have to work things out in my own way and my own time.'

'But I don't. Come here.' She put her arms around him. 'I've missed you so badly, Nish.'

'And I you – you're my dearest friend.' After a long moment he pulled away. 'Sorry – it's too hot.'

She sighed.

'Yggur will do something,' Irisis said a good while later.

'If they haven't got the air-floater already. There were three clankers, remember?'

'That's comforting.'

'Glad to be of assistance,' he grunted.

'It seems to be getting hotter every second,' she said after another long wait. 'Do you think they're still there?'

'We'd hear them move. Scavengers must be used to waiting.'

It was mid-afternoon now and Nish was parched. Unable to stand the suspense, he crept to the front end of the construct, peering warily around. A spear slammed into the dirt a finger's length from his nose. Shortly, the other two clankers thumped up.

'How long does it take to die of thirst?' Irisis asked casually. 'A few days, I'd imagine.'

'I don't—'

'What's that?' hissed Nish.

'It must be Yggur coming back in the air-floater.'

A shadow passed across the sun and soon the machine was hovering above the barrier, just out of javelard range.

'Now what?' said Nish. 'It can't come any lower, and we can't move without being shot.'

'We wait for dark.'

They did, interminably, but dark brought no relief. The scavengers raised a ramshackle tower from the top of the first clanker, from which, by some uncanny means, a beam of blinding light lit up the area around their refuge. The other two clankers did the same from the sides, leaving only a tiny pool of darkness behind the construct for Nish and Irisis to hide in. Camp fires were built, and shortly the smell of roasting meat drifted across.

'I could use a haunch of that, whatever it is,' Nish said in a cracked voice.

Irisis took his hand, giving it a hard squeeze. 'We've got to do something, Nish.'

Once Nish would have thought the same, but he was wiser now. 'There's nothing we can do. Leave it to Yggur. He'll have a plan and we might spoil it.'

'What if he doesn't? What if he's past it?'

He didn't reply.

'Can you hear something?' Irisis was on her feet. There was shouting off to the right, and one of the beams had gone out.

'Something's burning,' said Nish.

Another of the beams swung away. Nish peered from the dark side. 'One of their wagons is on fire.'

'Yggur's made a diversion,' said Irisis. 'Does he mean us to run for safety?'

'He hasn't come all this way to leave without the driver mechanism,' said Nish. 'Let's see if we can get it out.'

After further shouting, the third beam went out. They scampered round the exposed side and underneath, heaving and tugging, but hadn't moved the mechanism far before the beam swung back in their faces. They froze under the construct, trying to look like red dirt and black metal.

'If he realises we're here,' Irisis said out of the corner of her mouth, 'he can hardly miss.'

'Whoever he shoots won't know anything about it.' Nish shielded his eyes, but the beam was so dazzling he couldn't tell what was happening at the clankers.

As he was squinting off to his right, Nish saw a tiny spark drift down, as if attached to a piece of thistledown. It floated towards where the second of the clankers had been.

The explosion painted his retina red. The black cut-out of the clanker was lifted into the air and turned onto its side. His eardrums throbbed from the colossal boom and crash. There were cries of pain and terror, and the last beam swung away, crisscrossing the sky for the air-floater.

Feet pounded towards them. They shrank down into the dirt, then someone skidded under the construct. Flangers!

'Is this it?' he panted, indicating the mechanism.

'Yes, but we'll never lift it.'

'We don't have to.' They lugged it out from underneath. 'Round the back!' said Flangers, 'where they can't get such an easy shot at us.'

'What was that bang?' said Irisis.

'A big balloon full of floater gas, pulled down by sandbags. Went off nicely, didn't it?'

'We're not complaining,' Irisis said dryly.

'And before that, I dropped a burning jug of oil onto one of the wagons.'

'You're a dangerous man in an emergency,' said Nish. 'What's the plan?'

'Yggur's getting another balloon ready. As soon as it goes off, he'll lower a rope onto us and winch the mechanism up through a hole he's made in the barrier.'

'I'm not sure I want to be hanging in the air when the beams find us again.'

'We run,' said Flangers, 'and try to get out the way I came in.'

'Oh well,' said Irisis casually, 'if we don't get there, at least Yggur will have what he came for.'

'That's the way it is,' said Flangers, in a tone that suggested he'd be happy to make the sacrifice. He might have given his life into her keeping, but the soldier still wanted to do the only thing left to him.

Another explosion rocked the night, though this one did not do much damage. 'Get ready,' said Flangers.

The rope came hissing down, its last coils smacking into the ground just a few spans away. Flangers retrieved it, knotted it expertly around the mechanism, gave three sharp tugs and stepped back.

The rope tightened and the mechanism came up off the ground, but it rose only half a span before stopping, swaying back and forth.

'How's Yggur going to lift that by himself?' said Nish.

'A collection of pulleys,' said Flangers.

Someone shouted from the remaining clanker and the beam returned, picking up the rope, which shone like a vertical rod of light. The javelard fired.

'It's a difficult shot but if he hits the rope we're sunk,' said Flangers. 'We've got to make a diversion. Run, that way! Go separately. I'll come last.' The most dangerous position.

Irisis ran diagonally away from the clankers and the burning wagon. Nish went a few seconds later, followed by Flangers. The girl's voice called out a warning; the beam swung, fixed upon Irisis and tracked her.

'Down!' Flangers roared.

Running full tilt, she threw herself down, skidding on her front across the ground. *Thunnggg!* A spear went over her shoulders, ploughing the dirt beyond her, then she was up and haring off again.

Another beam fixed on the mechanism, now ten spans in the air. As Nish fled, he heard a spear clank off the outside and prayed it had done no damage. Another spear flew past Irisis's ear – he saw it flash like a silver snake through the beam – and they were beyond range of night shooting.

Flangers passed Nish, running easily. 'How far to go?' panted Nish, who had a stitch already.

'A thousand paces, more or less.'

'Less, I hope.'

The soldier drew level with Irisis, pointed a little to his left, then drew ahead. Irisis had begun to flag and Nish felt no better. After a day without food or water he had nothing left to give. He chanced a glance back and up. The clanker had one last shot at the rope, but missed. The mechanism was almost out of sight.

The clanker turned in their direction, following the other, which was moving slowly along the perimeter of the barrier. Ahead, Flangers was trotting, barely visible in the dark. As they caught up to him he had one hand out, searching for the opening Yggur had made for him earlier.

'Here!' he called in a low voice, pushing something invisible open and holding it for them.

'Which way?' gasped Irisis.

'Straight towards the north-western corner of the Snizort wall.' He indicated the direction with a finger.

Irisis jogged that way. Nish staggered after her, his throat so dry he could hear each breath rushing in and out. Flangers picked up a crossbow he'd left at the entrance and came last.

By the time they were halfway to the Snizort wall, the clankers, with at least thirty vengeful scavengers hanging off the top and sides, were thumping after them. The seeker girl must have been directing the pursuit for, no matter how they twisted and turned in the darkness, Irisis and Nish could not shake it off.

They topped a rise. To Irisis's dismay, the wall was a good half a league ahead. Flangers dropped to one knee and fired. Nish heard the bolt clang off the iron plates.

Just when he thought he could go no further, there was an explosion between the two clankers. They stopped in a scream of metal and the beams wavered across the sky, searching frantically, then went out.

The air-floater dropped out of the dark beside Irisis. They flopped over the side and it shot up and away.

FIFTY-ONE

Gilhaelith sent a messenger down to Oellyll, carrying another plea to the matriarch, for any world maps the lyrinx had made. Gyrull came up to see him that afternoon and again consented so readily to help that he wondered if she had an ulterior motive. But then, he knew she had an interest in his work.

'In our early days on Santhenar,' Gyrull said, 'before the war began, our best fliers crisscrossed the globe, mapping it from the air. We wanted to see if there were other lands we could go to, instead of fighting for a piece of Lauralin.'

'Did they find any?'

'Several. A small continent a long way to the west closely resembles the one marked on the far southern side of your geomantic globe. There are also a series of lands, well above the equator, that are wrongly depicted on your globe.'

No wonder it had let him down before. 'Do human peoples live there?'

'I don't know, Tetrarch. Those lands were so far away that only our best fliers could reach them, and they did not stay long. Such lands were of little interest to us, for the non-fliers, most of our population, would have had to sail there.' Jags flashed across her breast plates at the thought. 'The risk of sailing all that way was too great.' Her wings stirred in agitation. 'Better to die fighting for Meldorin and Lauralin than drown like dogs in the endless ocean. Our fliers did, however, make careful charts of the lands. I'll have a set of copies sent up.'

'What about nodes and fields?'

'We know where the most powerful ones lie, on land and undersea. We had to, to be able to fly to unknown lands. You may also see those charts. In return, you will permit me one use of your geomantic globe, should I request it.'

That night, four lyrinx carried up a great many rolled maps. Each was as large as a good-sized carpet, and each was drawn in meticulous detail in coloured ink on the softest leather Gilhaelith had ever seen. He unrolled the first map and recoiled. On the right-hand side, quite distinctly, was a navel, and above it a pair of large, dark nipples. It was made from human skin, evidently from women and several dozen skins had gone into each chart.

Once he got used to the idea, though, he discovered what a marvel the maps were. They showed the kind of detail that could only be observed from the air. Even with just a fraction of that information, the usefulness of his globe would be magnified a hundredfold.

Changing his world model, under the glass, was the most exquisitely painstaking work Gilhaelith had ever done. The lands and seas of the geomantic globe were marked so precisely that he required three pairs of lenses, mounted in a sliding frame, to resolve their finest structure. Once he had focussed on a particular point, Gilhaelith used the Art to change it, in three dimensions, to what was on the charts. Sometimes it took an hour to make one tiny alteration, for he might have to raise mountains, reduce highlands, correct the course of rivers or alter the shape of the coast. Hundreds of such modifications had to be made, not to mention creating an entire new continent in the northern hemisphere, complete with peninsulas, gulfs and archipelagos, and many islands large and small.

Immersed in this craftsmanship, it was almost possible to forget the slow decay of his mental faculties. Almost possible, save that each new task took longer and required more concentration. By evening he felt like a mat that had been hung over a rope and beaten. And the work took its toll. The slow leakage of power from those fragments of phantom crystal was steadily damaging him. The difference was not noticeable at the end of one day, or even a week, but after working on the globe for a month it was clear what he'd lost. His thoughts were sluggish and disconnected. His ability to concentrate, once effortless, now required the most anguished feats of willpower, while parts of the landscaping spell, which formerly he could have used without thinking, often faded from his mind midway and had to be done over and over again.

He knew Gyrull had set up hidden zygnadrs to spy on him but Gilhaelith pretended they weren't there. He'd known he would be watched. Besides, the geomantic globe was just a tool – it was what he planned to do with it that was important, and she couldn't know that.

It took two months of work, so all-consuming that Gilhaelith could do nothing else, before the globe was as true as he could make it. Finally, one rainy mid-autumn afternoon, he stood up, rubbing an aching neck, and allowed the globe to rotate on its cushion of freezing mist. It looked so real that he could have been seeing Santhenar from the void. Perhaps, in some strange duality, it was real – a perfect microcosm of the world, and a device he could use to probe its secrets, if he could probe and repair himself first.

Unfortunately it no longer depicted all the nodes he knew of, to say nothing of their individual natures. Sighing, he bent his head to the new task. He could never put all the known nodes on his globe; it would be the work of lifetimes. However, Gilhaelith did not think that would be required. As long as the greatest nodes were there, *the controlling ones* (now where had that thought come from?), the completed globe should enable him to reach a new understanding of the world.

Gilhaelith went back to the human-skin node charts. He had Tyal and another servant unroll them for him; he'd become squeamish about touching human leather lately. What if Gyrull killed him and made a map out of his skin? Disgusting!

He began to remove the existing nodes from the world surface and place them in a new layer, underneath the glass, that would allow him to include the nature of each node. For this task, he suspended the globe on its air cushion in a green-tinged nickel bowl on a platform of turned rosewood. Near the outer edge of the platform a series of concentric, graduated brass rings was inlaid into the timber. Slender pointers could be slid around inner rings to make the detailed measurements he required.

Weeks went by, but finally the task was done. Gilhaelith stood back, allowed the globe to rotate and brought a crystal close to the glass surface. A series of nodes lit up. The geomantic globe was as perfect a model of Santhenar as any man could make. It was the culmination of his life's work. Gilhaelith felt sure that, with it, he could finally understand how the world worked, and that would give him the key to the power of the nodes, if he wanted it. It should not take long now, if his strength held out and the accumulating mental damage did not prevent him.

'Masterly work, Tetrarch,' said Gyrull, behind him.

Gilhaelith spun around, seized by a sudden, blind panic. 'You've come for my globe,' he cried, trying to think of a way out and knowing there was none.

'*If* we wanted such a device we would make it ourselves,' she said with a curl of her leathery lip. 'But you can help me another way, Tetrarch. Indeed, you must, for you *owe* me.'

'The debt was discharged!' He put on an arrogant air to conceal his nervousness.

'On the contrary, it continues to accumulate. For your servants, the food and drink we provide you and them, and for your every other request that I have accommodated unquestioningly.'

'What do you want?'

'It's no great favour,' she said blandly. 'Just a series of measurements of the field, from a number of points overlooking the city.'

'You want me to go outside Alcifer? Didn't you say there are void beasts in the forests?' That sounded cowardly, but it wasn't. Having come so far, he grudged every moment spent away from his work. And having little time left, he couldn't afford to waste a minute.

Gyrull passed up the opportunity to mock him for cowardice. She was nobler than he'd thought. 'You're quite safe. Our boundaries extend some distance from Alcifer, and you'll have my guards with you.'

'Can't you take the measurements yourself?'

'We can, but I'm asking you to do it, as part-payment of your debt. We have much to do, presently. The measurements won't take much time at all. A few days, at most.'

Shortly after sunrise, Gilhaelith was taking sightings through a calibrated spyglass from a ridge high above the city, and noting field strengths on a map Gyrull had given him. The readings were to be done every half-hour all day, from this ridge, and from six other locations on succeeding days. Therefore the work would take a week, not the few days Gyrull had mentioned. There was no time for wondering why. No sooner was the first set of readings complete than it was time to start the second, and so it went all day, and the next. All twelve of his servants had been sent with him – keeping an eye on him for Gyrull, he assumed – and two guards were watching them.

On the third afternoon he was working on a higher ridge on the slope of the dormant volcano. He'd just moved the glass to a new position when a powerful distortion in the field led him to glance up the slope. The distortion seemed to be moving, but its source was masked or cloaked and it took quite an effort to see through it. To his astonishment, it was a thapter. The metal skin was undamaged, so it wasn't Tiaan's. Someone else had uncovered the secret. Soon, he supposed, the skies would be full of them.

The thapter drifted in his direction. Gilhaelith squinted at it, trying to identify the operator, but the machine was too far off. Whoever was inside it, human or Aachim, was a threat to him. He ducked under the trees, praying that it would turn aside.

Not so his servants, who began screaming and jumping up and down.

'Careful,' he called. 'Most likely it's Aachim in that flier.'

'Do they eat folk?' said the always irascible Tyal.

'Of course not.'

'Then they're a damn sight better than the enemy.'

If the Aachim found Gilhaelith he would certainly be imprisoned for keeping the thapter from them; he might even forfeit his life. Should the thapter be possessed by the scrutators, however, he would be swiftly tried for keeping it and the amplimet from Klarm, and as swiftly executed. That fate might await him from Gyrull, too, but surely not until he'd tested the globe. The decision took little time. Of his three possible fates, only remaining at Alcifer offered the chance to complete his life's work.

'Not for me,' muttered Gilhaelith, moving further into the shadows.

'So that's how it is,' roared Tyal. 'Look at him, hiding like the craven cur he is! His promises were lies. He's a traitor, as I've always said, and the scrutators will pay handsomely for him. Take Gilhaelith!'

Two of the male servants threw themselves on him, while the others took up cudgels and attacked the pair of lyrinx guards standing in the shade. The women began capering madly in the clearing, waving items of clothing at the thapter, but as Gilhaelith fell a cloaking spell renewed itself and the machine vanished.

Three of the male servants lay bleeding on the ground before the lyrinx were defeated. One was felled by an expertly thrown rock, the other went down under the weight of four humans. A cudgel blow knocked it unconscious.

Gilhaelith was dragged, struggling furiously, out into the open. Someone bound his wrists behind his back with a length of cord. Gilhaelith prayed that there were more lyrinx nearby, or he was finished.

FIFTY-TWO

Malien came to Tiaan's room that night, very late, looking rather drawn.

'I'm sorry,' she said on entering. 'I should have anticipated their reaction and kept our business till later.'

'Of course your people wouldn't want an outsider at their council,' said Tiaan, who had been watching the patterns ebb and flow in the translucent walls. 'I should have known better than to interrupt.'

'It's just that it showed up their fatal weakness – an inability to agree on anything.' Malien sat on the bed, a rhomboid frame of metal with a mattress as hard as a plank. The other furnishings were equally minimal and unornamented. In Tirthrax, every surface of every object had been decorated. 'It's worse than it was before the council began.'

'Are they like this in everything they do?'

Malien sighed. 'Unfortunately, when they deal with the outside world, yes. In the past we've allowed ourselves to be led to disaster because we lacked the courage to challenge a powerful, charismatic leader, or because we believed the unbelievable of him. The march of folly, I call it, and Tensor's folly became so seared into our consciousness that no one wishes to be leader any more. Every proposition is torn apart in the meeting room. We're so afraid of hubris that we won't act at all; not even when the outside world burns.'

'And Vithis is like Tensor, you said. Has Vithis been here?'

'His envoys have, though not recently. The country is too steep and rugged for constructs and, even from the lowlands of Kalar, west of these mountains, it takes weeks to walk into

Stassor. For the coming winter, which is six months long here, it can't be done at all.'

'Except by thapter. Do you know where Vithis is?' A long way away, Tiaan fervently hoped.

'He's gone north to the Foshorn, seized land there and closed the borders. No one knows what he's up to.'

'I was sure he would come after me,' Tiaan said softly.

'Another of our failings, in times of duress, is to retreat into our fastness and shut the world out.'

Tiaan sagged with relief. 'What are you going to do, Malien?'

'I don't know. I may return to Tirthrax, if Harjax will let me.'

'Why wouldn't he?'

'My people want the thapter. To gain such a prize, they may find the courage to act.'

'Are you in danger?'

'I hardly think so, though . . .'

Three nights later, Tiaan was lying awake in the dark when the room was shaken gently by an earth trembler. It wasn't the first she'd felt here, but the amplimet, which had hardly changed since she'd escaped from the Aachim's nets, began to blink rapidly. She sat up. The room shook again, violently enough to slide a metal goblet off the table. It rang on the stone floor like a distant alarm and the patterns in the walls went wild for a few seconds before returning to their previous progression. Tiaan thought about investigating the source of the trembler with geomancy, but that would require her to use the amplimet. She'd not touched it since Tirthrax and was reluctant to now. The feeling that it was waiting for something was stronger than ever.

She got out of bed to pick up the goblet, then reached for her hedron. As she touched it the field flashed into her mind, but it was all eaten away on one side as if something was taking massive amounts of power from it. Was this what the amplimet had been waiting for?

Without dressing, she fleeted down the hall to Malien's room. The stone was frigid underfoot, for the Aachim maintained their city at a temperature considerably lower than Tiaan found comfortable.

She rapped on the door. 'Enter!' said Malien.

Tiaan went in. Malien was sitting at the table with Bilfis, who had a glassy cube in his hands, like a model of Stassor. Coloured patterns moved within it, and on the outside. He was frowning.

Malien was making marks, in the Aachim script, on a complicated diagram. Bilfis rotated the edge of the cube, twisting it so that smaller cubes were revealed, twenty-five to each side. He moved the smaller cubes into a new pattern.

Malien made another series of marks. 'Worse!'

Bilfis set the divination cube down on the table and ran his hands through his hair.

'What is it, Tiaan?' said Malien.

'Just after the earth trembler, the amplimet began to blink, and now something is taking vast amounts of power from the Stassor node. I'm afraid—'

'It's not the amplimet,' said Bilfis. 'My people are building a great defence against attack by thapters or other kinds of flying machines.'

'That's all right then,' said Tiaan. 'Isn't it?'

'We're afraid they'll overload the node, or worse,' said Malien direly. 'If you recall, Tiaan, I mentioned this worry in Tirthrax. But my people won't listen. They're too afraid.'

'Of what?'

'Anyone and everyone. Once the secret of flight gets out, and surely that won't take long, Stassor will be vulnerable to attack by a fleet of thapters. Suddenly its isolation will be a disadvantage rather than a protection.'

'I see. And what could be worse than overloading the node?'

'Overloading *all* the nodes.'

Tiaan looked from one to the other. 'I don't understand.'

'We're not sure we do either,' said Bilfis, 'but we're

beginning to think that the nodes might not be separate, as has always been thought, but *linked.*'

'Through strong forces that can't be detected,' said Malien. 'Humanity has already seen the lyrinx drain nodes dry. They normally recover within days of the node-drainer being removed, though we don't understand how that can happen so quickly. It should take years for a node to regenerate the field by itself.'

'Unless,' said Bilfis, 'it's replenished from outside, from other nodes.'

'But that's good, isn't it?' Tiaan searched their faces.

'We thought so, until we heard about the death of the Snizort node,' said Bilfis. 'That's bothered me ever since I heard the news. I'm afraid . . .' He looked to Malien. She nodded.

'Yes?' said Tiaan.

'If the nodes *are* linked, it could be a problem.'

'What do you mean?'

'Every month humanity adds more clankers to the thousands they're already using, along with a myriad of other devices that draw power from the field. The lyrinx do the same, as does Vithis with his thousands of constructs. Now Stassor has embarked on this city-sized shield and just to build it will take much from the node. Maintaining it day after day, year after year, will require far more. It adds up to too much power, taken too quickly, and there's got to be a consequence. It may drain the node dry and, if the nodes are linked, the ones surrounding it as well. Perhaps even the ones surrounding *them*. You see the danger?'

'I think so . . .' said Tiaan.

'If many nodes fail at once, the great forces that create them will ultimately have to readjust. What's that going to do to the puny creatures clinging to Santhenar's fragile shell?'

'Are you saying that some of the nodes might explode, as at Snizort?' asked Tiaan.

'That's one possibility, and the explosive force could spread to the nodes surrounding them,' said Malien. 'Or the driving forces themselves could become unbalanced, tearing the crust of the world apart. No one knows enough geomancy to tell.'

'Is there any way to find out?'

'That's what we've been talking about.'

'Bilfis and I have put our concerns to the Aachim Syndic,' said Malien the following morning. 'That last earth trembler alarmed them, so we turned the screws. My people aren't happy, but they've agreed to give us what we want, in return for the secret of flight. They want to build their own thapters.'

'Is that wise?' said Tiaan, but regretted it as soon as she'd spoken. She had no right to question Malien.

'I had nothing else to bargain with.'

'What are they giving in return?'

'Everything they know about nodes.'

'You might have demanded that by right,' said Bilfis.

'And they might have stalled me for months,' said Malien. 'This way we can begin in a week.'

'To do what?' said Tiaan.

'To map the nodes near Stassor, so we can see how they're being affected.'

'Can I come too?' Tiaan was used to being busy but there would be nothing for her to do here. 'I'll do anything that needs doing.'

'I want you to come,' said Malien. 'Indeed, I can't do it without you.'

By the time the Aachim had released the thapter and made a start on building their own, weeks later, Tiaan, Malien and a mapmaker had gone through the archives and produced a series of charts of the mountains surrounding Stassor. These showed all nodes the Aachim knew about.

There were many kinds: weak nodes and strong, steady ones and those whose fields fluctuated wildly or unpredictably, or flared up only to die away to nothing. There were occasional double nodes and one triple – which Malien warned was too perilous to approach – as well as two anti-nodes which were even more dangerous. The anti-nodes may have grown by cannibalising the fields of others, but no one had ever dared approach close enough to find out.

Only then did Tiaan and Malien sit down, with a small glass of the Aachim liquor called syspial in hand, and consider their work. The nodes were not evenly distributed but fell into patterns, groups and aggregations, which in turn were organised into provinces. These often corresponded to geographic features like mountain chains, volcanoes, cliffs or ridges. Not always, though – some nodes were not related to anything on the surface of the earth.

Tiaan took a sip of her drink, which was the colour and flavour of sweet blackberry liqueur, but stingingly spicy-hot. 'Where do nodes come from, anyway?'

'No one has any idea,' said Malien, 'except, possibly, your friend Gilhaelith. He knows more about the natural philosophy of the world than anyone.'

'It's been his life's work.' She wondered if Gilhaelith was still alive; and if so, what he was up to.

The next step was to go out at night in the thapter, mapping the fields of the nodes while Malien flew a course by the moon or the stars, and Bilfis plotted the fields on the chart. Tiaan was forced to use the amplimet, which was always risky now. Once or twice she flew the thapter, and had to use the crystal for that as well. She did not have the talent to fly the thapter the way Malien did.

They spent a tedious month on this work, by which time they had created a map of the area within forty leagues of Stassor. It was very rough, but to refine it would have taken months more, for they learned something new every day: new fields and new nodes, even new kinds of nodes. Tiaan wished she understood them.

By that time, two teams, each one comprising hundreds of Aachim, working day and night, had built a pair of thapters, though only the second of them remained at Stassor: the other machine had flown west a fortnight ago. Tiaan suspected it had been sent on an embassy to Vithis, and she was not looking forward to its return.

The following morning she was in the front meeting room when there was a screeching whine outside and the missing thapter shot past a transparent section of wall, heading for the compressed-ice platform.

'Who's that?' Malien said sharply.

'Tormil,' said Harjax. 'I sent him to make contact with Vithis, and from his haste I'd say he has.' He bent his head to his papers.

Malien's left hand gripped Tiaan's knee under the table and squeezed hard – a warning. She wrote a note on a scrap of paper and passed it to Tiaan. 'Would you take this to Bilfis, please? He's in his room.'

'Of course,' said Tiaan. She rose, bowing to the Aachim, who ignored her as usual, and hurried out.

The operator was in such haste that he had flown his thapter right up to the cubular doors, which were spreading apart as Tiaan went by. He threw himself over the side, almost falling in his haste.

Tiaan made her way to Bilfis's room, and found him sitting at the table, poring over his field maps.

'Malien asked me to give you this.' She passed him the paper.

He scanned it, thrust it into his pocket, rolled the maps and sprang up. 'Take these to Malien's thapter. Act normally. Have you your amplimet?'

'Always.'

Scooping gear from the table, he thrust it into a small pack. A pile on the bed followed it and he tossed the pack over his shoulder.

'What's the matter?' said Tiaan.

'Don't ask stupid questions, just go!'

That alarmed her, for the Aachim of Stassor might be remote, condescending or aloof, but they were invariably polite.

'Walk calmly,' he went on. 'Don't attract attention.'

Easy to say, but she didn't know if he was helping or kidnapping her. Trust Malien, she told herself. Tiaan did her best to act normally, though it must have been obvious, had the passing Aachim glanced at her, that she was under a strain. Fortunately they took no more notice of her than at any other time.

They'd trudged the corridors and were halfway across the ice pavement outside when someone called out, 'Bilfis, can you spare me a moment?'

'Keep going, Tiaan,' Bilfis said softly. 'Get into the thapter and make it ready for flight. Don't get out no matter what happens, or what I say.' He turned. 'Harjax? I'm just checking some of the maps I left in the thapter.'

'Would you bring the old human back for interrogation, please?'

'Certainly. Tiaan,' he called, 'fetch the maps from the thapter, if you would.'

Tiaan risked a glance over her shoulder as she climbed the side. Harjax stood uncertainly outside the cubular doors, a victim of indecision and Aachim politeness. Tiaan slipped in, put the maps into their racks, carefully inserted the amplimet and made all ready. She felt ill. She'd only flown this thapter a couple of times, and then briefly. Its controls, different from those of her original thapter, could be temperamental. She prayed for a steady hand and a strong stomach.

'Would you fetch her please, Bilfis,' called Harjax, trying to be commanding without alerting his quarry. 'It's rather important.'

'Of course,' said Bilfis, 'if it's so urgent.' He strolled towards the thapter, a picture of unconcern. As he climbed the side he said quietly to Tiaan, 'Ready?'

'Yes.'

'Go, as fast as you possibly can. Fly around the side, then back to the east-facing door. Malien will be waiting there.' He jumped in.

The thapter sprang to life. Tiaan mentally worked the controls, praying she had them right.

Harjax, belatedly realising that something was wrong, began to run across the paving.

'Come on!' Bilfis snapped.

She jerked and twisted the yoke at the same time. The thapter lifted sharply, spinning on its axis, front down, so quickly that she couldn't see where she was going. Harjax sprang out of the way, shouted to the guards outside the doors but again hesitated, unwilling to fire on his own.

Tiaan turned the yoke back, a fraction too far, for the thapter now tumbled end for end while it was still spinning. At least it was slowly gaining height, though it was heading straight for the cubular doors.

'Do something!' Bilfis shouted.

She jerked the yoke, intuition guiding her hand, the machine straightened out and Tiaan took it up vertically. Harjax roared orders to fire but Tiaan sideslipped, hurtled towards the high north-western corner of Stassor, skimmed the flank of its peak and shot over the top, out of sight.

'Down, low to the roof!' hissed Bilfis. 'Weave about, just in case. They've weapons here that could shatter this machine like ice on an anvil, once they find the resolve to use them.'

Tiaan raced across the roof, dropped so sharply on the other side that Bilfis's feet lifted off the floor, corkscrewed around the north-eastern peak out of sight, then zipped back towards the eastern door. There was no one outside.

A shrill piping sounded within, a call to arms, and she saw a squad of soldiers racing down the hall. 'What do we do, Bilfis?'

Just as Tiaan was thinking that Malien wasn't coming, three people threw themselves through the doors. Tiaan slammed into a pancaking hover just to the right of the doors, so the guards could not shoot from inside the hall. The three Aachim flung themselves in and she shot up, piling them all onto the floor.

'Get over that far mountain, quick!' cried Malien, pointing to a range to their east. 'Fly like you've never flown before, or they'll melt us down to tallow.'

Crossbow bolts slammed into the sides. Tiaan spun down the ridge, across the glacier-filled valley and up the other side, towards a saddle between two rocky horns. As they were halfway up she felt the field draw down so hard that the thapter missed a beat. The patterns on the glass went wild and she could feel the amplimet flaring in sympathy.

'Over the saddle!' roared Malien. 'Get down into shelter, before it's too late.'

It was still a long way ahead, up a precipitous slope. Tiaan looked back. A tower at the top of the building had developed glowing crimson rings. The whole of the glassy cube of Stassor had gone black. A chill went up her spine. She hurled the thapter hard left, left again, right, up, then down and to the left once more.

The saddle approached, as sharp as a blade. She made for the middle of it, the lowest point. The rings were whirling up and down the tower, faster and faster. She could see them reflected on the glass of the binnacle.

Tiaan was almost to the saddle before she realised that it made the perfectly framed shot the Aachim were waiting for.

'Go left!' Malien's voice was a choked scream.

Tiaan was about to but, as her hand moved the yoke, an urgent sense of wrongness told her that the Aachim were expecting that. She flung the yoke hard the other way, veering right and shaving ice off the rising ridge crest with the base of the thapter.

The low point, as well as the left-hand side of the saddle, exploded in a spray of steam and molten rock, then they were over and hurtling down the sharp decline with an avalanche on their heels.

'Pull up,' said Malien, 'but keep well below the saddle. They might reflect the beam off the ice, even if they can't see us.'

Tiaan was already doing so. The Aachim picked themselves up from the floor, looking at each other. They were unharmed, apart from Bilfis, who had a fleck of blood on the back of his robes, below the right shoulder blade.

He rubbed it, examining his fingertip. 'Just a flying shard.'

'Where to?' asked Tiaan.

'We can't go to Tirthrax,' said Malien. 'Not for long, anyway.'

'Or to any of our other known refuges,' said Bilfis, 'since they'll look there in their thapters.'

Malien considered. 'We've got little food or drink, and only the clothes we're wearing. Head south and west, Tiaan, for the moment.'

'What happened back there?'

'Harjax was uncomfortable with the story of your escape,' said Malien. 'As soon as their first thapter was free, he sent it to the Foshorn, to Vithis. We had a feeling the news would be bad, so we were ready to flee. The urgency of the envoy's return was alarm enough.'

'And when he ordered the guards to fire on us,' added Bilfis, 'it confirmed the worst.'

Tiaan looked from one to the other. 'What news did he bear?'

'In your escape, you did more damage than you'd thought. Vithis suffered a broken arm and jaw, and three noble Aachim were killed in the construct that exploded underwater. But there was worse . . .'

'Minis!' Tiaan said, white-faced. 'I killed Minis.'

'You did worse than that, as far as Vithis is concerned.'

'How can anything be worse than death?'

'Oh, for some Aachim, there can be far worse,' Malien said grimly.

PART FIVE

AIR-DREADNOUGHT

FIFTY-THREE

'Death in life,' Malien explained sombrely. 'You maimed him, Tiaan. He lost a leg, three fingers, and his pelvis was crushed. He may never walk again; he'll never be without pain. But worse still, he's no longer *whole*, and every Aachim knows it. To their eyes Minis is a ruined man. If Vithis lives another thousand years he'll neither forgive nor forget. He's declared clan-vengeance against you and all who aid you in any way. Any Aachim who does so faces exile or death.'

'Even your people?' Tiaan whispered.

'Harjax's envoy bound us as well. Perhaps he felt it was a way of allying our sundered kind. Or perhaps he felt as aggrieved as Vithis. I didn't wait to find out.'

'And yet you three helped me, at the cost of your own lives.'

'It wasn't *just* for you,' said Malien. 'There's a higher danger and we can't do without you.'

'The nodes?' said Tiaan.

'The nodes. Bilfis has made a model of the ones near Stassor – those you've mapped – and they're more unstable than he'd imagined.'

'To put it at its bluntest,' said Bilfis, who was a pallid grey, and sweating despite the cold, 'I'm so terrified that I was prepared to break the code of clan-vengeance and become an outlaw. There is a higher duty, when the very world may be at stake.' Nodding formally to Tiaan, he went below.

The remaining Aachim seemed to be assessing her worth. The lean man was Talis the Mapmaker, whom Tiaan had met several times. The stocky one was called Forgre but she knew nothing about him. Without acknowledging her, he followed Bilfis and Talis below. A mutter of voices drifted up, in which she heard her own name several times, though she made out nothing more.

Tiaan looked up at Malien, who was staring at her. What was Malien thinking? Was she regretting giving up everything to save her, Tiaan? And poor, maimed Minis, condemned to a living death. Other tragedies, other disasters, though arising out of Tiaan's actions, had ultimately been caused by others. She had done this terrible wrong by herself, out of terror for her life. No, call it by its true name: cowardice. She had maimed the man who, for all his failings, had loved her. He'd been going to help her, she felt sure of that now, and in return she'd hurt him grievously and run away.

'Clan Elienor were blamed for allowing you to escape,' said Malien, 'and have suffered the greatest penalty Vithis could impose. They've been cast out, exiled and their constructs forfeited.'

Guilt overwhelmed Tiaan. The control yoke slipped in her hand and the construct dipped sharply.

'I think you'd better let me take over. Go below and lie down.' Within seconds Malien had ejected the amplimet and taken the yoke. Grim-faced, she flew between the unclimbable peaks.

The day faded. Tiaan lay dozing on her bunk. Malien flew on, torn half a dozen ways. Exile could not hurt her as it did her companions, for among her own people she'd been an outsider since the Forbidding was broken. Even so, to actively defy the entirety of her kind was no small thing. And now Tiaan's life had been laid in her hands – a precious, vital life if the nodes were fading, as Bilfis suspected. What was she to do about that?

Not to mention Clan Elienor. Though the clans had disappeared on Santhenar thousands of years ago, every Aachim knew their heritage. Malien's was the House of Elienor and she was a descendant of the great heroine. Now Clan Elienor were lost somewhere in Taltid. Their homes and means of travel had been confiscated and they had been abandoned to starve in a land stripped bare and plundered by lyrinx as well as human scavengers. Her duty was clear. She must do what she could for her people.

Malien knew roughly where Clan Elienor had to be. They had been left on the coast north-west of Snizort, where they could survive for a time by fishing and collecting seaweed, though when the fish migrated south to the Karama Malama in the winter their position would be dire. There was only one thing to be done. Around midnight, Malien turned south.

Tiaan woke wrapped in blankets but still cold. The thapter was whining furiously, and someone was coughing, over and over. She touched a globe to brightness. It was Bilfis, dabbing at his lips with a cloth that was stained red.

Seeing her staring, he said hoarsely, 'It's nothing. I suffer from mountain sickness. We're much higher than Stassor, here.'

She went up the ladder. It was mid-morning and Malien stood at the yoke, as she had all night.

'We're going back to Tirthrax,' said Malien.

'But you said we wouldn't be safe there.'

'Not for long, anyway,' Malien said tersely. 'We'll fill the thapter with provisions and other essential items, then head west.'

Tiaan, full of guilt and feeling that she was only here under sufferance, asked no questions.

'I plan to share my exile with Clan Elienor,' Malien went on. 'And ask them about the node problem, though they may not be able to help. The nodes of Santhenar must be very different from those of Aachan. It's lucky I have Bilfis. He's the most brilliant of all our field mancers and if anyone can solve this problem, he can.'

Tiaan took turns with her, winding through the passes night and day, and they reached Tirthrax on the third evening after fleeing Stassor. Malien flew inside and the Aachim got out. Bilfis, still coughing blood despite the lower altitude, came last.

'Stay here,' said Malien to Tiaan. 'Keep watch and make sure it's ready to go at a moment's notice. Forgre, would you set a sentinel at the entrance? I doubt if Harjax's thapters could reach here before this time tomorrow, since he has no relief pilots and they must stop to sleep, but we'd better be sure.'

They were gone many hours, during which Tiaan had ample time to reflect on her own problems, though not to find any resolution. The Aachim reappeared after midnight, wheeling trolleys filled with food and wine, bags and boxes of tools and equipment, a number of volumes of the Histories, plus atlases and charts of the western lands. It took until dawn to pack it all inside.

The sky was clear when they departed, and there was no sign of pursuit. Malien ordered Tiaan to set a course south-west, in the general direction of Snizort, and went below.

After an hour in which she got no sleep at all, Malien came back up. They were now flying over the north-western corner of Mirrilladell, a land of a million lakes and bogs. It looked pretty from the air but was scarcely inhabited, being bitterly cold in the long winter, and a mosquito-ridden hell in the short summer. Folktales told that the insects could bite through metal.

'Would you set down, Tiaan?' she said politely. 'Bilfis is no better. Even this height is troubling him.'

Tiaan settled the craft on a bare island in a braided stream milky with glacier-ground rock. They helped Bilfis out. He could not stop coughing.

'I begin to wonder if it *can* be mountain sickness,' said Malien. She unfastened his coat. 'Hold! What's that?'

There was a fresh stain on the back of his shirt. Bilfis raised a limp hand. 'It's nothing. A chip of stone hit me during the escape.'

'But that was days ago – let me see.' She tore off his shirt. Just below the shoulder blade a little green blister bulged out, leaking pale fluid.

'It's a flac!' said Malien in a rigidly controlled voice. 'Talis, my healer's bag, quickly!'

'What's a flac?' said Tiaan.

Malien did not answer.

'A tiny, burrowing dart,' Bilfis said weakly. 'It releases a slow poison into the blood that affects the breathing. It has to be cut out at once.'

'And never to be used against our own kind,' said Forgre grimly.

'It was intended for you, Tiaan,' said Bilfis, 'but you swerved unpredictably and I obviously took it instead. An irony, some might think.'

Talis raced up with the bag. Malien selected various bladed tools as well as a long thin pair of tweezers.

'It's too late,' Bilfis said. 'It'll be part-dissolved by now, Malien.'

'I have to try. Hold still.'

She began to cut into him. 'There, I see it,' she said after some time. 'Tweezers, Talis.'

He passed them across. 'This is a big risk, Bilfis,' said Malien. 'It's very fragile. I don't think I can get it out whole.'

'If it stays in, I die. If you break it, I die more quickly. It's designed so. I'm ready, either way.'

'It never occurred to me that they would use a flac against us,' said Malien, shaking her head.

'It's a forbidden weapon, even in clan-vengeance,' Forgre explained.

'But not against me,' said Tiaan.

'Not against the *lesser* species.' Malien wiped sweaty hands. Her lips moved in an exhortation, or a prayer. Slipping the tweezers into the slit, she took gentle hold of the end of the flac and tried to ease it out.

They all heard the sound, like rotten metal crunching. Bilfis jerked and his eyes went wide, then Malien was desperately, furiously raking the fragments from the wound and reaming out the residue, heedless of his pain.

Forgre held a white dish to Bilfis's back, probing the bloody residue with a forefinger. 'I think you may have got it,' he said.

Bilfis looked down at the dish and gave a rueful smile. 'I never thought—' He stiffened, gave the faintest of sighs and, with no other sign, he died.

'I wasn't quick enough.' Malien covered her face with her long fingers.

'No one ever is,' said Talis, closing the man's eyes.

Tiaan had expected them to take Bilfis's body to the Well of Echoes, but Malien was reluctant to do that given its unstable condition. They flew him up to the icefield on the high plateau, higher than Tiaan had ever been, where the cold was unrelenting. Malien melted a hole with the underside of the construct and slid the body in. Within a minute the water had frozen again, leaving him encased in ice as clear as glass. The Aachim sang a threnody in an archaic tongue.

'He loved the mountains,' said Malien, panting in the thin air. 'Bilfis would be happy that we've brought him here, where no other Aachim foot has ever trod.'

'No foot of any kind, I think,' said Talis the Mapmaker. 'No one could survive in such a high place.'

'Including us!' said Malien. 'A hundred thousand years from now he'll lie here unchanged. That would please him very much.' She headed for the thapter. 'But what are we going to do without him?'

They continued on to Snizort, flying long hours every day. It still took four days. Tiaan made measurements of the nodes whenever she got the chance, and marked them on the maps. Incessant work helped to keep her thoughts at bay. They passed by the battlefield, towards the Sea of Thurkad, and thence up the coast. The following afternoon they came upon a large encampment in a long but narrow inlet which had rocky ridges on either side. The camp was surrounded by a palisade of sharpened timber, the new home of exiled Clan Elienor. Tiaan saw no more of it, for as they approached Malien said, 'Go below.'

Tiaan searched Malien's lined face. 'Am I in danger here?'

'I don't know. It depends whether an outcast clan considers themselves bound by clan-vengeance. I won't risk it. Stay hidden while we unload the food and other supplies, and then we'll see.'

Tiaan spent the afternoon huddled under a blanket, trying to shut out the world. She could not erase her thoughts. The following morning Malien woke her. Talis and Forgre were there too.

'Stay where you are until we're in the air,' said Malien.

'Where are we going now?'

'West.'

'Across the sea to Meldorin?' said Tiaan. 'Where the lyrinx are?'

'We came at an opportune time. My people have just had vital news.'

'Oh?' said Tiaan.

'With Bilfis dead, only one person has the skills of geomancy and mathemancy to tell us how bad the node danger is, and how to avert it – the tetrarch, Gilhaelith. I now know where he's hiding.'

'Where is he?'

'He's north across the Sea of Thurkad, near a lyrinx city called Oellyll.'

Tiaan did not recognise the name, though it sent a shiver up her spine nonetheless. 'Is he a prisoner?'

'I don't think so. Word has it that he's made a deal with the enemy.'

FIFTY-FOUR

'What's the name of this place?' Tiaan asked as they were crossing the Sea of Thurkad.

Malien was at the controller. The sea here, almost eighty leagues north of the place where she had escaped from the Aachim nets, was more than twenty leagues across. In the distance she saw a gap in the range that ran down the east coast of Meldorin. The peaks were white, the flanks of the mountains dusted with an early fall of snow, for it was late autumn now. To the left, a steep-sided volcano fumed. There was no snow on its warm flanks, though similar dormant peaks to its north and south had caps of white.

Malien did not reply. She was frowning at the sullen water far below. 'Better go up; we could be seen at this height.' She lifted the thapter into the bumpy air inside the clouds.

'That's the Zarqa Gap,' said Talis, pointing, 'one of the few passes across these mountains, at least in the wintertime. See the ancient road?'

The thapter lurched. Tiaan caught another brief glimpse of the pass, then they were in opaque cloud again. Talis was silent until a second filmy gap appeared. 'It used to run all the way to the west coast, though already the forest is taking it back. The lyrinx eliminated the last people from these lands a generation ago.'

'Down south,' said Malien, 'further to our left, lie the ruins of Alcifer.'

There was nothing to see but cloud. 'I've heard that name,' said Tiaan. It gave her a shivery feeling.

'The city was designed by the brilliant architect Pitlis, for

584

Rulke, and Rulke's seduction of him is the greatest betrayal in the Histories. Many people say that Alcifer was the greatest creation of any of the human species, anywhere in the Three Worlds. It caused the downfall of my people, from which we have never recovered.'

The clouds broke and Tiaan pointed a spyglass where Malien had indicated. The mountains ran close to the sea there, and a flank of the volcano had been carved and sculpted to form the platform upon which Alcifer had been built. Great boulevards curved through it, and buildings great and small, their outlines just visible beneath aeons of growth, erosion and volcanic ash. From this distance no more detail could be seen.

On the slopes north of the city, the volcano had, long ago, formed a series of terraces covered in glittering crystalline salts, mud pools, geysers, fumaroles and the snaking lines of ancient lava tunnels whose tops had collapsed. Steam hung in wisps over the surface.

'That's chancy country,' said Talis, consulting an ancient gazetteer of the lands around Alcifer. 'When it rains, flows of mud and ash are dammed up against the edge of the terraces. They crust over. In the dry season, though if you tried to walk there you'd go straight through.'

'And slowly cook in hot mud,' said Forgre. 'Not how I'd choose to die.'

'In really wet years,' said Talis, reading from the gazetteer, 'the terrace walls burst and the hot slurry pours down the slope faster than a horse can gallop, sweeping trees and boulders away.'

'Chancy country indeed,' said Malien, rising into the clouds again.

'Is Alcifer in the Histories?' Tiaan asked.

'It's in the *Tale of Tar Gaarn*, which is in *our* Histories, but it's not much told these days. Rulke scarcely had the time to enjoy his creation, for soon after Alcifer was completed he was taken by the Council of Santhenar and cast into the Nightland; where he languished for a thousand years. Once freed, as far as is known, he never returned to Alcifer and it was never inhabited again. Who would dare?'

'Have *you* been there?'

Malien shivered. 'No, and I'm not looking forward to it. I feel the threat, even from here.'

Tiaan opened her mouth but closed it again. Malien was the most level-headed person she know. 'Where are we going now?'

'We'll fly across the range, then swing back and come on the place at night, on foot.'

The idea seemed absurd. How could they hope to find Gilhaelith in such a vast city, with so many lyrinx below and nearby? And if they did, how could they hope to free him?

They crossed the range north of the Zarqa Gap, at a pass that bore just a dusting of untracked snow. Keeping to what cloud they could find, they continued west over grassland and forest. The sun was sinking over the impassable swamp forests of Orist as they made a sweeping curve south and then east, approaching the range at its widest point, well south of Zarqa. Malien worked a set of concealed controls beneath the binnacle, then took the machine down as the sun set, cruising in the light of the stars, just above the treetops. It was eerie; everything was black and white and Tiaan found it difficult to measure distance. Trees and rocky peaks rushed at them out of nowhere.

'Aren't you worried about being spotted?' said Tiaan.

'I've just put a concealment on the thapter,' Malien said cryptically. 'It's quite effective from this distance, though I don't know how long I can keep it up.'

They floated above the treetops for hours, Talis and Forgre staring at their maps and conversing in whispers, before Talis said, 'Go down onto that bare spur, just to the left.'

Malien settled the thapter expertly on a shelf of some pale-coloured stone, shaped like the bowl of a spoon. A tree with a split trunk, black against the white bark, leaned out to over-hang the end of the ridge.

'This is as close as we dare go,' said Forgre, rubbing his

beardless cheek. 'We're but two leagues from Alcifer and Oellyll, the lyrinx city beneath it. Tens of thousands of lyrinx dwell there, and they hunt in these mountains.'

'Are we close to those terraces we saw yesterday?' said Tiaan. She could smell brimstone.

'They're that way,' said Talis, pointing towards the sea. 'They run east for leagues, then north high above the coast.'

'If you listen closely,' said Malien, 'you can hear the geysers going.'

No one spoke for a while, and in the distance Tiaan heard a rushing sound that built up to a muted roar before fading away.

'It seems a little *risky*, going down to Alcifer on foot,' she ventured.

'You mean insane and incomprehensible,' Malien observed dryly. 'I daren't take the thapter any closer. No concealment is perfect.'

'How are you going to find Gilhaelith in such a vast place?'

'We have certain information about his whereabouts.'

'How can you be sure it's reliable?'

'That's Forgre's job,' said Malien. 'He's our most gifted spy. Apparently the lyrinx shun Alcifer itself, so if Gilhaelith is there, using power, he won't be hard to find. Once Forgre discovers where he is, we'll fly down and snatch him.'

'Just like that?' said Tiaan.

'I hope so.'

'If Gilhaelith's in Alcifer, he must be trusted by the enemy.'

'He may be assisting them,' Forgre said, 'but I doubt they trust him.'

'From what I hear of Gilhaelith, he's always out for himself,' said Malien. 'I'd say they have some hold over him.'

Tiaan walked to the edge of the rock and stood looking down. The deep valley was like a pool of ink with a few pinpoints of light floating on it, starlight touching the tips of the tallest trees. She was so afraid, her knees would barely hold her up. Tiaan had sworn, after her captivity in Kalissin, that she would never go near the lyrinx again. But she had, and they'd put her into the patterners in Snizort. It was a horror she thought about every day.

Malien moved the thapter into deeper shelter and strengthened the concealment. 'That should be enough. It's a balance between doing enough to conceal the machine but not so much as to alert the enemy.'

'What if a lyrinx chances to walk past?'

'Any ordinary lyrinx could walk right into the thapter and just think it was rock. It hurts me to maintain it, though, so I hope it's not necessary for long.'

Malien turned into the forest. They followed silently, after an hour coming onto a narrow ridge that terminated in a cliff.

Malien peered over with her spyglass. 'Alcifer, look!' The hairs stood up on her nape.

Domes and spires rose out of woolly fog that hung in the hollows of the abandoned city like a bathtub full of kapok. How could a place abandoned so long ago still seem to hold such menace?

Forgre had been out several times. Tiaan had wondered how he could pass through the lyrinx guards into Alcifer, until she saw him in action. A master of the spying Art, he could blend into the background as well as any lyrinx, and when he moved it baffled the eye. It took a lot out of him, though; Forgre was always exhausted when he came back.

On their third day of watching, an air-floater appeared through a gap in the clouds and circled above Alcifer several times, before disappearing into the clouds again.

'What's that doing here?' hissed Malien.

'Oellyll is the greatest enemy city,' said Forgre. 'The scrutators often spy on it, now that they can fly above lyrinx height.'

'I can't imagine they'd see much from such an altitude.'

'It must be good for old-human morale.'

'Unfortunately for us, it'll make the lyrinx more watchful than ever,' said Malien.

'It may draw them away from us, at least.'

'Their fliers will be looking down as well as up.'

'Then we'll just have to be even more careful,' Forgre said wearily.

'Ah, I'm done in,' he said on his return from another mission. It was around midday on their fifth day of watching, and they were still camped by the lookout. The weather was cold and gloomy, with driven rain-showers, a chilly wind and occasional breaks of a watery sun that silvered the metal domes of Alcifer, far below.

Tiaan took up the spyglass and, as she had done a hundred times in the past days, swept it around and over the city. When the scudding showers passed, she could see slaves toiling in the lower gardens.

'Did you find him?' said Malien.

'No, though I know he's there.' Forgre looked down at his wiry hands, which were shaking. 'I'll have to rest awhile – my aftersickness is bad here.'

Tiaan looked through the spyglass again. 'He's *there*!'

'Forgre just said that,' Malien reminded her.

'*There*! Look!' Tiaan rose to her feet, pointing to a ridge east of theirs, which was rather lower. Its point, bare of trees, was momentarily exposed through the drifting mist.

Malien snatched the glass. 'I see six slaves, no, eight. They appear to be making readings of the field, at the direction of a very tall man. There could be more slaves in the shade of the trees.'

'It's Gilhaelith!' Tiaan whispered.

'Are you sure?'

'Positive.'

'How long have they been there?'

'I don't know. The mist has only just cleared.'

'They'll probably be taking readings for a while,' said Malien. 'This is the best chance we'll ever get. But how to do it?'

'Why not just fly there and grab him?' said Tiaan.

'The guards will hear the thapter long before we get there.

I can't conceal that. Once they do, the illusion will break and they'll vanish into the forest with him. We'll have to get to Gilhaelith on foot. Tiaan, slip back to the thapter and take it across, but hang further up the ridge, in the mist. My concealment will hold as long as you don't get too close.'

'What are you going to do?'

'We'll go across, also under concealment, and hide near the wall of the lowest terrace. I'll know when you're coming and take Gilhaelith. The instant I signal, race down and pick us up.'

'Are you sure you can do it?'

'Yes. You'd better get going.'

It all seemed suspiciously easy, but it would be presumptuous of her to challenge Malien's plan. As the Aachim disappeared beneath her concealment it occurred to Tiaan that Forgre's aftersickness had seemed really bad. She hoped he was up to it, because he certainly didn't look it.

FIFTY-FIVE

Tiaan headed up along the ridge and, with every step, the blockage in her chest seemed to grow. What if the lyrinx called down their fliers? What if the enemy had already found the thapter?

By the time she reached its hiding place, the clot had grown to half the size of her chest and fire was radiating from the point where she had broken her back. She clung to a tree, panting. She could not see the thapter anywhere.

She tried to remain calm. It was under a concealment, even from her. Malien had forgotten this, in the excitement at discovering Gilhaelith. It wasn't like her, and Tiaan's uneasiness grew. What if she couldn't find it?

She moved back towards the cliff, sweeping her head from side to side. Near the edge, from the very corner of her eye, a blocky shape appeared and disappeared between the trees, where there had been no shape previously. It *was* there.

She patted it with outstretched hands. It even felt like rock but, as Tiaan concentrated, the gritty surface smoothed out under her fingers. She went up the side in a rush, inserted the crystal in its socket and closed the hatch. Only then did she feel safe.

Bringing the thapter up to just below the tops of the trees, she wove her way between them, heading upslope of the exposed point where Gilhaelith had been, towards the terraces. It took a lot of concentration, and it was hard to be sure she was in the right place.

Tiaan circled for half an hour, feeling increasingly anxious about the mist, which might prevent Malien from seeing her;

the delay; and how well the concealment was holding. If Malien was signalling, how could she tell?

As the thapter eased up the terrace again, the screen began to fog over and Tiaan had to flip the hatch open to see. Strands of drifting mist swirled about her. She went higher but that made it worse. Holding her spyglass in one hand, she curved downhill again.

Edging the thapter over an outcrop of black rock furred with brilliantly green moss, she spotted a group of raggedly dressed people in the clearing, waving madly. The concealment must have parted. She turned away, hoping distance would renew it. There were violent movements in the undergrowth, then one of the slaves staggered out onto the rocks, bleeding from the belly. The attack had started, but where was the signal?

Tiaan made a tight circle, wondering what to do. Mist swept up the ridge, concealing everything, and when it broke some minutes later she saw Malien confronting a huge dark lyrinx. Neither looked up; the concealment had re-formed. Tiaan took the thapter sideways. Several bodies lay on the other side of the clearing, red and broken. She could not tell if they were Aachim, slaves or Gilhaelith. She went lower, turning in mid-air but not knowing what to do. She dared not land until she saw him.

And there he was, staggering across the rocks with two human slaves clinging to his arms. That didn't make sense either, though it was clear Malien's attack had failed. If she didn't do something, both Malien and Gilhaelith would be lost.

Tiaan sideslipped towards the point. The great lyrinx looked around, hearing the noise but unable to hold Malien and break the concealment at the same time. As Tiaan touched down, the lyrinx hurled Malien into the rocks, spun on the sole of one foot, its crest shimmering iridescently in the misty gloom, and raised its fist.

The thapter sang like a bundle of taut wires. Everyone on the ridge spun around, staring as it materialised in mid-air.

The creature raised its right arm and lyrinx burst out of the rocks, not stone-formed but camouflaged so perfectly there had been no trace of them. Tiaan's intuition had been right – it *was* a trap and it had already closed on Forgre. She recognised his broken body near the edge of the cliff.

She couldn't see Talis but Malien was on her feet, swaying as she worked her fingers in the air. The two slaves fell down. Gilhaelith tore the cords from around his wrists and raced for the trees.

'Gilhaelith!' Tiaan screamed. 'This way!'

His head whipped around. 'Tiaan?'

He took one step towards her, puzzled but not looking pleased. She was wondering why when a flying lyrinx swooped out of the mist, clamped its claws into his ribs and lifted him bodily.

Gilhaelith thrashed and it almost fell out of the air. Darting its open jaws at him, it gripped him around the top of the head until its teeth broke the skin. Tiaan was so close she could see the spots of blood. He went still and it pulled him in under the trees, out of sight, labouring under his weight.

Malien's attacker now rushed Tiaan, its spread wings darkening the sky. Its armour was as black as coal, its mighty crest a luminous gold. Many other lyrinx followed. They'd been after her, and the thapter, all along. The intelligence that Gilhaelith was at Alcifer must have been planted to lure her here, but it had been Malien who had taken the bait.

Tiaan slammed the hatch, twisting the lock as the first creature thudded onto the roof. Its claws tore at the metal but could find no grip, the seams were too perfect. Another lyrinx leapt onto the thapter, then half a dozen more, until the roof creaked under their weight. Between them she saw the black mancer-lyrinx, carrying a great bar with which to prise the hatch open. They could not use their Art, for the thapter was proof against it, but nothing could protect her from sheer physical force.

A glittering, luminous bubble burst against the black lyrinx's back but he shrugged it off. He did not turn to attack

Malien, whose magic it was, nor even to defend himself. It was an expression of contempt: you can't harm *me*.

Icy sweat oozed down Tiaan's back. The trap was closing fast. Forgre was dead, probably Talis as well. Gilhaelith had been removed. Now Malien fought alone against dozens of opponents, and surely could not last.

Running away was not a temptation – Tiaan wasn't going down that road again. The thumping against the shell of the thapter was deafening, and now it went dark inside as they covered the screen. She pulled up on the yoke, thinking to turn upside down and shake them off. The thapter vibrated so hard that her bones rattled, but did not lift; the weight of dozens of lyrinx was too much for it.

Tiaan tried to spin it on the spot but that didn't work either – the lyrinx must have linked arms with those on the ground, who dug in their claws and held it. She could not break their grip.

Cutting off the field, she sat back, panting. There had to be a way. The darkness broke as a small triangle of screen was cleared. A face appeared – the mancer-lyrinx. His anthracite skin glittered as if it had been sprinkled with diamond dust; the golden crest pulsed dark and bright. Power shimmered all around him like heat haze rising from a salt-pan.

He thrust his toothy head towards the screen, seeking her out. Tiaan kept away from the light, for he smouldered enough to burn her, and if his gaze locked on hers he might be able to command her to his will.

Tiaan could feel the command building. *Come into the light, where I can see you. Come. Come!*

Her hand shook. She wanted to go to him, to look into his eyes. It felt like the right thing to do. He wasn't her enemy. He would make it right for her.

What was she thinking? Tiaan moved back smartly, whacking her head on the back of the compartment. There had to be a way – she was a geomancer after all – and a brilliant one, according to Gilhaelith.

She'd not done any geomancy in ages. Since gaining the thapter, Tiaan had used its speed, its strength, and simply run away from her troubles. The great talents she'd begun to nurture had been neglected.

The golden-crested lyrinx jammed his bar into the join between the hatch and the shell of the thapter, and heaved. Metal screamed. If she was to save Malien, there was no time to lose.

Tiaan popped out the amplimet. Gripping it hard, she scanned the earth below the ridge, though not seeking power. She kept well away from the throbbing Alcifer node-within-a-node, which was far beyond her comprehension. She was looking for a way to use her fledgling geomancy; an attack they would never suspect.

She sensed many things – the aeons-slow creep of rocks under strain, the imperceptible rise of magma pools far below, the crackling of ancient lava fields surrounding the dormant volcano to the north. None were useful to her, nor the tension on a great faultline that curved beneath Alcifer. That held power beyond anyone's capacity to bear.

Metal squealed above her, as if the hatch were coming off. Ah, *there* was something! Seeping heat from the quiescent volcano had created the fuming, seething terraces above her, with their lines of hot springs and mud pools. She traced the paths of superheated fluid through the rocks nearby, seeking a weakness she could exploit to blast steam at the lyrinx, or create a minor landslide that might cause them to draw back in panic. She didn't need much.

The bar ground at the join of the hatch again and again, the shrill squeal tearing at her nerves. The black lyrinx's teeth were bared as it strained. There were so many paths of heat flowing through cracks and fissures; so many places where the superheated ground water was held tight. If she could find a weakness, and assist the rocks to give way there, the water must burst forth.

She found one but it was too far away. Another lay just above the ridge – too close and too powerful to take the risk.

A third pool had a fissure above it, sealed tight by crystallised salt, and it looked just right.

Tiaan explored its aura and field, seeking to know it, as she must. The fissure had been open many times in the past, making a spectacular geyser for weeks or months before the vent become blocked again.

Just a little extra pressure and the crystallised salt would crack like toffee. Tiaan put her fingers in her ears to block out the rasp of metal against metal as she hunted for a way that was within her capacity. She did not have the power to make the earth move. She had to use what was there, and fortunately the system was so delicately balanced that a small change could upset it.

She changed the field to direct a surge of heat into that lower chamber. The superheated water roiled, burst through a flimsy barrier and forced its way up. The lines of force changed colour; the salt plug cracked and was blasted away as the water forced its way up into a terrace filled with mud.

As the pressure was relieved, the water turned instantly to steam, boiling the mud and blasting a brown geyser upwards with a shriek that had the great lyrinx clapping his hands over his ears. He fell backwards, allowing Tiaan to see what she had done.

A circular wave of mud roared out from around the geyser, overtopping the banks that made a dam of the terrace, then tearing channels through them. A deluge of boiling mud began to pour over the slope above them like jam from the lip of a cooking pot.

The lyrinx hurled themselves out of the way, diving off the edges of the ridge and over the cliffs. Only the mancer-lyrinx held to his purpose, slamming his bar into the angle of the hatch yet again. He darted a glance over his shoulder, gave another prise that made metal squeal, then gave up the fight and lifted straight up in the air. The steam burst caught him, whirling him about then over the edge and out of sight.

Tiaan, limp-kneed and dripping perspiration, jerked up on the flight yoke. Nothing happened, for she still held the amplimet in her hand. It took some time to realise what the problem was. She banged it into its cavity, waited a second till it settled and jerked again.

The thapter shot into the air, buffeted by the steam blast as the wave of mud swept diagonally across the ridge, carrying trees, bushes and three unfortunate lyrinx with it, before pouring in a brown curtain over the cliff to her left. She'd overdone it yet again.

She hovered while it passed, looking for survivors. There was no sign of Malien and two-thirds of the ridge was covered in waist-deep sludge. The bodies of the fallen slaves, as well as Forgre, had been swept away. Five slaves cowered near the untouched end of the ridge, their faces scarlet from the steam.

Had she killed Gilhaelith? The lyrinx had taken him up the ridge into the forest, but that patch of trees had been swept away by the mudslide. She curved around the clifftops, just in case he'd got away. Yes, there he was. The lyrinx was just below the top of the cliff, still carrying him. Gilhaelith wasn't struggling. Surely he didn't *want* to go with it?

She turned towards them. The lyrinx caught an updraught and began to flap off, barely keeping Gilhaelith's weight in the air. As it passed below the point, heading for distant Alcifer, one of the slaves let out a furious cry of betrayal and hurled a rock, cracking it on the back of the skull. Its wing-beats faltered and it dropped sharply. *Now*, Tiaan thought.

She went round, passing close to the labouring beast to prevent it from getting away until she could think how to wrest Gilhaelith from it safely. Tiaan's brain fizzed from the power it was using.

It bared its teeth and one clawed hand struck out at the thapter. It was just a reflex, for she was too far away and the metal was proof against its claws. Its wings rippled. Gilhaelith shouted something but Tiaan could not make it out. Did he want her to attack, or keep well away? *As* she circled, the thapters wake buffeted the creature. Again it dropped; its wings missed a beat; its mouth hung open. She crept towards it, driving it to the cliff and the tall trees that reached two-thirds of the way to the top.

The lyrinx shuddered and its chameleon skin flared red, then white, then purple. It tried to duck in under the upper canopy of a tree but Tiaan smashed through the small branches after it. Its eyes were staring, its mouth opening and closing.

One wing struck a branch. The lyrinx fell, saved itself with a great flapping of leathery wings and crashed into the lower branches. Everything disappeared in a whirling cloud of leaves. When that cleared, the lyrinx came out on the underside of the canopy but it was no longer holding Gilhaelith.

Tiaan panicked, whirling the thapter this way and that, thinking he'd fallen. She was about to dart down the cliff when she heard a thin cry and spotted him clinging to the fork of a denuded branch.

Tiaan brought the thapter around and underneath, feeling quite desperately weary. Her hand shook on the controller; her spine throbbed mercilessly. Spans below, the lyrinx was struggling up through the foliage towards him.

She made the minute adjustments necessary to bring the hatch up beneath Gilhaelith, but he shook his head and began to crawl along the branch away from her. His trouser leg had been shredded, one boot was missing and he had blood down his side. And still he did not want to be rescued. What was the matter with him?

He raised his hands, out and up in the classic mancer's pose. He was drawing power against her! Without thinking, Tiaan rammed the branch from beneath. He lost his grip and fell through the hatch, landing so hard that it winded him. As the lyrinx beat its way towards her, Tiaan rotated the craft in the air and shot upwards.

Gilhaelith lay collapsed on the floor. The surviving lyrinx were converging on the untouched end of the ridge, where the remaining slaves huddled. Malien had survived, surrounded by a small protective bubble, though she was on her knees.

Tiaan raced the lyrinx there. As she settled the machine

next to Malien, the slaves surged forward then stopped, staring at the thapter. They could never have seen anything like it. Tiaan's head boiled over. The lyrinx that had abducted Gilhaelith was now circling some distance away, signalling furiously down.

Her eye was drawn down, down, to Alcifer. From behind the central dome a winged creature rose into the air, followed by a second and a third. Others joined them, leaping into the sky with their massive thighs. Dozens. Hundreds. A whole wall of them.

'Quick, Malien!' she shouted. 'They're coming.'

An ashen Malien dragged herself up over the side. The slaves moved tentatively towards the thapter.

'Where's Talis?' cried Tiaan.

Malien shook her head. 'He's gone. Forgre too.' Her voice was tight with grief.

The fizzing exploded in Tiaan's mind. She lifted the yoke and the thapter rose jerkily, though its whine hardly changed. Something was wrong.

'I've hardly any power,' she said. 'They must be using some kind of node-drainer.'

'Can't be,' slurred Malien. 'It's not stopping them from flying.'

The slaves began to run towards them, crying and holding out their arms. 'What about the slaves?' said Tiaan.

'Go, before it's too late.'

Tiaan looked into the desperate eyes of the slaves and wanted to weep. How could she leave them behind – she had been one herself. But there was no choice. Feeling like a murderer, she jerked up the yoke. The machine lifted sluggishly. Men and women with staring eyes clutched at the sides but there was nothing to hang on to. The thapter rose to half the height of the trees but would climb no higher, and it moved forward no faster than a running man. A wall of lyrinx were spiralling up from Alcifer, rolling into a flapping cylinder that was closing rapidly on her.

'What am I to do?' cried Tiaan. 'I can't get past them.'

There was no answer. Malien lay slumped on the floor on top of Gilhaelith. Tiaan fixed the field in her mind. There was plenty of power in it, but when she drew it, only a trickle came.

'I'll try to draw from another node,' she said to herself. She found one, more distant, latched onto it and the thapter shot up through the closing cylinder of lyrinx.

Gilhaelith shook Malien off and came to his feet, looking dazed. The thapter lurched and he fell through the hole to the lower level. He began to climb back up. Tiaan couldn't afford the distraction, for lyrinx were now rising out of Alcifer in their thousands. She dropped the hatch and kicked the bar across. Gilhaelith began to beat on the metal.

The lyrinx spread out to cut off her escape to the east, the south and the north. She had no alternative but to turn west. Within a minute the power began to fade, and shortly the thapter was back to its previous pace. The burst of speed had taken it west; snow-tipped peaks loomed ahead. She looked over her shoulder. The lyrinx were gaining rapidly.

There was still an hour to sunset, but that wouldn't save her. This close, the enemy could track her all night. She tried another node but the acceleration was less and did not last as long. They had anticipated her. She kept going, switching from one node to another as soon as the power began to fail, jerking and hopping across the sky but never getting far enough ahead to lose them.

The thapter passed over, or rather between, the mountains, for Tiaan dared not try for extra height. Beyond, a grass-covered plain extended into the distance. She continued west, now travelling swiftly with a strong tailwind. The lyrinx had spread out for leagues to north and south.

Malien stirred and rolled over onto her back, observing what Tiaan did without speaking.

'I can't get away,' Tiaan said. 'What if I were to turn back and fly straight at them?'

'They might take all your power,' said Malien hoarsely. She shook her head. 'It was a trap and I walked right into it. They lured us here. That's why Gilhaelith's whereabouts were common knowledge. I can't believe I didn't realise it.'

'You'd still have gone ahead,' said Tiaan.

'But more carefully. And Forgre and Talis might still be alive. Now I truly stand alone in the world.'

Tiaan did not have the words to comfort her. On they went, carving their staccato path, sometimes gaining, sometimes losing. They passed across the plain into swamp and forest. The thapter dipped sharply, as if it had lost power for a second, after which the hum resumed, though at a lower pitch.

'What was *that*?' said Malien, sitting up.

'It was as if, for a second, the controller wasn't working, though I could still see the field.'

Tiaan continued at a reduced pace. At sunset she looked back, but could not see the lyrinx at all. 'They've given up! They've turned back, Malien.'

Malien climbed onto the side, staring into the east. 'I believe you're right. I wonder why?'

'I suppose they realised that they'd never catch us.'

'Can you draw power now?'

'No more than before.'

'Curious,' said Malien to herself. 'Could they have attached a draining device to this machine?'

'Which way should I go, north or south?'

'Try south.'

Tiaan moved the lever in the required direction. Nothing happened. She tried again, then the other way.

'Malien!' she said in a panicky voice. 'It's not answering the controls.'

The song of the mechanism suddenly stopped and the thapter arced down towards the plains.

'Malien,' Tiaan screamed. 'I've got nothing. It must be the amplimet. It's trying to kill us.'

'But a crash would destroy it too.' Malien swayed on her feet, popped the crystal and took the controls. It made no difference; they kept plummeting earthwards.

'We're going to die,' said Tiaan. 'I never thought it would be like this.'

'I can see the field but I can't draw power from it either.'

'Why not?'

'I don't know. It just isn't working. Nothing's working.'

As abruptly, the song of the mechanism was back. The thapter lurched left, then jerked so hard to the right that Malien was thrown against the wall. The whole machine shuddered, before curving into level flight.

Malien moved the yoke every possible way, but it made no difference. She let go. The yoke moved left by itself. The thapter veered in the same direction, a little south of west, and the note of the machine went up a notch.

Tiaan sat on the floor, her chin resting on her knees. 'I don't know what's happening, Malien.'

'Someone . . . something has taken control of it and I can't get it back. So that's why the lyrinx gave up. They knew they could snatch it away from us whenever they wanted to.'

'Either that,' said Tiaan, 'or the amplimet is up to its treacherous work again.'

'But why now?' said Malien. 'Why *here*, after coming all this way?'

The thapter, whining gently, sped on.

'I suppose there's a node it wants to communicate with.'

FIFTY-SIX

'Xervish,' said Irisis one chilly night a few days after she'd come back from Snizort. They were sitting on either side of the fire after another of her masterly dinners. Everyone else had gone to bed. She was working on a piece of jewellery in silver filigree.

'Mm?' He was perusing a chart of central Lauralin, showing Nennifer and the surrounding mountains.

Flydd had been in a better humour since their return. He spent most of his time working in a large journal, either writing, sketching maps, charts and plans, or making endless lists and calculations. Only the relationship with Yggur was little changed. He circled Yggur, snapping and snarling, while Yggur maintained a chilly reserve. They could never be friends. It remained to be seen whether they could work together at all.

'How did you come to meet Eiryn Muss?'

'Why do you ask?' Flydd said without looking up.

'He's the strangest man I ever met. What does he want, or care about, or feel? No one knows.'

'He's the best spy there is – that's all I care about.'

His tone told Irisis to mind her own business, and for that reason she'd long delayed asking him, but she couldn't hold it in any longer.

'Did you know he's a morphmancer?'

'*What*!' he rose out of his chair. 'Where did you hear that?'

'I spied on him before we went into Jibstorn. He doesn't assume a disguise at all – he simply shapechanges, clothes and all, and it only takes him a minute.'

Flydd let out his breath so violently that the candle flames flickered and danced. 'I often wondered how he did it so perfectly, and so quickly.'

'And you never asked?'

'Every craft has its secrets. As long as the job's done, what does it matter how it's done? Why didn't you tell me this before?'

'You get cranky whenever I approach one of your precious mancer's secrets, Xervish.'

'Cranky, *me*? Is there anything else you want to get off your chest?'

'Well, er . . .'

'It's important, Irisis,' he said snappishly. He sat down again, pulling his chair closer to the fire.

'What else was Muss looking for in Snizort?'

'What do you mean?'

'Apart from the flesh-formed creatures, and the phynadr we stole?'

'That's all.' He seized her hands in his gnarled paws. 'Why do you ask?'

'After we'd found them, he was still looking for something. Muss didn't find it and was mightily put out.'

'Put out?'

'It's the only time I've ever seen him show emotion. He was really vexed.'

'What can he have been looking for?' Flydd began to pace back and forth on the worn flagstones. 'He's a morphmancer, a powerful adept. And he went to Gumby Marth just after the battle, defying my orders.' He paled. 'He must have been after the tears.'

'Did he know about them then?' said Irisis.

'I told him when he met me, after Troist picked me up . . .'

'So why was he looking for them at Snizort, weeks before?'

'I don't know. No one knew . . . Unless . . .'

'Xervish?'

'What if it was *him* all along?' Flydd breathed. 'Muss had charge of the device Ghorr gave me in Nennifer, to break the

604

node-drainer. And a morphmancer might easily overcome the scrutator magic that sealed the box. What if Muss tampered with the device, so as to *create* the tears?'

'If he did, why didn't he use it himself?'

'No one could predict what would happen. Safer to let you and me do it.'

'If it was Muss, why didn't he go directly to the node? Why was he looking for the tears in Snizort?'

'He must have thought they'd form at the node-drainer,' said Flydd. 'By the time he realised otherwise, the tears were gone. Jal-Nish had them.'

'And Muss has been hunting them ever since,' said Irisis. 'I wish you'd mentioned this before I sent him back to Lauralin.'

'Why does he want the tears anyway? Who *is* Muss?'

'He's been my faithful, meticulous spy for many, many years. It's hard to believe he could be otherwise.' He stood up. 'But one good thing has come out of your news, Irisis.'

'What's that, Xervish?'

'I feel inspired again.'

'No progress on the construct mechanism, Yggur?' Flydd said the following morning.

Yggur had just emerged from his workroom, looking as though he'd neither slept nor changed his clothes in days. On returning from Snizort he had taken the construct's mechanism to pieces and begun working on it by himself.

'I don't expect miracles. It's only been a few days.' He did look disappointed, though.

'I wonder how Tiaan managed it?' said Nish. 'It didn't take her long to make one fly.'

'Now there's a thought,' said Yggur. 'What happened to the flying construct after Vithis took Tiaan?'

'It burned. It was covered in tar.'

'Did you learn anything while you were in it? About how she made it fly, I mean?'

'It was Tirior's construct, but Tiaan made it go when Tiror

605

could not, using the amplimet to draw on a distant field. A little later, Tiaan had us blindfolded while she did something to the mechanisms, and after that it flew.'

'But *how* did she make it fly?' said Yggur to himself.

'Vithis had custody of her amplimet for a long time,' said Flydd, 'yet never succeeded in making any of his constructs fly. Which means . . .'

'That Tiaan alone knows the secret and he couldn't get it out of her,' said Nish.

'There must be more to it,' said Flydd.

'There's more,' said Yggur with a remote smile. 'I've had a full report come in by skeet. When Tiaan escaped from the Aachim she had the amplimet, but the construct didn't fly. Something vital must have been lost in the one that burned, and she couldn't replace it. We're getting closer.'

'And she's getting further away,' said Flydd.

'After flying a construct, merely hovering must be galling to her. She'll want to replace what was burned as quickly as possible.'

'She'll go back to Tirthrax,' said Flydd, bright-eyed, 'where she first discovered the secret, doubtless with Malien's aid. We can expect to see a flying machine again before too long.'

'Malien's still alive?' Yggur exclaimed. 'That *is* good news. What can you—?'

'Ask Nish,' said Flydd. 'He's met her!' It galled Flydd, for he'd desperately wanted to meet the legend when he had been in Tirthrax, but she hadn't shown herself.

'I had a couple of run-ins with her,' said Nish, looking down at his hands. 'Neither to my credit, though at the time I thought I was doing the right thing.'

'I'm beginning to see a possibility,' said Yggur. 'I've a mind to take the air-floater to Tirthrax and talk to Malien.'

'You can't have it!' said Flydd.

Yggur grew very still. 'You, a beggarly ex-scrutator, presume to tell me what I can do?'

'It's all we've got and if we lose it, we're finished,' said Flydd, daunted but defiant. 'And we *will* lose it. The lyrinx will be watching the skies, and so will the scrutators.'

'What's the point in having an air-floater if you haven't the courage to use it?'

'I need it for a plan of my own. Anyway, I thought you were going to make a flier with the construct mechanism?'

'It may take years to discover a secret that Tiaan or Malien could show us in a few minutes. What's your plan?'

Flydd hesitated. Secrecy was a way of life to him. His tired eyes searched Yggur's face, then he seemed to come to a decision. 'It also relies on a flying construct, though I'm not planning to build one. I'm going to track Tiaan down and ask her for the secret. Then, go to Tirthrax and make a flying construct from the damaged machines there.'

'And if that fails?'

'Attempt it at Snizort, where there are hundreds to choose from.'

'And once you have your flying machine, what then?'

Flydd studied his adversary. It was hard to overcome this instinctive rivalry, not to mention his dislike of a man who seemed so much more than he, in every respect, yet was reluctant to use his talents for the war.

With an effort, he put the feelings aside. 'Nennifer, the scrutators' secret bastion, isn't designed for defence against flying constructs. They'd never expect us to have one, or to attack them. I plan to go in at night, through the roof, and take them by surprise. In half an hour it could all be over.'

'Just you against eleven Council members and their thousands of guards and mancers?'

'I'll go alone, if no one will come with me,' said Flydd. 'The Council must be overthrown and I've sworn to do it, whatever it costs.'

Yggur regarded him, smiling faintly. 'You took your sweet time about it, but for once I agree. I will work with you, after all. First we must have flight. Once we have it, we bring down the Council and replace it. Only then can we plan how to end the war.'

Flydd stood up and shook his hand. 'I'll send Flangers out

in the air-floater, to contact Muss . . .' His eyes met Irisis's. 'Yes, Muss. If anybody can find Tiaan, he can.' *If he's still working for me*, he thought.

'And I'll send skeets to my factors, with the same message' said Yggur. 'It seems that we have the beginnings of a plan. While we wait to hear from our spies, I'll keep working on the construct mechanism. Nish will assist me and Flangers will be our labourer. Irisis and Inouye will work with me on a flight controller. You, Flydd, will refine your plan to take Nennifer and consider what you will do afterwards. If Malien or Tiaan *is* abroad in a flying construct, half the world will know of it.'

'What about the Numinator, surr?' Irisis said quietly to Flydd as they went back to the fire. 'Since he controls the Council, he won't appreciate you overthrowing it.'

'A masterly understatement,' said Flydd. 'Know your enemy, and I don't, so there's no way to prepare for him. But he dwells a long way south, so it'll be a while before he realises what has happened. I'll have that time to deal with him.'

'Or be dealt with,' Irisis added gloomily.

'Quite.'

A month went by. Though they made no secret of their dislike for each other, Flydd and Yggur had managed to achieve a working truce. At the end of that period they met to report progress.

'I haven't come up with much, I'm afraid.' Yggur touched the little beetle-shaped device that he had demonstrated before. With a faint hum it rose into the air. He moved his hands before him, sending the device whizzing down the room. It curved around in a series of spirals then floated back just below the ceiling. Another wave of his hands and it settled to the table without a sound. Yggur went pale and abruptly sat down.

'It flies,' he said hoarsely, 'but only for a few moments, and takes a great deal out of the user. What have you to report, Irisis?'

Irisis demonstrated her progress on a flight controller, but she could do no more without testing it in a full-sized flying machine.

'And you, Flydd?'

'The plan to attack Nennifer is coming along. I'll go through it with you in private later.'

'Did you manage to contact Muss, surr?' said Irisis.

'He's disappeared,' said Flydd with knotted jaw. 'Flangers could find no trace of him and he didn't reply to messages left at any of his rendezvous.'

'He's left you,' said Yggur. 'Muss has struck out on his own.'

By the scrutator's expression he thought so too, though he did not appreciate Yggur's pointing it out.

'Has either of you had news of the war?' Irisis asked.

'It's not *much* worse than before,' said Yggur. 'And with the coming of winter we can expect the situation to ease. The lyrinx breed at that time, avoiding conflict if they can.'

'They attacked our manufactory in winter, over and again,' said Irisis.

'Just small bands, I'll warrant, made up of lyrinx who had not yet mated.'

'Then let's pray for a long winter,' said Nish, 'and a vigorous mating season.'

'Judging by the early snowfalls,' said Yggur, 'it's going to be a hard winter. There'll be famine in Lauralin before spring.'

'Is it better to starve to death in the cold or be eaten by the enemy?' said Flydd. 'I think I'd probably choose the latter. If that's all, I'll go back to my work.'

'Ah!' Yggur held up a long finger. 'One more thing. A skeet came in the other day, bearing a message that's come in relays all the way from the east.' He looked pleased about it.

'Well?' Flydd snapped, not liking his own tricks being used on him.

'A flying construct was sighted over Stassor last week.'

'What!'

'It's true. It was seen on more than one occasion.'

'So Tiaan has gone to the Aachim.'

'It would appear so . . .'

Yggur looked as if he was holding something back, and Nish thought he knew what it was. 'I happened to be up on the wall at dawn this morning,' Nish said; 'I couldn't sleep. I saw another skeet come in.'

'It brought even better news. Just two days ago a second flying construct was seen above Stassor. It was a new design, quite different from Vithis's constructs.'

'So the secret is out!' breathed Flydd. 'If they can make two, they can make a thousand. And so, hopefully, can we.'

'What were they doing?' asked Nish.

'Good question,' said Yggur. 'The original one was flying a regular pattern over the mountains surrounding Stassor.'

'Really?' frowned Flydd.

'It flew slowly along a line, east-west, further than my informant could see, turned south for a league and flew back along a line parallel to the first. It did that all night. My spy was not able to find out what the flying construct was doing, though he did learn the identity of one of the people inside, as it turned for home in the morning. It was Tiaan.'

'She's surveying the nodes,' Irisis burst out. 'Even when she was a child, Tiaan used to map fields.'

'Interesting,' said Yggur, and there was a strange gleam in his eye. 'I'm getting an idea.'

They scarcely saw Yggur after that. He spent day and night in his workroom, labouring frantically on a project that he would not talk about, and rebuffed everyone who came to the door.

Irisis was insatiably curious. One day, being at an impasse in her work, she decided to find out what he was up to. She cooked another of her glorious meals, loaded up a tray and knocked at the door.

'Go away!' he roared, sounding more frosty than usual.

Irisis faltered, but she had not got this far without being strong of will and thick of hide, so she turned the handle and went in.

'Get out!' he said without looking up.

'I brought you something to eat,' she said softly. 'It'll be a change from the gruel your cook provides, the same thing day after day.'

'I like the same thing day after day.' He glanced at the tray, at her, back at the tray. He moistened his lips. 'Oh, very well, bring it here.'

She pushed the door shut with her foot and put the tray on the table, careful not to disturb his work. 'I've made—' she began.

'I can see! What do you want, Irisis?'

'I don't want anything . . .'

'I'm not stupid.'

'All right,' she said quietly. 'Let me be honest with you.'

'Why do those words always make me think I'm about to be conned?'

'I want to know what you're working on.'

'And I don't want to tell you.'

'Don't you trust me?'

'I don't trust anyone except the one person who has never let me down. Myself.'

'*I've* never let you down.'

'Ah, but you will. Everyone does, in the end.'

She laughed. 'You're a sad man, Yggur.'

'And you're making me sadder.'

'I'm doing you good. Anyway, I know what you're up to.'

Yggur selected a freshly baked roll, bit into it and leaned back in his chair, chewing reflectively. His black boots rested on the edge of the table. 'Go on.' He smiled, as if knowing she was going to make a fool of herself.

Perhaps she was. 'Until our last council of war, your door was always open and everyone could see what you were working on – either your little flying beetle, or the construct mechanism. You haven't touched them in weeks.'

'How do you know?'

She ran a fingertip over the iridescent surface of the beetle. 'Dust! The only devices free of it are the sphere of Golias the Mad, and this controller apparatus we took from the construct. And, judging by the way you've rebuilt the controller, I can tell what you're doing.'

'Really?' he said mockingly.

'You're trying to combine the two so you can seize control of a flying construct, should one ever come this way.' It was just a hunch, but a good one.

The chair fell forwards and his eyes met hers. 'Go to the door, check that there's no one outside, and lock it.'

She did so.

'Sit down,' he said fiercely. 'Who else knows?'

'No one.' Irisis took the chair at the end of the table, not entirely comfortable. She knew his reputation of long ago. Yggur was a hard man, not averse to riding over others to get what he wanted. If she was a threat to him, he might even decide to be rid of her. She didn't think so – Irisis was a good judge of character – but you could never tell with mancers. 'I worked it out just then. It was a flash of insight, really.'

'Explain!'

'When you first showed us Golias's sphere, your eyes were positively glowing with yearning. I've not seen you that inspired about anything else, not even your little flier. You want Golias's secret more than anything.'

'I've wanted it from the moment I saw the device.' He took the glass sphere in his big hands, turning it this way and that, staring through its outer layer at her.

Irisis had a momentary loss of confidence. Yggur had lived more than a thousand years, had seen everything this world had to offer, yet he looked no older than a hale and powerful fifty. All her life and experience were no more than the blink of an eye to him. But she must go on. 'And then, when you told us about Tiaan surveying the nodes the other day, I saw that look again.'

'Continue,' he said softly.

'The clincher is the way you've rebuilt this construct controller. Controllers are my life, Yggur. My mother had me pulling them to pieces and putting them back together before I could walk. See here and here and here,' she touched in turn the flat coils of metal that whorled out from the cup holding the powering crystal, and the reciprocating rods that extended in six directions, 'these are surely to channel power from the crystal to the controlling levers, and these to convey it to various parts of the construct—'

'You can tell all that so quickly? I've spent weeks puzzling it out.'

'I've been working with fields since I was an infant.'

'Even so . . .'

'A construct controller is nothing like the controllers I'm used to, but it does the same thing – it draws on the field and uses that force to power and control the machine.' She indicated other parts, where the reciprocating rods were surrounded by red concretions and a network of glass filaments. 'These modifications of yours have no place in a normal construct. They can only be for one purpose – to seize control of a flying construct from its operator.'

He nodded. 'That's exactly what I'm trying to do. Do you think it will work?'

She thought for a minute or two. 'No, because this array of crystals will cancel out the effect of this one, here. But if you were to network these crystals in this kind of arrangement, tightly coil these filaments around them thus . . .'

Irisis began to sketch swiftly on a large piece of paper with a stick of charcoal, covering it with lines, shapes and symbols. Yggur leaned forward, watching the design grow. She smeared out a number of lines with a fingertip, cocking her head as she redrew them. Finally satisfied, without a by-your-leave she took tools from his bench and began to pull his controller apart.

Yggur said nothing during the next hour, just watched the deft movement of her fingers as she completely rebuilt it, adding in new sections from the boxes of crystals and silver wires on his table. Finally she laid the controller down, brushed her yellow hair out of her eyes and looked up.

He studied the new arrangement for a good while, then suddenly smiled; it lit up his stern and craggy face. 'You're right, of course. Why couldn't I see that? You were going to say?'

'It'll work, assuming you've solved the other problem. How to communicate at a distance.' She rolled Golias's onion globe into her hand. It was as unfathomable as ever.

'I'm no further advanced than I was two hundred years ago. Do you have any ideas?'

She closed her hands over the globe. 'No. I can only think of one person who might, but—'

'Would that Tiaan were here,' he said shrewdly, 'rather than on the other side of the continent.'

Irisis pursed her lips, still feeling the rivalry after all this time. An idea occurred to her. 'Fyn-Mah scried out the scrutator in the middle of the Karama Malama, using only a crystal and a bowl of quicksilver—'

'To be correct, she scried out a special kind of lodestone he was carrying.'

'We might attune this controller to a flying construct's hedron in the same way.'

'I doubt it.'

'Let's ask Flydd.'

'What does Flydd know, pray?' Yggur said coolly.

'He knows more about the field, and devices to shape and use it, than anyone. For seven years he was in charge of the scrutators' secret project to develop new devices powered by the field.'

Yggur sat back with his eyes closed and fingers pressed to his temples. 'I can't bring myself to trust *any* scrutator, but in this emergency I suppose I must.' He put the globe away. 'Very well. On your say-so I'll ask to him. Anyone else?'

'Only me.'

Irisis was lying awake that night when she had another idea. She brought it up the following morning, as the group sat staring glumly at the controller.

'There are crystals,' she said thoughtfully, 'that can induce an aura around a hedron from some distance.'

'And some are natural,' Flydd added. 'Certain ore deposits caused problems with clanker controllers, back when they were first invented, until we discovered a way to shield them.'

'We're not getting anywhere with Golias's globe,' said Irisis. 'We might be better off trying to discover how such auras are generated, and how they can affect hedrons, and at what distance.'

'Let me see if I'm following your train of thought,' said Yggur. 'You're thinking that we should try to deliberately create such auras, even magnify them.'

'Yes. If we can find ones that work at a distance, perhaps we can imprint your controller aura onto them. I may be able to change your controller to do that.'

'Hmn,' Yggur said doubtfully. 'If by some chance we did manage to send such a signal, how would we take command of the controller of the flying construct? How would we control it? And how stop its operator from taking it back? The most likely result would be no effect at all. If it did work, the construct would doubtless fall out of the air, and all in it be destroyed.'

'We'll never know unless we try.'

The next couple of weeks were spent in the most tedious of labour, investigating hedrons of various types, and other kinds of crystals, to determine the nature of auras that could be induced from them. Irisis did most of this work, assisted somewhat uncomfortably by Fyn-Mah. And every time Flydd entered the room, she turned her dark eyes on him, gazing at him with that deferential longing that Irisis found so irritating. If you want him, she thought, go after him!

None of the rock crystals proved good enough, but one day Irisis discovered, in forgotten vats of brine in Yggur's cellars, crystals of various coloured salts that had grown slowly over a hundred years. One particular crystal had the most powerful aura of all. Using similar crystals grown painstakingly from special salt solutions, with layers of a second and third crystal grown over the top, she built a controller which, through a kind of ethyric transfer no one understood, would cause an ordinary controller in the next room to mimic it. Even Xervish Flydd was impressed.

'But will it work in the real world?' asked Yggur. 'That's the question.'

'We won't know until we try,' said Flydd. 'I'll have the air-floater loaded with supplies. We'll fly direct to Stassor, find Tiaan or the other flying construct, and test it.'

'What if the transfer controller fails?' said Yggur. 'The construct will fall out of the sky, destroying itself and everyone in it. We must test it here first, and know it will work perfectly, every time.'

FIFTY-SEVEN

Several days later, Yggur came striding down the hall, his stern face alive. 'Come into my workroom,' he said to Flydd, Nish and Irisis, who were warming their hands on mugs of tea beside an inadequate fire. 'I've something to show you.'

'What's the matter?' snapped the scrutator, whose own work was going badly. 'Surely you're not asking us for help?'

The chilly dignity took over again. 'Come inside.' Yggur caught Flydd by the arm, gesturing to Nish and Irisis with his other hand.

They followed him into his workroom. 'Flydd, would you operate this for me?' Yggur handed him the little beetle flier. 'It's much improved from the one I had when you came to Fiz Gorgo.'

The scrutator touched the device, which hummed to life and rose unsteadily in the air.

'Fly it around the room, any way you choose.' Yggur put the transfer controller in his pocket and went into the adjoining room. 'When I try to take over, fight hard against it.'

'It'll be a pleasure,' Flydd said with a wicked gleam in his eye. He moved his hands. The flier shot just over Nish's head, ruffling his hair. Flydd made a hasty gesture; it turned the other way. 'Stupid thing!' the scrutator said.

'Gentle movements,' said Irisis, who had spent long hours watching Yggur master the art of controlling the flier. 'You've got to have a calm mind.'

Remarkably, in a few minutes Flydd had gained enough control to keep it circling around the centre of the room, using just the movement of one hand. It was a strain, though; he had to sit down and his fingers had stiffened into hooked claws.

'Ready?' Yggur called.

Flydd massaged his fingers until they would straighten. 'Yes.'

The beetle flier kept circling, its pattern unchanged. Minutes passed.

'Knew it couldn't be done,' Flydd muttered. His gnarly hand was shaking. 'How much longer do I have to keep it up?'

Yggur put his head around the door. 'What's happening?'

'Absolutely nothing,' Flydd said with great cheer.

Yggur scowled. 'All right, bring it back to the table.'

'Can't you do that yourself?'

'It's keyed to you and your Art, until you release it or I break your hold.'

Flydd brought the flier down to the table. It landed on its side and thumped over onto its iridescent back. He touched it and the hum died.

'No luck?' said Flydd, not displeased that the great Yggur had failed in front of witnesses.

'You can leave now,' said Yggur evenly.

They hurried to the door. Irisis lingered, looking back at him. 'You too!' he said in a forbidding voice. 'I've not had a second's peace since you arrived.'

That afternoon Yggur called them back. There was no sign of his earlier euphoria. He sat with both elbows on the table, chin cupped in his hands, staring at the transfer controller.

'All right, let's try it again.' He went into the other room.

Flydd sent the flier up and circled it over their heads. There was silence from beyond the door. After a few minutes, the scrutator felt confident enough to try more complicated patterns: a series of vertical figure-eights, followed by a flat spiral down to the floor, another back up to the ceiling.

Yggur cursed and banged something on the wall. It sounded like his head, *thud-thud-thud*. The flier dipped sharply, flipped end for end and slammed into a stack of books on the table. It spun around on its curved back, making a whistling hum, struck a pile of papers and sent them whirling into the air. The hum died away.

Yggur burst through the doorway. 'What about that?'

'Fabulous!' said Irisis, running towards him. She stopped abruptly. 'What have you done to the scrutator?'

Xervish Flydd lay on his side behind the big table, his arms clutched to his chest. One knee was drawn up; the other leg kicked feebly, and his bloodshot eyes stared at the ceiling, unblinking.

Falling to her knees beside him, Irisis put her head on his chest. 'His heart's going like a racehorse but his eyes are blank. What have you done to him, Yggur?'

'Seizing control can be . . . traumatic to the mind,' said Yggur, who looked rather shaky himself. 'Both minds, as it happens. I thought he'd be strong enough to endure it.'

'Did you warn him, so that he could prepare himself?' she snapped. Irisis was a terrier when her friends were in trouble.

'I wanted his reactions to be as natural as possible. Anyway, he's been working with the Art for most of his life. He knew the risks.'

'I'd hate to be one of your enemies,' muttered Irisis, 'if this is the way you treat your friends.'

Yggur put his hands on Flydd's head, and then on his chest. 'I don't have any friends, thankfully. He'll recover in an hour or two. Take him to his room and let him sleep, and don't come back. I've got a lot of work to do before we try again.'

The scrutator recovered with no more harm than a piercing headache and a furious temper. He seemed to think that he had, somehow, been unmanned, which made Irisis even more livid. However, in the morning he was ready to try again.

'Are you sure you're prepared for this?' said Irisis. 'Do you want me to take your place?'

'I don't think that's such a good idea,' Flydd said without elaboration. 'I know what to expect now.'

They began again. The iridescent metal bug flew in

horizontal figure-eights about half a span below the ceiling. Flydd stood leaning against the table, his eyes following the flier, his fingers barely moving.

Time passed. Nothing happened. 'What's Yggur doing, do you think?' whispered Nish.

'I haven't got a clue.'

Flydd groaned and slipped to one knee, but his fingers kept moving and the flier held to its pattern. There came a cry from the next room, swiftly cut off.

Nish thought he detected a faint smile on the scrutator's face. 'He's not letting go this time,' he said quietly to Irisis. 'He's making Yggur work for it.'

'He's a proud fool,' said Irisis. 'Yggur is stronger than he'll ever be. He'll kill himself. I'm going to stop it.'

Nish caught her wrist as she passed. 'Never interfere in the affairs of mancers. Surely you know that?'

She swung her other hand at him, but he caught it as well. Irisis looked furious but it passed in a moment and she sat down, watching the scrutator. Flydd's other leg collapsed. He wobbled on his knees, his teeth bared, but his fingers still moved. While there was breath in his belly he was not going to give in to Yggur.

Another cry ripped through the door. Yggur let out a bellow and the flier dipped in the air.

'Ugh!' Flydd grunted, but regained control and flew another perfect figure-eight.

'Be damned!' roared Yggur, sounding as if he was thumping from one wall to another.

The air rushed out of the scrutator's lungs and he subsided gently to the floor, still smiling. His fingers stopped moving.

The flier turned sharply, bounced off the wall, jagged across the room, struck the door and disappeared through it.

'Ha!' cried Yggur. 'I knew I could do it.' Then silence.

Irisis lifted Flydd to his feet. 'I'm all right,' he said in a faint voice. 'I showed him a thing, didn't I?'

'Bloody idiot!' Letting him fall, Irisis hurried into the other room.

Yggur lay on the floor with the flier clutched in his hand, and he was actually smiling. 'We can do it. I never believed it would be possible.'

That evening, Irisis had just carried a tray into Yggur's room when a servant came running in, carrying a message pouch. 'It's from Uritz, surr, by skeet, and it's marked of the utmost urgency.'

Yggur dismissed the servant, pulled himself up in bed and broke the seal of the pouch. He still looked wan.

'Do you want me to leave?' said Irisis.

He did not answer. Yggur was staring at the paper as if he could not believe what was written there. Irisis felt her skin crawl. Another defeat? Was ruin imminent?

He threw the paper aside, slid the tray to the other side of the bed and levered himself out. Standing on shaky legs, he began to dress.

'What is it? You must rest, Yggur.'

'There's no time. It's come from a spy I have near Alcifer, sent this morning. The skeet must have burst its heart getting here so quickly. A flying construct came across the sea from the east yesterday, went well north of Alcifer, crossed the range and circled back after dark. It's now believed to be hidden in the forest somewhere near the abandoned city. This is our chance!'

'But you're not ready,' said Irisis. 'You could barely control that little flier, and it put you into your sickbed. How are you going to seize a construct?'

'I'll have to. I thought we'd have to go all the way to Stassor and try to find it, with all the risks that entails. Now it's right in my own territory. There'll never be another chance like this. But if *we* know about it, chances are the enemy do too. Call everyone together. We're going in the air-floater – tonight.'

In the end they did not get away until dawn, and with a head-wind made agonisingly slow progress, so that it was long after dark before they reached the vicinity of Alcifer. They turned

621

north, sitting the night out on a frigid mountain peak, and took off before sunrise the next morning.

'Stay higher than they can fly,' said Yggur to Pilot Inouye. 'Should a lyrinx come on us unexpectedly, the war could end right here.'

'They'll surely see us,' said Fyn-Mah. 'Their eyesight's not that bad.'

'I don't mind them knowing we're here. Ghorr often sends air-floaters over the lyrinx cities, spying. But keep to the clouds as much as possible. If the flying construct is still here, and pray that it is, we don't want to alert it.'

They circled high over Alcifer all day, examining the city and its surroundings with Yggur's spyglass, which was the best to be had. When the mist and rainclouds parted, they could see slaves working in the gardens, and their lyrinx guards, but there was no sign of a flying construct.

'Your spy must have been mistaken,' Flydd said at the end of a long, tedious day. He had spent most of it lying on the floor of the cabin holding his stomach.

They were flying within the base of the clouds, which made it difficult to see. 'Not Uritz—' Yggur broke off to train his spyglass on a lyrinx that was labouring up towards them, its wings straining in the thin air. It was not the first: half a dozen had already inspected them that day. 'That's an unusual beast. It's built more like a human than a lyrinx, and its skin's got no pigment at all.'

The lyrinx almost met their height. It circled just out of javelard range, watching them with its large eyes, before wheeling around and diving back towards Alcifer.

'If the flying construct *was* here,' said Flydd when the sun was about to disappear below the horizon, 'it isn't any longer. Let's go home.'

He broke into another fit of coughing, ending with a groan. The struggle with Yggur had hurt him more than he dared show.

'We're going nowhere,' said Yggur. 'They could be hiding, waiting for us to go away. After all, they'd assume that this air-floater belongs to the Council.'

They returned to their rocky peak for the night, and went back on station the following morning, though this time they floated so far from Alcifer that they would have been no more than a speck against the overcast. Again they saw nothing.

They were taking an early lunch on the third day of their watch when Flydd, who had been looking green all morning, stood up, groaned and collapsed against the rope mesh outside the cabin. He slid along the rope and had started to slip through, when Nish caught him by the arm and hauled him back. Irisis helped to carry him inside, where they laid him on the canvas bench at the front of the cabin.

Nish checked Flydd's pulse, which was fast and erratic. His skin was clammy. 'It's not good, Irisis.'

She stood up as Yggur came through the door. 'He's ill, Yggur.'

'We can't leave now. It's there somewhere.' Yggur paced to the fabric door and back. 'He'll be all right.'

'He looks bad.'

'He did this damage to himself, trying to prove he was as good as me. He's not, and I'm not turning back. If we can take this construct—'

'The damn thing's not here. And if it were, do you value the life of a scrutator less than some damned machine?'

'I wouldn't swap the flying construct for a hundred scrutators,' said Yggur.

'If I were a mancer, I'd blast you clear across the Sea of Thurkad,' she said furiously.

'Your loyalty outweighs your common sense, Artisan. A flying construct means the difference between certain defeat and possible victory. We're going nowhere until I'm satisfied that it's here, or gone.'

It was an unpleasant lunch. As they were finishing, the scrutator's groans gave way to a laboured panting.

'He's really ill,' Irisis wept as they circled towards the mud terraces again. 'Can't you do anything, Yggur?'

'I'm not a healer,' he replied.

'There's a good one in Old Hripton.'

'How did you know that?'

'I've been down there several times. Women's troubles.'

'Oh!' He wasn't going to ask about that. 'If we get back in time you may take him there.'

'Unless we go right away we *won't* be in time.'

He folded his arms across his chest. 'No man is worth more than humanity, as I'm sure Flydd would agree.'

Irisis had heard the scrutator say such things more than once. It made no difference – her friend and one-time lover was really ill. If she could have wrested control from Yggur, she would have. But that, of course, was impossible. She vented her fury at him as only she could. He ignored her.

They slid into a veil of high cloud that covered most of the sky. Nish took up a spyglass, though his mind was no longer on the search. Looking through the cloud was like peering through a silk scarf. Far below, mist clung to the ridges, and only the tips of the spires and domes of Alcifer rose above it.

'There's a lot of activity this afternoon,' he said after a while. There were at least a dozen lyrinx in the air.

Irisis cast a bitter glance towards the rotor, where Yggur stood with Inouye, and went inside to check on the scrutator. Nish followed her, blanched at the sight of Flydd and did not stay long.

'Something's going on,' Nish muttered a little later, peering through his spyglass.

The air-floater continued to circle within the base of the cloud. Irisis stalked from the watch to the cabin, and back to the watch, a dozen times. The mist thinned over Alcifer but still clung to the ridges. Scudding rain-showers obscured their view most of the time.

Irisis appeared in the doorway, breathing heavily. 'He's failing, Yggur. We've got to go *now*!'

'I've seen it!' snapped Yggur, staring through his spyglass.

Nish swung his own glass in the direction Yggur was looking, sweeping it back and forth as he tried to penetrate the mist. He could not see a flying construct, but its metal skin would not be easy to pick out against the mist-hung forest.

There were more lyrinx in the air than before, and yet more rising out of Alcifer.

'Where is it, Yggur?' he called.

'*You* mightn't see it – it's under some kind of concealment and I don't dare try breaking it from here.'

'He's failing, Yggur,' Irisis repeated. He didn't seem to hear her. She ran down and began beating him around the shoulders and head. He laid down the spyglass and caught her wrists, holding her easily. She tried to kick him.

'Stop it!' Yggur roared. He dragged her into the cabin, where Flydd lay panting on his bench.

Putting his hands to Flydd's belly, Yggur muttered a few words. The lines faded from the scrutator's face and his breathing eased. Yggur shook him, gently.

'Scrutator? Wake!'

Flydd's eyes opened. 'Yes?' he said in a scratchy voice.

'I've found the construct, but the lyrinx are rising and if we don't act now they must take it. And yet, Scrutator Flydd, you're very ill. Your resistance to the transfer controller must have burst something internally. I can ease the pain, as I just did, but I can't save you. Only a healer can.'

'Get on with it,' Flydd muttered, irascible to the last.

'But if we turn back now we must lose the construct, and all our plans fail with it. I give you the choice, Scrutator. What do you say?'

'You bastard!' said Irisis.

Flydd stared up at the ceiling.

'Do you understand what I'm saying, Scrutator?' said Yggur.

'I do,' he rasped.

'Well?'

'Of course you must take the flying construct. Why do you have to ask?' Flydd's head fell sideways and the laboured breathing renewed.

Yggur ran outside and focussed his spyglass. Not finding what he was looking for, he cursed and ran back, to lug out a wooden box.

'Hundreds of lyrinx are rising out of Alcifer,' he rapped.

'But where are they going? Flangers, you've got the best eyes, can you see the construct?' Handing him the spyglass, he began to unpack the transfer controller.

The rotor missed a beat. Inouye let out a frightened squawk.

'What the hell's going on?' said Yggur.

The mud terrace above the ridge erupted as a geyser roared thirty spans in the air. A roiling cloud of dirty steam burst out in all directions and they lost sight of the ridge, as well as the drama unfolding below.

'That can't have been an accident,' Fyn-Mah said quietly.

'Let's see what the result is,' said Yggur.

'The lyrinx are heading that way,' said Nish.

'*I can see the construct!*' Flangers hissed. 'There – at the end of that ridge. There are people around it, though I can't tell if it's on the ground or above it. No, it's flying. It's just gone out over the edge. There's a flying lyrinx there. Looks like it's carrying something. It's gone down into the trees. I think the construct's crashing. No, it's all right.'

Nish found it now, a shadow creeping in and out of the mist. Flangers was silent for a minute.

'It's coming up again,' said Flangers. 'It's landing on the ridge. Someone's getting in. Now it's lifting; it's moving very slowly. The enemy are coming fast, forming a circular wall around it.'

'Should I go down?' Inouye asked softly.

'Yes. No! Wait.' Yggur was uncharacteristically irresolute. 'No. They'll tear us to pieces. How is your power, Inouye?'

'Steady,' she said.

'Stay at this height.'

'Aren't you going to use your wonderful transfer controller?' Irisis ground the words out.

'When the time is right,' said Yggur. 'What do you see now, Flangers?'

'It's turned west, moving *very* slowly. They're going to catch it.' A long pause. Flangers adjusted the spyglass. 'No, it's shot up through the circle. It's leaving them behind.'

Yggur cursed. 'After it, Inouye! Stay in the clouds. We don't want them to see us.'

'Why not?' said Nish.

'It'll make it harder to seize control. Flangers?'

The air-floater turned, the rotor whirring, and soon a vigorous tailwind drove them swiftly west.

'It's slowing again,' said Flangers. 'The lyrinx are catching it.'

'They must be controlling its field,' said Yggur after they'd watched the construct's stop-start progress for some considerable time. 'I wonder how they're doing that? I don't dare try to take control while it's having trouble drawing power. All that's keeping it ahead of them is the skill of the pilot. I can't duplicate that from here.'

'If at all,' Irisis said under her breath, and turned back to the cabin.

'It's going the way we want,' she heard Yggur say as she went through the door. 'Keep shadowing it, Inouye.'

Flydd's knees were drawn up into his chest, his face wracked. His breathing was barely detectable. She took his hand. He was going to die, uselessly. Even if, by some miracle, Yggur did succeed in seizing control of the construct, he'd never fly it. He'd barely controlled his little flicr from the next room. The construct would fall out of the sky, destroying itself and everyone inside, and the lyrinx would feast on their remains.

She went out again. Far below, the situation was unchanged, though the construct seemed to have drawn a little further ahead. 'They're getting away,' Irisis said.

'I don't think so,' said Yggur, but it became clear the machine was outdistancing its pursuers, and shortly the lyrinx began to turn back. Soon there were none pursuing. The sun was just above the horizon.

'After them! Full speed, Inouye,' Yggur ordered.

He whipped the transfer controller from his pocket. It was an oval made of metal with holes in it like a colander, though larger, concealing the crystals and wires at its core. Thrusting his fingers through the holes, he held the device above his head, closed his eyes and strained.

'It's still drawing away,' said Flangers.

'Which direction?'

'Continuing west.'

Yggur strained again. Irisis focussed her spyglass through the veils of cloud. The construct dipped sharply before continuing on.

Yggur was panting. He kept trying, but without success He doesn't have the strength, Irisis thought. He *was* very old, despite his appearance. And, she reminded herself, he had not been tested in a long time.

'I can't help thinking that you're past it,' she said.

'The scrutator would have done the same, you know.'

Irisis knew it to be true, knew it to be the right thing to do, too, but it made no difference. Her loyalties were personal, not national.

'They're drawing further away,' called Flangers.

The sinews on Yggur's arms stood out. Still with eyes closed, he strained again. The construct sailed on, unaffected. He grunted with the effort. Sweat burst out on his forehead. The machine stalled, then dropped like a stone.

'I bloody well knew it!' Irisis raged. 'I knew this was all going to be for nothing.' She made a move towards him but thought better of it.

Yggur stood, hands straining above his head, eyelids bulging. They watched the construct plunge down and down. Irisis could imagine how the people inside must be feeling.

Yggur's eyes opened and closed again. He trembled from head to foot. A thread of saliva dribbled out of the corner of his mouth. 'Aaagh!' he cried, swinging the device around his head, then, 'Aah! I've got it.'

The construct fell unchecked.

'I've got it.'

There was no change in its downward plunge.

'I've got it!' Foam flew from his lips.

Irisis saw, through her spyglass, the fall become less

vertical. The construct swerved wildly but recovered. It curved away, away, away, rose slightly, flattened out and headed west.

'I've got it,' he whispered.

From inside the cabin, Flydd let out a groan that trailed off to nothing.

FIFTY-EIGHT

Gilhaelith had stopped pounding on the hatch long ago. Tiaan lifted it and looked down. He was sitting on the floor, eyes shut, rocking back and forth. She closed the hatch – putting off the confrontation for as long as possible.

'Hey, there's an air-floater behind us – really high up.'

'Is it the one we saw over Alcifer the other day?' said Malien.

'It looks the same.'

The air-floater disappeared in the clouds. The thapter was slowing now, as they began to pass over swamp forest. The sun went down. They continued in the dark for hours, having no idea where they were going. Finally, in pitch darkness, the whistling of the wind died away. The base of the thapter thumped hard against stone and sparks flew up.

A glowing globe blazed, revealing part of a dark wall and a wide doorway. All else was in darkness.

'What now?' said Tiaan.

'We wait,' Malien replied.

'This doesn't look like a lyrinx city.'

The air-floater ghosted down to their left. It was there one second, gone the next, as it went up in a rush. A tall man stood in the centre of the yard, a shadowed object in his left hand.

Malien said, 'Well, well. In a dozen lifetimes I wouldn't have expected this.'

'Who is it?'

She didn't answer.

'What do we do?' Tiaan squeaked.

'Go down. But keep your counsel, Tiaan. Let's find out what they want, first.'

Tiaan unfastened the lower hatch and quickly climbed down the side. Her back was aching but she managed to walk across to the steps without limping.

The man extended a hand. 'I am Yggur. Welcome to Fiz Gorgo.'

Had she been capable of rational thought, Tiaan would have assumed him dead centuries ago. 'Thank you. My name is Tiaan Liise-Mar.' She looked around but Malien wasn't in sight.

'Surely you're not alone?' he said.

'No.'

Malien had gone down the far side of the machine and now appeared out of the darkness without warning. 'Well met, Yggur. I imagine you no more expected to see me again than I did you.'

'Malien!' he exclaimed. 'It seems like it was only months ago I last saw you. And for all the change in you . . .'

'You flatter me. That was two centuries ago. It was in Chanthed, wasn't it, when Llian told his *Tale of the Mirror* and the masters voted that it become a Great Tale.'

'And he was banished from being a chronicler for seven years. No, Malien, we met for the last time in Gothryme, when the Charon sent Maigraith back through the gate.'

'Of course we did. My memory must be going. I wonder what—?'

He hastily interrupted her. 'Do you know what happened to Llian?'

'He would be dead a hundred and fifty years, even if he lived into grand old age.'

'And Karan too, no doubt.'

'We all have our time,' Malien said. 'I'll not complain when mine comes. The old must give way to the young.'

'Quite. Come inside,' said Yggur.

They went indoors, to a large chamber off the hall, where a fire blazed. Shortly Gilhaelith appeared in the doorway.

There were lines on his forehead, blood spots along his ribs, and his skin had a greenish cast. He was furious.

'Where did you come from, fellow?' said Yggur. 'I feel as though I ought to know something about you.' He did not offer to shake hands.

'I don't see why,' said Gilhaelith curtly. 'I'm a trader in odd commodities and a dabbler in the arts and sciences. My name is Gilhaelith and these wretches have just kidnapped me from Alcifer.'

'Ah, yes, Gilhaelith. The geomancer who trades with the enemy!' Yggur turned his back. 'Tiaan, I apologise for taking over your flier in such an . . . abrupt manner, but we need it desperately. We have a plan for the war.'

'I'm pleased to hear that someone has,' she said quietly. That terror of falling, of having control snatched away, would never leave her. 'But you're mistaken. The thapter belongs to Malien, not me.' She moved away from him, taking refuge by the fire. Thankfully Yggur did not follow, for she had no idea how to deal with such a legend.

Gilhaelith came up beside Tiaan. 'How dare you interfere in my life!'

She looked up at him, remembering how he might have come to her aid in Snizort, but had cared more about the amplimet. 'Do you mean to say you didn't *want* to be rescued?'

'I *chose* to be in Alcifer, and I was close to a breakthrough. Now all my precious instruments lie abandoned. You have destroyed the work of a lifetime.'

'I'm sure your friends the lyrinx will take good care of them!'

'What price did *you* pay, for them to repair your broken back?'

'Nothing I wasn't forced to. Unlike you, I've never dealt with the enemy for profit.'

'Why did Malien come after me?' he said in a low, quivering voice. '*Why me?*'

Tiaan saw no reason not to tell him. 'You're the greatest

geomancer and mathemancer in existence now, and no one else can help her.'

That mollified him a little. 'Certainly I am! Go on.'

'She's concerned that the nodes are being overdrawn and will soon fail, to the ruin of all.'

'What does it matter if one or two nodes fail?' he said.

'Because they're linked! Malien has discovered that a drained node is replenished from those surrounding nodes that are linked to it. Those, in turn, are replenished from nodes further away. If enough fail, all the nodes could collapse and the whole world—'

'*That's it!*' he whooped. 'The missing piece of the puzzle.'

'What do you mean, Gilhaelith?'

He strode away without answering, already so caught up in the problem that Tiaan was an irrelevance.

She ran and took him by the arm, so outraged by his arrogance that she wanted to unsettle him, shock him. 'The lyrinx were using you!' she cried. 'I can't believe you didn't realise that. You were just the bait to lure me and the thapter to Alcifer.'

His mouth opened and closed, and Tiaan could see the calculations running. He'd been manipulated from the beginning, all unknowing. Panic flared in his eyes but he controlled it and turned away.

Yggur took his place, and to Tiaan he seemed equally forbidding. 'May I ask what that dispute was about?' he said pleasantly.

'It seems that Gilhaelith *chose* to live in Alcifer, under the protection of the lyrinx, and I've ruined his life's work.'

Yggur frowned. 'Is that so? I'd hate to think I've allowed a cuckoo into my nest. What is his life's work?'

'To master geomancy and understand all the forces that move and shape the world.'

'To what end?'

'He maintains it's for the noblest purpose of all – simply to understand the material world – but Gilhaelith has a compulsion to control everything around him.'

'A dangerous man. You'd better tell me everything you know about Gilhaelith, Tiaan.'

The air-floater flew directly to Hripton, setting down outside the healer's house. Nish, Irisis and Flangers carried Flydd in. He was still breathing, though his chest barely moved and his lips were blue.

'What's the matter with him?' asked the healer, a woman of advanced years with a dowager's hump and white hair so thin that Irisis could see her scalp through it.

She explained as best she could without giving away any secrets. The healer lifted Flydd's shirt and drew in a sharp breath at the sight of his emaciated chest, practically bare of flesh, and the ancient scars crisscrossing his body. She laid hands on him, up and down. They turned him over and she did the same for his back.

'Something is damaged inside,' she said to Irisis. 'In his belly.'

'Is he going to die?' said Nish, who'd been silent for hours. He looked shattered.

'He may,' said the healer. 'Tonight will tell. He's dangerously ill.'

'Are there medicines? Potions? Herbs?' said Irisis. 'I have coin enough—'

'It's not a matter of coin,' replied the healer. 'He'll have the best treatment I can give, and besides, it will be to Fiz Gorgo's account. After that it will be up to him. Go now.'

'But I want to sit by him,' said Irisis.

'I can't work with people looking on. His life is wasting while I'm talking to you. Come back in the morning.'

They went out to the air-floater. 'You can fly,' Irisis said to Nish and Flangers. 'I'm going to walk. I need to think.'

Nish began to say something, searched her face then plodded across to the machine. He was taking it hard and Irisis could not comfort him. She just had to be alone. She headed down the road into the darkness.

Flangers spoke to Nish and Inouye, then the air-floater lifted off without him.

'Alone,' said Irisis. 'That means by myself.'

'You can't walk back by yourself at night. It's not safe.' Flangers eased his sword in its scabbard.

'In the mood I'm in, I could take on a lyrinx with either hand. All right, Flangers, but don't talk to me.'

They paced side by side along the rutted track that wound along the side of the bay towards Fiz Gorgo. It was so dark that they could not see each other. The many potholes were full of muddy water. She tramped through them, oblivious. Irisis could think of nothing but Flydd in that dingy little room, probably dying – and for what?

They passed by a pungent field of turnips, and another that reeked of freshly spread manure, before the track turned along the tidal flats. The tide was low and the strand stank of rotting seaweed and decaying fish.

'Flangers?' she said after they'd gone a good league.

'Yes, Irisis?'

'What if he dies? What are we going to do?'

'I'll be asking you to release me from my promise.'

'Does your honour mean so much to you?'

'I betrayed my oath, Irisis.'

She moved closer, taking his arm. 'He's a good man, Flangers. Without him, we're lost.'

'Do you love him?'

'As a friend and a guide.'

'I can't think of anyone better to have beside me in a dark hour,' said Flangers.

'Have you spoken to him?'

'What about?'

'Shooting down the air-floater.'

'How could I bother him about such a trivial thing?'

'It's your life, Flangers! He'd be angry if he knew you'd kept silent.'

'He'll never hear it from me. The scrutator will have enough problems of his own, *if* he recovers.'

'He'll hear from me the instant he's well enough.'

'No!' he cried.

'Then tell him. If you don't, I will.'

He did not reply. They trudged another league or two and, long after midnight, saw the gate lanterns of Fiz Gorgo in the distance.

'Flangers?'

'All right,' he said softly. 'I'll speak to him, *once he's well enough.*'

'You think he's going to die, don't you.'

'We're all going to die.'

Irisis rose before dawn, roused Inouye out of bed and they rotored back to Hripton. Irisis leapt out of the air-floater before it touched the ground and ran inside. Flydd's bed was empty. Her heart froze over. She stood there, staring down at his small indentation in the mattress.

'It's not what you think.' The healer had come in silently and the pouches under her eyes were like black bruises. She'd been up all night. 'I've moved him out the back. It's warmer there.'

'How is he?'

'A little better, though there's still some bleeding inside. He's not out of danger yet.'

'Can I see him?'

'Just for a minute.'

She led Irisis out to the back room. Flydd lay on the stretcher, staring blankly at the ceiling. He was so still that she thought he must have died after all, but then his eyes moved.

'You're an idiot,' she said fondly, taking his hand. 'Why did you go, when you'd done yourself such harm? You could have stayed behind.'

'I didn't realise I'd hurt myself.' His voice was like a breeze blowing through gossamer. 'When Yggur took over the little flier I felt a sharp pain in my belly, but it went away.'

'Why did you have to resist him? You're an overly proud man, Xervish.'

'I admit to a certain . . . rivalry,' he said hoarsely, 'but do you really think me so shallow? He asked me to fight him to the limit of my strength. It had to be a true test, otherwise he would not have known that he could take over the thapter when the time came.'

'That doesn't make up for his neglect of you,' she snapped.

'I meant what I said up there, Irisis. I would have done the same, even had it been you. What else could any good leader do? Would you not sacrifice one or two people, if by doing so you would be saving the whole of humanity?'

'I could not sacrifice my friends,' she said stubbornly. 'Not even for the sake of humanity.'

'That's the trouble with being a leader. You're always sacrificing someone. Or something.' He closed his eyes.

'Come away now,' said the healer. 'You can see him again tomorrow. He's got the constitution of a lyrinx. Two hours ago I'd have sworn he was dead, but he's looking better already.'

On her return, Irisis shook Nish awake. 'The healer thinks he's going to be all right.'

Nish sat up, rubbing red crusted eyes. He clutched her hands in silent thanks.

'You look as though you've had a hard night, Nish.' Despite only having a few hours' sleep she was as immaculate, and as beautiful, as ever.

'I've been having trouble sleeping lately. Flydd has been so good to me, Irisis. A hundred times he could have sent me to the front-lines for my follies, but he never did. He believed in me. Without him I'd be nothing. I couldn't face the thought of him dying.'

'Nor I – he's the anchor of all our lives. And our only hope. Come on, let's get some breakfast. I'm starving.'

They were walking down the corridor side by side when Tiaan turned the corner, coming the other way. She stopped dead, looking from Nish to Irisis in dismay.

Irisis had last seen Tiaan at the manufactory almost a year ago, just before she'd been diagnosed with incurable crystal fever and sent to the breeding factory. That, Irisis was ashamed to recall, had been partly due to her own scheming.

'What are you doing here?' Tiaan was trembling like a plucked wire.

'We came with Xervish Flydd, the scrutator,' said Irisis.

Tiaan relaxed a little. 'Where is he?' She looked ready to bolt.

'He's being treated by a healer. He's very ill.'

'Was that you flying the construct, Tiaan?' asked Nish. He took a step towards her and put out his hand, tentatively. 'Let me say how sorry—'

Tiaan backed away a step, her eyes darting from one to the other.

'We're on the same side, Tiaan,' said Irisis. 'We—'

'You betrayed me, both of you,' Tiaan hissed. 'Don't come near me.' She turned and headed back the way she had come, almost running.

'I suppose that was only to be expected,' said Irisis, not overly perturbed. 'A pity, though, since we'll have to work together.'

'Yes,' said Nish, staring after Tiaan. 'A great pity.'

Nish's unrequited passion for Tiaan had begun the whole affair, Irisis remembered as they continued down the hall. Surely he didn't still nurture some feeling for her? Even if he did, it couldn't come to anything. She was no more suited to him than Ullii had been.

Irisis bit her tongue in case she spoke without thinking, as was her wont. Nish was hers and he would realise it sooner or later. In the meantime she would watch over him, enjoy his friendship and say nothing about her own feelings. She would be patience itself. She might have to be.

FIFTY-NINE

Flydd was well enough to attend when they held their morning meeting two days later, though he had to be carried inside in his chair. The others present were Malien, Gilhaelith, Fyn-Mah, Tiaan, Irisis and Nish.

'I'm pleased to see you're better, Flydd,' said Yggur, 'though I didn't expect—'

'The council is sorely in need of my wisdom,' Flydd said with an ironical twitch of the mouth.

'I dare say,' Yggur answered, equally dryly. 'I salute your courage, Scrutator. I was wrong about you and I'm happy to admit it.'

'And I you, it seems. We'll best the enemy yet, Lord Yggur.'

Yggur quirked his lips but did not correct him. He turned to face the room. 'I begin without preamble. Faced with a resurgent enemy, and held back by a corrupt Council of Scrutators, humanity's situation is almost hopeless. But we've been debating, Flydd and I, what can be done. Would you care to set out our ideas, Scrutator.'

'I find I'm a little short of breath at the moment.'

Nish laughed. Irisis elbowed him in the ribs.

'We propose a simple plan,' said Yggur. 'We have neither the people, nor the resources, for anything else, and even this plan may be beyond us. But now that we have a thapter – or, should I say, since it belongs to Malien, the possibility of one – we may at least attempt it.'

'What is the plan?' growled Gilhaelith.

'To fly secretly to Nennifer, the scrutators' fortress that lies between the Great Mountains and the Desolation Sink. There to overthrow the Council of Scrutators and replace them with a body dedicated to winning the war, since it appears peace is not an option with the lyrinx.'

Gilhaelith began to laugh.

Yggur fixed him with a glare that would have stopped a volcanic eruption. 'If you don't share our objectives, you may leave this council. You will, of course, be kept in close confinement until the attack succeeds.'

He signalled with a finger to the back of the room, and Nish saw that, for the first time, a pair of armed guards waited inside the doors.

'Or fails,' scoffed Gilhaelith. 'Nennifer is the most closely guarded fortress in the world and you couldn't take it with an army of twenty thousand.'

'Rumour is the enemy of initiative,' said Yggur. 'Xervish Flydd spent years in Nennifer and knows every part of it, including its defences.'

'All but those installed since my departure five years ago,' Flydd qualified, 'and they could be many and various. Even if there are no new defences, this would be the most desperate venture in the Great Tales.' A spasm wracked him and he broke off to cough into a kerchief. 'The impregnable walls are guarded by two thousand men, hundreds of mancers and any number of bloody devices. Against such forces, we can bring no more than a dozen people, and Nennifer lies in the most inhospitable environment in the world. There's no cover of any kind. No food, no water, no shelter. And even in summer it's freezing outside at night.'

'We know it will be difficult,' said Tiaan. 'What are you going to do about it, supposing, of course, that Malien allows you the use of her thapter? And since that would constitute an act of aggression against humanity . . .'

'Thank you, Tiaan,' said Malien. 'I can speak for myself. Yet the point is a valid one, Yggur. I'll need much convincing, though I do feel sympathy for your cause.'

'I don't,' snapped Gilhaelith. 'It's a folly that can't succeed.'

'In that case,' said Yggur, 'I must restrain you for the duration. Would you come with me, please?'

Gilhaelith stood up slowly. 'You dare?'

Tiaan caught her breath. A duel between two great mancers could lay waste the room, if not the entirety of Fiz Gorgo.

'My guards will shoot before you can raise your hand,' said Yggur.

There was a taut instant of silence, then Gilhaelith held out his empty hands. Two guards bound him, while another two kept their crossbows aimed at his chest.

'I thought you'd be eager to help us,' Yggur resumed, 'since you're presently under a death sentence from the scrutators.'

'I was safe from them in Alcifer,' he said coldly as the guards took hold of him. 'I'm not about to commit suicide on your behalf. None of you will leave Nennifer alive.'

Yggur waved a hand and the guards led him away, unresisting.

'You were expecting that?' said Malien to Yggur.

'I spoke to Tiaan about him the other day. I wish he'd never come here. He's going to cause us trouble.'

'Yet we need him, for another purpose,' said Malien. 'The purpose for which I've come all the way from Stassor. Yggur, I must talk to you, alone.'

'Now?' said Yggur.

'I think so.'

'This meeting is adjourned,' Yggur said abruptly. 'Come to my quarters, Malien.' The others stared after them as they went out together. Yggur inclined his head. 'Would you care for some hot chard?'

'I prefer red wine, if you have it.'

'There are barrels of the stuff in my cellars, untapped these past fifty years.' He gave orders to his steward.

In his rooms, which were comfortable but austerely furnished, he lit the fire and drew two hard chairs up to it. A carafe of wine came, and a steaming pot of chard. He poured wine into a crystal goblet, orange chard into his bowl.

Malien held her goblet up to the flames. The wine was a deep purple, almost black. She warmed it in her hands, set it on a small side-table and turned to him.

'I never expected to see you again.'

'Nor I you. I came home to die, for there was nothing left in life that I wanted. Alas, life can be tenacious when you no longer value it, and here I am, two centuries older and hardly changed. I began to live again – not even my grief could out-last the centuries – but I don't know what to do with this endless existence. Oh, I'm active, and my mind is alert, but I've seen everything so many times before. Nothing surprises me and precious little entertains me.'

'To appreciate life again, you must put it at risk.'

'Wisely said, Malien. No doubt I will, in this hare-brained attack on Nennifer, which surely cannot succeed.'

'Yet you've committed to it.'

Yggur blew on his chard. He took a tentative sip, then blew on it again.

Malien tested the bouquet of the wine with a delicate sniff and smiled with pleasure. She sipped, rolling it back over her tongue. 'A truly great year, and a master winemaker.'

'Unobtainable now,' he said. 'The vineyards lie abandoned and covered in weeds.'

'Vines are long-lived,' Malien replied. 'Should the war end, with judicious pruning they'll yield again. And the oldest vines give the best fruit. I could spend a pleasant day in your cellars, Yggur, if only we had the leisure. You were saying?'

'I've realised that the world is worth saving, and who else but we can do it. What's your tale, Malien?'

'It has elements in common with your own. My line doesn't come from the long-lived Aachim, so I expected my end a hun-dred years ago. It never came. Since the Forbidding I've been an exile, revered for my place in the Histories but rejected for the independence of spirit that made my name. It's a hard thing to suffer when your own people won't have you. I'd had enough and was preparing to go to the Well when Tiaan came and shook me out of it. I too have begun to live again.'

'So here we are, two geriatrics – three if you count Flydd taking on the mighty. How the scrutators would roll about if they knew.'

She smiled. 'I dare say. Well, let's see if wisdom and ageless cunning are their match.'

He raised his bowl. 'To ageless cunning.'

They drank the toast, after which Yggur said curiously, 'Why do you need Gilhaelith?'

She explained her fears about the excessive drain on the world's nodes, the danger to the nodes themselves, and the wider threat that posed. 'Bilfis might have solved that problem, in time and with sufficiently good maps of the nodes. Now he's dead, I know of no one with the talents – geomancy plus the new Art of mathemancy – to do the same.'

'Except this miserable fellow I have in my dungeon,' said Yggur. 'I understand your concern. Profligacy is the curse of the modern age. Mancers no longer care for elegance, subtlety or economy in their Art. Nothing but raw power will do, and the more of it the better. Match power with greater power and simply blast your enemy away, no matter that it brings the whole world to ruin.'

'You're right, of course. Our age is well over, and lamenting it makes no difference. But who else has the vision to see where the world is heading?'

'The bigger picture,' he said approvingly. 'To me it's all part of the same picture. In the past we had our differences, Malien, but I trust you and I hope you feel the same way about me. I'll help you with the nodes, and even pressure this miserable worm Gilhaelith for you, though I doubt you'll find him cooperative. I know his type.'

'What do you require in return?'

'I require nothing,' he said, surprising her.

'Nothing?' He'd certainly changed from the single-minded Yggur of old, who had measured his debts to the last copper grint, and expected those who owed him to be equally exacting.

'You know what I want – the use of your thapter – but given freely. I would not make things worse by coming between you and your own kind.'

'We are already sundered,' said Malien, quaffing her wine. 'Vithis has declared clan-vengeance against Tiaan, for injuries done to his son during her escape. Since I helped her get away from Stassor, it applies equally to me.' In response to his quizzical glance, she told that tale.

'Astounding,' said Yggur at the end of it. 'And Tiaan is just a slip of a woman. Who would have thought she could do such marvels?'

'Other *slips* have,' Malien said dryly, 'going all the way back to my distant ancestor, Elienor. Not all heroes are big, sword-waving louts. Or tall, dark, wand-waving mancers, for that matter.'

'I forget the very Histories I've lived through.' He stared into the fire, remembering ancient days, but some thought must have caused him pain for he put his hands over his face, breathing heavily.

'Since I *am* exiled,' said Malien, 'no act of mine can further reflect on the Aachim. Therefore I offer my thapter to you, freely and unencumbered. Better yet, I will come with you to Nennifer. There may be a need for my talents.'

He did not react at once. Yggur rocked on his chair, then shook off his malaise and stood up. Malien did too.

'Thank you,' he said, bowing from the waist. 'You give me new hope. Shall we go back and plan the attack?'

'Walls have ears, even those as solid as your own. Let's keep the details to those who need to know, at least until we've lifted away from here.'

'Very wise,' he said. 'Just you, me and Xervish Flydd, then. We'll be on our way with the utmost speed. Who knows but Gilhaelith may find a way to reveal our secret, in time.'

'It feels as though we've gone back to last year,' Nish said to Irisis the following evening. 'Tiaan turns up and suddenly we're not trusted any more.'

Yesterday's meeting had been cancelled and they had been set to packing supplies and weapons and stowing them in the thapter, along with ropes, climbing irons, armour, tents and alpine sleeping pouches, and the myriad other things on Flydd's lists that they would need for an assault on the most closely guarded fortress in the known world.

'You're just feeling guilty for the way you treated her before,' said Irisis.

'I own it. I behaved shabbily to her. And so did you.'

Irisis shrugged. 'I've never denied it, but guilt isn't one of my afflictions.' That wasn't entirely true, but she didn't suffer from it the way Nish did. He was still having trouble coming to terms with Tiaan being here and, not knowing what to say, avoided her whenever possible. 'I can see why they'd want to keep it secret.'

Despite her words, she felt aggrieved at being left out. She'd helped to carry the crated and sealed items from Yggur's storeroom. They had to do with the Art, and with controllers too, and therefore came within her province, but she could discover nothing about what was inside, or what they were to be used for.

The attack would consist of Yggur, Flydd, Malien, Fyn-Mah, Inouye, Flangers, Nish, Irisis and Tiaan, plus three of Yggur's most experienced soldiers. They were leaving tomorrow afternoon, but had been told nothing more.

'It'll have to be one hell of a clever plan,' Nish persisted. 'The twelve of us against two thousand soldiers, hundreds of mancers, and everyone else in Nennifer.'

'Or a suicidal one,' said Irisis. 'If we fail, as seems likely, it'll be the end of any effective resistance in Lauralin.'

'That'll no longer be our worry.'

'Or our friends' or relatives',' she reminded him. 'The scrutators will destroy them all, down to the fourth cousins.'

He contemplated that in silence. 'And if we win, we'll have the Numinator after us.'

'I wish you hadn't mentioned that.'

'I wish I hadn't thought of it.'

'I dare say they'll tell us the plan on the way,' said Irisis. 'It'll take quite a few days to fly to Nennifer, so there'll be plenty of time for detailed planning. Better get a good night's sleep. It'll be your last in a proper bed for a while.'

SIXTY

The months had gone by slowly in the bastion of Nennifer, set in a highland where summer was short and cold, winter long and bitter and, in the shadow of towering mountains on all sides, it had not rained in twenty years. The ground was a barren grit less than the depth of Ullii's thumb, covered in black stones so smooth and shiny they appeared to have been melted in a furnace. Nothing grew there, save in the valleys where moisture from summer snowmelt supported the pastures, gardens and fish ponds that supplied Nennifer. Even the tallest mountains bore little snow, for higher ranges lay in every direction. The utter, uncompromising aridity suited the bleak souls of the scrutators.

Ullii hated Nennifer with all her angry little heart. There was nothing of beauty in the whole vast building, and little kindness either. The people who laboured there, whether mancers, artisans, artificers or common servants, were all of a type – cold, mechanical and closed off from their fellows. In all her time in the scrutators' citadel, Ullii saw no love, little passion save for their grim work, and precious little generosity or selflessness, just a desperate efficiency driven by terror. Everyone lived in fear of their superiors, and they of theirs, all the way up to the scrutators. And even the Council members, those who had not remained in Lybing to direct the war, kept one eye out for their dark and deadly chieftain.

Of all the people in Nennifer, Ullii was the only one who had any kind of freedom. Ghorr had tried to study and school her lattice-twisting talent, to understand how she had done such marvels in her previous escape with Irisis. Despite much labour and cunningly conceived punishments, it had proved an abject failure. Ullii could neither explain nor duplicate what she had previously done *in extremis*. Finally Ghorr passed the problem to his cleverest mancers and let her be. He had another use for Ullii and could not afford to damage her. Not yet.

He barely spoke to her for months afterwards, for she was too far beneath him to be worthy of his time. Ghorr was busy forging a mighty battle fleet, not to attack the enemy but to hunt Flydd to his refuge, whether in Meldorin or elsewhere, and to expunge him from the earth.

Though she was allowed outside, Ullii seldom went into the barrens. She loved nature in a romantic, idealised way, but there was no nature here, just cold desert. And as the seasons turned towards winter the land grew ever colder, windier and bleaker.

Once, Ullii's life of the mind had been all she'd needed, but the events of the past year had broken that mould. Other realities kept butting in, and other memories. Of Nish making love to her that day in the balloon basket, after she had driven off the nylatl. Of the nylatl attacking him again, after Scrutator Flydd had appeared in the air-floater. And her terror as Nish had blown the creature to bits with the flask of tar spirits, then been carried out of her life on what had been left of the balloon.

Something had died in her then – she'd seen it as an abandonment. For months Ullii had been sure that Nish was dead. When she finally found him again, at Snizort, he seemed to have forgotten her.

No matter how much she dwelt upon his previous kindnesses, Ullii kept coming back to that, and to the deaths of Myllii and Yllii. She blamed Nish for both and it constantly recharged her rage. She might be little and weak, but there was one thing she could do – take just retribution for her lost brother and son. It was all that kept her going.

Finally, in late autumn, the great battle fleet was ready. Ullii knew Ghorr was building one, but had no idea what form it would take. She had seen, in her lattice, the slow creation of all sorts of unpleasant machines and devices of war, but the testing had taken place in a vast walled yard. Only those who had business there were admitted through its guarded gates.

Everything had been planned to perfection. An army of clerks had checked the lists and made sure nothing that could possibly be required was left behind. Another small group of mancers and officers had been appointed to take every plan apart, to look at all the ways it could fail, and develop contingency plans for when it did.

Ullii was asleep when Ghorr came to her door. He flung it open so it crashed back against the wall, shocking her awake. She cowered under the covers, blocking her ears. He tore the blankets off.

'It's time for you to earn your keep, Seeker! Gather your gear.'

She had been provided with new clothes in Nennifer – half a dozen undersuits of the neck-to-knee spider-silk that protected her sensitive skin, as well as outer garments, coats, boots, scarves and hats. His artisans had made her several pairs of goggles and earmuffs, and all were to hand. Ullii stored all her possessions in two small packs beside her bed. It provided her with the only security she had.

A servant picked the packs up. Ullii snatched them from her and sat on them to get dressed. Already wearing an undersuit, she pulled on her boots, coat and hat, and made sure a set of goggles and earmuffs were in the pocket. While wearing the spider-silk undergarments she could better tolerate life's assaults on her other senses, though she still could not go out in the bright sunlight without her goggles.

'Follow me,' said Ghorr.

A swarm of knots grew in Ullii's lattice, like those made by the controllers of clankers or air-floaters, though these were much larger. Her stomach formed knots of its own.

Taking up her packs, Ullii trotted after Ghorr, up the stairs, along the corridors, out through the vast double doors and down the broad steps onto the paved area, as large as a parade ground, that ran from fortress Nennifer to the towering cliff that fell into the Desolation Sink. She stopped in shock.

The paved area was crammed with monstrous air-floaters, reaching above the topmost storey of Nennifer, which was five floors and a steep roof above the ground. Each was supported by no less than five cigar-shaped balloon bags as long as the trunk of a forest tree. Four were arranged at the corners of a diamond, one each at front and rear, another out to either side. A fifth, smaller balloon was suspended in the centre. The vessels slung beneath the balloons were more than twenty spans long and their side decks were packed with weapons whose design was unknown to her, though each looked deadly.

The machines were painted in brilliant reds and yellows, like poisonous reptiles, for they were intended to be seen and feared. Barbaric designs decorated their prows – vicious creatures with gnashing teeth and bloodstained tusks, or devices spitting fire or venom.

There were sixteen of the air-floaters, and drawn up at the front of each stood a squad of heavily armed soldiers, in a rank of five by five, with two officers before them. There were almost as many mancers, artisans, artificers and servants.

'What do you think of our air-dreadnoughts?' said Ghorr beside her. 'Aren't they the most magnificent sight you've ever seen?'

'I hate them,' she said fiercely, for their auras reeked of violence.

He smiled patronisingly. 'It doesn't matter what you think, little Ullii. Just find Flydd and Irisis, and we will have your revenge for you.'

In a flash she understood just how badly she had blundered. She didn't want revenge, but retribution, and it had to be with her own hands. Taking that away rendered it meaningless, vicious.

Ghorr shouted orders. People ran in all directions, in what appeared to be confusion but was carefully orchestrated, then she was urged up the ladder into the first air-dreadnought of the fleet, and ushered inside.

With a flourish of cornets, Ghorr's machine loosed its tethers. The great triple rotors began to tick, then whirr, its nose lifted and it rose into the sky. She could feel the drain on the field, which manifested itself as a swirling yellow pattern across her lattice.

The others followed, one by one, taking care to keep their distance. When all were in the air they manoeuvred into formation, signalled to each other with flags and then turned towards the west, to pick up the rest of the scrutators in Lybing. And then, on to the hunt.

The journey took days, though it was mostly uneventful, for which Ullii was glad. Used to shutting the world out, she found the proximity of so many hard, relentless people unbearable. She could not sleep in the great cabin, as the racket of chatter, snoring, belching and farting never stopped. On the second night she climbed onto the roof, found a recess sheltered from the wind and spent the night there, wrapped in blankets and coat. It was miserably cold but she was used to that. The air was fresh and the constant wailing of the wind blurred out the sounds of the fifty people below.

Only once during that journey did anything of note happen. It was about a week after they had departed Nennifer – Ullii did not count the days – and the fleet had just sailed high over the Sea of Thurkad, heading towards Meldorin Island and the ancient city of Thurkad, whose fall had heralded the loss of the west.

Ullii was standing at the bow, where the air streaming in her face protected her from the stink of unwashed humanity, when her keen hearing picked up Ghorr's voice, just outside the forward cabin door. He was talking to Scrutator Fusshte.

'Are you still going to give a demonstration?' Fusshte asked. His sibilant tones always made Ullii shiver, and the way he looked at her was worse.

'When I find the best target,' said Ghorr. 'I'll send a warning to our enemies not to take us too lightly.'

'And to our friends!' Fusshte chuckled nastily.

'Indeed,' said Ghorr. 'There's not a single person on Santhenar who should not know what I can do, *and beware.*'

Fusshte took a step backwards, just managing to control his alarm. 'Quite,' he said smoothly. 'People have come to doubt the power of the scrutators. After this, they'll be in no doubt at all.'

Ghorr called the captain of his personal guard. The man listened carefully, saluted, then gave orders to his signalman, who began to pull his coloured flags up and down. After checking the acknowledgment with a spyglass, he reported back to the captain.

The air-dreadnought turned slowly. The others followed it, maintaining their formation, until they were heading directly for the southern section of the city of Thurkad. Ghorr consulted a plan and gave further orders, which the signalman relayed.

'Just there,' he said to the captain, pointing. 'According to my intelligence, many lyrinx house themselves in that one.'

They were now close enough for the largest buildings of Thurkad to be distinguished. Ghorr's outstretched arm indicated one of a series of tall wooden warehouses, built on the edge of the wharf city that formed the seaward rim of the city proper. Lyrinx soared in the air though, as yet, none approached them. This mighty armada would be the match of hundreds of flying lyrinx, and flew above the height they could reach.

Artificers now pulled the cover off a large metal mirror, the best part of two spans across, and swung it out. But it was more than just a mirror, for it had a complicated controller apparatus at the back, and an operator to use it. On the other air-dreadnoughts, similar devices were being moved into position.

More signals were sent. At the bow, a young woman in a green and grey uniform turned over a minute-glass. The air-dreadnought floated ponderously towards the target. The operator made continual adjustments to his mirror, reflecting the sunlight in a narrow beam across the bay, and then at the wharves ahead. The beams of the other mirrors followed the first, making a tight cluster of bright dots.

'Ten,' called the young woman. A man behind her raised a series of signal flags, one after another, as she counted down the numbers. 'Five, four, three, two, one. *Now*!'

The signalman swept down his red flag. The mirror operator stood up on his toes, drew power into the mighty controller crystals and pulled down a lever. The air-dreadnought shuddered.

Ullii felt a sickening feeling in the pit of her stomach as the field – what was left of it – tried to tie itself in knots. For an instant the rotors stopped completely, and there was silence, apart from wind whistling through the ropes and wires.

The beams of all sixteen mirrors converged on a single point, the top floor of the warehouse Ghorr had indicated. Suddenly they were amplified a thousand times by the power from the controller crystals. The bright spot became incandescent, burning straight through the tiled roof. The timbers erupted in flames and within seconds the roof, fifty spans long and twenty wide, was gone.

The bright spot moved down inside, fire leaping up after it, before smoke belching from the warehouse blotted it out. A single lyrinx fled out through the roof, one wing aflame, before wheeling down to smack into the water beside the wharf.

The smoke sucked back down momentarily; then, in a colossal explosion, the walls of the warehouse blew out, raining burning debris everywhere and setting fire to the neighbouring buildings. Burning lyrinx fled through the doors and windows.

'Must have been an old store of naphtha barrels in there,' Ghorr said with a grim chuckle. 'But we won't mention that in our reports, eh, Fusshte? Let the world think we did it all.'

The mirror operator was standing up in his seat, helmet askew, mouth agape.

'Marvellous,' said Fusshte in a choked voice. He cast a sideways glance at Ghorr that told Ullii a lot. Suddenly, Fusshte was afraid of the chief scrutator.

Ullii became aware that the pilot was shouting. The rotors were still running irregularly and there was barely anything left in the field. Down below, a score of lyrinx tried to take to the air but none could get aloft.

Ghorr, Fusshte, and the pilot and operator had a hurried conference by the rail. With all the cheering, Ullii only caught part of it. They were worried by what had happened to the field.

'That'll have to be all,' Ghorr said regretfully. 'I'm not going to spoil a brilliant success by a failure. If there's no power there's no power. It'll look better if we just sail majestically on. Still, we've given them a shock they'll not forget.'

They drifted with the wind and, some leagues west of Thurkad, the operators picked up another field, though the rotors were still running irregularly. It appeared the surge of power had damaged something. Ullii was pleased about that. The ruin wrought by the mirrors had horrified her.

That night they passed over the mountains of Bannador, and the higher ranges beyond, which were covered in snow from top to bottom. 'Where do you think they are?' said Fusshte in the night. 'Shazmak? It lies south of our route.'

'Why would they go to Shazmak?' said Ghorr. 'They'll be somewhere where they can buy food, or hunt for it. Isolated towns survive in the north of Meldorin, I'm told, and on the west coast.'

In the morning they landed on a grassy plain, where they could see for leagues in any direction, though four of the air-dreadnoughts remained in the air, on watch.

'We're some little way north of the ruins of Chanthed,' said Ghorr, 'where the College of the Histories stood. The Plains of Folc lie north of us. To the west the plains run for fifty leagues into the Silbis Drylands. The western mountains lie beyond that, by the coast. Somewhere there we'll find them.

'Now,' he went on once the machine had settled on its

triple keels, 'it's your turn, Ullii. Find the traitor Flydd. Find Irisis Stirm, who lied to you and abandoned you. Find Cryl-Nish Hlar, the man who made you pregnant. The one who murdered your brother and destroyed your helpless baby. And then, lead us to them, so we can take your revenge for you.'

Ullii had had much time to dwell on her retribution on the journey here. Since the attack on Thurkad yesterday she'd thought about little else. Nish had done those terrible things, and deserved to be punished, but Ghorr was a wicked man, a brute and a liar. How could it be right to give up her former friends to him? She could not decide. She wanted to deceive him but did not know how. I won't give them up, she thought. But Nish does deserve to be punished . . .

'Well, Seeker?' growled Ghorr.

'I . . . can't see Flydd in my lattice,' she said. 'Nor Irisis.' It was the truth. Lately her lattice had been ever harder to see and she could no longer deny it. She dreaded that it would go completely, taking her unique life of the mind with it.

'Have you ever seen them, or any other sign of them, since we came west?'

'No.' Sweat prickled in her armpits, in spite of the chilly weather.

He skewered her with his all-seeing eyes. 'Then we must go up. We'll fly in a square, south, west, north and east, and you'll keep watch.'

'Yes,' she whispered.

They flew south. 'Can you see them?' Ghorr asked, halfway across the traverse.

'No,' she gulped.

They flew west. 'Can you see them now?'

Ullii shook her head. They headed north, then east, and ever Ghorr asked, and ever the answer was the same. By late that afternoon he was growing impatient. 'If all this has been for nothing . . .' he said menacingly.

Fusshte whispered in his ear. 'All right,' said Ghorr. 'You have my leave.'

Fusshte gave Ullii the look that always made her skin creep. Ghorr broke people like her, but Fusshte devoured them.

'Come inside the cabin with me, little Ullii,' Fusshte said in that voice as dry as the rustling of a snake's scales. 'I have some questions for you . . .'

'I'll try harder,' she squeaked.

'I thought you might,' said Ghorr. 'Go east another two leagues,' he said to the pilot, 'then turn south and keep going, expanding the square by two leagues each circuit. If they're anywhere on Meldorin, we'll find them.'

Fusshte looked like a viper who'd had his dinner stolen.

It wasn't until the following evening that Ullii picked up a trace. She let out a little gasp and tried vainly to conceal it, but the chief scrutator missed nothing. 'You've found them.'

'I can see *something*,' she said in a tiny voice.

Ghorr was on her in three powerful strides. 'Who, Seeker?'

'I don't recognise it.'

Ghorr and Fusshte exchanged glances. 'It's a trick,' Fusshte said in a low voice, but not too low for Ullii's keen ears. 'She's trying to protect them. If she picked up anyone, it would be Flydd. He's the strongest.'

'Maybe,' said Ghorr. 'And maybe not. Her talent defies analysis. It could be anything.' He turned back to the seeker. 'It's not lyrinx, is it?'

'No.'

'Not a node or field?'

'No.'

'It's human, isn't it?'

'Yes.' She barely exhaled the word.

'Where?' Ghorr seized her by the shoulders, but let her go at once. The time for threats was past. 'Which way, Seeker?' He put on a kindly voice but his eyes were like shards of glass.

Ullii gestured. 'A long way. As far as I can see.'

'South-south-west,' said the pilot.

'What's down that way?' said Ghorr.

The pilot consulted her map. 'We're here at the moment.' Her pointed fingernail, which was tinted yellow, marked a range of hills that ran west from the mountains almost all the way to the Silbis Drylands. 'Below us, according to the map, there used to be towns and scattered villages, running to forest in the east, up against the mountains. To the west it's just empty desert. Further south the desert passes into scrub and then into the swamp forests of Orist, which run on for fifty leagues, though much of that is said to be impassable.'

'Not to us,' said Ghorr. 'I need more, Ullii. Where on the map do you sense this person?'

Ullii, after much prompting, drew a large circle with her finger. It covered most of southern Meldorin.

'That's not good enough!' hissed Fusshte. 'Seeker—'

'Leave her,' said Ghorr. 'The talent only gives direction, not distance. Strong talents, or strong Arts, she may pick up from hundreds of leagues away, while insignificant ones could elude her from the other side of the hill. We'll follow her path until the destination becomes clear, then wait for night. I don't want to alert them – if it is them.'

'What does it matter?' said Fusshte. 'We've got power enough in these sixteen air-dreadnoughts to overcome any enemy. How can Flydd's ragtag band trouble us?'

'They've given us trouble aplenty over the past year,' snapped Ghorr. 'If Flydd realises we're coming, he may find a way of hiding, even from Ullii. Take nothing for granted, Scrutator.'

The hunt continued, but the next time she looked Ullii found nothing at all. It was not that their quarry had disappeared but, rather, as if something was blocking that part of the lattice. By now she was so worn out with seeking that there was no choice but to stop for the night. Ghorr was furious.

SIXTY-ONE

Gilhaelith had spent the previous day lying on his damp palliasse, brooding. It was an outrage that he should be controlled by such a collection of fools. He could not suffer it. The attack on Nennifer would certainly fail and the scrutators would come to Fiz Gorgo in force, to seize whatever Yggur had left behind. Finding Gilhaelith here, they would slay him out of hand.

It was clear that humanity was going to lose the war, so the safest place for him was Alcifer. He was going back, even if he had to slog all the way through the swamp forests of Orist. Nothing could stand in his way. Tiaan's remark about the nodes being linked had opened up a whole avenue of possibilities. The key to his project was not the nodes, as he'd always thought, but the way they were linked and force transferred between them. He was just a whisker away from his goal, but he needed the geomantic globe to prove it. And then, true mastery would be his. And real power too, if he wanted it – enough to heal himself; enough to ensure that he was never at the mercy of others again; enough to control the power available to other mancers, if he cared to; enough, just possibly, to protect the world he'd gone to such lengths to understand, from *all* mancers.

How to get away? He'd been stripped and searched carefully before they put him in this cell. The guards had taken his clothes and given him fresh ones, in case he'd had some device secreted about his person, as he had. He got up and began picking moodily at ice that had formed below a seeping crack in the wall. It was a dirty yellow colour, like urine. His breath steamed; it was miserably cold and he wasn't used to it.

Someone rapped at the door – a guard with his dinner. He rapped back, then moved to the rear of the cell. If he didn't, the brute would simply take it away. Two armed guards watched the whole time the door was open. The third guard placed the tray on the floor inside the door and went out.

Gilhaelith cast an eye over the meal. Clear soup, invariably lukewarm, a piece of overcooked fish, boiled vegetables and dry bread. Misery! He'd requested freshly salted live slugs, pickled pigs' ovaries and other delicacies he'd been used to in Nyriandiol, but the guard had given him a disgusted look and banged the door.

'Excuse me, Guard?' Gilhaelith said firmly. 'I'd like some salt, if you please.'

The guard checked with his fellows, who shrugged. He disappeared, shortly returning with a chunk of rock salt as big as a lemon, which he tossed to Gilhaelith. It was almost as hard as stone. The door clicked and was bolted on the outside.

Gilhaelith took up the bowl, slurping noisily at the soup, which wasn't lukewarm. It was cold, had a grey scum around the rim and was utterly tasteless. Prising off a piece of salt, Gilhaelith held it in his mouth and sucked the soup past it.

Something occurred to him. Spitting the rest of the soup back into the bowl, he took out the piece of salt and examined it in the dim light. It had crystal faces.

Salt was of little use in geomancy unless the crystals were perfectly formed, and even then it could take little power. But it was all he had. Using a tine of his fork, he picked away at the chunk of rock salt, trying to separate it into one or more crystals he could use. Gilhaelith was exquisitely careful, for the tiniest scratch on a crystal face would ruin it for mancery. He quite lost himself in his work, taking an hour to remove a flawed crystal as small as a grain of wheat.

The night passed, and the following morning. Gilhaelith laboured on, now holding the remaining crystals in a rag torn from his shirt, for even the moisture from his fingers would damage them. By the middle of the afternoon the last dross cleaved away and he had a single, perfect cube of salt, transparent and with a faint yellow tinge. He might be able to work some minor magic with it – slip the lock, douse the lights in the corridor, possibly even put the nearby guards to sleep, but that would be its limit.

Wiping a patch of floor, he set his forgotten dinner on it and carefully placed the crystal in the centre of the tray. A pair of guards passed down the corridor, talking quietly. Gilhaelith dropped his rag over the crystal and lay back on the palliasse, clenching his fists against the tension. The guards were watchful and intelligent. Anything might arouse their suspicion.

They looked in, saw nothing amiss and went by. He began at once. If the crystal did work, he would have to get it right first time, for Yggur would allow no second chances. It might be better to wait until he'd gone to Nennifer. No, Yggur could have special plans for Gilhaelith in his absence. Do it now.

Gilhaelith ever so gently drew power into the crystal – not enough to reveal himself, but enough for him to sense any auras elsewhere in Fiz Gorgo. They could be due to mancers or other sources of the Art best avoided. He picked up several: Yggur and Malien close together, Flydd elsewhere, and various devices presumably in Yggur's quarters. He wasn't worried about them, but something larger and more tenuous, further out, did bother him.

It was like a filmy cloud surrounding Fiz Gorgo, and he could detect nothing beyond it. It must be a protection of some sort, to keep the outside world from spying or even noticing that there were mancers here, or to keep people in.

Gilhaelith withdrew, considering. Invisible to sight and touch the protection might be, nonetheless it could prevent him from escaping. He probed it tentatively, to discover how it had been made, and its strength. To his surprise it did not resist him – it was set to protect from the outside, not from within.

He took a little more power but the phantom fragments stung his brain like sparklers. He lost control for a second and his probe went right through the protection, burning a small opening like an eye. He withdrew hastily and it closed over again. Too hastily! A final surge of power zipped through the cubic crystal, cleaving it down the middle. He cursed, crushed it underfoot and threw himself on the bed in disgust. He'd have to find another way.

Three times now, Ullii had thought she'd found them. Three times she'd rebuilt the lattice to try to uncover what had been hidden, but without success. Something was out there, a long way south, but she could neither pinpoint nor identify it. It pleased her that her failure was frustrating Ghorr and Fusshte, though she dreaded being punished for it.

'I don't like it,' said Ghorr. 'Is it deliberate, do you think?'

Ullii could not answer that. She simply saw what was in her lattice. She had no idea what was behind it.

In the mid-afternoon the fleet had set down on the plain south of Flumen, by a main road now partly reclaimed by grass and scrub, while he called the other scrutators into a conference. They spent an hour at it, all the while consulting instruments of their own, as Ullii squatted in the shadows waiting on their pleasure.

'They're hiding, but I don't think it's from *us*,' Ghorr concluded. 'Nothing suggests that they know we're coming, and we must strive to keep it that way. It's just a general cloaking, to conceal them from the lyrinx. We'll continue, more carefully.'

He turned to the seeker. 'Ullii, we *are* getting closer, are we not?'

'I can't tell.' Fear grew in her: fear that the lattice was failing, for it was harder to see each time; and fear of Ghorr and the scrutators, and what they would do once they'd captured their quarry and had no further need of her. She had to protect herself, which meant finding someone to look after her. But no one on these air-dreadnoughts cared if she lived or died, or how much she suffered.

She idly scanned her lattice, started, and again Ghorr noticed her flinch.

'Yes, Seeker?'

She didn't want to answer, but she had to. 'J – just then, for a second, I saw an opening like an eye.'

'An opening? In what?'

'I can't tell.'

'What else did you see? What was in the opening?'

'A strange knot.'

'Tell us more, Seeker,' said Fusshte.

'The knot shone out like someone peering from a hole cut in a cloud, then disappeared.'

'Did it now? Whose knot was it?'

'I don't know. It was strange but very strong. A mancer's knot.'

'Really?' he said. 'The cloud must be some kind of *protection*. That gives me an idea, Seeker.'

She waited numbly for his orders.

'Do you remember how you got Irisis out of her prison cell in Nennifer, Ullii?'

Of course she did. It was only the second brave thing she had done in her life. 'Yes,' she whispered.

'You held the magicked lock's knot in place and rotated the rest of your lattice around it, and that opened the door without breaking *my* magic.'

'Yes.' She felt faint just talking to him.

'What if you were to do that now? Hold that knot, what you remember of it, in place and redraw your lattice from the other side.'

'I'll try,' she said softly, 'though I don't see what—'

'Just do it,' he said. 'I won't punish you if you fail – only if you don't try hard enough.'

Ullii was so afraid that, at first, she could not see her lattice at all. When it finally appeared, more pale and ghostly than she had ever seen it, she recognised nothing but the bright knots made by Ghorr's scrutators and mancers, and the controllers that powered the air-dreadnoughts. Ghorr had to calm her, as unpleasant an operation as she could imagine, before she recovered the knot.

662

'You have it!' said Ghorr, dark eyes gleaming. 'Now, make your lattice anew, looking the other way.'

Ullii closed her eyes and put her hands over the goggles for good measure. Holding the image of that strange knot, she dissolved the rest of the lattice, turned the knot around in her mind and began to redraw the lattice from the other perspective. It became sprinkled with blotches, smudges and knots, near and far. The blotches were objects that used some form of the Art like controllers. The smudges were fields generated by nodes, while the knots indicated people who had some talent for the Art. A dim smudge was the cloud of protection but she could see through it now. Inside, she recognised several knots. Irisis was in the centre. Close by, Ullii saw Fyn-Mah, *and Flydd*, and other knots too, some very strong.

'I've found them.' She took her hands away from the goggles.

Ghorr's head swung around and his eyes glowed like broken glass melting from underneath.

'Where?' he hissed.

Her finger traced a line along the map until it encountered a dot with two small words beside it: Fiz Gorgo. 'There.'

Ghorr purred and called the scrutators. 'To the air! We can be there by three in the morning. Plan number seven.'

Nish went to bed early but tossed, turned and woke half a dozen times, uneasy, though he had no idea why. Deciding that he was never going to get back to sleep, he went down to the privy, relieved himself and headed back through the frigid corridors. Worms of ice, frozen seepage, oozed through the dark walls. Fiz Gorgo always seemed cold, even if it didn't have quite the perpetual dank frigidity of the manufactory, and Nish didn't mind it. He had grown up in such climes and Fiz Gorgo was more to his liking than the hot, parched plains of western Lauralin, where he had spent much of the past year.

Still wide awake, he turned up the narrow stone stairs to

Yggur's lookout. As he stepped out onto the crumbling stone balcony, he realised someone was standing there, leaning on the rail. Nish smelt an aroma like liquorice. Yggur!

'Worried about tomorrow, Nish?' said Yggur, not looking around.

'I've been through too much to bother about the future,' Nish said untruthfully. 'I can't sleep. My mind keeps going round and round, fretting in case I've forgotten something.'

'Mine too,' said Yggur. 'And no doubt you feel left out, and worried that we've planned this mission in haste and unjustifiable optimism.'

'We-e-e-ll . . .' said Nish.

'You can admit it. I'm not an ogre.'

'Is such secrecy really necessary, surr?'

'Probably not, but I'd rather not chance it. What do you think of the night?'

What a strange question. 'It's very still.'

'Aye, it can be at this time of the year. That's one of the things I like best about Fiz Gorgo. When the wind's not blowing, and the forest creatures are curled up in their holes, there's a stillness here that I've not felt anywhere else. It's why I've always come back. I like it when nothing is happening.'

'So do I,' said Nish. 'I'll leave you to it, then.'

'Stay a moment,' said Yggur. 'I . . . I feel . . . No, tell me what *you* feel.'

'Is something wrong, surr?'

'I feel uneasy tonight, though I can't say why. What about you?'

'An awful lot rests on this attack on Nennifer,' said Nish.

'Yes. And so, despite the risk, there really isn't any choice.'

'I suppose not.' Nish came to the rail, staring out. The darkness was complete, save for occasional lights winking on and off in the invisible forest. 'What's that?' he hissed.

Yggur chuckled. 'Not lyrinx, you can be sure. It's just fireflies in the swamp.'

They leaned on the rail for some time, not speaking. Yggur

offered Nish a piece of liquorice root. Nish chewed on it, reflectively. The night seemed to be brooding, even ominous, though the dark always encouraged such feelings in him.

Yggur spat over the rail. The aroma of liquorice filled the balcony. 'It was nothing. I'm a morbid fellow at the best of times, and sometimes my dark thoughts just go round and round. I'll bid you good night.'

'Goodnight,' said Nish. 'I'll stay a while. I can't sleep, anyway.'

Yggur's boots went down the steps. A cold breeze curled around the side of the wall and Nish pulled his coat tighter about his neck. The night lent itself to introspection. What would become of them? He wasn't just thinking of this suicidal mission. Every year of his life the losses of the war had been greater, until the lyrinx had seemed like a disease creeping across the world. The climax was rapidly approaching.

Even if they won at Nennifer, and replaced the Council, there was too little time to be ready. Once spring came, everything he knew and loved looked set to be swept away in a few weeks of violence. It was not a thought conducive to further sleep, but he had to be rested for the morrow, so Nish headed back to bed.

As he reached the lowest flight, feeling his way in pitch darkness, a great five-lobed shadow blotted out the stars to the north of Fiz Gorgo. Another moved in beside it, and a third, drifting down the wind, its rotors silent. More crept into position to the sides of Fiz Gorgo, and yet more. The night became so still that even the wind seemed to be holding its breath, waiting for the moment when all sixteen air-dreadnoughts were in place. Waiting for the order to attack.

Irisis rolled over in bed, trying to scrape the cobwebs from her brain. Something had disturbed her. Her heart was thudding as if she'd just run all the way to the top of Yggur's watchtower. Her throat was dry, her hands sweaty. What was the matter?

She was reaching for the short sword that she kept on the

chair beside her bed when she heard someone coming along the corridor. Irisis sat up, panic prickling the backs of her hands. Something was wrong. She slid her feet onto the frigid flagstones. Ah, it was so cold.

The footsteps came closer. She swung the sword back and forth, preparing to spring. The dark figure cleared its throat, she realised who it was and the panic seemed ridiculous.

'Nish!' she hissed, weak with relief. 'What the bloody hell are you doing? I was about to skewer you.'

'Irisis? What's the matter?'

She sensed him peering this way and that, trying to pick her out of the dark. 'Come in here.' She pulled him through the doorway of her room. 'What are you doing?'

'I couldn't sleep so I went for a pee. Is something wrong?'

Her knees went weak and she had to sit down on the bed, which annoyed her. 'Sorry, Nish. I thought you were an intruder, coming to slice open our gullets while we're asleep.'

'In Fiz Gorgo?' said Nish. 'This has to be the safest place in Santhenar. Even the lyrinx stay clear of it. What's the matter with you tonight?'

'I had a feeling of doom. I suppose it was a bad dream.'

'You're always having feelings of doom, Irisis.'

'Which surely means it's on it's way.'

'I was just up on the balcony with Yggur and I didn't see—'

'What was he doing up there?'

'I suppose he likes the solitude.'

'Well, I don't,' she muttered.

He sat on the bed beside her. 'I've never seen you so jumpy. At least, not since we were back at the manufactory, when—'

'I don't want to talk about that,' Irisis cut in more sharply than she intended. 'I've been having bad dreams lately.'

'What kind of dreams?'

'The kind where I come to a nasty end. I'm scared, Nish. We're not going to survive Nennifer.'

'You're being ridiculous. I can see you as a great-grandmother, with fifty grandchildren and great-grandchildren around you.'

'*I* can't, Nish. Not even one child, though I do so long for it.'

He put his arms around her. 'Hush. It's late, and dark, and you're just twitchy because things haven't been going well. It'll all be better tomorrow I'm going back to bed.'

'Stay with me, Nish. Just for a little while.'

She was warm and his bed was cold. And she was his dearest friend. 'Just a few minutes. I've got a lot to do in the morning.'

Nish lay on the bed, holding her but fretting. Eventually realising that Irisis was asleep, he eased himself out from her embrace, folded the covers over her and headed to his own cold bed. He still could not sleep.

The attack began not long before dawn, when the night was at its blackest. The sixteen air-dreadnoughts had manoeuvred themselves perfectly into position beforehand, fifteen surrounding the walls of Fiz Gorgo, the sixteenth on station high above, keeping watch for flying lyrinx. They did not expect to see any, and Ullii had spotted none in her lattice, but Chief Scrutator Ghorr was not a man to take chances where his own life was concerned.

Crossbow snipers checked the walls with hedron-enhanced night glasses, another new development from the workshops of Nennifer. There were only four guards on duty in Fiz Gorgo, for Yggur's walls protected him against anything short of an army. No land force could come at him through the swamp forests of Orist, even had they been able to evade the lyrinx further east.

The guards were identified before it was light enough for them to see the air-dreadnoughts, the snipers picking all four off in the same instant. Fiz Gorgo now lay unprotected save for certain defences Yggur had installed in the towers, but these were useless at such a distance. Besides, they were unmanned, for the protection had been broken without giving any warning.

In Ghorr's air-dreadnought, a quarter of a league away at the northern point of the compass, Ullii pinpointed each of Yggur's three defences.

'Very good,' said Ghorr, once the locations had been relayed to his troops. 'Ullii, I have here an ancient map of Fiz Gorgo. Mark out for me the positions of Xervish Flydd, Irisis Stirm and Perquisitor Fyn-Mah.'

Ullii studied the map. In the dim light she did not need to wear her goggles. She took hold of the paper. 'I don't understand it.'

Ghorr patiently turned the map around. It was beginning to get light. 'There's the tower on the left. See it? And this line is the outer wall.'

'I see it,' said Ullii.

'Where are they?'

Ullii shuddered. 'I – I—'

'Don't let me down now, Seeker.'

She said nothing. Ullii was in torment.

'You do know,' said Ghorr, 'how I treat those who fail me?'

'Yes!' she gasped.

'And remember, those who made you suffer so cruelly are traitors all. Remember what they did to your brother. They *hate* you, Ullii.'

She closed her eyes, as if that could hide her, then opened them again. 'Irisis is here.' She pointed to the map. 'Flydd along here. And Fyn-Mah,' she hesitated. Ullii had no quarrel with the perquisitor. 'She is here.'

'You're absolutely sure?'

'Yes,' she whispered.

'Very good. You may go.' She began to scuttle away. 'No, wait a moment.'

Ullii came creeping back. This was the moment she had been dreading.

'What else can you tell me about this place, Seeker? Can you see anything else in your lattice?'

'Yes,' she said faintly.

'What is it? You can see magical artefacts, can't you?'

'Hundreds!' she rushed out, greatly relieved.

'Hundreds?' Ghorr frowned. 'But of course, it must be the ancient trove of the great mancer Yggur, who dwelt here for centuries. You'll come with us, Seeker, to show us where the hoard is.'

He turned away, but something about her manner must have bothered him, for he swung back. 'Is there anything else I should know, Ullii?'

'O-other mancers, surr,' she stammered.

Giving Ullii an unpleasant smile, Ghorr lifted her onto the tips of her toes. 'What other mancers, Seeker?'

'I don't know who they are, but there are three, and each is very great. Greater – as great as you, surr,' she amended hastily.

'Really?' he whispered. 'What can you tell me about them?'

'Nothing, surr, but for one, an Aachim.'

'Aachim!' he ejaculated. 'What's an Aachim mancer doing *here*? This changes things,' Ghorr said to Fusshte. 'We don't want to upset the Aachim. Is that all, Seeker?'

Ullii stood there, frozen to the spot.

'You've been very helpful, Ullii,' Ghorr cajoled, 'and when we return home you shall have your reward – whatever you care to name. Just tell me what else you saw in your wonderful lattice, that no one else in the world can see.'

'Tiaan, surr,' she whispered. 'I can see Tiaan, and her amplimet, and a flying construct.'

Ghorr almost fell down in astonishment. He went to his knees, kissed the canvas deck then sprang up with a silent cry of exultation. Seizing Ullii's hand he kissed it as well.

She tore her hand free with a look of profound disgust, but he did not notice. Fate had just offered Ghorr the world and nothing was going to stand in his way. Calling Fusshte and his lieutenants together, he rapped out orders, then turned to his men.

Ghorr said, in a low but carrying voice, 'Soldiers and crew, below us lies the greatest prize in all of Lauralin, one I never dared to hope for – a prize that can win us the war. It is

Artisan Tiaan Liise-Mar, her precious amplimet, and the unique, marvellous flying construct. At all costs we must secure them, even if, in so doing, our enemies escape. But we will not let them escape, for they don't know we're here.'

He paused while signallers semaphored his words, with luminous coloured flags, to the soldiers assembled on the decks of the other air-dreadnoughts.

'They've got no army to protect them,' Ghorr continued, 'just a few guards. When I give the word, you will begin the attack. Watch all the escape routes. Let not a soul get away. For every person captured alive, there will be a reward beyond your dreams. We will make an example of these renegades that will be sung for a thousand years, and the whole of Santhenar must know of it.

'The evil traitor Xervish Flydd is worth ten thousand gold tells if captured alive and fit to stand trial, but *only one hundred dead*. There are two other mancers here as well. I don't know who they are, but clearly they are scoundrels and renegades. For each of them, the prize shall be two thousand gold tells if captured alive, but a mere for forty dead. And for the lesser villains: a thousand gold tells if alive, or twenty dead, for Cryl-Nish Hlar or Irisis Stirm; five hundred alive or ten dead for Perquisitor Fyn-Mah; and fifty tells alive or one dead for each of the ordinary folk. Do not fail me. Any man who does will go to a scrutators' quisitory, and I need not tell you—'

The sharp intake of breath was all he needed. Every man, woman and child in Lauralin knew what a scrutators' quisitory signified.

'But there is more,' said Ghorr. 'I'm advised that a great Aachim mancer is also here. He must be taken alive and unharmed, and treated with courtesy. He may be subdued if he struggles and, once taken, must be restrained hand and foot and his mouth stopped. Such a mancer may use his Art simply by the power of his voice. But once that's been done, take good care of him. The Aachim are not our enemies and we cannot survive if they declare war on us. He may not be harmed, on pain of death.

'My personal guard, you are charged with securing the construct. Those doing so will *each* receive two hundred gold tells. But should you lose it, each of you will be dismissed and sent to serve in the front-lines. So do not fail me.

'Finally, and most importantly of all, Artisan Tiaan Liise-Mar must be taken alive. She is a hero. I repeat, Tiaan is no renegade, but a hero worthy of the highest honour, and vital to the war. She must be taken alive and unharmed, though she too must be restrained until after the trials. Those who assist in taking her will share in twenty thousand gold tells. *Twenty thousand gold tells,*' he repeated. Ghorr looked around at his troops and his mancers, engaging with each of them in turn. His signallers stood behind him, relaying his words to each of the other air-dreadnoughts.

'But,' Ghorr went on, 'no matter how hard she struggles, any man who harms Artisan Tiaan, deliberately or accidentally, will be flayed alive. So have particular care. Master Artist, show everyone the sketches you have made. There must be no doubt of Tiaan's identity.'

A wizened little man covered in liver spots and flaking psoriasis hobbled down the line displaying his sketches. They bore a passable likeness to Tiaan. Her description was also relayed to the other craft.

Ghorr held up his hand. Everyone went still. He stared towards the east, tapping one foot. The arc of the sun crept above the horizon. Its first light fell on the powered mirrors and the operators did their work. Incandescent beams struck the three towers holding Yggur's defences. The towers erupted, their stone running like honey down the side of a jug. The defences were silent.

As the sun illuminated the mighty flying machines, Ghorr said, 'Go!'

The signalmen hoisted their flags, the great mirrors swung onto their targets, and the beams tore holes through the walls and towers. When all was chaos, the soldiers went down on ropes and stormed Fiz Gorgo.

Ghorr sat back in his chair, the other scrutators surrounding him. 'It's been a long wait, but today will make up for everything. We'll have the lot of them within the hour.'

'And the flying construct.' Fusshte rubbed his scaly hands together. 'This will make all the difference, Ghorr.'

Ghorr gave him an ambiguous glance. 'Indeed it will, Scrutator. All the difference in the world.'

SIXTY-TWO

Exploding stone and seething, boiling metal shocked Irisis awake. She shot up in bed, thinking she was back in the manufactory, under attack by the lyrinx. 'Nish?' she cried. 'Where are you?'

He was gone and the nightmare was back, but this time Irisis knew it was real. That crash was a battering-ram on the front doors. Those shrieks – the death screams of the servants who had foolishly run to see what was going on. This was it. Her long-anticipated doom had come at last.

She pulled on her clothes, tied her boots, grabbed the sword and peered out the door, expecting to see lyrinx everywhere. Soldiers were advancing methodically along the corridor, checking every door. For a fleeting second she relaxed, until it penetrated her fuzzy mind that they were human soldiers, wearing the black and scarlet uniform of the chief scrutator's personal guard, the most elite troops of all. It was worse than lyrinx, far worse. Ghorr had found them.

She could see at least a hundred soldiers and, from the racket in the other halls, many more were there. Doubtless there were mancers, too.

Against them, Yggur had merely twenty troops and Irisis was prepared to bet that the majority of them, stationed in the barracks outside, were dead. The battle was already lost, the only option to try to escape into the labyrinth of tunnels that honeycombed the rock underneath Fiz Gorgo. Unfortunately, though Irisis knew how to get into the labyrinth, she had never been down there. That was the problem with labyrinths, she thought wryly. They were so damned hard to get out of.

Ducking out the door, she ran towards the rear of the building. At the first corner, she stopped. Flydd's room was just to the left, Nish's a long way down the corridor to the right. There wasn't time to rouse both. After a second's hesitation, she turned left. Nish was a poor sleeper and was probably up already. If not, he'd be captured within seconds. It took a lot to rouse Flydd, so there was no choice. Ah, Nish love, I'm sorry.

Fleeting down the corridor in the dark, she pounded on Flydd's door. There was no answer so she kicked it open. Flydd was sitting up in bed, naked.

'What is it?' he said, only half-awake.

She dragged him out of bed. 'The scrutators are here, inside Fiz Gorgo, with hundreds of soldiers.'

He didn't move. 'Then we're done for. Run to the labyrinth. Hide. It's me they want.'

She found his boots, a knife, his clothes. 'I don't leave my friends behind. Get these on. Besides, they've come for the lot of us and they won't leave until they've torn this place apart, stone by stone. There's no point hiding unless you know a way out.'

'I expect I can find one.' He threw on his boots, buckled a belt around his waist, into which he thrust the knife, and tossed his satchel over his shoulder.

Irisis stood at the door, peering out into the dark corridor. The soldiers weren't yet in sight. There might just be time to run down to Nish's room. No, she could hear them coming from his direction. They'd have him already.

'You could at least tie on a loincloth,' she snapped. 'For dignity's sake.'

He tore a sheet off the bed and wrapped it around himself. 'At a time like this, dignity is the least of my worries.'

'It was my dignity I was thinking about,' she said.

'Oh!' He smiled. 'Right. Let's go.'

She opened the door. The corridor was now illuminated by

distant lantern light, and soldiers were advancing on them from both right and left. Past the junction of the corridors she saw people she recognised, struggling with their captors. Fyn-Mah went down under the weight of three men, who swiftly bound and gagged her. One soldier sufficed to subdue the tragic little pilot, Inouye, who just waited listlessly for her fate.

A great roar echoed along the hall, followed by a flash and a clap of thunder. Plaster rained down from the ceiling. It was Yggur, half-dressed and struggling furiously. A scarlet-robed mancer collapsed screaming and holding bloody ears. Another mancer reeled sideways, going face-first into the wall. Yggur let out another roar and, raising his arm, swung it like a scythe at his attackers. Black light streamed out in rippling beams and a group of soldiers fell. He swung it the other way, hurling aside another trio of armed men.

'He's going to do it,' she said, awed at Yggur's power.

The remaining soldiers broke and ran, abandoning their weapons.

'To me,' Yggur roared. 'Rally behind me. Flydd, make a—'

An unnoticed soldier behind Yggur brought the flat of his sword down on the mancer's head. The sword broke, but Yggur was driven to his knees. The soldier, gasping for breath, slammed the hilt into the side of Yggur's skull. He slid to the floor, stunned. The soldier pinioned his hands. The ones who had fled ran back, swarming over Yggur and binding him like a moth in a spider's web.

'That's it,' said Irisis.

'There's still a chance,' said Flydd. 'Gilhaelith and Malien each have the power to take on a brace of scrutators.'

'But not all of them together.' Irisis ducked back inside Flydd's room. '*And* their mancers at the same time. There's no way out, Xervish.' The room had no window.

Flydd was fumbling in his satchel and did not answer.

'Forget it, Xervish,' she said. 'There's far too many of them. There's nothing you can do.'

'Bar the door and shut up.'

She flung it shut, dropped the heavy bar and pushed the bed up against the door. 'What do you have in mind?' She didn't imagine he could do much, not being fully recovered yet.

'Close your eyes. Turn your back.'

'But—' she began, then obediently closed them and turned away. She'd been down that road before.

'One, two, three . . .' he said under his breath, then something cracked against the floor.

Sound enveloped the room, a roaring, crashing and crumbling. A piece of stone thumped her in the side so hard that it knocked the breath out of her.

He took her hand. 'You can look now.'

The room was full of whirling dust and there was a hole in the floor between them, large enough to have slid the bed down on its end. She could not see what lay below.

Flydd was already knotting the sheet and the blankets together and tying one end to a leg of the bed. 'Go down!' he said.

Something struck the door so hard that it shivered. Irisis grasped the blanket and slid through the hole to the first knot, then past it to the second, and the third. As she was dangling there her feet scraped the floor, though she still could not see anything. The room was in darkness.

Abandoning the makeshift rope, she sprang to one side. Flydd came sliding and bumping after her. He hit the floor hard, clutched at his middle and she steadied him.

'Are you all right?'

'Just a twinge.'

'Where to now?' said Irisis.

'I'm not sure. Feel around the walls for a door.'

He found it first, opening it into darkness. 'This way,' he whispered. 'Follow me.'

They eased through the door, tiptoed down a corridor and out into a wider hall that was also dark, though Irisis could feel a cold wind blowing along it. It was not far to the outside. They had a chance, though at the expense of leaving all their friends behind.

'Come on,' said Flydd. 'I think we're going to make it after all.' Irisis clutched her sword and followed, but they had not gone more than a dozen steps before brilliant lights came on before them, and behind.

'Xervish Flydd,' said a voice that was unpleasantly familiar. 'Irisis Stirm. I'm so pleased to see you both again.'

It was Chief Scrutator Ghorr, and he had at least a dozen soldiers with him. She looked the other way and recognised the malicious face of Scrutator Fusshte, with as many more troops, all armoured and heavily armed.

'These are the last,' said Fusshte. 'Let's get the trials under-way. The executioners are impatient.'

Their hands were bound behind them and they were marched out of the broken doors of Fiz Gorgo into the bleak yard. The thirty or so prisoners already there, each with their group of guards, were well separated. Yggur's servants and his few surviving guards were treated no differently. All were surrounded by four or five soldiers.

Irisis struggled all the way, suffering many a kick and a cuff across the face from the soldiers. It did not deter her. She fought them until the ropes had worn a collar of skin off each wrist and her raw flesh rasped against the wiry fibres.

'Cut it out,' said Flydd, who was still beside her. He looked up at the vast air-dreadnoughts, hanging in the sky around the walls in perfect formation. Already the attendants were teth-ering them in place with cables as thick as a man's arm. 'See what we're facing. They've spent half a year planning this. If I know Ghorr, he's left nothing to chance.'

'I'm not giving in,' she gritted. 'I'll never submit to them, Xervish.'

He shrugged. 'Do as you will. It won't make any differ-ence, either way.'

'What do you mean?'

'They made up their minds about us a long time ago. We've got as much time left as the trial takes, and that's the limit.'

For all her premonitions of doom, Irisis wasn't prepared for that. 'But surely they'll take us back to Nennifer. Or Lybing, or some other great city, to make a spectacle of our trial and punishment.'

'Ghorr won't risk it, in case any of us has a trick up our sleeves. Their air-dreadnoughts must contain a thousand people, and that's plenty to witness the spectacle. Among them will be tale-tellers and chroniclers enough to spread the word throughout all the lands of Santhenar. There have been too many humiliations, Irisis. The people are already questioning the scrutators' authority, so this operation has to be quick, brutal and complete. We must all die in the most drawn-out and horrible of ways, as a lesson to everyone else. I wonder what Ghorr's got planned for us?'

'How can you be so calm?' she said.

'To be a scrutator is to be impassive to the worst the world, and your fellows, can throw at you.'

'Impassive!' she murmured cheekily. 'I've seen the proud, imperious Flydd, the irascible, the querulous, and occasionally the mean and spiteful side of you, but I'd never call you impassive.'

'I'm just a man, with as many faults as any other, and I never claimed differently. It seems the worst brings out the best in me. Let me assure you, Irisis,' Flydd gave her the best smile he could manage, 'on the inside I'm quaking. I know what it's going to be like. I've been in their hands before, remember?'

The smile did not help. She'd been expecting to die for a year now, and had long ago inured herself to it. But this was going to be torment, inflicted by people who had made a science of agony.

'I'm really scared, Xervish.'

He rubbed his shoulder against hers, since his hands were tied behind his back and he could not reach her. 'You *should* be scared. Take comfort from one thing, though.'

'What's that?'

'We're all in it together, and we'll all be thinking of you, as you will be of us.'

'I don't see how that's going to make a difference,' she said bitterly. 'Oh, I suppose it does, in a way. I've suffered alone, and I've suffered with dear friends, and the latter is preferable.'

'Well, if that's little comfort,' said Flydd, 'here's something that should be: We'll all be dead by nightfall.'

'They'll draw our torment out for days. They like to make their prisoners suffer.'

'They won't dare, this deep in enemy territory. The air-dreadnoughts are a powerful force, none more so. And from what we heard earlier, they've got weapons no one has ever heard of before. But even so, air-dreadnoughts are as vulnerable as any other kind of air-floater. It only takes one lyrinx to tear the airbags, after all. In the daytime this fleet might fight off hundreds of flying lyrinx, but if they attacked in their thousands, enough would get through to bring down every machine and all the people in them. That would be the end of the Council, and Ghorr doesn't take chances like that. See how most of the guards up there have their weapons pointed out and up, rather than down at us.'

She did not look up. There was no point – to anything.

'And in the night,' Flydd went on, 'he won't dare land, for a handful of flying lyrinx could destroy all these air-dreadnoughts without being seen. Ghorr must finish his business with us and be high in the sky before nightfall. The only way to ensure the safety of such fragile craft is to fly higher than the lyrinx can reach. This Council will put their safety before anything else. No, it will all be over by dark, and that's a pity and a tragedy.'

'It's certainly a tragedy for us,' she said waspishly, 'and a pity we won't be around to mourn ourselves, since no one else will.'

'I meant for humanity. This victory spells the death-knell for humankind, and that's something I've fought my entire life to avoid.'

'Surely you've got a plan or two up your sleeve, Xervish? You always do. What about another of those embedded crystals, that you used to escape once before?'

'Sadly, no. I never thought Ghorr would dare come this deep into Meldorin. And even if I had a crystal or two, it wouldn't make a jot of difference. See up there?' He pointed with his elbow.

Each air-dreadnought held at least one robed mancer, watching the prisoners with a spyglass. Beside him were crossbowmen and javelard operators, whose weapons were trained on them.

'Ghorr has thought of everything,' said Flydd. 'Even if I could free myself with such a crystal, they'd shoot me down before I could move a dozen strides. That's why they've kept us in the middle of the yard, where we can be seen.'

'How did they find us?' said Irisis. 'I thought Yggur had a protection to hide Fiz Gorgo.'

'I don't know, but if they can track down mancers from so far away, what else can they do?'

Irisis didn't care to speculate. She was still thinking that there had to be a way to escape.

Flydd seemed to read her mind. 'Even were I Rulke himself, the greatest mancer that ever lived, there's no way out of here alive.'

'I refuse to give up. While there's a breath left in my lungs, I'll fight them.'

'By all means,' said Flydd. 'If that helps.'

Irisis looked around the yard. The other prisoners were surrounded by tall, burly guards so, in most cases, she could not identify who was in the middle. Over in the corner she made out the tall form of Yggur, tightly bound and his mouth stopped. He was swaying on his feet; a bloody bandage was wrapped around his skull. To his left, taller by his frizzled mass of sandy hair, Gilhaelith stood half a head above the biggest of the guards. Rags were bound across his mouth, in case he tried to speak mathemancy or any other kind of spell.

'Where's Malien?' said Irisis, still hoping that one of the company had escaped and would free them. If anyone had power to break the hold of the scrutators, it was Malien.

'Don't get your hopes up,' said Flydd. 'I saw her being

carried out, all trussed up like a chicken. She's over by the southern wall.'

Irisis made out someone slumped in the shadows, surrounded by at least twenty guards, and with a crystal-equipped mancer at either end. 'Surely they're not going to execute Malien?'

'They wouldn't dare. That would be as good as declaring war on the Aachim. But they've made sure she can't help us.'

Irisis scanned the yard. 'I don't see Tiaan anywhere.'

'You're clinging to the hope that she's got free and will single-handedly rescue us in the thapter.' Flydd chuckled mockingly.

'Why not?' she said, not liking his tone. 'The miracles Tiaan's performed in the past year, why can't I hope for one more?'

'Because they have her, too. She's there, strapped to the stretcher.' He nodded towards the western wall, in whose shadow a group of soldiers clustered around a prone figure, while a robed healer bent over it. 'Looks like she struggled and one of the soldiers struck her down. Besides, they've already secured the thapter. That would have been their first target. And you never know, it might *just* make the difference, in the war.'

'If they can get it to work,' said Irisis.

'Tiaan won't be on the execution list. They'll be taking good care of her. The soldier who struck her down will be lucky to keep his head.'

'Then there's no hope for us, Xervish.' It just drained out of her, turning her in an instant from hope to despair. Irisis was like that.

'You can always pray for a miracle. Say a wild storm that drives them off . . .'

'I've never seen the sky so clear.'

'Well, an attack by the lyrinx—'

'We're surrounded by swamp. They can only attack from the air,' said Irisis. 'The scrutators' spotters will see them half an hour before they get here. Plenty of time to take our heads off, in an emergency.'

681

'Suddenly you seem determined to establish that we've got no hope,' said Flydd.

'I'm a realist. I have to know the odds, but you've made me realise that there are no odds, because our chances are nil.'

'I'm really sorry about that, Irisis.'

Irisis took a few steps to her left, trying to identify who was being held by the soldiers over near the northern wall. Flangers, she thought, but couldn't be sure. The guards prodded her back to the centre of the circle.

'What's going to happen now?' They had been standing therefor the best part of an hour already. Irisis was only clad in indoor clothes and the yard was frigid. At this time of year, the sun never reached the ground inside the walls, and ice lingered there from autumn to spring.

Flydd was shivering too, and his scarred skin was mottled white and blue. He must be freezing in his sheet.

'They're preparing a special end for us. The scrutators do love their spectacles.'

SIXTY-THREE

They stood in the cold for hours, though it was some time before they realised just how extravagant the spectacle was going to be. Artificers and rope-crafters began by installing mounting rings atop the outside walls of Fiz Gorgo. Heavy cables were lowered from the moored air-dreadnoughts and fastened to the rings. Halfway up, thinner cables were stretched horizontally and knotted together to form a taut network rather like a horizontal spider's web.

Onto that frame they pulled vast rolls of canvas, extending them to create a platform, more than a hundred and fifty spans across, in the shape of a fourteen-sided figure. The platform was a good fifty spans above the ground but had neither walls nor rails. The canvas was lashed to the network of ropes and stretched to drum tightness. A small hole remained in the centre, of a size for a body to be dropped through. The canvas was so taut that a man standing on it made no depression.

'It's an aerial colosseum,' said Flydd, sounding genuinely admiring. 'What a clever idea! The audience, or witnesses, will stand around the outside, while we prisoners, along with our judges and executioners, will take our positions in the middle.'

The platform came together so quickly that the operation must have been practised many times, back in Nennifer. Well before noon it was complete. The prisoners were then hauled up in ropework baskets, arms and legs dangling through the mesh. The guards and scrutators were lifted, dignity intact, in canvas chairs. Within half an hour all the prisoners had been assembled in the centre of the platform. The soldiers prevented them from running to the rim, or the central hole, and leaping to their deaths.

The majority of the air-dreadnought crews and soldiers were lowered to the platform, to stand in arcs surrounding the prisoners. They were to be the witnesses. The pilots remained at their stations, however, and many guards at theirs, ever vigilant for signs of the enemy.

Soldiers were also placed at the bow and stern of each air-dreadnought with great axes, ready to cut the ropes should an emergency occur. The witnesses would have bare minutes to run to the walls of Fiz Gorgo before the platform collapsed. Anyone still on it when that happened would plummet fifty spans to the paved yard.

Rope chairs hung above each of the scrutators, of course, so they could be hauled up to safety. Irisis prayed that the enemy would attack. It would be worth anything to see Scrutator Ghorr swinging in terror on the end of a rope while a lyrinx slashed and clawed at him. Had there been any way of summoning the enemy, she would have done it without hesitation.

Anything, even the belly of a lyrinx, was better than the disgraceful death being planned for them. A host of chroniclers and tellers stood by to record the shameful scene. Beside them, at the front, were half a dozen artists at their easels. It was their job to portray every moment of the trial, and to capture the agony on the faces of the criminals as they were executed. For as long as they endured, the Histories of Santhenar, and the personal Histories of every family involved, would tell of their disgrace and ignominious end.

A horn blared. The master of the executions made the sign of a blade being drawn across a throat. Absolute silence fell. Chief Scrutator Ghorr came forward.

'Recorders and witnesses,' Ghorr said in that low, carrying voice, 'for these vile traitors there can be no formal inquisition. We are deep in enemy territory and cannot afford such niceties for those who would give comfort to the enemy.

Nevertheless, the process laid down for this situation will be followed to the letter.

'I must be brief, for even now the enemy could be on their way. The Council of Scrutators has appointed me to summarise the evidence. In each case, I assert that the prisoners are guilty of treason, and other capital crimes too numerous to list. The penalty for such wickedness is flaying, selective disembowelling while maintaining life, and, finally, dismemberment. Ultimately, the body parts shall be distributed to feed the lowest of carrion eaters.'

He paused to scowl at the prisoners, and then at the assembled witnesses, though to Irisis he seemed to be striking a pose for the tale-tellers and the artists. How she despised the man.

'However,' Ghorr went on, 'the formalities of trial must be preserved. Let it not be said that the scrutators are above the law.'

You stinking hypocrite, Irisis thought. A hundred thousand times, when it suited you, the scrutators have acted as judge, jury and executioner, so don't pretend otherwise for the sake of your own place in the Histories. She was drawing breath to scream it at the world when Flydd elbowed her in the ribs.

'Don't!' he hissed. 'It won't do you any good at all.'

'It'll give me the satisfaction!'

'The scrutators have unique forms of excruciation, should you prove recalcitrant. To make an example they may take *you* back east, tormenting you all the way—'

'It'd be worth it.'

'Oh, Irisis, you have no idea! Nothing is worth what they can do to you. Just shut your mouth and pray for the quickest possible death. I'm looking forward to mine,' he added in a low voice.

'Surr!' she whispered, shocked.

'I mean it. I've fought the long fight and been defeated. The present is a bitter failure, a reminder of a futile life. All my hopes, and all my work, have come to nothing. There's not a thing I can do now and I no longer have to carry the burden of the world. I can let it go at last and go to my death with dignity. I'll embrace it.'

'Embrace it?'

'Since the scrutators tortured me as a young man, I've not had a day without pain. Not even poppy syrup can cure it now. Death is the end of all pain and I long for its release.'

Irisis shivered and said no more.

'. . . therefore,' Ghorr was going on, 'before I pronounce sentence, I call upon the assembled witnesses to confirm the guilt of the prisoners. Witnesses, should any one of you disagree with the verdict, you must come down and state your case for the prisoner, after which the other witnesses shall vote on the merits of the case. The scrutators will, of course, abstain from the vote. Should the vote be for the prisoner, that prisoner will be freed. If the vote goes against the prisoner, guilt is confirmed and the sentence will be carried out as soon as the remaining trials are finished.'

Ghorr motioned to the master of the executions who, with a flourish, presented him with a scroll and bowed low.

'No, man, that's your job!' Ghorr's low voice carried as far as Irisis. 'Get on with it! We've a war to win.'

The master of the executions dropped the scroll and scrabbled on the canvas for it, looking uncomfortable. He held the scroll out in front of him. 'Pilot Inouye,' he said in a nervous whine, 'the Council of Scrutators, in formal assembly, has found you guilty of treason. Does any witness disagree with the verdict?'

'I beg leave—' Flydd began.

'Denied,' said Ghorr.

No one else spoke. After a lengthy pause, during which the master of the executions scanned the rows of witnesses, he turned to Ghorr and said, 'Since no witness has come forward to oppose the verdict, the sentence is confirmed.'

'Say it to the witnesses,' hissed Ghorr, 'not to me, you damn fool! The scrutators must appear impartial.'

Turning to the witnesses in front of him, the master of the executions said, rather more loudly than was necessary, 'Pilot

Inouye has been found guilty of treason. Take her to the place of execution to await her fate.'

The little pilot was dragged away to a pen surrounded by barbed ropes, plus at least twenty guards, weapons at the ready.

'Sergeant Flangers,' said the master of the executions. 'The Council of Scrutators, in formal assembly, has found you guilty of treason. Does any witness disagree with the verdict?'

After another lengthy pause there was a stir in the crowd and someone shouted, 'Sergeant Flangers is a war hero, awarded the Star of Valour for heroism beyond the call of duty during the Siege of Plimes. I contest the verdict.'

Ghorr scowled. 'Come down, witness. State your case for the defence.'

A soldier moved down through the ranks, wearing the uniform of a high officer. 'My name is General Galliman, and I was the commanding officer of the garrison at Plimes during the onslaught by the enemy two years ago. Sergeant Flangers was instrumental in saving the city. Ten times he fought off an attacking force of lyrinx, slaying nine of them and fighting alone for more than two hours when the remainder of his squad was dead. Though sorely wounded, he held the breach against the enemy for most of the day, and remained at his post until reinforcements broke through the enemy lines to relieve him. His Star of Valour was confirmed by the full Council, and it is not the only instance of his heroism, which should be an example to us all.'

The master of the executions turned to Ghorr for the rebuttal.

Ghorr smiled thinly. 'I am well aware of the case, for I personally awarded Sergeant Flangers the Star of Valour. But not even the greatest hero can be exempt from the justice of the scrutators. Sergeant Flangers has since turned on his own kind, conspiring in the escapes of Irisis Stirm and Fyn-Mah, and later, Xervish Flydd and the detestable Cryl-Nish Hlar. He fired on a Council air-floater and destroyed it, causing the deaths of many men and grievous injuries to Scrutator Klarm, here.' Ghorr indicated a big-headed dwarf of a man sitting to his left, one little leg supported by metal calipers. 'Scrutator Klarm only escaped death by a miracle. And Flangers committed this treasonous act even after his air-floater had been ordered to surrender.'

'As I understand it, surr,' said General Galliman, 'Sergeant Flangers was obeying a legitimate order from his superior, Perquisitor Fyn-Mah.'

'And as *I* understand it, General Galliman, Sergeant Flangers was aware that Perquisitor Fyn-Mah had been ordered to surrender her air-floater by a representative of her lawful superior, Acting Scrutator Jal-Nish Hlar, and that she had wilfully and treasonously disobeyed that order. Master of the Executions, put the judgment to the witnesses.'

'I beg leave to defend Sergeant Flangers,' said Flydd.

'Denied!' snapped Ghorr.

'I appeal to the witnesses,' said Flydd, turning to face them. 'Sergeant Flangers is a soldier with a perfect record. The Siege of Plimes was not the only battle where he displayed courage far beyond the call of duty. I can name a dozen other struggles, not least the fall of Thurkad, and the first battle for Nilkerrand, where he was equally bold, equally heroic. What say you, witnesses, may I speak for my man? Yea or nay?'

After a brief hesitation, there came a great roar of 'Yea!'

Ghorr was furious, but there was little he could do. He signalled to the master of the executions.

'You may speak,' said the master of the executions, 'but you have only one minute. Make it to the point.'

'One minute.' Flydd licked dry lips; he'd prepared a case but there was not the time to put it. 'My argument is simply this: Sergeant Flangers obeyed a direct order from Perquisitor Fyn-Mah, who was following written orders I had given her while scrutator and commander-in-chief of the army at Snizort. These orders took precedence over any orders from Acting Scrutator Jal-Nish, or Scrutator Klarm, whom I outranked. Equally, Flangers had no option but to follow her legitimate orders, for he is a man who loves his country and always does his duty, no matter the cost to himself. His action in shooting down the air-floater was correct in military law and therefore he is innocent.'

'Indeed it was not,' said Ghorr. 'You had been stripped of your rights and privileges the previous day, and therefore every order you had made was void.'

'Perquisitor Fyn-Mah cannot have known that,' Flydd said, 'and so my orders still held.'

'The law has been changed,' Ghorr said hastily. 'Ignorance is no longer an excuse—'

'When was the law changed?' Flydd thundered. 'Show us the chapter, the page, the line.'

'How dare you, a non-citizen, question me! It is as I have said. Besides, Fyn-Mah had been told of your fall and still disobeyed the representative of Jal-Nish, and subsequently Scrutator Klarm, who was in command of the air-floater she ordered to be shot down. Was that not so, Perquisitor Fyn-Mah?'

After a hesitation, she said, 'It was so.'

'I cannot—' Flydd began.

Ghorr cut him off. 'You've had your say, more than you were entitled to. Be silent or I'll have you silenced.'

Flydd met Flangers's eyes. Flangers gave a single shake of the head. Flydd bowed his own. He could do no more.

Ghorr motioned to the master of the executions to get on with it.

'Witnesses,' yelled the master of the executions, 'you have heard arguments for the defence by General Galliman, and the chief scrutator's telling rebuttal. You have heard Flydd's appeal dismissed. Raise your right hand if you disagree with the chief scrutator, and therefore deny the verdict.'

A considerable number of hands rose. 'The clerk of the executions will tally those who disagree,' said the master of the executions. Out of the corner of his mouth he added, 'Clerk, get their names.'

Once the clerk had done, the master said, 'Witnesses, raise your right hand if you agree with the chief scrutator and therefore confirm the verdict.'

A forest of hands rose. The clerk tallied them and handed his slate to the master of the executions.

He scanned the list, then said, 'The verdict is confirmed, by three hundred and eighty-one votes to two hundred and forty-four. Sergeant Flangers has been found guilty of treason. Take him to the place of execution to await his fate.'

An impassive Flangers bowed to the master of the executions, to the recorders and the witnesses, and finally to Flydd, before being led away by a group of soldiers who strode beside him like an honour guard.

In short order the remaining twenty-eight prisoners, including Yggur's guards and servants, an expressionless Fyn-Mah, a furiously struggling Gilhaelith and a coldly remote Yggur, were condemned and sent to the execution pen. Some wept, some cursed, some pleaded for their lives or invoked the names of beloved wives, aged mothers or little children. The witnesses were unmoved. Flydd attempted to speak for each of his people, but was denied every time, on the grounds that a prisoner could not be advocate for his fellows. No one spoke in their defence.

The only prisoners not on trial were Malien and Tiaan, but both were tightly bound, and Malien had been gagged as well, lest she use the undoubted power of her voice to attempt an escape.

Finally it was Irisis's turn for trial. For some reason, she clung to the fantasy that her sentence would be set aside.

It was not to be. Not a single witness came forward to defend her.

'I beg leave to defend Crafter Irisis Stirm,' said Flydd.

'Denied,' Ghorr replied. 'For the reasons already stated.'

The master of the executions raised his voice. 'Since no witness has spoken up to oppose the verdict, the sentence is confirmed. Crafter Irisis Stirm has been found guilty of treason. Take her to the place of execution to await her fate.'

The guards dragged her away. To her left a burly executioner was honing the blades of his flensing tools, so sharp and fine that they could, in the hands of a master such as he, remove the skin of a living human without nicking the flesh. Beside him, the master disemboweller polished the edges of his scalpels, gougers, slitters, reamers, renders, crushers, grinders and pluckers.

Last in the line, the master dismemberer rubbed at a speck of rust on one of his bone saws and frowned. Irisis was so struck by the sight – the men and the tools that would undo flesh and organs and part her sinews from their bones – that she did not even hear the sentence confirmed on Flydd.

Fyn-Mah cried out in anguish. Flydd looked up at her and the light finally dawned. He gave her a look of infinite tenderness, then made a sign to her with his left hand. Irisis could not read it but Fyn-Mah forced a smile.

The scrutator bore an ethereal expression as they dragged him across to join the others. Xervish Flydd had come to terms with his fate.

'Master Flenser,' he said, nodding to the first of the executioners, 'I trust you've a keen blade on those knives of yours. I'm a sensitive man and my skin is particularly thin, after the work your father did on me some decades back.'

'Never fear, old fellow,' said the master flenser. 'I'm an artist of rare skill, if I say so myself. I'll have the hide off you so quick you'll never know it's gone.'

'Oh, I'll know all right,' chuckled Flydd. 'Just don't let them make a handbag out of my backside. My dignity couldn't stand the strain.'

'Don't worry, surr,' said the master flenser. 'I'll treat you with the respect you deserve.' Irisis thought he was being ironic, until he added quietly, 'I'm sorry, surr. I'd rather peel anyone in the world than you, but your conviction is a legitimate one.' He spread his hairy hands as if to say, what's an honourable man to do?

'Of course you must do your duty, Master Flenser,' said Flydd. 'I would not ask anything else of you.'

Flydd was having similar jocular words with the master disemboweller and the master dismemberer when the master of the executions shouted, 'Quiet, if you please. The executions will now begin.' He consulted his list, saying, 'We will take them in order of the trial. The first will be Pilot Inouye.'

Two soldiers lifted Inouye under the arms. She was such a frail little figure that either of them could have carried her in one hand. They propelled her forwards, her feet skipping across the canvas. It appeared that she was going willingly to her death, though had they stood her up she would have fallen down again.

The master flenser was selecting his initiating knife when the master of the executions spun around, looking confused. Fusshte was shouting and waving at him. The master of the executions ran across, conferring with the scrutator, then called out to the soldiers, 'No, bring her back, lads.' To the witnesses he said, 'The scrutators bid me to execute the greatest criminal and traitor first, in case the enemy should attack.

'Ex-Scrutator Xervish Flydd,' he went on, politely, 'if you would be so kind as to step into the flensing trough.'

For a fleeting moment Flydd looked shocked, as though not expecting his end to come quite so soon. He nodded, raised his right hand in salute to the other prisoners, and then to Irisis, and stepped over the side. The flensing trough was like a long metal bathtub with a broad platform on either side. A pipe ran from below the plughole down through the hole in the centre of the canvas platform.

'Would you care to disrobe and take your place on the right-hand platform?' said the master flenser. 'On your back, if you please, with your legs spread. Take your time. Make yourself comfortable.'

Again that muffled wail from Fyn-Mah. Flydd's hand was shaking and his knees would scarcely hold him. He dropped the sheet, settled his scrawny backside on the platform and swung his legs up. Looking around, he caught Irisis's eye. Flydd attempted a smile, but not even he could pull it off at this moment.

Irisis's heart went out to the man, though her own end would come soon enough. 'Take heart, Xervish,' she said. 'It'll be over more quickly than you think.'

He gave a stifled, mirthless laugh. 'Somehow, that's not nearly as comforting as when I said it to you.'

'Begin, Master Flenser!' roared Ghorr, striking a pose for the artists and the chroniclers. 'I'll double your fee if you can take this scoundrel's skin off in one piece – I've a special use for it.'

The master flenser looked hurt. 'I don't need a bribe to do my best, surr.' He took up his knife, eyeing Flydd's prone figure as if choosing the best spot to begin, though both knew that the procedure was prescribed in the manuals of his art. Flensing began in the centre, at the most sensitive place, and worked out in all directions.

'Hold just a moment,' cried Fusshte. 'There's something wrong.'

'I've done everything exactly as set down in the rituals!' the master of the executions exclaimed.

'I'm not talking to you!' Fusshte snarled. He looked around wildly, then ran to Chief Scrutator Ghorr. 'One of the greatest villains of all is missing. Where the devil is the arch-traitor, Artificer Cryl-Nish Hlar?'

THE END
OF VOLUME THREE

VOLUME FOUR
CHIMAERA

concludes
THE WELL OF ECHOES QUARTET

GLOSSARY

Names (MAIN CHARACTERS IN ITALICS)

Aachim: The human species native to Aachan, once conquered and enslaved by a small force of invading Charon (the Hundred). The Aachim are great artisans and engineers, but melancholy or prone to hubris and arrogance. In ancient times, many were brought to Santhenar by Rulke in the fruitless hunt for the Golden Flute. The Aachim flourished on Santhenar but were later betrayed by Rulke and ruined in the Clysm. They then withdrew from the world to their hidden mountain cities. The ones remaining on Aachan gained their freedom after the Forbidding was broken, when the surviving Charon went back to the void. Two hundred years later, volcanic activity on Aachan had become so violent that it threatened to destroy all life on the planet. The Aachim sought for a way of escape and one of them, Minis, managed to contact Tiaan on Santhenar, because of her amplimet, and charmed her. The Aachim showed her how to open a gate between Aachan and Santhenar. She thought she was saving her beloved, Minis, and a small number of Aachim, but when they came through, they were a hundred and fifty thousand, a host ready for war, in eleven thousand mighty constructs.

Barkus: Deceased master crafter of controllers at the manufactory, uncle of Irisis, who allowed her to read his uncensored copies of the Great Tales.

Bilfis: A noble Aachim from Stassor, a brilliant mathemancer and geomancer.

Cryl-Nish Hlar: *A former scribe, prober in secret and reluctant artificer, generally known as Nish.*

Eiryn Muss: Halfwit; an air-moss grower and harmless pervert, he turned out to be the scrutator's prober (spy) in the manufactory, and vanished, but reappeared in the west.

Elienor (Clan): Elienor was a great Aachim heroine of ancient times, who almost defeated Rulke when the Hundred invaded Aachan. She was the founder of ostracised Clan Elienor.

Faellem: A long-lived human species who have passed out of the Histories, though some may still dwell in isolated parts of Santhenar.

Flammas: A kindly, forgetful mancer. Ullii spent five years in his dungeon, the most pleasant time of her life.

Flangers: A soldier and hero in past battles against the lyrinx.

Forgre: An Aachim and associate of Malien; a brilliant spy.

Fusshte: A treacherous member of the Council of Scrutators.

Fyn-Mah: The querist (chief of the municipal intelligence bureau) at Tiksi and a loyal supporter of Xervish Flydd.

Ghorr: Chief Scrutator and Flydd's enemy.

Gilhaelith: An eccentric, amoral geomancer and mathemancer who dwelt at Nyriandiol. Because of his dismal early years he is obsessed with controlling everyone and everything in his life. When unable to do this the stress causes him to have panic attacks. His overriding goal is to understand the nature of the physical world, so as to control it too.

Gyrull: Matriarch of the lyrinx city at Snizort. A powerful, far-sighted mancer, profoundly intelligent.

Haani: Tiaan's adopted sister, accidentally killed by the Aachim in Tirthrax.

Halie: A scrutator on the Council and former supporter of Flydd.

Inouye: The pilot of Jal-Nish's air-floater, stolen by Fyn-Mah.

Inthis: Vithis's clan of Aachim, since time immemorial first of the eleven clans (First Clan). All Clan Inthis, apart from Vithis and Minis, were lost in the void when the portal between Aachan and Tirthrax was opened.

Irisis Stirm: Crafter, originally in charge of the controller artisans at the manufactory; niece of Barkus; one time lover of Xervish Flydd, now a friend and comrade-in-arms.

Jal-Nish Hlar: Acting Scrutator; Nish's father. He suffered massive injuries from a lyrinx attack and begged to be allowed to die, but Nish and Irisis saved his life. Now, hideously maimed, he has a bitter loathing for them both, and an unquenchable desire to be the greatest scrutator of all.

Joeyn (Joe): An old miner, Tiaan's friend, who died in a roof fall.

Klarm: Scrutator for Borgistry. A handsome, cheerful man, despite his dwarfish stature.

Lemuir: A sergeant in Jal-Nish's army.

Liett: Gyrull's daughter, and a lyrinx with unarmoured skin and no chameleon ability; a talented flesh-former and brilliant flier who yearns to lead her people, even though she is regarded as incomplete. She has a turbulent relationship with Ryll.

Liliwen: Daughter of Troist and Yara, twin of Meriwen.

Luxor: A conciliatory Aachim clan leader.

Lyrinx: Massive winged humanoids who escaped from the void to Santhenar after the Forbidding was broken. Highly intelligent, many of them are able to use the Secret Art, most commonly for keeping their heavy bodies aloft in flight. They have armoured skin and a chameleon-like ability to change their colours and patterns, often used for communication (skin-speech). Some lyrinx are also flesh-formers: they can change small organisms into desired forms using the Art. In the void they used a similar ability to pattern their unborn young so as to survive in that harsh environment. As a consequence, they are not entirely comfortable in their powerful but much changed bodies. The lyrinx were forced to abandon their culture and heritage in the void. Their lives are entirely martial, and some of them are beginning to regret their loss and wonder what to do about it once they've won the war.

Maigraith: A great heroine of olden times, one-time lover of Yggur and the great love of Rulke's life.

Malien: A venerable but ostracised Aachim living in Tirthrax. A heroine from the time of the Mirror (also known as the Matah). She helped Tiaan make the thapter, or flying construct.

Meriwen: Daughter of Troist and Yara, twin of Liliwen.

Merryl: A slave who taught human languages to the lyrinx in Snizort; also known as Tutor. He was kind to Tiaan.

Minis: A young Aachim man of high status; foster-son of Vithis; Tiaan's dream lover who was forced to spurn her when the Aachim came through the gate to Tirthrax. He feels guilty about his treatment of her, yearns for her but is totally in the thrall of Vithis.

Mira: Yara's sister who dwells at Morgadis, embittered after the loss of her husband and her three sons in the war. She communicates by skeet with a coalition of like-minded people. Nish fled her home in fear of his life after an unfortunate liaison which ended with a misunderstanding.

M'lainte: Flydd's mechanician, in charge of balloon and air-floater construction.

Myllii: Ullii's long-lost twin brother for whom she has been searching all her life.

Nish: Cryl-Nish's nickname.

Numinator, the: A mysterious figure mentioned by Flydd when in his cups, said to control the Council of Scrutators.

Nylaitl, the: A malicious creature created by Ryll and Liett's flesh-forming. It killed Haani's aunts and attacked Tiaan. Nish destroyed it after it attacked him and Ullii near Tirthrax.

Ranii Mhel: An examiner; mother of Nish.

Rulke: The greatest of all the Charon, he created the first construct.

Ryll: An ostracised wingless lyrinx who captured Tiaan and subsequently used her in flesh-forming. He was an honourable lyrinx and after Tiaan saved his life he allowed her to escape from Kalissin. He later captured her again when she came to Snizort looking for Gilhaelith, and used her in the patterners.

Seeker: Ullii. Also, one who can sense the use of the Secret Art, or people who have that talent, or even enchanted objects.

Talis the Mapmaker: An Aachim and associate of Malien.

Tchlrrr: A young soldier in Troist's army.

Tiaan Liise-Mar: A young artisan; a visual thinker and talented controller-maker. With the amplimet, she picked up Minis's cry for help, fell in love with him and carried the amplimet all the way to Tirthrax, where she used it in opening a gate to Aachan, to save Minis and his people. She subsequently helped Malien make a thapter in Tirthrax, departed in it, attacked the Aachim camp and later crashed near Nyriandiol when the amplimet refused to do what she wanted. Her back was broken in the crash. She was taken to Nynandiol by Gilhaelith, who began to teach her geomancy. When he was kidnapped by Gyrull and taken to Snizort, she followed in the thapter but was captured and put to use in the patterners, to pattern torgnadrs or node-drainers. This was only partly successful, because of her broken back, so the lyrinx flesh-formed it to repair her spine. After Snizort was abandoned, Merryl helped Tiaan to escape the patterners.

Tirior: A manipulative Aachim clan leader.

Troist: An ambitious junior officer in the army destroyed by the lyrinx at Nilkerrand. He formed a smaller army out of the survivors. Troist became a general much loved by his troops. Nish rescued his daughters Liliwen and Meriwen from ruffians, and again when they were lost in an underground labyrinth.

Ullii: A hypersensitive seeker, used by Scrutator Flydd to track Tiaan and the amplimet. She accompanied Nish to Tirthrax in the balloon and found Tiaan, but Malien intervened. Nish and Ullii escaped in the balloon but a lyrinx tore it open and they landed in the trees. The nylatl attacked and Ullii helped to defend Nish, after which they made love in the balloon. But it attacked again and when Nish was carried away on the balloon, Ullii was devastated. Her talent failed her for a while, but subsequently she was used by Jal-Nish at the manufactory, before being rescued by Flydd and taken to Nennifer, then west to help in the war at Snizort. Flydd promised to help her find Myllii but lied to her about it, and Ullii is furious with him.

Vithis: Minis's foster-father; an Aachim from Aachan and the head of Inthis First Clan, who led the Aachim to Santhenar. When all First Clan (except Minis) were lost in the gate, he became angry and bitter. He forced Minis to repudiate Tiaan. He subsequently led the Aachim across Santhenar but did not hold to his original purpose, to seize land, instead pursuing Tiaan and her thapter across the continent of Lauralin.

Xabbier Frou: A lieutenant in Jal-Nish's army, and a long-lost childhood friend of Nish.

Xervish Flydd: *The scrutator (spymaster and master inquisitor) for Einunar. He is now commander-in-chief of all the scrutators' forces at Snizort, charged with defeating the lyrinx army there. Secretly, he was also required to sneak into Snizort and destroy the lyrinx's node-drainer. He, Irisis and Ullii succeeded but the device he'd been given was faulty, destroying both node-drainer and node in a cata-*

strophic explosion. The field vanished, rendering both the army's clankers and the Aachim's constructs useless, and the soldiers defenceless against the attacking lyrinx.

Yara: A brilliant advocate, wife to Troist.

Yggur: A great long-lived mancer of ancient times.

Major Artefacts, Forces and Powerful natural Places

Alcifer: The long-abandoned city of Rulke the Charon, in Meldorin. The entire city was held to have been a magical construct and it still has an aura of barely leashed power.

Amplimet: A rare hedron which, even in its natural state, can draw power from the force (the *field*) surrounding and permeating a node. Very powerful. Inexplicably, Tiaan's amplimet shows signs of a crystal instinct or purpose, for in Tirthrax it communicated with the node and woke the trapped Well of Echoes. It also communicated with nodes elsewhere, denied Tiaan control when she wanted to take the thapter places it did not want to go, and drew threads of force throughout Snizort, including to the node and to Gilhaelith.

Anthracism: Human internal combustion due to a mancer or an artisan drawing more power than their body can handle. Invariably fatal (gruesomely).

Booreah Ngrurle (the Burning Mountain): A large, double-cratered volcano in northern Worm Wood with a blue crater lake. It has a strange and powerful double node. Gilhaelith's home, Nyriandiol, is built on the inner rim of the crater.

Clanker: An armoured mechanical war cart with six, eight, ten or rarely twelve legs and an articulated body, driven by the Secret Art via a controller mechanism which is used by a trained operator. Armed with a rock-throwing catapult and a javelard (heavy spear-thrower) which are fired by a shooter riding on top. Clankers are made under supervision of a mechanician, artisan and weapons artificer. Emergency power is stored in a pair of heavy spinning flywheels, in case the field is interrupted.

Construct: A vehicle powered by the Secret Art, based on some of the secrets of Rulke's legendary vehicle. Unlike Rulke's, those made by the Aachim cannot fly, but only hover, and therefore cannot cross obstacles like deep, wide ditches, cliffs, very steep slopes or rugged terrain (see *Thapter*).

Controller: A mind-linked mechanical system of many flexible arms which draws power through a *hedron* and feeds it to the drive mechanisms of a *clanker*. A controller is attuned to a particular hedron, and the operator must be trained to use each controller, which takes time. Operators suffer withdrawal if removed from their machines for long periods, and inconsolable grief if their machines are destroyed, although this may be alleviated if the controller survives and can be installed in another clanker.

Crystal fever: A hallucinatory madness suffered by artisans and clanker operators, brought on by overuse of a *hedron*. Few recover from it. Mancers can suffer from related ailments.

Field: The diffuse (or weak) force surrounding and permeating (and presumably generated by) a *node*. It is the source of a mancer's power. Various strong forces are also known to exist, though no one knows how to tap them safely (see *Power*). Non-nodal stress-fields also exist, though on Santhenar these are weak and little used.

Flesh-forming: A branch of the Secret Art that only lyrinx can use. Developed to adapt themselves to the ever-mutable void they came from, it now involves the slow transformation of a living creature, tailoring it to suit some particular purpose. It is painful for both creature and lyrinx, and can only be employed on small creatures, though the lyrinx seek to change that.

Gate: A portal between one place (or one world) and another, connected by a trans-dimensional 'wormhole'

Geomancy: The most difficult and powerful of all the Secret Arts. An adept is able to draw upon the forces that move and shape the world. A most dangerous Art to the user.

Hedron: A natural or shaped crystal, formed deep in the earth from fluids circulating through a natural *node*. Trained artisans can tune a hedron to draw power from the field surrounding a node, via the ethyr. Rutilated quartz, that is, quartz, crystal containing dark needles of rutile, is commonly used. The artisan must first 'wake' the crystal using his or her *pliance*. Too far from a node, a hedron is unable to draw power and becomes useless. If a hedron is not used for long periods it may have to be rewoken by an artisan, though this can be hazardous.

Mathemancy: An Art developed by Gilhaelith, though since that time it has been discovered independently by other mancers, notably Bilfis.

Nennifer: The great bastion of the Council of Scrutators, on the escarpment over Kalithras, the Desolation Sink. Nennifer is home to countless mancers, artisans and artificers, all furiously working to design new kinds of Art-powered devices to aid the war against the lyrinx.

Nodes: Rare places in the world where the Secret Art works better. Once identified, a *hedron* (or a mancer) can sometimes draw *power* from the node's *field* through the ethyr, though the amount diminishes with distance, not always regularly. A *clanker* operator must be alert for the loss and ready to draw on another node, if available. The field can be drained, in which case the node may not be usable for years, or even centuries. Mancers have long sought the secret of drawing on the far greater power of a node itself (cf. *Power,* Nunar's *General Theory of Power*) but so far it has eluded them (or maybe those that succeeded did not live to tell about it).

There are also anti-nodes where the Art does not work at all, or is dangerously disrupted. Nodes and anti-nodes are frequently (though not always) associated with natural features or forces such as mountains, faults and hot spots.

Nyriandiol: Gilhaelith's home, fortress and laboratory on top of Booreah Ngurle; the entire building is a geomantic artefact designed to protect him, ensure his control and enhance his work.

Oellyll: A lyrinx city in Meldorin.

Patterner: A semi-organic device developed by the lyrinx to pattern *torgnadrs* and other artefacts used in their Art. The patterner essentially copies a particular human's talent into the growing torgnadr, greatly enhancing the talent and allowing it to be controlled by a lyrinx skilled in the Art.

Pliance: Device that enables an artisan to see the *field* and tune a *controller* to it.

Port-all: Tiaan's name for the device she makes in Tirthrax to open the gate.

Power: A mancer, Nunar, codified the laws of mancing, noting how limited it was, mainly because of lack of power. She recognised that mancing was held back because power came from diffuse and poorly understood sources. It all went through the mancer first, causing aftersickness that grew greater the more powerful it was. Eventually power, or after-sickness, would kill the mancer.

The traditional way around this was to charge up an arte-fact (such as a mirror or ring) with power over a long time, and to simply trigger it when needed. This had some advan-tages, though objects could be hard to control or become corrupted, and once discharged were essentially useless. Yet some of the ancients had used devices that held a charge, or perhaps replenished themselves. No one knew how, but it had to be so, else how could they maintain their power for hundreds if not thousands of years (for example, the Mirror of Aachan), or use quite prodigious amounts of power without becoming exhausted (Rulke's legendary construct)?

Nunar assembled a team of mancers utterly devoted to her project (no mean feat) and set out to answer these ques-tions. Mancing was traditionally secretive – people tried (often wasting their lives in dead ends) and usually failed alone. Only the desperate state of the war could have made them work together, sharing their discoveries, until the genius of Nunar put together the *Special Theory of Power* that described where the diffuse force came from and how a mancer actually tapped it, drawing not through the earthly elements but through the ultradimensional ethyr.

The ultimate goals of theoretical mancers are the *General Theory of Power*, which deals with how nodes work and how they might be tapped safely; and, ultimately, the *Unified Power Theory*, which reconciles all fields, weak and strong, in terms of a single force.

Secret Art: The use of magical or sorcerous powers (mancing).

Snizort: A place in Taltid with a potent and concentrated node, near the famous tar pits and seeps. The lyrinx took Gilhaelith there to help them find the remains of a village lost in the Great Seep thousands of years ago. When he did so, they exca-vated a tunnel into the seep by freezing the tar, and took out a number of crystals, other artefacts and long-dead human bodies. After the node exploded, the tar caught fire and Snizort had to be abandoned.

Strong Forces: Forces which are speculated to exist, though no mancer studying them has yet survived to prove their existence.

Thapter: Tiaan's name for the flying construct she and Malien created in Tirthrax.

Torgnadr: A device patterned by the lyrinx to drain a *field* dry, or to channel power from the field for their own purposes. Torgnadrs are extremely difficult to *pattern* and most attempts fail, though some result in weak devices such as phynadrs which can draw small amounts of power for a particular purpose. Tiaan was used, with her amplimet, to pattern particularly strong torgnadrs, though the patterning was not entirely successful.

Well of Echoes, the: An Aachim concept to do with the reverberation of time, memory and the Histories. Sometimes a place of death and rebirth (to the same cycling fate). Also a sense of being trapped in history, of being helpless to change collective fate (of a family, clan or species). Its origin is sometimes thought to be a sacred well on Aachan, sometimes on Santhenar. The term has become part of Aachim folklore. 'I have looked in the Well of Echoes.' 'I heard it at the Well.' 'I will go to the Well.' Possibly also a source; a great *node*.

The Well is represented by the three-dimensional symbol of infinity, the universe and nothingness. A Well of Echoes, trapped in Tirthrax, is held there only by the most powerful magic.

Look out for . . .

CHIMAERA
by
Ian Irvine

BOOK FOUR OF THE WELL OF ECHOES

www.orbitbooks.co.uk

A SHADOW ON THE GLASS

Ian Irvine

Volume One of
THE VIEW FROM THE MIRROR

Once there were three worlds, each with their own people.
Then, fleeing out of the void, on the edge of extinction,
came the Charon. And the balance changed forever.

Karan, a sensitive with a troubled past,
is forced to steal an ancient relic in payment for a
debt. But she is not told that the relic is the Mirror of
Aachan, a twisted, deceitful thing that remembers
everything it has seen.

Llian, meanwhile, a brilliant chronicler, is expelled
from his college for uncovering a perilous mystery.

Thrown together by fate,
Karen and Llian are hunted across a world at war,
for the Mirror contains a secret of incredible power.

A Shadow on the Glass is the first volume in
a sweeping epic fantasy of magic and adventure
by a sensational new storyteller.

THE TOWER ON THE RIFT

Ian Irvine

Volume Two of
THE VIEW FROM THE MIRROR

As war rages across the land, Tensor,
the desperate leader of the Aachim people, flees into
the wilderness, taking with him the ancient Mirror of
Aachan and the chronicler Llian.

Only Karan can save the chronicler,
though she's not sure she can help herself. Tensor
wants her dead, the other powers are hunting her
for her sensitive talents, and Rulke the Charon
broods over them all from his Nightland prison.

The Twisted Mirror holds knowledge that
the world can only dream about. But its
power may yet betray them all.

'The complex cultures, detailed geography,
and the palpable weight of history provides a solid
background to an intense story . . . this stands out as
a worldbuilding labour of love with some truly
original touches' *Locus*